THE CANTERBURY TALES

DOVER THRIFT EDITIONS

Geoffrey Chaucer

Rendered into Modern English by
J. U. Nicolson

DOVER PUBLICATIONS, INC.
MINEOLA, NEW YORK

DOVER THRIFT EDITIONS

GENERAL EDITOR: PAUL NEGRI
EDITOR OF THIS VOLUME: TOM CRAWFORD

Bibliographical Note

This Dover edition, first published in 2004 and reissued in 2015, is an unabridged republication of *Canterbury Tales: Rendered into Modern English by J. U. Nicolson*, published by Garden City Publishing Company, Garden City, New York, 1934.

Library of Congress Cataloging-in-Publication Data

Chaucer, Geoffrey, d. 1400.
    The Canterbury tales / Geoffrey Chaucer.
        p. cm. — (Dover giant thrift editions)
    Originally published: Garden City, N.Y. : Garden City Pub. Co., c1934.
    Rendered into modern English by J.U. Nicolson.
    ISBN-13: 978-0-486-43162-8
    ISBN-10: 0-486-43162-2 (pbk.)
        1. Christian pilgrims and pilgrimages—Poetry. 2. Canterbury (England)—Poetry.
3. Storytelling—Poetry. 4. Tales, Medieval. I. Nicolson, J. U. (John Urban), 1885–
II. Title.

PR1870.A1N5 2004
821'.1—dc22

2003060197

Manufactured in the United States by LSC Communications
43162204   2017
www.doverpublications.com

Note

> "This world nis but a thoroughfare full of woe,
> And we been pilgrims passing to and fro."

On a par with Boccaccio's *The Decameron,* which it resembles, Chaucer's *The Canterbury Tales* is not only by far the finest poem in Middle English, it is one of the greatest masterpieces of literature, timeless and universal in its depiction of a broad cross-section of English folk of the fourteenth century–knights, squires, monks and friars, millers, carpenters, scholars, wives, students, clerks, and many more.

Spanning a rich variety of genres — chivalric romances, bawdy *fabliaux,* religious parables, folk tales, legends, and other story forms, the tales are told by a group of thirty pilgrims on their way to the shrine of Thomas à Becket at Canterbury. As the pilgrims meet at the Tabard Inn in Southwark, the host, one Harry Bailly, proposes that to ease the boredom of the long journey, each pilgrim tell two tales on the outgoing trip, and two on the return. The teller of the best tale is to receive a free dinner at the Tabard when they get back. In Chaucer's overall scheme for the work, this would have resulted in 120 tales, but the poet only completed twenty-two before his death.

In a sense, Chaucer was the ideal man to write these stories, because his life encompassed acquaintance with many levels of society, from the lowest tradesman to the rarefied realms of royalty. The details of his life are scanty, but a few facts are part of the public record. He was born about 1343 into a family in royal service. He later participated in the English invasion of France in 1359, in which he was captured, and then ransomed in 1360. In 1366 he married Philippa, one of the queen's attendants. From 1368 to 1378, he appears to have made a series of secret diplomatic missions to France, as well as two to Italy, which brought him into contact with the works of Dante, Boccaccio and Petrarch.

Over the next two decades, Chaucer was appointed Controller of Customs, elected Justice of the Peace, and elected to Parliament. In addition, he was appointed Clerk of the King's Works in 1389, and made Deputy Forester of the Royal Forest in Somerset in 1391. These varied posts brought him into contact with a broad spectrum of human specimens, and sharp observer that he was, Chaucer drew upon his experience of people to create the rich variety of personalities found among his Canterbury pilgrims. Although most are imaginary, several of the people mentioned, including Harry Bailly, the proprietor of the Tabard (a real inn of the day) and the cook, Hodge of Ware, were actual people. In Chaucer's masterly treatment, both real and imagined personalities take on universal significance. From the rollicking earthiness of the Wife of Bath, to the coy pretensions of the Prioress, from the humble dignity of the Knight, to the pleasure-loving, hard-riding Monk, the Canterbury pilgrims come vividly to life as timeless types that have been part of the human family down through the ages. As Chaucer describes their appearances, clothing, physical attributes, occupations, personalities, strengths and failings, we are privy to an intimate, sympathetic and often tender look at the faults and foibles of fourteenth-century humanity.

It is thought that Chaucer began work on the General Prologue to *The Canterbury Tales* about 1387, and worked on the collection over the next thirteen years. By the early 1370s he had begun to abandon the octosyllabic couplets he used in such early works as *The House of Fame* and *The Book of the Duchess*, in favor of the decasyllabic couplet, which he employed in most of *The Canterbury Tales*, and which evolved into the heroic couplet. The language of the tales is the dialect of the south and east Midlands, used at Court and in the City of London. Thanks in part to Chaucer's mastery of the dialect (the ancestor of modern standard English), rich vocabulary and skillful and varied use of meter, his verse seemed rich and original to his contemporaries.

Today, we read Chaucer not only for his wonderful poetry, and an earthy look at a medieval world long gone, but for his ability to present and reconcile the contradictions of life's experiences; his humor and compassion, his combination of simplicity and worldliness—in short, we read him for his splendid and comprehensive humanity, beautifully captured in verse of the greatest richness and color.

Apologia

It is with much diffidence and after long hesitation that I offer to the public this version in modern English of the Tales of Canterbury—not indeed that I have felt myself less well equipped than another to perform the work, but that it may be called in question whether such a work, performed by anyone, is justifiable. For, after all is said, it remains a truth that Geoffrey Chaucer did not write in French, or in Latin, or in Gaelic, or in any other foreign language; he wrote in English. Why then (it may well be asked) should his lines need modernizing? For if they do, then it follows that a great deal of Shakespeare also may some day require the same treatment—which God forbid! Moreover, it may be further alleged that the principal reason for reading Chaucer at all is Chaucer's English. Those who are interested in him will gladly master the language in which he wrote; those to whom this presents too great a task, or who take no delight therein, will have small joy of their reading. Why, then, should any man permit himself to change, however slightly, the work of this old master, merely that it may be read with ease?

Yet it may be that such an argument is capable of being too rigorously conducted. It may be that many persons can delight in Chaucer's Tales who have not either time or opportunity wherein to master his spelling, his syntax and his pronunciation. It may be that it is as justifiable to render Chaucer into modern English as it is to translate Petronius from his crossroads Latin. Indeed it may be that there are those who, having tasted here the diluted flavour of his wine, will be prompted to re-fill their glasses with the unadulterated vintage.

It is because I believe in the validity of the reason last adduced that I have permitted my version of the Tales to be put in print. I hope that I shall not be accused of seeking to better Chaucer, as others have (seemingly) sought to do. My unwavering desire has been to offer that which may prove provocative of further interest upon the part of the reader.

With this apology, I set forth a diluted drink. May it arouse an enduring thirst for the older and more potent liquor.

J. U. N.

Riverside, 1931

Table of Contents

Group A

Group B

Group C

Group D

Group E

Group F

Group G

Group H

Group I

THE PROLOGUE

Here begins the Book of the Tales of Canterbury

When April with his showers sweet with fruit
The drought of March has pierced unto the root
And bathed each vein with liquor that has power
To generate therein and sire the flower;
When Zephyr also has, with his sweet breath,
Quickened again, in every holt and heath,
The tender shoots and buds, and the young sun
Into the Ram one half his course has run,
And many little birds make melody
That sleep through all the night with open eye
(So Nature pricks them on to ramp and rage) —
Then do folk long to go on pilgrimage,
And palmers to go seeking out strange strands,
To distant shrines well known in sundry lands.
And specially from every shire's end
Of England they to Canterbury wend,
The holy blessed martyr there to seek
Who helped them when they lay so ill and weak.

    Befell that, in that season, on a day
In Southwark, at the Tabard, as I lay
Ready to start upon my pilgrimage
To Canterbury, full of devout homage,
There came at nightfall to that hostelry
Some nine and twenty in a company
Of sundry persons who had chanced to fall
In fellowship, and pilgrims were they all
That toward Canterbury town would ride.
The rooms and stables spacious were and wide,
And well we there were eased, and of the best.
And briefly, when the sun had gone to rest,
So had I spoken with them, every one,
That I was of their fellowship anon,

1

And made agreement that we'd early rise
To take the road, as you I will apprise.
    But none the less, whilst I have time and space,
Before yet farther in this tale I pace,
It seems to me accordant with reason
To inform you of the state of every one
Of all of these, as it appeared to me,
And who they were, and what was their degree,
And even how arrayed there at the inn;
And with a knight thus will I first begin.

THE KNIGHT

A knight there was, and he a worthy man,
Who, from the moment that he first began
To ride about the world, loved chivalry,
Truth, honour, freedom and all courtesy.
Full worthy was he in his liege-lord's war,
And therein had he ridden (none more far)
As well in Christendom as heathenesse,
And honoured everywhere for worthiness.
    At Alexandria, he, when it was won;
Full oft the table's roster he'd begun
Above all nations' knights in Prussia.
In Latvia raided he, and Russia,
No christened man so oft of his degree.
In far Granada at the siege was he
Of Algeciras, and in Belmarie.[1]
At Ayas was he and at Satalye[2]
When they were won; and on the Middle Sea
At many a noble meeting chanced to be.
Of mortal battles he had fought fifteen,
And he'd fought for our faith at Tramissene[3]
Three times in lists, and each time slain his foe.
This self-same worthy knight had been also
At one time with the lord of Palatye[4]
Against another heathen in Turkey:
And always won he sovereign fame for prize.
Though so illustrious, he was very wise
And bore himself as meekly as a maid.
He never yet had any vileness said,

---

1. Benimarim (the name of a tribe), in Morocco.   2. Modern Adalia, in Asia Minor.
3. Modern Tlemçen, in Algeria.   4. Modern Balat.

In all his life, to whatsoever wight.
He was a truly perfect, gentle knight.
But now, to tell you all of his array,
His steeds were good, but yet he was not gay.
Of simple fustian wore he a jupon
Sadly discoloured by his habergeon;
For he had lately come from his voyage
And now was going on this pilgrimage.

THE SQUIRE

With him there was his son, a youthful squire,
A lover and a lusty bachelor,
With locks well curled, as if they'd laid in press.
Some twenty years of age he was, I guess.
In stature he was of an average length,
Wondrously active, aye, and great of strength.
He'd ridden sometime with the cavalry
In Flanders, in Artois, and Picardy,
And borne him well within that little space
In hope to win thereby his lady's grace.
Prinked out he was, as if he were a mead,
All full of fresh-cut flowers white and red.
Singing he was, or fluting, all the day;
He was as fresh as is the month of May.
Short was his gown, with sleeves both long and wide.
Well could he sit on horse, and fairly ride.
He could make songs and words thereto indite,
Joust, and dance too, as well as sketch and write.
So hot he loved that, while night told her tale,
He slept no more than does a nightingale.
Courteous he, and humble, willing and able,
And carved before his father at the table.

THE YEOMAN

A yeoman had he,[5] nor more servants, no,
At that time, for he chose to travel so;
And he was clad in coat and hood of green.
A sheaf of peacock arrows bright and keen
Under his belt he bore right carefully
(Well could he keep his tackle yeomanly:

---

5. That is, the Knight.

His arrows had no draggled feathers low),
And in his hand he bore a mighty bow.
A cropped head had he and a sun-browned face.
Of woodcraft knew he all the useful ways.
Upon his arm he bore a bracer gay,
And at one side a sword and buckler, yea,
And at the other side a dagger bright,
Well sheathed and sharp as spear point in the light;
On breast a Christopher[6] of silver sheen.
He bore a horn in baldric all of green;
A forester he truly was, I guess.

THE PRIORESS

There was also a nun, a prioress,
Who, in her smiling, modest was and coy;
Her greatest oath was but "By Saint Eloy!"
And she was known as Madam Eglantine.
Full well she sang the services divine,
Intoning through her nose, becomingly;
And fair she spoke her French, and fluently,
After the school of Stratford-at-the-Bow,
For French of Paris was not hers to know.
At table she had been well taught withal,
And never from her lips let morsels fall,
Nor dipped her fingers deep in sauce, but ate
With so much care the food upon her plate
That never driblet fell upon her breast.
In courtesy she had delight and zest.
Her upper lip was always wiped so clean
That in her cup was no iota seen
Of grease, when she had drunk her draught of wine.
Becomingly she reached for meat to dine.
And certainly delighting in good sport,
She was right pleasant, amiable — in short.
She was at pains to counterfeit the look
Of courtliness, and stately manners took,
And would be held worthy of reverence.
    But, to say something of her moral sense,
She was so charitable and piteous
That she would weep if she but saw a mouse
Caught in a trap, though it were dead or bled.

---

6. That is, an image of Saint Christopher.

She had some little dogs, too, that she fed
On roasted flesh, or milk and fine white bread.
But sore she'd weep if one of them were dead,
Or if men smote it with a rod to smart:
For pity ruled her, and her tender heart.
Right decorous her pleated wimple was;
Her nose was fine; her eyes were blue as glass;
Her mouth was small and therewith soft and red;
But certainly she had a fair forehead;
It was almost a full span broad, I own,
For, truth to tell, she was not undergrown.
Neat was her cloak, as I was well aware.
Of coral small about her arm she'd bear
A string of beads and gauded[7] all with green;
And therefrom hung a brooch of golden sheen
Whereon there was first written a crowned "A,"
And under, *Amor vincit omnia*.

THE NUN

Another little nun with her had she,

THE THREE PRIESTS

Who was her chaplain; and of priests she'd three.

THE MONK

A monk there was, one made for mastery,
An outrider,[8] who loved his venery;
A manly man, to be an abbot able.
Full many a blooded horse had he in stable:
And when he rode men might his bridle hear
A-jingling in the whistling wind as clear,
Aye, and as loud as does the chapel bell
Where this brave monk was master of the cell.[9]
The rule of Maurus or Saint Benedict,
By reason it was old and somewhat strict,
This said monk let such old things slowly pace
And followed new-world manners in their place.
He cared not for that text a clean-plucked hen
Which holds that hunters are not holy men;

---

7. In a rosary the beads marking divisions are called gauds.   8. Outrider: a monk privileged to ride abroad on the business of his order.   9. Cell: as here used, a small priory.

Nor that a monk, when he is cloisterless,
Is like unto a fish that's waterless;
That is to say, a monk out of his cloister.
But this same text he held not worth an oyster;
And I said his opinion was right good.
What? Should he study as a madman would
Upon a book in cloister cell? Or yet
Go labour with his hands and swink and sweat,
As Austin[10] bids? How shall the world be served?
Let Austin have his toil to him reserved.
Therefore he was a rider day and night;
Greyhounds he had, as swift as bird in flight.
Since riding and the hunting of the hare
Were all his love, for no cost would he spare.
I saw his sleeves were purfled at the hand
With fur of grey, the finest in the land;
Also, to fasten hood beneath his chin,
He had of good wrought gold a curious pin:
A love-knot in the larger end there was.
His head was bald and shone like any glass,
And smooth as one anointed was his face.
Fat was this lord, he stood in goodly case.
His bulging eyes he rolled about, and hot
They gleamed and red, like fire beneath a pot;
His boots were soft; his horse of great estate.
Now certainly he was a fine prelate:
He was not pale as some poor wasted ghost.
A fat swan loved he best of any roast.
His palfrey was as brown as is a berry.

THE FRIAR

A friar there was, a wanton and a merry,
A limiter,[11] a very festive man.
In all the Orders Four is none that can
Equal his gossip and his fair language.
He had arranged full many a marriage
Of women young, and this at his own cost.
Unto his order he was a noble post.[12]
Well liked by all and intimate was he
With franklins everywhere in his country,

---

10. Austin: Saint Augustine.   11. Limiter: a friar licensed to beg within a certain district—within limits.   12. That is, a pillar.

And with the worthy women of the town:
For at confessing he'd more power in gown
(As he himself said) than a good curate,
For of his order he was licentiate.
He heard confession gently, it was said,
Gently absolved too, leaving naught of dread.
He was an easy man to give penance
When knowing he should gain a good pittance;
For to a begging friar, money given
Is sign that any man has been well shriven.
For if one gave (he dared to boast of this),
He took the man's repentance not amiss.
For many a man there is so hard of heart
He cannot weep however pains may smart.
Therefore, instead of weeping and of prayer,
Men should give silver to poor friars all bare.
His tippet was stuck always full of knives
And pins, to give to young and pleasing wives.
And certainly he kept a merry note:
Well could he sing and play upon the rote.
At balladry he bore the prize away.
His throat was white as lily of the May;
Yet strong he was as ever champion.
In towns he knew the taverns, every one,
And every good host and each barmaid too-
Better than begging lepers, these he knew.
For unto no such solid man as he
Accorded it, as far as he could see,
To have sick lepers for acquaintances.
There is no honest advantageousness
In dealing with such poverty-stricken curs;
It's with the rich and with big victuallers.
And so, wherever profit might arise,
Courteous he was and humble in men's eyes.
There was no other man so virtuous.
He was the finest beggar of his house;
A certain district being farmed to him,
None of his brethren dared approach its rim;
For though a widow had no shoes to show,
So pleasant was his *In principio*,
He always got a farthing ere he went.
He lived by pickings, it is evident.
And he could romp as well as any whelp.

On love days[13] could he be of mickle help.
For there he was not like a cloisterer,
With threadbare cope as is the poor scholar,
But he was like a lord or like a pope.
Of double worsted was his semi-cope,
That rounded like a bell, as you may guess.
He lisped a little, out of wantonness,
To make his English soft upon his tongue;
And in his harping, after he had sung,
His two eyes twinkled in his head as bright
As do the stars within the frosty night.
This worthy limiter was named Hubert.

THE MERCHANT

There was a merchant with forked beard, and girt
In motley gown, and high on horse he sat,
Upon his head a Flemish beaver hat;
His boots were fastened rather elegantly.
His spoke his notions out right pompously,
Stressing the times when he had won, not lost.
He would the sea were held at any cost
Across from Middleburgh to Orwell town.
At money-changing he could make a crown.
This worthy man kept all his wits well set;
There was no one could say he was in debt,
So well he governed all his trade affairs
With bargains and with borrowings and with shares.
Indeed, he was a worthy man withal,
But, sooth to say, his name I can't recall.

THE CLERK

A clerk from Oxford was with us also,
Who'd turned to getting knowledge, long ago.
As meagre was his horse as is a rake,
Nor he himself too fat, I'll undertake,
But he looked hollow and went soberly.
Right threadbare was his overcoat; for he
Had got him yet no churchly benefice,
Nor was so worldly as to gain office.
For he would rather have at his bed's head

---

13. Love days: days appointed for the settling of disputes by arbitration.

Some twenty books, all bound in black and red,
Of Aristotle and his philosophy
Than rich robes, fiddle, or gay psaltery.
Yet, and for all he was philosopher,
He had but little gold within his coffer;
But all that he might borrow from a friend
On books and learning he would swiftly spend,
And then he'd pray right busily for the souls
Of those who gave him wherewithal for schools.
Of study took he utmost care and heed.
Not one word spoke he more than was his need;
And that was said in fullest reverence
And short and quick and full of high good sense.
Pregnant of moral virtue was his speech;
And gladly would he learn and gladly teach.

THE LAWYER

A sergeant[14] of the law, wary and wise,
Who'd often gone to Paul's walk to advise,
There was also, compact of excellence.
Discreet he was, and of great reverence;
At least he seemed so, his words were so wise.
Often he sat as justice in assize,
By patent or commission from the crown;
Because of learning and his high renown,
He took large fees and many robes could own.
So great a purchaser[15] was never known.
All was fee simple to him, in effect,
Wherefore his claims could never be suspect.
Nowhere a man so busy of his class,
And yet he seemed much busier than he was.
All cases and all judgments could he cite
That from King William's[16] time were apposite.
And he could draw a contract so explicit
Not any man could fault therefrom elicit;
And every statute he'd verbatim quote.
He rode but badly in a medley coat,
Belted in a silken sash, with little bars,
But of his dress no more particulars.

---

14. Sergeant: in English law, a barrister of the highest rank.   15. Purchaser: one who acquires lands by means other than descent or inheritance.   16. King William I.

THE FRANKLIN

There was a franklin in his company;
White was his beard as is the white daisy.
Of sanguine temperament by every sign,
He loved right well his morning sop in wine.
Delightful living was the goal he'd won,
For he was Epicurus' very son,
That held opinion that a full delight
Was true felicity, perfect and right.
A householder, and that a great, was he;
Saint Julian[17] he was in his own country.
His bread and ale were always right well done;
A man with better cellars there was none.
Baked meat was never wanting in his house,
Of fish and flesh, and that so plenteous
It seemed to snow therein both food and drink
Of every dainty that a man could think.
According to the season of the year
He changed his diet and his means of cheer.
Full many a fattened partridge did he mew,
And many a bream and pike in fish-pond too.
Woe to his cook, except the sauces were
Poignant and sharp, and ready all his gear.
His table, waiting in his hall alway,
Stood ready covered through the livelong day.
At county sessions was he lord and sire,
And often acted as a knight of shire.
A dagger and a trinket-bag of silk
Hung from his girdle, white as morning milk.
He had been sheriff and been auditor;
And nowhere was a worthier vavasor.[18]

THE HABERDASHER AND THE CARPENTER

A haberdasher and a carpenter,

THE WEAVER, THE DYER, AND THE ARRAS-MAKER

An arras-maker, dyer, and weaver
Were with us, clothed in similar livery,
All of one sober, great fraternity.

---

17. The patron saint of hospitality.   18. A sub-vassal, next in rank below a baron.

Their gear was new and well adorned it was;
Their weapons were not cheaply trimmed with brass,
But all with silver; chastely made and well
Their girdles and their pouches too, I tell.
Each man of them appeared a proper burgess
To sit in guildhall on a high dais.
And each of them, for wisdom he could span,
Was fitted to have been an alderman;
For chattels they'd enough, and, too, of rent;
To which their goodwives gave a free assent,
Or else for certain they had been to blame.
It's good to hear "Madam" before one's name,
And go to church when all the world may see,
Having one's mantle borne right royally.

THE COOK

A cook they had with them, just for the nonce,
To boil the chickens with the marrow-bones,
And flavour tartly and with galingale.
Well could he tell a draught of London ale.
And he could roast and seethe and broil and fry,
And make a good thick soup, and bake a pie.
But very ill it was, it seemed to me,
That on his shin a deadly sore had he;
For sweet blanc-mange,[19] he made it with the best.

THE SAILOR

There was a sailor, living far out west;
For aught I know, he was of Dartmouth town.
He sadly rode a hackney, in a gown,
Of thick rough cloth falling to the knee.
A dagger hanging on a cord had he
About his neck, and under arm, and down.
The summer's heat had burned his visage brown;
And certainly he was a good fellow.
Full many a draught of wine he'd drawn, I trow,
Of Bordeaux vintage, while the trader[20] slept.
Nice conscience was a thing he never kept.
If that he fought and got the upper hand,

huge wand on knee (festering)

---

19. Not akin to the modern dish, but a compound of minced capon, with cream, sugar and flour.   20. That is, his passenger.

By water he sent them home to every land.
But as for craft, to reckon well his tides,
His currents and the dangerous watersides,
His harbours, and his moon, his pilotage,
There was none such from Hull to far Carthage.
Hardy, and wise in all things undertaken,
By many a tempest had his beard been shaken.
He knew well all the havens, as they were,
From Gottland to the Cape of Finisterre,
And every creek in Brittany and Spain;
His vessel had been christened *Madeleine*.

THE PHYSICIAN

With us there was a doctor of physic;
In all this world was none like him to pick
For talk of medicine and surgery;
For he was grounded in astronomy.[21]
He often kept a patient from the pall
By horoscopes and magic natural.
Well could he tell the fortune ascendent
Within the houses for his sick patient.
He knew the cause of every malady,
Were it of hot or cold, of moist or dry,
And where engendered, and of what humour;
He was a very good practitioner.
The cause being known, down to the deepest root,
Anon he gave to the sick man his boot.[22]
Ready he was, with his apothecaries,
To send him drugs and all electuaries;
By mutual aid much gold they'd always won—
Their friendship was a thing not new begun.
Well read was he in Esculapius,
And Deiscorides, and in Rufus,
Hippocrates, and Hali, and Galen,
Serapion, Rhazes, and Avicen,
Averrhoës, Gilbert, and Constantine,
Bernard, and Gatisden, and John Damascene.
In diet he was measured as could be,
Including naught of superfluity,

---

21. Astronomy: Chaucer means the "science" we would now call astrology.
22. Boot: remedy, relief.

But nourishing and easy. It's no libel
To say he read but little in the Bible.
In blue and scarlet he went clad, withal,
Lined with a taffeta and with sendal;
And yet he was right chary of expense;
He kept the gold he gained from pestilence.
For gold in physic is a fine cordial,
And therefore loved he gold exceeding all.

THE WIFE OF BATH

There was a housewife come from Bath, or near,
Who—sad to say—was deaf in either ear.
At making cloth she had so great a bent
She bettered those of Ypres and even of Ghent.
In all the parish there was no goodwife
Should offering make before her, on my life;
And if one did, indeed, so wroth was she
It put her out of all her charity.
Her kerchiefs were of finest weave and ground;
I dare swear that they weighed a full ten pound
Which, of a Sunday, she wore on her head.
Her hose were of the choicest scarlet red,
Close gartered, and her shoes were soft and new.
Bold was her face, and fair, and red of hue.
She'd been respectable throughout her life,
With five churched husbands bringing joy and strife,
Not counting other company in youth;
But thereof there's no need to speak, in truth.
Three times she'd journeyed to Jerusalem;
And many a foreign stream she'd had to stem;
At Rome she'd been, and she'd been in Boulogne,
In Spain at Santiago, and at Cologne.
She could tell much of wandering by the way:
Gap-toothed was she, it is no lie to say.
Upon an ambler easily she sat,
Well wimpled, aye, and over all a hat
As broad as is a buckler or a targe;
A rug was tucked around her buttocks large,
And on her feet a pair of sharpened spurs.
In company well could she laugh her slurs.
The remedies of love she knew, perchance,
For of that art she'd learned the old, old dance.

THE PARSON

There was a good man of religion, too,
A country parson, poor, I warrant you;
But rich he was in holy thought and work.
He was a learned man also, a clerk,
Who Christ's own gospel truly sought to preach;
Devoutly his parishioners would he teach.
Benign he was and wondrous diligent,
Patient in adverse times and well content,
As he was ofttimes proven; always blithe,
He was right loath to curse to get a tithe,
But rather would he give, in case of doubt,
Unto those poor parishioners about,
Part of his income, even of his goods.
Enough with little, coloured all his moods.
Wide was his parish, houses far asunder,
But never did he fail, for rain or thunder,
In sickness, or in sin, or any state,
To visit to the farthest, small and great,
Going afoot, and in his hand, a stave.
This fine example to his flock he gave,
That first he wrought and afterwards he taught;
Out of the gospel then that text he caught,
And this figure he added thereunto—
That, if gold rust, what shall poor iron do?
For if the priest be foul, in whom we trust,
What wonder if a layman yield to lust?
And shame it is, if priest take thought for keep,
A shitty shepherd, shepherding clean sheep.
Well ought a priest example good to give,
By his own cleanness, how his flock should live.
He never let his benefice for hire,
Leaving his flock to flounder in the mire,
And ran to London, up to old Saint Paul's
To get himself a chantry there for souls,
Nor in some brotherhood did he withhold;
But dwelt at home and kept so well the fold
That never wolf could make his plans miscarry;
He was a shepherd and not mercenary.
And holy though he was, and virtuous,
To sinners he was not impiteous,
Nor haughty in his speech, nor too divine,

But in all teaching prudent and benign.
To lead folk into Heaven but by stress
Of good example was his busyness.
But if some sinful one proved obstinate,
Be who it might, of high or low estate,
Him he reproved, and sharply, as I know.
There is nowhere a better priest, I trow.
He had no thirst for pomp or reverence,
Nor made himself a special, spiced conscience,
But Christ's own lore, and His apostles' twelve
He taught, but first he followed it himself.[23]

THE PLOWMAN

With him there was a plowman, was his brother,
That many a load of dung, and many another
Had scattered, for a good true toiler, he,
Living in peace and perfect charity.
He loved God most, and that with his whole heart
At all times, though he played or plied his art,
And next, his neighbour, even as himself.
He'd thresh and dig, with never thought of pelf,
For Christ's own sake, for every poor wight,
All without pay, if it lay in his might.
He paid his taxes, fully, fairly, well,
Both by his own toil and by stuff he'd sell.
In a tabard he rode upon a mare.
    There were also a reeve[24] and miller there;
A summoner, manciple[25] and pardoner,
And these, beside myself, made all there were.

THE MILLER

The miller was a stout churl, be it known,
Hardy and big of brawn and big of bone;
Which was well proved, for when he went on lam
At wrestling, never failed he of the ram.[26]
He was a chunky fellow, broad of build;
He'd heave a door from hinges if he willed,
Or break it through, by running, with his head.

---

23. An old form of himself.   24. Reeve: a steward or bailiff of an estate.
25. Manciple: an officer who purchases victuals for a college.   26. Ram: a usual prize
in wrestling.

His beard, as any sow or fox, was red,
And broad it was as if it were a spade.
Upon the coping of his nose he had
A wart, and thereon stood a tuft of hairs,
Red as the bristles in an old sow's ears;
His nostrils they were black and very wide.
A sword and buckler bore he by his side.
His mouth was like a furnace door for size.
He was a jester and could poetize,
But mostly all of sin and ribaldries.
He could steal corn and full thrice charge his fees;
And yet he had a thumb of gold, begad.
A white coat and blue hood he wore, this lad.
A bagpipe he could blow well, be it known,
And with that same he brought us out of town.

THE MANCIPLE

There was a manciple from an inn of court,
To whom all buyers might quite well resort
To learn the art of buying food and drink;
For whether he paid cash or not, I think
That he so knew the markets, when to buy,
He never found himself left high and dry.
Now is it not of God a full fair grace
That such a vulgar man has wit to pace
The wisdom of a crowd of learned men?
Of masters had he more than three times ten,
Who were in law expert and curious;
Whereof there were a dozen in that house
Fit to be stewards of both rent and land
Of any lord in England who would stand
Upon his own and live in manner good,
In honour, debtless (save his head were wood),
Or live as frugally as he might desire;
These men were able to have helped a shire
In any case that ever might befall;
And yet this manciple outguessed them all.

THE REEVE

The reeve he was a slender, choleric man
Who shaved his beard as close as razor can.

His hair was cut round even with his ears;
His top was tonsured like a pulpiteer's.
Long were his legs, and they were very lean,
And like a staff, with no calf to be seen.
Well could he manage granary and bin;
No auditor could ever on him win.
He could foretell, by drought and by the rain,
The yielding of his seed and of his grain.
His lord's sheep and his oxen and his dairy,
His swine and horses, all his stores, his poultry,
Were wholly in this steward's managing;
And, by agreement, he'd made reckoning
Since his young lord of age was twenty years;
Yet no man ever found him in arrears.
There was no agent, hind, or herd who'd cheat
But he knew well his cunning and deceit;
They were afraid of him as of the death.
His cottage was a good one, on a heath;
By green trees shaded with this dwelling-place.
Much better than his lord could he purchase.
Right rich he was in his own private right,
Seeing he'd pleased his lord, by day or night,
By giving him, or lending, of his goods,
And so got thanked—but yet got coats and hoods.
In youth he'd learned a good trade, and had been
A carpenter, as fine as could be seen.
This steward sat a horse that well could trot,
And was all dapple-grey, and was named Scot.
A long surcoat of blue did he parade,
And at his side he bore a rusty blade.
Of Norfolk was this reeve of whom I tell,
From near a town that men call Badeswell.
Bundled he was like friar from chin to croup,
And ever he rode hindmost of our troop.

THE SUMMONER

A summoner was with us in that place,
Who had a fiery-red, cherubic face,
For eczema he had; his eyes were narrow
As hot he was, and lecherous, as a sparrow;
With black and scabby brows and scanty beard;

He had a face that little children feared.
There was no mercury, sulphur, or litharge,
No borax, ceruse, tartar, could discharge,
Nor ointment that could cleanse enough, or bite,
To free him of his boils and pimples white,
Nor of the bosses resting on his cheeks.
Well loved he garlic, onions, aye and leeks,
And drinking of strong wine as red as blood.
Then would he talk and shout as madman would.
And when a deal of wine he'd poured within,
Then would he utter no word save Latin.
Some phrases had he learned, say two or three,
Which he had garnered out of some decree;
No wonder, for he'd heard it all the day;
And all you know right well that even a jay
Can call out "Wat" as well as can the pope.
But when, for aught else, into him you'd grope,
'Twas found he'd spent his whole philosophy;
Just "*Questio quid juris*" would he cry.
He was a noble rascal, and a kind;
A better comrade 'twould be hard to find.
Why, he would suffer, for a quart of wine,
Some good fellow to have his concubine
A twelve-month, and excuse him to the full
(Between ourselves, though, he could pluck a gull).
And if he chanced upon a good fellow,
He would instruct him never to have awe,
In such a case, of the archdeacon's curse,
Except a man's soul lie within his purse;
For in his purse the man should punished be.
"The purse is the archdeacon's Hell," said he.
But well I know he lied in what he said;
A curse ought every guilty man to dread
  (For curse can kill, as absolution save),
And 'ware *significavit* to the grave.
In his own power had he, and at ease,
The boys and girls of all the diocese,
And knew their secrets, and by counsel led.
A garland had he set upon his head,
Large as a tavern's wine-bush on a stake;
A buckler had he made of bread they bake.

THE PARDONER

With him there rode a gentle pardoner
Of Rouncival, his friend and his compeer;
Straight from the court of Rome had journeyed he.
Loudly he sang "Come hither, love, to me,"
The summoner joining with a burden round;
Was never horn of half so great a sound.
This pardoner had hair as yellow as wax,
But lank it hung as does a strike of flax;
In wisps hung down such locks as he'd on head,
And with them he his shoulders overspread;
But thin they dropped, and stringy, one by one.
But as to hood, for sport of it, he'd none,
Though it was packed in wallet all the while.
It seemed to him he went in latest style,
Dishevelled, save for cap, his head all bare.
As shiny eyes he had as has a hare.
He had a fine veronica sewed to cap.
His wallet lay before him in his lap,
Stuffed full of pardons brought from Rome all hot.
A voice he had that bleated like a goat.
No beard had he, nor ever should he have,
For smooth his face as he'd just had a shave;
I think he was a gelding or a mare.
But in his craft, from Berwick unto Ware,
Was no such pardoner in any place.
For in his bag he had a pillowcase
The which, he said, was Our True Lady's veil:
He said he had a piece of the very sail
That good Saint Peter had, what time he went
Upon the sea, till Jesus changed his bent.
He had a latten cross set full of stones,
And in a bottle had he some pig's bones.
But with these relics, when he came upon
Some simple parson, then this paragon
In that one day more money stood to gain
Than the poor dupe in two months could attain.
And thus, with flattery and suchlike japes,
He made the parson and the rest his apes.
But yet, to tell the whole truth at the last,
He was, in church, a fine ecclesiast.

Well could he read a lesson or a story,
But best of all he sang an offertory;
For well he knew that when that song was sung,
Then might he preach, and all with polished tongue.
To win some silver, as he right well could;
Therefore he sang so merrily and so loud.

    Now have I told you briefly, in a clause,
The state, the array, the number, and the cause
Of the assembling of this company
In Southwark, at this noble hostelry
Known as the Tabard Inn, hard by the Bell.
But now the time is come wherein to tell
How all we bore ourselves that very night
When at the hostelry we did alight.
And afterward the story I engage
To tell you of our common pilgrimage.
But first, I pray you, of your courtesy,
You'll not ascribe it to vulgarity
Though I speak plainly of this matter here,
Retailing you their words and means of cheer;
Nor though I use their very terms, nor lie.
For this thing do you know as well as I:
When one repeats a tale told by a man,
He must report, as nearly as he can,
Every least word, if he remember it,
However rude it be, or how unfit;
Or else he may be telling what's untrue,
Embellishing and fictionizing too.
He may not spare, although it were his brother;
He must as well say one word as another.
Christ spoke right broadly out, in holy writ,
And, you know well, there's nothing low in it.
And Plato says, to those able to read:
"The word should be the cousin to the deed."
Also, I pray that you'll forgive it me
If I have not set folk, in their degree
Here in this tale, by rank as they should stand.
My wits are not the best, you'll understand.

    Great cheer our host gave to us, every one,
And to the supper set us all anon;
And served us then with victuals of the best.

Strong was the wine and pleasant to each guest.
A seemly man our good host was, withal,
Fit to have been a marshal in some hall;
He was a large man, with protruding eyes,
As fine a burgher as in Cheapside lies;
Bold in his speech, and wise, and right well taught,
And as to manhood, lacking there in naught.
Also, he was a very merry man,
And after meat, at playing he began,
Speaking of mirth among some other things,
When all of us had paid our reckonings;
And saying thus: "Now masters, verily
You are all welcome here, and heartily:
For by my truth, and telling you no lie,
I have not seen, this year, a company
Here in this inn, fitter for sport than now.
Fain would I make you happy, knew I how.
And of a game have I this moment thought
To give you joy, and it shall cost you naught.

"You go to Canterbury; may God speed
And the blest martyr soon requite your meed.
And well I know, as you go on your way,
You'll tell good tales and shape yourselves to play;
For truly there's no mirth nor comfort, none,
Riding the roads as dumb as is a stone;
And therefore will I furnish you a sport,
As I just said, to give you some comfort.
And if you like it, all, by one assent,
And will be ruled by me, of my judgment,
And will so do as I'll proceed to say,
Tomorrow, when you ride upon your way,
Then, by my father's spirit, who is dead,
If you're not gay, I'll give you up my head.
Hold up your hands, nor more about it speak."

Our full assenting was not far to seek;
We thought there was no reason to think twice,
And granted him his way without advice,
And bade him tell his verdict just and wise,

"Masters," quoth he, "here now is my advice;
But take it not, I pray you, in disdain;
This is the point, to put it short and plain,
That each of you, beguiling the long day,
Shall tell two stories as you wend your way

To Canterbury town; and each of you
On coming home, shall tell another two,
All of adventures he has known befall.
And he who plays his part the best of all,
That is to say, who tells upon the road
Tales of best sense, in most amusing mode,
Shall have a supper at the others' cost
Here in this room and sitting by this post,
When we come back again from Canterbury.
And now, the more to warrant you'll be merry,
I will myself, and gladly, with you ride
At my own cost, and I will be your guide.
But whosoever shall my rule gainsay
Shall pay for all that's bought along the way.
And if you are agreed that it be so,
Tell me at once, or if not, tell me no,
And I will act accordingly. No more."

   This thing was granted, and our oaths we swore,
With right glad hearts, and prayed of him, also,
That he would take the office, nor forgo
The place of governor of all of us,
Judging our tales; and by his wisdom thus
Arrange that supper at a certain price,
We to be ruled, each one, by his advice
In things both great and small; by one assent,
We stood committed to his government.
And thereupon, the wine was fetched anon;
We drank, and then to rest went every one,
And that without a longer tarrying.

   Next morning, when the day began to spring,
Up rose our host, and acting as our cock,
He gathered us together in a flock,
And forth we rode, a jog-trot being the pace,
Until we reached Saint Thomas' watering-place.
And there our host pulled horse up to a walk,
And said: "Now, masters, listen while I talk.
You know what you agreed at set of sun.
If even-song and morning-song are one,
Let's here decide who first shall tell a tale.
And as I hope to drink more wine and ale,
Whoso proves rebel to my government
Shall pay for all that by the way is spent.
Come now, draw cuts, before we farther win,

And he that draws the shortest shall begin.
Sir knight," said he, "my master and my lord,
You shall draw first as you have pledged your word.
Come near," quoth he, "my lady prioress:
And you, sir clerk, put by your bashfulness,
Nor ponder more; out hands, now, every man!"

  At once to draw a cut each one began,
And, to make short the matter, as it was,
Whether by chance or whatsoever cause,
The truth is, that the cut fell to the knight,
At which right happy then was every wight.
Thus that his story first of all he'd tell,
According to the compact, it befell,
As you have heard. Why argue to and fro?
And when this good man saw that it was so,
Being a wise man and obedient
To plighted word, given by free assent,
He said: "Since I must then begin the game,
Why, welcome be the cut, and in God's name!
Now let us ride, and hearken what I say."

  And at that word we rode forth on our way;
And he began to speak, with right good cheer,
His tale anon, as it is written here.

HERE ENDS THE PROLOGUE OF THIS BOOK
AND HERE BEGINS THE FIRST TALE,
WHICH IS THE KNIGHT'S TALE

THE KNIGHT'S TALE

*Iamque domos patrias, Scithice post aspera gentis Prelia,
laurigero, etc.*
—STATIUS, *Theb.*, XII, 519.

Once on a time, as old tales tell to us,
There was a duke whose name was Thesëus:
Of Athens he was lord and governor,
And in his time was such a conqueror
That greater was there not beneath the sun.
Full many a rich country had he won;
What with his wisdom and his chivalry
He gained the realm of Femininity,
That was of old time known as Scythia.
There wedded he the queen, Hippolyta,
And brought her home with him to his country.
In glory great and with great pageantry,
And, too, her younger sister, Emily.
And thus, in victory and with melody,
Let I this noble duke to Athens ride
With all his armed host marching at his side.

   And truly, were it not too long to hear,
I would have told you fully how, that year,
Was gained the realm of Femininity
By Thesëus and by his chivalry;
And all of the great battle that was wrought
Where Amazons and the Athenians fought;
And how was wooed and won Hippolyta,
That fair and hardy queen of Scythia;
And of the feast was made at their wedding,
And of the tempest at their home-coming;
But all of that I must for now forbear.
I have, God knows, a large field for my share,
And weak the oxen, and the soil is tough.

24

The remnant of the tale is long enough.
I will not hinder any, in my turn;
Let each man tell his tale, until we learn
Which of us all the most deserves to win;
So where I stopped, again I'll now begin.
  This duke of whom I speak, of great renown,
When he had drawn almost unto the town,
In all well-being and in utmost pride,
He grew aware, casting his eyes aside,
That right upon the road, as suppliants do,
A company of ladies, two by two,
Knelt, all in black, before his cavalcade;
But such a clamorous cry of woe they made
That in the whole world living man had heard
No such a lamentation, on my word;
Nor would they cease lamenting till at last
They'd clutched his bridle reins and held them fast.
  "What folk are you that at my home-coming
Disturb my triumph with this dolorous thing?"
Cried Theseus. "Do you so much envy
My honour that you thus complain and cry?
Or who has wronged you now, or who offended?
Come, tell me whether it may be amended;
And tell me, why are you clothed thus, in black?"
  The eldest lady of them answered back,
After she'd swooned, with cheek so deathly drear
That it was pitiful to see and hear,
And said: "Lord, to whom Fortune has but given
Victory, and to conquer where you've striven,
Your glory and your honour grieve not us;
But we beseech your aid and pity thus.
Have mercy on our woe and our distress.
Some drop of pity, of your gentleness,
Upon us wretched women, oh, let fall!
For see, lord, there is no one of us all
That has not been a duchess or a queen;
Now we are captives, as may well be seen:
Thanks be to Fortune and her treacherous wheel,
There's none can rest assured of constant weal.
And truly, lord, expecting your return,
In Pity's temple, where the fires yet burn,
We have been waiting through a long fortnight;
Now help us, lord, since it is in your might.

"I, wretched woman, who am weeping thus,
Was once the wife of King Capanëus,
Who died at Thebes, oh, cursed be the day!
And all we that you see in this array,
And make this lamentation to be known,
All we have lost our husbands at that town
During the siege that round about it lay.
And now the old Creon, ah welaway!
The lord and governor of Thebes city,
Full of his wrath and all iniquity,
He, in despite and out of tyranny,
To do the dead a shame and villainy,
Of all our husbands, lying among the slain,
Has piled the bodies in a heap, amain,
And will not suffer them, nor give consent,
To buried be, or burned, nor will relent,
But sets his dogs to eat them, out of spite."
    And on that word, at once, without respite,
They all fell prone and cried out piteously:
"Have on us wretched women some mercy,
And let our sorrows sink into your heart!"
    This gentle duke down from his horse did start
With heart of pity, when he'd heard them speak.
It seemed to him his heart must surely break,
Seeing them there so miserable of state,
Who had been proud and happy but so late.
And in his arms he took them tenderly,
Giving them comfort understandingly:
And swore his oath, that as he was true knight,
He would put forth so thoroughly his might
Against the tyrant Creon as to wreak
Vengeance so great that all of Greece should speak
And say how Creon was by Thesëus served,
As one that had his death full well deserved.
This sworn and done, he no more there abode;
His banner he displayed and forth he rode
Toward Thebes, and all his host marched on beside;
Nor nearer Athens would he walk or ride,
Nor take his ease for even half a day,
But onward, and in camp that night he lay;
And thence he sent Hippolyta the queen
And her bright sister Emily, I ween,
Unto the town of Athens, there to dwell

While he went forth. There is no more to tell.
　The image of red Mars, with spear and shield,
So shone upon his banner's snow-white field
It made a billowing glitter up and down;
And by the banner borne was his pennon,
On which in beaten gold was worked, complete,
The Minotaur, which he had slain in Crete.
Thus rode this duke, thus rode this conqueror,
And in his host of chivalry the flower,
Until he came to Thebes and did alight
Full in the field where he'd intent to fight.
But to be brief in telling of this thing,
With Creon, who was Thebes' dread lord and king,
He fought and slew him, manfully, like knight,
In open war, and put his host to flight;
And by assault he took the city then,
Levelling wall and rafter with his men;
And to the ladies he restored again
The bones of their poor husbands who were slain,
To do for them the last rites of that day.
But it were far too long a tale to say
The clamour of great grief and sorrowing
Those ladies raised above the bones burning
Upon the pyres, and of the great honour
That Thesëus, the noble conqueror,
Paid to the ladies when from him they went;
To make the story short is my intent.
When, then, this worthy duke, this Thesëus
Had slain Creon and won Thebes city thus,
Still on the field he took that night his rest,
And dealt with all the land as he thought best.
　In searching through the heap of enemy dead,
Stripping them of their gear from heel to head,
The busy pillagers could pick and choose,
After the battle, what they best could use;
And so befell that in a heap they found,
Pierced through with many a grievous, bloody wound,
Two young knights lying together, side by side,
Bearing one crest, wrought richly, of their pride,
And of those two Arcita was the one,
The other knight was known as Palamon.
Not fully quick, nor fully dead they were,
But by their coats of arms and by their gear

The heralds readily could tell, withal,
That they were of the Theban blood royal,
And that they had been of two sisters born.
Out of the heap the spoilers had them torn
And carried gently over to the tent
Of Thesëus; who shortly had them sent
To Athens, there in prison cell to lie
For ever, without ransom, till they die.
And when this worthy duke had all this done,
He gathered host and home he rode anon,
With laurel crowned again as conqueror;
There lived he in all joy and all honour
His term of life; what more need words express?
And in a tower, in anguish and distress,
Palamon and Arcita, day and night,
Dwelt whence no gold might help them to take flight.

    Thus passed by year by year and day by day,
Till it fell out, upon a morn in May,
That Emily, far fairer to be seen
Than is the lily on its stalk of green,
And fresher than is May with flowers new
(For with the rose's colour strove her hue,
I know not which was fairer of the two),
Before the dawn, as was her wont to do,
She rose and dressed her body for delight;
For May will have no sluggards of the night.
That season rouses every gentle heart
And forces it from winter's sleep to start,
Saying: "Arise and show thy reverence."
So Emily remembered to go thence
In honour of the May, and so she rose.
Clothed, she was sweeter than any flower that blows,
Her yellow hair was braided in one tress
Behind her back, a full yard long, I guess.
And in the garden, as the sun up-rose,
She sauntered back and forth and through each close,
Gathering many a flower, white and red,
To weave a delicate garland for her head;
And like a heavenly angel's was her song.
The tower tall, which was so thick and strong,
And of the castle was the great donjon,
(Wherein the two knights languished in prison,
Of whom I told and shall yet tell, withal),

Was joined, at base, unto the garden wall
Whereunder Emily went dallying.
Bright was the sun and clear that morn in spring,
And Palamon, the woeful prisoner,
As was his wont, by leave of his gaoler,
Was up and pacing round that chamber high,
From which the noble city filled his eye,
And, too, the garden full of branches green,
Wherein bright Emily, fair and serene,
Went walking and went roving up and down.
This sorrowing prisoner, this Palamon,
Being in the chamber, pacing to and fro,
And to himself complaining of his woe,
Cursing his birth, he often cried "Alas!"
And so it was, by chance or other pass,
That through a window, closed by many a bar
Of iron, strong and square as any spar,
He cast his eyes upon Emilia,
And thereupon he blenched and cried out "Ah!"
As if he had been smitten to the heart.
And at that cry Arcita did up-start,
Asking: "My cousin, why what ails you now
That you've so deathly pallor on your brow?
Why did you cry out? Who's offended you?
For God's love, show some patience, as I do,
With prison, for it may not different be;
Fortune has given this adversity.
Some evil disposition or aspect
Of Saturn did our horoscopes affect
To bring us here, though differently 'twere sworn;
But so the stars stood when we two were born;
We must endure it; that, in brief, is plain."
  This Palamon replied and said again:
"Cousin, indeed in this opinion now
Your fancy is but vanity, I trow.
It's not our prison that caused me to cry.
But I was wounded lately through the eye
Down to my heart, and that my bane will be.
The beauty of the lady that I see
There in that garden, pacing to and fro,
Is cause of all my crying and my woe.
I know not if she's woman or goddess;
But Venus she is verily, I guess."

And thereupon down on his knees he fell,
And said: "O Venus, if it be thy will
To be transfigured in this garden, thus
Before me, sorrowing wretch, oh now help us
Out of this prison to be soon escaped.
And if it be my destiny is shaped,
By fate, to die in durance, in bondage,
Have pity, then, upon our lineage
That has been brought so low by tyranny."

    And on that word Arcita looked to see
This lady who went roving to and fro.
And in that look her beauty struck him so
That, if poor Palamon is wounded sore,
Arcita is as deeply hurt, and more.
And with a sigh he said then, piteously:
"The virgin beauty slays me suddenly
Of her that wanders yonder in that place;
And save I have her pity and her grace,
That I at least may see her day by day,
I am but dead; there is no more to say."

    This Palamon, when these words he had heard,
Pitilessly he watched him, and answered:
"Do you say this in earnest or in play?"

    "Nay," quoth Arcita, "earnest, now, I say!
God help me, I am in no mood for play!"

    Palamon knit his brows and stood at bay.
"It will not prove," he said, "to your honour
After so long a time to turn traitor
To me, who am your cousin and your brother,
Sworn as we are, and each unto the other,
That never, though for death in any pain,
Never, indeed, till death shall part us twain,
Either of us in love shall hinder other,
No, nor in any thing, O my dear brother;
But that, instead, you shall so further me
As I shall you. All this we did agree.
Such was your oath and such was mine also.
You dare not now deny it, well I know.
Thus you are of my party, beyond doubt.
And now you would all falsely go about
To love my lady, whom I love and serve,
And shall while life my heart's blood may preserve.
Nay, false Arcita, it shall not be so.

I loved her first, and told you all my woe,
As to a brother and to one that swore
To further me, as I have said before.
For which you are in duty bound, as knight,
To help me, if the thing lie in your might,
Or else you're false, I say, and downfallen."
    Then this Arcita proudly spoke again:
"You shall," he said, "be rather false than I;
And that you're so, I tell you utterly;
For *par amour* I loved her first, you know.
What can you say? You know not, even now,
Whether she is a woman or goddess!
Yours is a worship as of holiness,
While mine is love, as of a mortal maid;
Wherefore I told you of it, unafraid,
As to my cousin and my brother sworn.
Let us assume you loved her first, this morn;
Know you not well the ancient writer's saw
Of 'Who shall give a lover any law?'
Love is a greater law, aye by my pan,[1]
Than man has ever given to earthly man.
And therefore statute law and such decrees
Are broken daily and in all degrees.
A man must needs have love, maugre his head.
He cannot flee it though he should be dead,
And be she maid, or widow, or a wife.
And yet it is not likely that, in life,
You'll stand within her graces; nor shall I;
For you are well aware, aye verily,
That you and I are doomed to prison drear
Perpetually; we gain no ransom here.
We strive but as those dogs did for the bone;
They fought all day, and yet their gain was none.
Till came a kite while they were still so wroth
And bore the bone away between them both.
And therefore, at the king's court, O my brother,
It's each man for himself and not for other.
Love if you like; for I love and aye shall;
And certainly, dear brother, that is all.
Here in this prison cell must we remain
And each endure whatever fate ordain."

---

1. Pan: the brain-pan; the skull.

Great was the strife, and long, betwixt the two,
If I had but the time to tell it you,
Save in effect. It happened on a day
(To tell the tale as briefly as I may),
A worthy duke men called Pirithous,
Who had been friend unto Duke Theseüs
Since each had been a little child, a chit,
Was come to visit Athens and visit
His play-fellow, as he was wont to do,
For in this whole world he loved no man so;
And Theseüs loved him as truly—nay,
So well each loved the other, old books say,
That when one died (it is but truth I tell),
The other went and sought him down in Hell;
But of that tale I have no wish to write.
Pirithous loved Arcita, too, that knight,
Having known him in Thebes full many a year;
And finally, at his request and prayer,
And that without a coin of ransom paid,
Duke Theseüs released him out of shade,
Freely to go where'er he wished, and to
His own devices, as I'll now tell you.

The compact was, to set it plainly down,
As made between those two of great renown:
That if Arcita, any time, were found,
Ever in life, by day or night, on ground
Of any country of this Theseüs,
And he were caught, it was concerted thus,
That by the sword he straight should lose his head.
He had no choice, so taking leave he sped
Homeward to Thebes, lest by the sword's sharp edge
He forfeit life. His neck was under pledge.
How great a sorrow is Arcita's now!
How through his heart he feels death's heavy blow,
He weeps, he wails, he cries out piteously;
He thinks to slay himself all privily.
Said he: "Alas, the day that I was born!
I'm in worse prison, now, and more forlorn;
Now am I doomed eternally to dwell
No more in Purgatory, but in Hell.
Alas, that I have known Pirithous!
For else had I remained with Theseüs,
Fettered within that cell; but even so

Then had I been in bliss and not in woe.
Only the sight of her that I would serve,
Though I might never her dear grace deserve,
Would have sufficed, oh well enough for me!
O my dear cousin Palamon," said he,
"Yours is the victory, and that is sure,
For there, full happily, you may endure.
In prison? Never, but in Paradise!
Oh, well has Fortune turned for you the dice,
Who have the sight of her, I the absence.
For possible it is, in her presence,
You being a knight, a worthy and able,
That by some chance, since Fortune's changeable.
You may to your desire sometime attain.
But I, that am in exile and in pain,
Stripped of all hope and in so deep despair
That there's no earth nor water, fire nor air,
Nor any creature made of them there is
To help or give me comfort, now, in this —
Surely I'll die of sorrow and distress;
Farewell, my life, my love, my joyousness!

    "Alas! Why is it men so much complain
Of what great God, or Fortune, may ordain,
When better is the gift, in any guise,
Than men may often for themselves devise?
One man desires only that great wealth
Which may but cause his death or long ill-health.
One who from prison gladly would be free,
At home by his own servants slain might be.
Infinite evils lie therein, 'tis clear;
We know not what it is we pray for here.
We fare as he that's drunken as a mouse;
A drunk man knows right well he has a house,
But he knows not the right way leading thither;
And a drunk man is sure to slip and slither.
And certainly, in this world so fare we;
We furiously pursue felicity,
Yet we go often wrong before we die.
This may we all admit, and specially I,
Who deemed and held, as I were under spell,
That if I might escape from prison cell,
Then would I find again what joy might heal,
Who now am only exiled from my weal.

For since I may not see you, Emily,
I am but dead; there is no remedy."
    And on the other hand, this Palamon,
When that he found Arcita truly gone,
Such lamentation made he, that the tower
Resounded of his crying, hour by hour.
The very fetters on his legs were yet
Again with all his bitter salt tears wet.
"Alas!" said he, "Arcita, cousin mine,
With all our strife, God knows, you've won the wine.
You're walking, now, in Theban streets, at large,
And all my woe you may from mind discharge.
You may, too, since you've wisdom and manhood,
Assemble all the people of our blood
And wage a war so sharp on this city
That by some fortune, or by some treaty,
You shall yet have that lady to your wife
For whom I now must needs lay down my life.
For surely 'tis in possibility,
Since you are now at large, from prison free,
And are a lord, great is your advantage
Above my own, who die here in a cage.
For I must weep and wail, the while I live,
In all the grief that prison cell may give,
And now with pain that love gives me, also,
Which doubles all my torment and my woe."
    Therewith the fires of jealousy up-start
Within his breast and burn him to the heart
So wildly that he seems one, to behold,
Like seared box tree, or ashes, dead and cold.
Then said he: "O you cruel Gods, that sway
This world in bondage of your laws, for aye,
And write upon the tablets adamant
Your counsels and the changeless words you grant,
What better view of mankind do you hold
Than of the sheep that huddle in the fold?
For man must die like any other beast,
Or rot in prison, under foul arrest,
And suffer sickness and misfortune sad,
And still be ofttimes guiltless, too, by gad!
    "What management is in this prescience
That, guiltless, yet torments our innocence?
And this increases all my pain, as well,

That man is bound by law, nor may rebel,
For fear of God, but must repress his will,
Whereas a beast may all his lust fulfill.
And when a beast is dead, he feels no pain;
But, after death, man yet must weep amain,
Though in this world he had but care and woe:
There is no doubt that it is even so.
The answer leave I to divines to tell,
But well I know this present world is hell.
Alas! I see a serpent or a thief,
That has brought many a true man unto grief,
Going at large, and where he wills may turn,
But I must lie in gaol, because Saturn,
And Juno too, both envious and mad,
Have spilled out well-nigh all the blood we had
At Thebes, and desolated her wide walls.
And Venus slays me with the bitter galls
Of fear of Arcita, and jealousy."

    Now will I leave this Palamon, for he
Is in his prison, where he still must dwell,
And of Arcita will I forthwith tell.

    Summer being passed away and nights grown long,
Increased now doubly all the anguish strong
Both of the lover and the prisoner.
I know not which one was the woefuller.
For, to be brief about it, Palamon
Is doomed to lie for ever in prison,
In chains and fetters till he shall be dead;
And exiled (on the forfeit of his head)
Arcita must remain abroad, nor see,
For evermore, the face of his lady.

    You lovers, now I ask you this question:
Who has the worse, Arcita or Palamon?
The one may see his lady day by day,
But yet in prison must he dwell for aye.
The other, where he wishes, he may go,
But never see his lady more, ah no.
Now answer as you wish, all you that can.
For I will speak right on as I began.

Explicit prima pars.
Sequitur pars secunda.

Now when Arcita unto Thebes was come,

He lay and languished all day in his home,
Since he his lady nevermore should see,
But telling of his sorrow brief I'll be.
Had never any man so much torture,
No, nor shall have while this world may endure.
Bereft he was of sleep and meat and drink,
That lean he grew and dry as shaft, I think.
His eyes were hollow and ghastly to behold,
His face was sallow, all pale and ashen-cold,
And solitary kept he and alone,
Wailing the whole night long, making his moan.
And if he heard a song or instrument,
Then he would weep ungoverned and lament;
So feeble were his spirits, and so low,
And so changed was he, that no man could know
Him by his words or voice, whoever heard.
And in this change, for all the world he fared
As if not troubled by malady of love,
But by that humor dark and grim, whereof
Springs melancholy madness in the brain,
And fantasy unbridled holds its reign.
And shortly, all was turned quite upside-down,
Both habits and the temper all had known
Of him, this woeful lover, Dan Arcite.

Why should I all day of his woe indite?
When he'd endured all this a year or two,
This cruel torment and this pain and woe,
At Thebes, in his own country, as I said,
Upon a night, while sleeping in his bed,
He dreamed of how the winged God Mercury
Before him stood and bade him happier be.
His sleep-bestowing wand he bore upright;
A hat he wore upon his ringlets bright.
Arrayed this god was (noted at a leap)
As he'd been when to Argus he gave sleep.
And thus he spoke: "To Athens shall you wend;
For all your woe is destined there to end."
And on that word Arcita woke and started.
"Now truly, howsoever sore I'm smarted,"
Said he, "to Athens right now will I fare;
Nor for the dread of death will I now spare
To see my lady, whom I love and serve;
I will not reck of death, with her, nor swerve."

And with that word he caught a great mirror,
And saw how changed was all his old colour,
And saw his visage altered from its kind.
And right away it ran into his mind
That since his face was now disfigured so,
By suffering endured (as well we know),
He might, if he should bear him low in town,
Live there in Athens evermore, unknown,
Seeing his lady well-nigh every day.
And right anon he altered his array,
Like a poor labourer in mean attire,
And all alone, save only for a squire,
Who knew his secret heart and all his case,
And who was dressed as poorly as he was,
To Athens was he gone the nearest way.
And to the court he went upon a day,
And at the gate he proffered services
To drudge and drag, as any one devises.
And to be brief herein, and to be plain,
He found employment with a chamberlain
Was serving in the house of Emily;
For he was sharp and very soon could see
What every servant did who served her there.
Right well could he hew wood and water bear,
For he was young and mighty, let me own,
And big of muscle, aye and big of bone,
To do what any man asked, in a trice.
A year or two he was in this service,
Page of the chamber of Emily the bright;
He said "Philostrates" would name him right.
But half so well beloved a man as he
Was never in that court, of his degree;
His gentle nature was so clearly shown,
That throughout all the court spread his renown.
They said it were but kindly courtesy
If Theseüs should heighten his degree
And put him in more honourable service
Wherein he might his virtue exercise.
And thus, anon, his name was so up-sprung,
Both for his deeds and sayings of his tongue,
That Theseüs had brought him nigh and nigher
And of the chamber he had made him squire,
And given him gold to maintain dignity.

Besides, men brought him, from his own country,
From year to year, clandestinely, his rent;
But honestly and slyly it was spent,
And no man wondered how he came by it.
And three years thus he lived, with much profit,
And bore him so in peace and so in war
There was no man that Theseüs loved more.
And in such bliss I leave Arcita now,
And upon Palamon some words bestow.

In darksome, horrible, and strong prison
These seven years has now sat Palamon,
Wasted by woe and by his long distress.
Who has a two-fold evil heaviness
But Palamon? whom love yet tortures so
That half out of his wits he is for woe;
And joined thereto he is a prisoner,
Perpetually, not only for a year.
And who could rhyme in English, properly,
His martyrdom? Forsooth, it is not I;
And therefore I pass lightly on my way.

It fell out in the seventh year, in May,
On the third night (as say the books of old
Which have this story much more fully told),
Were it by chance or were it destiny
(Since, when a thing is destined, it must be),
That, shortly after midnight, Palamon,
By helping of a friend, broke from prison,
And fled the city, fast as he might go;
For he had given his guard a drink that so
Was mixed of spice and honey and certain wine
And Theban opiate and anodyne,
That all that night, although a man might shake
This gaoler, he slept on, nor could awake.
And thus he flees as fast as ever he may.
The night was short and it was nearly day,
Wherefore he needs must find a place to hide;
And to a grove that grew hard by, with stride
Of furtive foot, went fearful Palamon.
In brief, he'd formed his plan, as he went on,
That in the grove he would lie fast all day,
And when night came, then would he take his way
Toward Thebes, and there find friends, and of them pray
Their help on Theseüs in war's array;

And briefly either he would lose his life,
Or else win Emily to be his wife;
This is the gist of his intention plain.
    Now I'll return to Arcita again,
Who little knew how near to him was care
Till Fortune caught him in her tangling snare.
    The busy lark, the herald of the day,
Salutes now in her song the morning grey;
And fiery Phoebus rises up so bright
That all the east is laughing with the light,
And with his streamers dries, among the greves,[2]
The silver droplets hanging on the leaves.
And so Arcita, in the court royal
With Theseüs, and his squire principal,
Is risen, and looks on the merry day.
And now, to do his reverence to May,
Calling to mind the point of his desire,
He on a courser, leaping high like fire,
Is ridden to the fields to muse and play,
Out of the court, a mile or two away;
And to the grove, whereof I lately told,
By accident his way began to hold,
To make him there the garland that one weaves
Of woodbine leaves and of green hawthorn leaves.
And loud he sang within the sunlit sheen:
"O May, with all thy flowers and all thy green,
Welcome be thou, thou fair and freshening May:
I hope to pluck some garland green today."
And from his courser, with a lusty heart,
Into the grove right hastily did start,
And on a path he wandered up and down,
Near which, and as it chanced, this Palamon
Lay in the thicket, where no man might see,
For sore afraid of finding death was he.
He knew not that Arcita was so near:
God knows he would have doubted eye and ear,
But it has been a truth these many years
That "Fields have eyes and every wood has ears."
It's well for one to bear himself with poise;
For every day unlooked-for chance annoys.
And little knew Arcita of his friend,

2. Greves: groves.

Who was so near and heard him to the end,
Where in the bush he sat now, keeping still.
　Arcita, having roamed and roved his fill,
And having sung his rondel, lustily,
Into a study fell he, suddenly,
As do these lovers in their strange desires,
Now in the trees, now down among the briers,
Now up, now down, like bucket in a well.
Even as on a Friday, truth to tell,
The sun shines now, and now the rain comes fast,
Even so can fickle Venus overcast
The spirits of her people; as her day
Is changeful, so she changes her array.
Seldom is Friday quite like all the week.
　Arcita, having sung, began to speak,
And sat him down, sighing like one forlorn.
"Alas," said he, "the day that I was born!
How long, O Juno, of thy cruelty,
Wilt thou wage bitter war on Thebes city?
Alas! Confounded beyond all reason
The blood of Cadmus and of Amphion;
Of royal Cadmus, who was the first man
To build at Thebes, and first the town began,
And first of all the city to be king;
Of his lineage am I, and his offspring,
By true descent, and of the stock royal:
And now I'm such a wretched serving thrall,
That he who is my mortal enemy,
I serve him as his squire, and all humbly.
And even more does Juno give me shame,
For I dare not acknowledge my own name;
But whereas I was Arcita by right,
Now I'm Philostrates, not worth a mite.
Alas, thou cruel Mars! Alas, Juno!
Thus have your angers all our kin brought low,
Save only me, and wretched Palamon,
Whom Theseüs martyrs yonder in prison.
And above all, to slay me utterly,
Love has his fiery dart so burningly
Struck through my faithful and care-laden heart,
My death was patterned ere my swaddling-shirt.
You slay me with your two eyes, Emily;
You are the cause for which I now must die.

For on the whole of all my other care
I would not set the value of a tare,
So I could do one thing to your pleasure!"
And with that word he fell down in a trance
That lasted long; and then he did up-start.

This Palamon, who thought that through his heart
He felt a cold and sudden sword blade glide,
For rage he shook, no longer would he hide.
But after he had heard Arcita's tale,
As he were mad, with face gone deathly pale,
He started up and sprang out of the thicket,
Crying: "Arcita, oh you traitor wicked,
Now are you caught, that crave my lady so,
For whom I suffer all this pain and woe,
And are my blood, and know my secrets' store,
As I have often told you heretofore,
And have befooled the great Duke Thesëus,
And falsely changed your name and station thus:
Either I shall be dead or you shall die.
You shall not love my lady Emily,
But I will love her, and none other, no;
For I am Palamon, your mortal foe.
And though I have no weapon in this place,
Being but out of prison by God's grace,
I say again, that either you shall die
Or else forgo your love for Emily.
Choose which you will, for you shall not depart."

This Arcita, with scornful, angry heart,
When he knew him and all the tale had heard,
Fierce as a lion, out he pulled a sword,
And answered thus: "By God that sits above!
Were it not you are sick and mad for love,
And that you have no weapon in this place,
Out of this grove you'd never move a pace,
But meet your death right now, and at my hand.
For I renounce the bond and its demand
Which you assert that I have made with you.
What, arrant fool, love's free to choose and do,
And I will have her, spite of all your might!
But in as much as you're a worthy knight
And willing to defend your love, in mail,
Hear now this word: tomorrow I'll not fail
(Without the cognizance of any wight)

To come here armed and harnessed as a knight,
And to bring arms for you, too, as you'll see;
And choose the better and leave the worse for me.
And meat and drink this very night I'll bring,
Enough for you, and clothes for your bedding.
And if it be that you my lady win
And slay me in this wood that now I'm in,
Then may you have your lady, for all of me."
    This Palamon replied: "I do agree."
And thus they parted till the morrow morn,
When each had pledged his honour to return.
    O Cupido, that know'st not charity!
O despot, that no peer will have with thee!
Truly, 'tis said, that love, like all lordship,
Declines, with little thanks, a partnership.
Well learned they that, Arcite and Palamon.
    Arcita rode into the town anon,
And on the morrow, ere the dawn, he bore,
Secretly, arms and armour out of store,
Enough for each, and proper to maintain
A battle in the field between the twain.
So on his horse, alone as he was born,
He carried out that harness as he'd sworn;
And in the grove, at time and place they'd set,
Arcita and this Palamon were met.
Each of the two changed colour in the face.
For as the hunter in the realm of Thrace
Stands at the clearing with his ready spear,
When hunted is the lion, or the bear,
And through the forest hears him rushing fast,
Breaking the boughs and leaves, and thinks aghast,
"Here comes apace my mortal enemy!
Now, without fail, he must be slain, or I;
For either I must kill him ere he pass,
Or he will make of me a dead carcass" —
So fared these men, in altering their hue,
So far as each the strength of other knew.
There was no "good-day" given, no saluting,
But without word, rehearsal, or such thing,
Each of them helping, so they armed each other
As dutifully as he were his own brother;
And afterward, with their sharp spears and strong,
They thrust each at the other wondrous long.

You might have fancied that this Palamon,
In battle, was a furious, mad lion,
And that Arcita was a tiger quite:
Like very boars the two began to smite,
Like boars that froth for anger in the wood.
Up to the ankles fought they in their blood.
And leaving them thus fighting fast and fell,
Forthwith of Theseus I now will tell.

    Great destiny, minister-general,
That executes in this world, and for all,
The needs that God foresaw ere we were born,
So strong it is that, though the world had sworn
The contrary of a thing, by yea or nay,
Yet sometime it shall fall upon a day,
Though not again within a thousand years.
For certainly our wishes and our fears,
Whether of war or peace, or hate or love,
All, all are ruled by that Foresight above.
This show I now by mighty Theseus,
Who to go hunting is so desirous,
And specially of the hart of ten, in May,
That, in his bed, there dawns for him no day
That he's not clothed and soon prepared to ride
With hound and horn and huntsman at his side.
For in his hunting has he such delight,
That it is all his joy and appetite
To be himself the great hart's deadly bane:
For after Mars, he serves Diana's reign.

    Clear was the day, as I have told ere this,
When Theseus, compact of joy and bliss,
With his Hippolyta, the lovely queen,
And fair Emilia, clothed all in green,
A-hunting they went riding royally.
And to the grove of trees that grew hard by,
In which there was a hart, as men had told,
Duke Theseus the shortest way did hold.
And to the glade he rode on, straight and right,
For there the hart was wont to go in flight,
And over a brook, and so forth on his way.
This duke would have a course at him today,
With such hounds as it pleased him to command.

    And when this duke was come upon that land,
Under the slanting sun he looked, anon,

And there saw Arcita and Palamon,
Who furiously fought, as two boars do;
The bright swords went in circles to and fro
So terribly, that even their least stroke
Seemed powerful enough to fell an oak;
But who the two were, nothing did he note.
This duke his courser with the sharp spurs smote,
And in one bound he was between the two,
And lugged his great sword out, and cried out: "Ho!
No more, I say, on pain of losing head!
By mighty Mars, that one shall soon be dead
Who smites another stroke that I may see!
But tell me now what manner of men ye be
That are so hardy as to fight out here
Without a judge or other officer,
As if you rode in lists right royally?"
    This Palamon replied, then, hastily,
Saying: "O Sire, what need for more ado?
We have deserved our death at hands of you.
Two woeful wretches are we, two captives
That are encumbered by our own sad lives;
And as you are a righteous lord and judge,
Give us not either mercy or refuge,
But slay me first, for sacred charity;
But slay my fellow here, as well, with me.
Or slay him first; for though you learn it late,
This is your mortal foe, Arcita—wait!—
That from the land was banished, on his head.
And for the which he merits to be dead.
For this is he who came unto your gate,
Calling himself Philostrates—nay, wait!—
Thus has he fooled you well this many a year,
And you have made him your chief squire, I hear:
And this is he that loves fair Emily.
For since the day is come when I must die,
I make confession plainly and say on,
That I am that same woeful Palamon
Who has your prison broken, viciously.
I am your mortal foe, and it is I
Who love so hotly Emily the bright
That I'll die gladly here within her sight.
Therefore do I ask death as penalty,
But slay my fellow with the same mercy,

For both of us deserve but to be slain."
　This worthy duke presently spoke again,
Saying: "This judgment needs but a short session:
Your own mouth, aye, and by your own confession,
Has doomed and damned you, as I shall record.
There is no need for torture, on my word.
But you shall die, by mighty Mars the red!"
　But then the queen, whose heart for pity bled,
Began to weep, and so did Emily
And all the ladies in the company.
Great pity must it be, so thought they all,
That ever such misfortune should befall:
For these were gentlemen, of great estate,
And for no thing, save love, was their debate.
They saw their bloody wounds, so sore and wide,
And all cried out—greater and less, they cried:
"Have mercy, lord, upon us women all!"
And down upon their bare knees did they fall,
And would have kissed his feet there where he stood,
Till at the last assuaged was his high mood;
For soon will pity flow through gentle heart.
And though he first for ire did shake and start,
He soon considered, to state the case in brief,
What cause they had for fighting, what for grief;
And though his anger still their guilt accused,
Yet in his reason he held them both excused;
In such wise: he thought well that every man
Will help himself in love, if he but can,
And will himself deliver from prison;
And, too, at heart he had compassion on
Those women, for they cried and wept as one;
And in his gentle heart he thought anon,
And softly to himself he said then: "Fie
Upon a lord that will have no mercy,
But acts the lion, both in word and deed,
To those repentant and in fear and need,
As well as to the proud and pitiless man
That still would do the thing that he began!
That lord must surely in discretion lack
Who, in such case, can no distinction make,
But weighs both proud and humble in one scale."
And shortly, when his ire was thus grown pale,
He looked up to the sky, with eyes alight,

And spoke these words, as he would promise plight:
"The god of love, ah *benedicite!*
How mighty and how great a lord is he!
Against his might may stand no obstacles,
A true god is he by his miracles;
For he can manage, in his own sweet wise,
The heart of anyone as he devise.
Lo, here, Arcita and this Palamon,
That were delivered out of my prison,
And might have lived in Thebes right royally,
Knowing me for their mortal enemy,
And also that their lives lay in my hand;
And yet their love has wiled them to this land,
Against all sense, and brought them here to die!
Look you now, is not that a folly high?
Who can be called a fool, except he love?
And see, for sake of God who sits above,
See how they bleed! Are they not well arrayed?
Thus has their lord, the god of love, repaid
Their wages and their fees for their service!
And yet they are supposed to be full wise
Who serve love well, whatever may befall!
But this is yet the best jest of them all,
That she for whom they have this jollity
Can thank them for it quite as much as me;
She knows no more of all this fervent fare,
By God! than knows a cuckoo or a hare.
But all must be essayed, both hot and cold,
A man must play the fool, when young or old;
I know it of myself from years long gone:
For of love's servants I've been numbered one.
And therefore, since I know well all love's pain,
And know how sorely it can man constrain,
As one that has been taken in the net,
I will forgive your trespass, and forget,
At instance of my sweet queen, kneeling here,
Aye, and of Emily, my sister dear.
And you shall presently consent to swear
That nevermore will you my power dare,
Nor wage war on me, either night or day,
But will be friends to me in all you may;
I do forgive this trespass, full and fair."
    And then they swore what he demanded there,

And, of his might, they of his mercy prayed,
And he extended grace, and thus he said:
"To speak for royalty's inheritress,
Although she be a queen or a princess,
Each of you both is worthy, I confess,
When comes the time to wed: but nonetheless,
I speak now of my sister Emily,
The cause of all this strife and jealousy—
You know yourselves she may not marry two,
At once, although you fight or what you do:
One of you, then, and be he loath or lief,
Must pipe his sorrows in an ivy leaf.
That is to say, she cannot have you both,
However jealous one may be, or wroth.
Therefore I put you both in this decree,
That each of you shall learn his destiny
As it is cast; and hear, now, in what wise
The word of fate shall speak through my device.

   "My will is this, to draw conclusion flat,
Without reply, or plea, or caveat
(In any case, accept it for the best),
That each of you shall follow his own quest,
Free of all ransom or of fear from me;
And this day, fifty weeks hence, both shall be
Here once again, each with a hundred knights,
Armed for the lists, who stoutly for your rights
Will ready be to battle, to maintain
Your claim to love. I promise you, again,
Upon my word, and as I am a knight,
That whichsoever of you wins the fight,
That is to say, whichever of you two
May with his hundred, whom I spoke of, do
His foe to death, or out of boundary drive,
Then he shall have Emilia to wive
To whom Fortuna gives so fair a grace.
The lists shall be erected in this place.
And God so truly on my soul have ruth
As I shall prove an honest judge, in truth.
You shall no other judgment in me waken
Than that the one shall die or else be taken.
And if you think the sentence is well said,
Speak your opinion, that you're well repaid.
This is the end, and I conclude hereon."

Who looks up lightly now but Palamon?
Who leaps for you but Arcita the knight?
And who could tell, or who could ever write
The jubilation made within that place
Where Thesëus has shown so fair a grace?
But down on knee went each one for delight
And thanked him there with all his heart and might,
And specially those Thebans did their part.
And thus, with high hopes, being blithe of heart,
They took their leave; and homeward did they ride
To Thebes that sits within her old walls wide.

Explicit secunda pars.
Sequitur pars tercia.

I think that men would deem it negligence
If I forgot to tell of the expense
Of Thesëus, who went so busily
To work upon the lists, right royally;
For such an amphitheatre he made,
Its equal never yet on earth was laid.
The circuit, rising, hemmed a mile about,
Walled all of stone and moated deep without.
Round was the shape as compass ever traces,
And built in tiers, the height of sixty paces,
That those who sat in one tier, or degree,
Should hinder not the folk behind to see.
    Eastward there stood a gate of marble white,
And westward such another, opposite.
In brief, no place on earth, and so sublime,
Was ever made in so small space of time;
For in the land there was no craftsman quick
At plane geometry or arithmetic,
No painter and no sculptor of hard stone,
But Thesëus pressed meat and wage upon
To build that amphitheatre and devise.
And to observe all rites and sacrifice,
Over the eastern gate, and high above,
For worship of Queen Venus, god of love,
He built an altar and an oratory;
And westward, being mindful of the glory
Of Mars, he straightway builded such another
As cost a deal of gold and many a bother.
And northward, in a turret on the wall,

Of alabaster white and red coral,
An oratory splendid as could be,
In honour of Diana's chastity,
Duke Theseüs wrought out in noble wise.

    But yet have I forgot to advertise
The noble carvings and the portraitures,
The shapes, the countenances, the figures
That all were in these oratories three.

    First, in the fane of Venus, one might see,
Wrought on the wall, and piteous to behold,
The broken slumbers and the sighing cold,
The sacred tears and the lamenting dire,
The fiery throbbing of the strong desire,
That all love's servants in this life endure;
The vows that all their promises assure;
Pleasure and hope, desire, foolhardiness,
Beauty, youth, bawdiness, and riches, yes,
Charms, and all force, and lies, and flattery,
Expense, and labour; aye, and Jealousy
That wore of marigolds a great garland
And had a cuckoo sitting on her hand;
Carols and instruments and feasts and dances,
Lust and array, and all the circumstances
Of love that I may reckon or ever shall,
In order they were painted on the wall,
Aye, and more, too, than I have ever known.
For truly, all the Mount of Citheron,
Where Venus has her chief and favoured dwelling,
Was painted on that wall, beyond my telling,
With all the gardens in their loveliness.
Nor was forgot the gate-guard Idleness,
Nor fair Narcissus of the years long gone,
Nor yet the folly of King Solomon,
No, nor the giant strength of Hercules,
Nor Circe's and Medea's sorceries,
Nor Turnus with his hardy, fierce courage,
Nor the rich Croesus, captive in his age.
Thus may be seen that wisdom, nor largess,
Beauty, nor skill, nor strength, nor hardiness,
May with Queen Venus share authority;
For as she wills, so must the whole world be.
Lo, all these folk were so caught in her snare
They cried aloud in sorrow and in care.

Here let suffice examples one or two,
Though I might give a thousand more to you.
    The form of Venus, glorious as could be,
Was naked, floating on the open sea,
And from the navel down all covered was
With green waves, bright as ever any glass.
A citole in her small right hand had she,
And on her head, and beautiful to see,
A garland of red roses, sweet smelling;
Above her swirled her white doves, fluttering.
Before her stood her one son, Cupido,
Whose two white wings upon his shoulders grow;
And blind he was, as it is often seen;
A bow he bore, and arrows bright and keen.
    Why should I not as well, now, tell you all
The portraiture that was upon the wall
Within the fane of mighty Mars the red?
In length and breadth the whole wall was painted
Like the interior of that grisly place,
The mighty temple of great Mars in Thrace,
In that same cold and frosty region where
Mars to his supreme mansion may repair.
    First, on the wall was limned a vast forest
Wherein there dwelt no man nor any beast,
With knotted, gnarled, and leafless trees, so old
The sharpened stumps were dreadful to behold;
Through which there ran a rumbling, even now,
As if a storm were breaking every bough;
And down a hill, beneath a sharp descent,
The temple stood of Mars armipotent,
Wrought all of burnished steel, whereof the gate
Was grim like death to see, and long, and strait.
And therefrom raged a wind that seemed to shake
The very ground, and made the great doors quake.
The northern light in at those same doors shone,
For window in that massive wall was none
Through which a man might any light discern.
The doors were all of adamant eterne,
Rivetted on both sides, and all along,
With toughest iron; and to make it strong,
Each pillar that sustained this temple grim
Was thick as tun, of iron bright and trim.
    There saw I first the dark imagining

Of felony, and all the compassing;
And cruel anger, red as burning coal;
Pickpurses, and the dread that eats the soul;
The smiling villain, hiding knife in cloak;
The farm barns burning, and the thick black smoke;
The treachery of murder done in bed;
The open battle, with the wounds that bled;
Contest, with bloody knife and sharp menace;
And loud with creaking was that dismal place.
The slayer of himself, too, saw I there,
His very heart's blood matted in his hair;
The nail that's driven in the skull by night;
The cold plague-corpse, with gaping mouth upright.
In middle of the temple sat Mischance,
With gloomy, grimly woeful countenance.
And saw I Madness laughing in his rage;
Armed risings, and outcries, and fierce outrage;
The carrion in the bush, with throat wide carved;
A thousand slain, nor one by plague, nor starved.
The tyrant, with the spoils of violent theft;
The town destroyed, in ruins, nothing left.
And saw I burnt the ships that dance by phares;
The hunter strangled by the fierce wild bears;
The sow chewing the child right in the cradle;
The cook well scalded, spite of his long ladle.
Nothing was lacking of Mars' evil part:
The carter over-driven by his cart,
Under a wheel he lay low in the dust.
There were likewise in Mars' house, as needs must,
The surgeon, and the butcher, and the smith
Who forges sharp swords and great ills therewith.
And over all, depicted in a tower,
Sat Conquest, high in honour and in power,
Yet with a sharp sword hanging o'er his head
But by the tenuous twisting of a thread.
Depicted was the death of Julius,
Of Nero great, and of Antonius;
And though at that same time they were unborn,
There were their deaths depicted to adorn
The menacing of Mars, in likeness sure;
Things were so shown, in all that portraiture,
As are fore-shown among the stars above,
Who shall be slain in war or dead for love.

Suffice one instance from old plenitude,
I could not tell them all, even if I would.
   Mars' image stood upon a chariot,
Armed, and so grim that mad he seemed, God wot;
And o'er his head two constellations shone
Of stars that have been named in writings known,
One being Puella, and one Rubeus.
This god of armies was companioned thus:
A wolf there was before him, at his feet,
Red-eyed, and of a dead man he did eat.
A cunning pencil there had limned this story
In reverence of Mars and of his glory.
   Now to the temple of Diana chaste,
As briefly as I can, I'll pass in haste,
To lay before you its description well.
In pictures, up and down, the wall could tell
Of hunting and of modest chastity.
There saw I how Callisto fared when she
(Diana being much aggrieved with her)
Was changed from woman into a she-bear,
And after, made into the lone Pole Star;
There was it; I can't tell how such things are.
Her son, too, is a star, as men may see.
There saw I Daphne turned into a tree
(I do not mean Diana, no, but she,
Penëus' daughter, who was called Daphne).
I saw Actaeon made a hart all rude
For punishment of seeing Diana nude;
I saw, too, how his fifty hounds had caught
And him were eating, since they knew him not.
And painted farther on, I saw before
How Atalanta hunted the wild boar;
And Meleager, and many another there,
For which Diana wrought him woe and care.
There saw I many another wondrous tale
From which I will not now draw memory's veil.
This goddess on an antlered hart was set,
With little hounds about her feet, and yet
Beneath her perfect feet there was a moon,
Waxing it was, but it should wane full soon.
In robes of yellowish green her statue was,
She'd bow in hand and arrows in a case.
Her eyes were downcast, looking at the ground,

Where Pluto in his dark realm may be found.
Before her was a woman travailing,
Who was so long in giving birth, poor thing,
That pitifully Lucina did she call,
Praying, "Oh help, for thou may'st best of all!"
Well could he paint, who had this picture wrought,
With many a florin he'd his colours bought,
     But now the lists were done, and Theseüs,
Who at so great cost had appointed thus
The temples and the circus, as I tell,
When all was done, he liked it wondrous well.
But hold I will from Theseüs, and on
To speak of Arcita and Palamon.
     The day of their return is forthcoming,
When each of them a hundred knights must bring
The combat to support, as I have told;
And into Athens, covenant to uphold,
Has each one ridden with his hundred knights,
Well armed for war, at all points, in their mights.
And certainly, 'twas thought by many a man
That never, since the day this world began,
Speaking of good knights hardy of their hands,
Wherever God created seas and lands,
Was, of so few, so noble company.
For every man that loved all chivalry,
And eager was to win surpassing fame,
Had prayed to play a part in that great game;
And all was well with him who chosen was.
For if there came tomorrow such a case,
You know right well that every lusty knight
Who loves the ladies fair and keeps his might,
Be it in England, aye or otherwhere,
Would wish of all things to be present there
To fight for some fair lady. *Ben'cite!*
'Twould be a pleasant goodly sight to see!
     And so it was with those with Palamon.
With him there rode of good knights many a one;
Some would be armoured in a habergeon
And in a breastplate, under light jupon;
And some wore breast- and back-plates thick and large;
And some would have a Prussian shield, or targe;
Some on their very legs were armoured well,
And carried axe, and some a mace of steel.

There is no new thing, now, that is not old.
And so they all were armed, as I have told,
To his own liking and design, each one.
  There might you see, riding with Palamon,
Lycurgus' self, the mighty king of Thrace;
Black was his beard and manly was his face.
The eyeballs in the sockets of his head,
They glowed between a yellow and a red.
And like a griffon glared he round about
From under bushy eyebrows thick and stout.
His limbs were large, his muscles hard and strong.
His shoulders broad, his arms both big and long,
And, as the fashion was in his country,
High in a chariot of gold stood he,
With four white bulls in traces, to progress.
Instead of coat-of-arms above harness,
With yellow claws preserved and bright as gold,
He wore a bear-skin, black and very old.
His long combed hair was hanging down his back,
As any raven's feather it was black:
A wreath of gold, arm-thick, of heavy weight,
Was on his head, and set with jewels great,
Of rubies fine and perfect diamonds.
About his car there circled huge white hounds,
Twenty or more, as large as any steer,
To hunt the lion or the antlered deer;
And so they followed him, with muzzles bound,
Wearing gold collars with smooth rings and round.
A hundred lords came riding in his rout,
All armed at point, with hearts both stern and stout
  With Arcita, in tales men call to mind,
The great Emetrëus, a king of Ind,
Upon a bay steed harnessed all in steel,
Covered with cloth of gold, all diapered well,
Came riding like the god of arms, great Mars.
His coat-of-arms was cloth of the Tartars,
Begemmed with pearls, all white and round and great.
Of beaten gold his saddle, burnished late;
A mantle from his shoulders hung, the thing
Close-set with rubies red, like fire blazing.
His crisp hair all in bright ringlets was run,
Yellow as gold and gleaming as the sun.
His nose was high, his eyes a bright citrine,

His lips were full, his colouring sanguine.
And a few freckles on his face were seen,
None either black or yellow, but the mean;
And like a lion he his glances cast.
Not more than five-and-twenty years he'd past.
His beard was well beginning, now, to spring;
His voice was as a trumpet thundering.
Upon his brows he wore, of laurel green,
A garland, fresh and pleasing to be seen.
Upon his wrist he bore, for his delight,
An eagle tame, as any lily white.
A hundred lords came riding with him there,
All armed, except their heads, in all their gear,
And wealthily appointed in all things.
For, trust me well, that dukes and earls and kings
Were gathered in this noble company
For love and for increase of chivalry.
About this king there ran, on every side,
Many tame lions and leopards in their pride.
And in such wise these mighty lords, in sum,
Were, of a Sunday, to the city come
About the prime, and in the town did light.
    This Theseus, this duke, this noble knight,
When he'd conducted them to his city,
And quartered them, according to degree,
He feasted them, and was at so much pains
To give them ease and honour, of his gains,
That men yet hold that never human wit,
Of high or low estate, could better it.
The minstrelsy, the service at the feast,
The great gifts to the highest and the least,
The furnishings of Theseus' rich palace,
Who highest sat or lowest on the dais,
What ladies fairest were or best dandling,
Or which of them could dance the best, or sing,
Or who could speak most feelingly of love,
Or what hawks sat upon the perch above,
Or what great hounds were lying on the floor—
Of all these I will make no mention more;
But tell my tale, for that, I think, is best;
Now comes the point, and listen if you've zest.
    That Sunday night, ere day began to spring,
When Palamon the earliest lark heard sing,

Although it lacked two hours of being day,
Yet the lark sang, and Palamon sang a lay.
With pious heart and with a high courage
He rose, to go upon a pilgrimage
Unto the blessed Cytherea's shrine
(I mean Queen Venus, worthy and benign).
And at her hour he then walked forth apace
Out to the lists wherein her temple was,
And down he knelt in manner to revere,
And from a full heart spoke as you shall hear.

"Fairest of fair, O lady mine, Venus,
Daughter of Jove and spouse to Vulcanus,
Thou gladdener of the Mount of Citheron,
By that great love thou borest to Adon,
Have pity on my bitter tears that smart
And hear my humble prayer within thy heart.
Alas! I have no words in which to tell
The effect of all the torments of my hell;
My heavy heart its evils can't bewray;
I'm so confused I can find naught to say.
But mercy, lady bright, that knowest well
My heart, and seëst all the ills I feel,
Consider and have ruth upon my sore
As truly as I shall, for evermore,
Well as I may, thy one true servant be,
And wage a war henceforth on chastity.
If thou wilt help, thus do I make my vow,
To boast of knightly skill I care not now,
Nor do I ask tomorrow's victory,
Nor any such renown, nor vain glory
Of prize of arms, blown before lord and churl,
But I would have possession of one girl,
Of Emily, and die in thy service;
Find thou the manner how, and in what wise.
For I care not, unless it better be,
Whether I vanquish them or they do me,
So I may have my lady in my arms.
For though Mars is the god of war's alarms,
Thy power is so great in Heaven above,
That, if it be thy will, I'll have my love.
In thy fane will I worship always, so
That on thine altar, where'er I ride or go,
I will lay sacrifice and thy fires feed.

And if thou wilt not so, O lady, cede,
I pray thee, that tomorrow, with a spear,
Arcita bear me through the heart, just here.
For I'll care naught, when I have lost my life,
That Arcita may win her for his wife.
This the effect and end of all my prayer,
Give me my love, thou blissful lady fair."
   Now when he'd finished all the orison,
His sacrifice he made, this Palamon,
Right piously, with all the circumstance,
Albeit I tell not now his observance.
But at the last the form of Venus shook
And gave a sign, and thereupon he took
This as acceptance of his prayer that day.
For though the augury showed some delay,
Yet he knew well that granted was his boon;
And with glad heart he got him home right soon.
   Three hours unequal[3] after Palamon
To Venus' temple at the lists had gone,
Up rose the sun and up rose Emily,
And to Diana's temple did she hie.
Her maidens led she thither, and with them
They carefully took fire and each emblem,
And incense, robes, and the remainder all
Of things for sacrifice ceremonial.
There was not one thing lacking; I'll but add
The horns of mead, as was a way they had.
In smoking temple, full of draperies fair,
This Emily with young heart debonnaire,
Her body washed in water from a well;
But how she did the rite I dare not tell,
Except it be at large, in general;
And yet it was a thing worth hearing all;
When one's well meaning, there is no transgression;
But it is best to speak at one's discretion.
Her bright hair was unbound, but combed withal;
She wore of green oak leaves a coronal
Upon her lovely head. Then she began
Two fires upon the altar stone to fan,
And did her ceremonies as we're told

---

3. Hours unequal: hours formed by dividing the daylight by twelve. Hence, in May, hours of longer duration than sixty minutes.

In Statius' *Thebaid* and books as old.
When kindled was the fire, with sober face
Unto Diana spoke she in that place.
   "O thou chaste goddess of the wildwood green,
By whom all heaven and earth and sea are seen,
Queen of the realm of Pluto, dark and low,
Goddess of maidens, that my heart dost know
For all my years, and knowest what I desire,
Oh, save me from thy vengeance and thine ire
That on Actaeon fell so cruelly.
Chaste goddess, well indeed thou knowest that I
Desire to be a virgin all my life,
Nor ever wish to be man's love or wife.
I am, thou know'st, yet of thy company,
A maid, who loves the hunt and venery,
And to go rambling in the greenwood wild,
And not to be a wife and be with child.
I do not crave the company of man.
Now help me, lady, since thou may'st and can,
By the three beings who are one in thee.
For Palamon, who bears such love to me,
And for Arcita, loving me so sore,
This grace I pray thee, without one thing more,
To send down love and peace between those two,
And turn their hearts away from me: so do
That all their furious love and their desire,
And all their ceaseless torment and their fire
Be quenched or turned into another place;
And if it be thou wilt not show this grace,
Or if my destiny be moulded so
That I must needs have one of these same two,
Then send me him that most desires me.
Behold, O goddess of utter chastity,
The bitter tears that down my two cheeks fall.
Since thou art maid and keeper of us all,
My maidenhead keep thou, and still preserve,
And while I live a maid, thee will I serve."
   The fires blazed high upon the altar there,
While Emily was saying thus her prayer,
But suddenly she saw a sight most quaint,
For there, before her eyes, one fire went faint,
Then blazed again; and after that, anon,
The other fire was quenched, and so was gone.

And as it died it made a whistling sound,
As do wet branches burning on the ground,
And from the brands' ends there ran out, anon,
What looked like drops of blood, and many a one;
At which so much aghast was Emily
That she was near dazed, and began to cry,
For she knew naught of what it signified;
But only out of terror thus she cried
And wept, till it was pitiful to hear.
But thereupon Diana did appear,
With bow in hand, like any right huntress,
And said: "My daughter, leave this heaviness.
Among the high gods it has been affirmed,
And by eternal written word confirmed,
That you shall be the wife of one of those
Who bear for you so many cares and woes;
But unto which of them I may not tell.
I can no longer tarry, so farewell.
The fires that on my altar burn incense
Should tell you everything, ere you go hence,
Of what must come of love in this your case."

     And with that word the arrows of the chase
The goddess carried clattered and did ring,
And forth she went in mystic vanishing;
At which this Emily astonished was,
And said she then: "Ah, what means this, alas!
I put myself in thy protection here,
Diana, and at thy disposal dear."

     And home she wended, then, the nearest way.
This is the purport; there's no more to say.

     At the next hour of Mars, and following this,
Arcita to the temple walked, that is
Devoted to fierce Mars, to sacrifice
With all the ceremonies, pagan-wise.
With sobered heart and high devotion, on
This wise, right thus he said his orison.

     "O mighty god that in the regions cold
Of Thrace art honoured, where thy lordships hold,
And hast in every realm and every land
The reins of battle in thy guiding hand,
And givest fortune as thou dost devise,
Accept of me my pious sacrifice.
If so it be that my youth may deserve,

And that my strength be worthy found to serve
Thy godhead, and be numbered one of thine,
Then pray I thee for ruth on pain that's mine.
For that same pain and even that hot fire
Wherein thou once did'st burn with deep desire,
When thou did'st use the marvelous beauty
Of fair young wanton Venus, fresh and free,
And had'st her in thine arms and at thy will
(Howbeit with thee, once, all the chance fell ill,
And Vulcan caught thee in his net, whenas
He found thee lying with his wife, alas!)—
For that same sorrow that was in thy heart,
Have pity, now, upon my pains that smart.
I'm young, and little skilled, as knowest thou,
With love more hurt and much more broken now
Than ever living creature was, I'm sure;
For she who makes me all this woe endure,
Whether I float or sink cares not at all,
And ere she'll hear with mercy when I call,
I must by prowess win her in this place;
And well I know, too, without help and grace
Of thee, my human strength shall not avail.
Then help me, lord, tomorrow not to fail,
For sake of that same fire that once burned thee,
The which consuming fire so now burns me;
And grant, tomorrow, I have victory.
Mine be the toil, and thine the whole glory!
Thy sovereign temple will I honour most
Of any spot, and toil and count no cost
To pleasure thee and in thy craft have grace,
And in thy fane my banner will I place,
And all the weapons of my company;
And evermore, until the day I die,
Eternal fire shalt thou before thee find.
Moreover, to this vow myself I bind:
My beard, my hair that ripples down so long,
That never yet has felt the slightest wrong
Of razor or of shears, to thee I'll give,
And be thy loyal servant while I live.
Now, lord, have pity on my sorrows sore;
Give me the victory. I ask no more."

  With ended prayer of Arcita the young,
The rings that on the temple door were hung,

And even the doors themselves, rattled so fast
That this Arcita found himself aghast.
The fires blazed high upon the altar bright,
Until the entire temple shone with light;
And a sweet odour rose up from the ground;
And Arcita whirled then his arm around,
And yet more incense on the fire he cast,
And did still further rites; and at the last
The armour of God Mars began to ring,
And with that sound there came a murmuring,
Low and uncertain, saying: "Victory!"
For which he gave Mars honour and glory.
And thus in joy and hope, which all might dare,
Arcita to his lodging then did fare,
Fain of the fight as fowl is of the sun.

    But thereupon such quarrelling was begun,
From this same granting, in the heaven above,
'Twixt lovely Venus, goddess of all love,
And Mars, the iron god armipotent,
That Jove toiled hard to make a settlement;
Until the sallow Saturn, calm and cold,
Who had so many happenings known of old,
Found from his full experience the art
To satisfy each party and each part.
For true it is, age has great advantage;
Experience and wisdom come with age;
Men may the old out-run, but not out-wit.
Thus Saturn, though it scarcely did befit
His nature so to do, devised a plan
To quiet all the strife, and thus began:

    "Now my dear daughter Venus," quoth Saturn,
"My course, which has so wide a way to turn,
Has power more than any man may know.
Mine is the drowning in the sea below;
Mine is the dungeon underneath the moat;
Mine is the hanging and strangling by the throat;
Rebellion, and the base crowd's murmuring,
The groaning and the private poisoning,
And vengeance and amercement—all are mine,
While yet I dwell within the Lion's sign.
Mine is the ruining of all high halls,
And tumbling down of towers and of walls
Upon the miner and the carpenter.

I struck down Samson, that pillar shaker;
And mine are all the maladies so cold,
The treasons dark, the machinations old;
My glance is father of all pestilence.
Now weep no more. I'll see, with diligence,
That Palamon, who is your own true knight,
Shall have his lady, as you hold is right.
Though Mars may help his man, yet none the less
Between you two there must come sometime peace,
And though you be not of one temperament,
Causing each day such violent dissent,
I am your grandsire and obey your will;
Weep then no more, your pleasure I'll fulfill."
  Now will I cease to speak of gods above,
Of Mars and Venus, goddess of all love,
And tell you now, as plainly as I can,
The great result, for which I first began.

Explicit tercia pars.
Sequitur pars quarta.

Great was the fête in Athens on that day,
And too, the merry season of the May
Gave everyone such joy and such pleasance
That all that Monday they'd but joust and dance,
Or spend the time in Venus' high service.
But for the reason that they must arise
Betimes, to see the heralded great fight,
All they retired to early rest that night.
And on the morrow, when that day did spring,
Of horse and harness, noise and clattering,
There was enough in hostelries about.
And to the palace rode full many a rout
Of lords, bestriding steeds and on palfreys.
There could you see adjusting of harness,
So curious and so rich, and wrought so well
Of goldsmiths' work, embroidery, and of steel;
The shields, the helmets bright, the gay trappings,
The gold-hewn casques, the coats-of-arms, the rings,
The lords in vestments rich, on their coursers,
Knights with their retinues and also squires;
The rivetting of spears, the helm-buckling,
The strapping of the shields and thong-lacing—
In their great need, not one of them was idle;

The frothing steeds, champing the golden bridle,
And the quick smiths, and armourers also,
With file and hammer spurring to and fro;
Yeoman, and peasants with short staves were out,
Crowding as thick as they could move about;
Pipes, trumpets, kettledrums, and clarions,
That in the battle sound such grim summons;
The palace full of people, up and down,
Here three, there ten, debating the renown
And questioning about these Theban knights,
Some put it thus, some said, "It's so by rights."
Some held with him who had the great black beard,
Some with the bald-heads, some with the thick-haired;
Some said, "He looks grim, and he'll fight like hate;
He has an axe of twenty pound in weight."
And thus the hall was full of gossiping
Long after the bright sun began to spring.

   The mighty Theseüs, from sleep awakened
By songs and all the noise that never slackened,
Kept yet the chamber of this rich palace,
Till the two Theban knights, with equal grace
And honour, were ushered in with flourish fitting.
Duke Theseüs was at a window sitting,
Arrayed as he were god upon a throne.
Then pressed the people thitherward full soon,
To see him and to do him reverence,
Aye, and to hear commands of sapience.

   A herald on a scaffold cried out "Ho!"
Till all the people's noise was stilled; and so,
When he observed that all were fallen still,
He then proclaimed the mighty ruler's will.

   "The duke our lord, full wise and full discreet,
Holds that it were but wanton waste to meet
And fight, these gentle folk, all in the guise
Of mortal battle in this enterprise.
Wherefore, in order that no man may die,
He does his earlier purpose modify.
No man, therefore, on pain of loss of life,
Shall any arrow, pole-axe, or short knife
Send into lists in any wise, or bring;
Nor any shortened sword, for point-thrusting,
Shall a man draw, or bear it by his side.
Nor shall a knight against opponent ride,

Save one full course, with any sharp-ground spear;
Unhorsed, a man may thrust with any gear.
And he that's overcome, should this occur,
Shall not be slain, but brought to barrier,
Whereof there shall be one on either side;
Let him be forced to go there and abide.
And if by chance the leader there must go,
Of either side, or slay his equal foe,
No longer, then, shall tourneying endure.
God speed you; go forth now, and lay on sure.
With long sword and with maces fight your fill.
Go now your ways; this is the lord duke's will."
    The voices of the people rent the skies,
Such was the uproar of their merry cries:
"Now God save such a lord, who is so good
He will not have destruction of men's blood!"
Up start the trumpets and make melody.
And to the lists rode forth the company,
In marshalled ranks, throughout the city large,
All hung with cloth of gold, and not with serge.
Full like a lord this noble duke did ride,
With the two Theban knights on either side;
And, following, rode the queen and Emily,
And, after, came another company
Of one and other, each in his degree.
And thus they went throughout the whole city,
And to the lists they came, all in good time.
The day was not yet fully come to prime
When throned was Theseüs full rich and high,
And Queen Hippolyta and Emily,
While other ladies sat in tiers about.
Into the seats then pressed the lesser rout.
And westward, through the gate of Mars, right hearty,
Arcita and the hundred of his party
With banner red is entering anon;
And in that self-same moment, Palamon
Is under Venus, eastward in that place,
With banner white, and resolute of face.
In all the world, searching it up and down,
So equal were they all, from heel to crown,
There were no two such bands in any way.
For there was no man wise enough to say
How either had of other advantage

In high repute, or in estate, or age,
So even were they chosen, as I guess.
And in two goodly ranks they did then dress.
And when the name was called of every one,
That cheating in their number might be none,
Then were the gates closed, and the cry rang loud:
"Now do your devoir, all you young knights proud!"
  The heralds cease their spurring up and down;
Now ring the trumpets as the charge is blown;
And there's no more to say, for east and west
Two hundred spears are firmly laid in rest;
And the sharp spurs are thrust, now, into side.
Now see men who can joust and who can ride!
Now shivered are the shafts on bucklers thick;
One feels through very breast-bone the spear's prick;
Lances are flung full twenty feet in height;
Out flash the swords like silver burnished bright.
Helmets are hewed, the lacings ripped and shred;
Out bursts the blood, gushing in stern streams red.
With mighty maces bones are crushed in joust.
One through the thickest throng begins to thrust.
There strong steeds stumble now, and down goes all.
One rolls beneath their feet as rolls a ball.
One flails about with club, being overthrown,
Another, on a mailed horse, rides him down.
One through the body's hurt, and haled, for aid.
Spite of his struggles, to the barricade,
As compact was, and there he must abide;
Another's captured by the other side.
At times Duke Theseüs orders them to rest,
To eat a bite and drink what each likes best.
And many times that day those Thebans two
Met in the fight and wrought each other woe;
Unhorsed each has the other on that day.
No tigress in the vale of Galgophey,[4]
Whose little whelp is stolen in the light,
Is cruel to the hunter as Arcite
For jealousy is cruel to Palamon;
Nor in Belmarie, when the hunt is on
Is there a lion, wild for want of food,
That of his prey desires so much the blood

---

4. Probably the vale of Gargaphie, where Actæon was turned into a stag.

As Palamon the death of Arcite there.
Their jealous blows fall on their helmets fair;
Out leaps the blood and makes their two sides red.
    But sometime comes the end of every deed;
And ere the sun had sunk to rest in gold,
The mighty King Emetrëus did hold
This Palamon, as he fought with Arcite,
And made his sword deep in the flesh to bite;
And by the force of twenty men he's made,
Unyielded, to withdraw to barricade.
And, trying hard to rescue Palamon,
The mighty King Lycurgus is borne down;
And King Emetrëus, for all his strength,
Is hurled out of the saddle a sword's length,
So hits out Palamon once more, or ere
(But all for naught) he's brought to barrier.
His hardy heart may now avail him naught;
He must abide there now, being fairly caught
By force of arms, as by provision known.
    Who sorrows now but woeful Palamon,
Who may no more advance into the fight?
And when Duke Thesëus had seen this sight,
Unto the warriors fighting, every one,
He cried out: "Hold! No more! For it is done!
Now will I prove true judge, of no party.
Theban Arcita shall have Emily,
Who, by his fortune, has her fairly won."
    And now a noise of people is begun
For joy of this, so loud and shrill withal,
It seems as if the very lists will fall.
    But now, what can fair Venus do above?
What says she now? What does this queen of love
But weep so fast, for thwarting of her will,
Her tears upon the lists begin to spill.
She said: "Now am I shamed and over-flung."
But Saturn said: "My daughter, hold your tongue.
Mars has his will, his knight has all his boon,
And, by my head, you shall be eased, and soon."
    The trumpeters and other minstrelsy,
The heralds that did loudly yell and cry,
Were at their best for joy of Arcita.
But hear me further while I tell you—ah!—
The miracle that happened there anon.

This fierce Arcita doffs his helmet soon,
And mounted on a horse, to show his face,
He spurs from end to end of that great place,
Looking aloft to gaze on Emily;
And she cast down on him a friendly eye
(For women, generally speaking, go
Wherever Fortune may her favor show)
And she was fair to see, and held his heart.
But from the ground infernal furies start,
From Pluto sent, at instance of Saturn,
Whereat his horse, for fear, began to turn
And leap aside, all suddenly falling there;
And Arcita before he could beware
Was pitched upon the ground, upon his head,
And lay there, moving not, as he were dead,
His chest crushed in upon the saddle-bow.
And black he lay as ever coal, or crow,
So ran the surging blood into his face.
Anon they carried him from out that place,
With heavy hearts, to Theseüs' palace.
There was his harness cut away, each lace,
And swiftly was he laid upon a bed,
For he was yet alive and some words said,
Crying and calling after Emily.
    Duke Theseüs, with all his company,
Is come again to Athens, his city,
With joyous heart and great festivity.
And though sore grieved for this unhappy fall,
He would not cast a blight upon them all.
Men said, too, that Arcita should not die,
But should be healed of all his injury.
And of another thing they were right fain,
Which was, that of them all no one was slain,
Though each was sore, and hurt, and specially one
Who'd got a lance-head thrust through his breastbone.
For other bruises, wounds and broken arms,
Some of them carried salves and some had charms;
And medicines of many herbs, and sage
They drank, to keep their limbs from hemorrhage.
In all of which this duke, as he well can,
Now comforts and now honours every man,
And makes a revelry the livelong night
For all these foreign lords, as was but right.

Nor was there held any discomfiting,
Save from the jousts and from the tourneying.
For truly, there had been no cause for shame,
Since being thrown is fortune of the game;
Nor is it, to be led to barrier,
Unyielded, and by twenty knights' power,
One man alone, surrounded by the foe,
Driven by arms, and dragged out, heel and toe,
And with his courser driven forth with staves
Of men on foot, yeomen and serving knaves—
All this imputes to one no kind of vice,
And no man may bring charge of cowardice.

For which, anon, Duke Theseus bade cry,
To still all rancour and all keen envy,
The worth, as well of one side as the other,
As equal both, and each the other's brother;
And gave them gifts according to degree,
And held a three days' feast, right royally;
And then convoyed these kings upon their road
For one full day, and to them honour showed.
And home went every man on his right way.
There was naught more but "Farewell" and "Good-day."
I'll say no more of war, but turn upon
My tale of Arcita and Palamon.

Swells now Arcita's breast until the sore
Increases near his heart yet more and more.
The clotted blood, in spite of all leech-craft,
Rots in his bulk, and there it must be left,
Since no device of skillful blood-letting,
Nor drink of herbs, can help him in this thing.
The power expulsive, or virtue animal
Called from its use the virtue natural,
Could not the poison void, nor yet expel.
The tubes of both his lungs began to swell,
And every tissue in his breast, and down,
Is foul with poison and all rotten grown.
He gains in neither, in his strife to live,
By vomiting or taking laxative;
All is so broken in that part of him,
Nature retains no vigour there, nor vim.
And certainly, where Nature will not work,
It's farewell physic, bear the man to kirk!
The sum of all is, Arcita must die,

And so he sends a word to Emily,
And Palamon, who was his cousin dear;
And then he said to them as you shall hear.
   "Naught may the woeful spirit in my heart
Declare one point of how my sorrows smart
To you, my lady, whom I love the most;
But I bequeath the service of my ghost
To you above all others, this being sure
Now that my life may here no more endure.
Alas, the woe! Alas, the pain so strong
That I for you have suffered, and so long!
Alas for death! Alas, my Emily!
Alas, the parting of our company!
Alas, my heart's own queen! Alas, my wife!
My soul's dear lady, ender of my life!
What is this world? What asks a man to have?
Now with his love, now in the cold dark grave
Alone, with never any company.
Farewell, my sweet foe! O my Emily!
Oh, take me in your gentle arms, I pray,
For love of God, and hear what I will say.
   "I have here, with my cousin Palamon,
Had strife and rancour many a day that's gone,
For love of you and for my jealousy.
May Jove so surely guide my soul for me,
To speak about a lover properly,
With all the circumstances, faithfully—
That is to say, truth, honour, and knighthood,
Wisdom, humility and kinship good,
And generous soul and all the lover's art—
So now may Jove have in my soul his part
As in this world, right now, I know of none
So worthy to be loved as Palamon,
Who serves you and will do so all his life.
And if you ever should become a wife,
Forget not Palamon, the noble man."
   And with that word his speech to fail began,
For from his feet up to his breast had come
The cold of death, making his body numb.
And furthermore, from his two arms the strength
Was gone out, now, and he was lost, at length.
Only the intellect, and nothing more,
Which dwelt within his heart so sick and sore,

Began to fail now, when the heart felt death,
And his eyes darkened, and he failed of breath.
But on his lady turned he still his eye,
And his last word was, "Mercy, Emily!"
His spirit changed its house and went away.
As I was never there, I cannot say
Where; so I stop, not being a soothsayer;
Of souls here naught shall I enregister;
Nor do I wish their notions, now, to tell
Who write of them, though they say where they dwell.
Arcita's cold; Mars guides his soul on high;
Now will I speak forthwith of Emily.

    Shrieked Emily and howled now Palamon,
Till Thesëus his sister took, anon,
And bore her, swooning, from the corpse away.
How shall it help, to dwell the livelong day
In telling how she wept both night and morrow?
For in like cases women have such sorrow,
When their good husband from their side must go,
And, for the greater part, they take on so,
Or else they fall into such malady
That, at the last, and certainly, they die.

    Infinite were the sorrows and the tears
Of all old folk and folk of tender years
Throughout the town, at death of this Theban;
For him there wept the child and wept the man;
So great a weeping was not, 'tis certain,
When Hector was brought back, but newly slain,
To Troy. Alas, the sorrow that was there!
Tearing of cheeks and rending out of hair.
"Oh why will you be dead," these women cry,
"Who had of gold enough, and Emily?"
No man might comfort then Duke Thesëus,
Excepting his old father, Ægëus,
Who knew this world's mutations, and men's own.
Since he had seen them changing up and down,
Joy after woe, and woe from happiness:
He showed them, by example, the process.

    "Just as there never died a man," quoth he,
"But he had lived on earth in some degree,
Just so there never lived a man," he said,
"In all this world, but must be sometime dead.
This world is but a thoroughfare of woe,

And we are pilgrims passing to and fro;
Death is the end of every worldly sore."
And after this, he told them yet much more
To that effect, all wisely to exhort
The people that they should find some comfort.
  Duke Thesëus now considered and with care
What place of burial he should prepare
For good Arcita, as it best might be,
And one most worthy of his high degree.
And at the last concluded, hereupon,
That where at first Arcita and Palamon
Had fought for love, with no man else between,
There, in that very grove, so sweet and green,
Where he mused on his amorous desires
Complaining of love's hot and flaming fires,
He'd make a pyre and have the funeral
Accomplished there, and worthily in all.
And so he gave command to hack and hew
The ancient oaks, and lay them straight and true
In split lengths that would kindle well and burn.
His officers, with sure swift feet, they turn
And ride away to do his whole intent.
And after this Duke Theseus straightway sent
For a great bier, and had it all o'er-spread
With cloth of gold, the richest that he had.
Arcita clad he, too, in cloth of gold;
White gloves were on his hands where they did fold;
Upon his head a crown of laurel green,
And near his hand a sword both bright and keen.
Then, having bared the dead face on the bier,
The duke so wept, 'twas pitiful to hear.
And, so that folk might see him, one and all,
When it was day he brought them to the hall,
Which echoed of their wailing cries anon.
  Then came this woeful Theban, Palamon,
With fluttery beard and matted, ash-strewn hair,
All in black clothes wet with his tears; and there,
Surpassing all in weeping, Emily,
The most affected of the company.
And so that every several rite should be
Noble and rich, and suiting his degree,
Duke Thesëus commanded that they bring
Three horses, mailed in steel all glittering,

And covered with Arcita's armour bright.
Upon these stallions, which were large and white,
There rode three men, whereof one bore the shield,
And one the spear he'd known so well to wield;
The third man bore his Turkish bow, nor less
Of burnished gold the quiver than harness;
And forth they slowly rode, with mournful cheer,
Toward that grove, as you shall further hear.
     The noblest Greeks did gladly volunteer
To bear upon their shoulders that great bier,
With measured pace and eyes gone red and wet,
Through all the city, by the wide main street,
Which was all spread with black, and, wondrous high,
Covered with this same cloth were houses nigh.
Upon the right hand went old Ægëus,
And on the other side Duke Thesëus,
With vessels in their hands, of gold right fine,
All filled with honey, milk, and blood, and wine;
And Palamon with a great company;
And after that came woeful Emily,
With fire in hands, as use was, to ignite
The sacrifice and set the pyre alight.
     Great labour and full great apparelling
Went to the service and the fire-making,
For to the skies that green pyre reached its top,
And twenty fathoms did the arms out-crop,
That is to say, the branches went so wide.
Full many a load of straw they did provide.
But how the fire was made to climb so high;
Or what names all the different trees went by.
As oak, fir, birch, asp, alder, poplar, holm,
Willow, plane, ash, box, chestnut, linden, elm,
Laurel, thorn, maple, beech, yew, dogwood tree,
Or how they were felled, sha'n't be told by me.
Nor how the wood-gods scampered up and down,
Driven from homes that they had called their own,
Wherein they'd lived so long at ease, in peace,
The nymphs, the fauns, the hamadryades;
Nor how the beasts, for fear, and the birds, all
Fled, when that ancient wood began to fall;
Nor how aghast the ground was in the light,
Not being used to seeing the sun so bright;
Nor how the fire was started first with straw,

And then with dry wood, riven thrice by saw,
And then with green wood and with spicery,
And then with cloth of gold and jewellery,
And garlands hanging with full many a flower,
And myrrh, and incense, sweet as rose in bower;
Nor how Arcita lies among all this,
Nor what vast wealth about his body is;
Nor how this Emily, as was their way,
Lighted the sacred funeral fire, that day,
Nor how she swooned when men built up the fire,
Nor what she said, nor what was her desire;
No, nor what gems men on the fire then cast,
When the white flame went high and burned so fast;
Nor how one cast his shield, and one his spear,
And some their vestments, on that burning bier,
With cups of wine, and cups of milk, and blood,
Into that flame, which burned as wild-fire would;
Nor how the Greeks, in one huge wailing rout,
Rode slowly three times all the fire about,
Upon the left hand, with a loud shouting,
And three times more, with weapons clattering,
While thrice the women there raised up a cry;
Nor how was homeward led sad Emily;
Nor how Arcita burned to ashes cold;
Nor aught of how the lichwake they did hold
All that same night, nor how the Greeks did play
Who, naked, wrestled best, with oil anointed,
Nor who best bore himself in deeds appointed.
I will not even tell how they were gone
Home, into Athens, when the play was done;
But briefly to the point, now, will I wend
And make of this, my lengthy tale, an end.

   With passing in their length of certain years,
All put by was the mourning and the tears
Of Greeks, as by one general assent;
And then it seems there was a parliament
At Athens, upon certain points in case;
Among the which points spoken of there was
The ratifying of alliances
That should hold Thebes from all defiances.
Whereat this noble Theseüs, anon,
Invited there the gentle Palamon,
Not telling him what was the cause, and why;

But in his mourning clothes, and sorrowfully,
He came upon that bidding, so say I.
And then Duke Thesëus sent for Emily.
When they were seated and was hushed the place,
And Thesëus had mused a little space,
Ere any word came from his full wise breast,
His two eyes fixed on whoso pleased him best,
Then with a sad face sighed he deep and still,
And after that began to speak his will.

"The Primal Mover and the Cause above,
When first He forged the goodly chain of love,
Great the effect, and high was His intent;
Well knew He why, and what thereof He meant;
For with that goodly chain of love He bound
The fire, the air, the water, and dry ground
In certain bounds, the which they might not flee;
That same First Cause and Mover," then quoth he,
"Has stablished in this base world, up and down,
A certain length of days to call their own
For all that are engendered in this place,
Beyond the which not one day may they pace,
Though yet all may that certain time abridge;
Authority there needs none, I allege,
For it is well proved by experience,
Save that I please to clarify my sense.
Then may men by this order well discern
This Mover to be stable and eterne.
Well may man know, unless he be a fool,
That every part derives but from the whole.
For Nature has not taken his being
From any part and portion of a thing,
But from a substance perfect, stable aye,
And so continuing till changed away.
And therefore, of His Wisdom's Providence,
Has He so well established ordinance
That species of all things and all progressions,
If they'd endure, it must be by successions,
Not being themselves eternal, 'tis no lie:
This may you understand and see by eye.

"Lo now, the oak, that has long nourishing
Even from the time that it begins to spring,
And has so long a life, as we may see,
Yet at the last all wasted is the tree.

"Consider, too, how even the hard stone
Under our feet we tread each day upon
Yet wastes it, as it lies beside the way.
And the broad river will be dry some day.
And great towns wane; we see them vanishing.
Thus may we see the end to everything.
   "Of man and woman just the same is true:
Needs must, in either season of the two,
That is to say, in youth or else in age,
All men perish, the king as well as page;
Some in their bed, and some in the deep sea,
And some in the wide field—as it may be;
There's naught will help; all go the same way. Aye,
Then may I say that everything must die.
Who causes this but Jupiter the King?
He is the Prince and Cause of everything,
Converting all back to that primal well
From which it was derived, 'tis sooth to tell.
And against this, for every thing alive,
Of any state, avails it not to strive.
   "Then is it wisdom, as it seems to me,
To make a virtue of necessity,
And calmly take what we may not eschew,
And specially that which to all is due.
Whoso would balk at aught, he does folly,
And thus rebels against His potency.
And certainly a man has most honour
In dying in his excellence and flower,
When he is certain of his high good name;
For then he gives to friend, and self, no shame.
And gladder ought a friend be of his death
When, in much honour, he yields up his breath,
Than when his name's grown feeble with old age;
For all forgotten, then, is his courage.
Hence it is best for all of noble name
To die when at the summit of their fame.
The contrary of this is wilfulness.
Why do we grumble? Why have heaviness
That good Arcita, chivalry's fair flower,
Is gone, with honour, in his best-lived hour.
Out of the filthy prison of this life?
Why grumble here his cousin and his wife
About his welfare, who loved them so well?

Can he thank them? Nay, God knows, not! Nor tell
How they his soul and their own selves offend,
Though yet they may not their desires amend.

"What may I prove by this long argument
Save that we all turn to merriment,
After our grief, and give Jove thanks for grace.
And so, before we go from out this place,
I counsel that we make, of sorrows two,
One perfect joy, lasting for aye, for you;
And look you now, where most woe is herein,
There will we first amend it and begin.

"Sister," quoth he, "you have my full consent,
With the advice of this my Parliament,
That gentle Palamon, your own true knight,
Who serves you well with will and heart and might,
And so has ever, since you knew him first—
That you shall, of your grace, allay his thirst
By taking him for husband and for lord:
Lend me your hand, for this is our accord.
Let now your woman's pity make him glad.
For he is a king's brother's son, by gad;
And though he were a poor knight bachelor,
Since he has served you for so many a year,
And borne for you so great adversity,
This ought to weigh with you, it seems to me,
For mercy ought to dominate mere right."

Then said he thus to Palamon the knight:
"I think there needs but little sermoning
To make you give consent, now, to this thing.
Come near, and take your lady by the hand."

Between them, then, was tied that nuptial band,
Which is called matrimony or marriage,
By all the council and the baronage.
And thus, in all bliss and with melody,
Has Palamon now wedded Emily.
And God, Who all this universe has wrought,
Send him His love, who has it dearly bought.
For now has Palamon, in all things, wealth,
Living in bliss, in riches, and in health;
And Emily loved him so tenderly,
And he served her so well and faithfully,
That never word once marred their happiness,
No jealousy, nor other such distress.

Thus ends now Palamon and Emily;
And may God save all this fair company! Amen.

HERE ENDS THE KNIGHT'S TALE

THE MILLER'S PROLOGUE

The Words between the Host and the Miller

Now when the knight had thus his story told,
In all the rout there was nor young nor old
But said it was a noble story, well
Worthy to be kept in mind to tell;
And specially the gentle folk, each one.
Our host, he laughed and swore, "So may I run,
But this goes well; unbuckled is the mail;[1]
Let's see now who can tell another tale:
For certainly the game is well begun.
Now shall you tell, sir monk, if't can be done,
Something with which to pay for the knight's tale."

    The miller, who with drinking was all pale,
So that unsteadily on his horse he sat,
He would not take off either hood or hat,
Nor wait for any man, in courtesy,
But all in Pilate's voice began to cry,
And by the Arms and Blood and Bones he swore,
"I have a noble story in my store,
With which I will requite the good knight's tale."

    Our host saw, then, that he was drunk with ale,
And said to him: "Wait, Robin, my dear brother,
Some better man shall tell us first another:
Submit and let us work on profitably."

    "Now by God's soul," cried he, "that will not I!
For I will speak, or else I'll go my way."

    Our host replied: "Tell on, then, till doomsday!
You are a fool, your wit is overcome."

    "Now hear me," said the miller, "all and some!
But first I make a protestation round

---

1. Mail (male, in the original): a bag.

That I'm quite drunk, I know it by my sound:
And therefore, if I slander or mis-say,
Blame it on ale of Southwark, so I pray;
For I will tell a legend and a life
Both of a carpenter and of his wife,
And how a scholar set[2] the good wright's cap."

The reeve replied and said: "Oh, shut your trap,
Let be your ignorant drunken ribaldry!
It is a sin, and further, great folly
To asperse any man, or him defame,
And, too, to bring upon a man's wife shame.
There are enough of other things to say."

This drunken miller spoke on in his way,
And said: "Oh, but my dear brother Oswald,
The man who has no wife is no cuckold.
But I say not, thereby, that you are one:
Many good wives there are, as women run,
And ever a thousand good to one that's bad,
As well you know yourself, unless you're mad.
Why are you angry with my story's cue?
I have a wife, begad, as well as you,
Yet I'd not, for the oxen of my plow,
Take on my shoulders more than is enow,
By judging of myself that I am one;
I will believe full well that I am none.
A husband must not be inquisitive
Of God, nor of his wife, while she's alive.
So long as he may find God's plenty there,
For all the rest he need not greatly care."

What should I say, except this miller rare
He would forgo his talk for no man there,
But told his churlish tale in his own way:
I think I'll here re-tell it, if I may.
And therefore, every gentle soul, I pray
That for God's love you'll hold not what I say
Evilly meant, but that I must rehearse,
All of their tales, the better and the worse,
Or else prove false to some of my design.
Therefore, who likes not this, let him, in fine,
Turn over page and choose another tale:
For he shall find enough, both great and small,

2. Set: to set a cap, i.e., to befool, to make a cuckold of.

Of stories touching on gentility,
And holiness, and on morality;
And blame not me if you do choose amiss.
The miller was a churl, you well know this;
So was the reeve, and many another more,
And ribaldry they told from plenteous store.
Be then advised, and hold me free from blame;
Men should not be too serious at a game.

HERE ENDS THE PROLOGUE

THE MILLER'S TALE

Once on a time was dwelling in Oxford
A wealthy lout who took in guests to board,
And of his craft he was a carpenter.
A poor scholar was lodging with him there,
Who'd learned the arts, but all his phantasy
Was turned to study of astrology;
And knew a certain set of theorems
And could find out by various stratagems,
If men but asked of him in certain hours
When they should have a drought or else have showers,
Or if men asked of him what should befall
To anything—I cannot reckon them all.
This clerk was called the clever Nicholas;
Of secret loves he knew and their solace;
And he kept counsel, too, for he was sly
And meek as any maiden passing by.
He had a chamber in that hostelry,
And lived alone there, without company,
All garnished with sweet herbs of good repute;
And he himself sweet-smelling as the root
Of licorice, valerian, or setwall.
His *Almagest*, and books both great and small,
His astrolabe, belonging to his art,
His algorism stones[3]—all laid apart
On shelves that ranged beside his lone bed's head;
His press was covered with a cloth of red.

---

3. Algorism stones: counting stones.

And over all there lay a psaltery
Whereon he made an evening's melody,
Playing so sweetly that the chamber rang;
And *Angelus ad virginem* he sang;
And after that he warbled the *King's Note:*[4]
Often in good voice was his merry throat.
And thus this gentle clerk his leisure spends
Supported by some income and his friends.

    This carpenter had lately wed a wife
Whom he loved better than he loved his life;
And she was come to eighteen years of age.
Jealous he was and held her close in cage.
For she was wild and young and he was old,
And deemed himself as like to be cuckold.
He knew not Cato, for his lore was rude:
That vulgar man should wed similitude.
A man should wed according to estate,
For youth and age are often in debate.
But now, since he had fallen in the snare,
He must endure, like other folk, his care.

    Fair was this youthful wife, and therewithal
As weasel's was her body slim and small.
A girdle wore she, barred and striped, of silk.
An apron, too, as white as morning milk
About her loins, and full of many a gore;
White was her smock, embroidered all before
And even behind, her collar round about,
Of coal-black silk, on both sides, in and out;
The strings of the white cap upon her head
Were, like her collar, black silk worked with thread;
Her fillet was of wide silk worn full high:
And certainly she had a lickerish eye.
She'd thinned out carefully her eyebrows two,
And they were arched and black as any sloe.
She was a far more pleasant thing to see
Than is the newly budded young pear-tree;
And softer than the wool is on a wether.
Down from her girdle hung a purse of leather,
Tasselled with silk, with latten beading sown.
In all this world, searching it up and down,
So gay a little doll, I well believe,

---

4. King's note: the name of a tune.

Or such a wench, there's no man can conceive.
Far brighter was the brilliance of her hue
Than in the Tower the gold coins minted new.
And songs came shrilling from her pretty head
As from a swallow's sitting on a shed.
Therewith she'd dance too, and could play and sham
Like any kid or calf about its dam.
Her mouth was sweet as bragget or as mead
Or hoard of apples laid in hay or weed.
Skittish she was as is a pretty colt,
Tall as a staff and straight as cross-bow bolt.
A brooch she wore upon her collar low,
As broad as boss of buckler did it show;
Her shoes laced up to where a girl's legs thicken.
She was a primrose, and a tender chicken
For any lord to lay upon his bed,
Or yet for any good yeoman to wed.

   Now, sir, and then, sir, so befell the case,
That on a day this clever Nicholas
Fell in with this young wife to toy and play,
The while her husband was down Osney way,
Clerks being as crafty as the best of us;
And unperceived he caught her by the puss,
Saying: "Indeed, unless I have my will,
For secret love of you, sweetheart, I'll spill."
And held her hard about the hips, and how!—
And said: "O darling, love me, love me now,
Or I shall die, and pray you God may save!"

   And she leaped as a colt does in the trave,[5]
And with her head she twisted fast away,
And said: "I will not kiss you, by my fay!
Why, let go," cried she, "let go, Nicholas!
Or I will call for help and cry 'alas!'
Do take your hands away, for courtesy!"

   This Nicholas for mercy then did cry,
And spoke so well, importuned her so fast
That she her love did grant him at the last,
And swore her oath, by Saint Thomas of Kent,
That she would be at his command, content,
As soon as opportunity she could spy.
   "My husband is so full of jealousy,

---

5. Trave: a frame for confining a horse or colt for shoeing.

Unless you will await me secretly,
I know I'm just as good as dead," said she.
"You must keep all quite hidden in this case."

  "Nay, thereof worry not," said Nicholas,
"A clerk has lazily employed his while
If he cannot a carpenter beguile."

  And thus they were agreed, and then they swore
To wait a while, as I have said before.
When Nicholas had done thus every whit
And patted her about the loins a bit,
He kissed her sweetly, took his psaltery,
And played it fast and made a melody.

  Then fell it thus, that to the parish kirk,
The Lord Christ Jesus' own works for to work,
This good wife went, upon a holy day;
Her forehead shone as bright as does the May,
So well she'd washed it when she left off work.

  Now there was of that church a parish clerk
Whose name was (as folk called him) Absalom.
Curled was his hair, shining like gold, and from
His head spread fanwise in a thick bright mop;
'Twas parted straight and even on the top;
His cheek was red, his eyes grey as a goose;
With Saint Paul's windows cut upon his shoes,
He stood in red hose fitting famously.
And he was clothed full well and properly
All in a coat of blue, in which were let
Holes for the lacings, which were fairly set.
And over all he wore a fine surplice
As white as ever hawthorn spray, and nice.
A merry lad he was, so God me save,
And well could he let blood, cut hair, and shave,
And draw a deed or quitclaim, as might chance.
In twenty manners could he trip and dance,
After the school that reigned in Oxford, though,
And with his two legs swinging to and fro;
And he could play upon a violin;
Thereto he sang in treble voice and thin;
And as well could he play on his guitar.
In all the town no inn was, and no bar,
That he'd not visited to make good cheer,
Especially were lively barmaids there.
But, truth to tell, he was a bit squeamish

Of farting and of language haughtyish.
  This Absalom, who was so light and gay,
Went with a censer on the holy day,
Censing the wives like an enthusiast;
And on them many a loving look he cast,
Especially on this carpenter's goodwife.
To look at her he thought a merry life,
She was so pretty, sweet, and lickerous.
I dare well say, if she had been a mouse
And he a cat, he would have mauled her some.
  This parish clerk, this lively Absalom
Had in his heart, now, such a love-longing
That from no wife took he an offering,
For courtesy, he said, he would take none.
The moon, when it was night, full brightly shone,
And his guitar did Absalom then take,
For in love-watching he'd intent to wake.
And forth he went, jolly and amorous,
Until he came unto the carpenter's house
A little after cocks began to crow;
And took his stand beneath a shot-window[6]
That was let into the good wood-wright's wall.
He sang then, in his pleasant voice and small,
"Oh now, dear lady, if your will it be,
I pray that you will have some ruth on me,"
The words in harmony with his string-plucking.
This carpenter awoke and heard him sing,
And called unto his wife and said, in sum:
"What, Alison! Do you hear Absalom,
Who plays and sings beneath our bedroom wall?"
  And she said to her husband, therewithal:
"Yes, God knows, John, I hear it, truth to tell."
  So this went on; what is there better than well?
From day to day this pretty Absalom
So wooed her he was woebegone therefrom.
He lay awake all night and all the day;
He combed his spreading hair and dressed him gay;
By go-betweens and agents, too, wooed he,
And swore her loyal page he'd ever be.
He sang as tremulously as nightingale;
He sent her sweetened wine and well-spiced ale

6. A window opening (or containing a division that opens) on a hinge.

And waffles piping hot out of the fire,
And, she being town-bred, mead for her desire.
For some are won by means of money spent,
And some by tricks, and some by long descent.
Once, to display his versatility,
He acted Herod on a scaffold high.

   But what availed it him in any case?
She was enamoured so of Nicholas
That Absalom might go and blow his horn;
He got naught for his labour but her scorn.
And thus she made of Absalom her ape,
And all his earnestness she made a jape.
For truth is in this proverb, and no lie,
Men say well thus: It's always he that's nigh
That makes the absent lover seem a sloth.
For now, though Absalom be wildly wroth,
Because he is so far out of her sight,
This handy Nicholas stands in his light.

   Now bear you well, you clever Nicholas!
For Absalom may wail and sing "Alas!"
And so it chanced that on a Saturday
This carpenter departed to Osney;
And clever Nicholas and Alison
Were well agreed to this effect: anon
This Nicholas should put in play a wile
The simple, jealous husband to beguile;
And if it chanced the game should go a-right,
She was to sleep within his arms all night,
For this was his desire, and hers also.
Presently then, and without more ado,
This Nicholas, no longer did he tarry,
But softly to his chamber did he carry
Both food and drink to last at least a day,
Saying that to her husband she should say—
If he should come to ask for Nicholas—
Why, she should say she knew not where he was,
For all day she'd not seen him, far or nigh;
She thought he must have got some malady,
Because in vain her maid would knock and call;
He'd answer not, whatever might befall.

   And so it was that all that Saturday
This Nicholas quietly in chamber lay,
And ate and slept, or did what pleased him best,

Till Sunday when the sun had gone to rest.
   This simple man with wonder heard the tale,
And marvelled what their Nicholas might ail,
And said: "I am afraid, by Saint Thomas,
That everything's not well with Nicholas.
God send he be not dead so suddenly!
This world is most unstable, certainly;
I saw, today, the corpse being borne to kirk
Of one who, but last Monday, was at work.
Go up," said he unto his boy anon,
"Call at his door, or knock there with a stone,
Learn how it is and boldly come tell me."
   The servant went up, then, right sturdily,
And at the chamber door, the while he stood,
He cried and knocked as any madman would—
"What! How! What do you, Master Nicholay?
How can you sleep through all the livelong day?"
   But all for naught, he never heard a word;
A hole he found, low down upon a board,
Through which the house cat had been wont to creep;
And to that hole he stooped, and through did peep,
And finally he ranged him in his sight.
This Nicholas sat gaping there, upright,
As if he'd looked too long at the new moon.
Downstairs he went and told his master soon
In what array he'd found this self-same man.
   This carpenter to cross himself began,
And said: "Now help us, holy Frideswide!
Little a man can know what shall betide.
This man is fallen, with his astromy,[7]
Into some madness or some agony;
I always feared that somehow this would be!
Men should not meddle in God's privity.
Aye, blessed always be the ignorant man,
Whose creed is all he ever has to scan!
So fared another clerk with astromy;
He walked into the meadows for to pry
Into the stars, to learn what should befall,
Until into a clay-pit he did fall;
He saw not that. But yet, by Saint Thomas,
I'm sorry for this clever Nicholas.

---

7. The carpenter's corruption.

He shall be scolded for his studying,
If not too late, by Jesus, Heaven's King!
    "Get me a staff, that I may pry before,
The while you, Robin, heave against the door.
We'll take him from this studying, I guess."
    And on the chamber door, then, he did press.
His servant was a stout lad, if a dunce,
And by the hasp he heaved it up at once;
Upon the floor that portal fell anon.
This Nicholas sat there as still as stone,
Gazing, with gaping mouth, straight up in air.
This carpenter thought he was in despair,
And took him by the shoulders, mightily,
And shook him hard, and cried out, vehemently:
"What! Nicholay! Why how now! Come, look down!
Awake, and think on Jesus' death and crown!
I cross you from all elves and magic wights!"
    And then the night-spell said he out, by rights,
At the four corners of the house about,
And at the threshold of the door, without:—
    "O Jesus Christ and good Saint Benedict,
Protect this house from all that may afflict,
For the night hag the white Paternoster!—
Where hast thou gone, Saint Peter's sister?"
And at the last this clever Nicholas
Began to sigh full sore, and said: "Alas!
Shall all the world be lost so soon again?"
    This carpenter replied: "What say you, then?
What! Think on God, as we do, men that swink."
    This Nicholas replied: "Go fetch me drink;
And afterward I'll tell you privately
A certain thing concerning you and me;
I'll tell it to no other man or men."
    This carpenter went down and came again,
And brought of potent ale a brimming quart;
And when each one of them had drunk his part,
Nicholas shut the door fast, and with that
He drew a seat and near the carpenter sat.
    He said: "Now, John, my good host, lief and dear,
You must upon your true faith swear, right here,
That to no man will you this word betray;
For it is Christ's own word that I will say,
And if you tell a man, you're ruined quite;

This punishment shall come to you, of right,
That if you're traitor you'll go mad—and should!"

"Nay, Christ forbid it, for His holy blood!"
Said then this simple man: "I am no blab,
Nor, though I say it, am I fond of gab.
Say what you will, I never will it tell
To child or wife, by Him that harried Hell!"

"Now, John," said Nicholas, "I will not lie;
But I've found out, from my astrology,
As I have looked upon the moon so bright,
That now, come Monday next, at nine of night,
Shall fall a rain so wildly mad as would
Have been, by half, greater than Noah's flood.
This world," he said, "in less time than an hour,
Shall all be drowned, so terrible is this shower;
Thus shall all mankind drown and lose all life."

This carpenter replied: "Alas, my wife!
And shall she drown? Alas, my Alison!"
For grief of this he almost fell. Anon
He said: "Is there no remedy in this case?"

"Why yes, good luck," said clever Nicholas,
"If you will work by counsel of the wise;
You must not act on what your wits advise.
For so says Solomon, and it's all true,
'Work by advice and thou shalt never rue.'
And if you'll act as counselled and not fail,
I undertake, without a mast or sail,
To save us all, aye you and her and me.
Haven't you heard of Noah, how saved was he,
Because Our Lord had warned him how to keep
Out of the flood that covered earth so deep?"

"Yes," said this carpenter, "long years ago."

"Have you not heard," asked Nicholas, "also
The sorrows of Noah and his fellowship
In getting his wife to go aboard the ship?
He would have rather, I dare undertake,
At that time, and for all the weather black,
That she had one ship for herself alone.
Therefore, do you know what would best be done?
This thing needs haste, and of a hasty thing
Men must not preach nor do long tarrying.

"Presently go, and fetch here to this inn
A kneading-tub, or brewing vat, and win

One each for us, but see that they are large,
Wherein we may swim out as in a barge,
And have therein sufficient food and drink
For one day only; that's enough, I think.
The water will dry up and flow away
About the prime of the succeeding day.
But Robin must not know of this, your knave,
And even Jill, your maid, I may not save;
Ask me not why, for though you do ask me,
I will not tell you of God's privity.
Suffice you, then, unless your wits are mad,
To have as great a grace as Noah had.
Your wife I shall not lose, there is no doubt,
Go, now, your way, and speedily get about,
But when you have, for you and her and me,
Procured these kneading-tubs, or beer-vats, three,
Then you shall hang them near the roof-tree high,
That no man our purveyance may espy.
And when you thus have done, as I have said,
And have put in our drink and meat and bread,
Also an axe to cut the ropes in two
When the flood comes, that we may float and go,
And cut a hole, high up, upon the gable,
Upon the garden side, over the stable,
That we may freely pass forth on our way
When the great rain and flood are gone that day—
Then shall you float as merrily, I'll stake,
As does the white duck after the white drake.
Then I will call, 'Ho, Alison! Ho, John!
Be cheery, for the flood will pass anon.'
And you will say, 'Hail, Master Nicholay!
Good morrow, I see you well, for it is day!'
And then shall we be barons all our life
Of all the world, like Noah and his wife.
    "But of one thing I warn you now, outright.
Be well advised, that on that very night
When we have reached our ships and got aboard,
Not one of us must speak or whisper word,
Nor call, nor cry, but sit in silent prayer;
For this is God's own bidding, hence—don't dare!
    "Your wife and you must hang apart, that in
The night shall come no chance for you to sin
Either in looking or in carnal deed.

These orders I have told you, go, God speed!
Tomorrow night, when all men are asleep,
Into our kneading-tubs will we three creep
And sit there, still, awaiting God's high grace.
Go, now, your way, I have no longer space
Of time to make a longer sermoning.
Men say thus: 'Send the wise and say no thing.'
You are so wise it needs not that I teach;
Go, save our lives, and that I do beseech."
    This silly carpenter went on his way.
Often he cried "Alas!" and "Welaway!"
And to his wife he told all, privately;
But she was better taught thereof than he
How all this rigmarole was to apply.
Nevertheless she acted as she'd die,
And said: "Alas! Go on your way anon,
Help us escape, or we are lost, each one;
I am your true and lawfully wedded wife;
Go, my dear spouse, and help to save our life."
    Lo, what a great thing is affection found!
Men die of imagination, I'll be bound,
So deep an imprint may the spirit take.
This hapless carpenter began to quake;
He thought now, verily, that he could see
Old Noah's flood come wallowing like the sea
To drown his Alison, his honey dear.
He wept, he wailed, he made but sorry cheer,
He sighed and made full many a sob and sough.
He went and got himself a kneading-trough
And, after that, two tubs he somewhere found
And to his dwelling privately sent round,
And hung them near the roof, all secretly.
With his own hand, then, made he ladders three,
To climb up by the rungs thereof, it seems,
And reach the tubs left hanging to the beams;
And those he victualled, tubs and kneading-trough,
With bread and cheese and good jugged ale, enough
To satisfy the needs of one full day.
But ere he'd put all this in such array,
He sent his servants, boy and maid, right down
Upon some errand into London town.
And on the Monday, when it came on night,
He shut his door, without a candle-light,

And ordered everything as it should be.
And shortly after up they climbed, all three;
They sat while one might plow a furlong-way.

"Now, by Our Father, hush!" said Nicholay,
And "Hush!" said John, and "Hush!" said Alison.

This carpenter, his loud devotions done,
Sat silent, saying mentally a prayer,
And waiting for the rain, to hear it there.

The deathlike sleep of utter weariness
Fell on this wood-wright even (as I guess)
About the curfew time, or little more;
For travail of his spirit he groaned sore,
And soon he snored, for badly his head lay.
Down by the ladder crept this Nicholay,
And Alison, right softly down she sped.
Without more words they went and got in bed
Even where the carpenter was wont to lie.
There was the revel and the melody!
And thus lie Alison and Nicholas,
In joy that goes by many an alias,
Until the bells for lauds began to ring
And friars to the chancel went to sing.

This parish clerk, this amorous Absalom,
Whom love has made so woebegone and dumb,
Upon the Monday was down Osney way,
With company, to find some sport and play;
And there he chanced to ask a cloisterer,
Privately, after John the carpenter.
This monk drew him apart, out of the kirk,
And said: "I have not seen him here at work
Since Saturday; I think well that he went
For timber, that the abbot has him sent;
For he is wont for timber thus to go,
Remaining at the grange a day or so;
Or else he's surely at his house today;
But which it is I cannot truly say."

This Absalom right happy was and light,
And thought: "Now is the time to wake all night;
For certainly I saw him not stirring
About his door since day began to spring.
So may I thrive, as I shall, at cock's crow,
Knock cautiously upon that window low
Which is so placed upon his bedroom wall.

To Alison then will I tell of all
My love-longing, and thus I shall not miss
That at the least I'll have her lips to kiss.
Some sort of comfort shall I have, I say,
My mouth's been itching all this livelong day;
That is a sign of kissing at the least.
All night I dreamed, too, I was at a feast.
Therefore I'll go and sleep two hours away
And all this night then will I wake and play."

And so when time of first cock-crow was come,
Up rose this merry lover, Absalom,
And dressed him gay and all at point-device,
But first he chewed some licorice and spice
So he'd smell sweet, ere he had combed his hair.
Under his tongue some bits of true-love rare,[8]
For thereby thought he to be more gracious.
He went, then, to the carpenter's dark house.
And silent stood beneath the shot-window;
Unto his breast it reached, it was so low;
And he coughed softly, in a low half tone:
"What do you, honeycomb, sweet Alison?
My cinnamon, my fair bird, my sweetie,
Awake, O darling mine, and speak to me!
It's little thought you give me and my woe,
Who for your love do sweat where'er I go.
Yet it's no wonder that I faint and sweat;
I long as does the lamb for mother's teat.
Truly, sweetheart, I have such love-longing
That like a turtle-dove's my true yearning;
And I can eat no more than can a maid."

"Go from the window, jack-a-napes," she said,
"For, s'help me God, it is not 'come kiss me.'
I love another, or to blame I'd be,
Better than you, by Jesus, Absalom!
Go on your way, or I'll stone you therefrom,
And let me sleep, the fiends take you away!"

"Alas," quoth Absalom, "and welaway!
That true love ever was so ill beset!
But kiss me, since you'll do no more, my pet,
For Jesus' love and for the love of me."

"And will you go, then, on your way?" asked she.

---

8. True-love: probably herb paris.

"Yes truly, darling," said this Absalom.
"Then make you ready," said she, "and I'll come!"
And unto Nicholas said she, low and still:
"Be silent now, and you shall laugh your fill."
    This Absalom plumped down upon his knees,
And said: "I am a lord in all degrees;
For after this there may be better still!
Darling, my sweetest bird, I wait your will."
    The window she unbarred, and that in haste.
"Have done," said she, "come on, and do it fast,
Before we're seen by any neighbour's eye."
    This Absalom did wipe his mouth all dry;
Dark was the night as pitch, aye dark as coal,
And through the window she put out her hole.
And Absalom no better felt nor worse,
But with his mouth he kissed her naked arse
Right greedily, before he knew of this.
    Aback he leapt—it seemed somehow amiss,
For well he knew a woman has no beard;
He'd felt a thing all rough and longish haired,
And said, "Oh fie, alas! What did I do?"
    "Teehee!" she laughed, and clapped the window to;
And Absalom went forth a sorry pace.
    "A beard! A beard!" cried clever Nicholas,
"Now by God's *corpus*, this goes fair and well!"
    This hapless Absalom, he heard that yell,
And on his lip, for anger, he did bite;
And to himself he said, "I will requite!"
    Who vigorously rubbed and scrubbed his lips
With dust, with sand, with straw, with cloth, with chips,
But Absalom, and often cried "Alas!
My soul I give now unto Sathanas,
For rather far than own this town," said he,
"For this despite, it's well revenged I'd be.
Alas," said he, "from her I never blenched!"
    His hot love was grown cold, aye and all quenched;
For, from the moment that he'd kissed her arse,
For paramours he didn't care a curse,
For he was healed of all his malady;
Indeed all paramours he did defy,
And wept as does a child that has been beat.
With silent step he went across the street
Unto a smith whom men called Dan Jarvis,

Who in his smithy forged plow parts, that is
He sharpened shares and coulters busily.
This Absalom he knocked all easily,
And said: "Unbar here, Jarvis, for I come."

   "What! Who are you?"

                          "It's I, it's Absalom."

   "What! Absalom! For Jesus Christ's sweet tree,
Why are you up so early? *Ben'cite!*
What ails you now, man? Some gay girl, God knows,
Has brought you on the jump to my bellows;
By Saint Neot, you know well what I mean."

   This Absalom cared not a single bean
For all this play, nor one word back he gave;
He'd more tow on his distaff, had this knave,
Than Jarvis knew, and said he: "Friend so dear,
This red-hot coulter in the fireplace here,
Lend it to me, I have a need for it,
And I'll return it after just a bit."

   Jarvis replied: "Certainly, were it gold
Or a purse filled with yellow coins untold,
Yet should you have it, as I am true smith;
But eh, Christ's foe! What will you do therewith?"

   "Let that," said Absalom, "be as it may;
I'll tell you all tomorrow, when it's day"—
And caught the coulter then by the cold steel
And softly from the smithy door did steal
And went again up to the wood-wright's wall.
He coughed at first, and then he knocked withal
Upon the window, as before, with care.

   This Alison replied: "Now who is there?
And who knocks so? I'll warrant it's a thief."

   "Why no," quoth he, "God knows, my sweet roseleaf,
I am your Absalom, my own darling!
Of gold," quoth he, "I have brought you a ring;
My mother gave it me, as I'll be saved;
Fine gold it is, and it is well engraved;
This will I give you for another kiss."

   This Nicholas had risen for a piss,
And thought that it would carry on the jape
To have his arse kissed by this jack-a-nape.
And so he opened window hastily,
And put his arse out thereat, quietly,
Over the buttocks, showing the whole bum;

And thereto said this clerk, this Absalom,
"O speak, sweet bird, I know not where thou art."
This Nicholas just then let fly a fart
As loud as it had been a thunder-clap,
And well-nigh blinded Absalom, poor chap;
But he was ready with his iron hot
And Nicholas right in the arse he got.

Off went the skin a hand's-breadth broad, about,
The coulter burned his bottom so, throughout,
That for the pain he thought that he should die.
And like one mad he started in to cry,
"Help! Water! Water! Help! For God's dear heart!"

This carpenter out of his sleep did start,
Hearing that "Water!" cried as madman would,
And thought, "Alas, now comes down Noel's[9] flood!"
He struggled up without another word
And with his axe he cut in two the cord,
And down went all; he did not stop to trade
In bread or ale till he'd the journey made,
And there upon the floor he swooning lay.

Up started Alison and Nicholay
And shouted "Help!" and "Hello!" down the street.
The neighbours, great and small, with hastening feet
Swarmed in the house to stare upon this man,
Who lay yet swooning, and all pale and wan;
For in the falling he had smashed his arm.
He had to suffer, too, another harm,
For when he spoke he was at once borne down
By clever Nicholas and Alison.
For they told everyone that he was odd;
He was so much afraid of "Noel's" flood,
Through fantasy, that out of vanity
He'd gone and bought these kneading-tubs, all three,
And that he'd hung them near the roof above;
And that he had prayed them, for God's dear love,
To sit with him and bear him company.

The people laughed at all this fantasy;
Up to the roof they looked, and there did gape,
And so turned all his injury to a jape.
For when this carpenter got in a word,
'Twas all in vain, no man his reasons heard;

9. The carpenter's corruption.

With oaths impressive he was so sworn down,
That he was held for mad by all the town;
For every clerk did side with every other.
They said: "The man is crazy, my dear brother."
And everyone did laugh at all this strife.
    Thus futtered was the carpenter's goodwife,
For all his watching and his jealousy;
And Absalom has kissed her nether eye;
And Nicholas is branded on the butt.
This tale is done, and God save all the rout!

HERE ENDS THE MILLER'S TALE

THE REEVE'S PROLOGUE

When folk had laughed their fill at this nice pass
Of Absalom and clever Nicholas,
Then divers folk diversely had their say;
And most of them were well amused and gay,
Nor at this tale did I see one man grieve,
Save it were only old Oswald the reeve,
Because he was a carpenter by craft.
A little anger in his heart was left,
And he began to grouse and blame a bit.
    "S' help me," said he, "full well could I be quit
With blearing of a haughty miller's eye,
If I but chose to speak of ribaldry.
But I am old; I will not play, for age;
Grass time is done, my fodder is rummage,
This white top advertises my old years,
My heart, too, is as mouldy as my hairs,
Unless I fare like medlar, all perverse.
For that fruit's never ripe until it's worse,
And falls among the refuse or in straw.
We ancient men, I fear, obey this law:
Until we're rotten, we cannot be ripe;
We dance, indeed, the while the world will pipe.
Desire sticks in our nature like a nail
To have, if hoary head, a verdant tail,
As has the leek; for though our strength be gone,
Our wish is yet for folly till life's done.
For when we may not act, then will we speak;
Yet in our ashes is there fire to reek
    "Four embers have we, which I shall confess:
Boasting and lying, anger, covetousness;
These four remaining sparks belong to eld.
Our ancient limbs may well be hard to wield,
But lust will never fail us, that is truth.

97

And yet I have had always a colt's tooth,
As many years as now are past and done
Since first my tap of life began to run.
For certainly, when I was born, I know
Death turned my tap of life and let it flow;
And ever since that day the tap has run
Till nearly empty now is all the tun.
The stream of life now drips upon the chime;[1]
The silly tongue may well ring out the time
Of wretchedness that passed so long before;
For oldsters, save for dotage, there's no more."

   Now when our host had heard this sermoning,
Then did he speak as lordly as a king;
He said: "To what amounts, now, all this wit?
Why should we talk all day of holy writ?
The devil makes a steward for to preach,
And of a cobbler, a sailor or a leech.
Tell forth your tale, and do not waste the time.
Here's Deptford! And it is half way to prime.
There's Greenwich town that many a scoundrel's in;
It is high time your story should begin."

   "Now, sirs," then said this Oswald called the reeve,
"I pray you all, now, that you will not grieve
Though I reply and somewhat twitch his cap;
It's lawful to meet force with force, mayhap.

   "This drunken miller has related here
How was beguiled and fooled a carpenter—
Perchance in scorn of me, for I am one.
So, by your leave, I'll him requite anon;
All in his own boor's language will I speak.
I only pray to God his neck may break.
For in my eye he well can see the mote,
But sees not in his own the beam, you'll note."

THE REEVE'S TALE

At Trumpington, not far from Cambridge town,
There is a bridge wherethrough a brook runs down,

---

1. Chime (or chimb): the edge or rim of a cask, formed by the projecting ends of the staves.

Upon the side of which brook stands a mill;
And this is very truth that now I tell.
A miller dwelt there, many and many a day;
As any peacock he was proud and gay.
He could mend nets, and he could fish, and flute,
Drink and turn cups, and wrestle well, and shoot;
And in his leathern belt he did parade
A cutlass with a long and trenchant blade.
A pretty dagger had he in his pouch;
There was no man who durst this man to touch.
A Sheffield whittler bore he in his hose;
Round was his face and turned-up was his nose.
As bald as any ape's head was his skull;
He was a market-swaggerer to the full.
There durst no man a hand on him to lay,
Because he swore he'd make the beggar pay.
A thief he was, forsooth, of corn and meal,
And sly at that, accustomed well to steal.
His name was known as arrogant Simpkin.
A wife he had who came of gentle kin;
The parson of the town her father was.
With her he gave full many a pan of brass,[2]
To insure that Simpkin with his blood ally.
She had been bred up in a nunnery;
For Simpkin would not have a wife, he said,
Save she were educated and a maid
To keep up his estate of yeomanry.
And she was proud and bold as is a pie.
A handsome sight it was to see those two;
On holy days before her he would go
With a broad tippet bound about his head;
And she came after in a skirt of red,
While Simpkin's hose were dyed to match that same.
There durst no man to call her aught but dame;
Nor was there one so hardy, in the way,
As durst flirt with her or attempt to play,
Unless he would be slain by this Simpkin
With cutlass or with knife or with bodkin.
For jealous folk are dangerous, you know,
At least they'd have their wives to think them so.
Besides, because she was a dirty bitch,

---

2. Brass: money of brass, bronze or copper.

She was as high as water in a ditch;
And full of scorn and full of back-biting.
She thought a lady should be quite willing
To greet her for her kin and culture, she
Having been brought up in that nunnery.

A daughter had they got between the two,
Of twenty years, and no more children, no,
Save a boy baby that was six months old;
It lay in cradle and was strong and bold.
This girl right stout and well developed was,
With nose tip-tilted and eyes blue as glass,
With buttocks broad, and round breasts full and high,
But golden was her hair, I will not lie.

The parson of the town, since she was fair,
Was purposeful to make of her his heir,
Both of his chattels and of his estate,
But all this hinged upon a proper mate.
He was resolved that he'd bestow her high
Into some blood of worthy ancestry;
For Holy Church's goods must be expended
On Holy Church's blood, as it's descended.
Therefore he'd honour thus his holy blood,
Though Holy Church itself became his food.

Large tolls this miller took, beyond a doubt,
With wheat and malt from all the lands about;
Of which I'd specify among them all
A Cambridge college known as Soler Hall;
He ground their wheat and all their malt he ground.

And on a day it happened, as they found,
The manciple got such a malady
That all men surely thought that he should die.
Whereon this miller stole both flour and wheat
A hundredfold more than he used to cheat;
For theretofore he stole but cautiously,
But now he was a thief outrageously,
At which the warden scolded and raised hell;
The miller snapped his fingers, truth to tell,
And cracked his brags and swore it wasn't so.

There were two poor young clerks, whose names I know,
That dwelt within this Hall whereof I say.
Willful they were and lusty, full of play,
And (all for mirth and to make revelry)
After the warden eagerly did they cry

To give them leave, at least for this one round,
To go to mill and see their produce ground;
And stoutly they proclaimed they'd bet their neck
The miller should not steal one half a peck
Of grain, by trick, nor yet by force should thieve;
And at the last the warden gave them leave.
John was the one and Alain was that other;
In one town were they born, and that called Strother,
Far in the north, I cannot tell you where.

This Alain, he made ready all his gear,
And on a horse loaded the sack anon.
Forth went Alain the clerk, and also John,
With good sword and with buckler at their side.
John knew the way and didn't need a guide,
And at the mill he dropped the sack of grain.
"Ah, Simon, hail, good morn," first spoke Alain.
"How fares it with your fair daughter and wife?"

"Alain! Welcome," said Simpkin, "by my life,
And John also. How now? What do you here?"

"Simon," said John, "by God, need makes no peer;
He must himself serve who's no servant, eh?
Or else he's but a fool, as all clerks say.
Our manciple—I hope he'll soon be dead,
So aching are the grinders in his head—
And therefore am I come here with Alain
To grind our corn and carry it home again;
I pray you speed us thither, as you may."

"It shall be done," said Simpkin, "by my fay.
What will you do the while it is in hand?"

"By God, right by the hopper will I stand,"
Said John, "and see just how the corn goes in;
I never have seen, by my father's kin,
Just how the hopper waggles to and fro."

Alain replied: "Well, John, and will you so?
Then will I get beneath it, by my crown,
To see there how the meal comes sifting down
Into the trough; and that shall be my sport.
For, John, in faith, I must be of your sort;
I am as bad a miller as you be."

The miller smiled at this, their delicacy,
And thought: "All this is done but for a wile;
They think there is no man may them beguile;
But, by my thrift, I will yet blear their eyes,

For all the tricks in their philosophies.
The more odd tricks and stratagems they make,
The more I'll steal when I begin to take.
In place of flour I'll give them only bran.
'The greatest clerk is not the wisest man,'
As once unto the grey wolf said the mare.
But all their arts—I rate them not a tare."

Out of the door he went, then, secretly,
When he had seen his chance, and quietly;
He looked up and looked down, until he found
The clerks' horse where it stood, securely bound.
Behind the mill, under an arbour green;
And to the horse he went, then, all unseen;
He took the bridle off him and anon,
When the said horse was free, why he was gone
Toward the fen, for wild mares ran therein,
And with a neigh he went, through thick and thin.

This miller straight went back and no word said,
But did his business and with these clerks played,
Until their corn was fairly, fully ground.
But when the flour was sacked and the ears bound,
This John went out, to find his horse away,
And so he cried: "Hello!" and "Weladay!
Our horse is lost! Alain, for Jesus' bones
Get to your feet, come out, man, now, at once!
Alas, our warden's palfrey's lost and lorn!"

This Alain forgot all, both flour and corn,
Clean out of mind was all his husbandry,
"What? Which way did he go?" began to cry.

The wife came bounding from the house, and then
She said: "Alas! Your horse went to the fen,
With the wild mares, as fast as he could go.
A curse light on the hand that tied him so,
And him that better should have knotted rein!"

"Alas!" quoth John, "Alain, for Jesus' pain,
Lay off your sword, and I will mine also;
I am as fleet, God knows, as is a roe;
By God's heart, he shall not escape us both!
Why didn't you put him in the barn? My oath!
Bad luck, by God, Alain, you are a fool!"

These foolish clerks began to run and roll
Toward the marshes, both Alain and John.

And when the miller saw that they were gone,

He half a bushel of their flour did take
And bade his wife go knead it and bread make.
He said: "I think those clerks some trickery feared;
Yet can a miller match a clerkling's beard,
For all his learning; let them go their way.
Look where they go, yea, let the children play,
They'll catch him not so readily, by my crown!"

Those simple clerks went running up and down
With "Look out! Halt! Halt! Down here! 'Ware the rear!
Go whistle, you, and I will watch him here!"
But briefly, till it came to utter night,
They could not, though they put forth all their might,
That stallion catch, he always ran so fast,
Till in a ditch they trapped him at the last.

Weary and wet, as beast is in the rain,
Came foolish John and with him came Alain.
"Alas," said John, "the day that I was born!
Now are we bound toward mockery and scorn.
Our corn is stolen, folk will call us fools,
The warden and the fellows at the schools,
And specially this miller. Weladay!"

Thus John complained as he went on his way
Toward the mill, with Bayard[3] once more bound.
The miller sitting by the fire he found,
For it was night, and farther could they not;
But, for the love of God, they him besought
For shelter and for supper, for their penny.

The miller said to them: "If there be any,
Such as it is, why you shall have your part.
My house is small, but you have learned your art;
You can, by metaphysics, make a place
A full mile wide in twenty feet of space.
Let us see now if this place will suffice,
Or make more room with speech, by some device."

"Now, Simon," said John, "by Saint Cuthbert's beard,
You're always merry and have well answered.
As I've heard, man shall take one of two things:
Such as he finds, or take such as he brings.
But specially, I pray you, mine host dear,
Give us some meat and drink and some good cheer,
And we will pay you, truly, to the full.

---

3. Bayard: the horse, any horse.

With empty hand no man takes hawk or gull;
Well, here's our silver, ready to be spent."
    This miller to the town his daughter sent
For ale and bread, and roasted them a goose,
And tied their horse, that it might not go loose;
And then in his own chamber made a bed,
With sheets and with good blankets fairly spread,
Not from his bed more than twelve feet, or ten.
The daughter made her lone bed near the men,
In the same chamber with them, by and by;
It could not well be bettered, and for why?
There was no larger room in all the place.
They supped and talked, and gained some small solace,
And drank strong ale, that evening, of the best.
Then about midnight all they went to rest.
    Well had this miller varnished his bald head,
For pale he was with drinking, and not red.
He hiccoughed and he mumbled through his nose,
As he were chilled, with humours lachrymose.
To bed he went, and with him went his wife.
As any jay she was with laughter rife,
So copiously was her gay whistle wet.
The cradle near her bed's foot-board was set,
Handy for rocking and for giving suck.
And when they'd drunk up all there was in crock,
To bed went miller's daughter, and anon
To bed went Alain and to bed went John.
There was no more; they did not need a dwale.[4]
This miller had so roundly bibbed his ale
That, like a horse, he snorted in his sleep,
While of his tail behind he kept no keep.
His wife joined in his chorus, and so strong,
Men might have heard her snores a full furlong;
And the girl snored, as well, for company.
    Alain the clerk, who heard this melody,
He poked at John and said: "Asleep? But how?
Did you hear ever such a song ere now?
Lo, what a compline is among them all!
Now may the wild-fire on their bodies fall!
Who ever heard so outlandish a thing?
But they shall have the flour of ill ending.

---

4. Dwale: an opiate, a sleeping potion.

Through this long night there'll be for me no rest;
But never mind, 'twill all be for the best.
For, John," said he, "so may I ever thrive,
As, if I can, that very wench I'll swive.
Some recompense the law allows to us;
For, John, there is a statute which says thus,
That if a man in one point be aggrieved,
Yet in another shall he be relieved.
Our corn is stolen, to that there's no nay,
And we have had an evil time this day.
But since I may not have amending, now,
Against my loss I'll set some fun—and how!
By God's great soul it shan't be otherwise!"
    This John replied: "Alain, let me advise.
The miller is a dangerous man," he said,
"And if he be awakened, I'm afraid
He may well do us both an injury."
    But Alain said: "I count him not a fly."
And up he rose and to the girl he crept.
This wench lay on her back and soundly slept,
Until he'd come so near, ere she might spy,
It was too late to struggle, then, or cry;
And, to be brief, these two were soon as one.
Now play, Alain! For I will speak of John.
    This John lay still a quarter-hour, or so,
Pitied himself and wept for all his woe.
"Alas," said he, "this is a wicked jape!
Now may I say that I am but an ape.
Yet has my friend, there, something for his harm;
He has the miller's daughter on his arm.
He ventured, and his pains are now all fled,
While I lie like a sack of chaff in bed;
And when this jape is told, another day,
I shall be held an ass, a milksop, yea!
I will arise and chance it, by my fay!
'Unhardy is unhappy,' as they say."
    And up he rose, and softly then he went
To find the cradle for expedient,
And bore it over to his own foot-board.
    Soon after this the wife no longer snored,
But woke and rose and went outside to piss,
And came again and did the cradle miss,
And groped round, here and there, but found it not.

"Alas!" thought she, "my way I have forgot.
I nearly found myself in the clerks' bed.
Eh, *ben'cite*, but that were wrong!" she said.
And on, until by cradle she did stand.
And, groping a bit farther with her hand,
She found the bed, and thought of naught but good,
Because her baby's cradle by it stood,
And knew not where she was, for it was dark;
But calmly then she crept in by the clerk,
And lay right still, and would have gone to sleep.
But presently this John the clerk did leap,
And over on this goodwife did he lie.
No such gay time she'd known in years gone by.
He pricked her hard and deep, like one gone mad.
And so a jolly life these two clerks had
Till the third cock began to crow and sing.
   Alain grew weary in the grey dawning,
For he had laboured hard through all the night;
And said: "Farewell, now, Maudy, sweet delight!
The day is come, I may no longer bide;
But evermore, whether I walk or ride,
I am your own clerk, so may I have weal."
   "Now, sweetheart," said she, "go and fare you well!
But ere you go, there's one thing I must tell.
When you go walking homeward past the mill,
Right at the entrance, just the door behind,
You shall a loaf of half a bushel find
That was baked up of your own flour, a deal
Of which I helped my father for to steal.
And, darling, may God save you now and keep!"
And with that word she almost had to weep.
   Alain arose and thought: "Ere it be dawn,
I will go creep in softly by friend John."
And found the cradle with his hand, anon.
"By God!" thought he, "all wrong I must have gone;
My head is dizzy from my work tonight,
And that's why I have failed to go aright.
I know well, by this cradle, I am wrong,
For here the miller and his wife belong."
And on he went, and on the devil's way,
Unto the bed wherein the miller lay.
He thought to have crept in by comrade John,
So, to the miller, in he got anon,

And caught him round the neck, and softly spake,
Saying: "You, John, you old swine's head, awake,
For Christ's own soul, and hear a noble work,
For by Saint James, and as I am a clerk,
I have, three times in this short night, no lack,
Swived that old miller's daughter on her back,
While you, like any coward, were aghast."

"You scoundrel," cried the miller, "you trespassed?
Ah, traitor false and treacherous clerk!" cried he,
"You shall be killed, by God's own dignity!
Who dares be bold enough to bring to shame
My daughter, who is born of such a name?"

And by the gullet, then, he caught Alain.
And pitilessly he handled him amain,
And on the nose he smote him with his fist.
Down ran the bloody stream upon his breast;
And on the floor, with nose and mouth a-soak,
They wallowed as two pigs do in a poke.
And up they came, and down they both went, prone,
Until the miller stumbled on a stone,
And reeled and fell down backwards on his wife,
Who nothing knew of all this silly strife;
For she had fallen into slumber tight
With John the clerk, who'd been awake all night.
But at the fall, from sleep she started out.
"Help, holy Cross of Bromholm!" did she shout,
"In *manus tuas*, Lord, to Thee I call!
Simon, awake, the Fiend is on us all
My heart is broken, help, I am but dead!
There lies one on my womb, one on my head!
Help, Simpkin, for these treacherous clerks do fight!"

John started up, as fast as well he might,
And searched along the wall, and to and fro,
To find a staff; and she arose also,
And knowing the room better than did John,
She found a staff against the wall, anon;
And then she saw a little ray of light,
For through a hole the moon was shining bright;
And by that light she saw the struggling two,
But certainly she knew not who was who,
Except she saw a white thing with her eye.
And when she did this same white thing espy,
She thought the clerk had worn a nightcap here.

And with the staff she nearer drew, and near,
And, thinking to hit Alain on his poll,
She fetched the miller on his bald white skull,
And down he went, crying out, "Help, help, I die!"
The two clerks beat him well and let him lie;
And clothed themselves, and took their horse anon.
And got their flour, and on their way were gone.
And at the mill they found the well-made cake
Which of their meal the miller's wife did bake.

Thus is the haughty miller soundly beat,
And thus he's lost his pay for grinding wheat,
And paid for the two suppers, let me tell,
Of Alain and of John, who've tricked him well.
His wife is taken, also his daughter sweet;
Thus it befalls a miller who's a cheat.
And therefore is this proverb said with truth,
"An evil end to evil man, forsooth."
The cheater shall himself well cheated be.
And God, Who sits on high in majesty,
Save all this company, both strong and frail!
Thus have I paid this miller with my tale.

HERE IS ENDED THE REEVE'S TALE

THE COOK'S PROLOGUE

The cook from London, while the reeve yet spoke,
Patted his back with pleasure at the joke.
"Ha, ha!" laughed he, "by Christ's great suffering,
This miller had a mighty sharp ending
Upon his argument of harbourage!
For well says Solomon, in his language,
'Bring thou not every man into thine house;'
For harbouring by night is dangerous.
Well ought a man to know the man that he
Has brought into his own security.
I pray God give me sorrow and much care
If ever, since I have been Hodge[1] of Ware,
Heard I of miller better brought to mark.
A wicked jest was played him in the dark.
But God forbid that we should leave off here;
And therefore, if you'll lend me now an ear,
From what I know, who am but a poor man,
I will relate, as well as ever I can,
A little trick was played in our city."
    Our host replied: "I grant it readily.
Now tell on, Roger; see that it be good;
For many a pasty have you robbed of blood,
And many a Jack of Dover[2] have you sold
That has been heated twice and twice grown cold.
From many a pilgrim have you had Christ's curse,
For of your parsley they yet fare the worse,
Which they have eaten with your stubble goose;[3]
For in your shop full many a fly is loose.
Now tell on, gentle Roger, by your name.

---

1. Hodge: a nickname for Roger. 2. Jack of Dover: a slang term for a meat pie which, not being sold the day it was cooked, the gravy was drawn off. 3. Stubble goose: an old goose fed on stubble, not on grain.

But yet, I pray, don't mind if I make game,
A man may tell the truth when it's in play."
   "You say the truth," quoth Roger, "by my fay!
But 'true jest, bad jest' as the Fleming saith.
And therefore, Harry Bailey, on your faith,
Be you not angry ere we finish here,
If my tale should concern an inn-keeper.
Nevertheless, I'll tell not that one yet,
But ere we part your jokes will I upset."
   And thereon did he laugh, in great good cheer,
And told his tale, as you shall straightway hear.

THUS ENDS THE PROLOGUE OF THE COOK'S TALE

THE COOK'S TALE

There lived a 'prentice, once, in our city,
And of the craft of victuallers was he;
Happy he was as goldfinch in the glade,
Brown as a berry, short, and thickly made,
With black hair that he combed right prettily.
He could dance well, and that so jollily,
That he was nicknamed Perkin Reveller.
He was as full of love, I may aver,
As is a beehive full of honey sweet;
Well for the wench that with him chanced to meet.
At every bridal would he sing and hop,
Loving the tavern better than the shop.
   When there was any festival in Cheap,
Out of the shop and thither would he leap,
And, till the whole procession he had seen,
And danced his fill, he'd not return again.
He gathered many fellows of his sort
To dance and sing and make all kinds of sport.
And they would have appointments for to meet
And play at dice in such, or such, a street.
For in the whole town was no apprentice
Who better knew the way to throw the dice
Than Perkin; and therefore he was right free
With money, when in chosen company.
His master found this out in business there;

For often-times he found the till was bare.
For certainly a revelling bond-boy
Who loves dice, wine, dancing, and girls of joy—
His master, in his shop, shall feel the effect,
Though no part have he in this said respect;
For theft and riot always comrades are,
And each alike he played on gay guitar.
Revels and truth, in one of low degree,
Do battle always, as all men may see.

　　This 'prentice shared his master's fair abode
Till he was nigh out of his 'prenticehood,
Though he was checked and scolded early and late,
And sometimes led, for drinking, to Newgate;
But at the last his master did take thought,
Upon a day, when he his ledger sought,
On an old proverb wherein is found this word:
"Better take rotten apple from the hoard
Than let it lie to spoil the good ones there."
So with a drunken servant should it fare;
It is less ill to let him go, apace,
Than ruin all the others in the place.
Therefore he freed and cast him loose to go
His own road unto future care and woe;
And thus this jolly 'prentice had his leave.
Now let him riot all night long, or thieve.

　　But since there's never thief without a buck
To help him waste his money and to suck
All he can steal or borrow by the way,
Anon he sent his bed and his array
To one he knew, a fellow of his sort,
Who loved the dice and revels and all sport,
And had a wife that kept, for countenance,
A shop, and whored to gain her sustenance.

OF THIS COOK'S TALE CHAUCER MADE NO MORE

INTRODUCTION
TO THE LAWYER'S PROLOGUE

The Words of the Host to the Company

Our good host saw well that the shining sun
The arc of artificial day[1] had run
A quarter part, plus half an hour or more;
And though not deeply expert in such lore,
He reckoned that it was the eighteenth day
Of April, which is harbinger to May;
And saw well that the shadow of each tree
Was, as to length, of even quantity
As was the body upright causing it.
And therefore by the shade he had the wit
To know that Phoebus, shining there so bright,
Had climbed degrees full forty-five in height;
And that, that day, and in that latitude,
It was ten of the clock, he did conclude,
And suddenly he put his horse about.

    "Masters," quoth he, "I warn all of this rout,
A quarter of this present day is gone;
Now for the love of God and of Saint John,
Lose no more time, or little as you may;
Masters, the time is wasting night and day,
And steals away from us, what with our sleeping
And with our sloth, when we awake are keeping,
As does the stream, that never turns again,
Descending from the mountain to the plain.
And well may Seneca, and many more,
Bewail lost time far more than gold in store.
'For chattels lost may yet recovered be,
But time lost ruins us for aye,' says he.

---

1. From sunrise to sunset.

It will not come again, once it has fled,
Not any more than will Mag's maidenhead
When she has lost it in her wantonness;
Let's not grow mouldy thus in idleness.
"Sir Lawyer," said he, "as you have hope of bliss,
Tell us a tale, as our agreement is;
You have submitted, by your free assent,
To stand, in this case, to my sole judgment;
Acquit yourself, keep promise with the rest,
And you'll have done your duty, at the least."
    "Mine host," said he, "by the gods, I consent;
To break a promise is not my intent.
A promise is a debt, and by my fay
I keep all mine; I can no better say.
For such law as man gives to other wight,
He should himself submit to it, by right;
Thus says our text; nevertheless, 'tis true
I can relate no useful tale to you,
But Chaucer, though he speaks but vulgarly
In metre and in rhyming dextrously,
Has told them in such English as he can,
In former years, as knows full many a man.
For if he has not told them, my dear brother,
In one book, why he's done so in another.
For he has told of lovers, up and down,
More than old Ovid mentions, of renown,
In his *Epistles*, that are now so old.
Why should I then re-tell what has been told?
In youth he told of Ceyx and Alcyon,
And has since then spoken of everyone—
Of noble wives and lovers did he speak.
And whoso will that weighty volume seek
Called *Legend of Good Women*, need not chide;
There may be ever seen the large wounds wide
Of Lucrece, Babylonian Thisbe;
Dido's for false Aeneas when fled he;
Demophoon and Phyllis and her tree;
The plaint of Deianira and Hermione;
Of Ariadne and Hypsipyle;
The barren island standing in the sea;
The drowned Leander and his fair Hero;
The tears of Helen and the bitter woe
Of Briseis and that of Laodomea;

The cruelty of that fair Queen Medea,
Her little children hanging by the neck
When all her love for Jason came to wreck!
O Hypermnestra, Penelope, Alcestis,
Your wifehood does he honour, since it best is!
    "But certainly no word has written he
Of that so wicked woman, Canace,
Who loved her own blood brother sinfully.
Of suchlike cursed tales, I say 'Let be!'
Nor yet of Tyrian Apollonius;
Nor how the wicked King Antiochus
Bereft his daughter of her maidenhead
(Which is so horrible a tale to read),
When down he flung her on the paving stones.
And therefore he, advisedly, truth owns,
Would never write, in one of his creations,
Of such unnatural abominations.
And I'll refuse to tell them, if I may.
    "But for my tale, what shall I do this day?
Any comparison would me displease
To Muses whom men call Pierides
(The *Metamorphoses* show what I mean).
Nevertheless, I do not care a bean
Though I come after him with my plain fare.
I'll stick to prose. Let him his rhymes prepare."
    And thereupon, with sober face and cheer,
He told his tale, as you shall read it here.

THE LAWYER'S PROLOGUE

O Hateful evil! State of Poverty!
With thirst, with cold, with hunger so confounded!
To ask help shameth thy heart's delicacy;
If none thou ask, by need thou art so wounded
That need itself uncovereth all the wound hid!
Spite of thy will thou must, for indigence,
Go steal, or beg, or borrow thine expense.

Thou blamest Christ, and thou say'st bitterly,
He misdistributes riches temporal;
Thy neighbour dost thou censure, sinfully,

Saying thou hast too little and he hath all.
"My faith," sayest thou, "sometime the reckoning shall
Come on him, when his tail shall burn for greed,
Not having helped the needy in their need."

Hear now what is the judgment of the wise:
"Better to die than live in indigence;"
"Thy very pauper neighbours thee despise."
If thou be poor, farewell thy reverence!
Still of the wise man take this full sentence:
"The days of the afflicted are all sin."
Beware, therefore, that thou come not therein!

"If thou be poor, thy brother hateth thee,
And all thy friends will flee from thee, alas!"
O wealthy merchants, full of weal ye be,
O noble, prudent folk in happier case!
Your dice-box doth not tumble out ambsace,[1]
But with *six-cinq*[2] ye throw against your chance;[3]
And so, at Christmas, merrily may ye dance!

Ye search all land and sea for your winnings,
And, as wise folk, ye know well the estate
Of all realms; ye are sires of happenings
And tales of peace and tales of war's debate.
But I were now of tales all desolate,
Were 't not a merchant, gone this many a year,
Taught me the story which you now shall hear.

THE LAWYER'S TALE

In Syria, once, there dwelt a company
Of traders rich, all sober men and true,
That far abroad did send their spicery,
And cloth of gold, and satins rich in hue;
Their wares were all so excellent and new
That everyone was eager to exchange
With them, and sell them divers things and strange.

---

1. Double-ace.   2. Six and five.   3. Chance: similar to the "point" in the modern game of craps.

It came to pass, the masters of this sort
Decided that to Rome they all would wend,
Were it for business or for only sport;
No other message would they thither send,
But went themselves to Rome; this is the end.
And there they found an inn and took their rest
As seemed to their advantage suited best.

Sojourned have now these merchants in that town
A certain time, as fell to their pleasance.
And so it happened that the high renown
Of th' emperor's daughter, called the fair Constance,
Reported was, with every circumstance,
Unto these Syrian merchants, in such wise,
From day to day, as I will now apprise.

This was the common voice of every man:
"Our emperor of Rome, God save and see,
A daughter has that since the world began,
To reckon as well her goodness as beauty,
Was never such another as is she;
I pray that God her fame will keep, serene,
And would she were of all Europe the queen.

"In her is beauty high, and without pride;
Youth, without crudity or levity;
In all endeavours, virtue is her guide;
Meekness in her has humbled tyranny;
She is the mirror of all courtesy;
Her heart's a very shrine of holiness;
Her hand is freedom's agent for largess."

And all this voice said truth, as God is true.
But to our story let us turn again.
These merchants all have freighted ships anew,
And when they'd seen the lovely maid, they fain
Would seek their Syrian homes with all their train,
To do their business as they'd done of yore,
And live in weal; I cannot tell you more.

Now so it was, these merchants stood in grace
Of Syria's sultan; and so wise was he
That when they came from any foreign place
He would, of his benignant courtesy,
Make them good cheer, inquiring earnestly

For news of sundry realms, to learn, by word,
The wonders that they might have seen and heard.

Among some other things, especially
These merchants told him tales of fair Constance;
From such nobility, told of earnestly,
This sultan caught a dream of great pleasance,
And she so figured in his remembrance
That all his wish and all his busy care
Were, throughout life, to love that lady fair.

Now peradventure, in that mighty book
Which men call heaven, it had come to pass,
In stars, when first a living breath he took,
That he for love should get his death, alas!
For in the stars, far clearer than is glass,
Is written, God knows, read it he who can,—
And truth it is—the death of every man.

In stars, full many a winter over-worn,
Was written the death of Hector, Achilles,
Of Pompey, Julius, long ere they were born;
The strife at Thebes; and of great Hercules,
Of Samson, of Turnus, of Socrates,
The death to each; but men's wits are so dull
There is no man may read this to the full.

This sultan for his privy-council sent,
And, but to tell it briefly in this place,
He did to them declare his whole intent,
And said that, surely, save he might have grace
To gain Constance within a little space,
He was but dead; and charged them, speedily
To find out, for his life, some remedy.

By divers men, then, divers things were said;
They reasoned, and they argued up and down;
Full much with subtle logic there they sped;
They spoke of spells, of treachery in Rome town;
But finally, as to an end foreknown,
They were agreed that nothing should gainsay
A marriage, for there was no other way.

Then saw they therein so much difficulty,
When reasoning of it (to make all plain,
Because such conflict and diversity

Between the laws of both lands long had lain)
They held: "No Christian emperor were fain
To have his child wed under our sweet laws,
Given us by Mahomet for God's cause."

But he replied: "Nay, rather then than lose
The Lady Constance, I'll be christened, yes!
I must be hers, I can no other choose.
I pray you let be no rebelliousness;
Save me my life, and do not be careless
In getting her who thus alone may cure
The woe whereof I cannot long endure."

What needs a copious dilation now?
I say: By treaties and by embassy,
And the pope's mediation, high and low,
And all the Church and all the chivalry,
That, to destruction of Mahometry
And to augmenting Christian faith so dear,
They were agreed, at last, as you shall hear.

The sultan and his entire baronage
And all his vassals, they must christened be,
And he shall have Constance in true marriage,
And gold (I know not in what quantity),
For which was found enough security;
This, being agreed, was sworn by either side.
Now, Constance fair, may great God be your guide!

Now would some men expect, as I may guess,
That I should tell of all the purveyance
The emperor, of his great nobleness,
Has destined for his daughter, fair Constance.
But men must know that so great ordinance
May no one tell within a little clause
As was arrayed there for so high a cause.

Bishops were named who were with her to wend,
Ladies and lords and knights of high renown,
And other folk—but I will make an end,
Except that it was ordered through the town
That everyone, with great devotion shown,
Should pray to Christ that He this marriage lead
To happy end, and the long voyage speed.

The day is come, at last, for leave-taking,

I say, the woeful, fatal day is come,
When there may be no longer tarrying,
But to go forth make ready all and some;
Constance, who was with sorrow overcome,
Rose, sad and pale, and dressed herself to wend;
For well she saw there was no other end.

Alas! What wonder is it that she wept?
She shall be sent to a strange country, far
From friends that her so tenderly have kept,
And bound to one her joy to make or mar
Whom she knows not, nor what his people are.
Husbands are all good, and have been of yore,
That know their wives, but I dare say no more.

"Father," she said, "your wretched child, Constance,
Your daughter reared in luxury so soft,
And you, my mother, and my chief pleasance,
Above all things, save Christ Who rules aloft,
Constance your child would be remembered oft
Within your prayers, for I to Syria go,
Nor shall I ever see you more, ah no!

"Unto the land of Barbary[4] my fate
Compels me now, because it is your will;
But Christ, Who died to save our sad estate,
So give me grace, His mandates I'll fulfill;
I, wretched woman, though I die, 'tis nil.
Women are born to slave and to repent,
And to be subject to man's government."

I think, at Troy, when Pyrrhus broke the wall;
When Ilium burned; when Thebes fell, that city;
At Rome, for all the harm from Hannibal,
Who vanquished Roman arms in campaigns three —
I think was heard no weeping for pity
As in the chamber at her leave-taking;
Yet go she must, whether she weep or sing.

O primal-moving, cruel Firmament,
With thy diurnal pressure, that doth sway
And hurl all things from East to Occident,

---

4. Barbary: (Barbre, in original); from F. *barbarie*, barbarous, but with especial reference to Saracens or pagans. Hence confused with Ar. *Barbar*, the people of Barbary.

Which otherwise would hold another way,
Thy pressure set the heavens in such array,
At the beginning of this wild voyage,
That cruel Mars hath murdered this marriage.

Unfortunate ascendant tortuous,
Of which the lord has helpless fall'n, alas,
Out of his angle to the darkest house!
O Mars! O Atazir in present case![5]
O feeble Moon, unhappy is thy pace!
Thou'rt in conjunction where thou'rt not received,
And where thou should'st go, thou hast not achieved.

Imprudent emperor of Rome, alas!
Was no philosopher[6] in all thy town?
Is one time like another in such case?
Indeed, can there be no election shown,
Especially to folk of high renown,
And when their dates of birth may all men know?
Alas! We are too ignorant or too slow.

To ship is brought this fair and woeful maid,
Full decorously, with every circumstance.
"Now Jesus Christ be with you all," she said;
And there's no more, save "Farewell, fair Constance!"
She strove to keep a cheerful countenance,
And forth I let her sail in this manner,
And turn again to matters far from her.

The mother of the sultan, well of vices,
Has heard the news of her son's full intent,
How he will leave the ancient sacrifices;
And she at once for her own council sent;
And so they came to learn what thing she meant.
And when they were assembled, each compeer,
She took her seat and spoke as you shall hear.

"My lords," said she, "you know well, every man,
My son intends to forgo and forget
The holy precepts of our Alkoran,
Given by God's own prophet, Mahomet.
But I will make one vow to great God yet:

---

5. Atazir: the influence of a star on other stars or on men.   6. Philosopher: astrologer in the present instance.

The life shall rather from my body start
Than Islam's laws out of my faithful heart!

"What should we get from taking this new creed
But thralldom for our bodies and penance?
And afterward, be drawn to Hell, indeed,
For thus denying our faith's inheritance?
But, lords, if you will give your sustenance,
And join me for the wisdom I've in store,
I swear to save us all for evermore."

They swore and they assented, every man,
To live by her and die, and by her stand;
And each of them, in what best wise he can,
Shall gather friends and followers into band;
And she shall take the enterprise in hand,
The form of which I soon will you apprise,
And to them all she spoke, then, in this wise.

"We will first feign the Christian faith to take;
Cold water will not harm us from the rite;
And I will such a feast and revel make
As will, I trust, to lull be requisite.
For though his wife be christened ever so white,
She shall have need to wash away the red,
Though a full font of water be there sped."

O sultana, root of iniquity!
Virago, you Semiramis second!
O serpent hid in femininity,
Just as the Serpent deep in Hell is bound!
O pseudo-woman, all that may confound
Virtue and innocence, through your malice,
Is bred in you, the nest of every vice!

O Satan, envious since that same day
When thou wert banished from our heritage,
Well know'st thou unto woman thine old way!
Thou made'st Eve bring us into long bondage.
Thou wilt destroy this Christian marriage.
Thine instrument—ah welaway the while!—
Make'st thou of woman when thou wilt beguile!

Now this sultana whom I blame and harry,
Let, secretly, her council go their way.
Why should I longer in my story tarry?

She rode unto the sultan, on a day,
And told him she'd renounce her old faith, yea,
Be christened at priests' hands, with all the throng,
Repentant she'd been heathen for so long.

Beseeching him to do her the honour
To let her have the Christian men to feast:
"To entertain them will be my labour."
The sultan said: "I'll be at your behest."
And, kneeling, thanked her for that fair request,
So glad he was he knew not what to say;
She kissed her son, and homeward went her way.

Explicit prima pars.
Sequitur pars secunda.

Arrived now are these Christian folk at land,
In Syria, with a great stately rout,
And hastily this sultan gave command,
First to his mother and all the realm about,
Saying his wife was come, beyond a doubt,
And prayed her that she ride to meet the queen,
That all due honour might be shown and seen.

Great was the crush and rich was the array
Of Syrians and Romans, meeting here;
The mother of the sultan, rich and gay,
Received her open-armed, with smiling cheer,
As any mother might a daughter dear;
And to the nearest city, with the bride,
At gentle pace, right festively they ride.

I think the triumph of great Julius,
Whereof old Lucan make so long a boast,
Was not more royal nor more curious
Than was the assembling of this happy host.
But this same Scorpion, this wicked ghost—
The old sultana, for all her flattering,
Chose in that sign full mortally to sting.

The sultan came himself, soon after this,
So regally 'twere wonderful to tell,
And welcomed her into all joy and bliss.
And thus in such delight I let them dwell.
The fruit of all is what I now shall tell.
When came the time, men thought it for the best

Their revels cease, and got them home to rest.

The time came when this old sultana there
Has ordered up the feast of which I told,
Whereto the Christian folk did them prepare,
The company together, young and old.
There men might feast and royalty behold,
With dainties more than I can e'en surmise;
But all too dear they've bought it, ere they rise.

O sudden woe! that ever will succeed
On worldly bliss, infused with bitterness;
That ends the joy of earthly toil, indeed;
Woe holds at last the place of our gladness.
Hear, now, this counsel for your certainness:
Upon your most glad day, bear then in mind
The unknown harm and woe that come behind.

For, but to tell you briefly, in one word—
The sultan and the Christians, every one,
Were all hewed down and thrust through at the board,
Save the fair Lady Constance, she alone.
This old sultana, aye, this cursed crone
Has, with her followers, done this wicked deed,
For she herself would all the nation lead.

There was no Syrian that had been converted,
Being of the sultan's council resolute,
But was struck down, ere from the board he'd started.
And Constance have they taken now, hot-foot,
And on a ship, of rudder destitute,
They her have placed, bidding her learn to sail
From Syria to Italy—or fail.

A certain treasure that she'd brought, they add,
And, truth to tell, of food great quantity
They have her given, and clothing too she had;
And forth she sails upon the wide salt sea.
O Constance mine, full of benignity,
O emperor's young daughter, from afar
He that is Lord of fortune be your star!

She crossed herself, and in a pious voice
Unto the Cross of Jesus thus said she:
"O bright, O blessed Altar of my choice,
Red with the Lamb's blood full of all pity,

That washed the world from old iniquity,
Me from the Fiend and from his claws, oh keep
That day when I shall drown within the deep!

"Victorious Tree, Protection of the true,
The only thing that worthy was to bear
The King of Heaven with His wounds so new,
The White Lamb Who was pierced through with the spear,
Driver of devils out of him and her
Who on Thine arms do lay themselves in faith,
Keep me and give me grace before my death!"

For years and days drifted this maiden pure,
Through all the seas of Greece and to the strait
Of dark Gibraltar did she adventure;
On many a sorry meal now may she bait;
Upon her death full often may she wait
Before the wild waves and the winds shall drive
Her vessel where it shall some day arrive.

Men might well ask: But why was she not slain?
And at that feast who could her body save?
And I reply to that demand, again:
Who saved young Daniel in the dreadful cave
Where every other man, master and knave,
Was killed by lions ere he might up-start?
No one, save God, Whom he bore in his heart.

God willed to show this wondrous miracle
Through her, that we should see His mighty works;
And Christ Who every evil can dispel,
By certain means does oft, as know all clerks,
Do that whereof the end in darkness lurks
For man's poor wit, which of its ignorance
Cannot conceive His careful purveyance.

Now, since she was not slain at feast we saw,
Who kept her that she drowned not in the sea?
But who kept Jonah in the fish's maw
Till he was spewed forth there at Nineveh?
Well may men know it was no one but He
Who saved the Hebrew people from drowning
When, dry-shod, through the sea they went walking.

Who bade the four great spirits of tempest,
That power have to harry land and sea,

"Not north, nor south, nor yet to east, nor west
Shall ye molest the ocean, land, or tree"?
Truly, the Captain of all this was He
Who from the storm has aye this woman kept,
As well when waking as in hours she slept.

Where might this woman get her drink and meat?
Three years and more, how lasted her supply?
Who gave Egyptian Mary food to eat
In cave or desert? None but Christ, say I.
Five thousand folk, the gospels testify,
On five loaves and two fishes once did feed.
And thus God sent abundance for her need.

Forth into our own ocean then she came,
Through all our wild white seas, until at last,
Under a keep, whose name I cannot name,
Far up Northumberland, her ship was cast,
And on the sands drove hard and stuck so fast
That thence it moved not, no, for all the tide,
It being Christ's will that she should there abide.

The warden of the castle down did fare
To view this wreck, and through the ship he sought
And found this weary woman, full of care;
He found, also, the treasure she had brought.
In her own language mercy she besought
That he would help her soul from body win
To free her from the plight that she was in.

A kind of bastard Latin did she speak,
But, nevertheless, these folk could understand;
The constable no longer thought to seek,
But led the sorrowing woman to the land;
There she knelt down and thanked God, on the sand,
But who or what she was, she would not say,
For threat or promise, though she died that day.

She said she'd been bewildered by the sea,
And had lost recollection, by her truth;
The warden had for her so great pity,
As had his wife, that both they wept for ruth.
She was so diligent to toil, in sooth,
To serve and please all folk within that place,
That all loved her who looked upon her face.

This warden and Dame Hermengild, his wife,
Were pagans, and that country, everywhere;
But Hermengild now loved her as her life,
And Constance has so long abided there,
And prayed so oft, with many a tearful prayer,
That Jesus has converted, through His grace,
Dame Hermengild, the lady of that place.

In all that land no Christian dared speak out
All Christians having fled from that country,
For pagan men had conquered all about
The regions of the north, by land and sea;
To Wales was fled the Christianity
Of the old Britons dwelling in this isle;
That was their refuge in the wild meanwhile.

Yet ne'er were Christian Britons so exiled
But some of them assembled, privately,
To honour Christ, and heathen folk beguiled;
And near the castle dwelt of such men three.
But one of them was blind and could not see,
Save with the inner optics of his mind,
Wherewith all men see after they go blind.

Bright was the sun upon that summer's day
When went the warden and his wife also,
And Constance, down the hill, along the way
Toward the sea, a furlong off, or so,
To frolic and to wander to and fro;
And in their walk on this blind man they came,
With eyes fast shut, a creature old and lame.

"In name of Christ!" this blind old Briton cried,
"Dame Hermengild, give me my sight again."
But she was frightened of the words, and sighed,
Lest that her husband, briefly to be plain,
Should have her, for her love of Jesus, slain;
Till Constance strengthened her and bade her work
The will of God, as daughter of His kirk.

The warden was confounded by that sight,
And asked: "What mean these words and this affair?"
Constance replied: "Sir, it is Jesus' might
That helps all poor folk from the foul Fiend's snare."
And so far did she our sweet faith declare

That she the constable, before 'twas eve,
Converted, and in Christ made him believe.

This constable, though not lord of that place
Where he'd found Constance, wrecked upon the sand,
Had held it well for many a winter's space,
For Alla, king of all Northumberland,
Who was full wise and hardy of his hand
Against the Scots, as men may read and hear,
But I will to my tale again—give ear.

Satan, that ever waits, men to beguile,
Saw now, in Constance, all perfection grown,
And wondering how to be revenged the while,
He made a young knight, living in the town,
Love her so madly, with foul passion flown,
That verily he thought his life should spill,
Save that, of her, he once might have his will.

He wooed her, but it all availed him naught;
She would not sin in any wise or way;
And, for despite, he plotted in his thought
To make her die a death of shame some day.
He waited till the warden was away,
And, stealthily by night, he went and crept
To Hermengild's bed-chamber, while she slept.

Weary with waking for her orisons,
Slept Constance, and Dame Hermengild also.
This knight, by Satan's tempting, came at once
And softly to the bedside he did go.
And cut the throat of Hermengild, and so
Laid the hot reeking knife by fair Constance,
And went his way—where God give him mischance!

Soon after came the warden home again,
And with him Alla, king of all that land,
And saw his wife so pitilessly slain,
For which he wept and cried and wrung his hand;
And in the bed the bloody dagger, and
The Lady Constance. Ah! What could she say?
For very woe her wits went all away.

King Alla was apprised of this sad chance,
And told the time, and where, and in what wise
Was found in a wrecked ship the fair Constance,

As heretofore you've heard my tale apprise.
But in the king's heart pity did arise
When he saw so benignant a creature
Fallen in distress of such misadventure.

For as the lamb unto his death is brought,
So stood this innocent before the king;
And the false knight that had this treason wrought,
He swore that it was she had done this thing.
Nevertheless, there was much sorrowing
Among the people, saying, "We cannot guess
That she has done so great a wickedness.

"For we have seen her always virtuous,
And loving Hermengild as she loved life."
To this bore witness each one in that house,
Save he that slew the victim with his knife.
The gentle king suspected motive rife
In that man's heart; and thought he would inquire
Deeper therein, the truth to learn entire.

Alas, Constance! You have no champion,
And since you cannot fight, it's welaway!
But He Who died for us the cross upon,
And Satan bound (who lies yet where he lay),
So be your doughty Champion this day!
For, except Christ a miracle make known,
You shall be slain, though guiltless, and right soon.

She dropped upon her knees and thus she prayed:
"Immortal God, Who saved the fair Susanna
From lying blame, and Thou, O gracious Maid
(Mary, I mean, the daughter of Saint Anna),
Before whose Child the angels sing hosanna,
If I be guiltless of this felony,
My succour be, for otherwise I die!"

Have you not sometime seen a pallid face
Among the crowd, of one that's being led
Toward his death—one who had got no grace?
And such a pallor on his face was spread
All men must mark it, full of horrid dread,
Among the other faces in the rout.
So stood fair Constance there and looked about.

O queens that live in all prosperity,

Duchesses, and you ladies, every one,
Have pity, now, on her adversity;
An emperor's young daughter stands alone;
She has no one to whom to make her moan.
O royal blood that stands there in such dread,
Far are your friends away in your great need!

This King Alla has such compassion shown
(Since gentle heart is full of all pity),
That from his two eyes ran the tears right down.
"Now hastily go fetch a book," quoth he,
"And if this knight will swear that it was she
Who slew the woman, then will we make clear
The judge we shall appoint the case to hear."

A book of Gospels writ in British tongue
Was brought, and on this Book he swore anon
Her guilt; but then the people all among
A clenched hand smote him on the shoulder-bone,
And down he fell, as stunned as by a stone,
And both his eyes burst forth out of his face
In sight of everybody in that place.

A voice was heard by all that audience,
Saying: "You have here slandered the guiltless
Daughter of Holy Church, in high Presence;
Thus have you done, and further I'll not press."
Whereat were all the folk aghast, no less;
As men amazed they stand there, every one,
For dread of vengeance, save Constance alone.

Great was the fear and, too, the repentance
Of those that held a wrong suspicion there
Against this simple innocent Constance;
And by this miracle so wondrous fair,
And by her mediation and her prayer,
The king, with many another in that place,
Was there converted, thanks to Christ His grace!

This lying knight was slain for his untruth,
By sentence of King Alla, hastily;
Yet Constance had upon his death great ruth.
And after this, Jesus, of His mercy,
Caused Alla take in marriage, solemnly,
This holy maiden, so bright and serene,

And thus has Christ made fair Constance a queen.

But who was sad, if I am not to lie,
At this but Lady Donegild, she who
Was the king's mother, full of tyranny?
She thought her wicked heart must burst in two;
She would he'd never thought this thing to do;
And so she hugged her anger that he'd take
So strange a wife as this creature must make.

Neither with chaff nor straw it pleases me
To make a long tale, here, but with the corn.
Why should I tell of all the royalty
At that wedding, or who went first, well-born,
Or who blew out a trumpet or a horn?
The fruit of every tale is but to say,
They eat and drink and dance and sing and play.

They went to bed, as was but just and right,
For though some wives are pure and saintly things,
They must endure, in patience, in the night,
Such necessaries as make pleasurings
To men whom they have wedded well with rings,
And lay their holiness a while aside;
There may no better destiny betide.

On her he got a man-child right anon;
And to a bishop and the warden eke
He gave his wife to guard, while he was gone
To Scotland, there his enemies to seek;
Now Constance, who so humble is, and meek,
So long is gone with child that, hushed and still,
She keeps her chamber, waiting on Christ's will.

The time was come, a baby boy she bore;
Mauritius they did name him at the font;
This constable sent forth a messenger
And wrote unto King Alla at the front
Of all this glad event, a full account,
And other pressing matters did he say.
He took the letter and went on his way.

This messenger, to forward his own ends,
To the king's mother rode with swiftest speed,
Humbly saluting her as down he bends:
"Madam," quoth he, "be joyful now indeed!

To God a hundred thousand thanks proceed.
The queen has borne a child, beyond all doubt,
To joy and bliss of all this land about.

"Lo, here are letters sealed that say this thing,
Which I must bear with all the speed I may;
If you will send aught to your son, the king,
I am your humble servant, night and day."
Donegild answered: "As for this time, nay;
But here tonight I'd have you take your rest;
Tomorrow I will say what I think best."

This messenger drank deep of ale and wine,
And stolen were his letters, stealthily,
Out of his box, while slept he like a swine;
And counterfeited was, right cleverly,
Another letter, wrought full sinfully,
Unto the king, of this event so near,
All from the constable, as you shall hear.

The letter said, the queen delivered was
Of such a fiendish, horrible creature,
That in the castle none so hardy as
Durst, for a lengthy time, there to endure.
The mother was an elf or fairy, sure,
Come there by chance of charm, or sorcery,
And all good men hated her company.

Sad was the king when this letter he'd seen;
But to no man he told his sorrows sore,
But with his own hand he wrote back again:
"Welcome what's sent from Christ, for evermore,
To me, who now am learned in His lore;
Lord, welcome be Thy wish, though hidden still,
My own desire is but to do Thy will.

"Guard well this child, though foul it be or fair,
And guard my wife until my home-coming;
Christ, when He wills it, may send me an heir
More consonant than this with my liking."
This letter sealed, and inwardly weeping,
To the same messenger 'twas taken soon,
And forth he went; there's no more to be done.

O messenger, possessed of drunkenness,
Strong is your breath, your limbs do falter aye,

And you betray all secrets, great and less;
Your mind is gone, you jangle like a jay;
Your face is mottled in a new array!
Where drunkenness can reign, in any rout,
There is no counsel kept, beyond a doubt.

O Donegild, there is no English mine
Fit for your malice and your tyranny!
Therefore you to the Fiend I do resign,
Let him go write of your foul treachery!
Fie, mannish women! Nay, by God, I lie!
Fie, *fiendish spirit*, for I dare well tell,
Though you walk here, your spirit is in Hell!

This messenger came from the king again,
And at the king's old mother's court did light,
And she was of this messenger full fain
To please him in whatever way she might.
He drank until his girdle was too tight,
He slept and snored and mumbled, drunken-wise,
All night, until the sun began to rise.

Again were his letters stolen, every one,
And others counterfeited, in this wise:
"The king commands his constable, anon,
On pain of hanging by the high justice,
That he shall suffer not, in any guise,
Constance within the kingdom to abide
Beyond three days and quarter of a tide.

"But in the ship wherein she came to strand
She and her infant son and all her gear
Shall be embarked and pushed out from the land,
And charge her that she never again come here."
O Constance mine, well might your spirit fear,
And, sleeping, in your dream have great grievance
When Donegild arranged this ordinance.

This messenger, the morrow, when he woke,
Unto the castle held the nearest way,
And to the constable the letter took;
And when he'd read and learned what it did say,
Often he cried "Alas!" and "Welaway!
Lord Christ," quoth he, "how may this world endure?
So full of sin is many a bad creature.

"O mighty God, and is it then Thy will?
Since Thou art righteous judge, how can it be
That innocence may suffer so much ill
And wicked folk reign in prosperity?
O good Constance, alas! Ah, woe is me
That I must be your torturer, or die
A shameful death! There is no other way."

Wept both the young and old of all that place
Because the king this cursed letter sent,
And Constance, with a deathly pallid face,
Upon the fourth day to the ship she went.
Nevertheless, she took as good intent
The will of Christ, and kneeling on the strand,
She said: "Lord, always welcome Thy command!

"He that did keep me from all lying blame
The while I lived among you, sun and snow,
He can still guard me from all harm and shame
Upon salt seas, albeit I see not how.
As strong as ever He was, so is He now.
In Him I trust and in His Mother dear,
He is my sail, the star by which I steer."

Her little child lay crying in her arm,
And kneeling, piteously to him she said:
"Peace, little son, I will do you no harm."
With that the kerchief took she from her braid,
And binding it across his eyes, she laid
Again her arm about and lulled him fast
Asleep, and then to Heaven her eyes up-cast.

"Mother," she said, "O Thou bright Maid, Mary,
True is it that through woman's incitement
Mankind was banished and is doomed to die,
For which Thy Son upon the cross was rent;
Thy blessed eyes saw all of His torment;
Wherefore there's no comparison between
Thy woe and any woe of man, though keen.

"Thou sawest them slay Thy Son before Thine eyes;
And yet lives now my little child, I say!
O Lady bright, to Whom affliction cries,
Thou glory of womanhood, O Thou fair May,
Haven of refuge, bright star of the day,

Pity my child, Who of Thy gentleness
Hast pity on mankind in all distress!

"O little child, alas! What is your guilt,
Who never wrought the smallest sin? Ah me,
Why will your too hard father have you killed?
Have mercy, O dear constable!" cried she,
"And let my little child bide, safe from sea;
And if you dare not save him, lest they blame,
Then kiss him once in his dear father's name!"

Therewith she gazed long backward at the land,
And said: "Farewell, my husband merciless!"
And up she rose and walked right down the strand
Toward the ship; followed her all the press;
And ever she prayed her child to cry the less;
And took her leave; and with a high intent
She crossed herself; and aboard ship she went.

Victualled had been the ship, 'tis true—indeed
Abundantly—for her, and for long space;
Of many other things that she should need
She had great plenty, thanks be to God's grace!
Through wind and weather may God find her place
And bring her home! I can no better say;
But out to sea she stood upon her way.

Explicit secunda pars.
Sequitur pars tercia.

Alla the king came home soon after this
Unto his castle, of the which I've told,
And asked for wife and child, whom he did miss.
The constable about his heart grew cold,
And plainly all the story he then told,
As you have heard, I cannot tell it better,
And showed the king his seal and the false letter.

And said: "My lord, as you commanded me,
On pain of death, so have I done—in vain!"
The messenger was tortured until he
Made known the facts to all men, full and plain,
From night to night, in what beds he had lain.
And thus, by dint of subtle questioning,
'Twas reasoned out from whom this harm did spring.

The hand was known, now, that the letter wrote,
And all the venom of this cursed deed,
But in what wise I certainly know not,
The effect is this, that Alla, for her meed,
His mother slew, as men may plainly read,
She being false to her sworn allegiance,
And thus old Donegild ended with mischance.

The sorrow that this Alla, night and day,
Felt for his wife, and for his child also,
There is no human tongue on earth to say.
But now will I back to fair Constance go,
Who drifted on the seas, in pain and woe,
Five years and more, as was Lord Christ's command,
Before her ship approached to any land.

Under a heathen castle, at the last,
Whereof the name not in my text I find,
Constance and her young son the sea did cast.
Almighty God, Redeemer of mankind,
Have Constance and her little child in mind!
Who must fall into heathen hands and soon
Be near to death, as I shall tell anon.

Down from the castle came full many a wight
To stare upon the ship and on Constance.
But briefly, from the castle, on a night,
The warden's steward—God give him mischance!—
A thief who had renounced allegiance
To Christ, came to the ship and said he should
Possess her body, whether or not she would.

Woe for this wretched woman then began,
Her child cried out and she cried, piteously;
But blessed Mary helped her soon; the man
With whom she struggled well and mightily,
This thief fell overboard all suddenly,
And in the sea was drowned by God's vengeance;
And thus has Christ unsullied kept Constance.

O foul desire of lechery, lo thine end!
Not only dost thou cripple a man's mind,
But verily dost thou his body rend;
The end of all thy work and thy lusts blind
Is bitterness; how many may we find

That not for actions but for mere intent
To do this sin, to shame or death are sent.

How could this poor weak woman have the strength
To keep herself against that renegade?
Goliath of immeasurable length,
How could young David such a death have made,
So slight and without armour? How arrayed
Himself to look upon that dreadful face?
Men may well see, it was but God's own grace!

Who gave to Judith courage all reckless
To slay him, Holofernes, in his tent,
And to deliver out of wretchedness
The folk of God? I say, for this intent
That just as God a soul of vigour sent
To them, and saved them out of their mischance,
So sent He might and vigour to Constance.

Forth went her ship and through the narrow mouth
Of Ceuta and Gibraltar, on its way,
Sometimes to west, and sometimes north or south,
Aye and sometimes east, many a weary day,
Until Christ's Mother (blest be She for aye!)
Did destine, out of good that is endless,
To make an end of Constance' heaviness.

But let us leave this Constance now, and turn
To speak of that same Roman emperor
Who does, from Syria, by letters, learn
The slaughter of Christians and the dishonour
Done to his daughter by a vile traitor—
I mean that old sultana, years ago,
Who, at the feast, slew all men, high and low.

For which this emperor did send anon
A senator, with royal ordinance,
And other lords, God knows, and many a one,
On Syrians to take full high vengeance.
They burn, they slay, they give them all mischance
Through many a day; but, briefly to make end,
Homeward to Rome, at last, the victors wend.

This senator returned with victory
To Rome again, sailing right royally,
And spoke the ship (so goes the old story)

In which our Constance sat so piteously,
Nothing he knew of who she was, or why
She was in such a plight; nor would she say
Aught of herself, though she might die that day.

He took her into Rome, and to his wife
Gave her in charge, and her young son also;
And in his house she lived awhile her life.
Thus can Our Lady bring from deepest woe
Most woeful Constance, aye and more, we know.
And for a long time dwelt she in that place,
Engaged in God's good works, such was her grace.

The senator's good wife her own aunt was,
Yet for all that she knew her never the more;
I will no longer tarry in this case,
But to King Alla, whom we left, of yore,
Weeping for his lost wife and sighing sore.
I will return, and I will leave Constance
Under the senator's roof and governance.

King Alla, who had had his mother slain,
Upon a day fell to such repentance,
That, but to tell it briefly and be plain,
To Rome he came to pay his just penance
And put himself in the pope's ordinance,
In high and low; and Jesus Christ he sought
To pardon all the wicked deeds he'd wrought.

The news anon through all Rome town was borne,
How King Alla would come on pilgrimage,
By harbingers that unto him were sworn;
Whereat the senator, as was usage,
Rode out to him, with many of his lineage,
As well to show his own magnificence
As do to any king a reverence.

Great welcome gave this noble senator
To King Alla, and he to him also;
Each of them showed the other much honour;
And so befell that, in a day or so,
This senator to King Alla did go
To feast, and briefly, if I may not lie,
Constance' young son went in his company.

Some men would say, 'twas instance of Constance

That sent him with the senator to feast;
I cannot tell you every circumstance,
Be it as may be, he was there, at least.
But truth is that, at his mother's behest,
Before the king, during the banquet's space,
The child stood, looking in King Alla's face.

This child aroused within the king great wonder,
And to the senator he said, anon:
"Whose is the fair child that is standing yonder?"
"I know not," quoth he, "by God and Saint John!
A mother he has, but father has he none
That I know of"—and briefly, at a bound,
He told King Alla how this child was found.

"But God knows," said this senator, as well,
"So virtuous a liver, in my life
I never saw, as she is, nor heard tell
Of earthly woman, maiden, no nor wife.
I dare say, she would rather have a knife
Thrust through her breast than play a female trick;
There is no man could bring her to the prick."

Now this boy was as like unto Constance
As it was possible for one to be.
Alla had kept the face in remembrance
Of Dame Constance, and thereon now mused he:
Mayhap the mother of the child was she
Who was his wife. And inwardly he sighed,
And left the table with a hasty stride.

"In faith," thought he, "a phantom's in my head!
I ought to hold, by any right judgment,
That in the wide salt sea my wife is dead."
And afterward he made this argument:
"How know I but that Christ has hither sent
My wife by sea, as surely as she went
To my own land, the which was evident?"

And, after noon, home with the senator
Went Alla, all to test this wondrous chance.
The senator did Alla great honour,
And hastily he sent for fair Constance.
But, trust me, she was little fain to dance
When she had heard the cause of that command.

Scarcely upon her two feet could she stand.

When Alla saw his wife, he greeted her,
Then wept till it was a sad thing to see.
For, at the first glance, when she entered there,
He knew full verily that it was she.
And she for grief stood dumb as ever tree;
So was her heart shut up in her distress
When she remembered his unkindliness.

Twice did she swoon away there, in his sight;
He wept and he protested piteously.
"Now God," quoth he, "and all His angels bright
So truly on my spirit have mercy
As of your ills all innocent am I,
As is Maurice, my son, so like your face,
Or may the foul Fiend take me from this place!"

Long was the sobbing and the bitter pain
Before their woeful hearts could find surcease;
Great was the pity to hear them complain,
Whereof their sorrows surely did increase.
I pray you all my labour to release;
I cannot tell their grief until tomorrow,
I am so weary, speaking long of sorrow.

But, truth being known and all doubt now dismissed,
And Alla proven guiltless of her woe,
I think a hundred times they must have kissed,
And such great bliss there was between the two
That, save the joy that nevermore shall go,
There was naught like it, present time or past,
Nor shall be, ever, while the world shall last.

Then prayed she of her husband, all meekly,
As for her pain a splendid anodyne,
That he would pray her father, specially,
That, of his majesty, he would incline
And that, some day, would come with him to dine;
She prayed him, also, he should in no way
Unto her father one word of her say.

Some men would say, it was the child Maurice
Did bear this message to the emperor;
But, as I guess, King Alla was too nice
In etiquette to one of such honour

As he that was of Christendom the flower,
To send a child; and it is best to deem
He went himself, and so it well may seem.

This emperor has granted, graciously,
To come to dinner, as he's been besought,
And, well I think, he pondered busily
Upon the child, and on his daughter thought.
Alla went to his inn, and, as he ought,
Made ready for the feast in every wise
As far as his experience could devise.

The morrow came, and Alla rose to dress,
And, too, his wife, the emperor to meet;
And forth they rode in joy and happiness.
And when she saw her father in the street,
She lighted down, and falling at his feet,
"Father," quoth she, "your young child, your Constance,
Is now gone clean out of your remembrance.

"I am your daughter Constance," then said she,
"That once you sent to Syria. 'Tis I.
It is I, father, who, on the salt sea,
Was sent, alone to drift and doomed to die.
But now, good father, mercy must I cry:
Send me no more to heathendom, godless,
But thank my lord, here, for his kindliness."

But all the tender joy, who'll tell it all
That was between the three who thus are met?
But of my tale, now, make an end I shall;
The day goes fast, I will no longer fret.
These happy folk at dinner are all set,
And there, in joy and bliss, I let them dwell;
Happier a thousand fold than I can tell.

This child Maurice was, since then, emperor
Made by the pope, and lived right christianly.
Unto Christ's Church he did a great honour;
But I let all his story pass me by.
Of Constance is my tale, especially.
In ancient Roman histories men may find
The life of Maurice; I've it not in mind.

This King Alla, when came the proper day,
With his Constance, his saintly wife so sweet,

To England went again, by the straight way,
Where they did live in joy and quiet meet.
But little while it lasts us, thus complete.
Joy of this world, for time will not abide;
From day to day it changes as the tide.

Who ever lived in such delight one day
That was not stirred therefrom by his conscience,
Desire, or anger, or some kindred fray,
Envy, or pride, or passion, or offense?
I say but to one ending this sentence:
That but a little while in joy's pleasance
Lasted the bliss of Alla and Constance.

For death, that takes from high and low his rent,
When but a year had passed, as I should guess,
Out of the world King Alla quickly sent,
For whom Constance felt heavy wretchedness.
Now let us pray that God his soul will bless!
And of Dame Constance, finally to say,
Towards the town of Rome she took her way.

To Rome is come this holy one and pure,
And finds that all her friends are safe and sound;
For now she's done with all her adventure;
And when she'd come there, and her father found,
Down on her two knees fell she to the ground,
Weeping but joyful gave she God her praise
A hundred thousand times for all His ways.

In virtue, and with alms and holy deed,
They all live there, nor ever asunder wend;
Till death does part them, such a life they lead.
And fare now well, my tale is at an end.
And Jesus Christ, Who of His might may send
Joy after woe, govern us by His grace
And keep us all that now are in this place! Amen.

HERE ENDS THE LAWYER'S TALE;
NEXT FOLLOWS THE SAILOR'S PROLOGUE

THE SAILOR'S PROLOGUE

Our host upon his stirrups stood, anon,
And said: "Good men, now hearken, every one;
This was a useful story, for the nonce!
Sir parish priest," quoth he, "for God His bones.
Tell us a tale, as you agreed before.
I see well that you learned men of lore
Have learned much good, by God's great dignity!"
   The parson answered: "*Benedicite!*
What ails the man, so sinfully to swear?"
   Our host replied: "Ho, Jenkin, are you there?
I smell a Lollard in the wind," quoth he.
"Ho, good men!" said our host, "now hearken me;
Wait but a bit, for God's high passion do,
For we shall have a sermon ere we're through;
This Lollard here will preach to us somewhat."
   "Nay, by my father's soul, that shall he not!"
Replied the sailor; "Here he shall not preach,
Nor comment on the gospels here, nor teach.
We all believe in the great God," said he,
"But he would sow among us difficulty,
Or sprinkle cockles in our good clean corn;
And therefore, host, beforehand now, I warn
My jolly body shall a story tell
And I will clink for you so merry a bell
That it shall waken all this company;
But it shall not be of philosophy,
Nor yet of physics, nor quaint terms of law;
There is but little Latin in my maw."

HERE ENDS THE SAILOR'S PROLOGUE

THE SAILOR'S TALE

A merchant, dwelling, once, at Saint Denis,
Was rich, for which men held him wise, and he
Had got a wife of excellent beauty,
And very sociable and gay was she,
Which is a thing that causes more expense
Than all the good cheer and the deference
That men observe at festivals and dances;
Such salutations and masked countenances
Pass by as does a shadow on the wall;
But woe to him that must pay for it all.
The foolish husband, always he must pay;
He must buy clothes and other fine array,
And all for his own worship, wealthily,
In which, indeed, women dance jollily.
And if he cannot thus, peradventure,
Or cares not such expenses to endure,
But thinks his money wasted or quite lost,
Why then another man must pay the cost,
Or else lend gold, and that is dangerous.
     This noble merchant had a worthy house,
To which, each day, so many did repair,
Since he was generous and his wife was fair,
'Twas to be wondered at; but hear my tale.
Among his many guests of great and small
There was a monk, a handsome man and bold,
I think that he was thirty winters old,
Who was for ever coming to that place.
This youthful monk, who was so fair of face,
Was so far intimate with the worthy man,
And had been since their friendship first began,
That in the house familiar was he
As it is possible for friend to be.
     And in as much as this same goodly man
And too, this monk of whom I first began,
Were both born in the village they'd lived in,
The monk claimed him for cousin, or such kin;
And he again, he never said him nay,
But was as glad thereof as bird of day;
For to his heart it was a great pleasance.
Thus they were knit by endless alliance,
And each of them did other one assure

Of brotherhood the while their lives endure.
     Free was Dan John with money and expense
When in that house; and full of diligence
To please all there, whatever be his age.
He ne'er forgot to tip the humblest page
In all that house; according to degree
He gave the master, then the company,
Whene'er he came, some kind of honest thing;
For which they were as glad of his coming
As bird is glad when the new sun up-rises.
No more of all this now, for it suffices.
     It so befell, this merchant, on a day,
Prepared to make all ready his array,
Since to the town of Bruges he was to fare
To purchase there a quantity of ware;
To which end he'd to Paris sent someone
With messages, and he had prayed Dan John
That he should come to Saint-Denis to pay
Him and his wife a visit for a day,
Said 'twas a thing he certainly must do.
     This noble monk, whereof I'm telling you,
Had from his abbot, when he wished, license,
Because he was a man of great prudence,
An officer, indeed, who out did ride
To see to barns and granges, far and wide;
And now to Saint-Denis he came anon.
Who was so welcome as my lord Dan John,
Our cousin dear, so full of courtesy?
With him he brought a jug of rare malmsey,
And still another full of fine vernage,[1]
And wild fowls, too, as was his long usage.
And so I let them eat and drink and play,
This monk and merchant, for a night and day.
     Upon the third day this good trader rises,
And on his needs discreetly he advises;
And up into his counting-house goes he
To reckon up his books, as well may be,
For the past year, to learn how matters stood
And what he'd spent, and whether it were good,
And whether he were wealthier than before.
His books and bags, all that he had in store,

---

1. Vernage: an old wine of Italy.

He put before him on his counting-board;
He was right rich in goods and rich in hoard,
For the which cause he bolted fast his door;
He'd have no one disturb him while before
Him stood his books and monies at that time;
And thus he sat till it was well past prime.

Dan John had risen with the dawn, also,
And in the garden wandered to and fro,
Having said all his prayers full reverently.

Then came this goodwife, walking secretly
Into the garden, walking slow and soft.
And kissed him in salute, as she'd done oft.
A little girl came walking at her side,
Was in her charge to govern and to guide,
For yet beneath the rod was this small maid.

"O my dear cousin, O Dan John," she said,
"What ails you that so early you arise?"

"Dear niece," said he, "surely it should suffice
To sleep for five full hours of any night,
Unless 'twere for some old and languid wight,
As are these married men, who doze and dare
About as in the form the weary hare,
Worn all distraught by hounds both great and small.
But, my dear niece, just why are you so pale?
I must suppose of course that our good man
Has you belaboured since the night began,
And you were forced to sleep but scantily."

And with that word he laughed right merrily,
And, what of his own thoughts, he blushed all red.

This pretty wife began to shake her head,
And answered thus: "Aye, God knows all!" said she:
"Nay, cousin mine, it stands not so with me.
For by that God Who gave me soul and life,
In all the realm of France there is no wife
Who has less lust for that same sorry play.
For I may sing 'Alas!' and 'Welaway
That I was born!' but to no man," said she,
"Dare I to tell how this thing stands with me.
Wherefore I'm thinking from this land to wend,
Or else of my own life to make an end,
I am so fearful and so full of care."

This monk began, then, at the wife to stare,
And said: "Alas, my niece, may God forbid

That you, for any care or fear morbid,
Destroy yourself! But tell me of your grief;
Perhaps I may, whatever the mischief,
Counsel or help, and therefore do tell me
All the annoyance, for 'twill secret be;
For on my breviary I make oath
That never in my life, though lief or loath,
Shall I your secret whisper or betray."

"The same to you again," said she, "I say;
By God and by this breviary, I swear,
Though men this body of mine a-pieces tear,
No I will never, though I go to Hell,
Betray a single word that you may tell,
And this, not for our kinship and alliance,
But verily for love and true reliance."

Thus are they sworn, and thereupon they kissed,
And each told other such things as they list.

"Cousin," said she, "if I had time and space,
As I have not, and specially in this place,
Then would I tell a legend of my life,
What I have suffered since I've been a wife,
From my husband, though he is your cousin."

"Nay," quoth the monk, "by God and Saint Martin,
He is no more a cousin unto me
Than is this leaf a-hanging on the tree!
I call him so, by Saint-Denis of France,
To have but better reason to advance
With you, whom I have loved especially
Above all other women, and truly;
I swear this to you on the faith I own.
Tell me your grief before your man comes down,
Come, hasten now, and go your way anon."

"My dearest love," said she, "O my Dan John,
Right glad I were this counsel for to hide,
But it must out, I can't it more abide.
To me my husband is the poorest man
That ever was, since first the world began.
But since I am a wife, becomes not me
To tell a living soul our privity,
Either abed or in some other place;
God guard that I should tell it, of His grace!
For wife must never talk of her husband,
Save to his honour, as I understand.

But now to you thus much I can and shall:
So help me God, he is not worth, at all,
In any wise, the value of a fly.
But yet this grieves me most—he's niggardly;
And well you know that women naturally
Desire six things, and even so do I.
For women all would have their husbands be
Hardy, and wise, and rich, and therewith free,
Obedient to the wife, and fresh in bed.
But by that very Lord Who for us bled,
Though in his honour, myself to array
On Sunday next, I must yet go and pay
A hundred francs, or else be but forlorn.
Yet would I rather never have been born
Than have a scandal or disgrace, say I.
And if my husband such a thing should spy,
I were but lost, and therefore do I pray,
Lend me this sum, or else I perish, yea!
Dan John, I say, lend me these hundred francs;
By gad, I will not fail to give you thanks,
If only you will do the thing I pray.
For on a certain day I will repay,
And give to you what pleasure and service
I can give, aye, just as you may devise.
And if I don't, God take on me vengeance
As foul as once on Ganelon of France!"

    This gentle monk replied as you shall hear.
"Now truthfully, my own sweet lady dear,
I have," said he, "on you so great a ruth
That I do swear and promise you, in truth,
That when your husband goes to Flanders there,
I will deliver you from all this care;
For I will bring to you a hundred francs."

    And with that word he caught her by the flanks
And hugged her to him hard and kissed her oft.
"Go now your way," he said, "all still and soft,
And let us dine as soon as ever we may,
For by my dial it's the prime of day.
Go now, and be as true as I shall be."

    "Now all else God forbid, sir," then said she.
And in she went as jolly as a pie,
And bade the cooks that they to kitchen hie,
So that her men might dine, and that anon.

Up to her husband is this wife then gone,
And knocked upon his counting-room boldly.
    "*Qui est là?*" asked he.

                        "Peter![2] It is I,"
Said she; "What, sir, and how long will you fast?
How long time will you reckon up and cast
Your sums and books and other tiresome things?
The devil take away such reckonings!
You have enough, by gad, of God's mercy;
Come down today, and let your gold-bags be.
Why, are you not ashamed that our Dan John
Has fasted miserably all morning gone?
What! Let us hear a Mass and then go dine."

    "Wife," said this man, "little can you divine
The curious businesses that merchants have.
As for us traders, as may God me save,
And by that lord that all we call Saint Yve,
Among twelve merchants scarcely two shall thrive
Continually, and lasting into age.
We must keep open house and blithe visage,
While goes the world as it may chance to be,
And hold all our affairs in secrecy
Till we are dead; or else we must go play
At pilgrimage, or else go clean away.
And therefore have I great necessity
That on this curious world advised I be;
For evermore we merchants stand in dread
Of chance and mishap as our ways we tread.

    "To Flanders go I at the break of day,
And I'll come back as soon as ever I may.
For which, my dearest wife, your aid I seek
To be, to all, both courteous and meek,
And to maintain our wealth be studious,
And govern honourably and well our house.
You have enough in every sort of wise
That, to a thrifty household, should suffice.
You've clothes and food, I've seen to each detail,
And silver in your purse shall never fail."

    And with that word his counting-door he shut
And down he went, no longer tarrying, but
Right hastily a Mass for them was said,

---

2. Peter: that is, Saint Peter.

And speedily the tables there were spread,
And to the dinner swiftly all they sped;
And richly then the monk this merchant fed.
    After the dinner Dan John soberly
This merchant took aside, and privately
He said to him, "Cousin, it stands just so,
For I see well that you to Bruges will go.
God and good Saint Augustine speed and guide!
I pray you, cousin, that you'll wisely ride;
Guard your health well, and govern your diet
Temperately, especially in this heat.
Neither of us requires outlandish fare;
Farewell, dear cousin; God shield you from care.
If anything there be, by day or night,
If it lie in my power and my might,
That you would have me do, in any wise,
It shall be done, just as you may devise.
    "One thing, before you go, if it may be,
I pray you do, and that is, to lend me
A hundred francs, for but a week or two,
For certain cattle I must buy, to do
The stocking of a little place of ours.
So help me God, I would that it were yours!
I will not fail you, come next settling day,
Not for a thousand francs, a mile away.
But let this thing be secret, pray, for I,
Even tonight, must go these beasts to buy;
And farewell now, my own good cousin dear.
And many thanks for entertainment here."
    This noble merchant, civilly, anon,
Answered and said: "O cousin mine, Dan John,
Now surely this is but a small request;
My gold is yours and aye at your behest.
And not gold only, no but all my ware;
Take what you like, God shield that you should spare.
    "There's but one thing, which you know well enow
Of traders, for their money is their plow.
We may on credit trade, while we've a name,
But to be goldless is to lose the game.
Pay it again when you are at your ease;
In all I can, full fain am I to please."
    These hundred francs he went and got anon,
And privately he gave them to Dan John.

No one in all the world knew of this loan,
Saving this merchant and Dan John alone.
They drink, and talk, and walk awhile, and play,
Until Dan John sets out for his abbey.

The morrow came and forth this merchant rides
Toward Flanders; and his apprentice guides
Until he came to Bruges all happily.
Now went this merchant fast and busily
About his trade, and bought, and borrowed gold;
He neither played at dice nor danced, I'm told,
But like a merchant, briefly here to tell,
He led his life, and there I let him dwell.

On the first Sunday after he was gone,
To Saint-Denis is come again Dan John,
With face and tonsure shining from a shave.
In all the house was not so small a knave,
Nor any other, but was right glad, then,
Because my lord Dan John was come again.
And coming briefly to the point, anon
This lovely wife agreed with her Dan John
That for these hundred francs he should, all night,
Have her within his arms and bolt upright;
And this agreement was performed in bed.
In mirth all night a busy life they led
Till it was dawn, when Dan John went his way,
Bidding the household "Farewell!" and "Good-day!"
For none of them, nor any in the town,
Had of Dan John the least suspicion shown.
So forth he rode, home to his own abbey,
Or where he wished; no more of him I say.

This merchant, when all ended was the fair,
To Saint-Denis made ready to repair;
And with his wife he feasted and made cheer,
And told her that, since goods were very dear,
He needs must get more cash at his command,
For he was bound by his own note of hand
To pay some twenty thousand crowns anon.
For which this merchant is to Paris gone
To borrow there, from certain friends he had,
Some certain francs unto his own to add.
And when he'd come at length into the town,
Out of great friendship never yet outgrown,
Unto Dan John he went first, there to play,

Not to talk business, nor ask money, nay,
But to inquire and see to his welfare,
And, too, to tell about his Flemish ware,
As friends are wont when come from far or near.
Dan John made him a feast and merry cheer;
And he told him again, and specially,
How he had purchased well and luckily—
Thanks be to God!—all of his merchandise.
Save that he must, nor fail in any wise,
Obtain a loan, at least it would be best,
And then he'd have some time for joy and rest.

    Dan John replied: "No gladness do I feign
That sound in health you are come home again.
And if I were but rich, as I have bliss,
These twenty thousand crowns you should not miss,
Since you so kindly, but the other day,
Lent me some gold; and as I can and may,
I thank you, by the Lord and by Saint James!
Nevertheless, to no hand but our dame's,
Your wife at home, I gave the gold again
Upon your counter; she'll remember when
By certain tokens that I gave to her.
Now, by your leave, I must get up and stir,
Our abbot will be leaving town anon;
And in his company I must be gone.
Greet well our dame, your wife and my niece sweet,
And farewell, cousin dear, until we meet."

    This merchant, being a man full wary-wise,
Has got his loan and paid there in Paris,
To certain Lombards, ready in their hand,
The sum of gold, and got his note back, and
Now home he goes as merry as a jay.
For well he knew he stood in such array
That now he needs must make, with nothing lost,
A thousand francs above his total cost.

    His wife, all ready, met him at the gate,
As she was wont, though he came soon or late,
And all that night with pleasure did they pet,
For he was rich and cleanly out of debt.
When it was day, this merchant did embrace
His wife anew, and kissed her on her face,
And up he goes and makes it rather tough.

    "No more," cried she, "by God, you've had enough!"

And wantonly again with him she played,
Till, at the last, this merchant sighed and said:
"By God," said he, "I am a little wroth
With you, my wife, though to be so I'm loath.
And know you why? By God, and as I guess,
You've been the causing of some small strangeness
Between me and my cousin, dear Dan John.
You should have warned me, really, ere I'd gone,
That he to you a hundred francs had paid
In cash; he was put out, I am afraid,
Because I spoke to him of loans, by chance,
At least I judged so by his countenance.
Nevertheless, by God our Heavenly King,
I never thought to ask him such a thing.
I pray you, wife, never again do so;
But always tell me, ere away I go,
If any debtor has, in my absence,
Repaid to you, lest through your negligence
I might demand a sum already paid."

This wife was not astounded nor afraid,
But boldly she spoke up and that anon:
"Marry, I challenge that false monk, Dan John!
I kept, of all his coins, not one to tell.
He brought me certain gold—that know I well!
What! Ill success upon his friar's snout!
For God knows that I thought, with never a doubt,
That he had given it me because of you,
To advance thus my honour, and yours too,
In cousinhood, and for the merry cheer
That he has found so many a time right here.
But since I see our peace is thus disjoint,
I'll answer you but briefly, to the point.
You have far slacker debtors than am I!
For I will pay you well and readily
From day to day; and if it be I fail
I am your wife, tally it on my tail,
And I will pay as soon as ever I may.
For by my truth I have, on new array,
And not on rubbish, spent it, every sou.
And since so well I've spent it, all for you,
All for your honour, for God's sake, I say,
Do not be angry, but let's laugh and play.
My jolly body's yours in pledge," she said,

"By God, I will not pay you, save in bed!
Forgive me, then, my own sweet husband dear;
Let us be happy now—turn over here!"
    This merchant saw there was no remedy,
And, thought he, chiding were but great folly,
Since that the thing might not amended be.
    "Now wife," he said, "I do forgive, you see;
But on your life, don't run so far at large;
Conserve our wealth hereafter, so I charge."
    Thus ends my tale, and may the good God send
Tales fair enough until our lives shall end! Amen.

HERE ENDS THE SAILOR'S TALE

THE PRIORESS'S PROLOGUE

*The Merry Words of the Host to the Sailor
and to My Lady Prioress*

"Well said, by *corpus dominus*," said our host,
"Now long time may you sail along the coast,
Sir gentle master, gentle mariner!
God give this monk a thousand years bitter!
Aha, comrades, beware of such a jape!
The monk put into that man's hood an ape,
And in the wife's too, by Saint Augustine!
Invite no more monks to your house or inn.

   "But let that pass, and let us look about
To see who shall be next, of all this rout,
To tell a tale."

                  And after that he said,
As courteously as it had been a maid:
"My lady prioress, and by your leave,
So that I knew I should in no way grieve,
I would opine that tell a tale you should,
The one that follows next if you but would.
Now will you please vouchsafe it, lady dear?"
   "Gladly," said she, and spoke as you shall hear.

Explicit

THE PRIORESS'S INVOCATION

Domine, dominus noster.

"O Lord, Our Lord, Thy name how marvelous
Is spread through all this mighty world," said she;
"For not alone Thy praise so glorious

154

Is given by men of worth and dignity,
But from the mouths of children Thy bounty
Is hymned, yea, even sucklings at the breast
Do sometimes Thy laudation manifest.

"Wherefore in praise, as best I can or may,
Of Thee and of that pure white Lily-flower
Who bore Thee, and is yet a maid alway,
I tell a tale as best is in my power,
Not that I may increase Her heavenly dower,
For She Herself is honour and the one
From Whom spring wealth and goodness, next Her Son.

"O Mother-Maid! O Maiden-Mother free!
O bush unburnt, burning in Moses' sight,
Who ravished so the Soul of Deity,
With Thy meekness, the Spirit of the Light,
That His virtue, which was Thy soul's delight,
Conceived in Thee the Father's wise Essence,
Help me to speak now with all reverence!

"Lady, Thy goodness and Thy generous grace,
Thy virtue and Thy great humility—
No tongue may say, no pen may fully trace;
For sometimes, Lady, ere men pray to Thee,
Thou goest before, of Thy benignity,
And givest us the true light, by Thy prayer,
To guide us all unto Thy Son so dear.

"I cannot bear the burden, blessed Queen,
Of fitly praising all Thy worthiness,
My wisdom and my knowledge are too mean;
But as a child of twelve months old, or less,
That scarcely any word can well express,
So fare I now, and therefore do I pray,
Guide Thou that song of Thee which I shall say!"

Explicit

THE PRIORESS'S TALE

In Asia, in a city rich and great
There was a Jewry set amidst the town,

Established by a rich lord of the state
For usury and gain of ill renown,
Hateful to Christ and those who are His own;
And through that street a man might ride or wend,
For it was free[1] and open at each end.

A little school for Christian folk there stood,
Down at the farther end, in which there were
A many children born of Christian blood,
Who learned in that same school, year after year,
Such teachings as with men were current there,
Which is to say, to sing well and to read,
As children do of whatsoever creed.

Among these children was a widow's son,
A little choir boy, seven years of age,
Who went to school as days passed one by one,
And who, whenever saw he the image
Of Jesus' Mother, it was his usage,
As he'd been taught, to kneel down there and say
Ave Maria, ere he went his way.

Thus had this widow her small son well taught
Our Blessed Lady, Jesus' Mother dear,
To worship always, and he ne'er forgot,
For simple child learns easily and clear;
But ever, when I muse on matters here,
Saint Nicholas stands aye in my presence,
For he, when young, did do Christ reverence.

This little child, his little lesson learning,
Sat at his primer in the school, and there,
While boys were taught the antiphons, kept turning,
And heard the *Alma redemptoris* fair,
And drew as near as ever he did dare,
Marking the words, remembering every note,
Until the first verse he could sing by rote.

He knew not what this Latin meant to say,
Being so young and of such tender age,
But once a young school-comrade did he pray
To expound to him the song in his language,
Or tell him why the song was in usage;

---

1. The third Council of Lateran (1179) had prohibited Christians from lodging even transiently in a ghetto.

Asking the boy the meaning of the song,
On his bare knees he begged him well and long.

His fellow was an older lad than he,
And answered thus: "This song, as I've heard say,
Was made to praise Our Blessed Lady free,
Her to salute and ever Her to pray
To be our help when comes our dying day.
I can expound to you only so far;
I've learned the song; I know but small grammar."

"And is this song made in all reverence
Of Jesus' Mother?" asked this innocent;
"Now truly I will work with diligence
To learn it all ere Christmas sacrament,
Though for my primer I take punishment
And though I'm beaten thrice within the hour,
Yet will I learn it by Our Lady's power!"

His fellow taught him on their homeward way
Until he learned the antiphon by rote.
Then clear and bold he sang it day by day,
Each word according with its proper note;
And twice each day it welled from out his throat,
As schoolward went he and as homeward went;
On Jesus' Mother was his fixed intent.

As I have said, as through the Jewry went
This little school-boy, out the song would ring,
And joyously the notes he upward sent;
O *Alma redemptoris* would he sing;
To his heart's core it did the sweetness bring
Of Christ's dear Mother, and, to Her to pray,
He could not keep from singing on his way.

Our primal foe, the serpent Sathanas,
Who has in Jewish heart his hornets' nest,
Swelled arrogantly: "O Jewish folk, alas!
Is it to you a good thing, and the best,
That such a boy walks here, without protest,
In your despite and doing such offense
Against the teachings that you reverence?"

From that time forth the Jewish folk conspired
Out of the world this innocent to chase;
A murderer they found, and thereto hired,

Who in an alley had a hiding-place;
And as the child went by at sober pace,
This cursed Jew did seize and hold him fast,
And cut his throat, and in a pit him cast.

I say, that in a cesspool him they threw,
Wherein these Jews did empty their entrails.
O cursed folk of Herod, born anew,
How can you think your ill intent avails?
Murder will out, 'tis sure, nor ever fails,
And chiefly when God's honour vengeance needs.
The blood cries out upon your cursed deeds.

"O martyr firm in thy virginity,
Now mayest thou sing, and ever follow on
The pure white Lamb Celestial"—quoth she—
"Whereof the great evangelist, Saint John,
In Patmos wrote, saying that they are gone
Before the Lamb, singing a song that's new,
And virgins all, who never woman knew."

This widow poor awaited all that night
Her child's return to her, but he came not;
For which, so soon as it was full daylight,
With pale face full of dread, and busy thought,
At school she sought and everywhere she sought,
Until, at last, from all her questioning she
Learned that he last was seen in the Jewry.

With mother's pity in her breast enclosed
She ran, as she were half out of her mind,
To every place where it might be supposed,
In likelihood, that she her son should find;
And ever on Christ's Mother meek and kind
She called until, at last, Our Lady wrought
That amongst the cursed Jews the widow sought.

She asked and she implored, all piteously,
Of every Jew who dwelt in that foul place,
To tell her where her little child could be.
They answered "Nay." But Jesus, of His grace,
Put in her mind, within a little space,
That after him in that same spot she cried
Where he'd been cast in pit, or near beside.

O Thou great God, Who innocents hast called

To give Thee praise, now shown is Thy great might!
This gem of chastity, this emerald,
Of martyrdom the ruby clear and bright,
Began, though slain and hidden there from sight,
The *Alma redemptoris* loud to sing,
So clear that all the neighbourhood did ring.

The Christian folk that through the ghetto went
Came running for the wonder of this thing,
And hastily they for the provost sent;
He also came without long tarrying,
And gave Christ thanks, Who is of Heaven King,
And, too, His Mother, honour of mankind;
And after that the Jews there did he bind.

This child, with piteous lamentation, then
Was taken up, singing his song alway;
And, honoured by a great concourse of men,
Carried within an abbey near, that day.
Swooning, his mother by the black bier lay,
Nor easily could people who were there
This second Rachel carry from the bier.

With torture and with shameful death, each one,
The provost did these cursed Hebrews serve
Who of the murder knew, and that anon;
From justice to the villains he'd not swerve.
Evil shall have what evil does deserve.
And therefore, with wild horses, did he draw,
And after hang, their bodies, all by law.

Upon the bier lay this poor innocent
Before the altar, while the mass did last,
And after that the abbot and monks went
About the coffin for to close it fast;
But when the holy water they did cast,
Then spoke the child, at touch of holy water,
And sang, "O *Alma redemptoris mater!*"

This abbot, who was a right holy man,
As all monks are, or as they ought to be,
The dead young boy to conjure then began,
Saying: "O dear child, I do beg of thee,
By virtue of the Holy Trinity,
Tell me how it can be that thou dost sing

After thy throat is cut, to all seeming?"

"My throat is cut unto the spinal bone,"
Replied the child. "By nature of my kind
I should have died, aye, many hours agone,
But Jesus Christ, as you in books shall find,
Wills that His glory last in human mind;
Thus for the honour of His Mother dear,
Still may I sing 'O *Alma*' loud and clear.

"This well of mercy, Jesus' Mother sweet,
I always loved, after my poor knowing;
And when came time that I my death must meet,
She came to me and bade me only sing
This anthem in the pain of my dying,
As you have heard, and after I had sung,
She laid a precious pearl upon my tongue.

"Wherefore I sing, and sing I must, 'tis plain,
In honour of that blessed Maiden free,
Till from my tongue is taken away the grain;
And afterward she said thus unto me:
'My little child, soon will I come for thee,
When from thy tongue the little bead they take;
Be not afraid, thee I will not forsake.'"

The holy monk, this abbot, so say I,
The tongue caught out and took away the grain,
And he gave up the ghost, then, easily,
And when the abbot saw this wonder plain,
The salt tears trickled down his cheeks like rain,
And humbly he fell prone upon the ground,
Lying there still as if he had been bound.

And all the monks lay there on the pavement,
Weeping and praising Jesus' Mother dear,
And after that they rose and forth they went,
Taking away this martyr from his bier,
And in a tomb of marble, carved and clear,
Did they enclose his little body sweet;
Where he is now—God grant us him to meet!

O you young Hugh of Lincoln,[2] slain also
By cursed Jews, as is well known to all,
Since it was but a little while ago,
Pray you for us, sinful and weak, who call,
That, of His mercy, God will still let fall
Something of grace, and mercy multiply,
For reverence of His Mother dear on high. Amen.

HERE ENDS THE PRIORESS'S TALE

2. Referring to a murder that had attracted much attention in England during the reign of Henry III.

PROLOGUE TO SIR THOPAS

The Merry Words of the Host to Chaucer

When told was all this miracle, every man
So sober fell 'twas wonderful to see,
Until our host in jesting wise began,
And for the first time did he glance at me,
Saying, "What man are you?"—'twas thus quoth he—
"You look as if you tried to find a hare,
For always on the ground I see you stare.

"Come near me then, and look up merrily.
Now make way, sirs, and let this man have place;
He in the waist is shaped as well as I;
This were a puppet in an arm's embrace
For any woman, small and fair of face.
Why, he seems absent, by his countenance,
And gossips with no one for dalliance.

"Since other folk have spoken, it's your turn;
Tell us a mirthful tale, and that anon."
"Mine host," said I, "don't be, I beg, too stern,
For of good tales, indeed, sir, have I none,
Save a long rhyme I learned in years agone."
"Well, that is good," said he; "now shall we hear
It seems to me, a thing to bring us cheer."

Explicit

SIR THOPAS

The First Fit

Listen, lords, with good intent,
I truly will a tale present

Of mirth and of solace;
All of a knight was fair and gent[1]
In battle and in tournament.
His name was Sir Thopas.

Born he was in a far country,
In Flanders, all beyond the sea,
And Poperinghe the place;
His father was a man full free,
And lord he was of that countree,
As chanced to be God's grace.

Sir Thopas was a doughty swain,
White was his brow as paindemaine,[2]
His lips red as a rose;
His cheeks were like poppies in grain,
And I tell you, and will maintain,
He had a comely nose.

His hair and beard were like saffron
And to his girdle reached adown,
His shoes were of cordwain;[3]
From Bruges were come his long hose brown,
His rich robe was of ciclatoun[4]—
And cost full many a jane.[5]

Well could he hunt the dim wild deer
And ride a-hawking by river,
With grey goshawk on hand;
Therewith he was a good archer,
At wrestling was there none his peer
Where any ram[6] did stand.

Full many a maiden, bright in bower,
Did long for him for paramour
When they were best asleep;
But chaste he was, no lecher sure,
And sweet as is the bramble-flower
That bears a rich red hepe.[7]

---

1. Gent: of gentle birth.   2. Paindemaine: white bread of the finest quality.
3. Cordwain: Cordovan leather.   4. Ciclatoun: a costly kind of thin cloth.   5. Jane: a
Genoese coin, current in England in the 14th century.   6. Ram: the usual prize in
wrestling.   7. Modern, hip.

And so befell, upon a day,
In truth, as I can tell or may,
    Sir Thopas out would ride;
He mounted on his stallion grey,
And held in hand a lance, I say,
    With longsword by his side.

He spurred throughout a fair forest
Wherein was many a dim wild beast,
    Aye, both the buck and hare;
And as he spurred on, north and east,
I tell you now he had, in breast,
    A melancholy care.

There herbs were springing, great and small,
The licorice blue and white setwall,
    And many a gillyflower,
And nutmeg for to put in ale,
All whether it be fresh or stale,
    Or lay in chest in bower.

The birds they sang, upon that day,
The sparrow-hawk and popinjay,
    Till it was joy to hear;
The missel thrush he made his lay,
The tender stockdove on the spray,
    She sang full loud and clear.

Sir Thopas fell to love-longing
All when he heard the throstle sing,
    And spurred as madman would:
His stallion fair, for this spurring,
Did sweat till men his coat might wring,
    His two flanks were all blood.

Sir Thopas grown so weary was
With spurring on the yielding grass,
    So fierce had been his speed,
That down he laid him in that place
To give the stallion some solace
    And let him find his feed.

"O holy Mary, *ben'cite!*
What ails my heart that love in me
    Should bind me now so sore?
For dreamed I all last night, pardie,

An elf-queen shall my darling be,
    And sleep beneath my gore.[8]

"An elf-queen will I love, ywis,[9]
For in this world no woman is
    Worthy to be my make
                    In town;
All other women I forsake,
And to an elf-queen I'll betake
    Myself, by dale and down!"

Into his saddle he climbed anon
And spurred then over stile and stone,
    An elf-queen for to see,
Till he so far had ridden on
He found a secret place and won
    The land of Faëry
                    So wild;
For in that country was there none
That unto him dared come, not one,
    Not either wife or child.

Until there came a great giant,
Whose name it was Sir Oliphant,[10]
    A dangerous man indeed;
He said: "O Childe, by Termagant,
Save thou dost spur from out my haunt,
    Anon I'll slay thy steed
                    With mace.
For here the queen of Faëry,
With harp and pipe and harmony,
    Is dwelling in this place."

The Childe said: "As I hope to thrive,
We'll fight the morn, as I'm alive,
    When I have my armour;
For well I hope, and *par ma fay*,
That thou shalt by this lance well pay,
    And suffer strokes full sore;
                    Thy maw
Shall I pierce through, and if I may,

---

8. Gore: the gore of his garment.   9. Ywis: truly, certainly.   10. Oliphant: an old form of elephant.

Ere it be fully prime of day,
　Thou'lt die of wounds most raw."

Sir Thopas drew aback full fast;
This giant at him stones did cast
　Out of a fell staff-sling;
But soon escaped was Childe Thopas,
And all it was by God's own grace,
　And by his brave bearing.

And listen yet, lords, to my tale,
Merrier than the nightingale,
　Whispered to all and some,
How Sir Thopas, with pride grown pale,
Hard spurring over hill and dale,
　Came back to his own home.

His merry men commanded he
To make for him both game and glee,
　For needs now must he fight
With a great giant of heads three,
For love in the society
　Of one who shone full bright.

"Do come," he said, "my minstrels all,
And jesters, tell me tales in hall
　Anon in mine arming;
Of old romances right royal,
Of pope and king and cardinal,
　And e'en of love-liking."

They brought him, first, the sweet, sweet wine,
And mead within a maselyn,[11]
　And royal spicery
Of gingerbread that was full fine,
Cumin and licorice, I opine,
　And sugar so dainty.

He drew on, next his white skin clear,
Of finest linen, clean and sheer,
　His breeches and a shirt;
And next the shirt a stuffed acton,[12]

---

11. Maselyn: a maple bowl.　12. Acton: a quilted jacket.

And over that a habergeon[13]
   'Gainst piercing of his heart.

And over that a fine hauberk[14]
That was wrought all of Jewish work
   And reinforced with plate;
And over that his coat-of-arms,
As white as lily-flower that charms,
   Wherein he will debate.

His shield was all of gold so red,
And thereon was a wild boar's head
   A carbuncle beside;
And now he swore, by ale and bread,
That soon "this giant shall be dead,
   Betide what may betide!"

His jambeaux[15] were of cuir-bouilli,[16]
His sword sheath was of ivory,
   His helm of latten[17] bright,
His saddle was of rewel[18] bone,
And as the sun his bridle shone,
   Or as the full moonlight.

His spear was of fine cypress wood,
That boded war, not brotherhood,
   The head full sharply ground;
His steed was all a dapple grey
Whose gait was ambling, on the way,
   Full easily and round
           In land.
Behold, my lords, here is a fit![19]
If you'll have any more of it,
   You have but to command.

The Second Fit

Now hold your peace, *par charitee,*
Both knight and lady fair and free,
   And hearken to my spell;

---

13. Habergeon: a short coat of mail. 14. Hauberk: a long coat of mail. 15. Jambeaux: leg armour. 16. Cuir-bouilli: hardened leather. 17. Latten: a brass-like alloy. 18. Rewel bone: probably whale or walrus ivory. 19. Fit: a part of a ballad.

Of battle and of chivalry
And all of ladies' love-drury[20]
   Anon I will you tell.

Romances men recount of price,
Of King Horn and of Hypotis,
   Of Bevis and Sir Guy,
Of Sir Libeaux and Plain-d'Amour;
But Sir Thopas is flower sure
   Of regal chivalry.

His good horse all he then bestrode,
And forth upon his way he rode
   Like spark out of a brand;
Upon his crest he bore a tower
Wherein was thrust a lily-flower;
   God grant he may withstand!

He was a knight adventurous,
Wherefore he'd sleep within no house,
   But lay down in his hood;
His pillow was his helmet bright,
And by him browsed his steed all night
   On forage fine and good.

Himself drank water of the well,
As did the knight Sir Percival,
   So worthy in his weeds,
Till on a day . . .

HERE THE HOST HALTED CHAUCER
IN HIS TALE OF THOPAS

---

20. Love-drury: love, passion.

PROLOGUE TO MELIBEUS

"No more of this, for God's high dignity!"
Exclaimed our host, "For you, sir, do make me
So weary with your vulgar foolishness
That, as may God so truly my soul bless,
My two ears ache from all your worthless speech;
Now may such rhymes the devil have, and each!
This sort of thing is doggerel," said he.

    "Why so?" I asked, "Why will you hinder me
In telling tales more than another man,
Since I have told the best rhyme that I can?"

    "By God!" cried he, "now plainly, in a word,
Your dirty rhyming is not worth a turd;
You do naught else but waste and fritter time.
Sir, in one word, you shall no longer rhyme.
Let's see if you can use the country verse,
Or tell a tale in prose—you might do worse—
Wherein there's mirth or doctrine good and plain."

    "Gladly," said I, "by God's sweet tears and pain,
I will relate a little thing in prose
That ought to please you, or so I suppose,
For surely, else, you're contumelious.
It is a moral tale, right virtuous,
Though it is told, sometimes, in different wise
By different folk, as I shall you apprise.
As thus: You know that each evangelist
Who tells the passion of Lord Jesus Christ
Says not in all things as his fellows do,
But, nonetheless, each gospel is all true,
And all of them accord in their essence,
Howbeit there's in telling difference.
For some of them say more and some say less
When they His piteous passion would express;

169

I mean now Mark and Matthew, Luke and John;
Yet, without doubt, their meaning is all one.
And therefore, masters all, I do beseech,
If you should think I vary in my speech,
As thus: That I do quote you somewhat more
Of proverbs than you've ever heard before,
Included in this little treatise here,
To point the morals out, as they appear,
And though I do not quite the same words say
That you have heard before, yet now, I pray,
You'll blame me not; for in the basic sense
You will not find a deal of difference
From the true meaning of that tale polite
After the which this happy tale I write.
And therefore hearken now to what I say,
And let me tell you all my tale, I pray."

Explicit

THE TALE OF MELIBEUS

A young man named Melibeus, mighty and rich, begot on Prudence, his wife, a daughter who was called Sophie.

It happened one day that, for his amusement he went into the fields to play. His wife and daughter remained at home, the doors of his house being all fast shut and locked. But three of his old enemies, having spied out the state of things, set ladders to the wall of the house and entered therein by a window; and they beat the wife and wounded the daughter with five dangerous wounds in five different places; that is to say, in her feet, in her hands, in her ears, in her nose, and in her mouth; and they left her for dead and went away.

When Melibeus returned to his house and saw all this mischief, he, like a madman, rending his clothes, began to weep and cry.

Prudence his wife, so far as she dared, besought him to cease his weeping; nevertheless he wept and cried but the more.

This noble wife Prudence remembered then the opinion of Ovid, in his book *The Remedy for Love*, wherein he says: "He is but a fool who interferes with the mother weeping for the death of her child, until she shall have wept her fill, and for a certain time; and only then may a man be diligent, with kind words, to comfort her, and pray her to forgo her tears." For which reason this noble wife Prudence suffered her husband to weep and cry for a time; and when she saw her opportunity, she spoke to him. "Alas, my lord!" said she, "Why do you allow yourself to act like a fool? For truly it becomes not a wise man to show such sorrow. Your daughter, by the grace of God, shall be healed and will recover. And were she dead even now, you ought not, for this, to destroy yourself. Seneca says: 'The wise man will not take too sorrowfully to heart the death of his children, but will suffer it with patience, just as he awaits the death of his own body.'"

Melibeus answered, saying: "What man should cease his weeping who has so great a cause to weep? Jesus Christ Our Lord Himself wept for the death of His friend Lazarus."

Prudence replied: "Indeed, well do I know that moderate weeping is not forbidden to anyone who sorrows, among sorrowing folk; but, rather, it is permitted him to weep. The Apostle Paul writes unto the Romans: 'Rejoice with them that do rejoice, and weep with them that weep.' But though a tempered weeping may be granted, excessive weeping certainly is forbidden. Moderation in grief should be considered, according to the teaching of Seneca. 'When your friend is dead,' says he, 'let not your eyes be too wet with tears, nor yet too dry; and though your tears rise to the eyes, let them not fall.' So, when you have given over your friend, be diligent in procuring another; and this is wiser than to weep for the friend who is lost; for therein is no profit. And therefore, if you govern yourself with wisdom, put away sorrow out of your heart. Remember how Jesus son of Sirach says: 'A joyous and glad heart makes a man flourish in his age; but truly a sorrowful heart drieth the bones.' He says also that sorrow hath killed many a man. Solomon says that as moths in the sheep's fleece annoy the clothes, and as small worms the tree, so sorrow annoys the heart. Wherefore we ought to be patient, not less for the death of our children than for the loss of worldly goods.

"Remember the patient Job, when he had lost his children and his substance, and had in his body received and endured many a grievous tribulation, yet said he thus: 'The Lord gave, and the Lord hath taken away; blessed be the name of the Lord.'"

To these things Melibeus answered, saying to Prudence his wife: "All your words are true, and likewise profitable, but verily my heart is troubled so grievously with this sorrow that I know not what to do."

"Call, then," said Prudence, "all of your true friends and those of your kindred who are wise; tell them your trouble and hearken to what they say in council; and then govern yourself according to their advice. Says Solomon: 'Do nothing without advice, and thou shalt never repent.'"

Then, upon the advice of his wife Prudence, Melibeus called together a great gathering of people, old and young; and some among them were surgeons and physicians; and some were of his old enemies who seemed to have become reconciled to him; and there came some of his neighbours who respected him more out of fear than of love, as often happens; there came also a great many subtle flatterers; and there were wise advocates learned in the law.

And when all these folks were assembled together, Melibeus, with sorrowful words and mien, told them his trouble; and by the manner of his speech it appeared that in his heart he bore a savage anger, ready to take vengeance upon his foes, and was desirous that the war upon them should quickly come. Nevertheless, he asked their advice upon this matter. Then a surgeon, by leave and voice of all present who were wise, rose up and spoke to Melibeus as you shall hear.

"Sir," said he, "as for us surgeons, it belongs to us that we do for everyone the best that we can, when we have been retained, and that we do no harm to our patients. Wherefore it happens, many times and oft, that when two men have wounded one another, the same surgeon heals them both. Therefore it does not become us to foment warfare nor to support factions. And certainly, as to the healing of your daughter, although she is dangerously wounded, we will be so attentive, by day and by night, that, with God's grace, she shall be made sound and whole again, and that as soon as may be possible."

Almost in the same words the physicians answered, save that they added: "Just as diseases are cured by their contraries, so shall men cure war by vengeance."

His neighbours, full of envy, his false friends who feigned to be reconciled to him, and his flatterers, made a semblance of weeping; and they greatly aggravated the matter by praising Melibeus, speaking of his might, his power, his wealth, and his friends, and disparaging the strength of his enemies; and they said outright, that very swiftly he should begin the war and wreak vengeance upon his foes.

Then arose an advocate, a wise man, by leave and advice of others who were wise, and said: "Masters, the matter for which we are assembled here is a heavy thing, and a high, what with the wrong and wickedness that have been done, and by reason of the great evil that may follow hereafter from this same cause; and, too, by reason of the great wealth and power of both parties. For all of these reasons it were dangerous indeed to err in this matter. Wherefore, Melibeus, this is our judgment: we counsel you above all things, that, without delay, you take steps to guard your own person in such wise that you shall lack neither spy nor watchman. And we counsel, that in your house you establish a sufficient garrison, so that the house may be as well defended as you yourself. But, to say truth, as to initiating warfare in order to obtain a sudden revenge, we can give no opinion, in so short a time, on whether such a move will be profitable. Therefore we ask for leisure and time wherein to deliberate upon the matter more fully. For the common proverb runs 'Resolve in haste, in haste repent.' And besides, men hold that he is a wise judge who quickly understands a case and leisurely pronounces thereupon. For though delay may be annoying, nevertheless it is not to be blamed when it is a question of rendering just judgments, or of securing vengeance, when the delay is both sufficient and reasonable. And that was shown, in example, by Our Lord Jesus Christ. For when the woman taken in adultery was brought into His presence, in order to learn what He would have them to do with her, though He well knew what He would thereafter answer, yet would He not answer quickly, but deliberated; and He stooped down and wrote twice upon the ground. For all these reasons, we ask time in which to deliberate, and thereafter we will counsel you, by the grace of God, as to the most profitable course."

Up started, then, all of the young folk, at once, and the greater part of them scorned the counsel of the old wise men; and they raised a clamour and said: that just as it is well to strike while the iron is hot, so should men wreak their vengeance while they are fresh in anger. And they all cried loudly, "War, war!"

Upon this, one of the old wise ones arose, and with his hand commanding silence and attention, he said: "Masters, there is many a man to cry 'War, War!' who yet knows but little of the meaning of it. War, in the beginning, has so high an entrance, and so wide, that every man may enter when he pleases, and may find war easily. But truly, what the end of war shall be is not so easy to know. For when a war is once begun, many an unborn child shall die in the womb because of the strife, or else shall be born into sorrow and die in wretchedness. Therefore, ere any war begins, men should take much counsel together and act only after much deliberation."

But when this old man thought to reinforce his words with reasons, then well-nigh all the younger folk arose and began to heckle him and to break up his argument, bidding him cut short his remarks. For indeed, he that preaches to those who have ears but hear not, makes of himself a nuisance. As Jesus son of Sirach says: "A tale out of season is as musick in mourning." Which is to say, it avails as much to speak to folk to whom the speech is annoying as to sing before one who weeps. And when this wise man understood that he lacked an audience, he sat down again, much confused. For Solomon says: "When there is none will hear thee, cease to speak." "I see well," said this wise man, "that the proverb says truth, which runs, 'Good counsel is wanting when it is most needed.'"

Again, Melibeus had in his council many men who said one thing in his private ear and spoke otherwise in general audience.

When Melibeus heard that the greater part of his councillors were agreed on war, straightway he showed himself in accord with them and confirmed their judgment. Then Dame Prudence, seeing that her husband shaped his course for war and revenge, humbly and after biding her time, said to him: "My lord, I beseech you as earnestly as I dare and can, that you go not too hastily in this matter; and for your own good give me a hearing. For Petrus Alfonsus says: 'And if one man do to another any good or any evil, let there be no haste to repay it in kind; for then will the friend remain friendly, while the enemy shall but the longer fear.' The proverb has it: 'He hastens well who wisely can delay.' And in foolish haste there is no profit."

This Melibeus answered Prudence his wife: "I purpose not to work by your counsel, for many causes and reasons. For truly every man would then take me for a fool; by which I mean: if I by your advising, should change things that have been ordained and confirmed by so many wise men. Secondly, I say that all women are evil and none good. 'Behold, this have I found (saith the Preacher), counting one by one, to find out the account; which yet my soul seeketh, but I found not: one man among a thousand have I found; but a woman among all those have I not found.' And certainly, if I were to be governed by your counsel, it would appear as if I had given over to you my sovereignty; and may God forbid that such a thing should ever be. For Jesus son of Sirach says: 'A woman, if she maintain her husband, is full of anger, impudence, and much reproach.' And Solomon says: 'Give not thy son and wife, thy brother and friend, power over thee while thou livest, and give not thy goods to another: lest it repent thee, and thou entreat for the same again. As long as thou livest and hast breath in thee, give not thyself over to any. For better it is that thy children should seek to thee, than that thou shouldest stand to their courtesy.' And also, if I were to work according to your counselling, certain it is that my counsels must be kept secret until the proper time to make them known; and this could not thus be. For it is written that 'The chattering of women can conceal nothing except that which they do not know.' Furthermore, the philosopher says: 'In evil counsel women surpass men.' And for all these reasons I will not follow your advice."

When Dame Prudence, very affably and with great patience, had heard all that her husband chose to say, then she asked of him leave to speak, and said: "My lord, as to your first reason, surely it may readily be answered. For I say that it is no folly to over-rule counsel when circumstances are changed, or when the cause appears otherwise than at the first. And, moreover, I say that though you have sworn and war-

ranted to perform your enterprise, nevertheless, should you refuse for
just cause to perform it, men will not therefore say that you are a liar
and forsworn. For the book says that the wise man deals not falsely
when he changes his first purpose for a better one. And although your
undertaking be ordained and established by a great many men, yet you
need not accomplish it, unless you like. For the truth of things, and the
profit thereof, are found rather among a few folk who are wise and rea-
sonable than among the multitude, where every man cries and gabbles
as he likes. Truly such a crowd is not worthy of honour. As to the sec-
ond reason, wherein you say that all women are evil, then certainly, sav-
ing your grace, you must despise all women by so saying; and he that
despises all displeases all, as the book says. And Seneca says that
'Whoso has sapience will not any man dispraise; but he will gladly im-
part such knowledge as he can, and that without presumption and
pride. And for such things as he knows not, he will not be ashamed to
inquire of and learn from lesser folk.' And, sir, that there has been many
a good woman may be easily proved. For certainly, sir, Our Lord Jesus
Christ would never have condescended to be born of a woman if all
women had been evil. And thereafter, for the great worth that is in
women, Our Lord Jesus Christ, when He had risen from death unto
life, appeared to a woman, rather than to His disciples. And although
Solomon says that he never found good in any woman, it follows not,
therefore, that all women are wicked. For, though he may never have
found a good woman, surely many another man has found full many a
woman to be both good and true. Or perchance Solomon's meaning
was this: that so far as the highest virtue is concerned, he found no such
woman; which is to say, that there is no one who has sovereign good-
ness and worth, save God alone, as He Himself has caused to be
recorded in His gospels. For there is no creature so good that he is not
somehow wanting in the perfection of God, Who is his Maker. Your
third reason is this: You say that if you were to be governed by my coun-
sel, it should appear as if you had given over to me the mastery and sov-
ereignty of your person. Sir, saving your presence, it is not so. For, if it
were true, then, in order that no man should ever be advised, save by
those who had mastery over his person, men could not so often be ad-
vised. For truly, every man who asks counsel concerning any purpose
yet retains his freedom to choose whether he will or will not proceed
by that counselling. And as to your fourth reason, wherein you say that
the chattering of women can hide things of the which they are not
aware, as one might say that a woman cannot hide what she knows —
sir, these words are only to be understood of women who are both evil
and gossipy; of which women men say that three things will drive a
man out of his own house: smoke, and the dripping of rain, and a

wicked wife. And further, of such women, Solomon says: 'It were bet-
ter to dwell in a corner of the housetop than with a brawling woman in
a wide house.' And, sir, by your leave, that I am not; for you have often
enough tested my ability to keep silence, and tried my patience, and
even how I can hide and conceal matters that men ought to keep se-
cret. And, in good truth, as to your fifth reason, wherein you say that in
evil counsel women surpass men, God knows that this reason has no
standing here. For understand now, you ask counsel to do wickedness;
and if your will is to work wickedness, and your wife restrains such an
ill purpose and overcomes you by reason and good counsel given, then,
certainly, your wife ought rather to be praised than blamed. Thus
should you understand the saw of the philosopher who says that in evil
counsel women surpass their husbands. And whereas you blame all
women and their reasonings, I will show you, by many examples, that
many women have been good and are yet, and have given counsel both
wholesome and profitable. True, some men have said that the advice
of women is either too dear or too cheap in price. But, be it that many
a woman is bad, and her counsel vile and worthless, yet men have
found many a good woman, full wise and full discreet in giving coun-
sel. Behold how Jacob, by following the good advice of his mother
Rebecca, won the blessing of Isaac, his father, and came to authority
over all his brethren. Judith, by her good counsel, delivered the city of
Bethulia, wherein she dwelt, out of the hands of Holofernes, who be-
sieged it and who would have completely destroyed it. Abigail deliv-
ered her husband Nabal from David the king, who would have slain
him, and appeased the anger of the king by her wit and good advising.
Esther, by her good counsel, greatly exalted the people of God in the
reign of King Ahasuerus. And men may tell much of the same excel-
lence of good advice in many a good woman. Moreover, when Our
Lord had created Adam, our forefather, he said thus: 'It is not good that
the man should be alone: I will make him a help meet for him.' Here
you may see that, if women were not good, and their counsels good and
profitable, Our Lord God of Heaven would never have wrought them,
nor called them the help of man, but, rather, the confusion of man.
And once a writer said, in two verses: 'What is better than gold? Jasper.
What is better than jasper? Wisdom. What is better than wisdom?
Woman. And what is better than woman? Nothing.'[1] And, sir, by many
other examples you may see that women are good and their coun-

---

1. *Quid melius auro? Iaspis. Quid iaspide? Sensus. Quid sensu? Ratio. Quid ratione?*
Deus. But there is an alternative reading: *Quid melius auro? Iaspis. Quid iaspide?*
Sensus. Quid sensu? Mulier. Quid muliere? Nihil. —Ebrardi Bituniensis Graecismus,
cum comm. Vincentii Metulini, fol. C, 1.

selling both good and profitable. And thereupon, sir, if you will trust to my advice, I will restore to you your daughter whole and sound. And moreover, I will do for you so much that you shall come out of this affair with honour."

When Melibeus had listened to the words of his wife Prudence, he said: "I see well that the word of Solomon is true. He says, 'Pleasant words are as a honeycomb, sweet to the soul and health to the bones.' And, wife, because of your sweet words, and because, moreover, I have tried and proved your great wisdom and your great truthfulness, I will be governed in all things by your counsels."

"Now, sir," said Dame Prudence, "since you give yourself to be governed by my advice, I will tell you how to choose your councillors. You shall first, in all your works, meekly pray to the high God that He will be your adviser, and you shall mould your understanding in such wise that He may give you counsel and comfort, as Tobit taught his son, that is to say: 'Bless the Lord thy God always, and desire of Him that thy ways may be directed and that all thy paths and counsels may prosper.' And look to it that all your counsels are in Him for evermore. Saint James, also, says: 'If any of you lack wisdom, let him ask of God.' And after that, then shall you take counsel within yourself, and examine well your thoughts, concerning all things that seem to be the best for your own profit. And then shall you drive from your heart three things that are opposed to the following of good counsel, and they are anger, and covetousness, and hastiness.

"First, he that takes counsel within himself, certainly he must be free from anger, and this for many reasons. The first one is this: He that has great ire and wrath within himself thinks always that he is capable of doing things that he cannot do. Secondly, he that is angry and full of wrath cannot think or judge well, and he that cannot judge well cannot well advise. The third reason is this: That 'He that is angry,' as says Seneca, 'can speak only to berate and blame.' And thus with his vicious words he drives others into a like state.

"And too, sir, you must drive covetousness out of your heart. For the Apostle says that 'The love of money is the root of all evil.' And, trust me, a covetous man cannot judge correctly, nor can he think well, save only to the furtherance of his covetousness; and that, in truth, can never really be accomplished, because the richer he becomes, the greater desire has he for yet a larger abundance.

"And, sir, you must drive hastiness out of your inmost heart. For certain it is that you cannot hold to be best the sudden thought that comes into your heart, but you must weigh it and advise upon it. For, as you have heard before, the common proverb has it that he who resolves in haste soon repents. Sir, you are not always in like mood and of a like disposition; for surely that which at one time seems good to you, at another appears to be quite the contrary.

"When you have taken counsel within yourself, and have, after due deliberation, deemed such, or such, a thing to be for the best, then, I advise you, keep it secret. Reveal not your intentions to any person, save to such as you may certainly know will be of help to render your position more tenable through such revelation. For Jesus son of Sirach says: 'Whether it be to a friend or a foe, talk not of other men's lives; and if thou canst without offense, reveal them not. For he heard and observed thee, and when time cometh he will hate thee.' And another writer says: 'Hardly shalt thou find one person who can keep secrets.' The Book says: 'While thou dost keep thy counsel in thine own heart, thou keepest it imprisoned; and when thou revealest it to anyone, he holdeth thee imprisoned.' And therefore it is better that you hide your thoughts within your own heart, than pray to him to whom you have told them that he will be close and keep silence. For Seneca says: 'If thou canst not keep thine own counsel, how darest thou beg of another that he will do so?' But, nevertheless, if you deem certainly that the revealing of your secret to anyone will better your condition, then tell it to him in this wise. First, you shall give no indication whether you prefer peace or war, or this or that, and show him not your determination and intent; for, trust me, councillors are commonly flatterers, especially the councillors of great lords. For they are at pains always to speak pleasantly, inclining toward the lord's desire, rather than to use words that are, in themselves, true and profitable. And therefore men say that the rich man rarely receives good counsel, save as he has it from himself. And after that, you shall consider your friends and your enemies. Touching your friends, you must consider which of them are most old and faithful, and wisest, and most approved in counselling. And of them shall you ask advice, as the event requires.

"I say that first you must call into council such of your friends as are true. For Solomon says: 'Ointment and perfume rejoice the heart; so doth the sweetness of a man's friend by hearty counsel.' He says also: 'Nothing doth countervail a faithful friend, and his excellency is invaluable.' For certain it is that neither gold nor silver are worth so much as the goodwill of a true friend. Again he says: 'A faithful friend is a strong defence: and he that hath found such an one hath found a treasure.'

"Then, too, shall you consider whether your real friends are discreet and wise. For the Book says: 'Stand in the multitude of the elders, and cleave unto him that is wise.' And for this reason you should call to your council, of your friends that have arrived at a proper age, those who have seen and experienced many things, and who have been approved in parliaments. For the Book says: 'With the ancient is wisdom; and in length of days understanding.' And Tullius says: 'Great things are not accomplished by strength and activity of body, but by counsel, authority, and knowledge; and these things do not become enfeebled with age, but rather grow stronger and increase day after day.'

"And then you shall keep this for a general rule. First, you shall call to your council but a few of your most special friends. For Solomon says: 'Have thou many friends, but of a thousand choose but one to be thy councillor.' And although you should, at the first, tell your secrets to but a few, afterward you may tell them to others, if there be need. But look to it always that your councillors have the three attributes that I have mentioned, namely: that they are true, wise, and experienced. And act not always, and in every need, by the advice of one councillor alone; for sometimes it is well to have the advice of many. Says Solomon: 'Without counsel purposes are disappointed: but in the multitude of councillors they are established.'

"Now that I have told you of the sort of folk by whom you should be counselled, I will teach you which sort of counsel you ought to eschew. First, you shall avoid the counselling of fools. For Solomon says: 'Consult not with a fool, for he cannot keep counsel.' It is said in a book that the characteristic of a fool is this: he readily believes evil of everyone, and as readily believes all good of himself. You shall also eschew the counselling of all flatterers, such as force themselves rather to praise your person than to tell you the truth about things.

"Wherefore Tullius says, that of all the pestilences of friendship, the greatest is flattery. And so it is more needful that you eschew and fear flatterers than any other kind of men. The Book says that one should rather flee from and fear the sweet words of flatterers than the earnest words of the friend who tells one the truth. Solomon says that the words of a flatterer are a snare wherewith to catch innocents. He says also, that he who speaks sweet words to his friend, sets before his feet a net to catch him. And therefore says Tullius Cicero: 'Incline not thine ears to flatterers, nor take counsel of flattering words.' And Cato says: 'Be well advised, and avoid sweet and pleasant words.' And you must also eschew the counsels of such of your former enemies as have become reconciled to you. The Book says that no one can safely trust to the goodwill of a former enemy. And Aesop says: 'Trust not to those with whom you have been sometime at war or in enmity, neither tell them of your intentions.' And Seneca tells us the reason for this. 'It may not be,' says he, 'that, where fire has long existed there shall remain no vapour of heat.' And thereto says Solomon: 'The kisses of an enemy are deceitful.' For, certainly, though your enemy may be reconciled, and appear before you in all humility, and bow his head to you, you should never trust him. Surely he feigns this humility more for his advantage than for any love of you; for he thinks to gain some victory over you by such feigning, the which he could not gain by strife of open war. And Petrus Alfonsus says: 'Have no fellowship with ancient foes; for if you do good to them, they will pervert it into evil.' And, too, you must eschew the advice of those who are your own servants and bear themselves toward you with all reverence; for perchance they speak more out of fear than for love. And therefore says a philosopher thus: "There is no one perfectly true to him of whom he is afraid.' And Tullius says: 'There is no power of any emperor, fitted to endure, save it be founded more in the love of the people than in the fears.' You must also avoid the counselling of drunkards; for they can retain nothing. Solomon says that there is no secrecy where drunkenness reigns. You should also suspect the counsels of such as advise you privately to one thing and to a contrary thing in public. For Cassiodorus says that it is but an artifice to hinder when a man does one thing openly and its contrary in private. You should also hold suspect the counselling of the wicked. For the Book says that the advice of the wicked is always full of fraud. And David says that he is a happy man who has not followed the counselling of villains. You should also avoid and shun the advice of the young; for their judgments are not mature.

"And now, sir, that I have shown you as to the folk from whom you may take counsel, and what counsel you may accept and follow, now will I teach you how that counsel should be examined, according to the doctrines of Tullius. In bringing a councillor to the test, you must consider many things. First, you should consider that, in this very thing that you purpose, and upon which you are in need of advice, only the truth may be told; that is to say, state your case truthfully. For he that lies or prevaricates may not well be counselled, at least in so far as he has deceived. And after this, you must consider the things that agree with your purpose in council; whether reason agrees therewith; and whether you have power to attain your purpose; and whether the major and the better part of your council agree with it. Then shall you consider the probable result of acting upon all your advices: as hate, peace, war, honour, gain, loss, and many other things. And in all these things you must choose the best and avoid all else. Then must you take into consideration the root whereof is grown the matter of your counselling, and what fruit it may engender. Then, too, you shall consider all of the causes and examine into the causes of causes. And when you have examined your counselling as I have outlined to you, and have determined which part of it is the better and more profitable, and have found it to be approved by many wise and elderly men: then shall you consider whether you have power to carry it to a good end. For surely reason will not permit a man to begin a thing, save he carry it through as he should. Nor should anyone take upon himself a burden so heavy that he cannot bear it. For says the proverb: He that too much embraces, confines but little. And Cato says: 'Attempt only what thou hast power to do, lest the great task so oppress thee that it shall behoove thee to forgo that which thou hast begun.' And if it be that you are in doubt whether you can perform a thing, choose rather to suffer than to begin. For Petrus Alfonsus says: 'If you have power to do any thing which you must later regret, it is better to say nay than yea.' That is to say, it is better to keep silence than to speak. Then may you apprehend, and for stronger reasons, that if you have the ability to carry out any work whereof it is likely that later you must repent, then it is better to suffer it to remain undone than to begin it. Well do they speak who forbid a man to attempt a thing of which he has doubt of his ability to perform it. And afterward, when you have thoroughly examined your counsels, as I have set forth, and are convinced that you can carry through your enterprise to its goal, conform to it, then, gravely and carefully to the end.

"Now it is time that I instruct you when and for what you may change your intention without reproach. For truly a man may change purpose and plan when the cause for them is removed, or when a new condition arises. For the law says that new conditions demand new counsels. And Seneca says: 'If thy plan be come to the ears of thine enemy, change thy plan.' You may also change your plan if it develops that, through error or for other reason, harm will ensue from following it. Also, if your counselling is dishonest, or comes of a false premise, change your plan. For the laws provide that all dishonest mandates are invalid. And plans may be altered if they are impossible of fulfilment, or may not well be performed.

"And take this for a general rule: That every counsel that is so rigorously established that it cannot be altered, for any condition that may arise, I say that that counsel is vicious."

This Melibeus, when he had heard all the doctrines of his wife, Dame Prudence, answered her thus: "Dame, so far you have well and agreeably taught me, in a general way, how I should govern myself in the choosing and in the rejecting of councillors. But now I would fain have you descend to the particular, and tell me how you like them and how they appear to you—I mean, the councillors who have been already chosen in the present need."

"My lord," said she, "I beg of you, in all humility, that you will not wilfully object to my reasons, nor allow anger to enter your heart, even though I should say things that must displease you. For God knows that, as for my intention, I speak to your best interest, your honour, and your advantage. And, truly, I hope that your benignity will take it all in patience. Trust me, your counselling in this case should not be called counselling, properly speaking, but only a motion to do folly; and you have erred in many ways.

"First and foremost, you have erred in the method and manner of assembling your councillors. For you should have called, at first, but a few, and thereafter, had there arisen a need, you might have called in more. But, indeed, you have suddenly called into council a great multitude of persons, all very burdensome and all very tiresome to hear. Also, you have erred thus: whereas you should have called into council only your true friends, elderly and wise, you have gathered here many strange men, and young men, false flatterers, reconciled enemies, and men who do you reverence without love. Again, you have erred in that you have brought with you into council anger, covetousness, and hastiness, the which three things are antagonistic to every honest and profitable parliament; nor have you voided nor destroyed them, either in yourself or in your councillors, as you ought to have done. You have erred, again, in that you have revealed your wishes to your councillors, and your desire to make war and obtain vengeance; they have learned from your speeches the thing toward which you incline. Therefore, they have advised you agreeably to your wishes, rather than to your profit. You have erred, also, in that it appears to have sufficed you to be counselled by these councillors only, and with little advising; whereas, in so great and high a matter, it was really encumbent upon you to have procured more councillors and to have deliberated longer upon the means of performing your enterprise. Again you have erred, for you have not examined and tested your council in the manner aforesaid, nor in any manner required by the cause. You have erred, again, in that you have made no division between your councillors; that is to say, between your true friends and your feigned; nor have you learned the desire of your true friends, the elderly and wise of them; but you have cast the words of every man into a hotchpot, and you have then inclined your heart toward the majority, and upon that side have you stooped to folly. And since you well know that men must always exhibit, in any gathering, a greater number of fools than of wise heads, therefore in those councils composed of large numbers, where rather is considered the will of the majority than the wisdom of individuals, you may see easily enough that in such cases the fools must have the mastery."

Melibeus answered her again, saying: "I grant that I have erred; but since you have already told me that he is not to blame who changes councillors under certain conditions and for just causes, I stand ready to change mine, just as you shall prompt. The proverb runs: To err is human, but to persist in sin is the work of the devil."

To this replied Dame Prudence: "Examine your council, and let us see which of them have spoken most reasonably and given the best advice. And since such an examination is necessary, let us begin with the surgeons and physicians who spoke the first in this cause. I say that the surgeons and physicians have spoken discreetly, as they should; and they wisely spoke when they said that to their profession belongs the duty of dealing honourably with every man, and to his profit, and to harm no one; and, according to their skill, to set diligently about the healing of those under their care. And sir, since they have answered wisely and discreetly, I advise that they be richly and nobly rewarded for their noble speech, and, too, that they may be the more attentive to the healing of your dear daughter. For, though they are your friends, you must not suffer it that they serve you for nothing; you ought, indeed, but the more to reward them and to give them largess. And, touching the proposition that the physicians introduced into this case, namely, that, in diseases, the thing is cured by its contrary, I would fain learn how you understand that saying and what is your opinion of it."

"Indeed," said Melibeus, "I understand it thus: That just as they have done me an injury, so should I do them another. For just as they have revenged themselves upon me, and have thereby done me a wrong, so shall I now take my revenge and do them a wrong. And then shall I have cured one contrary by another."

"Lo, lo," exclaimed Dame Prudence, "how easily is every man inclined toward his own desire and to the securing of his own pleasure! Surely the words of the physicians should not have been interpreted in this sense. For, indeed, wickedness is not the contrary of wickedness, nor is vengeance of vengeance, nor wrong of wrong; but they are their likenesses. And therefore one vengeance is not to be cured by another vengeance, nor one wrong by another wrong; but, rather, each of them fructifies and engenders upon the other. But the words of the physicians should be understood in this wise: good and evil are opposites, and peace and war, revenge and forgiveness, discord and concord, and many others. But, certainly, wickedness shall be cured by goodness, discord by concord, war by peace, and so on of other things. And with this Saint Paul the Apostle accords in many places. Says he: 'See that none render evil for evil unto any man; but ever follow that which is good, both among yourselves, and to all men.' And in many other places he admonishes to peace and harmony.

"But now will I speak of the counselling that was given by the lawyers and suchlike wise men, who were all of one accord, as you heard: to the effect that, above all else, you should be diligent in guarding your person and in garrisoning and provisioning your house. And they held, also, that in these matters you ought to act advisedly and after much deliberation. Sir, as to the first point, which touches upon the safety of your person, you must understand that he who is at war should meekly and devoutly pray, above all things, that Jesus Christ, of His great mercy, will keep him under His protection and be his sovereign and very present help in time of need. For assuredly, in this world there is no man who can be safeguarded by advice, save and except he be within the keeping of Our Lord Jesus Christ. With this opinion agrees the prophet David, who says: 'Except the Lord keep the city, the watchman wakes but in vain.' Now then, sir, you shall commit the guarding of your person to your true friends, approved and well known; for of them only should you ask such help. For Cato says: 'If thou hast need of aid, ask it of thy friends; for there is no physician so valuable as thy true friend.' And hereafter you must keep always from all strange folk, and from liars, and hold them always suspect. For Petrus Alfonsus says: 'Never take company of a strange man, on the way, unless it is that you have known him longer than the present moment. And if it be that he fall in with you by accident, and without your assent, inquire then, as subtly as you may, into his conversation and into his life, and do you dissemble for yourself; say that you are going where you do not intend to go; and if he carry a spear, walk upon the right side of him, and if he bear a sword, walk on his left.' And hereafter shall you wisely hold yourself verily aloof from the sorts of people I have described, and eschew both them and their counsel. And you shall not presume so much upon your strength that you are led to despise and hold as naught the might of your adversary, thus endangering your person by this presumption; for every wise man fears his enemy. And Solomon says that it is well for him that suspects all others; for verily he that, because of the courage of his heart and the strength of his body, presumes too much upon them—him shall evil befall. Then, you should guard always against all ambushments and all espionage. For Seneca says: 'The wise man that fears danger avoids danger; he does not fall into peril who peril shuns.' And though it may seem that you are secure in a place, yet shall you be always upon your guard; that is to say, be not negligent either before your greatest enemy or your least. Seneca says: 'A man that is well advised dreads his weakest foe.' Ovid says that the little weasel may kill the great bull and the wild hart. And the Book says that a little thorn may sorely prick a great king; and that a hound will hold the wild boar. But, nevertheless, I do not say that you are to be so cowardly as to be afraid where there is no just cause for fear. It is said in a book that some folk have a great wish to deceive, who yet fear deception. But you shall fear poisoning, and withhold yourself from the company of scoffers. For the Book says that with the scoffer one should have no fellowship, and should avoid his words as venom.

"Now, as to the second point, wherein your wise councillors have advised you to provision and garrison your house, I would know how you understand their words, and what is your opinion of them."

Melibeus answered and said: "Verily, I understand them in this wise: that I am to equip my house with towers, such as castles have, and other such buildings, and with armour and with artilleries; by means of which I may keep my house and may so defend and keep my person that my enemies will not dare to approach me."

To this judgment Prudence then replied: "The garrisoning, provisioning, and equipping of high towers is sometimes but the pandering to pride. And it sometimes happens that even when men build high towers and great fortresses, at much cost and with untold labour, when they are completed they are not worth a straw, unless they be defended by true friends, who are both old and wise. And understand well that the greatest and strongest garrison a powerful man may have, as well to defend his person as his property, is the love of his vassals and his neighbours. For Tullius says that there is a kind of garrison which no man can vanquish or disperse, and that is the love of a lord's own citizens and people.

"Now, sir, as to the third point, whereof your older and wiser councillors averred that you ought not suddenly and hastily to proceed in this matter, but that you should provide for and array yourself with great diligence and after much careful thought, indeed I think that they spoke wisely and truthfully. For Tullius says: 'In every act, or ever thou begin it, array thyself with great diligence.' Then, say I, in seeking vengeance, in war, in battle, and in making arrangements, before you begin you must thoroughly prepare yourself and do it with much forethought. For Tullius says that a swift victory is the result of long preparation. And Cassiodorus says that the garrison is the stronger for being well prepared.

"But let us now speak of the counsel that was given by your neighbours, those who do you reverence without love; by your old reconciled enemies; by your flatterers who counselled you privately to certain things and openly to quite others; and by the younger men, also, who advised a speedy taking of vengeance and an immediate opening of hostilities. And certainly, sir, as I have said before, you were greatly in error in calling such folk into your council; such councillors are sufficiently discredited by the reasons hitherto adduced. But, nonetheless, let us descend to the particular. You should first proceed after the teaching of Tullius. Certainly the truth of this matter, or of this counselling, needs no long inquiry. For we know well who they are that have done to you this injury and this villainy, and how many offenders there are, and in what manner they have wrought against you this wrong and harm. And after this, then shall you examine the second condition which this same Tullius added. For Tullius puts forth a condition which he calls 'complying,' by which he means: who they are, and how many of them, that complied with your wishes to do hasty vengeance on your enemies, as you expressed it in council. And let us consider, also, who they are and how many, that complied with the wishes of your adversaries. As to the first group, it is well known who they are that complied with your hasty wilfulness; for truly all those who counselled you to make a sudden war are not your friends. Let us now consider who they are that you hold so steadfastly to be friends of your person. For though you are a mighty man, and a rich, true it is that you do but stand alone. For you have no child, save a daughter; nor have you any brothers, or cousins, or other near kinsmen for the dread of whom your enemies might forgo treating with you or attempting to destroy your person. You know also that your wealth, when apportioned out, will be distributed to a few men not closely related to you; and when each of them shall have received his share, then he will have but little incentive to avenge your death. But your enemies are three, and they have many children, brothers, cousins, and other near kinsmen; and though it were that you had slain two or three of them, yet there should remain enough to avenge those deaths by killing you. And though it were that your own kindred are true and more steadfast than those of your enemies, yet, nevertheless, your own kinsmen are but distantly related to you, whereas the kinsmen of your adversaries are closely sib to them. And, certainly, as for that, their condition is better than yours. Then let us consider, also, whether the advice of those who urged you to a sudden vengeance accords with reason. Certainly you know here that the answer is nay. For you know well that there is no man who may take vengeance upon anyone, save the judge who has proper jurisdiction, and when it has been granted to him to take such vengeance, hastily or slowly, as the law requires. And, moreover, as to that same word which Tullius calls 'complying,' you should consider whether your might and power may consent to comply with your wilfulness and that of your councillors. And, surely, to that also you must answer no. For indeed, properly speaking, we should do nothing save such things as we may do rightfully. And, in truth, rightfully you may take no vengeance as of your own authority. Thus you may see that your power does not rightfully consent to comply with your wilfulness. Let us now examine the third point, which Tullius calls the 'consequence.' You must understand that the vengeance which you purpose is the consequence. And from that follows another vengeance, another peril, and another war, and further injuries and damages without number whereof we are not at this time aware. And, touching the fourth point, which Tullius calls 'engendering,' you should consider that this wrong done to you was engendered of the hate of your enemies; and of the vengeance taken on that evil would be begotten another vengeance, and therewithal much sorrow and wastage of wealth, as I have pointed out.

"Now, sir, as to the point which Tullius calls 'causes,' which is the last point to consider, you must understand that the wrong that has been done you had certain causes, the which scholars call *Oriens* and *Efficens*, and *Causa longinqua* and *Causa propinqua*, which is to say, the ultimate cause and the proximate cause. The ultimate cause is Almighty God, Who is the Cause of all things. The proximate cause is your three enemies. The accidental cause is hate. The material cause is the five wounds of your daughter. The formal cause is the method of their working who brought ladders and climbed in at your windows. The final cause was the wish to slay your daughter; it hindered them not, in so far as they did their best. But, to speak now of the ultimate cause, as to what end they shall reach, or what shall finally betide your enemies in this case, I cannot judge, save in conjecture and supposition. Yet we may suppose that they shall come to an evil end, for the *Book of Decrees* says: 'Seldom, and only with great pain, are causes brought to a good end, when they have been badly begun.'

"Now, sir, if men ask me why God has suffered men to do this villainy, certainly I can answer nothing in any reliable language. For the Apostle says that the wisdom and the judgments of Our Lord God Almighty are very deep, whereof no man may comprehend anything, nor search into them. Nevertheless, by certain presumptions and conjecturings, I hold and believe that God, Who is justice and righteousness, has permitted this villainy upon a just and reasonable cause.

"Your name is Melibee, which is to say, a man who drinks honey.[2] You have drunk so much of the sweet honey of mundane riches and delights and honours that you are intoxicated therewith, and have forgotten Jesus Christ, your Creator: you have not honoured Him as you should have done, nor have you showed Him a proper reverence. Nor have you well observed those words of Ovid, who says: 'Under the honey of the good things of the flesh is hidden the venom that slays the soul.' And Solomon says that if you have found honey, eat of it only a sufficiency; for if you eat of it overmuch, you shall vomit, and so be again hungry and in want. And perchance Christ holds you in scorn, and has turned away His face from you, and shut up the ears of His mercy; and also He has suffered it that you have been punished in that manner in which you have sinned. You have sinned against Our Lord

---

2. Meliboeus, a shepherd in Vergil's First Eclogue. Chaucer's tale was translated from the old French tale called *Le livre de Melibee et Dame Prudence*.

Christ; for, certainly, those three enemies of mankind, the world, the flesh, and the devil, you have wilfully suffered to enter into your heart through the windows of your body, and you have not sufficiently defended yourself against their assaults and temptations, so that they have wounded your soul in five different places; that is to say, the deadly sins that have entered into your heart through your five senses. In the same manner Our Lord Christ has willed and permitted it that your three enemies have entered your house through the windows thereof, and have wounded your daughter in the manner whereof you know."

"Certainly," said Melibeus, "I see well that you so strengthen your arguments that I shall not revenge myself upon my enemies, showing me thus the perils and the evils that may result from this taking of vengeance. But if everyone were to consider, in every revenge, the dangers and ills that might ensue therefrom, no man would ever take vengeance, and that would be harmful; for by vengeance-taking the wicked are set apart from the good men. And they that have the will to do wickedly restrain their evil purpose when they see the punishment and chastisement of other wrongdoers."

To this replied Dame Prudence: "Surely," said she, "I grant that much good and much evil come of vengeance; but vengeance-taking does not belong to everyone, but only to judges and such as have a proper jurisdiction and authority over wrongdoers. And I say, further, that just as an individual sins in wreaking vengeance upon another man, so sins the judge if he does not fully exact payment from those who have deserved to be punished. For Seneca says: 'That is a good master who convicts criminals.' And as Cassiodorus says: 'A man shrinks from crime when he understands and knows that it angers the judges and the sovereigns.' And yet another says: 'The judge who fears to deal justly makes criminals of men.' And Saint Paul the apostle says in his Epistle to the Romans that not without reason are the fasces borne before the magistrates. For they are borne to punish criminals and miscreants, and for the security of good and just men. If, then, you would have revenge upon your enemies, you should turn to and have recourse unto the judge having a proper jurisdiction over them; and he will punish them as the law demands and requires."

"Ah!" exclaimed Melibeus. "This idea of vengeance is no longer to my liking. I remember, now, how Fortune has nourished me from my childhood, helping me over many a difficult place. I give heed to this; and now will I make trial of her again, believing that, with God's help, she will aid me to avenge my shame."

"Indeed," said Prudence, "if you will act according to my advice, you shall not make trial of Fortune in any way; you shall not bow down before her. For, to quote Seneca: 'Things done foolishly and in the hope of Fortune, shall never come to any good end.' And as the same Seneca says: 'The clearer and the more shining Fortune appears, the more brittle she is and the more easily broken.' Trust not in her, for she is neither steadfast nor stable; for when you believe yourself to be most secure and most certain of her help, she will deceive and fail you. And whereas you say that Fortune has nourished you from your childhood, I say that by so much the less should you trust now to her and to her ingenuity. For Seneca says: 'As for the man who is nursed by Fortune, she will make of him a great fool.' Now then, since you desire and demand vengeance, and since the sort of vengeance that is to be had according to law and before a judge is not to your taste, and since the vengeance that is attempted in reliance upon Fortune is dangerous and uncertain, then remains to you no other remedy than to have recourse unto the sovereign Judge Who punishes all villainies and avenges all wrongs. And He will avenge you, as He Himself promises, for 'Vengeance is mine, saith the Lord.'"

Melibee answered: "If I do not revenge myself for the injury that men have done to me, I invite and advertise to those who have injured me, and to all others, that they are free to do me another wrong. For it is written: 'If thou take no revenge for an old injury, thou invitest thine enemies to do thee a new evil.' And also, what of my sufferance, men would do to me so much of villainy that I could neither endure it nor sustain it; and I should be held in contempt. For men say: 'In patient sufferance shall many things happen to one, the which one may not grin and bear.'"

"Certainly," said Prudence, "I grant you that too much of sufferance is not a good thing; but yet it follows not therefrom that every person to whom men do a rascality may take vengeance for it; for that is the duty of and belongs only to the proper judges. Wherefore the two authorities that you have quoted are only to be understood as speaking to and of the judges; for when they suffer overmuch that wrong and crime remain unpunished, they not only invite new injury and wrong, but they command that they be done. Also a wise man says: 'The judge who does not chasten the sinner, bids him to sin again.' And it is conceivable that the judges and sovereigns of any realm might show so much leniency to criminals and evil-doers that, from such sufferance, in process of time, they might so wax in power as to turn out the judges and the monarchs from their places, and thus, at last, deprive them of the mastery.

"But now let us assume that you have a proper leave to avenge yourself. I say that you have not now the power to avenge yourself. For if you will compare your own with the power and might of your adversaries, you shall find, in many ways, as I have previously pointed out, that their condition is better than yours. And therefore say I that it is well, as for this time, to suffer your injuries in patience.

"Furthermore, you know well the common saw: It is madness in a man to strive with one who is stronger than himself; and to strive with a man of even strength is dangerous; but to strive with a weaker man is foolish. And for this reason a man should avoid all strife, in so far as he may. For Solomon says that it is to a man's honour if he withhold himself from noise and strife. And if it so happen that a man of greater power or strength does you an injury, make it your business to study how to stop the pain of it, rather than how to avenge it. For Seneca says: 'He puts himself into great peril who strives with a greater than himself.' And Cato says: 'If a man of higher degree or estate, or one more mighty than thou do thee an annoyance or grievance, tolerate him; for he that once has grieved thee, at another time he may relieve and help.' Yet I am assuming that you have both the power and the license to avenge yourself. I say, nevertheless, that there are very many things which ought to constrain you to withhold your punishment, and make you rather incline toward sufferance and to have patience under whatever may have been done to you. First and foremost, if you will, consider the faults in your own person, for which defects God has permitted that you have this tribulation, as I said before. For the poet says that we ought patiently to endure the tribulations that come to us when we think upon and well consider that we have deserved them. And Saint Gregory says: 'When a man considers well the multitude of his faults and sins, the trials and tribulations that he suffers will seem but the lighter to be borne; and just in so much as he holds his sins to be the more heavy and grievous, in so much will seem his pains the lighter and the easier to be borne.' Also, you ought to incline and bow down your heart to observe and learn the patience of Our Lord Jesus Christ, as Saint Peter says in his Epistle. 'Jesus Christ,' he says, 'hath suffered for us, and hath given example to every man to follow Him and to pray unto Him; for He did never sin, nor ever came there a vicious word out of His mouth; when men cursed Him, he cursed them not, and when men belaboured Him with blows, He would not menace them.' Also, the great patience which the saints in Paradise showed in bearing the tribulations of this world, and all without their deserving or their guilt—this ought greatly to prompt you to patience. Furthermore, you should enforce patience upon yourself when you consider that the tribulations of this world can but a little while endure, being soon over and ended. But the happiness that a man looks to receive by bearing tribulations patiently is perdurable, as the apostle says in his Epistle. 'The joy of God,' he says, 'is perdurable.' Which is to say, it is everlasting. Also, hold and believe steadfastly that he is neither well bred nor well taught who cannot have patience, or will not receive training in patience. For Solomon says that the belief and the knowledge of a man are known by his patience. And in another place he says that he who is patient will govern himself prudently. And this same Solomon says that the angry and wrathful man is noisy, while the patient man moderates and quiets noise. He says, also, that it is better to be patient than to be very strong; and he that governeth his own heart is more praiseworthy than he that taketh a city. And thereto says Saint James in his Epistle: 'Let patience have her perfect work.'"

"Surely," said Melibeus, "I will grant you, Dame Prudence, that patience is a great virtue of perfection; but every man may not attain to the perfection that you seek; nor am I of the number of perfect men, for my heart will never find peace until I have revenged myself. And though it was dangerous to my enemies to do me an injury in taking vengeance upon me, yet took they no heed of their own peril, but fulfilled their evil purpose. And therefore it seems to me that men ought not to find fault with me if I incur a little peril in taking vengeance, even though I go to great excess, that is to say, that I avenge one outrage with another."

"Ah," said Dame Prudence, "you speak out of your purpose as you desire it to happen; but never in this world should any man commit an outrage or go to excess to obtain his vengeance. For Cassiodorus says: 'As much evil does he who avenges himself by outrage as did he who first committed outrage.' And therefore you must avenge yourself in an orderly manner, and rightfully, that is to say, according to law, and not by excess nor by outrage. For if you avenge yourself in any other way, you sin. And thereupon Seneca says: 'A man must not avenge villainy with villainy.' If you say that right demands that a man defend himself violently against violence, and fightingly against fighting, certainly you speak but the truth, when the fighting is done immediately, without interval of tarrying or delay, and simply for defence and not for vengeance. And it behooves a man that he conduct his defence with such moderation that men will have no cause to accuse him of excess and outrage; for otherwise the thing were unreasonable. By God, you know well that you are not now defending yourself, but are going to revenge yourself; and so it follows that you have no wish to do your deed with moderation. That is why I hold that patience would be good for you. For Solomon says: 'He that is not patient shall endure great evil.'"

"Certainly," said Melibeus, "I grant you that when a man is impatient and wroth because of that which touches him not, and in no way concerns him, if he be harmed thereby it is not to be wondered at. For the law provides that he is culpable who interferes or meddles with what does not concern him. And Solomon says that he who interferes in the strife of other men is like one who seizes a hound by the ears. For just as he who takes a strange dog by the ears is likely to be bitten, just so is it reasonable to suppose that he may be injured who, by his impatience, meddles in the strife of other men, when it does not concern him. But you know well that this deed, that is to say, my grief and unrest, touches me closely. Therefore, if I am angry and impatient, it is no marvel. And, saving your presence, I cannot see wherein it can greatly harm me if I wreak my revenge: for I am richer and stronger than are my enemies. And well do you know that with money and great possessions are governed all the matters of this world. Solomon says that all things obey great wealth."

When Prudence had heard her husband boast thus of his possessions and money, despising the power of his enemies, she answered and said: "Surely, dear sir, I grant that you are mighty and rich, and that wealth is a good thing for those who have acquired it honestly and know well how to use it. For just as the body of man cannot live without the soul, neither can it exist without worldly goods. And by means of riches a man may acquire powerful friends. Thereupon says Pamphilius: 'If a cowherd's daughter be rich, she may make choice of a thousand men, which she will take for her husband; for, of a thousand, not one will forsake or refuse her.' And this Pamphilius also says: 'If thou be very happy, that is to say, if thou be very rich, thou shalt find a great many comrades and friends. And if thy fortune change, so that thou become poor, then farewell fellowship and friendship; for thou shalt be left alone, without any company, save it be the company of the poor.' And still further says Pamphilius: 'Those who are thralls and born of bondmen's blood shall be made worthy and noble by wealth.' And just as from riches come many good things, so from poverty come many ills and evils. For deep poverty forces a man into evil deeds. Therefore Cassiodorus calls poverty the 'mother of ruin,' which is to say, the mother of overthrowing or of falling down. And thereupon says Petrus Alfonsus: 'One of the greatest adversities of this world is when a man free by kindred and birth is constrained by poverty to eat of the alms of his enemy.' And the same thing is said by Innocent in one of his books, for he says: 'Sorrowful and unhappy is the condition of the poor beggar; for if he beg not his food, he dies of hunger; and if he beg it, he dies of shame; and yet necessity constrains him to beg.' And thereupon Solomon says that it is better to die than to live in poverty. And this same Solomon says that it is better to die the bitter death than to live in such wise. For these reasons that I have given, and for many others that I could adduce, I grant you that riches are good for those who have well acquired them, and for those who use them well. And therefore will I show you how you should bear yourself in acquiring wealth, and how you should use it.

"First, you should get it without any great desire, and leisurely, and gradually, and not over eagerly. For the man who is too desirous of gathering riches abandons himself first to theft and to all other evils. And thereupon says Solomon: 'A merchant shall hardly keep himself from doing wrong, and a huckster shall not be freed from sin.' He says also: 'The wealth that cometh hastily unto a man goeth soon and passeth lightly away from him; but the wealth that cometh by a little and a little waxeth alway and multiplieth.' And, sir, you shall acquire riches by your wisdom and by your labour to your own profit; and that without wronging or doing harm to any other person. For the law provides that no man shall legally become rich who injures another in the process; that is to say, that Nature forbids, and rightfully, that a man acquire wealth at another's expense. And Tullius says: 'No sorrow, no fear of death, nay nothing that may befall a man, is so much against Nature as for a man to increase and take his profit at the expense of another. And though the great man and the mighty man acquire riches more easily than thou, yet be not idle nor slow in gaining thine own profit; for thou must, in all things, avoid idleness.' For Solomon says that idleness teaches a man to do many evil things. And the same Solomon says that he that labours and busies himself to till his land shall eat bread; but he that is given over to idleness and has no business or occupation shall fall into poverty and die of hunger. And he that is idle and slow can never find a convenient time wherein to transact his business. For there is a versifier who says: 'The lazy man excuses himself in winter because of the great cold, and in summer because of the great heat.' For these reasons Cato says: 'Wake, and be not overly inclined toward sleep; for a superfluity of rest causes and nourishes many vices.' And thereupon says Saint Jerome: 'Do some good deeds, that the Devil, our Enemy, find you not unoccupied. For the Devil takes not easily into his service those whom he finds occupied in good deeds.'

"Thus, then, in getting riches, you must avoid idleness. And afterward you shall use the wealth, which you have acquired by your knowledge and by your labour, in such manner that men will not hold you to be too stingy, or too sparing, or too foolishly generous, that is to say, too great a spendthrift. For just as men blame an avaricious man for his meanness and penuriousness, in the same wise is he to be blamed that spends too freely. Thereupon says Cato: 'Use the wealth which thou hast acquired in such manner that men shall have no reason to call thee either wretch or niggard; for it is shameful for a man to have a poor heart and a rich purse.' He says also: 'Use the wealth which thou hast measureably.' That is to say, spend it within measure; for those who foolishly spend and waste what riches they have, when they have no longer any property of their own, scheme then to take that of another man. I say, then, that you shall flee avarice; using your riches in such manner that men shall not say that you have buried them, but that you hold them in your power and at your wielding. For a wise man reproves an avaricious man thus, in two verses: 'Wherefore and why does a man bury his wealth, of his great avarice, when he knows well that he must needs die; for death is the end of every man in this present life? And for what cause or occasion does he join or knit himself so closely to his goods that all his wit may not dissever or part him therefrom; when he knows, or ought to know, that when he is dead he shall have borne with him nothing at all from this world? Thereupon says Saint Augustine: 'The avaricious man is like unto Hell; for the more it swallows the more desire has it to swallow and devour.' And just as you would hate to be called an avaricious man, or a stingy, just so should you govern yourself that men will not call you a spendthrift. Therefore says Tullius: 'The riches of thy house should not be hid, nor should they be kept so closely that they may not be opened by pity and good will.' That is to say, in order to give a part to those in need. 'But yet thy wealth should not be so openly exposed as to become the goods of every man.' Afterward, in getting your wealth and in using it, you should have always three things in mind, that is to say, Our Lord God, conscience, and your own good name. First, you should have God in your heart, and for the sake of no riches at all should you do anything which may in any manner displease God, Who is your Creator and Maker. For, after the word of Solomon: Better it is to have little and therewith the love of God, than great riches and treasure and the loss of God's love thereby. And the prophet says that it is better to be held for a good man and to have but little of the wealth and treasure of this world, than to be held for a villain and have great riches. And yet say I still, that you should always do your business in the gathering of wealth so that you gather it with a good conscience. And the apostle says that there is not anything in all this world whereof a man should have so great a joy as when his conscience bears a good witness unto himself. And the wise man says that the substance a man has is righteous when sin lies not upon the conscience of that man. Afterward, in gathering your riches and in the using them, you must busy yourself and be diligent to observe that your good name be kept and conserved. For Solomon says: 'A good name is rather to be chosen than great riches.' And thereupon he says elsewhere: 'Do thy diligence in keeping of thy friend and of thine own good name; for these shall abide longer than any treasure, be it never so precious.' And surely he should not be called a good man who, after God and his own conscience, in all things else is not diligent in the business of maintaining his good name. Cassiodorus says: 'It is a sign of a good heart in a man when he loves and desires to have and to keep an honoured name.' And thereupon says Saint Augustine: 'Two things there be which are necessary and needful, and they are: good conscience and a good name; that is to say, a good conscience for the sake of thy soul, and a good name for the sake of thy neighbour.' And he who will trust so much in his own good conscience that he recks not of displeasing and setting at naught the value of his neighbour's opinion of his good name, and cares nothing if he keep not his good name toward his neighbour—he is but a boor.

"My lord, now have I showed you how you should act in acquiring riches, and how you should employ them; and well I understand that, because of the faith you rest in your wealth you will move toward war and battle. I counsel you that you begin no war upon faith in the continuance of your wealth; for your wealth is not sufficient to maintain war. Wherefore says a philosopher: 'He who intrigues for and will always have war, shall never have sufficient funds; for the richer he is, the more must his expenses be, always providing he wants respect and victory.' And Solomon says that the greater a man's riches the more leeches hang upon him. And, dear sir, though because of your wealth you may have many followers, yet it behooves you not, nor is it a good thing, to initiate a war when you may have a peace, and that to your own honour and profit. For victory in battle in this world lies not in a great multitude of people, neither lies it in the virtue of man; but it lies alone within the will and in the hands of Our Lord God Almighty. And therefore Judas Maccabeus, God's own knight, when called upon to fight against an adversary greatly superior in numbers and stronger than his own people, comforted his little army, saying: 'As easily may Our Lord God Almighty give victory unto a few as unto a multitude; for the fortune of war lieth not in numbers, but cometh solely from Our Lord God of Heaven.' And, dear sir, for as much as there is no man certain whether he be worthy that God give him the victory, any more than he can be certain whether he is worthy of the love of God, therefore Solomon says that every man should greatly fear to begin a war. Also, in battle, many perils befall, and many chances of evil, and therein is a great man as easily slain as a poor; and thereupon is it written in the *Second Book of the Kings* that the issue of battle is all at chance and is not to be known beforehand; for as easily hurt with a spear is one man as any other. And since there lies great peril in war, therefore should a man flee and eschew warfare, in so far as he may with honour. For Solomon says: 'He that liveth by the sword shall perish by the sword.'"

After Dame Prudence had spoken in this manner, Melibeus answered and said: "I see well, Dame Prudence, that by your fair words and by the reasons you have adduced before me, you are not in favour of war; but I have not yet heard you advise as to what course I ought to pursue in this extremity."

"Certainly," quoth she, "I counsel you that you accord with your adversaries, and that you have peace with them. For Saint James says in his Epistle that by concord and peace little fortunes grow great, and by discord and warfare are great fortunes brought low. And well you know that one of the greatest things there is in all this world is unity and peace. Wherefore says Our Lord Jesus Christ in this wise to His disciples: 'Blessed are the peacemakers, for they shall be called the children of God.'"

"Ah," said Melibee, "now do I see well that you love neither my honour nor my reputation. You know well that my adversaries have begun this quarrel and contention by their outrage; and you see well that they neither require nor ask peace from me, nor even do they ask to be reconciled. Will you, then, that I go and show myself meek and make myself humble before them, and cry mercy of them? Forsooth that were not to my honour. For just as men say that too much familiarity breeds contempt, so fares it with overmuch humility or meekness."

Then began Dame Prudence to make a show of wrath, and she said: "Certainly, sir, saving your grace, I love your honour and your profit as I do my own, and so have I ever; nor have you or any other hitherto said anything to the contrary. And yet, if I had said that you should have bought a peace and a reconciliation, I had not been much mistaken nor said very far amiss. For the wise man says that dissension begins with another, but reconciliation with oneself. And the prophet says: 'Flee evil and do good; seek peace and follow it.' Yet say I not that you shall rather sue to your enemies than they to you; for well I know that you are so hard-hearted that you will do nothing for me. And Solomon says that he that is too hard of heart shall in the end have evil fortune."

When Melibee had heard Dame Prudence show anger thus, he said: "Dame, I pray you that you be not displeased at things I say, for you know well that I am in my angry mood, and that it is no wonder; and that those who are angry cannot judge well of what they say or do. Wherefore the prophet says: 'The troubled eyes have no clear sight.' But speak to and counsel me as you like; for I am ready to do as you wish; and if you reprove me for my folly I am but bound the more to love you and praise you. For Solomon says that he that reproves him who has done a folly shall have more grace than he that deceives him with sweet words."

Then said Dame Prudence: "I make no show of wrath or anger save for your great profit. For Solomon says that more worth is he who reproves and chides a fool for his folly than is he that supports him and praises him and laughs at his foolishness. And this same Solomon says that by the sorrowful visage of a man (that is to say, by the sorry and heavy countenance of a man) the fool corrects and amends himself."

Then said Melibee: "I shall not know how to answer so many fair and good reasons as you show and lay before me. Speak out briefly your counsel and your wish, for I am ready to fulfill and to perform it."

Then Dame Prudence showed him all her wish and desire, saying: "I counsel you, above all things, that you make peace with God and become reconciled to Him and to His grace. For, as I have heretofore said, God has suffered you to have this tribulation and unrest because of your sins. And if you do as I tell you to do, God will send your adversaries unto you and make them fall at your feet, ready to do your will and to obey your commands. For Solomon says that when the condition of a man is pleasant and to God's liking, He changes the hearts of that man's enemies and constrains them to seek peace of him, and grace. And I pray you, let me have private speech with your adversaries; for they shall not know that it is done with your consent. And then, when I have learned their whole intent and will, I may the more surely counsel you."

"Dame," quoth Melibee, "do your whole will and whatsoever pleases you. For I put myself entirely at your disposal and command."

Then Dame Prudence, when she saw the goodwill of her husband, deliberated and took advice of herself how she might bring this whole matter to a good end. And when she saw her time, she sent for these adversaries to come to her privately; and truly showed them the great good to be gained from peace and the great harms and dangers that are in war; and told them in a gracious manner that they ought to be repentant for the injury and wrong they had done to Melibee, her lord, and to herself, and to her daughter.

And when they heard the gracious words of Dame Prudence they were so taken by surprise and so ravished with delight of her, that it was wonderful to tell. "Ah, lady," they said, "you have showed us the 'blessings of sweetness' in the words of David the prophet; for the reconciliation we are in no way worthy of, though we ought but in the greater contrition and humility to ask it—this, of your goodness, you have offered to us. Now see we well that the wisdom and knowledge of Solomon are true indeed, for he says that sweet words multiply and increase friends and cause villains to become courteous and humble.

"Certainly," said they, "we will put our actions and all our matter and cause wholly in your good keeping; and we stand ready to obey the word and command of Lord Melibee. Therefore, dear and benign lady, we pray and beseech you, as humbly as we can, that it shall please you, in your great goodness, to fulfill your goodly words in deeds; for we consider and acknowledge that we have offended and grieved Lord Melibee beyond measure; so far indeed that it lies not within our power to make him any amends. Therefore we obligate and bind ourselves and our friends to do whatsoever he commands. But perchance he has for us such a heaviness of wrath, what of our offense, that he will impose upon us so great a pain of punishment that we shall not be able to bear it. And therefore, noble lady, we beseech you of your womanly pity to take such advisement in this need that we, and our friends, shall not be disinherited and destroyed because of our folly."

"Certainly," said Prudence, "it is a hard thing, and a dangerous, for a man to put himself utterly into the arbitrament and judgment and into the might and power of his enemies. For Solomon says: 'Give not thy son and wife, thy brother and friend, power over thee while thou livest, and give not thy goods to another: lest it repent thee, and thou entreat for the same again. As long as thou livest and hast breath in thee, give not thyself over to any.' Now, since he counsels that a man give not even to a brother or a friend the power over his body, by a stronger reason he forbids a man to give himself over to his enemy. Nevertheless, I counsel you that you mistrust not my lord. For I know well and truly that he is kindly and meek, large-hearted, courteous, and nothing desirous nor covetous of goods and riches. For there is nothing in all the world that he desires, save only respect and honour. Furthermore, I know well and am right sure that he will do nothing in this case without my counsel. And I shall so work therein that, by the grace of Our Lord God, you shall be reconciled unto us."

Then said they with one voice: "Worshipful lady, we put ourselves and our property all fully at your command and disposal; and we are ready to come, upon whatever day is agreeable to your goodness, to make and give our obligation and bond, and that as strong as your goodness may desire: all that we may fulfill your will and that of Lord Melibee."

When Dame Prudence had heard the answers of these men, she sent them away again, secretly. And she returned to Lord Melibee and reported to him how she had found these adversaries ready to suffer pain and punishment, praying him, however, for mercy and pity.

"Then," said Melibee, "he is well worthy of pardon and to have his sins forgiven who excuses not his crime but acknowledges it and repents, asking indulgence. For Seneca says: 'There is the remission and the forgiveness where confession is.' For confession is neighbour to innocence. And he says in another place: 'He that is ashamed for his sin and acknowledges it, is worthy of remission.' Therefore I assent to peace; but it is best that we do this with the advice and consent of our friends."

Then was Dame Prudence right glad and joyful, and she said: "Certainly, sir, you have well answered. For just as by the counsel, assent, and help of your friends you have been stirred to avenge yourself and go to war, just so you should not, without their consent, accord and make peace with your adversaries. For the law says: There is nothing so good in kind as that a thing shall be unbound by him by whom it was bound."

And then Dame Prudence, without delay or tarrying, sent messengers for their kindred and for their old friends who were true and wise, and told them in detail and in order, in the presence of Melibee, all of this matter, as it has been here expressed and declared; and she prayed them that they would advise and counsel what best were to be done in this need. And when Melibee's friends had taken their advices in this said matter, and had examined into it with diligence, they gave their counsel for peace and rest; and that Melibee should receive, with good heart, the prayers of his adversaries for forgiveness and mercy.

And when Dame Prudence had heard the assent of her lord, Melibee, and the counsel of these friends, how they accorded with her will and intention, she was wonderfully glad of heart; and she said: "There is an old proverb which advises that the goodness you may do this day, do it; and delay it not until the morrow. Therefore I counsel you that you send wise and discreet messengers to your adversaries, bidding them that, if they are still minded to treat with you of peace and concord, they come hither to us without delay or tarrying."

Which thing was done. And when these trespassers and repentant folk, that is to say, the adversaries of Melibeus, had heard the messengers' words, they were right glad and joyful, and they replied full meekly and favourably, yielding grace and giving thanks to their Lord Melibee and to all his party; and they made ready, without delay, to accompany the messengers in obedience to the command of Lord Melibee.

Soon, then, they took their way toward Melibee's court, and they took with them some of their true friends to stand as sureties for them, and as hostages. And when they were come into the presence of Melibee, he spoke to them as follows: "It stands thus, and true it is, that you, without just cause, and without right or reason, have done great injury and wrong to me, to my wife Prudence, and to my daughter also. For you have entered my house with violence, and you did such outrage here that all men know well enough that you have fully deserved death; therefore do I ask of you whether you will leave the punishment, the chastisement, and the vengeance of this thing to me and to my wife Prudence? Or will you not?"

Then the wisest of these three answered for all of them, saying: "Sir, we know well that we are unworthy to come into the court of so great and so worthy a lord as you are. For we have so greatly erred, and have offended guiltily in such wise against your lordship, that verily we have been deserving of death. But yet, for the great goodness and kindness that all the world witnesses in your person, we submit ourselves to the excellence and benignity of your gracious lordship, and stand ready to obey all your commands, beseeching you, that of your mercy and pity you will consider our great repentance and humble submission, and will grant us forgiveness for our outrageous trespass and offence. For well we know that your liberal grace and mercy reach out farther into goodness than reach our outrageous guilts and trespasses into wickedness; and this despite the fact that we have wickedly and damnably offended against your high lordship."

Then Melibee took them benignly up from the ground, and received their obligations and bonds, by their oaths, and their pledges and sureties and hostages, and assigned a day for their reappearance before his court to receive and accept his sentence and judgment, the which he should impose; and after this, each man returned to his own home.

And when Dame Prudence saw her opportunity, she asked her lord, Melibee, what vengeance he purposed taking on these adversaries.

To which Melibee replied: "Surely I think and fully purpose to confiscate all that they have and to strip them out of their inheritances, and then to send them into perpetual banishment."

"Certainly," said Dame Prudence, "that were a cruel sentence and much against reason. For you are rich enough, and have no need of other men's property. And you could easily in this way acquire a name for covetousness, which is a vicious thing and ought to be avoided by every good man. For, after the word of the apostle, covetousness is the root of all evil. Therefore were it better for you to lose an equal property of your own than to take theirs from them in this manner. For better it is to lose goods with honour than to win them by villainy and shame. And every man ought to be diligent about getting and keeping a good name. And he should not only busy himself with the keeping of a good name, but he should impose upon himself the constant task of renewing it. For it is written that 'The good fame or good name of a man is soon passed and forgotten, unless it be renewed.' And touching what you say, that you will exile your adversaries, that seems to me much against reason and out of all measure, considering how they have placed themselves within your power. And it is written that 'He deserves to lose his privilege who abuses and misuses the might and the power that are given to him.' And I submit that, even if you might impose upon them that pain by right and by law, which I think that you could not, I say that you might not be able to put it into execution, by some chance, and then were you as likely to fall again into war as you were before. Therefore, if you would have men render you obedience, you must judge more courteously, that is to say, you must give more easy sentences. For it is written that 'He who most courteously commands, men most readily obey.' Therefore I pray you that in this need you contrive to conquer your own heart. For Seneca says: 'He that overcomes his own heart, conquers twice.' And Tullius says: 'There is nothing so commendable in a great lord as when he is kindly and meek and easily satisfied.' And I pray you that you will forgo your vengeance in this manner, in order that your good name may be kept and preserved; and that men may have cause and reason to praise you for pity and for mercy, and that you yourself shall not have cause to repent for what you have done. For Seneca says: 'He conquers but evilly who repents of his victory.' Wherefore, I pray you, let there be mercy in your mind and in your heart, to the end that God Almighty may have mercy upon you at His last judgment. For Saint James says in his Epistle: 'For he shall have judgment without mercy, who hath showed no mercy.'"

When Melibee had heard the great arguments and reasons of Dame Prudence, and her wise information and teaching, his heart began to incline toward the desire of his wife, considering her true intent; and he conformed his will to hers and assented fully to her counselling. And he thanked God, from Whom proceeds all virtue and goodness, that He had sent him a wife of so very great discretion.

And when the day arrived for his adversaries to appear before him, he spoke to them kindly, in this wise: "Howbeit that of your pride and presumption and folly, and in your negligence and ignorance, you have borne yourselves badly and have trespassed against me, yet for as much as I see and behold your great humility and that you are sorry and repentant for your crimes, it constrains me to show you grace and mercy. Therefore do I receive you into my grace and forgive you utterly all the offences, injuries, and wrongs that you have done against me and mine; to this effect and to this end: that God of His endless mercy will, at our dying day, forgive us our sins that we have sinned against Him in this wretched world. For doubtless, if we be sorry and repentant for the sins and crimes which we have committed in the sight of Our Lord, He is so free and so merciful that He will forgive us our guilt and bring us into His everlasting bliss. Amen."

HERE ENDS CHAUCER'S TALE OF MELIBEE
AND OF DAME PRUDENCE

THE MONK'S PROLOGUE

The Merry Words of the Host to the Monk

When ended was my tale of Melibee
And of Prudence and her benignity,
Our host remarked: "As I am faithful man,
And by the precious *corpus Madrian*,
I'd rather than a barrel of good ale
That my wife Goodlief could have heard this tale!
For she has no such patience, I'll avow,
As had this Melibeus' Prudence, now.
By God's own bones! When I do beat my knaves
She fetches forth the stoutest gnarly staves
And cries out: 'Slay the damned dogs, every one!
And break their bones, backbone and every bone!'
And if but any neighbour, aye, of mine
Will not, in church, bow to her and incline,
Or happens to usurp her cherished place,
Why, she comes home and ramps right in my face,
Crying, 'False coward, go avenge your wife!
By *corpus* bones! Come, let me have your knife,
And you shall take my distaff and go spin!'
From day to day like this will she begin:
'Alas!' she cries, 'that ever fate should shape
My marriage with a milksop coward ape
That may be overborne by every wight!
You dare not stand up for your own wife's right!'
This is my life, unless I choose to fight;
And through the door anon I must take flight,
Or else I'm lost, unless, indeed, that I
Be like a young wild lion, foolhardy.
I know well she will make me kill, one day,
Some neighbour man and have to run away.

For I am dangerous with a knife in hand,
Albeit that I dare not her withstand;
For she's big of arm, and wickedly inclined,
As anyone who crosses her will find.
But let us leave that doleful subject here.
    "My lord the monk," said he, "be of good cheer,
For you shall tell a tale, and verily.
Lo, Rochester is standing there hard by!
Ride up, my own liege lord, break not our game,
But, by my truth, I do not know your name,
Whether I ought to call you lord Don John,
Or Don Thomas, or else Don Albion?
Of what house are you, by your father's kin?
I vow to God you have a right fair skin;
It is a noble pasture where you're most;
You are not like a penitent or ghost.
Upon my faith, you are some officer,
Some worthy sexton, or a cellarer,
For by my father's soul, I guess, in sum,
You are a master when you are at home.
No cloisterer or novice can you be:
A wily governor you seem to me,
And therewithal a man of brawn and bone.
A person of some consequence you've grown.
I pray that God confound the silly fool
That put you first in a religious school;
You would have been a hen-hopper, all right!
Had you as good a chance as you have might
To work your lust in good engendering,
Why, you'd beget full many a mighty thing.
Alas! Why do you wear so wide a cope?
God give me sorrow but, if I were pope,
Not only you, but every mighty man,
Though he were shorn full high upon the pan,
Should have a wife. For all the world's forlorn!
Religion, why it's gathered all the corn
Of treading, and we laymen are but shrimps!
From feeble trees there come but wretched imps.
That's why our heirs are all so very slender
And feeble that they may not well engender.
That's why our goodwives always will essay
Religious folk, for you may better pay
With Venus' payments than we others do;

God knows, in no light weight of coin pay you!
But be not wroth, my lord, because I play;
Full oft in jest have I heard truth, I say."
    This worthy monk took all with sober sense,
And said: "I will do all my diligence,
So far as it accords with decency,
To tell to you a tale, or two, or three.
And if you care to hear, come hitherward,
And I'll repeat the life of Saint Edward;
Or rather, first some tragedies I'll tell,
Whereof I have a hundred in my cell.
Tragedy is to say a certain story
From ancient books which have preserved the glory
Of one that stood in great prosperity
And is now fallen out of high degree
In misery, where he ends wretchedly.
Such tales are versified most commonly
In six feet, which men call hexameter.
In prose are many written; some prefer
A quantitative metre, sundry wise.
Lo, this short prologue will enough suffice.
    "Now hearken, if you'd like my speech to hear;
But first I do beseech, let it be clear
That I, in order, tell not all these things,
Be it of popes, of emperors, or kings,
Each in his place, as men in writings find,
But I put some before and some behind,
As they to memory may come by chance;
Hold me excused, pray, of my ignorance."

Explicit

THE MONK'S TALE

De Casibus Virorum Illustrium

I will bewail in manner of tragedy
The ills of those that stood in high degree
And fell so far there was no remedy
To bring them out of their adversity;
For certain 'tis, when Fortune wills to flee,

There may no man the course of her withhold;
Let no man trust in blind prosperity;
Be warned by these examples true and old.

LUCIFER

With Lucifer, though he was angel fair
And not a man, with him will I begin;
For though Fortune may not an angel dare,
From high degree yet fell he for his sin
Down into Hell, and he lies yet therein.
O Lucifer, brightest of angels all,
Now art thou Satan, and thou may'st not win
From misery wherein thou far did'st fall!

ADAM

Lo, Adam, in the garden Damascene,
By God Almighty's finger wrought was he,
And not begotten of man's sperm unclean;
He ruled all Paradise, except one tree.
Had never earthly man so high degree
As Adam, till he, for misgovernance,
Was driven from his high prosperity
To labour, and to Hell, and to mischance.

SAMSON

Lo, Samson, whose birth was annunciated
By angel, long ere his nativity,
And was to God Almighty consecrated,
And had nobility while he could see.
Was never such another as was he
For body's strength, and therewith hardiness;
But to his wives he told his privity,
Whereby he slew himself for wretchedness.

Samson, this noble mighty champion,
Without a weapon in his hands, I say,
He slew and rent in two a young lion,
While to his wedding walking in the way.
His false wife could so please him, she did pray
Till she his secret held, when she, untrue,
Unto his foes that secret did betray
And him forsook for other loves and new.

Three hundred foxes Samson took, for ire,
And bound their brushes well together, and
Then set those foxes' tails alight with fire,
For he to every one had fixed a brand;
And they burned all the corn of all that land
And all the olive trees and vines, each one.
A thousand men he slew with his own hand,
With no weapon save an ass's jaw-bone.

When they were slain, he thirsted so that he
Was well nigh lost, for which he prayed, say I,
That God would on his pain have some pity
And send him drink, or must he surely die;
And from that ass's jaw-bone, then but dry,
Out of a tooth there sprang anon a well,
Whereof he drank his fill and laid it by.
Thus helped him God, as *Judges*, fifteen, tell.

By very force at Gaza, on a night,
Maugre Philistines of that said city,
The great gates of the town he took with might,
And on his shoulders carried them, did he,
High on a hill where every man might see.
O noble mighty Samson, lief and dear,
Had'st thou not woman told thy privity,
In all this world had never been thy peer.

This Samson never liquor drank, nor wine,
Nor on his head came razor, nor a shear,
Obeying thus the angel's word divine,
For all his forces in his long locks were;
And fully twenty winters, year by year,
He held of Israel the governance.
But all too soon should he weep many a tear,
For women should betray him to mischance!

Delilah being his darling, her he told
That in his unshorn locks all his strength lay,
And him to foemen then she falsely sold.
For, sleeping in her bosom, on a day,
She clipped and sheared all his long hair away,
Then showed his state unto his enemies,
And when they found him lying in this array
They bound him fast and put out both his eyes.

Before his hair was sheared and shaven close,
There were no bonds wherewith men might him bind;
But now he lies in prison cell, morose,
And labours, when at mill they make him grind.
O noble Samson, strongest of mankind,
O judge, but late, in glory measureless,
Now may'st thou shed hot tears from thine eyes blind,
For thou from wealth art fallen to wretchedness.

This captive's end was as I now shall say;
His foes they made a feast upon a day,
And made him as their fool before them play,
All in a temple great, of rich array.
But at the last he made a stern affray;
For he two pillars took and caused them fall,
And down came roof and all, and there it lay,
Killing himself and enemies, each and all.

That is to say, those princes, every one,
And full three thousand others who were slain
By falling of that temple built of stone.
To Samson now I'll not revert again.
Be warned by this example old and plain.
Men should not tell their business to their wives
In such things as of secrecy they're fain,
And if it touch their limbs or touch their lives.

HERCULES

Of Hercules, the sovereign conquering power,
Sing his deeds' praise and sing his high renown;
For in his time of strength he was the flower.
He slew, and made a lion's skin his own;
Of centaurs laid he all the boastings down;
He killed the cruel Harpies, those birds fell;
Brought golden apples from the dragon thrown;
And he stole Cerberus, the hound of Hell.

He slew the cruel tyrant Busiris
And made his horses eat him, flesh and bone;
To a fiery, venomous worm he wrote finis;
Achelous had two horns, but he broke one;
Cacus he slew within his cave of stone;
He slew the giant Anthaeus the strong;
He killed the Erymanthian boar anon;

And bore the heavens upon his shoulders long.

Was never man, since this old world began,
That slew so many monsters as did he.
Throughout all earth's wide realms his honour ran,
What of his strength and his high chivalry,
And every kingdom went he out to see.
He was so strong no man could hinder him;
At both ends of the world, as says Trophy,
In lieu of limits he set pillars grim.

A darling had this noble champion,
Deianira, sweet as is the May;
And as these ancient writers say, each one,
She sent to him a new shirt, fresh and gay.
Alas that shirt, alas and welaway!
Envenomed was so cunningly withal
That, ere he'd worn the thing but half a day,
It made the flesh from off his bones to fall.

Yet are there writers who do her excuse
Because of Nessus, who the shirt had made;
Howe'er it be, I will not her accuse;
But all his naked back this poison flayed
Until the flesh turned black, and torn, and frayed.
And when he saw no other remedy,
Upon a pyre of hot brands he was laid,
For of no poison would he deign to die.

Thus died this mighty worthy, Hercules.
Lo, who may trust to Fortune any throw?
And he who seeks on earth for fame and case
Ere he's aware, he's often brought down low.
Right wise is he that can his own heart know.
Beware, when Fortune may her smile disclose,
She lies in wait her man to overthrow,
And in such wise as he would least suppose.

NEBUCHADNEZZAR

The precious treasure and the mighty throne,
The glorious sceptre and royal majesty
That Nebuchadnezzar counted as his own
With tongue or pen not easily told may be.
Twice of Jerusalem the victor he;

The Temple's vessels took he and was glad.
And Babylon was the ancient sovereign see
Wherein his glory and delight he had.

The fairest children of the blood royal
Of Israel, he gelded them anon,
And made each one of them to be his thrall.
Among the number Daniel thus was one,
Of all the youth the nation's wisest son;
For he the dreams of the great king expounded
When in Chaldea wise clerk was there none
Who knew to what end those dreams were propounded.

This proud king made a statue of pure gold
Full sixty cubits long by seven wide,
Unto which image both the young and old
Commanded he to bow down, nor deride,
Else in a furnace full of flames go bide
And burn to ashes, who would not obey.
But no assent to that, whate'er betide,
Would Daniel and his pair of comrades say.

This king of kings right proud was and elate,
And thought that God, Who sits in majesty,
Could not bereave him of his high estate:
Yet suddenly he lost all dignity,
And like a brute beast then he seemed to be,
And ate hay like an ox, and lay without;
In rain and storm with all wild beasts walked he,
Until a certain time was come about.

And like an eagle's feathers were his hairs,
His nails like any bird's claws hookèd were;
Till God released him after certain years
And gave him sense; and then, with many a tear,
He gave God thanks; thereafter all in fear
He lived of doing ever again trespass,
And till the time they laid him on his bier,
He knew that God was full of might and grace.

BELSHAZZAR

His son, called Belshazzar, or Balthasar,
Who held the realm after his father's day,
He for his father's fate would not beware,

For proud he was of heart and of array;
He was a worshipper of idols aye.
His high estate assured him in his pride.
But Fortune cast him down and there he lay,
And suddenly his kingdom did divide.

A feast he made unto a thousand lords,
Upon a time, and bade them merry be.
Then to his officers he said these words:
"Go fetch me forth the vessels all," said he,
"Of which my father, in prosperity,
The temple in Jerusalem bereft,
And unto our high gods give thanks that we
Retain the honour that our elders left."

His wife, his lords, and all his concubines,
They drank then, while that mighty feast did last,
Out of those noble vessels sundry wines.
But on a wall this king his eyes did cast
And saw an armless hand that wrote full fast,
For fear whereof he shook with trouble sore.
This hand that held Belshazzar so aghast
Wrote *Mene, mene, tekel,* and no more.

In all that land magician was there none
Who could explain what thing this writing meant;
But when they sent for Daniel it was done,
Who said: "O king, God to your father lent
Glory and honour, treasure, government,
And he was proud, nor feared God, being mad,
Wherefore Lord God great misery on him sent,
And him bereft of all the realm he had.

"He was cast out of human company;
With asses was his habitation known;
He ate hay like a beast, through wet and dry,
Until he learned, by grace and reason shown,
That Heaven's God has dominion, up and down,
Over all realms and everything therein;
And then did God to him compassion own
And gave him back his kingdom and his kin.

"Now you, who are his son, are proud also,
Though you knew all these things, aye verily;
You are a rebel and you are God's foe.

You drank from out His vessels boastfully;
Your wife and all your wenches sinfully
Drank from those sacred vessels sundry wines,
And praised false gods, and hailed them, wickedly;
Whereof toward you the wrath of God inclines.

"That hand was sent from God which on the wall
Wrote *Mene, mene, tekel.* Oh, trust me,
Your reign is done, you have no worth at all,
Divided is your realm, and it shall be
To Medes and Persians given now," said he.
And that night went the king to fill death's maw,
And so Darius took his high degree,
Though he thereto had naught of right in law.

Masters, therefrom a moral may you take,
That in dominion is no certainness;
For when Fortune will any man forsake,
She takes his realm and all he may possess,
And all his friends, too, both the great and less;
For when a man has friends that Fortune gave,
Mishap but turns them enemies, as I guess:
This word is true for king as well as slave.

ZENOBIA

Zenobia, of all Palmyra queen
(As write old Persians of her nobleness),
So mighty was in warfare, and so keen,
That no man her surpassed in hardiness,
Nor yet in lineage, nor in gentleness.
Of blood of Persia's kings she was descended;
I say not she had greatest beauteousness,
But of her figure naught could be amended.

From childhood on I find that she had fled
Duties of women, and to wildwood went;
And many a wild hart's blood therein she shed
With arrows broad that she within them sent.
So swift she was, she ran them down all spent;
And when she was grown older she would kill
Lions and leopards, and bears too she rent,
And in her arms she broke them at her will.

She even dared the wild beasts' dens to seek,

And ran upon the mountains all the night,
Sleeping beneath a bush; and, nothing weak,
Wrestled by very force and very might
With any man, however brave in fight;
For there was nothing in her arms could stand.
She kept her maidenhead from every wight,
And unto no man would she yield her hand.

But at the last her friends did make her marry
Odenathus, a prince of that country,
Albeit she long waited and did tarry;
And you must understand that also he
Held to the same queer fancies as had she.
Nevertheless, when wedded, 'twould appear
They lived in joy and all felicity,
For each of them held other lief and dear.

But to one thing she never would consent,
For any prayers, that he should near her lie
Save one night only, when 'twas her intent
To have a child, since men should multiply;
Yet when she learned she'd got no pregnancy
From that night's work together on her bed,
Then would she suffer him again to try,
But only once indeed, and then with dread.

And when she was with child, all at the last,
Then no more might he play at that same game
Till fully forty days were gone and past;
Then would she once more suffer him the same
And were Odenathus grown wild or tame,
He got no more of her; for thus she'd say:
"In wives it is but lechery and shame
When, oftener, men with their bodies play."

Two sons by this Odenathus had she,
The which she bred in virtue and learning;
But now again unto our tale turn we.
I say, so worshipful a young being,
Wise, and right generous in everything,
Careful in war and courteous as well,
And hardy in the field, and full daring,
Was not in all the world where men do dwell.

Her rich array may not be rightly told,

Either of vessels or of fine clothing;
She was clad all in jewels and in gold;
And she did never cease, despite hunting,
To gain of divers tongues a full knowing,
Whenever she had time; she did intend
To learn from books, which were to her liking,
How she in virtue might her whole life spend.

And briefly of this story now to treat,
So doughty was her husband, as was she,
That they two conquered many kingdoms great
Throughout the East, with many a fair city
That did pertain unto the majesty
Of Rome; and with strong hands they held them fast;
Nor might a foe escape by trying to flee
The while Odenathus' good days did last.

Her battles all (as whoso wills may read)
Against Sapor the king and others too,
And all her story as it fell, indeed,
Why she was victor and had right thereto,
And, after, all her misfortune and woe,
How they besieged her and at last did take,
Let him unto my master Petrarch go,
Who wrote the whole of this, I undertake.

Now when Odenathus was dead, then she
The kingdom held within her own strong hand;
Against her foes she fought so bitterly
There was no king or prince in all that land
But was right glad, if mercy make her bland,
That she turned not against him her array;
With her they made alliance, bond and band,
To keep the peace and let her ride and play.

The emperor of Rome, one Claudius
(His predecessor, Galien too, that man),
Had never courage to oppose her thus;
Nor was Egyptian nor Armenian,
Nor Syrian, nor yet Arabian
That dared against her in the field to fight,
For fear that at her hands they might be slain,
Or by her army put to sudden flight.

In kingly habit went her sons also,

As being heirs to their sire's kingdoms all,
Athenodorus and Thymalao
Their names were (or the Greeks did so them call).
But Fortune's honey is aye mixed with gall;
This mighty queen could no great while endure.
And Fortune from her high throne made her fall
To wretchedness and into ways obscure.

Aurelian, when Roman governance
Came to his two strong hands, made no delay,
But swore that on this queen he'd wreak vengeance,
And so with mighty legions took his way
Against Zenobia; let me briefly say
He made her flee; and at the last he sent
And fettered her and her two sons one day,
And won the land, and home to Rome he went.

Among the other booty Asian
Her chariot was, of gold and jewellery,
And this great Roman, this Aurelian,
He carried it away for men to see.
Before his car in triumph then walked she
With golden chains upon her neck hanging;
Crowned was she, too, to show her high degree,
And full of priceless gems was her clothing.

Alas, Fortune! She that but lately was
The scourge of kings and emperors and powers,
Now may the rabble gape at her, alas!
And she that, armed, rode where grim battle lowers
And took by force great cities and strong towers,
Must wear a cap now while her two eyes weep;
And she that bore the sceptre of carved flowers
May bear a distaff and thus earn her keep.

PEDRO, KING OF SPAIN

O noble Pedro, glory once of Spain,
Whom Fortune held so high in majesty,
Well ought men read thy piteous death with pain!
Out of thy land thy brother made thee flee;
And later, at a siege, by scheme crafty,
Thou wert betrayed, and led into his tent,
Where he then, and with his own hand, slew thee,
Succeeding to thy realm and government.

The field of snow, with eagle black therein,[1]
Caught by the lime-rod, coloured as the gleed,
He brewed this wickedness and all this sin.
The "Wicked Nest"[2] was worker of this deed;
Not that Charles Oliver who aye took heed
Of truth and honour, but the Armorican
Ganelon Oliver, corrupt for mead,
Brought low this worthy king by such a plan.

PETER, KING OF CYPRUS

O noble Peter, Cyprus' lord and king,
Which Alexander won by mastery,
To many a heathen ruin did'st thou bring;
For this thy lords had so much jealousy,
That, for no crime save thy high chivalry,
All in thy bed they slew thee on a morrow.
And thus does Fortune's wheel turn treacherously
And out of happiness bring men to sorrow.

BERNABO OF LOMBARDY

Of Milan, great Bernabo Visconti,
God of delight and scourge of Lombardy,
Why should I tell not of thy misery,
Since in all power thou did'st climb so high?
Thy brother's son, and doubly thine ally,
For he thy nephew was and son-in-law,
Within his prison shut thee up to die,
But I know not how death to thee did draw.

UGOLINO, COUNT OF PISA

Of Ugolino, Count of Pisa's woe
No tongue can tell the half for hot pity.
Near Pisa stands a tower, and it was so
That to be there imprisoned doomed was he,
While with him were his little children three,
The eldest child was scarce five years of age.
Alas, Fortune! It was great cruelty
To lock such birds up into such a cage!

---

1. The arms of Bertrand du Guesclin.   2. Wicked Nest: Chaucer puts this for OF. *mau ni*, meaning thereby Sir Oliver Mauny.

Condemned was he to die in that prison,
Since Ruggieri, Pisa's bishop, twice
Had lied, intrigued, and egged old passions on,
Whereby the people did against him rise,
And thrust him into prison in such wise
As you have heard; and meat and drink he had
So little that it could not long suffice,
And was, moreover, very poor and bad.

And on a day befell it, at the hour
When commonly to him his food was brought,
The gaoler shut the great doors of the tower.
He heard it well enough, but he said naught,
And to his heart anon there came the thought
That they by hunger would leave him to die.
"Alas," said he, "that ever I was wrought!"
And thereupon the tears fell from his eye.

His youngest son, who three years was of age,
Unto him said: "Father, why do you weep?
When will the gaoler bring us out pottage?
Is there no crumb of bread that you did keep?
I am so hungry that I cannot sleep.
Now would God that I might sleep on for aye!
Then should not hunger through my belly creep;
For nothing more than bread I'd rather pray."

Thus, day by day, this little child did cry,
Till on his father's breast at length he lay
And said: "Farewell, my father, I must die."
And kissed the man and died that very day.
And when the father saw it dead, I say,
For grief his arms gnawed he until blood came,
And said: "Alas, Fortune and welaway,
It is thy treacherous wheel that I must blame!"

His children thought that it for hunger was
He gnawed his arms, and not that 'twas for woe,
And cried: "O father, do not thus, alas!
But rather eat our young flesh, even so;
This flesh you gave us; take it back and go
And eat enough!" 'Twas thus those children cried,
And after that, within a day or two,
They laid themselves upon his knees and died.

Himself, despairing, all by hunger starved,
Thus ended this great count of Pisa's cries;
All his vast riches Fortune from him carved.
Of his fate tragic let thus much suffice.
Whoso would hear it told in longer wise,
Let him read the great bard of Italy
Whom men call Dante; seen through Dante's eyes
No point is slurred, nor in one word fails he.

NERO

Though viciousness had Nero in overplus,
As ever fiend that's low in torment thrown,
Yet he, as tells us old Suetonius,
This whole wide world held subject; aye, did own,
East, west, south, north, wherever Rome was known.
Of rubies, sapphires, and of great pearls white
Were all his garments broidered up and down,
For he in jewels greatly did delight.

More delicate, more pompous of array,
More proud was never emperor than he;
That toga which he wore on any day,
After that time he nevermore would see.
Nets of gold thread he had in great plenty
To fish in Tiber when he pleased to play.
His lusts were all the laws in his decree,
For Fortune was his friend and would obey.

He burned Rome for his delicate profligacy;
Some senators he slew upon a day
Only to learn how men might weep and cry;
He killed his brother and with his sister lay.
His mother put he into piteous way,
For he her belly ripped up just to see
Where he had been conceived; alack-a-day,
That but so little for her life cared he!

No tear out of his two eyes for that sight
Came, but he said: "A woman fair was she."
Great wonder is it how he could or might
Pass judgment thus upon her dead beauty.
Wine to be brought him then commanded he
And drank anon; no other sign he made.
When might is wedded unto cruelty,

Alas, too deep its venom will pervade!

A master had, in youth, this emperor,
To teach him letters and all courtesy,
For of morality he was the flow'r
In his own time, unless the old books lie;
And while this master held his mastery,
So well he taught him wiles and subtle ways
That ere could tempt him vice or tyranny
Was, it is said, the length of many days.

This Seneca, of whom I do apprise,
By reason Nero held him in such dread,
Since he for vices spared not to chastise,
Discreetly, though, by word and not by deed—
"Sir," would he say, "an emperor must need
Be virtuous and hate all tyranny"—
For which, in bath, did Nero make him bleed
From both his arms until he had to die.

This Nero had, though, out of arrogance,
Been wont, in youth, against the rod to rise,
Which afterward he thought a great grievance;
Wherefore he made him perish in this wise.
Nevertheless, this Seneca the wise
Chose in a bath to die, as you did hear,
Rather than suffer in some other guise;
And thus did Nero slay his master dear.

Now it befell that Fortune cared no longer
To Nero's high pride to be accomplice;
For though he might be strong, yet she was stronger;
She thought thus: "By God, I am none too nice,
Setting a man who is but filled with vice
In high degree, emperor over all.
By God, up from his seat I will him trice;
When he least thinks of it, then shall he fall."

The people rose against him, on a night,
For all his faults; and when he it espied,
Out of the doors he went and took to flight
Alone; and where he thought he was allied
He knocked; but always, and the more he cried
The faster did they bar the doors, aye all;
Then learned he well he'd been his own worst guide,

And went his way, nor longer dared to call.

The people cried and rumbled up and down,
And, having ears, he heard the thing they said:
"Where's this false tyrant Nero, where's he flown?"
For fear almost out of his wits he strayed,
And to his gods, then, piously he prayed
For succour, but no help might him betide.
For fear of this he wished himself unmade,
And ran into a garden, there to hide.

And in this garden were two fellows, yea,
Who sat before a great fire and a red,
And to those fellows he began to pray
That they would slay him and strike off his head,
But of his body, after he was dead,
They should do nothing to its further shame.
Himself he slew, no better counsel sped,
Whereat Dame Fortune laughed and made a game.

HOLOFERNES

Was never captain, no, of any king's
That had more kingdoms in subjection thrown,
Nor stronger was, in field, above all things,
Nor in his time a greater of renown,
Nor had more pomp with high presumption shown,
Than Holofernes, whom Dame Fortune kissed
Right lecherously, and led him up and down
Until his head was off before 'twas missed.

Not only did this world hold him in awe
For taking all its wealth and liberty,
But he made every man renounce old law.
"Nebuchadnezzar is your god," said he,
"And now no other god shall worshipped be."
Against his order no man dared to stand,
Save in Bethulia, a strong city,
Where Eliachim priest was of the land.

But from the death of Holofernes learn.
Amidst his host he lay drunk, on a night,
Within his tent, as large as ever barn,
And yet, for all his pomp and all his might,
Judith, a woman, as he lay upright,

Sleeping, smote off his head and from his tent
Stole secretly away from every wight,
And with the head to her own town she went.

ANTIOCHUS EPIPHANES

What needs it, as for King Antiochus,
To tell his high and royal majesty,
His great pride and his deeds so venomous?
There never was another such as he.
Go read what's said of him in Maccabee,
And all the haughty sayings that he said,
And how he fell from high prosperity,
And on a hill how wretchedly lay dead.

Fortune had so enhanced the man's great pride
That verily he thought he might attain
Unto the utter stars on every side,
And in a balance weigh the high mountain,
And all the flood-tides of the sea restrain.
And God's own people held he most in hate.
Them would he slay with torment and with pain,
Thinking that God his pride would not abate.

And because Nicanor and Timothy
Were vanquished by the Jews so mightily,
Unto all Jews so great a hate had he
That he bade bring his chariot hastily,
And swore an oath and said, impiteously,
That to Jerusalem he'd go ere noon
To wreak his ire on it full cruelly;
But from his purpose he was turned, and soon.

God, for this menace, smote him then full sore
With wound invisible, incurable,
For in his guts he was so carved, aye more,
The pain of it was insupportable.
And certainly the thing was reasonable,
For many a man's guts he had caused to pain;
But from his purpose, cursed, damnable,
In spite of all he would not him restrain.

He gave command to marshal his great host,
And suddenly, or ere he was aware,
God daunted all his pride and all his boast.

For he so heavily fell from his car
That from his very bones the flesh did tear,
So that he might not either walk or ride,
But in a litter men were forced to bear
Him with them, bruised upon the back and side.

The wrath of God smote him so cruelly
That through his body loathsome maggots crept;
And therewithal he stank so horribly
That none of those that round his person kept,
Whether he lay awake or whether slept,
Could, for the very stench of him, endure.
In this foul state he wailed and howled and wept;
That God was Lord of all he then was sure.

To all his host and to himself also
Full loathsome was his carrion, one great blain;
There were no men could bear him to and fro.
And in this stink and in this horrid pain
He died full wretchedly on a mountain.
Thus had this robber and this homicide,
Who made so many men weep and complain,
Such guerdon as belongs to too great pride.

ALEXANDER

Alexander's tale is so well known a tune
That everyone who is not simple grown
Has heard somewhat, or all, of his fortune
This whole wide world, to state conclusion known,
He won by strength, or else for his renown
Right gladly men to sue for peace did send.
The pride of man and beast he tumbled down
Where'er he went, and that was the world's end.

Comparison might never yet be staked
Upon a single similar conquering power;
For all this world in dread of him has quaked.
He was of knighthood and of freedom flower;
Fortune made him her heir to honour's bower;
Save wine and women, nothing might assuage
His high intent in arms; all men must cower,
So filled he was of leonine courage.

What praise were it to him, though 'gain were told

Darius' tale or of others brought low—
Of kings and dukes and earls and princes bold,
The which he conquered and brought down to woe?
I say, as far as man may ride or go
The world was his, to tell it in a trice.
For though I wrote or told you always, so,
Of his knighthood, the time would not suffice.

Twelve years he reigned, as tells us Maccabee;
And Philip's son of Macedon he was,
Who first was king of Greece, the whole country.
O noble Alexander, O alas!
That ever you should come to such a pass!
For poisoned by your very own you were;
Your six did Fortune turn into an ace,
And yet for you she never wept a tear!

Who shall give me the tears now to complain
For death of gentle blood and high franchise?
He all the world did wield as one domain,
And yet he thought it could not long suffice,
So full his heart was of high enterprise.
Alas! And who shall help me to indict
False Fortune, and all poison to despise?
For these I blame for all the woe I write.

JULIUS CAESAR

By wisdom, manhood, and by great labour,
From humble bed to royal majesty
Up rose he, Julius the conqueror,
Who won the Occident by land and sea,
By force of arms, or else by clear treaty,
And unto Rome made all this tributary;
And then of Rome the emperor was he,
Till Fortune came to be his adversary.

O mighty Caesar, who in Thessaly
Against great Pompey, father of yours in law,
That of the East had all the chivalry
From farthest places that the sun e'er saw,
You, by your knighthood broke them for death's maw,
Save those few men who thence with Pompey fled,
Whereby you put the Orient in awe.
Thank Fortune now that you so well have sped.

But now a little while I will bewail
This Pompey, this so noble governor
Of Rome, who fled when battle's chance did fail;
I say, one of his men, a false traitor,
Smote off his head to win himself favour
With Julius, and there the head he brought.
Alas, Pompey! Of Orient conqueror,
That Fortune such an end for thee hath wrought!

To Rome again repaired great Julius,
To have his triumph, laureate full high;
But on a time Brutus and Cassius,
Who ever had of great estate envy,
Full secretly did lay conspiracy
Against this Julius, in subtle wise,
And fixed the place at which he soon should die
By dagger thrusts, as I shall you apprise.

This Julius, to the Capitol he went
Upon a day, as he'd been wont to go,
And there they seized on him, as well they meant,
This treacherous Brutus and each other foe,
And struck him with their daggers, high and low,
And gave him many a wound and let him die;
But never groaned he, save at one stroke, no
(Or two perchance), unless his legend lie.

So manly was this Julius in his heart,
And so well loved he stately decency,
That, though his deadly wounds did burn and smart,
His mantle yet about his hips cast he,
That no man there should see his privity.
And as he lay there, dying, in a trance,
And knew that he was dying, verily,
Of decency yet had he remembrance.

Lucan to tell this story I commend,
Suetonius too, Valerius also,
Who of the tale have written to the end
And told how, of these mighty conquerors two,
Fortune was first the friend and then the foe.
No man may trust in Fortune's favour long,
But as one fearing ambush must he go.
Witness the end of all these conquerors strong.

CROESUS

The wealthy Croesus, Lydia's sometime king,
Of which Croesus King Cyrus had such dread,
Yet was he taken, in his pride swelling,
And to be burned upon a pyre was led.
But such a rain down from the clouds was shed
As quenched the fire and let him there escape;
But to be warned, no grace was in him spread
Till Fortune on the gallows made him gape.

When he'd escaped, not changed was his intent
To march at once into new wars again.
He thought right well 'twas Fortune that had sent
Such chance that he'd escape because of rain,
And that by foes he never should be slain;
And then a vision in the night he met,
At which he waxed so proud and grew so fain
That upon vengeance all his heart was set.

Upon a tree he was, or so he thought,
Where Jupiter did wash him, back and side,
And Phoebus, then, a fair white towel brought
To dry him with and thereby swell his pride;
And to his daughter, who stood there beside,
And well, he knew, in knowledge did abound,
He bade interpret what it signified,
And she his dream in this wise did expound.

"The tree," she said, "the gallows is to mean,
And Jupiter betokens snow and rain,
While Phoebus with his towel white and clean,
That is the sunbeams beating down amain;
You shall be hanged, O father, 'tis certain;
The rain shall wash you and the sun shall dry."
And thus she gave him warning flat and plain,
His daughter, who was Phania, say I.

So hanged was Croesus, that proud Lydian king,
His royal throne could nothing then avail.
Tragedy is no other kind of thing;
Nor can the singer cry aught, or bewail,
But that Dame Fortune always will assail
With unwarned stroke those great ones who are proud;

For when men trust her most, then will she fail
And cover her bright face as with a cloud.

Explicit tragedia

HERE THE KNIGHT HALTED THE MONK IN HIS TALE

THE PROLOGUE
TO THE NUN'S PRIEST'S TALE

"Hold!" cried the knight. "Good sir, no more of this,
What you have said is right enough, and is
Very much more; a little heaviness
Is plenty for the most of us, I guess.
For me, I say it's saddening, if you please,
As to men who've enjoyed great wealth and ease,
To hear about their sudden fall, alas!
But the contrary's joy and great solace,
As when a man has been in poor estate
And he climbs up and waxes fortunate,
And there abides in all prosperity.
Such things are gladsome, as it seems to me,
And of such things it would be good to tell."
   "Yea," quoth our host, "and by Saint Paul's great bell,
You say the truth; this monk, his clapper's loud.
He spoke how 'Fortune covered with a cloud'
I know not what, and of a 'tragedy,'
As now you heard, and gad! no remedy
It is to wail and wonder and complain
That certain things have happened, and it's pain.
As you have said, to hear of wretchedness.
Sir monk, no more of this, so God you bless!
Your tale annoys the entire company;
Such talking is not worth a butterfly;
For in it is no sport nor any game.
Wherefore, sir monk, Don Peter by your name,
I pray you heartily tell us something else,
For truly, but for clinking of the bells
That from your bridle hang on either side,
By Heaven's king, Who for us all has died,
I should, ere this, have fallen down for sleep,
Although the mud had never been so deep;
Then had your story all been told in vain.

For certainly, as all these clerks complain,
'Whenas a man has none for audience,
It's little help to speak his evidence.'
And well I know the substance is in me
To judge of things that well reported be.
Sir, tell a tale of hunting now, I pray."
    "Nay," said this monk, "I have no wish to play;
Now let another tell, as I have told."
    Then spoke our host out, in rude speech and bold,
And said he unto the nun's priest anon:
"Come near, you priest, come hither, you Sir John,
Tell us a thing to make our hearts all glad;
Be blithe, although you ride upon a jade.
What though your horse may be both foul and lean?
If he but serves you, why, don't care a bean;
Just see your heart is always merry. So."
    "Yes, sir," said he, "yes, host, so may I go,
For, save I'm merry, I know I'll be blamed."
    And right away his story has he framed,
And thus he said unto us, every one,
This dainty priest, this goodly man, Sir John.

Explicit

THE NUN'S PRIEST'S TALE

OF THE COCK AND HEN, CHANTICLEER AND PERTELOTE

A widow poor, somewhat advanced in age,
Lived, on a time, within a small cottage
Beside a grove and standing down a dale.
This widow, now, of whom I tell my tale,
Since that same day when she'd been last a wife
Had led, with patience, her strait simple life,
For she'd small goods and little income-rent;
By husbanding of such as God had sent
She kept herself and her young daughters twain.
Three large sows had she, and no more, 'tis plain,
Three cows and a lone sheep that she called Moll.
Right sooty was her bedroom and her hall,
Wherein she'd eaten many a slender meal.

Of sharp sauce, why she needed no great deal,
For dainty morsel never passed her throat;
Her diet well accorded with her coat.
Repletion never made this woman sick;
A temperate diet was her whole physic,
And exercise, and her heart's sustenance.
The gout, it hindered her nowise to dance,
Nor apoplexy spun within her head;
And no wine drank she, either white or red;
Her board was mostly garnished, white and black,
With milk and brown bread, whereof she'd no lack,
Broiled bacon and sometimes an egg or two,
For a small dairy business did she do.
  A yard she had, enclosed all roundabout
With pales, and there was a dry ditch without,
And in the yard a cock called Chanticleer.
In all the land, for crowing, he'd no peer.
His voice was merrier than the organ gay
On Mass days, which in church begins to play;
More regular was his crowing in his lodge
Than is a clock or abbey horologe.
By instinct he'd marked each ascension down
Of equinoctial value in that town;
For when fifteen degrees had been ascended,
Then crew he so it might not be amended.
His comb was redder than a fine coral,
And battlemented like a castle wall.
His bill was black and just like jet it shone;
Like azure were his legs and toes, each one;
His spurs were whiter than the lily flower;
And plumage of the burnished gold his dower.
This noble cock had in his governance
Seven hens to give him pride and all pleasance,
Which were his sisters and his paramours
And wondrously like him as to colours,
Whereof the fairest hued upon her throat
Was called the winsome Mistress Pertelote.
Courteous she was, discreet and debonnaire,
Companionable, and she had been so fair
Since that same day when she was seven nights old,
That truly she had taken the heart to hold
Of Chanticleer, locked in her every limb;
He loved her so that all was well with him.

But such a joy it was to hear them sing,
Whenever the bright sun began to spring,
In sweet accord, "My love walks through the land."
For at that time, and as I understand,
The beasts and all the birds could speak and sing.

   So it befell that, in a bright dawning,
As Chanticleer 'midst wives and sisters all
Sat on his perch, the which was in the hall,
And next him sat the winsome Pertelote,
This Chanticleer he groaned within his throat
Like man that in his dreams is troubled sore.
And when fair Pertelote thus heard him roar,
She was aghast and said: "O sweetheart dear,
What ails you that you groan so? Do you hear?
You are a sleepy herald. Fie, for shame!"

   And he replied to her thus: "Ah, *madame*,
I pray you that you take it not in grief:
By God, I dreamed I'd come to such mischief,
Just now, my heart yet jumps with sore affright.
Now God," cried he, "my vision read aright
And keep my body out of foul prison!
I dreamed, that while I wandered up and down
Within our yard, I saw there a strange beast
Was like a dog, and he'd have made a feast
Upon my body, and have had me dead.
His colour yellow was and somewhat red;
And tipped his tail was, as were both his ears,
With black, unlike the rest, as it appears;
His snout was small and gleaming was each eye.
Remembering how he looked, almost I die;
And all this caused my groaning, I confess."

   "Aha," said she, "fie on you, spiritless!
Alas!" cried she, "for by that God above,
Now have you lost my heart and all my love;
I cannot love a coward, by my faith.
For truly, whatsoever woman saith,
We all desire, if only it may be,
To have a husband hardy, wise, and free,
And trustworthy, no niggard, and no fool,
Nor one that is afraid of every tool,
Nor yet a braggart, by that God above!
How dare you say, for shame, unto your love
That there is anything that you have feared?

Have you not man's heart, and yet have a beard?
Alas! And are you frightened by a vision?
Dreams are, God knows, a matter for derision.
Visions are generated by repletions
And vapours and the body's bad secretions
Of humours overabundant in a wight.
Surely this dream, which you have had tonight,
Comes only of the superfluity
Of your bilious irascibility,
Which causes folk to shiver in their dreams
For arrows and for flames with long red gleams,
For great beasts in the fear that they will bite,
For quarrels and for wolf whelps great and slight;
Just as the humour of melancholy
Causes full many a man, in sleep, to cry,
For fear of black bears or of bulls all black,
Or lest black devils put them in a sack.
Of other humours could I tell also,
That bring, to many a sleeping man, great woe;
But I'll pass on as lightly as I can.
    "Lo, Cato, and he was a full wise man,
Said he not, we should trouble not for dreams?
Now, sir," said she, "when we fly from the beams,
For God's love go and take some laxative;
On peril of my soul, and as I live,
I counsel you the best, I will not lie,
That both for choler and for melancholy
You purge yourself; and since you shouldn't tarry,
And on this farm there's no apothecary,
I will myself go find some herbs for you
That will be good for health and pecker too;
And in our own yard all these herbs I'll find,
The which have properties of proper kind
To purge you underneath and up above.
Forget this not, now, for God's very love!
You are so very choleric of complexion.
Beware the mounting sun and all dejection,
Nor get yourself with sudden humours hot;
For if you do, I dare well lay a groat
That you shall have the tertian fever's pain,
Or some ague that may well be your bane.
A day or two you shall have digestives
Of worms before you take your laxatives

Of laurel, centuary, and fumitory,
Or else of hellebore purificatory,
Or caper spurge, or else of dogwood berry,
Or herb ivy, all in our yard so merry;
Peck them just as they grow and gulp them in.
Be merry, husband, for your father's kin!
Dread no more dreams. And I can say no more."
　　"Madam," said he, "gramercy for your lore.
Nevertheless, not running Cato down,
Who had for wisdom such a high renown,
And though he says to hold no dreams in dread,
By God, men have, in many old books, read
Of many a man more an authority
That ever Cato was, pray pardon me,
Who say just the reverse of his sentence,
And have found out by long experience
That dreams, indeed, are good significations,
As much of joys as of all tribulations
That folk endure here in this life present.
There is no need to make an argument;
The very proof of this is shown indeed.
　　"One of the greatest authors that men read
Says thus: That on a time two comrades went
On pilgrimage, and all in good intent;
And it so chanced they came into a town
Where there was such a crowding, up and down,
Of people, and so little harbourage,
That they found not so much as one cottage
Wherein the two of them might sheltered be.
Wherefore they must, as of necessity,
For that one night at least, part company;
And each went to a different hostelry
And took such lodgment as to him did fall.
Now one of them was lodged within a stall,
Far in a yard, with oxen of the plow;
That other man found shelter fair enow,
As was his luck, or was his good fortune,
Whatever 'tis that governs us, each one.
　　"So it befell that, long ere it was day,
This last man dreamed in bed, as there he lay,
That his poor fellow did unto him call,
Saying: 'Alas! For in an ox's stall
This night shall I be murdered where I lie.

Now help me, brother dear, before I die.
Come in all haste to me.' 'Twas thus he said.
This man woke out of sleep, then, all afraid;
But when he'd wakened fully from his sleep,
He turned upon his pillow, yawning deep,
Thinking his dream was but a fantasy.
And then again, while sleeping, thus dreamed he.
And then a third time came a voice that said
(Or so he thought): 'Now, comrade, I am dead;
Behold my bloody wounds, so wide and deep!
Early arise tomorrow from your sleep,
And at the west gate of the town,' said he,
A wagon full of dung there shall you see,
Wherein is hid my body craftily;
Do you arrest this wagon right boldly.
They killed me for what money they could gain.
And told in every point how he'd been slain,
With a most pitiful face and pale of hue.
And trust me well, this dream did all come true;
For on the morrow, soon as it was day,
Unto his comrade's inn he took the way;
And when he'd come into that ox's stall,
Upon his fellow he began to call.

   "The keeper of the place replied anon,
And said he: 'Sir, your friend is up and gone;
As soon as day broke he went out of town.'
This man, then, felt suspicion in him grown,
Remembering the dream that he had had,
And forth he went, no longer tarrying, sad,
Unto the west gate of the town, and found
A dung-cart on its way to dumping-ground,
And it was just the same in every wise
As you have heard the dead man advertise;
And with a hardy heart he then did cry
Vengeance and justice on this felony:
'My comrade has been murdered in the night,
And in this very cart lies, face upright.
I cry to all the officers,' said he
'That ought to keep the peace in this city.
Alas, alas, here lies my comrade slain!'
   "Why should I longer with this tale detain?
The people rose and turned the cart to ground,
And in the center of the dung they found

The dead man, lately murdered in his sleep.
   "O Blessed God, Who art so true and deep!
Lo, how Thou dost turn murder out alway!
Murder will out, we see it every day.
Murder's so hateful and abominable
To God, Who is so just and reasonable,
That He'll not suffer that it hidden be;
Though it may skulk a year, or two, or three,
Murder will out, and I conclude thereon.
Immediately the rulers of that town,
They took the carter and so sore they racked
Him and the host, until their bones were cracked,
That they confessed their wickedness anon,
And hanged they both were by the neck, and soon.
   "Here may men see that dreams are things to dread.
And certainly, in that same book I read,
Right in the very chapter after this
(I spoof not, as I may have joy and bliss),
Of two men who would voyage oversea,
For some cause, and unto a far country,
If but the winds had not been all contrary,
Causing them both within a town to tarry,
Which town was builded near the haven-side.
But then, one day, along toward eventide,
The wind did change and blow as suited best.
Jolly and glad they went unto their rest.
And were prepared right early for to sail;
But unto one was told a marvelous tale.
For one of them, a-sleeping as he lay,
Did dream a wondrous dream ere it was day.
He thought a strange man stood by his bedside
And did command him, he should there abide,
And said to him: 'If you tomorrow wend,
You shall be drowned; my tale is at an end.'
He woke and told his fellow what he'd met
And prayed him quit the voyage and forget;
For just one day he prayed him there to bide.
His comrade, who was lying there beside,
Began to laugh and scorned him long and fast.
'No dream,' said he, 'may make my heart aghast,
So that I'll quit my business for such things.
I do not care a straw for your dreamings,
For visions are but fantasies and japes.

Men dream, why, every day, of owls and apes,
And many a wild phantasm therewithal;
Men dream of what has never been, nor shall.
But since I see that you will here abide,
And thus forgo this fair wind and this tide,
God knows I'm sorry; nevertheless, good day!'
    "And thus he took his leave and went his way.
But long before the half his course he'd sailed,
I know not why, nor what it was that failed,
But casually the vessel's bottom rent,
And ship and men under the water went,
In sight of other ships were there beside,
The which had sailed with that same wind and tide.
    "And therefore, pretty Pertelote, my dear,
By such old-time examples may you hear
And learn that no man should be too reckless
Of dreams, for I can tell you, fair mistress,
That many a dream is something well to dread.
    "Why in the 'Life' of Saint Kenelm I read
(Who was Kenelphus' son, the noble king
Of Mercia), how Kenelm dreamed a thing;
A while ere he was murdered, so they say,
His own death in a vision saw, one day.
His nurse interpreted, as records tell,
That vision, bidding him to guard him well
From treason; but he was but seven years old,
And therefore 'twas but little he'd been told
Of any dream, so holy was his heart.
By God! I'd rather than retain my shirt
That you had read this legend, as have I.
Dame Pertelote, I tell you verily,
Macrobius, who wrote of Scipio
The African a vision long ago,
He holds by dreams, saying that they have been
Warnings of things that men have later seen.
    "And furthermore, I pray you to look well
In the Old Testament at Daniel,
Whether he held dreams for mere vanity.
Read, too, of Joseph, and you there shall see
Where dreams have sometimes been (I say not all)
Warnings of things that after did befall.
Consider Egypt's king, Dan Pharaoh,
His baker and his butler, these also,

Whether they knew of no effect from dreams.
Whoso will read of sundry realms the themes
May learn of dreams full many a wondrous thing.
Lo, Croesus, who was once of Lydia king,
Dreamed he not that he sat upon a tree,
Which signified that hanged high he should be?
Lo, how Andromache, great Hector's wife,
On that same day when Hector lost his life,
She dreamed upon the very night before
That Hector's life should be lost evermore,
If on that day he battled, without fail.
She warned him, but no warning could avail;
He went to fight, despite all auspices,
And so was shortly slain by Achilles.
But that same tale is all too long to tell,
And, too, it's nearly day, I must not dwell
Upon this; I but say, concluding here,
That from this vision I have cause to fear
Adversity; and I say, furthermore,
That I do set by laxatives no store,
For they are poisonous, I know it well.
Them I defy and love not, truth to tell.
    "But let us speak of mirth and stop all this;
My lady Pertelote, on hope of bliss,
In one respect God's given me much grace;
For when I see the beauty of your face,
You are so rosy-red beneath each eye,
It makes my dreadful terror wholly die.
For there is truth in *In principio*
Mulier est hominis confusio
(Madam, the meaning of this Latin is,
Woman is man's delight and all his bliss).
For when I feel at night your tender side,
Although I cannot then upon you ride,
Because our perch so narrow is, alas!
I am so full of joy and all solace
That I defy, then, vision, aye and dream."
    And with that word he flew down from the beam,
For it was day, and down went his hens all;
And with a cluck he them began to call,
For he had found some corn within the yard.
Regal he was, and fears he did discard.
He feathered Pertelote full many a time

And twenty times he trod her ere 'twas prime.
He looked as if he were a grim lion
As on his toes he strutted up and down;
He deigned not set his foot upon the ground.
He clucked when any grain of corn he found,
And all his wives came running at his call.
Thus regal, as a prince is in his hall,
I'll now leave busy Chanticleer to feed,
And with events that followed I'll proceed.

When that same month wherein the world began,
Which is called March, wherein God first made man,
Was ended, and were passed of days also,
Since March began, full thirty days and two,
It fell that Chanticleer, in all his pride,
His seven wives a-walking by his side,
Cast up his two eyes toward the great bright sun
(Which through the sign of Taurus now had run
Twenty degrees and one, and somewhat more),
And knew by instinct and no other lore
That it was prime, and joyfully he crew,
"The sun, my love," he said, "has climbed anew
Forty degrees and one, and somewhat more.
My lady Pertelote, whom I adore,
Mark now these happy birds, hear how they sing,
And see all these fresh flowers, how they spring;
Full is my heart of revelry and grace."

But suddenly he fell in grievous case;
For ever the latter end of joy is woe.
God knows that worldly joys do swiftly go;
And if a rhetorician could but write,
He in some chronicle might well indite
And mark it down as sovereign in degree.
Now every wise man, let him hark to me:
This tale is just as true, I undertake,
As is the book of *Launcelot of the Lake*,
Which women always hold in such esteem.
But now I must take up my proper theme.

A brant-fox, full of sly iniquity,
That in the grove had lived two years, or three,
Now by a fine premeditated plot
That same night, breaking through the hedge, had got
Into the yard where Chanticleer the fair
Was wont, and all his wives too, to repair;

And in a bed of greenery still he lay
Till it was past the quarter of the day,
Waiting his chance on Chanticleer to fall,
As gladly do these killers one and all
Who lie in ambush for to murder men.
O murderer false, there lurking in your den!
O new Iscariot, O new Ganelon!
O false dissimulator, Greek Sinon
That brought down Troy all utterly to sorrow!
O Chanticleer, accursed be that morrow
When you into that yard flew from the beams!
You were well warned, and fully, by your dreams
That this day should hold peril damnably.
But that which God foreknows, it needs must be,
So says the best opinion of the clerks.
Witness some cleric perfect for his works,
That in the schools there's a great altercation
In this regard, and much high disputation
That has involved a hundred thousand men.
But I can't sift it to the bran with pen,
As can the holy Doctor Augustine,
Or Boethius, or Bishop Bradwardine,
Whether the fact of God's great foreknowing
Makes it right needful that I do a thing
(By needful, I mean, of necessity);
Or else, if a free choice he granted me,
To do that same thing, or to do it not,
Though God foreknew before the thing was wrought;
Or if His knowing constrains never at all,
Save by necessity conditional.
I have no part in matters so austere;
My tale is of a cock, as you shall hear,
That took the counsel of his wife, with sorrow,
To walk within the yard upon that morrow
After he'd had the dream whereof I told.
Now women's counsels oft are ill to hold;
A woman's counsel brought us first to woe,
And Adam caused from Paradise to go,
Wherein he was right merry and at ease.
But since I know not whom it may displease
If woman's counsel I hold up to blame,
Pass over, I but said it in my game.
Read authors where such matters do appear,

And what they say of women, you may hear.
These are the cock's words, they are none of mine;
No harm in women can I e'er divine.
    All in the sand, a-bathing merrily,
Lay Pertelote, with all her sisters by,
There in the sun; and Chanticleer so free
Sang merrier than a mermaid in the sea
(For Physiologus says certainly
That they *do* sing, both well and merrily).
And so befell that, as he cast his eye
Among the herbs and on a butterfly,
He saw this fox that lay there, crouching low.
Nothing of urge was in him, then, to crow;
But he cried "Cock-cock-cock" and did so start
As man who has a sudden fear at heart.
For naturally a beast desires to flee
From any enemy that he may see,
Though never yet he's clapped on such his eye.
    When Chanticleer the fox did then espy,
He would have fled but that the fox anon
Said: "Gentle sir, alas! Why be thus gone?
Are you afraid of me, who am your friend?
Now, surely, I were worse than any fiend
If I should do you harm or villainy.
I came not here upon your deeds to spy;
But, certainly, the cause of my coming
Was only just to listen to you sing.
For truly, you have quite as fine a voice
As angels have that Heaven's choirs rejoice;
Boethius to music could not bring
Such feeling, nor do others who can sing.
My lord your father (God his soul pray bless!)
And too your mother, of her gentleness,
Have been in my abode, to my great ease;
And truly, sir, right fain am I to please.
But since men speak of singing, I will say
(As I still have my eyesight day by day),
Save you, I never heard a man so sing
As did your father in the grey dawning;
Truly 'twas from the heart, his every song.
And that his voice might ever be more strong,
He took such pains that, with his either eye,
He had to blink, so loudly would he cry,

A-standing on his tiptoes therewithal,
Stretching his neck till it grew long and small.
And such discretion, too, by him was shown,
There was no man in any region known
That him in song or wisdom could surpass.
I have well read, in *Dan Burnell the Ass*,
Among his verses, how there was a cock,
Because a priest's son gave to him a knock
Upon the leg, while young and not yet wise,
He caused the boy to lose his benefice.
But, truly, there is no comparison
With the great wisdom and the discretion
Your father had, or with his subtlety.
Now sing, dear sir, for holy charity,
See if you can your father counterfeit."
    This Chanticleer his wings began to beat,
As one that could no treason there espy,
So was he ravished by this flattery.
Alas, you lords! Full many a flatterer
Is in your courts, and many a cozener,
That please your honours much more, by my fay,
Than he that truth and justice dares to say.
Go read the Ecclesiast on flattery;
Beware, my lords, of all their treachery!
    This Chanticleer stood high upon his toes,
Stretching his neck, and both his eyes did close,
And so did crow right loudly, for the nonce;
And Russel Fox, he started up at once,
And by the gorget grabbed our Chanticleer,
Flung him on back, and toward the wood did steer,
For there was no man who as yet pursued.
O destiny, you cannot be eschewed!
Alas, that Chanticleer flew from the beams!
Alas, his wife recked nothing of his dreams!
And on a Friday fell all this mischance.
O Venus, who art goddess of pleasance,
Since he did serve thee well, this Chanticleer,
And to the utmost of his power here,
More for delight than cocks to multiply,
Why would'st thou suffer him that day to die?
O Gaufred,[1] my dear master sovereign,

---

1. Gaufred de Vinsauf, who is here satirized.

Who, when King Richard Lionheart was slain
By arrow, sang his death with sorrow sore,
Why have I not your faculty and lore
To chide Friday, as you did worthily?
(For truly, on a Friday slain was he).
Then would I prove how well I could complain
For Chanticleer's great fear and all his pain.

    Certainly no such cry and lamentation
Were made by ladies at Troy's desolation,
When Pyrrhus with his terrible bared sword
Had taken old King Priam by the beard
And slain him (as the Aeneid tells to us),
As made then all those hens in one chorus
When they had caught a sight of Chanticleer.
But fair Dame Pertelote assailed the ear
Far louder than did Hasdrubal's good wife
When that her husband bold had lost his life,
And Roman legionaries burned Carthage;
For she so full of torment was, and rage,
She voluntarily to the fire did start
And burned herself there with a steadfast heart.
And you, O woeful hens, just so you cried
As when base Nero burned the city wide
Of Rome, and wept the senators' stern wives
Because their husbands all had lost their lives,
For though not guilty, Nero had them slain.
Now will I turn back to my tale again.

    This simple widow and her daughters two
Heard these hens cry and make so great ado,
And out of doors they started on the run
And saw the fox into the grove just gone,
Bearing upon his back the cock away.
And then they cried, "Alas, and weladay!
Oh, oh, the fox!" and after him they ran,
And after them, with staves, went many a man;
Ran Coll, our dog, ran Talbot and Garland,
And Malkin with a distaff in her hand;
Ran cow and calf and even the very hogs,
So were they scared by barking of the dogs
And shouting men and women all did make,
They all ran so they thought their hearts would break.
They yelled as very fiends do down in Hell;
The ducks they cried as at the butcher fell;

The frightened geese flew up above the trees;
Out of the hive there came the swarm of bees;
So terrible was the noise, ah *ben'cite!*
Certainly old Jack Straw[2] and his army
Never raised shouting half so loud and shrill
When they were chasing Flemings for to kill,
As on that day was raised upon the fox.
They brought forth trumpets made of brass, of box,
Of horn, of bone, wherein they blew and pooped,
And therewithal they screamed and shrieked and whooped;
It seemed as if the heaven itself should fall!
    And now, good men, I pray you hearken all.
Behold how Fortune turns all suddenly
The hope and pride of even her enemy!
This cock, which lay across the fox's back,
In all his fear unto the fox did clack
And say: "Sir, were I you, as I should be,
Then would I say (as God may now help me!),
'Turn back again, presumptuous peasants all!
A very pestilence upon you fall!
Now that I've gained here to this dark wood's side,
In spite of you this cock shall here abide.
I'll eat him, by my faith, and that anon!'"
    The fox replied: "In faith, it shall be done!"
And as he spoke that word, all suddenly
This cock broke from his mouth, full cleverly,
And high upon a tree he flew anon.
And when the fox saw well that he was gone,
"Alas," quoth he, "O Chanticleer, alas!
I have against you done a base trespass
In that I frightened you, my dear old pard,
When you I seized and brought from out that yard;
But, sir, I did it with no foul intent;
Come down, and I will tell you what I meant.
I'll tell the truth to you, God help me so!"
    "Nay then," said he, "beshrew us both, you know,
But first, beshrew myself, both blood and bones,
If you beguile me, having done so once,
You shall no more, with any flattery,
Cause me to sing and close up either eye.
For he who shuts his eyes when he should see,

---

2. Jack Straw: one of the leaders in Wat Tyler's rebellion, 1381.

And wilfully, God let him ne'er be free!"
  "Nay," said the fox, "but God give him mischance
Who is so indiscreet in governance
He chatters when he ought to hold his peace."
  Lo, such it is when watch and ward do cease,
And one grows negligent with flattery.
But you that hold this tale a foolery,
As but about a fox, a cock, a hen,
Yet do not miss the moral, my good men.
For Saint Paul says that all that's written well
Is written down some useful truth to tell.
Then take the wheat and let the chaff lie still.
  And now, good God, and if it be Thy will,
As says Lord Christ, so make us all good men
And bring us into His high bliss. Amen.

HERE ENDS THE NUN'S PRIEST'S TALE

EPILOGUE
TO THE NUN'S PRIEST'S TALE

"Sir nun's priest," said our host, and that anon,
"Now blessed be your breech and every stone!
This was a merry tale of Chanticleer.
But, truth, if you were secular, I swear
You would have been a hen-hopper, all right!
For if you had the heart, as you have might,
You'd need some hens, I think it will be seen,
And many more than seven times seventeen.
For see what muscles has this noble priest,
So great a neck and such a splendid chest!
He's got a hawk's fierce fire within his eye;
And certainly he has no need to dye
His cheeks with any stain from Portugal.
Sir, for your tale, may blessings on you fall!"
  And after that he, with right merry cheer,
Spoke to another one, as you shall hear.

THE PHYSICIAN'S TALE

There was, as tells us Titus Livius,
A knight whose name was called Virginius,
Fulfilled of honour and of worthiness,
Who many friends and much wealth did possess.
　　This knight had had a daughter by his wife,
Nor children more had he in all his life.
Fair was this maid, in excellent beauty
Above all others that a man may see;
For Nature had, with sovereign diligence,
Moulded her to so great an excellence
She seemed to say: "Behold now, I, Nature,
Thus can I form and paint a creature pure
When I desire. Who can it counterfeit?
Pygmalion? Nay, not though he forge and beat,
Or curve, or paint; and I dare say again,
Apelles, Zeuxis too, should work in vain,
Either to carve or paint, or forge or beat,
If they presumed my work to counterfeit.
For He Who is Creator Principal
Has made of me His Vicar General
To form and colour earthly creatures all,
Just as I like, for they're mine, great and small
Under the moon, the which may wax and wane;
And for my work I ask no payment vain;
My Lord and I are of one sole accord;
I made her in the worship of my Lord.
So do I other fair or foul creatures,
What colours though they have, or what figures."
It seems to me that Nature thus would say.
　　This maid was fourteen years of age, this may
In whom Dame Nature had so great delight.
For just as she can paint a lily white

243

Or redden rose, even with such a stroke
She did this creature by her art evoke
Ere she was born, painting her sweet limbs free
In such true colours as they'd come to be;
And Phoebus dyed her long hair with such gold
As have his burning streamers manifold.
But if right excellent was her beauty,
A thousand-fold more virtuous was she.
In her there lacked not one condition known
That's praiseworthy when by discretion shown.
As well in soul as body chaste was she;
For which she flowered in virginity
With all humility and abstinence,
And with all temperance and with patience,
And with a modest bearing and array.
Discreet in her replies she was alway;
Though she was wise as Pallas, and not vain,
Her speech was always womanly and plain,
No highfalutin pretty words had she
To ape deep knowledge; after her degree
She spoke, and all her words, greater and less,
Tended to virtue and to gentleness.
Modest she was, with maiden bashfulness,
Constant of heart, and full of busyness
To keep her from all idle sluggardry.
Bacchus had of her mouth no mastery;
For wine and youth help Venus to increase,
As when on fire is scattered oil or grease.
And of her virtue, free and unconstrained,
She had ofttimes some little illness feigned
In order to avoid a company
Which likely was to do some great folly,
As people do at revels and at dances,
Which are occasions when young folk take chances.
Such things but make young men and maidens be
Too ripe and bold, as everyone may see,
Which is right dangerous, as 'twas of yore.
For all too soon a virgin learns the lore
Of wantonness when she becomes a wife.
    You governesses, who in older life
Have great lords' daughters in your governance,
Take from my words no foolish petulance;
Remember you've been set to governings

Of lords' daughters for but one of two things:
Either that you have kept your honesty,
Or else that you've succumbed to your frailty,
And having learned the measures of love's dance,
Have now forsaken such ways of mischance
For evermore; therefore, for Jesus' sake,
See that you teach them virtue, nor mistake.
A poacher of the deer, who has reformed,
Left wicked ways and been by goodness warmed,
Can guard a forest best of any man.
So guard them well, for if you will you can;
Look that to no vice do you give assent,
Lest you be damned for your so vile intent;
For who does thus is traitor, that's certain.
And take good care that I speak not in vain;
Of treacheries all, the sovereign pestilence
Is when adults betray young innocence.

    You fathers and you mothers fond, also,
If you have children, be it one or two,
Yours is the burden of their wise guidance
The while they are within your governance.
Beware that not from your own lax living,
Or by your negligence in chastening
They fall and perish; for I dare well say,
If that should chance you'll dearly have to pay.
Under a shepherd soft and negligent
Full many a sheep and lamb by wolf is rent.
Suffice one instance, as I give it here,
For I must in my story persevere.

    This maid, of whom I do this praise express,
Guarded herself, nor needed governess;
For in her daily life all maids might read,
As in a book, every good word or deed
That might become a maiden virtuous;
She was so prudent and so bounteous.
From all this grew the fame on every side
Of both her beauty and her goodness wide;
Throughout that land they praised her, every one
That virtue loved; and Envy stood alone,
That sorry is when others live in weal
And for their woe will ever gladness feel.
(Doctor Augustine's are these words, I own).

    This maid, upon a day, went into town

Unto a temple, with her mother dear,
As the wont is of young maids everywhere.
  Now there was then a justice in that town
Was governor of all the region known.
And so befell, this judge his two eyes cast
Upon this maid, noting her beauty fast,
As she went by the place wherein he stood.
Swiftly his heart was altered, and his mood,
He was so caught by beauty of the maid,
And to his own dark secret heart he said:
"She shall be mine in spite of any man!"
  Anon the Fiend into his bosom ran
And taught him swiftly how, by treachery,
The maiden to his purpose might win he.
For truly not to bribery or force
Would it avail, he thought, to have recourse,
Since she had many friends, and was so good,
So strong in virtue, that he never could
By any subtle means her favour win
And make her give her body unto sin.
Therefore, and with great scheming up and down,
He sent to find a fellow of the town,
Which man, he knew, was cunning and was bold.
And unto this man, when the judge had told
His secret, then he made himself right sure
That it should come to ears of no creature,
For if it did the fellow'd lose his head.
And when assent to this crime had been said,
Glad was the judge, and then he made great cheer
And gave the fellow precious gifts and dear.
  When plotted out was their conspiracy,
From point to point, how all his lechery
Should have its will, performing craftily,
As you shall hear it now told openly,
Home went the churl, whose name was Claudius.
This false judge, who was known as Appius
(Such was his name, for this is no fable,
But an historical event I tell,
At least the gist is true, beyond a doubt)—
This false judge goes now busily about
To hasten his delight in all he may.
And so befell soon after, on a day,
This false judge, as recounts the ancient story,

As he was wont, sat in his auditory
And gave his judgment upon every case.
Forthwith the wicked churl advanced a pace,
And said: "Your honour, if it be your will,
Then give me justice prayed for in this bill
Of my complaint against Virginius.
And if he claim the matter stands not thus,
I will so prove, by many a good witness,
That truth is what my bill does here express."
    The judge replied: "On this, in his absence,
I may not give definitive sentence.
Let him be called and I will gladly hear;
You shall have all your right, and no wrong, here."
    Virginius came to learn the judge's will,
And then was read to him this wicked bill,
The substance of it being as you shall hear.
    "To you, Judge Appius, may it so appear
That comes and says your servant Claudius,
How that a knight, by name Virginius,
Against the law, against all equity,
Holds, expressly against the will of me,
My servant who is slave to me by right,
Who from my house was stolen, on a night,
While yet she was but young; this will I prove,
My lord, by witness competent thereof.
She's not his child, whatever he may say;
Wherefore to you, my lord the judge, I pray,
Yield me my slave, if that it be your will."
Lo, this was all the substance of his bill.
    Virginius' eyes the churl's began to hold,
But hastily, before his tale he'd told,
Ready to prove it, as befits a knight,
And by the evidence of many a wight,
That false was this charge of his adversary.
The wicked judge, he would no moment tarry,
Nor hear a word more from Virginius,
But gave his judgment then and there, as thus:
"I do decree in favour of the churl:
No longer shall you hold this servant girl.
Go bring her here and leave her as my ward.
This man shall have his slave, as my award."
    And when this noble knight Virginius,
By judgment of this Justice Appius,

Must now, perforce, his darling daughter give
Unto the judge, in lechery to live,
He did go home and sat down in his hall,
And gave command his daughter there to call;
And, with a face dead white and ashen cold,
Her modest mien his eyes did then behold,
With father's pity striking through his heart,
Though from his purpose he would not depart.

   "Daughter," said he, "Virginia by your name,
There are two ways, for either death or shame
You now must suffer. Ah, that I was born!
For you have not deserved to be thus lorn,
To die by means of sword or any knife.
O my dear daughter, ender of my life,
Whom I have bred up with so deep pleasance
That you were never from my remembrance!
O daughter who are now my final woe,
Aye, and in life my final joy also,
O gem of chastity, in brave patience
Receive your death, for that is my sentence.
For love and not for hate you must be dead;
My pitying hand must strike your innocent head.
Alas! That ever Appius saw you! Nay,
Thus has he falsely judged of you today."—
And told her all the case, as you before
Have heard; there is no need to tell it more.

   "O mercy, my dear father," said this maid,
And with that word both of her arms she laid
About his neck, as she was wont to do;
Then broke the bitter tears from her eyes two.
She said: "O my good father, must I die?
Is there no grace? Is there no remedy?"

   "No, truly, darling daughter mine," said he.

   "Then give me leisure, father mine," quoth she,
"But to lament my death a little space;
For even Jephtha gave his daughter grace
To weep a little ere he slew, alas!
And God knows that in naught did she trespass,
Save that she ran to be the first to see
And welcome him with greetings, merrily."

   And with that word she fell into a swoon,
And after, when the faint was past and gone,
She rose up and unto her father said:

"Praise be to God that I shall die a maid.
Give me my death before I come to shame;
Do with your child your will, and in God's name!"
    And then she prayed him, as he was expert,
He'd strike her swiftly, lest the blow should hurt,
Whereon again a-swooning down she fell.
Her father, with a heavy heart and will,
Struck off her head, and bore it by the hair
Straight to the judge and did present it there
While yet he sat on bench in auditory.
And when the judge saw this, so says the story,
He bade them take him out and swiftly hang.
But then a thousand people rose and sprang
To save the knight, for ruth and for pity,
For known was now the false iniquity.
The people had suspected some such thing,
By the churl's manner in his challenging,
That it was done to please this Appius;
They knew right well that he was lecherous.
Wherefore they ran this Appius upon
And cast him into prison cell anon,
Wherein he slew himself; and Claudius,
Who had been creature of this Appius,
Was sentenced to be hanged upon a tree;
But then Virginius, of his great pity,
So pleaded for him that he was exiled,
For, after all, the judge had him beguiled.
The rest were hanged, the greater and the less,
Who had been parties to this wickedness.
    Here may men see how sin has its desert!
Beware, for no man knows whom God will hurt,
Nor how profoundly, no, nor in what wise
The hidden worm of conscience terrifies
The wicked soul, though secret its deeds be
And no one knows thereof but God and he.
For be he ignorant or learned, yet
He cannot know when fear will make him sweat.
Therefore I counsel you, this counsel take:
Forsake your sin ere sin shall you forsake.

HERE ENDS THE PHYSICIAN'S TALE

THE WORDS OF THE HOST
TO THE PHYSICIAN
AND THE PARDONER

Our host began to swear as madman would:
"Halloo!" he cried, "now by the Nails and Blood!
This was a false churl and a false justice!
As shameful death as thinking may devise
Come to such judge who such a helper has!
And so this luckless maid is slain, alas!
Alas, too dearly paid she for beauty!
Wherefore I always say, as men may see,
That Fortune's gifts, or those of Dame Nature,
Are cause of death to many a good creature.
Her beauty was her death, I say again;
Alas, so pitiably she there was slain!
From both the kinds of gift I speak of now
Men often take more harm than help, I vow.
But truly, my own master lief and dear,
This is a very pitiful tale to hear,
Yet let us pass it by as of no force.
I pray to God to save your gentle corse,
Your urinals and all your chamberpots,
Your hippocras and medicines and tots
And every boxful of electuary;
God bless them, and Our Lady, holy Mary!
So may I prosper, you're a proper man,
And like a prelate too, by Saint Ronan!
Said I not well? I can't speak in set terms;
But well I know my heart with grief so warms
That almost I have caught a cardiac pain.
Body and Bones! Save I some remedy gain,
Or else a draught of fresh-drawn, malty ale,
Or save I hear, anon, a merry tale,

My heart is lost for pity of this maid.
You, *bon ami*, you pardoner," he said,
"Tell us some pleasant tale or jest, anon."

"It shall be done," said he, "by Saint Ronan!
But first," he said, "just here, at this ale-stake,
I will both drink and eat a bite of cake."

But then these gentle folk began to cry:
"Nay, let him tell us naught of ribaldry;
Tell us some moral thing, that we may hear
Wisdom, and then we gladly will give ear."

"I grant it, aye," said he, "but I must think
Upon some seemly tale the while I drink."

THE PROLOGUE
OF THE PARDONER'S TALE

Radix malorum est Cupiditas:
Ad Thimotheum, sexto.

"Masters," quoth he, "in churches, when I preach,
I am at pains that all shall hear my speech,
And ring it out as roundly as a bell,
For I know all by heart the thing I tell.
My theme is always one, and ever was:
'Radix malorum est cupiditas.'
    "First I announce the place whence I have come,
And then I show my pardons, all and some.
Our liege-lord's seal on my patent perfect,
I show that first, my safety to protect,
And then no man's so bold, no priest nor clerk,
As to disturb me in Christ's holy work;
And after that my tales I marshal all.
Indulgences of pope and cardinal,
Of patriarch and bishop, these I do
Show, and in Latin speak some words, a few,
To spice therewith a bit my sermoning
And stir men to devotion, marvelling.
Then show I forth my hollow crystal-stones,
Which are crammed full of rags, aye, and of bones;
Relics are these, as they think, every one.
Then I've in latten box a shoulder bone
Which came out of a holy Hebrew's sheep.
'Good men,' say I, 'my words in memory keep;
If this bone shall be washed in any well,
Then if a cow, calf, sheep, or ox should swell
That's eaten snake, or been by serpent stung,
Take water of that well and wash its tongue,

And 'twill be well anon; and furthermore,
Of pox and scab and every other sore
Shall every sheep be healed that of this well
Drinks but one draught; take heed of what I tell.
And if the man that owns the beasts, I trow,
Shall every week, and that before cock-crow,
And before breakfast, drink thereof a draught,
As that Jew taught of yore in his priestcraft,
His beasts and all his store shall multiply.
And, good sirs, it's a cure for jealousy;
For though a man be fallen in jealous rage,
Let one make of this water his pottage
And nevermore shall he his wife mistrust,
Though he may know the truth of all her lust,
Even though she'd taken two priests, aye, or three.
    "'Here is a mitten, too, that you may see.
Who puts his hand therein, I say again,
He shall have increased harvest of his grain,
After he's sown, be it of wheat or oats,
Just so he offers pence or offers groats.
    "'Good men and women, one thing I warn you,
If any man be here in church right now
That's done a sin so horrible that he
Dare not, for shame, of that sin shriven be,
Or any woman, be she young or old,
That's made her husband into a cuckold,
Such folk shall have no power and no grace
To offer to my relics in this place.
But whoso finds himself without such blame,
He will come up and offer, in God's name,
And I'll absolve him by authority
That has, by bull, been granted unto me.'
    "By this fraud have I won me, year by year,
A hundred marks, since I've been pardoner.
I stand up like a scholar in pulpit,
And when the ignorant people all do sit,
I preach, as you have heard me say before,
And tell a hundred false japes, less or more.
I am at pains, then, to stretch forth my neck,
And east and west upon the folk I beck,
As does a dove that's sitting on a barn.
With hands and swift tongue, then, do I so yarn
That it's a joy to see my busyness.

Of avarice and of all such wickedness
Is all my preaching, thus to make them free
With offered pence, the which pence come to me.
For my intent is only pence to win,
And not at all for punishment of sin.
When they are dead, for all I think thereon
Their souls may well black-berrying have gone!
For, certainly, there's many a sermon grows
Ofttimes from evil purpose, as one knows;
Some for folks' pleasure and for flattery,
To be advanced by all hypocrisy,
And some for vainglory, and some for hate.
For, when I dare not otherwise debate,
Then do I sharpen well my tongue and sting
The man in sermons, and upon him fling
My lying defamations, if but he
Has wronged my brethren or—much worse—wronged me.
For though I mention not his proper name,
Men know whom I refer to, all the same,
By signs I make and other circumstances.
Thus I pay those who do us displeasances.
Thus spit I out my venom under hue
Of holiness, to seem both good and true.
    "But briefly my intention I'll express;
I preach no sermon, save for covetousness.
For that my theme is yet, and ever was,
'*Radix malorum est cupiditas*.'
Thus can I preach against that self-same vice
Which I indulge, and that is avarice.
But though myself be guilty of that sin,
Yet can I cause these other folk to win
From avarice and really to repent.
But that is not my principal intent.
I preach no sermon, save for covetousness;
This should suffice of that, though, as I guess.
    "Then do I cite examples, many a one,
Out of old stories and of time long gone,
For vulgar people all love stories old;
Such things they can re-tell well and can hold.
What? Think you that because I'm good at preaching
And win me gold and silver by my teaching
I'll live of my free will in poverty?
No, no, that's never been my policy!

For I will preach and beg in sundry lands;
I will not work and labour with my hands,
Nor baskets weave and try to live thereby,
Because I will not beg in vain, say I.
I will none of the apostles counterfeit;
I will have money, wool, and cheese, and wheat,
Though it be given by the poorest page,
Or by the poorest widow in village,
And though her children perish of famine.
Nay! I will drink good liquor of the vine
And have a pretty wench in every town.
But hearken, masters, to conclusion shown:
Your wish is that I tell you all a tale.
Now that I've drunk a draught of musty ale,
By God, I hope that I can tell something
That shall, in reason, be to your liking.
For though I am myself a vicious man,
Yet I would tell a moral tale, and can,
The which I'm wont to preach more gold to win.
Now hold your peace! my tale I will begin."

THE PARDONER'S TALE

In Flanders, once, there was a company
Of young companions given to folly,
Riot and gambling, brothels and taverns;
And, to the music of harps, lutes, gitterns,
They danced and played at dice both day and night.
And ate also and drank beyond their might,
Whereby they made the devil's sacrifice
Within that devil's temple, wicked wise,
By superfluity both vile and vain.
So damnable their oaths and so profane
That it was terrible to hear them swear;
Our Blessed Saviour's Body did they tear;
They thought the Jews had rent Him not enough;
And each of them at others' sins would laugh.
Then entered dancing-girls of ill repute,
Graceful and slim, and girls who peddled fruit,
Harpers and bawds and women selling cake,
Who do their office for the Devil's sake,

To kindle and blow the fire of lechery,
Which is so closely joined with gluttony;
I call on holy writ, now, to witness
That lust is in all wine and drunkenness.
　　Lo, how the drunken Lot unnaturally
Lay with his daughters two, unwittingly;
So drunk he was he knew not what he wrought.
　　Herod, as in his story's clearly taught,
When full of wine and merry at a feast,
Sitting at table idly gave behest
To slay John Baptist, who was all guiltless.
　　Seneca says a good word too, doubtless;
He says there is no difference he can find
Between a man that's quite out of his mind
And one that's drunken, save perhaps in this
That when a wretch in madness fallen is,
The state lasts longer than does drunkenness.
O gluttony; full of all wickedness,
O first cause of confusion to us all,
Beginning of damnation and our fall,
Till Christ redeemed us with His blood again!
Behold how dearly, to be brief and plain,
Was purchased this accursed villainy;
Corrupt was all this world with gluttony!
　　Adam our father, and his wife also,
From Paradise to labour and to woe
Were driven for that vice, no doubt; indeed
The while that Adam fasted, as I read,
He was in Paradise; but then when he
Ate of the fruit forbidden of the tree,
Anon he was cast out to woe and pain.
O gluttony, of you we may complain!
Oh, knew a man how many maladies
Follow on excess and on gluttonies,
Surely he would be then more moderate
In diet, and at table more sedate.
Alas! The throat so short, the tender mouth,
Causing that east and west and north and south,
In earth, in air, in water men shall swink
To get a glutton dainty meat and drink!
Of this same matter Paul does wisely treat:
"Meat for the belly and belly for the meat:
And both shall God destroy," as Paul does say.

Alas! A foul thing is it, by my fay,
To speak this word, and fouler is the deed,
When man so guzzles of the white and red
That of his own throat makes he his privy,
Because of this cursed superfluity.
  The apostle, weeping, says most piteously:
"For many walk, of whom I've told you, aye,
Weeping I tell you once again they're dross,
For they are foes of Christ and of the Cross,
Whose end is death, whose belly is their god."
O gut! O belly! O you stinking cod,
Filled full of dung, with all corruption found!
At either end of you foul is the sound.
With how great cost and labour do they find
Your food! These cooks, they pound and strain and grind;
Substance to accident they turn with fire,
All to fulfill your gluttonous desire!
Out of the hard and riven bones knock they
The marrow, for they throw nothing away
That may go through the gullet soft and sweet;
With spicery, with leaf, bark, root, replete
Shall be the sauces made for your delight,
To furnish you a sharper appetite.
But truly, he that such delights entice
Is dead while yet he wallows in this vice.
  A lecherous thing is wine, and drunkenness
Is full of striving and of wretchedness.
O drunken man, disfigured is your face,
Sour is your breath, foul are you to embrace,
And through your drunken nose there comes a sound
As if you snored out "Samson, Samson" round;
And yet God knows that Samson drank no wine.
You fall down just as if you were stuck swine;
Your tongue is loose, your honest care obscure;
For drunkenness is very sepulture
Of any mind a man may chance to own.
In whom strong drink has domination shown
He can no counsel keep for any dread.
Now keep you from the white and from the red,
And specially from the white wine grown at Lepe
That is for sale in Fish Street or in Cheap.
This wine of Spain, it mixes craftily
With other wines that chance to be near by,

From which there rise such fumes, as well may be,
That when a man has drunk two draughts, or three,
And thinks himself to be at home in Cheap,
He finds that he's in Spain, and right at Lepe,—
Not at Rochelle nor yet at Bordeaux town,
And then will he snore out "Samson, Samson."

But hearken, masters, one word more I pray:
The greatest deeds of all, I'm bold to say,
Of victories in the old testament,
Through the True God, Who is omnipotent,
Were gained by abstinence and after prayer:
Look in the Bible, you may learn this there.

Lo, Attila, the mighty conqueror,
Died in his sleep, in shame and dishonour,
And bleeding at the nose for drunkenness;
A great captain should live in soberness.
Above all this, advise yourself right well
What was commanded unto Lemuel—
Not Samuel, but Lemuel, say I—
The Bible's words you cannot well deny:
Drinking by magistrates is called a vice.
No more of this, for it may well suffice.

And now that I have told of gluttony,
I'll take up gambling, showing you thereby
The curse of chance, and all its evils treat;
From it proceeds false swearing and deceit,
Blaspheming, murder, and—what's more—the waste
Of time and money; add to which, debased
And shamed and lost to honour quite is he,
Who once a common gambler's known to be.
And ever the higher one is of estate,
The more he's held disgraced and desolate.
And if a prince plays similar hazardry
In all his government and policy,
He loses in the estimate of men
His good repute, and finds it not again.

Chilon, who was a wise ambassador,
Was sent to Corinth, all in great honour,
From Lacedaemon, to make alliance.
And when he came, he noticed there, by chance,
All of the greatest people of the land
Playing at hazard there on every hand.
Wherefore, and all as soon as it might be,

He stole off home again to his country,
And said: "I will not thus debase my name;
Nor will I take upon me so great shame
You to ally with common hazarders.
Send, if you will, other ambassadors;
For, by my truth, I say I'd rather die
Than you with gamblers like to them ally.
For you that are so glorious in honours
Shall never ally yourselves with hazarders
By my consent, or treaty I have made."
This wise philosopher, 'twas thus he said.

   Let us look, then, at King Demetrius.
The king of Parthia, as the book tells us,
Sent him a pair of golden dice, in scorn,
Because the name of gambler he had borne;
Wherefore he marked his reputation down
As valueless despite his wide renown.
Great lords may find sufficient other play
Seemly enough to while the time away.

   Now will I speak of oaths both false and great
A word or two, whereof the old books treat.
Great swearing is a thing abominable,
And vain oaths yet more reprehensible.
The High God did forbid swearing at all,
As witness Matthew; but in especial
Of swearing says the holy Jeremiah,
"Thou shalt not swear in vain, to be a liar,
But swear in judgment and in righteousness";
But idle swearing is a wickedness.
Behold, in the first table of the Law,
That should be honoured as High God's, sans flaw,
This second one of His commandments plain:
"Thou shalt not take the Lord God's name in vain."
Nay, sooner He forbids us such swearing
Than homicide or many a wicked thing;
I say that, as to order, thus it stands;
'Tis known by him who His will understands
That the great second law of God is that.
Moreover, I will tell you full and flat,
That retribution will not quit his house
Who in his swearing is too outrageous.
"By God's own precious heart, and by His nails,
And by the blood of Christ that's now at Hales,

Seven is my chance,[1] and yours is five and trey!"
"By God's good arms, if you do falsely play,
This dagger through your heart I'll stick for you!"
Such is the whelping of the bitched bones two:
Perjury, anger, cheating, homicide.
Now for the love of Christ, Who for us died,
Forgo this swearing oaths, both great and small;
But, sirs, now will I tell to you my tale.

    Now these three roisterers, whereof I tell,
Long before prime was rung by any bell,
Were sitting in a tavern for to drink;
And as they sat they heard a small bell clink
Before a corpse being carried to his grave;
Whereat one of them called unto his knave:
"Go run," said he, "and ask them civilly
What corpse it is that's just now passing by,
And see that you report the man's name well."

    "Sir," said the boy, "it needs not that they tell.
I learned it, ere you came here, full two hours;
He was, by gad, an old comrade of yours;
And he was slain, all suddenly, last night,
When drunk, as he sat on his bench upright;
An unseen thief, called Death, came stalking by,
Who hereabouts makes all the people die,
And with his spear he clove his heart in two
And went his way and made no more ado.
He's slain a thousand with this pestilence;
And, master, ere you come in his presence,
It seems to me to be right necessary
To be forewarned of such an adversary:
Be ready to meet him for evermore.
My mother taught me this, I say no more."

    "By holy Mary," said the innkeeper,
"The boy speaks truth, for Death has slain, this year,
A mile or more hence, in a large village,
Both man and woman, child and hind and page.
I think his habitation must be there;
To be advised of him great wisdom 'twere,
Before he did a man some dishonour."

    "Yea, by God's arms!" exclaimed this roisterer,
"Is it such peril, then, this Death to meet?

---

1. Chance: akin to the point in the modern game of craps.

I'll seek him in the road and in the street,
As I now vow to God's own noble bones!
Hear, comrades, we're of one mind, as each owns;
Let each of us hold up his hand to other
And each of us become the other's brother,
And we three will go slay this traitor Death;
He shall be slain who's stopped so many a breath,
By God's great dignity, ere it be night."

Together did these three their pledges plight
To live and die, each of them for the other,
As if he were his very own blood brother.
And up they started, drunken, in this rage,
And forth they went, and towards that village
Whereof the innkeeper had told before.
And so, with many a grisly oath, they swore
And Jesus' blessed body once more rent—
"Death shall be dead if we find where he went."

When they had gone not fully half a mile,
Just as they would have trodden over a stile,
An old man, and a poor, with them did meet.
This ancient man full meekly them did greet,
And said thus: "Now, lords, God keep you and see!"

The one that was most insolent of these three
Replied to him: "What? Churl of evil grace,
Why are you all wrapped up, except your face?
Why do you live so long in so great age?"

This ancient man looked upon his visage
And thus replied: "Because I cannot find
A man, nay, though I walked from here to Ind,
Either in town or country who'll engage
To give his youth in barter for my age;
And therefore must I keep my old age still,
As long a time as it shall be God's will.
Not even Death, alas! my life will take;
Thus restless I my wretched way must make,
And on the ground, which is my mother's gate,
I knock with my staff early, aye, and late,
And cry: 'O my dear mother, let me in!
Lo, how I'm wasted, flesh and blood and skin!
Alas! When shall my bones come to their rest?
Mother, with you fain would I change my chest,
That in my chamber so long time has been,
Aye! For a haircloth rag to wrap me in!'

But yet to me she will not show that grace,
And thus all pale and withered is my face.
    "But, sirs, in you it is no courtesy
To speak to an old man despitefully,
Unless in word he trespass or in deed.
In holy writ you may, yourselves, well read
'Before an old man, hoar upon the head,
You should arise.' Which I advise you read,
Nor to an old man any injury do
More than you would that men should do to you
In age, if you so long time shall abide;
And God be with you, whether you walk or ride.
I must pass on now where I have to go."
    "Nay, ancient churl, by God it sha'n't be so,"
Cried out this other hazarder, anon;
"You sha'n't depart so easily, by Saint John!
You spoke just now of that same traitor Death,
Who in this country stops our good friends' breath.
Hear my true word, since you are his own spy,
Tell where he is or you shall rue it, aye
By God and by the holy Sacrament!
Indeed you must be, with this Death, intent
To slay all us young people, you false thief."
    "Now, sirs," said he, "if you're so keen, in brief,
To find out Death, turn up this crooked way,
For in that grove I left him, by my fay,
Under a tree, and there he will abide;
Nor for your boasts will he a moment hide.
See you that oak? Right there you shall him find.
God save you, Who redeemed all humankind,
And mend your ways!"—thus said this ancient man.
    And every one of these three roisterers ran
Till he came to that tree; and there they found,
Of florins of fine gold, new-minted, round,
Well-nigh eight bushels full, or so they thought.
No longer, then, after this Death they sought,
But each of them so glad was of that sight,
Because the florins were so fair and bright,
That down they all sat by this precious hoard.
The worst of them was first to speak a word.
    "Brothers," said he, "take heed to what I say;
My wits are keen, although I mock and play.
This treasure here Fortune to us has given

That mirth and jollity our lives may liven,
And easily as it's come, so will we spend.
Eh! By God's precious dignity! Who'd pretend,
Today, that we should have so fair a grace?
But might this gold be carried from this place
Home to my house, or if you will, to yours—
For well we know that all this gold is ours—
Then were we all in high felicity.
But certainly by day this may not be;
For men would say that we were robbers strong,
And we'd, for our own treasure, hang ere long.
This treasure must be carried home by night
All prudently and slyly, out of sight.
So I propose that cuts among us all
Be drawn, and let's see where the cut will fall;
And he that gets the short cut, blithe of heart
Shall run to town at once, and to the mart,
And fetch us bread and wine here, privately.
And two of us shall guard, right cunningly,
This treasure well; and if he does not tarry,
When it is night we'll all the treasure carry
Where, by agreement, we may think it best."

That one of them the cuts brought in his fist
And bade them draw to see where it might fall;
And it fell on the youngest of them all;
And so, forth toward the town he went anon.
And just as soon as he had turned and gone,
That one of them spoke thus unto the other:
"You know well that you are my own sworn brother,
So to your profit I will speak anon.
You know well how our comrade is just gone;
And here is gold, and that in great plenty,
That's to be parted here among us three.
Nevertheless, if I can shape it so
That it be parted only by us two,
Shall I not do a turn that is friendly?"

The other said: "Well, now, how can that be?
He knows well that the gold is with us two.
What shall we say to him? What shall we do?"

"Shall it be secret?" asked the first rogue, then,
"And I will tell you in eight words, or ten,
What we must do, and how bring it about."

"Agreed," replied the other, "Never doubt,

That, on my word, I nothing will betray."
  "Now," said the first, "we're two, and I dare say
The two of us are stronger than is one.
Watch when he sits, and soon as that is done
Arise and make as if with him to play;
And I will thrust him through the two sides, yea,
The while you romp with him as in a game,
And with your dagger see you do the same;
And then shall all this gold divided be,
My right dear friend, just between you and me;
Then may we both our every wish fulfill
And play at dice all at our own sweet will."
And thus agreed were these two rogues, that day
To slay the third, as you have heard me say.

  This youngest rogue who'd gone into the town,
Often in fancy rolled he up and down
The beauty of those florins new and bright.
"O Lord," thought he, "if so be that I might
Have all this treasure to myself alone,
There is no man who lives beneath the throne
Of God that should be then so merry as I."

  And at the last the Fiend, our enemy,
Put in his thought that he should poison buy
With which he might kill both his fellows; aye,
The Devil found him in such wicked state,
He had full leave his grief to consummate;
For it was utterly the man's intent
To kill them both and never to repent.
And on he strode, no longer would he tarry,
Into the town, to an apothecary,
And prayed of him that he'd prepare and sell
Some poison for his rats, and some as well
For a polecat that in his yard had lain,
The which, he said, his capons there had slain,
And fain he was to rid him, if he might,
Of vermin that thus damaged him by night.

  The apothecary said: "And you shall have
A thing of which, so God my spirit save,
In all this world there is no live creature
That's eaten or has drunk of this mixture
As much as equals but a grain of wheat,
That shall not sudden death thereafter meet;
Yea, die he shall, and in a shorter while

Than you require to walk but one short mile;
This poison is so violent and strong."
    This wicked man the poison took along
With him boxed up, and then he straightway ran
Into the street adjoining, to a man,
And of him borrowed generous bottles three;
And into two his poison then poured he;
The third one he kept clean for his own drink.
For all that night he was resolved to swink
In carrying the florins from that place.
And when this roisterer, with evil grace,
Had filled with wine his mighty bottles three,
Then to his comrades forth again went he.
    What is the need to tell about it more?
For just as they had planned his death before,
Just so they murdered him, and that anon.
And when the thing was done, then spoke the one:
"Now let us sit and drink and so be merry,
And afterward we will his body bury."
    And as he spoke, one bottle of the three
He took wherein the poison chanced to be
And drank and gave his comrade drink also,
For which, and that anon, lay dead these two.
    I feel quite sure that Doctor Avicena
Within the sections of his *Canon* never
Set down more certain signs of poisoning
Than showed these wretches two at their ending.
Thus ended these two homicides in woe;
Died thus the treacherous poisoner also.
    O cursed sin, full of abominableness!
O treacherous homicide! O wickedness!
O gluttony, lechery, and hazardry!
O blasphemer of Christ with villainy,
And with great oaths, habitual for pride!
Alas! Mankind, how may this thing betide
That to thy dear Creator, Who thee wrought,
And with His precious blood salvation bought,
Thou art so false and so unkind, alas!
    Now, good men, God forgive you each trespass,
And keep you from the sin of avarice.
My holy pardon cures and will suffice,
So that it brings me gold, or silver brings,
Or else, I care not—brooches, spoons or rings.

Bow down your heads before this holy bull!
Come up, you wives, and offer of your wool!
Your names I'll enter on my roll, anon,
And into Heaven's bliss you'll go, each one.
For I'll absolve you, by my special power,
You that make offering, as clean this hour
As you were born.
         And lo, sirs, thus I preach.
And Jesus Christ, who is our souls' great leech,
So grant you each his pardon to receive;
For that is best; I will not you deceive.
   But, sirs, one word forgot I in my tale;
I've relics in my pouch that cannot fail,
As good as England ever saw, I hope,
The which I got by kindness of the pope.
If gifts your change of heart and mind reveal,
You'll get my absolution while you kneel.
Come forth, and kneel down here before, anon,
And humbly you'll receive my full pardon;
Or else receive a pardon as you wend,
All new and fresh as every mile shall end,
So that you offer me each time, anew,
More gold and silver, all good coins and true.
It is an honour to each one that's here
That you may have a competent pardoner
To give you absolution as you ride,
For all adventures that may still betide.
Perchance from horse may fall down one or two,
Breaking his neck, and it might well be you.
See what insurance, then, it is for all
That I within your fellowship did fall,
Who may absolve you, both the great and less,
When soul from body passes, as I guess.
I think our host might just as well begin,
For he is most enveloped in all sin.
Come forth, sir host, and offer first anon,
And you shall kiss the relics, every one,
Aye, for a groat! Unbuckle now your purse."
   "Nay, nay," said he, "then may I have Christ's curse!
It sha'n't be," said he, "as I've hope for riches,
Why, you would have me kissing your old breeches,
And swear they were the relics of a saint,
Though with your excrement 'twere dabbed like paint.

By cross Saint Helen found in Holy Land,
I would I had your ballocks in my hand
Instead of relics in a reliquary;
Let's cut them off, and them I'll help you carry;
They shall be shrined within a hog's fat turd."

    This pardoner, he answered not a word;
So wrathy was he no word would he say.

    "Now," said our host, "I will no longer play
With you, nor any other angry man."

    But at this point the worthy knight began,
When that he saw how all the folk did laugh:
"No more of this, for it's gone far enough;
Sir pardoner, be glad and merry here;
And you, sir host, who are to me so dear,
I pray you that you kiss the pardoner.
And, pardoner, I pray you to draw near,
And as we did before, let's laugh and play."
And then they kissed and rode forth on their way.

        HERE IS ENDED THE PARDONER'S TALE

THE WIFE OF BATH'S PROLOGUE

Experience, though no authority
Were in this world, were good enough for me,
To speak of woe that is in all marriage;
For, masters, since I was twelve years of age,
Thanks be to God Who is for aye alive,
Of husbands at church door have I had five;
For men so many times have wedded me;
And all were worthy men in their degree.
But someone told me not so long ago
That since Our Lord, save once, would never go
To wedding (that at Cana in Galilee),
Thus, by this same example, showed He me
I never should have married more than once.
Lo and behold! What sharp words, for the nonce,
Beside a well Lord Jesus, God and man,
Spoke in reproving the Samaritan:
'For thou hast had five husbands,' thus said He,
'And he whom thou hast now to be with thee
Is not thine husband.' Thus He said that day,
But what He meant thereby I cannot say;
And I would ask now why that same fifth man
Was not husband to the Samaritan?
How many might she have, then, in marriage?
For I have never heard, in all my age,
Clear exposition of this number shown,
Though men may guess and argue up and down.
But well I know and say, and do not lie,
God bade us to increase and multiply;
That worthy text can I well understand.
And well I know He said, too, my husband
Should father leave, and mother, and cleave to me;
But no specific number mentioned He,

Whether of bigamy or octogamy;
Why should men speak of it reproachfully?
   Lo, there's the wise old king Dan Solomon;
I understand he had more wives than one;
And now would God it were permitted me
To be refreshed one half as oft as he!
Which gift of God he had for all his wives!
No man has such that in this world now lives.
God knows, this noble king, it strikes my wit,
The first night he had many a merry fit
With each of them, so much he was alive!
Praise be to God that I have wedded five!

1 {
   Of whom I did pick out and choose the best
   Both for their nether purse and for their chest.
   Different schools make divers perfect clerks,
   Different methods learned in sundry works
   Make the good workman perfect, certainly.
   Of full five husbands tutoring am I.

Welcome the sixth whenever come he shall.
Forsooth, I'll not keep chaste for good and all;
When my good husband from the world is gone,
Some Christian man shall marry me anon;
For then, the apostle says that I am free
To wed, in God's name, where it pleases me.
He says that to be wedded is no sin;
Better to marry than to burn within.
What care I though folk speak reproachfully
Of wicked Lamech and his bigamy?
I know well Abraham was holy man,
And Jacob, too, as far as know I can;
And each of them had spouses more than two;
And many another holy man also.
Or can you say that you have ever heard
That God has ever by His express word
Marriage forbidden? Pray you, now, tell me;
Or where commanded He virginity?
I read as well as you no doubt have read
The apostle when he speaks of maidenhead;
He said, commandment of the Lord he'd none.
Men may advise a woman to be one,
But such advice is not commandment, no;

---

1. Genuine lines carried in some manuscripts.

He left the thing to our own judgment so.
For had Lord God commanded maidenhood,
He'd have condemned all marriage as not good;
And certainly, if there were no seed sown,
Virginity—where then should it be grown?
Paul dared not to forbid us, at the least,
A thing whereof his Master'd no behest.
The dart is set up for virginity;
Catch it who can; who runs best let us see.
      "But this word is not meant for every wight,
But where God wills to give it, of His might.
I know well that the apostle was a maid;
Nevertheless, and though he wrote and said
He would that everyone were such as he,
All is not counsel to virginity;
And so to be a wife he gave me leave
Out of permission; there's no shame should grieve
In marrying me, if that my mate should die,
Without exception, too, of bigamy.
And though 'twere good no woman's flesh to touch,
He meant, in his own bed or on his couch;
For peril 'tis fire and tow to assemble;
You know what this example may resemble.
This is the sum: he held virginity
Nearer perfection than marriage for frailty.
And frailty's all, I say, save he and she
Would lead their lives throughout in chastity.
      "I grant this well, I have no great envy
Though maidenhood's preferred to bigamy;
Let those who will be clean, body and ghost,
Of my condition I will make no boast.
For well you know, a lord in his household,
He has not every vessel all of gold;
Some are of wood and serve well all their days.
God calls folk unto Him in sundry ways,
And each one has from God a proper gift,
Some this, some that, as pleases Him to shift.
      "Virginity is great perfection known,
And continence e'en with devotion shown.
But Christ, Who of perfection is the well,
Bade not each separate man he should go sell
All that he had and give it to the poor
And follow Him in such wise going before.

He spoke to those that would live perfectly;
And, masters, by your leave, such am not I.
I will devote the flower of all my age
To all the acts and harvests of marriage.
   "Tell me also, to what purpose or end
The genitals were made, that I defend,
And for what benefit was man first wrought?
Trust you right well, they were not made for naught.
Explain who will and argue up and down
That they were made for passing out, as known,
Of urine, and our two belongings small
Were just to tell a female from a male,
And for no other cause—ah, say you no?
Experience knows well it is not so;
And, so the clerics be not with me wroth,
I say now that they have been made for both,
That is to say, for duty and for ease
In getting, when we do not God displease.
Why should men otherwise in their books set
That man shall pay unto his wife his debt?
Now wherewith should he ever make payment,
Except he used his blessed instrument?
Then on a creature were devised these things
For urination and engenderings.
   "But I say not that every one is bound,
Who's fitted out and furnished as I've found,
To go and use it to beget an heir;
Then men would have for chastity no care.
Christ was a maid, and yet shaped like a man,
And many a saint, since this old world began,
Yet has lived ever in perfect chastity.
I bear no malice to virginity;
Let such be bread of purest white wheat-seed,
And let us wives be called but barley bread;
And yet with barley bread (if Mark you scan)
Jesus Our Lord refreshed full many a man.
In such condition as God places us
I'll persevere, I'm not fastidious.
In wifehood I will use my instrument
As freely as my Maker has it sent.
If I be niggardly, God give me sorrow!
My husband he shall have it, eve and morrow,
When he's pleased to come forth and pay his debt.

I'll not delay, a husband I will get
Who shall be both my debtor and my thrall
And have his tribulations therewithal
Upon his flesh, the while I am his wife.
I have the power during all my life
Over his own good body, and not he.
For thus the apostle told it unto me;
And bade our husbands that they love us well.
And all this pleases me whereof I tell."

Up rose the pardoner, and that anon.
"Now dame," said he, "by God and by Saint John,
You are a noble preacher in this case!
I was about to wed a wife, alas!
Why should I buy this on my flesh so dear?
No, I would rather wed no wife this year."

"But wait," said she, "my tale is not begun;
Nay, you shall drink from out another tun
Before I cease, and savour worse than ale.
And when I shall have told you all my tale
Of tribulation that is in marriage,
Whereof I've been an expert all my age,
That is to say, myself have been the whip,
Then may you choose whether you will go sip
Out of that very tun which I shall broach.
Beware of it ere you too near approach;
For I shall give examples more than ten.
Whoso will not be warned by other men
By him shall other men corrected be.
The self-same words has written Ptolemy;
Read in his Almagest and find it there."

"Lady, I pray you, if your will it were,"
Spoke up this pardoner, "as you began,
Tell forth your tale, nor spare for any man,
And teach us younger men of your technique."

"Gladly," said she, "since it may please, not pique.
But yet I pray of all this company
That if I speak from my own phantasy,
They will not take amiss the things I say;
For my intention's only but to play.

"Now, sirs, now will I tell you forth my tale.
And as I may drink ever wine and ale,
I will tell truth of husbands that I've had,
For three of them were good and two were bad.

The three were good men and were rich and old:
Not easily could they the promise hold
Whereby they had been bound to cherish me.
You know well what I mean by that, pardie!
So help me God, I laugh now when I think
How pitifully by night I made them swink;
And by my faith I set by it no store.
They'd given me their gold, and treasure more;
I needed not do longer diligence
To win their love, or show them reverence.
They all loved me so well, by God above,
I never did set value on their love!
A woman wise will strive continually
To get herself loved, when she's not, you see.
But since I had them wholly in my hand,
And since to me they'd given all their land,
Why should I take heed, then, that I should please,
Save it were for my profit or my ease?
I set them so to work, that, by my fay,
Full many a night they sighed out 'Welaway!'
The bacon was not brought them home, I trow,
That some men have in Essex at Dunmowe.
I governed them so well, by my own law,
That each of them was happy as a daw,
And fain to bring me fine things from the fair.
And they were right glad when I spoke them fair;
For God knows that I nagged them mercilessly.

   "Now hearken how I bore me properly,
All you wise wives that well can understand.

   "Thus shall you speak and wrongfully demand;
For half so brazenfacedly can no man
Swear to his lying as a woman can.
I say not this to wives who may be wise,
Except when they themselves do misadvise.
A wise wife, if she knows what's for her good,
Will swear the crow is mad, and in this mood
Call up for witness to it her own maid;
But hear me now, for this is what I said.

   "'Sir Dotard, is it thus you stand today?
Why is my neighbour's wife so fine and gay?
She's honoured over all where'er she goes;
I sit at home, I have no decent clo'es.
What do you do there at my neighbour's house?

Is she so fair? Are you so amorous?
Why whisper to our maid? *Benedicite!*
Sir Lecher old, let your seductions be!
And if I have a gossip or a friend,
Innocently, you blame me like a fiend
If I but walk, for company, to his house!
You come home here as drunken as a mouse,
And preach there on your bench, a curse on you!
You tell me it's a great misfortune, too,
To wed a girl who costs more than she's worth;
And if she's rich and of a higher birth,
You say it's torment to abide her folly
And put up with her pride and melancholy.
And if she be right fair, you utter knave,
You say that every lecher will her have;
She may no while in chastity abide
That is assailed by all and on each side.

    "'You say, some men desire us for our gold,
Some for our shape and some for fairness told:
And some, that she can either sing or dance,
And some, for courtesy and dalliance;
Some for her hands and for her arms so small;
Thus all goes to the devil in your tale.
You say men cannot keep a castle wall
That's long assailed on all sides, and by all.

    "'And if that she be foul, you say that she
Hankers for every man that she may see;
For like a spaniel will she leap on him
Until she finds a man to be victim;
And not a grey goose swims there in the lake
But finds a gander willing her to take.
You say, it is a hard thing to enfold
Her whom no man will in his own arms hold.
This say you, worthless, when you go to bed;
And that no wise man needs thus to be wed,
No, nor a man that hearkens unto Heaven.
With furious thunder-claps and fiery levin
May your thin, withered, wrinkled neck be broke!

    "'You say that dripping eaves, and also smoke,
And wives contentious, will make men to flee
Out of their houses; ah, *benedicite!*
What ails such an old fellow so to chide?

    "'You say that all we wives our vices hide

Till we are married, then we show them well;
That is a scoundrel's proverb, let me tell!
  "'You say that oxen, asses, horses, hounds
Are tried out variously, and on good grounds;
Basins and bowls, before men will them buy,
And spoons and stools and all such goods you try.
And so with pots and clothes and all array;
But of their wives men get no trial, you say,
Till they are married, base old dotard you!
And then we show what evil we can do.
  "'You say also that it displeases me
Unless you praise and flatter my beauty,
And save you gaze always upon my face
And call me "lovely lady" every place;
And save you make a feast upon that day
When I was born, and give me garments gay;
And save due honour to my nurse is paid
As well as to my faithful chambermaid,
And to my father's folk and his allies—
Thus you go on, old barrel full of lies!
  "'And yet of our apprentice, young Jenkin,
For his crisp hair, showing like gold so fine,
Because he squires me walking up and down,
A false suspicion in your mind is sown;
I'd give him naught, though you were dead tomorrow.
  "'But tell me this, why do you hide, with sorrow,
The keys to your strong-box away from me?
It is my gold as well as yours, pardie.
Why would you make an idiot of your dame?
Now by Saint James, but you shall miss your aim,
You shall not be, although like mad you scold,
Master of both my body and my gold;
One you'll forgo in spite of both your eyes;
Why need you seek me out or set on spies?
I think you'd like to lock me in your chest!
You should say: "Dear wife, go where you like best.
Amuse yourself, I will believe no tales;
You're my wife Alis true, and truth prevails."
We love no man that guards us or gives charge
Of where we go, for we will be at large.
  "'Of all men the most blessed may he be,
That wise astrologer, Dan Ptolemy,
Who says this proverb in his Almagest:

"Of all men he's in wisdom the highest
That nothing cares who has the world in hand."
And by this proverb shall you understand:
Since you've enough, why do you reck or care
How merrily all other folks may fare?
For certainly, old dotard, by your leave,
You shall have cunt all right enough at eve.
He is too much a niggard who's so tight
That from his lantern he'll give none a light.
For he'll have never the less light, by gad;
Since you've enough, you need not be so sad.

"'You say, also, that if we make us gay
With clothing, all in costliest array,
That it's a danger to our chastity;
And you must back the saying up, pardie!
Repeating these words in the apostle's name:
"In habits meet for chastity, not shame,
Your women shall be garmented," said he,
"And not with broidered hair, or jewellery,
Or pearls, or gold, or costly gowns and chic;"
After your text and after your rubric
I will not follow more than would a gnat.
You said this, too, that I was like a cat;
For if one care to singe a cat's furred skin,
Then would the cat remain the house within;
And if the cat's coat be all sleek and gay,
She will not keep in house a half a day,
But out she'll go, ere dawn of any day,
To show her skin and caterwaul and play.
This is to say, if I'm a little gay,
To show my rags I'll gad about all day.

"'Sir Ancient Fool, what ails you with your spies?
Though you pray Argus, with his hundred eyes,
To be my body-guard and do his best,
Faith, he sha'n't hold me, save I am modest;
I could delude him easily—trust me!

"'You said, also, that there are three things—three—
The which things are a trouble on this earth,
And that no man may ever endure the fourth:
O dear Sir Rogue, may Christ cut short your life!
Yet do you preach and say a hateful wife
Is to be reckoned one of these mischances.
Are there no other kinds of resemblances

That you may liken thus your parables to,
But must a hapless wife be made to do?
    "'You liken woman's love to very Hell,
To desert land where waters do not well.
You liken it, also, unto wildfire;
The more it burns, the more it has desire
To consume everything that burned may be.
You say that just as worms destroy a tree,
Just so a wife destroys her own husband;
Men know this who are bound in marriage band.'
    "Masters, like this, as you must understand,
Did I my old men charge and censure, and
Claim that they said these things in drunkenness;
And all was false, but yet I took witness
Of Jenkin and of my dear niece also.
O Lord, the pain I gave them and the woe,
All guiltless, too, by God's grief exquisite!
For like a stallion could I neigh and bite.
I could complain, though mine was all the guilt,
Or else, full many a time, I'd lost the tilt.
Whoso comes first to mill first gets meal ground;
I whimpered first and so did them confound.
They were right glad to hasten to excuse
Things they had never done, save in my ruse.
    "With wenches would I charge him, by this hand,
When, for some illness, he could hardly stand.
Yet tickled this the heart of him, for he
Deemed it was love produced such jealousy.
I swore that all my walking out at night
Was but to spy on girls he kept outright;
And under cover of that I had much mirth.
For all such wit is given us at birth;
Deceit, weeping, and spinning, does God give
To women, naturally, the while they live.
And thus of one thing I speak boastfully,
I got the best of each one, finally,
By trick, or force, or by some kind of thing,
As by continual growls or murmuring;
Especially in bed had they mischance,
There would I chide and give them no pleasance;
I would no longer in the bed abide
If I but felt his arm across my side,
Till he had paid his ransom unto me;

Then would I let him do his nicety.
And therefore to all men this tale I tell,
Let gain who may, for everything's to sell.
With empty hand men may no falcons lure;
For profit would I all his lust endure,
And make for him a well-feigned appetite;
Yet I in bacon never had delight;
And that is why I used so much to chide.
For if the pope were seated there beside
I'd not have spared them, no, at their own board.
For by my truth, I paid them, word for word.
So help me the True God Omnipotent,
Though I right now should make my testament,
I owe them not a word that was not quit.
I brought it so about, and by my wit,
That they must give it up, as for the best,
Or otherwise we'd never have had rest.
For though he glared and scowled like lion mad,
Yet failed he of the end he wished he had.
    "Then would I say: 'Good dearie, see you keep
In mind how meek is Wilkin, our old sheep;
Come near, my spouse, come let me kiss your cheek!
You should be always patient, aye, and meek,
And have a sweetly scrupulous tenderness,
Since you so preach of old Job's patience, yes.
Suffer always, since you so well can preach;
And, save you do, be sure that we will teach
That it is well to leave a wife in peace.
One of us two must bow, to be at ease;
And since a man's more reasonable, they say,
Than woman is, you must have patience aye.
What ails you that you grumble thus and groan?
Is it because you'd have my cunt alone?
Why take it all, lo, have it every bit;
Peter! Beshrew you but you're fond of it!
For if I would go peddle my *belle chose*,
I could walk out as fresh as is a rose;
But I will keep it for your own sweet tooth.
You are to blame, by God I tell the truth.'
    "Such were the words I had at my command.
Now will I tell you of my fourth husband.
    "My fourth husband, he was a reveller,
That is to say, he kept a paramour;

And young and full of passion then was I,
Stubborn and strong and jolly as a pie.
Well could I dance to tune of harp, nor fail
To sing as well as any nightingale
When I had drunk a good draught of sweet wine.
Metellius, the foul churl and the swine,
Did with a staff deprive his wife of life
Because she drank wine; had I been his wife
He never should have frightened me from drink;
For after wine, of Venus must I think:
For just as surely as cold produces hail,
A liquorish mouth must have a lickerish tail.
In women wine's no bar of impotence,
This know all lechers by experience.
   "But Lord Christ! When I do remember me
Upon my youth and on my jollity,
It tickles me about my heart's deep root.
To this day does my heart sing in salute
That I have had my world in my own time.
But age, alas! that poisons every prime,
Has taken away my beauty and my pith;
Let go, farewell, the devil go therewith!
The flour is gone, there is no more to tell,
The bran, as best I may, must I now sell;
But yet to be right merry I'll try, and
Now will I tell you of my fourth husband.
   "I say that in my heart I'd great despite
When he of any other had delight.
But he was quit, by God and by Saint Joce!
I made, of the same wood, a staff most gross;
Not with my body and in manner foul,
But certainly I showed so gay a soul
That in his own thick grease I made him fry
For anger and for utter jealousy.
By God, on earth I was his purgatory,
For which I hope his soul lives now in glory.
For God knows, many a time he sat and sung
When the shoe bitterly his foot had wrung.
There was no one, save God and he, that knew
How, in so many ways, I'd twist the screw.
He died when I came from Jerusalem,
And lies entombed beneath the great rood-beam,
Although his tomb is not so glorious

As was the sepulchre of Darius,
The which Apelles wrought full cleverly;
'Twas waste to bury him expensively.
Let him fare well. God give his soul good rest,
He now is in the grave and in his chest.

"And now of my fifth husband will I tell.
God grant his soul may never get to Hell!
And yet he was to me most brutal, too;
My ribs yet feel as they were black and blue,
And ever shall, until my dying day.
But in our bed he was so fresh and gay,
And therewithal he could so well impose,
What time he wanted use of my *belle chose*,
That though he'd beaten me on every bone,
He could re-win my love, and that full soon.
I guess I loved him best of all, for he
Gave of his love most sparingly to me.
We women have, if I am not to lie,
In this love matter, a quaint fantasy;
Look out a thing we may not lightly have,
And after that we'll cry all day and crave.
Forbid a thing, and that thing covet we;
Press hard upon us, then we turn and flee.
Sparingly offer we our goods, when fair;
Great crowds at market make for dearer ware,
And what's too common brings but little price;
All this knows every woman who is wise.

"My fifth husband, may God his spirit bless!
Whom I took all for love, and not riches,
Had been sometime a student at Oxford,
And had left school and had come home to board
With my best gossip, dwelling in our town,
God save her soul! Her name was Alison.
She knew my heart and all my privity
Better than did our parish priest, s'help me!
To her confided I my secrets all.
For had my husband pissed against a wall,
Or done a thing that might have cost his life,
To her and to another worthy wife,
And to my niece whom I loved always well,
I would have told it—every bit I'd tell,
And did so, many and many a time, God wot,
Which made his face full often red and hot

For utter shame; he blamed himself that he
Had told me of so deep a privity.

"So it befell that on a time, in Lent
(For oftentimes I to my gossip went,
Since I loved always to be glad and gay
And to walk out, in March, April, and May,
From house to house, to hear the latest malice),
Jenkin the clerk, and my gossip Dame Alis,
And I myself into the meadows went.
My husband was in London all that Lent;
I had the greater leisure, then, to play,
And to observe, and to be seen, I say,
By pleasant folk; what knew I where my face
Was destined to be loved, or in what place?
Therefore I made my visits round about
To vigils and processions of devout,
To preaching too, and shrines of pilgrimage,
To miracle plays, and always to each marriage,
And wore my scarlet skirt before all wights.
These worms and all these moths and all these mites,
I say it at my peril, never ate;
And know you why? I wore it early and late.

"Now will I tell you what befell to me.
I say that in the meadows walked we three
Till, truly, we had come to such dalliance,
This clerk and I, that, of my vigilance,
I spoke to him and told him how that he,
Were I a widow, might well marry me.
For certainly I say it not to brag,
But I was never quite without a bag
Full of the needs of marriage that I seek.
I hold a mouse's heart not worth a leek
That has but one hole into which to run,
And if it fail of that, then all is done.

"I made him think he had enchanted me;
My mother taught me all that subtlety.
And then I said I'd dreamed of him all night,
He would have slain me as I lay upright,
And all my bed was full of very blood;
But yet I hoped that he would do me good,
For blood betokens gold, as I was taught.
And all was false, I dreamed of him just—naught,
Save as I acted on my mother's lore,

As well in this thing as in many more.

    "But now, let's see, what was I going to say?
Aha, by God, I know! It goes this way.

    "When my fourth husband lay upon his bier,
I wept enough and made but sorry cheer,
As wives must always, for it's custom's grace,
And with my kerchief covered up my face;
But since I was provided with a mate,
I really wept but little, I may state.

    "To church my man was borne upon the morrow
By neighbours, who for him made signs of sorrow;
And Jenkin, our good clerk, was one of them.
So help me God, when rang the requiem
After the bier, I thought he had a pair
Of legs and feet so clean-cut and so fair
That all my heart I gave to him to hold.
He was, I think, but twenty winters old,
And I was forty, if I tell the truth;
But then I always had a young colt's tooth.
Gap-toothed I was, and that became me well;
I had the print of holy Venus' seal.
So help me God, I was a healthy one,
And fair and rich and young and full of fun;
And truly, as my husbands all told me,
I had the silkiest *quoniam* that could be.
For truly, I am all Venusian
In feeling, and my brain is Martian.
Venus gave me my lust, my lickerishness,
And Mars gave me my sturdy hardiness.
Taurus was my ascendant, with Mars therein.
Alas, alas, that ever love was sin!
I followed always my own inclination
By virtue of my natal constellation;
Which wrought me so I never could withdraw
My Venus-chamber from a good fellow.
Yet have I Mars's mark upon my face,
And also in another private place.
For God so truly my salvation be
As I have never loved for policy,
But ever followed my own appetite,
Though he were short or tall, or black or white;
I took no heed, so that he cared for me,
How poor he was, nor even of what degree.

"What should I say now, save, at the month's end,
This jolly, gentle, Jenkin clerk, my friend,
Had wedded me full ceremoniously,
And to him gave I all the land in fee
That ever had been given me before;
But later I repented me full sore.
He never suffered me to have my way.
By God, he smote me on the ear, one day,
Because I tore out of his book a leaf,
So that from this my ear is grown quite deaf.
Stubborn I was as is a lioness,
And with my tongue a very jay, I guess,
And walk I would, as I had done before,
From house to house, though I should not, he swore.
For which he oftentimes would sit and preach
And read old Roman tales to me and teach
How one Sulpicius Gallus left his wife
And her forsook for term of all his life
Because he saw her with bared head, I say,
Looking out from his door, upon a day.

"Another Roman told he of by name
Who, since his wife was at a summer-game
Without his knowing, he forsook her eke.
And then would he within his Bible seek
That proverb of the old Ecclesiast
Where he commands so freely and so fast
That man forbid his wife to gad about;
Then would he thus repeat, with never doubt:
'Whoso would build his whole house out of sallows,
    And spur his blind horse to run over fallows,
    And let his wife alone go seeking hallows,
    Is worthy to be hanged upon the gallows.'
But all for naught, I didn't care a haw
For all his proverbs, nor for his old saw,
Nor yet would I by him corrected be.
I hate one that my vices tells to me,
And so do more of us—God knows!—than I.
This made him mad with me, and furiously,
That I'd not yield to him in any case.

"Now will I tell you truth, by Saint Thomas,
Of why I tore from out his book a leaf,
For which he struck me so it made me deaf.

"He had a book that gladly, night and day,

For his amusement he would read alway.
He called it 'Theophrastus' and 'Valerius',
At which book would he laugh, uproarious.
And, too, there sometime was a clerk at Rome,
A cardinal, that men called Saint Jerome,
Who made a book against Jovinian;
In which book, too, there was Tertullian,
Chrysippus, Trotula, and Heloïse
Who was abbess near Paris' diocese;
And too, the *Proverbs* of King Solomon,
And Ovid's *Art*, and books full many a one.
And all of these were bound in one volume.
And every night and day 'twas his custom,
When he had leisure and took some vacation
From all his other worldly occupation,
To read, within this book, of wicked wives.
He knew of them more legends and more lives
Than are of good wives written in the Bible.
For trust me, it's impossible, no libel,
That any cleric shall speak well of wives,
Unless it be of saints and holy lives,
But naught for other women will they do.
Who painted first the lion, tell me who?[2]
By God, if women had but written stories,
As have these clerks within their oratories,
They would have written of men more wickedness
Than all the race of Adam could redress.
The children of Mercury and of Venus
Are in their lives antagonistic thus;
For Mercury loves wisdom and science,
And Venus loves but pleasure and expense.
Because they different dispositions own,
Each falls when other's in ascendant shown.
And God knows Mercury is desolate
In Pisces, wherein Venus rules in state;
And Venus falls when Mercury is raised;
Therefore no woman by a clerk is praised.
A clerk, when he is old and can naught do
Of Venus' labours worth his worn-out shoe,
Then sits he down and writes, in his dotage,
That women cannot keep vow of marriage!

---

2. Referring to one of Æsop's fables.

"But now to tell you, as I started to,
Why I was beaten for a book, *pardieu*.
Upon a night Jenkin, who was our sire,
Read in his book, as he sat by the fire,
Of Mother Eve who, by her wickedness,
First brought mankind to all his wretchedness,
For which Lord Jesus Christ Himself was slain,
Who, with His heart's blood, saved us thus again.
Lo here, expressly of woman, may you find
That woman was the ruin of mankind.

"Then read he out how Samson lost his hairs,
Sleeping, his leman cut them with her shears;
And through this treason lost he either eye.

"Then read he out, if I am not to lie,
Of Hercules, and Deianira's desire
That caused him to go set himself on fire.

"Nothing escaped him of the pain and woe
That Socrates had with his spouses two;
How Xantippe threw piss upon his head;
This hapless man sat still, as he were dead;
He wiped his head, no more durst he complain
Than 'Ere the thunder ceases comes the rain.'

"Then of Pasiphaë, the queen of Crete,
For cursedness he thought the story sweet;
Fie! Say no more—it is an awful thing—
Of her so horrible lust and love-liking.

"Of Clytemnestra, for her lechery,
Who caused her husband's death by treachery,
He read all this with greatest zest, I vow.

"He told me, too, just when it was and how
Amphiaraus at Thebes lost his life;
My husband had a legend of his wife
Eriphyle who, for a brooch of gold,
In secrecy to hostile Greeks had told
Whereat her husband had his hiding place,
For which he found at Thebes but sorry grace.

"Of Livia and Lucia told he me,
For both of them their husbands killed, you see,
The one for love, the other killed for hate;
Livia her husband, on an evening late,
Made drink some poison, for she was his foe.
Lucia, lecherous, loved her husband so
That, to the end he'd always of her think,

She gave him such a philtre, for love-drink,
That he was dead or ever it was morrow;
And husbands thus, by same means, came to sorrow.
   "Then did he tell how one Latumius
Complained unto his comrade Arrius
That in his garden grew a baleful tree
Whereon, he said, his wives, and they were three,
Had hanged themselves for wretchedness and woe.
'O brother,' Arrius said, 'and did they so?
Give me a graft of that same blessed tree
And in my garden planted it shall be!'
   "Of wives of later date he also read,
How some had slain their husbands in their bed
And let their lovers shag them all the night
While corpses lay upon the floor upright.
And some had driven nails into the brain
While husbands slept and in such wise were slain.
And some had given them poison in their drink.
He told more evil than the mind can think.
And therewithal he knew of more proverbs
Than in this world there grows of grass or herbs.
'Better,' he said, 'your habitation be
With lion wild or dragon foul,' said he,
'Than with a woman who will nag and chide.'
'Better,' he said, 'on the housetop abide
Than with a brawling wife down in the house;
Such are so wicked and contrarious
They hate the thing their husband loves, for aye.'
He said, 'a woman throws her shame away
When she throws off her smock,' and further, too:
'A woman fair, save she be chaste also,
Is like a ring of gold in a sow's nose.'
Who would imagine or who would suppose
What grief and pain were in this heart of mine?
   "And when I saw he'd never cease, in fine,
His reading in this cursed book at night,
Three leaves of it I snatched and tore outright
Out of his book, as he read on; and eke
I with my fist so took him on the cheek
That in our fire he reeled and fell right down.
Then he got up as does a wild lion,
And with his fist he struck me on the head,
And on the floor I lay as I were dead.

And when he saw how limp and still I lay,
He was afraid and would have run away,
Until at last out of my swoon I made:
'Oh, have you slain me, you false thief?' I said,
'And for my land have you thus murdered me?
Kiss me before I die, and let me be.'
    "He came to me and near me he knelt down,
And said: 'O my dear sister Alison,
So help me God, I'll never strike you more;
What I have done, you are to blame therefor.
But all the same forgiveness now I seek!'
And thereupon I hit him on the cheek,
And said: 'Thief, so much vengeance do I wreak!
Now will I die; I can no longer speak!'
But at the last, and with much care and woe,
We made it up between ourselves. And so
He put the bridle reins within my hand
To have the governing of house and land;
And of his tongue and of his hand, also;
And made him burn his book, right then, oho!
And when I had thus gathered unto me
Masterfully, the entire sovereignty,
And he had said: 'My own true wedded wife,
Do as you please the term of all your life,
Guard your own honour and keep fair my state'—
After that day we never had debate.
God help me now, I was to him as kind
As any wife from Denmark unto Ind,
And also true, and so was he to me.
I pray to God, Who sits in majesty,
To bless his soul, out of His mercy dear!
Now will I tell my tale, if you will hear."

BEHOLD THE WORDS BETWEEN THE SUMMONER AND THE FRIAR

The friar laughed when he had heard all this.
"Now dame," said he, "so have I joy or bliss
This is a long preamble to a tale!"
    And when the summoner heard this friar's hail,
"Lo," said the summoner, "by God's arms two!

A friar will always interfere, mark you.
Behold, good men, a housefly and a friar
Will fall in every dish and matters higher.
Why speak of preambling, you in your gown?
What! Amble, trot, hold peace, or go sit down;
You hinder our diversion thus to inquire."

   "Aye, say you so, sir summoner?" said the friar,
"Now by my faith I will, before I go,
Tell of a summoner such a tale, or so,
That all the folk shall laugh who're in this place."

   "Otherwise, friar, I beshrew your face,"
Replied this summoner, "and beshrew me
If I do not tell tales here, two or three,
Of friars ere I come to Sittingbourne,
That certainly will give you cause to mourn,
For well I know your patience will be gone."

   Our host cried out, "Now peace, and that anon!"
And said he: "Let the woman tell her tale.
You act like people who are drunk with ale.
Do, lady, tell your tale, and that is best."

   "All ready, sir," said she, "as you request,
If I have license of this worthy friar."

   "Yes, dame," said he, "to hear you's my desire."

HERE THE WIFE OF BATH ENDS HER PROLOGUE

THE TALE OF THE WIFE OF BATH

Now in the olden days of King Arthur,
Of whom the Britons speak with great honour,
All this wide land was land of faëry.
The elf-queen, with her jolly company,
Danced oftentimes on many a green mead;
This was the old opinion, as I read.
I speak of many hundred years ago;
But now no man can see the elves, you know.
For now the so-great charity and prayers
Of limiters and other holy friars
That do infest each land and every stream
As thick as motes are in a bright sunbeam,
Blessing halls, chambers, kitchens, ladies' bowers,

Cities and towns and castles and high towers,
Manors and barns and stables, aye and dairies—
This causes it that there are now no fairies.
For where was wont to walk full many an elf,
Right there walks now the limiter himself
In noons and afternoons and in mornings,
Saying his matins and such holy things,
As he goes round his district in his gown.
Women may now go safely up and down,
In every copse or under every tree;
There is no other incubus than he,
And would do them nothing but dishonour.

And so befell it that this King Arthur
Had at his court a lusty bachelor
Who, on a day, came riding from river;[3]
And happened that, alone as she was born,
He saw a maiden walking through the corn,
From whom, in spite of all she did and said,
Straightway by force he took her maidenhead;
For which violation was there such clamour,
And such appealing unto King Arthur,
That soon condemned was this knight to be dead
By course of law, and should have lost his head,
Peradventure, such being the statute then;
But that the other ladies and the queen
So long prayed of the king to show him grace,
He granted life, at last, in the law's place,
And gave him to the queen, as she should will,
Whether she'd save him, or his blood should spill.

The queen she thanked the king with all her might,
And after this, thus spoke she to the knight,
When she'd an opportunity, one day:
"You stand yet," said she, "in such poor a way
That for your life you've no security.
I'll grant you life if you can tell to me
What thing it is that women most desire.
Be wise, and keep your neck from iron dire!
And if you cannot tell it me anon,
Then will I give you license to be gone
A twelvemonth and a day, to search and learn
Sufficient answer in this grave concern.

---

3. From river: that is, from hawking for waterfowl beside a stream or mere.

And your knight's word I'll have, ere forth you pace,
To yield your body to me in this place."

    Grieved was this knight, and sorrowfully he sighed;
But there! he could not do as pleased his pride.
And at the last he chose that he would wend,
And come again upon the twelvemonth's end,
With such an answer as God might purvey;
And so he took his leave and went his way.

    He sought out every house and every place
Wherein he hoped to find that he had grace
To learn what women love the most of all;
But nowhere ever did it him befall
To find, upon the question stated here,
Two persons who agreed with statement clear.

    Some said that women all loved best riches,
Some said, fair fame, and some said, prettiness;
Some, rich array, some said 'twas lust abed
And often to be widowed and re-wed.

    Some said that our poor hearts are aye most eased
When we have been most flattered and thus pleased.
And he went near the truth, I will not lie;
A man may win us best with flattery;
And with attentions and with busyness
We're often limed, the greater and the less.

    And some say, too, that we do love the best
To be quite free to do our own behest,
And that no man reprove us for our vice,
But saying we are wise, take our advice.
For truly there is no one of us all,
If anyone shall rub us on a gall,
That will not kick because he tells the truth.
Try, and he'll find, who does so, I say sooth.
No matter how much vice we have within,
We would be held for wise and clean of sin.

    And some folk say that great delight have we
To be held constant, also trustworthy,
And on one purpose steadfastly to dwell,
And not betray a thing that men may tell.
But that tale is not worth a rake's handle;
By God, we women can no thing conceal,
As witness Midas. Would you hear the tale?

    Ovid, among some other matters small,
Said Midas had beneath his long curled hair,

Two ass's ears that grew in secret there,
The which defect he hid, as best he might,
Full cunningly from every person's sight,
And, save his wife, no one knew of it, no.
He loved her most, and trusted her also;
And he prayed of her that to no creature
She'd tell of his disfigurement impure.

    She swore him: Nay, for all this world to win
She would do no such villainy or sin
And cause her husband have so foul a name;
Nor would she tell it for her own deep shame.
Nevertheless, she thought she would have died
Because so long the secret must she hide;
It seemed to swell so big about her heart
That some word from her mouth must surely start;
And since she dared to tell it to no man,
Down to a marsh, that lay hard by, she ran;
Till she came there her heart was all afire,
And as a bittern booms in the quagmire,
She laid her mouth low to the water down:
"Betray me not, you sounding water blown,"
Said she, "I tell it to none else but you:
Long ears like asses' has my husband two!
Now is my heart at ease, since that is out;
I could no longer keep it, there's no doubt."
Here may you see, though for a while we bide,
Yet out it must; no secret can we hide.
The rest of all this tale, if you would hear,
Read Ovid: in his book does it appear.

    This knight my tale is chiefly told about
When what he went for he could not find out,
That is, the thing that women love the best,
Most saddened was the spirit in his breast;
But home he goes, he could no more delay.
The day was come when home he turned his way;
And on his way it chanced that he should ride
In all his care, beneath a forest's side,
And there he saw, a-dancing him before,
Full four and twenty ladies, maybe more;
Toward which dance eagerly did he turn
In hope that there some wisdom he should learn.
But truly, ere he came upon them there,
The dancers vanished all, he knew not where.

No creature saw he that gave sign of life,
Save, on the greensward sitting, an old wife;
A fouler person could no man devise.
Before the knight this old wife did arise,
And said: "Sir knight, hence lies no travelled way.
Tell me what thing you seek, and by your fay.
Perchance you'll find it may the better be;
These ancient folk know many things," said she.

"Dear mother," said this knight assuredly,
"I am but dead, save I can tell, truly,
What thing it is that women most desire;
Could you inform me, I'd pay well your hire."

"Plight me your troth here, hand in hand," said she,
"That you will do, whatever it may be,
The thing I ask if it lie in your might;
And I'll give you your answer ere the night."

"Have here my word," said he. "That thing I grant."

"Then," said the crone, "of this I make my vaunt,
Your life is safe; and I will stand thereby,
Upon my life, the queen will say as I.
Let's see which is the proudest of them all
That wears upon her hair kerchief or caul,
Shall dare say no to that which I shall teach;
Let us go now and without longer speech."

Then whispered she a sentence in his ear,
And bade him to be glad and have no fear.

When they were come unto the court, this knight
Said he had kept his promise as was right,
And ready was his answer, as he said.
Full many a noble wife, and many a maid,
And many a widow, since they are so wise,
The queen herself sitting as high justice,
Assembled were, his answer there to hear;
And then the knight was bidden to appear.

Command was given for silence in the hall,
And that the knight should tell before them all
What thing all worldly women love the best.
This knight did not stand dumb, as does a beast,
But to this question presently answered
With manly voice, so that the whole court heard:
"My liege lady, generally," said he,
"Women desire to have the sovereignty
As well upon their husband as their love,

And to have mastery their man above;
This thing you most desire, though me you kill
Do as you please, I am here at your will."

In all the court there was no wife or maid
Or widow that denied the thing he said,
But all held, he was worthy to have life.

And with that word up started the old wife
Whom he had seen a-sitting on the green.
"Mercy," cried she, "my sovereign lady queen!
Before the court's dismissed, give me my right.
'Twas I who taught the answer to this knight;
For which he did plight troth to me, out there
That the first thing I should of him require
He would do that, if it lay in his might.
Before the court, now, pray I you, sir knight,"
Said she, "that you will take me for your wife;
For well you know that I have saved your life.
If this be false, say nay, upon your fay!"

This knight replied: "Alas and welaway!
That I so promised I will not protest.
But for God's love pray make a new request.
Take all my wealth and let my body go."

"Nay then," said she, "beshrew us if I do!
For though I may be foul and old and poor,
I will not, for all metal and all ore
That from the earth is dug or lies above,
Be aught except your wife and your true love."

"My love?" cried he, "nay, rather my damnation!
Alas! that any of my race and station
Should ever so dishonoured foully be!"

But all for naught; the end was this, that he
Was so constrained he needs must go and wed,
And take his ancient wife and go to bed.

Now, peradventure, would some men say here,
That, of my negligence, I take no care
To tell you of the joy and all the array
That at the wedding feast were seen that day.
Make a brief answer to this thing I shall;
I say, there was no joy or feast at all;
There was but heaviness and grievous sorrow;
For privately he wedded on the morrow,
And all day, then, he hid him like an owl;
So sad he was, his old wife looked so foul.

Great was the woe the knight had in his thought
When he, with her, to marriage bed was brought;
He rolled about and turned him to and fro.
His old wife lay there, always smiling so,
And said: "O my dear husband, *ben'cite!*
Fares every knight with wife as you with me?
Is this the custom in King Arthur's house?
Are knights of his all so fastidious?
I am your own true love and, more, your wife;
And I am she who saved your very life;
And truly, since I've never done you wrong,
Why do you treat me so, this first night long?
You act as does a man who's lost his wit;
What is my fault? For God's love tell me it,
And it shall be amended, if I may."

    "Amended!" cried this knight, "Alas, nay, nay!
It will not be amended ever, no!
You are so loathsome, and so old also,
And therewith of so low a race were born,
It's little wonder that I toss and turn.
Would God my heart would break within my breast!"

    "Is this," asked she, "the cause of your unrest?"

    "Yes, truly," said he, "and no wonder 'tis."

    "Now, sir," said she, "I could amend all this,
If I but would, and that within days three,
If you would bear yourself well towards me.

    "But since you speak of such gentility
As is descended from old wealth, till ye
Claim that for that you should be gentlemen,
I hold such arrogance not worth a hen.
Find him who is most virtuous alway,
Alone or publicly, and most tries aye
To do whatever noble deeds he can,
And take him for the greatest gentleman.
Christ wills we claim from Him gentility,
Not from ancestors of landocracy.
For though they give us all their heritage,
For which we claim to be of high lineage,
    ...y not bequeath, in anything,
    ...s, their virtuous living,
    ...men say they had gentility,
    ...s follow them in like degree.
    ...es that poet wise of great Florence,

Called Dante, speak his mind in this sentence;
Somewhat like this may it translated be:
'Rarely unto the branches of the tree
Doth human worth mount up: and so ordains
He Who bestows it; to Him it pertains.'[4]
For of our fathers may we nothing claim
But temporal things, that man may hurt and maim.

"And everyone knows this as well as I,
If nobleness were implanted naturally
Within a certain lineage, down the line,
In private and in public, I opine,
The ways of gentleness they'd alway show
And never fall to vice and conduct low.

"Take fire and carry it in the darkest house
Between here and the Mount of Caucasus,
And let men shut the doors and from them turn;
Yet will the fire as fairly blaze and burn
As twenty thousand men did it behold;
Its nature and its office it will hold,
On peril of my life, until it die.

"From this you see that true gentility
Is not allied to wealth a man may own,
Since folk do not their deeds, as may be shown,
As does the fire, according to its kind.
For God knows that men may full often find
A lord's son doing shame and villainy;
And he that prizes his gentility
In being born of some old noble house,
With ancestors both noble and virtuous,
But will himself do naught of noble deeds
Nor follow him to whose name he succeeds,
He is not gentle, be he duke or earl;
For acting churlish makes a man a churl.
Gentility is not just the renown
Of ancestors who have some greatness shown,
In which you have no portion of your own.
Your own gentility comes from God alone;
Thence comes our true nobility by grace,
It was not willed us with our rank and place.

"Think how noble, as says Valerius,

---

4. Dante, *Purgat*, VII, 122, 123. The quotation is from Cary's translation, slightly altered to fit the exigency of rhyme.

Was that same Tullius Hostilius,
Who out of poverty rose to high estate.
Seneca and Boethius inculcate,
Expressly (and no doubt it thus proceeds),
That he is noble who does noble deeds;
And therefore, husband dear, I thus conclude:
Although my ancestors mayhap were rude,
Yet may the High Lord God, and so hope I,
Grant me the grace to live right virtuously.
Then I'll be gentle when I do begin
To live in virtue and to do no sin.

   "And when you me reproach for poverty,
The High God, in Whom we believe, say I,
In voluntary poverty lived His life.
And surely every man, or maid, or wife
May understand that Jesus, Heaven's King,
Would not have chosen vileness of living.
Glad poverty's an honest thing, that's plain,
Which Seneca and other clerks maintain.
Whoso will be content with poverty,
I hold him rich, though not a shirt has he.
And he that covets much is a poor wight,
For he would gain what's all beyond his might.
But he that has not, nor desires to have,
Is rich, although you hold him but a knave.

   "True poverty, it sings right naturally;
Juvenal gaily says of poverty:
'The poor man, when he walks along the way,
Before the robbers he may sing and play.'
Poverty's odious good, and, as I guess,
It is a stimulant to busyness;
A great improver, too, of sapience
In him that takes it all with due patience.
Poverty's this, though it seem misery—
Its quality may none dispute, say I.
Poverty often, when a man is low,
Makes him his God and even himself to know.
And poverty's an eye-glass, seems to me,
Through which a man his loyal friends may see.
Since you've received no injury from me,
Then why reproach me for my poverty.

   "Now, sir, with age you have upbraided me;
And truly, sir, though no authority

Were in a book, you gentles of honour
Say that men should the aged show favour,
And call him father, of your gentleness;
And authors could I find for this, I guess.

"Now since you say that I am foul and old,
Then fear you not to be made a cuckold;
For dirt and age, as prosperous I may be,
Are mighty wardens over chastity.
Nevertheless, since I know your delight,
I'll satisfy your worldly appetite.

"Choose, now," said she, "one of these two things, aye,
To have me foul and old until I die,
And be to you a true and humble wife,
And never anger you in all my life;
Or else to have me young and very fair
And take your chance with those who will repair
Unto your house, and all because of me,
Or in some other place, as well may be.
Now choose which you like better and reply."

This knight considered, and did sorely sigh,
But at the last replied as you shall hear:
"My lady and my love, and wife so dear,
I put myself in your wise governing;
Do you choose which may be the more pleasing,
And bring most honour to you, and me also.
I care not which it be of these things two;
For if you like it, that suffices me."

"Then have I got of you the mastery,
Since I may choose and govern, in earnest?"

"Yes, truly, wife," said he, "I hold that best."

"Kiss me," said she, "we'll be no longer wroth,
For by my truth, to you I will be both;
That is to say, I'll be both good and fair.
I pray God I go mad, and so declare,
If I be not to you as good and true
As ever wife was since the world was new.
And, save I be, at dawn, as fairly seen
As any lady, empress, or great queen
That is between the east and the far west,
Do with my life and death as you like best.
Throw back the curtain and see how it is."

And when the knight saw verily all this,
That she so very fair was, and young too,

For joy he clasped her in his strong arms two,
His heart bathed in a bath of utter bliss;
A thousand times, all in a row, he'd kiss.
And she obeyed his wish in everything
That might give pleasure to his love-liking.
    And thus they lived unto their lives' fair end,
In perfect joy; and Jesus to us send
Meek husbands, and young ones, and fresh in bed,
And good luck to outlive them that we wed.
And I pray Jesus to cut short the lives
Of those who'll not be governed by their wives;
And old and querulous niggards with their pence,
And send them soon a mortal pestilence!

HERE ENDS THE WIFE OF BATH'S TALE

THE FRIAR'S PROLOGUE

This worthy limiter, this noble friar,
He turned always a lowering face, and dire,
Upon the summoner, but for courtesy
No rude and insolent word as yet spoke he.
But at the last he said unto the wife:
"Lady," said he, "God grant you a good life!
You have here touched, as I may prosperous be,
Upon school matters of great difficulty;
You have said many things right well, I say;
But, lady, as we ride along our way,
We need but talk to carry on our game,
And leave authorities, in good God's name,
To preachers and to schools for clergymen.
But if it pleases all this company, then,
I'll tell you of a summoner, to make game.
By God, you could surmise it by the name
That of a summoner may no good be said;
I pray that no one will be angry made.
A summoner is a runner up and down
With summonses for fornication known,
And he is beaten well at each town's end."

    Our host then spoke: "O sir, you should attend
To courtesy, like man of your estate;
In company here we will have no debate.
Tell forth your tale and let the summoner be."

    "Nay," said the summoner, "let him say to me
What pleases him; when it falls to my lot,
By God I'll then repay him, every jot.
I'll then make plain to him what great honour
It is to be a flattering limiter;
I'll certainly tell him what his business is."

    Our host replied: "Oh peace, no more of this!"
And after that he said unto the friar:
"Tell now your tale to us, good master dear."

HERE ENDS THE FRIAR'S PROLOGUE

299

THE FRIAR'S TALE

Once on a time there dwelt in my country
An archdeacon, a man of high degree,
Who boldly executed the Church's frown
In punishment of fornication known,
And of witchcraft and of all known bawdry,
And defamation and adultery
Of church-wardens, and of fake testaments
And contracts, and the lack of sacraments,
And still of many another kind of crime
Which need not be recounted at this time,
And usury and simony also.
But unto lechers gave he greatest woe;
They should lament if they were apprehended;
And payers of short tithes to shame descended.
If anyone informed of such, 'twas plain
He'd not escape pecuniary pain.
For all short tithes and for small offering
He made folk pitifully to howl and sing.
For ere the bishop caught them with his crook,
They were already in the archdeacon's book.
Then had he, by his competent jurisdiction,
Power to punish them by such infliction.
He had a summoner ready to his hand,
A slyer rogue was not in all England;
For cunningly he'd espionage to trail
And bring reports of all that might avail.
He could protect of lechers one or two
To learn of four and twenty more, mark you.
For though this man were wild as is a hare,
To tell his evil deeds I will not spare;
For we are out of his reach of infliction;
They have of us no competent jurisdiction,
Nor ever shall for term of all their lives.

"Peter! So are the women of the dives,"
The summoner said, "likewise beyond my cure!"

"Peace, with mischance and with misadventure!"
Thus spoke our host, "and let him tell his tale.
Now tell it on, despite the summoner's wail,
Nor spare in anything, my master dear."

This false thief, then, this summoner (said the friar)
Had always panders ready to his hand,

For any hawk to lure in all England,
Who told him all the scandal that they knew;
For their acquaintances were nothing new.
They were all his informers privily;
And he took to himself great gain thereby;
His master knew not how his profits ran.
Without an order, and an ignorant man,
Yet would he summon, on pain of Christ's curse,
Those who were glad enough to fill his purse
And feast him greatly at the taverns all.
And just as Judas had his purses small
And was a thief, just such a thief was he.
His master got but half of every fee.
He was, if I'm to give him proper laud,
A thief, and more, a summoner, and a bawd.
He'd even wenches in his retinue,
And whether 'twere Sir Robert, or Sir Hugh,
Or Jack, or Ralph, or whosoever 'twere
That lay with them, they told it in his ear;
Thus were the wench and he in partnership.
And he would forge a summons from his scrip,
And summon to the chapter-house those two
And fleece the man and let the harlot go.
Then would he say: "My friend, and for your sake,
Her name from our blacklist will I now take;
Trouble no more for what this may entail;
I am your friend in all where 'twill avail."
He knew more ways to fleece and blackmail you
Than could be told in one year or in two.
For in this world's no dog trained to the bow
That can a hurt deer from a sound one know
Better than this man knew a sly lecher,
Or fornicator, or adulterer.
And since this was the fruit of all his rent,
Therefore on it he fixed his whole intent.

    And so befell that once upon a day
This summoner, ever lurking for his prey,
Rode out to summon a widow, an old rip,
Feigning a cause, for her he planned to strip.
It happened that he saw before him ride
A yeoman gay along a forest's side.
A bow he bore, and arrows bright and keen;
He wore a short coat of the Lincoln green,

And hat upon his head, with fringes black.
    "Sir," said the summoner, "hail and well met, Jack!"
    "Welcome," said he, "and every comrade good!
Whither do you ride under this greenwood?"
Said this yeoman, "Will you go far today?"
    This summoner replied to him with: "Nay,
Hard by this place," said he, "'tis my intent
To ride, sir, to collect a bit of rent
Pertaining to my lord's temporality."
    "And are you then a bailiff?"
                          "Aye," said he.
He dared not, no, for very filth and shame,
Say that he was a summoner, for the name.
    "In God's name," said this yeoman then, "dear brother,
You are a bailiff and I am another.
I am a stranger in these parts, you see;
Of your acquaintance I'd be glad," said he,
"And of your brotherhood, if 'tis welcome.
I've gold and silver in my chest at home.
And if you chance to come into our shire,
All shall be yours, just as you may desire."
    "Many thanks," said this summoner, "by my faith!"
    And they struck hands and made their solemn oath
To be sworn brothers till their dying day.
Gossiping then they rode upon their way.
    This summoner, who was as full of words
As full of malice are these butcher birds,
And ever enquiring after everything,
"Brother," asked he, "where now is your dwelling,
If some day I should wish your side to reach?"
    This yeoman answered him in gentle speech,
"Brother," said he, "far in the north country,
Where, as I hope, some day you'll come to me.
Before we part I will direct you so
You'll never miss it when that way you go."
    "Now, brother," said this summoner, "I pray
You'll teach me, while we ride along our way,
Since that you are a bailiff, as am I,
A trick or two, and tell me faithfully
How, in my office, I may most coin win;
And spare not for nice conscience, nor for sin,
But as my brother tell your arts to me."
    "Now by my truth, dear brother," then said he,

If I am to relate a faithful tale,
My wages are right scanty, and but small.
My lord is harsh to me and niggardly,
My job is most laborious, you see;
And therefore by extortion do I live.
Forsooth, I take all that these men will give;
By any means, by trick or violence,
From year to year I win me my expense.
I can no better tell you faithfully."

   "Now truly," said this summoner, "so do I.
I never spare to take a thing, God wot,
Unless it be too heavy or too hot.
What I get for myself, and privately,
No kind of conscience for such things have I.
But for extortion, I could not well live,
Nor of such japes will I confession give.
Stomach nor any conscience have I, none;
A curse on father-confessors, every one.
Well are we met, by God and by Saint James!
But, my dear brother, tell your name or names."
Thus said the summoner, and in meanwhile
The yeoman just a little began to smile.

   "Brother," said he, "and will you that I tell?
I am a fiend, my dwelling is in Hell.
But here I ride about in hope of gain
And that some little gift I may obtain.
My only income is what so is sent.
I see you ride with much the same intent
To win some wealth, you never care just how;
Even so do I, for I would ride, right now,
Unto the world's end, all to get my prey."

   "Ah," cried he, "ben'cite! What do you say?
I took you for a yeoman certainly.
You have a human shape as well as I;
Have you a figure then determinate
In Hell, where you are in your proper state?"

   "Nay," said he, "there of figure we have none;
But when it pleases us we can take one,
Or else we make you think we have a shape,
Sometimes like man, or sometimes like an ape;
Or like an angel can I seem, you know.
It is no wondrous thing that this is so;
A lousy juggler can deceive, you see,

And by gad, I have yet more craft than he."
  "Why," asked the summoner, "ride you then, or go,
In sundry shapes, and not in one, you know?"
  "Because," said he, "we will such figures make
As render likely that our prey we'll take."
  "What causes you to have all this labour?"
  "Full many a cause, my dear sir summoner,"
Replied the fiend, "but each thing has its time.
The day is short, and it is now past prime,
And yet have I won not a thing this day.
I will attend to winning, if I may,
And not our different notions to declare.
For, brother mine, your wits are all too bare
To understand, though I told mine fully.
But since you ask me why thus labour we—
Well, sometimes we are God's own instruments
And means to do His orders and intents,
When so He pleases, upon all His creatures,
In divers ways and shapes, and divers features.
Without Him we've no power, 'tis certain,
If He be pleased to stand against our train.
And sometimes, at our instance, have we leave
Only the body, not the soul, to grieve;
As witness Job, to whom we gave such woe.
And sometimes have we power of both, you know,
That is to say, of soul and body too.
And sometimes we're allowed to search and do
That to a man which gives his soul unrest,
And not his body, and all is for the best.
And when one does withstand all our temptation,
It is the thing that gives his soul salvation;
Albeit that it was not our intent
He should be saved; we'd have him impotent.
And sometimes we are servants unto man,
As to that old archbishop, Saint Dunstan,
And to the apostles servant once was I."
  "Yet tell me," said the summoner, "faithfully,
Make you yourselves new bodies thus alway
Of elements?"
                    The fiend replied thus: "Nay.
Sometimes we feign them, sometimes we arise
In bodies that are dead, in sundry wise,
And speak as reasonably and fair and well

As to the witch at En-dor Samuel.
And yet some men maintain it was not he;
I do not care for your theology.
But of one thing I warn, nor will I jape,
You shall in all ways learn our proper shape;
You shall hereafter come, my brother dear,
Where you'll not need to ask of me, as here.
For you shall, of your own experience,
In a red chair have much more evidence
Than Virgil ever did while yet alive,
Or ever Dante; now let's swiftly drive.
For I will hold with you my company
Till it shall come to pass you part from me."
    "Nay," said the other, "that shall not betide;
"I am a bailiff, known both far and wide;
My promise will I keep in this one case.
For though you were the devil Sathanas,
My troth will I preserve to my dear brother,
As I have sworn, and each of us to other,
That we will be true brothers in this case;
And let us both about our business pace.
Take your own part, of what men will you give,
And I will mine; and thus may we both live.
And if that either of us gets more than other,
Let him be true and share it with his brother."
    "Agreed, then," said the devil, "by my fay."
    And with that word they rode upon their way.
As they drew near the town—it happened so—
To which this summoner had planned to go,
They saw a cart that loaded was with hay,
The which a carter drove along the way.
Deep was the mire; for which the cart now stood.
The carter whipped and cried as madman would,
"Hi, Badger, Scot! What care you for the stones?
The Fiend," he cried, "take body of you and bones,
As utterly as ever you were foaled!
More trouble you've caused me than can be told!
Devil take all, the horses, cart, and hay!"
    This summoner thought, "Here shall be played a play."
And near the fiend he drew, as naught were there,
And unobserved he whispered in his ear:
"Listen, my brother, listen, by your faith;
Hear you not what the carter says in wrath?

Take all, at once, for he has given you
Both hay and cart, and this three horses too."
"Nay," said the devil, "God knows, never a bit.
It is not his intention, trust to it.
Ask him yourself, if you believe not me,
Or else withhold a while, and you shall see."

This carter stroked his nags upon the croup,
And they began in collars low to stoop.
"Hi now!" cried he, "May Jesus Christ you bless
And all His creatures, greater, aye and less!
That was well pulled, old horse, my own grey boy!
I pray God save you, and good Saint Eloy!
Now is my cart out of the slough, by gad!"

"Lo, brother," said the fiend, "what said I, lad?
Here may you see, my very own dear brother,
The peasant said one thing, but thought another.
Let us go forth upon our travellers' way;
Here win I nothing I can take today."

When they had come a little out of town,
This summoner whispered, to his brother drawn,
"Brother," said he, "here lives an ancient crone
Who'd quite as gladly lose her neck as own
She must give up a penny, good or bad.
But I'll have twelvepence, though it drive her mad,
Or I will summon her to our office;
And yet God knows I know of her no vice.
But since you cannot, in this strange country,
Make your expenses, here take note of me."

This summoner knocked on the widow's gate.
"Come out," cried he, "you old she-reprobate!
I think you've got some friar or priest there, eh?"

"Who knocks then?" said the widow. "*Ben'cite!*
God save you, master, what is your sweet will?"

"I have," said he, "a summons here, a bill;
On pain of excommunication be
Tomorrow morn at the archdeacon's knee
To answer to the court for certain things."

"Now, lord," said she, "Christ Jesus, King of kings,
So truly keep me as I cannot; nay,
I have been sick, and that for many a day.
I cannot walk so far," said she, "nor ride,
Save I were dead, such aches are in my side.
Will you not give a writ, sir summoner,

And let my proctor for me there appear
To meet this charge, whatever it may be?"
 "Yes," said this summoner, "pay anon—let's see—
Twelvepence to me, and I'll have you acquitted.
Small profit there for me, be it admitted;
My master gets the profit, and not I.
Come then, and let me ride on, speedily;
Give me twelvepence, I may no longer tarry."
 "Twelvepence!" cried she, "Our Lady Holy Mary
So truly keep me out of care and sin,
And though thereby I should the wide world win,
I have not twelvepence in my house all told.
You know right well that I am poor and old;
Show mercy unto me, a poor old wretch!"
 "Nay, then," said he, "the foul Fiend may me fetch
If I excuse you, though your life be spilt!"
 "Alas!" cried she, "God knows I have no guilt!"
 "Pay me," he cried, "or by the sweet Saint Anne
I'll take away with me your brand-new pan
For debt that you have owed to me of old,
When you did make your husband a cuckold;
I paid at home that fine to save citation."
 "You lie," she cried then, "by my own salvation!
Never was I, till now, widow or wife,
Summoned unto your court in all my life;
Nor ever of my body was I untrue!
Unto the Devil rough and black of hue
Give I your body and my pan also!"
 And when the devil heard her cursing so
Upon her knees, he said to her just here:
"Now, Mabely, my own old mother dear,
Is this your will, in earnest, that you say?"
 "The Devil," said she, "take him alive today,
And pan and all, unless he will repent!"
 "Nay, you old heifer, it's not my intent,"
The summoner said, "for pardon now to sue
Because of aught that I have had from you;
I would I had your smock and all your clo'es."
 "Nay, brother," said the devil, "easy goes;
Your body and this pan are mine by right.
And you shall come to Hell with me tonight,
Where you shall learn more of our privity
Than any doctor of divinity."

And with that word this foul fiend to him bent;
Body and soul he with the devil went
Where summoners have their rightful heritage.
And God, Who made after His own image
Mankind, now save and guide us, all and some;
And grant that summoners good men become!

Masters, I could have told you, said this friar,
Were I not pestered by this summoner dire,
After the texts of Christ and Paul and John,
And of our other doctors, many a one,
Such torments that your hearts would shake with dread,
Albeit by no tongue can half be said,
Although I might a thousand winters tell,
Of pains in that same cursed house of Hell.
But all to keep us from that horrid place,
Watch, and pray Jesus for His holy grace,
And so reject the tempter Sathanas.
Hearken this word, be warned by this one case;
The lion lies in wait by night and day
To slay the innocent, if he but may.
Dispose your hearts in grace, that you withstand
The Fiend, who'd make you thrall among his band.
He cannot tempt more than beyond your might;
For Christ will be your champion and knight.
And pray that all these summoners repent
Of their misdeeds, before the Fiend torment.

HERE ENDS THE FRIAR'S TALE

THE SUMMONER'S PROLOGUE

High in his stirrups, then, the summoner stood;
Against the friar his heart, as madman's would,
Shook like a very aspen leaf, for ire.
  "Masters," said he, "but one thing I desire;
I beg of you that, of your courtesy,
Since you have heard this treacherous friar lie,
You suffer it that I my tale may tell!
This friar he boasts he knows somewhat of Hell,
And God He knows that it is little wonder;
Friars and fiends are never far asunder.
For, by gad, you have oftentimes heard tell
How such a friar was snatched down into Hell
In spirit, once, and by a vision blown;
And as an angel led him up and down
To show the pains and torments that there were,
In all the place he saw no friar there.
Of other folk he saw enough in woe;
And to the angel then he questioned so:
  "'Now, sir,' said he, 'have friars such a grace
That none of them shall come into this place?'
  "'Nay,' said the angel, 'millions here are thrown!'
And unto Sathanas he led him down.
"'And now has Sathanas,' said he, 'a tail
Broader than of a galleon is the sail.
Hold up thy tail, thou Sathanas!' said he,
"'Show forth thine arse and let the friar see
Where is the nest of friars in this place!'
And ere one might go half a furlong's space,
Just as the bees come swarming from a hive,
Out of the Devil's arse-hole there did drive
Full twenty thousand friars in a rout,
And through all Hell they swarmed and ran about,

And came again, as fast as they could run,
And in his arse they crept back, every one.
He clapped his tail to and then lay right still.
This friar, when he'd looked at length his fill
Upon the torments of that sorry place,
His spirit God restored, of His high grace,
Into his body, and he did awake;
Nevertheless for terror did he quake
So was the Devil's arse-hole in his mind,
Which is his future home, and like in kind.
God save all but this cursed friar here;
My prologue ends thus; to my tale give ear.

HERE ENDS THE PROLOGUE OF THE SUMMONER'S TALE

THE SUMMONER'S TALE

Masters, there is in Yorkshire, as I guess,
A marshy region that's called Holderness,
Wherein there went a limiter about
To preach, and to beg too, beyond a doubt.
And so befell that on a day this friar
Had preached in church in his own manner dire,
And specially, and above everything,
Incited he the people, by preaching,
To trentals,[1] and to give, for God's own sake,
The means wherewith men might new churches make,
That there the services of God might flower,
And not to them who waste and wealth devour,
Nor where there's no necessity to give,
As to the monks, who easily may live—
Thanks be to God!—and need no wealth to gain.
"Trentals," said he, "deliver from their pain
The souls of friends who're dead, the old and young,
Yea, even when they have been hastily sung;
Not that I hold as frivolous and gay,
A priest who only sings one mass a day.
"Act quickly now," said he, "their souls redeem,
For hard it is, with spikes and hooks, I deem,

---

1. Trentals: series of thirty Masses for the dead.

To be so torn, aye, or to burn or bake;
Now speed you all to this, for Christ's own sake!"
And when this friar had said all that he meant,
With *cui cum patre* on his way he went.
    When folk in church had given at his behest,
He went his way, no longer would he rest,
With scrip and ferruled staff and skirts tucked high;
In every house he went to peer and pry,
And beg for flour and cheese, or else for corn.
His fellow had a staff was tipped with horn,
A set of tablets all of ivory,
And stylus that was polished elegantly,
And wrote the names down always as he stood,
Of those that gave him anything of good,
As if for them he later meant to pray.
"Give us of wheat or malt or rye," he'd say,
"A bushel; or a God's cake; or some cheese;
We may not choose, so give us what you please;
Give us God's halfpenny or a mass-penny,
Or give us of your brawn, if you have any;
A small piece of your blanket, my dear dame,
Our sister dear, lo, here I write your name;
Bacon or beef, or such thing as you find."
    A sturdy menial went these two behind—
The servant of their host—and bore a sack,
And what men gave them, laid it on his back.
And when they'd left the house, why, then anon
He planed away the names of folk, each one,
That he before had written on his tables;
And thus he served them mockeries and fables.
    ("Nay, there you lie, you summoner!" cried the friar.
"Peace, for Christ's Mother's sake, call no one liar!"
Our host said. "Tell your tale, nor spare at all."
"So thrive I," said this summoner, "that I shall.")
    Along he went from house to house, till he
Came to a house where he was wont to be
Refreshed more than in hundred places round.
And sick the goodman of the place he found;
Bedridden on a couch he prostrate lay.
    "*Deus hic*," said he. "Thomas, my friend, good day,"
Said he, this friar, courteously and soft.
"Thomas," said he, "may God repay you! Oft
Have I sat on this bench and fared right well.

Here have I eaten many a merry meal."
      And from the bench he drove away the cat,
And laid down there his steel-tipped staff and hat
And his scrip, too, and sat him softly down.
His fellow had gone walking into town,
With the said menial, to a hostelry
Wherein he thought that very night to lie.
      "O my dear master," whispered this sick man,
"How have you fared since this month March began?
"I've seen you not this fortnight, aye or more."
      "God knows," said he, "that I have toiled full sore;
And very specially for your salvation
Have I said precious prayers, and at each station,
And for our other friends, whom may God bless!
I have today been to your church, at Mass,
And preached a sermon after my poor wit,
Not wholly from the text of holy writ,
For that is hard and baffling in the main;
And therefore all its meaning I'll explain.
Glosing's a glorious thing, and that's certain,
For letters kill, as scholars say with pain.
Thus have I taught them to be charitable,
And spend their money reasonably, as well.
And there I saw your dame—ah, where is she?"
      "Yonder within the yard I think she'll be,"
Said this sick man, "and she will come anon."
      "Eh, master! Welcome be you, by Saint John!"
Exclaimed the wife. "How fare you, heartily?"
      The friar arose, and that full courteously,
And her embraced within his two arms narrow,
And kissed her sweetly, chirping like a sparrow
With his two lips. "Ah, dame," said he, "right well,
As one that is your servant, let me tell,
Thanks be to God Who gave you soul and life,
For saw I not this day so fair a wife
In all the congregation, God save me!"
      "Yea, God correct all faults, sir," answered she,
"But you are always welcome, by my fay!"
      "Many thanks, dame, this have I found alway.
But of your innate goodness, by your leave,
I'd beg of you you won't be cross or grieve
If I with Thomas speak a little now.
These curates are right negligent and slow

In searching tenderly into conscience.
To preach confession is my diligence,
And I do study Peter's words and Paul's.
I walk and fish for Christian persons' souls
To yield to Jesus Christ His increment;
To spread His gospel is my whole intent."
    "Now, by your leave, O my dear sir," said she,
"Berate him well, for Holy Trinity.
He is as crabbed as an old pismire,
Though he has everything he can desire.
Though him I cover at night, and make him warm,
And lay my leg across him, or my arm,
He grunts and groans like our old boar in sty
And other sport—just none from him have I.
I cannot please him, no, in any case."
    "O Thomas, *je vous dis*, Thomas, Thomas!
This is the Fiend's work, this must be amended.
Anger's a thing that makes High God offended,
And thereof will I speak a word or two."
    "Now, master," said the wife, "before I go,
What will you eat? I will about it scoot."
    "Now, dame," said he then, "*je vous dis, sans doute,*
Had I of a fat capon but the liver,
And of your soft white bread naught but a sliver,
And after that a pig's head well roasted
(Save that I would no beast for me were dead),
Then had I with you plain sufficiency.
I am a man of little gluttony.
My spirit has its nourishment in the Bible.
My body is so inured and so pliable
To watching, that my appetite's destroyed.
I pray you, lady, be you not annoyed
Though I so intimately my secret show;
By God, I would reveal it to but few."
    "Now, sir," said she, "but one word ere I go;
My child has died within this fortnight—oh,
Soon after you left town last, it did die."
    "His death saw I by revelation, aye,"
Replied this friar, "at home in dormitory
Less than an hour, I dare say, ere to glory,
After his death, I saw him borne in bliss
In vision mine, may God me guide in this!
So did our sexton and infirmarian,

Who have been true friars fifty years, each man;
And may now, God be thanked for mercy shown,
Observe their jubilee and walk alone.
And I rose up and did my brothers seek,
With many a tear down trickling on my cheek,
And without noise or clashing of the bells;
Te deum was our song and nothing else,
Save that to Christ I said an orison,
And thanked Him for the vision he had shown.
For, sir and dame, trust me full well in all,
Our orisons are more effectual,
And more we see of Christ's own secret things
Than folk of the laity, though they were kings.
We live in poverty and abstinence,
And laymen live in riches and expense
Of meat and drink, and in their gross delight.
This world's desires we hold in great despite.
Dives and Lazarus lived differently,
And different recompense they had thereby.
Whoso would pray, he must fast and be clean,
Fatten his soul and keep his body lean.
We fare as says the apostle; clothes and food
Suffice us, though they be not over-good.
The cleanness and the fasting of us friars
Result in Christ's accepting all our prayers.
    "Lo, Moses forty days and forty nights
Fasted before the mightiest God of mights
Spoke with him on the Mountain of Sinai.
With empty belly, fasting long, say I,
Received he there the law that had been writ
By God's hand; and Elias (you know of it)
On Mount Horeb, ere he had any speech
With the High God, Who is our spirits' leech,
He fasted long and deep his contemplation.
    "Aaron, who ruled the temple of his nation,
And all the other great priests, every one,
When they into the temple would be gone
To pray there for the folk and do their rites,
They would not drink of that which man excites
And makes him drunk or stirs in any way,
But there in abstinence they'd watch and pray
Lest they should die—to what I say take heed!—
Were they not sober when they prayed, indeed.

Beware my words. No more! for it suffices.
Our Lord Christ, as the holy writ apprises,
Gave us example of fasting and of prayers.
Therefore we mendicants, we simple friars,
Are sworn to poverty and continence,
To charity, meekness, and abstinence,
To persecution for our righteousness,
To weeping, pity, and to cleanliness.
And therefore may you see that all our prayers—
I speak of us, we mendicants, we friars—
Are to the High God far more acceptable
Than yours, with all the feasts you make at table.
From Paradise, if I am not to lie,
Was man chased out because of gluttony;
And chaste was man in Paradise, that's plain.
    "But hear now, Thomas, lest I speak in vain.
I have no text for it, I must admit,
But by analogy the words will fit,
That specially our sweet Lord Christ Jesus
Spoke of the begging friars when He said thus:
'Blest are the poor in spirit.' So said He,
And so through all the gospel may you see
Whether the Word fit better our profession
Or theirs, the monks', who swim in rich possession.
Fie on their pomp and on their gluttony!
And for their lewdness do I them defy.
    "It seems to me they're like Jovinian,
Fat as a whale and waddling as a swan;
As full of wine as bottle in the spence.
Their prayers are always of great reverence,
When they for souls that psalm of David say:
'Cor meum eructavit—bouf!'—that way!
Who follow Christ's Word going on before
But we who are so humble, chaste, and poor,
And doers of God's Word, not hearers, merely?
As falcons rise to heaven, just so clearly
Spring up into the air the holy prayers
Of charitable and chaste and toiling friars
Make their way upward into God's ears two.
Thomas, O Thomas! As I ride or go,
And by that lord whom all we call Saint Yve,
Were you not brother to us, you'd not thrive!
In our chapter we pray both day and night

To Christ, that He will send you health and might
To move about again, and speedily."
    "God knows," said he, "nothing thereof feel I;
So help me Christ as I, these last few years,
Have spent on divers friars, it appears,
Full many a pound; and I'm no better yet.
Truly my wealth have I almost upset.
Farewell my gold! for it has slipped away."
    The friar replied: "Ah, Thomas, so you say!
But why need you to different friars reach?
Why should he need, who has a perfect leech,
To call in other leeches from the town?
Your trouble from your fickleness has grown.
Think you that I, or at least our convent,
Could not suffice to pray? That's what I meant.
Thomas, your feeble joke's not worth a tittle;
Your illness lasts because you've given too little.
    "'Ah, give that convent bushels four of oats!'
'Ah, give that convent four and twenty groats!'
'Ah, give that friar a penny and let him go!'
    "Nay, nay, Thomas, the thing should not be so!
What is a farthing worth, when split twelve ways?
A thing in its integrity displays
Far greater strength than does a unit scattered.
Thomas, by me you shall not here be flattered;
You would you had our labour all for naught.
But the High God, Who all this world has wrought,
Says that the workman's worthy of his hire.
Thomas! Naught of your treasure I desire
As for myself, but that all our convent
To pray for you is always diligent,
And also to build up Christ's holy kirk.
Thomas! If you will learn the way to work,
Of building up of churches you may find
(If it be good) in Thomas' life, of Inde.
You lie here, full of anger and of ire,
Wherewith the Devil set your heart afire,
And you chide here this hapless innocent,
Your wife, who is so meek and so patient.
And therefore, Thomas, trust me if you please,
Scold not your wife, who tries to give you ease;
And bear this word away now, by your faith,
Touching this thing, lo what the wise man saith:

'Within thy house do not the lion play,
Oppress thy subjects in no kind of way,
Nor cause thine equals and thy friends to flee.'
And Thomas, yet again I charge you, be
Wary of her that in your bosom sleeps;
Beware the serpent that so slyly creeps
Under the grass and stings so treacherously.
Beware, my son, and hear this patiently,
That twenty thousand men have lost their lives
For quarrelling with their sweet ones, and their wives.
Now, since you have so holy and meek a wife,
Why need you, Thomas, so to stir up strife?
There is, indeed, no serpent so cruel,
When man treads on his tail, nor half so fell,
As woman is when she is filled with ire;
Vengeance is then the whole of her desire.
Anger's a sin, one of the deadly seven,
Abominable unto the God of Heaven;
And it is sure destruction unto one.
This every vulgar vicar or parson
Can say, how anger leads to homicide.
Truth, anger's the executant of pride.
I could of anger tell you so much sorrow
My tale should last until it were tomorrow.
And therefore I pray God both day and night,
An ireful man, God send him little might!
It is great harm and truly great pity
To set an ireful man in high degree.
    "For once there was an ireful potentate,
(As Seneca says) and while he ruled the state,
Upon a day out riding went knights two,
And as Dame Fortune willed it, it was so
That one of them came home, and one did not.
Anon that knight before the judge was brought,
Who said thus: 'Sir, you have your fellow slain,
For which I doom you to the death, amain.'
And to another knight commanded he,
'Go lead him to his death, so I charge ye.'
It happened, as they went along their way,
Toward the place where he must die that day,
They met the knight that men had thought was dead.
Then thought they, it were best not go ahead,
And so led both unto the judge again.

They said: 'O lord, this knight, he has not slain
His fellow; for he stands here sound, alive.'
'You shall die then,' he cried, 'so may I thrive!
That is to say, you shall all die, all three!'
And then to the first knight 'twas thus said he:
'I doomed you, and therefore you must be dead.
And you, also, must needs now lose your head,
Since you're the causing of your fellow's end.'
And then on the third knight did he descend:
'You have not done what I ordained should be!'
And thus he did away with all the three.

"Ireful Cambyses was a drunkard too,
And much delighted dirty deeds to do.
And so befell, a lord of his household,
Who loved all moral virtue, we are told,
Said on a day, when they were talking, thus:
'A lord is lost if he be too vicious;
And drunkenness is foul thing to record
Of any man, and specially of a lord.
There is full many an eye and many an ear
Waiting upon a lord, nor knows he where.
For God's dear love, sir, drink more moderately;
Wine causes man to lose, and wretchedly,
His mind, and his limbs' usage, every one.'

"'The opposite you'll see,' said he, 'anon;
And you'll prove, by your own experience,
That wine does not to men such foul offence.
There is no wine can rob me of my might
Of hand or foot, nor yet of my eyesight!'
And for despite he drank much wine the more,
A hundred times, than he had drunk before;
And then anon this ireful wicked wretch
Sent one this knight's young son to go and fetch,
And ordered that before him he should stand.
And suddenly he took his bow in hand,
And drew the string thereof up to his ear,
And with an arrow slew the child right there.
'Now tell me whether I've sure hand, or none!'
He said, 'And are my might and mind all gone?
Has wine deprived me of my good eyesight?'

"How shall I tell the answer of the knight?
His son was slain, there is no more to say.
Beware, therefore, with lords look how you play.

But sing *placebo*, and 'I shall, if I can,'
Unless it be unto a helpless man.
To a poor man men should his vices tell,
But to a lord, no, though he go to Hell.
    "Lo, ireful Cyrus, that great Persian king,
Destroyed the river Gyndes at its spring,
Because a horse of his was drowned therein
When he went forth old Babylon to win.
He caused the river to become so small
That women could go wading through it all.
    "Lo, what said he whose teaching all commend?
'An angry man take never for a friend,
Nor with a madman walk along the way,
Lest you repent.' There is no more to say.
    "Now, Thomas, my dear brother, leave your ire;
You shall find me as just as is a squire.
Hold not the Devil's knife against your heart;
Your anger does too sorely burn and smart;
But show me all, now, in confession, son."
    "Nay," said the sick man, "by Saint Simeon!
I have been shriven today by my curate;
I have him told the whole truth of my state;
There's no more need to speak of it," said he,
"Save as I please, of my humility."
    "Then give me of your gold to build our cloister,"
Said he, "for many a mussel and an oyster,
When other men have been well at their ease,
Have been our food, that building should not cease,
And yet, God knows, is finished nothing more
Than the foundation, while of all the floor
There's not a tile yet laid to call our own;
By God, we owe full forty pounds for stone!
Now help, Thomas, for Him that harried Hell!
Else must we turn about and our books sell.
And if you laymen lack our high instruction,
Then will the world go all to its destruction.
For whoso shall deny us right to live,
So may God save me, Thomas, by your leave,
He'll have deprived the whole world of the sun.
For who can teach and work as we have done?
And that's not been for little time," said he;
"Elias and Elisha used to be
Friars, you'll find the scriptures do record,

And beggars too, thanks be to the good Lord!
Now, Thomas, help for holy charity!"
And down he went then, kneeling on one knee.
　　This sick man, he went well-nigh mad for ire;
He would have had that friar set afire
For the hypocrisy that he had shown.
"Such things as I possess and are my own,"
Said he, "those may I give you and no other.
You tell me that I am as your own brother?"
　　"Yea, truly," said the friar, "trust me well;
I gave your wife a letter with our seal."
　　"That's well," said he, "and something will I give
Unto your holy convent while I live,
And right anon you'll have it in your hand,
On this condition only, understand,
That you divide it so, my own dear brother,
That every friar shall have as much as other.
This shall you swear upon the faith you own,
And without fraud or cavil, be it known."
　　"I swear it," said this friar, "on my faith!"
And on the sick man's laid his hand therewith.
"Lo, hear my oath! In me shall truth not lack."
　　"Now then, come put your hand right down my back,"
Replied this man, "and grope you well behind;
For underneath my buttocks shall you find
A thing that I have hid in privity."
　　"Ah," thought the friar, "this shall go with me!"
And down he thrust his hand right to the cleft,
In hope that he should find there some good gift.
And when the sick man felt the friar here
Groping about his hole and all his rear,
Into his hand he let the friar a fart.
There is no stallion drawing loaded cart
That might have let a fart of such a sound.
　　The friar leaped up as with wild lion's bound:
"Ah, treacherous churl," he cried, "by God's own bones,
I'll see that he who scorns me thus atones;
You'll suffer for this fart—I'll find a way!"
　　The servants, who had heard all this affray,
Came leaping in and chased the friar out;
And forth he scowling went, with angry shout,
And found his fellow, where he'd left his store.
He glared about as he were some wild boar;

He ground and gnashed his teeth, so wroth was he.
He quickly sought the manor, there to see
The lord thereof, whose honour was the best,
And always to the friar he confessed;
This worthy man was lord of that village.
The friar came, as he were in a rage,
Where sat the lord at dinner at his board.
And hardly could the friar speak a word,
Till at the last he said, "God be with ye!"
    This lord looked up and said then, *"Ben'cite!*
What, Friar John! What kind of world is this?
I see right well that something is amiss.
You look as if the wood were full of thieves,
Sit down, and tell me what it is that grieves,
And it shall be amended, if I may."
    "I have," said he, "insulted been today—
May God reward you!—down in your village.
And in this world is not so poor a page
As would not feel the insult, if 'twere thrown
At him, that I have suffered in your town.
Yet nothing grieves me in this matter more
Than that this peasant, with his long locks hoar,
Has thus blasphemed our holy convent too."
    "Now, master," said his lordship, "I pray you—"
    "No master, sir," said he, "but servitor,
Though true, I had in school such honour, sir.
But rabbi—God's not pleased that men so call
Us, in the public square or your wide hall."
    "No matter," said he, "tell me all your grief."
    "Sir," said this friar, "an odious mischief
Was this day done to my order and me,
And so, *per consequens,* to each degree
Of Holy Church, may God it soon amend!"
    "Sir," said the lord, "the story I attend.
As my confessor, pray your wrath control;
Salt of the earth are you—the savour whole.
For love of God, I beg you patience hold;
Tell me your grievance."
                                            And anon he told
As you have heard before, you know well what.
    The lady of the house right silent sat
Till she had heard all that the friar said:
"Eh, by God's Mother," cried she, "Blessed Maid!

Is there aught else? A point that we did miss?"
　　"Madam," asked he, "what do you think of this?"
　　"What do I think?" she asked, "So God me speed,
I say, a churl has done a churlish deed.
What should I say? May God desert him! See—
Why his sick head is full of vanity.
The man, no doubt, is more or less insane."
　　"Madam," said he, "I will not lie or feign:
If otherwise I cannot vengeance wreak,
I will defame him wheresoe'er I speak,
This false blasphemer who has dared charge me
Thus to divide what won't divided be,
To every man alike, and with mischance!"
　　The lord sat still as he were in a trance,
And in his mind he rolled it up and down:
"How had this churl imagination grown
To pose so fine a problem to the friar?
I never heard the like, or I'm a liar;
I think the devil stuck it in his mind.
And in arithmetic did no man find,
Before this day, such puzzling question shown.
Who could be able, now, to make it known
How every man should have an equal part
Of both the sound and savour of a fart?
O scrupulous proud churl, beshrew his face!
Lo, sirs," this lord said then, with hard grimace,
"Who ever heard of such a thing ere now?
To every man alike? But tell me how!
Why it's impossible, it cannot be!
Exacting churl, God give him never glee!
The rumbling of a fart, and every sound,
Is but the air's reverberation round,
And ever it wastes, by little and little, away.
There is no man can judge, aye, by my fay,
Whether it were divided equally.
Behold, my churl! And yet how cursedly
To my confessor has he made this crack!
I hold him surely a demoniac!
Now eat your meat and let the churl go play,
Let him go hang himself, the devil's way!"
　　Now the lord's squire stood ready near the board
To carve his meat, and he heard, word for word,
All of the things that I to you have said.

"My lord," said he, "be not ill pleased indeed;
For I could tell, for cloth to make a gown,
To you, sir friar, so you do not frown,
How this said fart evenly doled could be
Among your fellows, if the thing pleased me."

"Tell," said the lord, "and you shall have anon
Cloth for a gown, by God and by Saint John!"

"My lord," said he, "when next the weather's fair,
And there's no wind to stir the quiet air,
Let someone bring a cartwheel to this hall,
But see there are no missing spokes at all.
Twelve spokes a cartwheel has, sir, commonly.
And bring me then twelve friars, and know you why?
Because a convent's thirteen, as I guess.
The present confessor, for his worthiness,
He shall complete the tale of this convent.
Then shall they all kneel down, by one assent,
And at each spoke's end, in this manner, sire,
Let the nose be laid firmly of a friar.
Your noble sir confessor, whom God save,
Shall hold his nose upright beneath the nave.
Then shall this churl, with belly stiff and taut
As any tabour—let him here be brought;
And set him on the wheel of this same cart,
Upon the hub, and make him let a fart.
And you shall see, on peril of my life,
With proof so clear that there shall be no strife,
That equally the sound of it will wend,
And the stink too, to each spoke's utter end;
Save that this worthy man, your confessor,
Because he is a man of great honour,
Shall have first fruits, as reasonable it is;
The noble custom of all friars is this,
The worthy men of them shall be first served;
And certainly this has he well deserved.
He has today taught us so much of good,
With preaching in the pulpit where he stood,
That for my part I gladly should agree,
He might well have the first smell of farts three,
And so would all his convent, generously,
He bears himself so well and holily."

The lord, the lady, and each man, save the friar,
Agreed that Jenkin spoke, as classifier,

As well as Euclid or as Ptolemy.
Touching the churl, they said that subtlety
And great wit taught him how to make his crack.
He was no fool, nor a demoniac.
And Jenkin by this means has won a gown.
My tale is done, we're almost into town.

HERE ENDS THE SUMMONER'S TALE

THE CLERK'S PROLOGUE

"Sir clerk of Oxford," our good host then said,
"You ride as quiet and still as is a maid
But newly wedded, sitting at the board;
This day I've heard not from your tongue a word.
Perhaps you mull a sophism that's prime,
But Solomon says, each thing to its own time.

"For God's sake, smile and be of better cheer,
It is no time to think and study here.
Tell us some merry story, if you may;
For whatsoever man will join in play,
He needs must to the play give his consent.
But do not preach, as friars do in Lent,
To make us, for our old sins, wail and weep,
And see your tale shall put us not to sleep.

"Tell us some merry thing of adventures.
Your terms, your colours, and your speech-figures,
Keep them in store till so be you indite
High style, as when men unto kings do write.
Speak you so plainly, for this time, I pray,
That we can understand what things you say."

This worthy clerk, benignly he answered.
"Good host," said he, "I am under your yard;
You have of us, for now, the governance,
And therefore do I make you obeisance
As far as reason asks it, readily.
I will relate to you a tale that I
Learned once, at Padua, of a worthy clerk,
As he proved by his words and by his work.
He's dead, now, and nailed down within his chest,
And I pray God to give his soul good rest!

"Francis Petrarch, the laureate poet,
Was this clerk's name, whose rhetoric so sweet
Illumed all Italy with poetry,

325

As did Lignano with philosophy,
Or law, or other art particular;
But Death, that suffers us not very far,
Nor more, as 'twere, than twinkling of an eye,
Has slain them both, as all of us shall die.

"But forth, to tell you of this worthy man,
Who taught this tale to me, as I began,
I say that first, with high style he indites,
Before the body of his tale he writes,
A proem to describe those lands renowned,
Saluzzo, Piedmont, and the region round,
And speaks of Apennines, those hills so high
That form the boundary of West Lombardy,
And of Mount Viso, specially, the tall,
Whereat the Po, out of a fountain small,
Takes its first springing and its tiny source
That eastward ever increases in its course
Toward Emilia, Ferrara, and Venice;
The which is a long story to devise.
And truly, in my judgment reluctant
It is a thing not wholly relevant,
Save that he introduces thus his gear:
But this is his tale, which you now may hear."

THE CLERK'S TALE

There is, in the west side of Italy,
Down at the foot of Mount Viso the cold,
A pleasant plain that yields abundantly,
Where many a tower and town one may behold,
That were there founded in the times of old.
With many another fair delightful sight;
Saluzzo is this noble region bright.

A marquis once was lord of all that land,
As were his noble ancestors before;
Obedient and ready to his hand
Were all his lieges, both the less and more.
Thus in delight he lived, and had of yore,
Beloved and feared, through favour of Fortune,
Both by his lords and by the common run.

Therewith he was, to speak of lineage,
Born of the noblest blood of Lombardy,
With person fair, and strong, and young of age,
And full of honour and of courtesy;
Discreet enough to lead his nation, he,
Save in some things wherein he was to blame,
And Walter was this young lord's Christian name.

I blame him thus, that he considered naught
Of what in coming time might him betide,
But on his present wish was all his thought,
As, he would hunt and hawk on every side;
Well-nigh all other cares would he let slide,
And would not, and this was the worst of all,
Marry a wife, for aught that might befall.

That point alone his people felt so sore
That in a flock one day to him they went,
And one of them, the wisest in all lore,
Or else because the lord would best consent
That he should tell him what the people meant,
Or else that he could make the matter clear,
He to the marquis spoke as you shall hear.

"O noble marquis, your humanity
Assures us, aye, and gives us hardiness
As often as there is necessity
That we to you may tell our heaviness.
Accept, lord, now of your great nobleness
That we with sincere hearts may here complain,
Nor let your ears my humble voice disdain.

"Though I have naught to do in this matter
More than another man has in this place,
Yet for as much as you, most honoured sir,
Have always showed me favour and much grace,
I dare the more to ask of you a space
Of audience, to set forth our request,
And you, my lord, will do as you like best.

"For truly, lord, so well do we like you
And all your works (and ever have), that we —
We could not, of ourselves, think what to do
To make us live in more felicity,
Save one thing, lord, and if your will it be,

That to be wedded man you hold it best,
Then were your people's hearts at utter rest.

"But bow your neck beneath that blessed yoke
Of sovereignty and not of hard service,
The which men call espousal or wedlock;
And pray think, lord, among your thoughts so wise,
How our days pass and each in different guise;
For though we sleep or wake or roam or ride,
Time flies, and for no man will it abide.

"And though your time of green youth flower as yet,
Age creeps in always, silent as a stone;
Death threatens every age, nor will forget
For any state, and there escapes him none:
And just as surely as we know, each one,
That we shall die, uncertain are we all
What day it is when death shall on us fall.

"Accept then of us, lord, the true intent,
That never yet refused you your behest,
And we will, lord, if you will give consent,
Choose you a wife without delay, at least,
Born of the noblest blood and the greatest
Of all this land, so that it ought to seem
Honour to God and you, as we shall deem.

"Deliver us from all our constant dread
And take yourself a wife, for High God's sake;
For if it so befell, which God forbid,
That by your death your noble line should break
And that a strange successor should come take
Your heritage, woe that we were alive!
Wherefore we pray you speedily to wive."

Their humble prayer and their so earnest cheer
Roused in the marquis' heart great sympathy.
"You'd have me," he replied, "my people dear,
Do what I've never yet thought necessary.
I have rejoiced in my fond liberty,
That men so seldom find in their marriage;
Where I was free, I must be in bondage.

"Nevertheless, I see your true intent,
And know there's always sense in what you say;
Wherefore of my free will will I consent

To wed a wife, as soon as ever I may.
But whereas you have offered here today
To choose a wife for me, I you release
From that, and pray that you thereof will cease.

"For God knows well that children oft retain
Naught of their worthy elders gone before;
Goodness comes all from God, not of the strain
Whereof they were engendered; furthermore
I trust in God's great goodness, and therefore
My marriage and my state and all my ease
I leave to Him to do with as He please.

"Let me alone in choosing of my wife,
That burden on my own back I'll endure;
But I pray you, and charge you on your life,
That what wife I may take, me you'll assure
You'll honour her throughout her life's tenure,
In word and deed, both here and everywhere,
As if she were an emperor's daughter fair.

"And furthermore, this shall you swear, that you
Against my choice shall neither grouse nor strive;
Since I'm forgoing liberty, and woo
At your request, so may I ever thrive
As, where my heart is set, there will I wive;
And save you give consent in such manner,
I pray you speak no more of this matter."

With hearty will they swore and gave assent
To all this, and no one of them said nay;
Praying him, of his grace, before they went,
That he would set for them a certain day
For his espousal, soon as might be; yea,
For still the people had a little dread
Lest that the marquis would no woman wed.

He granted them the day that pleased him best
Whereon he would be married, certainly,
And said he did all this at their request;
And they with humble hearts, obediently,
Kneeling upon their knees full reverently,
All thanked him there, and thus they made an end
Of their design and homeward did they wend.

And thereupon he to his officers

Ordered that for the fête they should provide,
And to his household gentlemen and squires,
Such charges gave as pleased him to decide;
And all obeyed him: let him praise or chide,
And each of them did all his diligence
To show unto the fête his reverence.

Explicit prima pars.
Incipit secunda pars.

Not far from that same honoured palace where
This marquis planned his marriage, at this tide,
There stood a hamlet, on a site most fair,
Wherein the poor folk of the countryside
Stabled their cattle and did all abide,
And where their labour gave them sustenance
After the earth had yielded abundance.

Amongst these humble folk there dwelt a man
Who was considered poorest of them all;
But the High God of Heaven sometimes can
Send His grace to a little ox's stall;
Janicula men did this poor man call.
A daughter had he, fair enough to sight;
Griselda was this young maid's name, the bright.

If one should speak of virtuous beauty,
Then was she of the fairest under sun;
Since fostered in dire poverty was she,
No lust luxurious in her heart had run;
More often from the well than from the tun
She drank, and since she would chaste virtue please,
She knew work well, but knew not idle ease.

But though this maiden tender was of age,
Yet in the breast of her virginity
There was enclosed a ripe and grave courage;
And in great reverence and charity
Her poor old father fed and fostered she;
A few sheep grazing in a field she kept,
For she would not be idle till she slept.

And when she homeward came, why she would bring
Roots and green herbs, full many times and oft,
The which she'd shred and boil for her living,
And made her bed a hard one and not soft;

Her father kept she in their humble croft
With what obedience and diligence
A child may do for father's reverence.

Upon Griselda, humble daughter pure,
The marquis oft had looked in passing by,
As he a-hunting rode at adventure;
And when it chanced that her he did espy,
Not with the glances of a wanton eye
He gazed at her, but all in sober guise,
And pondered on her deeply in this wise:

Commending to his heart her womanhood,
And virtue passing that of any wight,
Of so young age in face and habitude.
For though the people have no deep insight
In virtue, he considered all aright
Her goodness, and decided that he would
Wed only her, if ever wed he should.

The day of wedding came, but no one can
Tell who the woman is that bride shall be;
At which strange thing they wondered, many a man,
And they said, marvelling, in privacy:
"Will not our lord yet leave his vanity?
Will he not wed? Alas, alas, the while!
Why will he thus himself and us beguile?"

Nevertheless, this marquis has bade make,
Of jewels set in gold and in rich azure,
Brooches and rings, all for Griselda's sake,
And for her garments took he then the measure
By a young maiden of her form and stature,
And found all other ornaments as well
That for such wedding would be meet to tell.

The time of mid-morn of that very day
Approached when this lord's marriage was to be;
And all the palace was bedecked and gay,
Both hall and chambers, each in its degree;
With kitchens stuffed with food in great plenty,
There might one see the last and least dainty
That could be found in all of Italy.

This regal marquis, splendidly arrayed,
With lords and ladies in his company

(Who to attend the feasting had been prayed),
And of his retinue the bachelory,
With many a sound of sundry melody,
Unto the village whereof I have told,
In this array the nearest way did hold.

Griselda who, God knows, was innocent
That for her sake was all this fine array,
To fetch some water, to a fountain went,
Yet she returned soon, did this lovely may,
For she had heard it said that on this day
The marquis was to wed, and if she might,
She was full fain to see the glorious sight.

She thought: "With other maidens I will stand
(Who are my friends) within our door, and see
The marchioness, and therefore I'll turn hand
To do at home, as soon as it may be,
The household work that's waiting there for me;
And then I'll be at leisure to behold
Her, if they this way to the castle hold."

And as across her threshold she'd have gone,
The marquis came, and for her did he call;
And she set down her water jar anon
Beside the threshold, in an ox's stall,
And down upon her two knees did she fall
And, kneeling, with grave countenance, was still
Till she had heard what was his lordship's will.

This thoughtful marquis spoke unto this maid
Full soberly, and said in this manner:
"Griselda, where's your father?" so he said.
And she, with reverence and with humble cheer,
Answered: "My lord, he is but inside here."
And in she went without more tarrying
And to the marquis did her father bring.

He by the hand then took this ancient man
And said, when he had led him well aside:
"Janicula, I neither will nor can
Conceal my love, nor my heart's longing hide.
If you but acquiesce, whate'er betide,
Your daughter will I take, before I wend,
To be my wife until her life's dear end.

"You love me, and I know it well today,
And are my faithful liege, and were of yore;
And all that pleases me, I dare well say,
Pleases you too; especially therefore
Assure me on the point I made before—
Can we together in this compact draw,
And will you take me as your son-in-law?"

This sudden word the man astonished so
That red he grew, abashed, and all quaking
He stood; nor could he answer further, no,
Than but to say: "O Lord, I am willing
To do your will; but against your liking
I'll do no thing; you are my lord so dear
That what you wish governs this matter here."

"Then I will," said this marquis, quietly,
"That in your chamber you and I and she
Have consultation, and do you know why?
Because I'd ask her if her will it be
To be my wife and so be ruled by me;
And all this shall be done in your presence,
I will not speak without your audience."

And while in chamber they three were about
Their business, whereof you'll hereafter hear,
The people crowded through the house without
And wondered by what honest method there
So carefully she'd kept her father dear.
But more Griselda wondered, as she might,
For never before that saw she such a sight.

No wonder, though, astonishment she felt
At seeing so great a guest within that place;
With people of his sort she'd never dealt,
Wherefore she looked on with a pallid face.
But briefly through the matter now to race,
These are the very words the marquis said
To this most modest, truly constant maid.

"Griselda," said he, "You shall understand
It's pleasing to your father and to me
That I wed you, and even it may stand,
As I suppose, that you would have it be.
But these demands must I first make," said he,

"And since it shall be done in hasty wise,
Will you consent, or will you more advise?

"I say this: Are you ready with good heart
To grant my wish, and that I freely may,
As I shall think best, make you laugh or smart,
And you to grumble never, night or day?
And too, when I say 'yea' you say not 'nay'
By word or frown to what I have designed.
Swear this, and here I will our contract bind."

Wondering upon this word, quaking for fear,
She said: "My lord, unsuited, unworthy
Am I to take the honour you give me here;
But what you'd have, that very thing would I.
And here I swear that never willingly,
In deed or thought, will I you disobey,
To save my life, and I love life, I say."

"This is enough, Griselda mine," cried he.
And forth he went then with full sober cheer
Out at the door, and after him came she,
And to the people who were waiting near,
"This is my wife," he said, "who's standing here.
Honour her, all, and love her, all, I pray,
Who love me; and there is no more to say."

And so that nothing of her former gear
She should take with her to his house, he bade
That women strip her naked then and there;
Whereat these ladies were not over-glad
To handle clothes wherein she had been clad.
Nevertheless, this maiden bright of hue
From head to foot they clothed her all anew.

Her hair they combed and brushed, which fell untressed
All artlessly, and placed a coronal
With their small fingers on her head, and dressed
Her robes with many jewels great and small;
Of her array how shall I tell withal?
Scarcely the people knew her for fairness,
So transformed was she in her splendid dress.

This marquis her has married with a ring
Brought for the purpose there; and then has set
Upon a horse, snow-white and well ambling,

And to his palace, without longer let,
With happy following folk and more they met,
Convoyed her home, and thus the day they spent
In revelry until the sun's descent.

And briefly forth throughout this tale to chase,
I say that unto this new marchioness
God has such favour sent her, of His grace,
It seemed in no way true, by likeliness,
That she was born and bred in humbleness,
As in a hovel or an ox's stall,
But rather nurtured in an emperor's hall.

To everyone she soon became so dear
And worshipful, that folk where she had dwelt
And from her birth had known her, year by year,
Although they could have sworn it, scarcely felt
That to Janicula, with whom I've dealt,
She really was a daughter, for she seemed
Another creature now, or so they deemed.

For though she ever had been virtuous,
She was augmented by such excellence
Of manners based on noble goodness thus,
And so discreet and wise of eloquence,
So gentle and so worthy reverence,
And she could so the people's hearts embrace,
That each her loved that looked upon her face.

Not only in Saluzzo, in the town,
Was published wide the goodness of her name,
But throughout many a land where she'd renown
If one said well, another said the same;
So widespread of her goodness was the fame
That men and women came; the young and old
Went to Saluzzo, her but to behold.

Thus Walter lowly, nay, but royally,
Wedded, by Fortune's grace, right honourably,
In the good peace of God lived easily
At home, and outward grace enough had he;
And since he saw that under low degree
Is virtue often hid, the people fairly
Held him a prudent man, and that's done rarely.

Not only this Griselda through her wit

Knew how with wifely arts her home to bless,
But also, when there was a need for it,
The people's wrongs she knew how to redress.
There was no discord, rancour, heaviness
In all that land that she could not appease,
And wisely bring them all to rest and ease.

Although her husband from the court were gone,
If gentlemen, or less, of her country
Were angered, she would bring them all at one;
So wise and so mature of speech was she,
And judgments gave of so great equity,
Men felt that God from Heaven her did send
People to save and every wrong to amend.

Not long Griselda had, it seems, been wed
Before a daughter to her lord she bore,
Though of a son she'd rather have gone to bed.
Glad were the marquis and the folk therefor;
For though a girl-child came thus all before,
She might well to a boy-child yet attain,
Since barren she was not, it now was plain.

Explicit secunda pars.
Incipit tercia pars.

It happened, as it has sometimes before,
That when this child had sucked a month or so,
This marquis in his heart such longing bore
To test his wife, her patience thus to know,
He could not in his heart the chance forgo
This marvelous desire his wife to try;
'Twas needless, God knows, thus to peek and pry.

He had sufficiently tried her before
And found her ever good; what needed it
That he should test her ever more and more?
Though some men praise it for a subtle wit,
Yet I say that to him 'twas no credit
To try his wife when there was never need,
Putting her heart to anguish and to dread.

In doing which the marquis took this turn:
He came alone by night to where she lay
And with a troubled look and features stern
He said to her: "Griselda mine, that day

When I removed you from your poor array
And placed you in a state of nobleness—
You have not all forgotten that, I guess.

"I say, Griselda, this your dignity
Wherein I have so placed you, as I trow,
Has not made you forgetful now to be
That I raised you from poor estate and low
For any good you might then have or know.
Take heed of every word that now I say,
There's no one else shall hear it, by my fay.

"You know and well enough how you came here
Into this house, it is not long ago,
And though to me you are both lief and dear,
Unto my nobles you are not; and so
They say that unto them 'tis shame and woe
To be your subjects and compelled to serve
You who are village-born and naught deserve.

"And specially, since that girl-child you bore,
These things they've said—of this there is no doubt;
But I desire, as I have done before,
To live at peace with all the folk about;
I cannot in this matter leave them out.
I must do with your daughter what is best,
Not as I would, but under men's behest.

"And yet, God knows, the act is hard for me;
And only with your knowledge would I bring
The deed to pass, but this I would," said he,
"That you assent with me to this one thing.
Show now that patience in your life's dealing
You told me of and swore to in your village
The day that marked the making of our marriage."

When she had heard all this, this she received
With never a word or change of countenance;
For, as it seemed, she was in no way grieved.
She said: "Lord, all lies at your own pleasance;
My child and I, with hearty obeisance,
Are all yours, and you may save us or kill
That which is yours; do you what thing you will.

"There is no thing, and so God my soul save,
That you may like displeasing unto me;

I do not wish a single thing to have,
Nor dread a thing to lose, save only ye;
This will is in my heart and aye shall be,
Nor length of time nor death may this deface,
Nor turn my passion to another place."

Glad was this marquis of her answering,
And yet he feigned as if he were not so;
All dreary were his face and his bearing
When it came time from chamber he should go.
Soon after this, a quarter-hour or so,
He privily told all of his intent
Unto a man, whom to his wife he sent.

A kind of sergeant was this serving man,
Who had proved often faithful, as he'd found,
In matters great, and such men often can
Do evil faithfully, as can a hound.
The lord knew this man loved him and was bound;
And when this sergeant learned his lordship's will
He stalked into the chamber, grim and still.

"Madam," said he, "you must forgive it me,
Though I do that to which I am constrained;
You are so wise you know well, it may be,
That a lord's orders may not well be feigned;
They may be much lamented or complained,
But men must needs their every wish obey,
And thus will I; there is no more to say.

"This child I am commanded now to take"—
And spoke no more, but seized that innocent
Pitilessly, and did a gesture make
As if he would have slain it ere he went,
Griselda, she must suffer and consent;
And so, meek as a lamb, she sat there, still,
And let this cruel sergeant do his will.

Suspicious of repute was this same man,
Suspect his face, suspect his word also,
Suspect the time when this thing he began,
Alas! Her daughter that she had loved so,
She thought he'd slay it right there, whether or no.
Nevertheless, she neither wept nor sighed,
Doing the marquis' liking though she died.

At last she found her voice and thus began
And meekly to the sergeant then she prayed
That, as he was a worthy, gentle man,
She might kiss her child once before his blade;
And on her breast this little child she laid,
With sad face, and so kissed it and did press
And lulled it and at last began to bless.

And thus she said in her benignant voice:
"Farewell, my child that I no more shall see;
But now I've crossed you thus, I will rejoice
That of the Father blessed may you be,
Who died for us upon the bitter tree.
Your soul, my little child, to Him I give;
This night you die for my sake—though I live."

I think that to a nurse in such a case
It had been hard this pitiful thing to see;
Well might a mother then have cried "Alas!"
But so steadfastly serious was she
That she endured all her adversity,
And to the sergeant she but meekly said:
"I give you now again your little maid.

"Go now," said she, "and do my lord's behest,
But one thing will I pray you, of your grace,
That, save my lord forbade you, at the least
Bury this little body in some place
Where beasts nor birds will tear its limbs and face."
But no word to that purpose would he say,
But took the child and went upon his way.

This sergeant went unto his lord again
And of Griselda's words and of her cheer
He told him point by point, all short and plain,
And so presented him his daughter dear.
A little pity felt the marquis here;
Nevertheless, he held his purpose still,
As great lords do when they will have their will;

And bade the sergeant that he privily
Should softly swaddle the young child and wrap
With all the necessaries, tenderly,
And in a coffer or some garment lap;
But upon pain his head should meet mishap

No man should know the least of his intent,
Nor whence he came, nor whither that he went;

But to Bologna, to his sister dear
Who then was of Panago the countess,
He should take it, and tell of matters here,
Asking of her she do her busyness
This child to foster in all nobleness;
And whose the child was, that he bade her hide
From everyone, for aught that might betide.

The sergeant goes and has fulfilled this thing;
But to this marquis now return must we;
For soon he went to see her, wondering
If by his wife's demeanour he might see,
Or by her conversation learn that she
Were changed in aught; but her he could not find
Other than ever serious and kind.

As glad, as humble, as busy in service,
And even in love, as she was wont to be,
Was she to him at all times in each wise;
And of her daughter not a word spoke she.
No strange nor odd look of adversity
Was seen in her, and her dear daughter's name
She never named in earnest nor in game.

Explicit tercia pars.
Sequitur pars quarta.

In this way over them there passed four years
Ere she with child was; but as High God would,
A boy-child then she bore, as it appears,
By Walter, fair and pleasing to behold.
And when folk this word to the father told,
Not only he but all the people raised
Their joyous hymns to God and His grace praised.

When he was two years old and from the breast
Weaned by his nurse, it chanced upon a day
This marquis had another wish to test
And try his wife yet further, so they say.
Oh, needless her temptation in this way!
But wedded men no measure can observe
When they've a wife who's patient and will serve.

"Wife," said this marquis, "you have heard before,
My people bear our marriage with ill-will;
Particularly since my son you bore
Now it is worse than ever, all this ill.
Their murmurs all my heart and courage kill,
For to my ears come words so aimed to smart
That they have well-nigh broken all my heart.

"Now they say this: 'When Walter's dead and gone.
Then shall Janicula's base blood succeed
And be our lord, for other have we none!'
Such words my people say, 'tis true, indeed!
Well ought I of such murmurs to take heed;
For truly do I fear the populace,
Though they say nothing plainly to my face.

"I would exist in peace, if that I might;
Wherefore I am determined utterly
That as his sister served I, and by night,
Just so will I serve him full secretly;
And thus I warn you, that not suddenly
Out of yourself for woe you start or stray;
Be patient in this sorrow, so I pray."

"I have," said she, "said thus, and ever shall:
I'll have no thing, or not have, that's certain,
Save as you wish; nothing grieves me at all,
Even though my daughter and my son are slain
At your command, and that, I think, is plain.
I have had no part in my children twain
But sickness first, and after, woe and pain.

"You are our master; do with your own thing
Just as you like; no counsel ask of me.
For, as I left at home all my clothing
When first I came to you, just so," said she,
"Left I my will and all my liberty,
And took your clothing; wherefore do I pray
You'll do your pleasure, I'll your wish obey.

"For certainly, if I had prescience
Your will to know ere you your wish had told,
I would perform it without negligence;
But now I know the wish that you unfold,
To do your pleasure firmly will I hold;

For knew I that my death would give you ease,
Right gladly would I die, lord, you to please.

"For death can offer no loss that is known
Compared to your love's loss." And when, I say,
He saw his wife's great constancy, then down
He cast his eyes, and wondered at the way
She would in patience all his will obey;
And forth he went with dreary countenance,
But in his heart he knew a great pleasance.

This ugly sergeant in the very wise
That he her daughter took away, so he
(Or worse, if worse than this men could devise)
Has taken her son, the child of such beauty.
And always yet so all-patient was she
That she no sign gave forth of heaviness,
But kissed her son and so began to bless;

Save this: She prayed him that, and if he might,
Her son he'd bury in an earthen grave,
His tender limbs, so delicate to sight,
From ravenous birds and from all beasts to save.
But she no answer out of him could have.
He went his way as if he cared nor thought,
But to Bologna tenderly 'twas brought.

This marquis wondered ever more and more
Upon her patience; and indeed if he
Had not known truly in her years before
That she had loved her children perfectly,
He would have thought that out of subtlety
And malice, or from some urge more savage
She suffered this with calm face and courage.

But well he knew that, next himself, 'twas plain
She loved her children best in every wise.
But now to ask of women I am fain,
Whether these trials should not the man suffice?
What could an obdurate husband more devise
To prove her wifehood and her faithfulness,
And he continuing in his stubbornness?

But there are folk to such condition grown
That, when they do a certain purpose take,
They cannot quit the intent they thus own,

But just as they were bound unto a stake
They will not from that first hard purpose shake.
Just so this marquis fully was purposed
To test his wife, as he was first disposed.

He watched her, if by word or countenance
She show a change toward him, or in courage;
But never could he find a variance.
She was aye one in heart and in visage;
And aye the farther that she went in age,
The more true, if such thing were possible,
She was in love, and painstaking, as well.

From which it seemed that, as between those two,
There was but one will, for, to Walter's quest,
The same thing was her sole desire also,
And—God be thanked!—all fell out for the best.
She showed well that, in all this world's unrest,
A wife, of her volition, nothing should
Will to be done, save as her husband would.

The scandal of this Walter widely spread,
That, of his cruel heart, he'd wickedly
(Because a humble woman he had wed)
Murdered his two young children secretly.
Such murmurs went among them commonly.
No wonder, either, for to people's ear
There came no word but they'd been murdered there.

For which, whereas the people theretofore
Had loved him, now the scandal of such shame
Caused them to hate where they had loved before;
To be a murderer brings a hateful name.
Nevertheless, in earnest nor in game
Would he from this his cruel plan be bent;
To test his wife was all his fixed intent.

Now when his daughter was twelve years of age,
He to the court of Rome (in subtle wise
Informed of his design) sent his message,
Commanding them such bulls they should devise
As for his cruel purpose would suffice,
How that the pope, for Walter's people's rest,
Bade him to wed another, and the best.

I say, he ordered they should counterfeit

A papal bull and set it forth therein
That he had leave his first wife now to quit,
By papal dispensation, with no sin,
To stop all such dissension as did win
Between his folk and him; thus said the bull,
The which thing they did publish to the full.

The ignorant people, as no wonder is,
Supposed of course that things were even so;
But when Griselda's ears caught word of this,
I judge that then her heart was filled with woe.
But she, for ever steadfast, still did show
Herself disposed, this humble meek creature,
The adversity of Fortune to endure.

Abiding ever his wish and pleasure still,
To whom she had been given, heart and all,
He was her worldly hope, for good or ill;
But to tell all this briefly, if I shall,
This marquis wrote, in letter personal,
The devious working of his whole intent
And secretly 'twas to Bologna sent.

Unto Panago's count, who had, we know,
Wedded his sister, prayed he specially
To bring him home again his children two,
In honourable estate, all openly.
But one more thing he prayed him, utterly,
That he to no one, whoso should inquire,
Would tell who was their mother or their sire,

But say: The maiden married was to be
Unto Saluzzo's marquis, and anon.
And as this count was asked, so then did he;
For on day set he on his way was gone
Toward Saluzzo, with lords many a one,
In rich array, this maiden there to guide,
With her young brother riding at her side.

So toward her marriage went this fresh young maid
Clad richly and bedecked with jewels clear;
Her brother with her, boyishly arrayed,
And all anew, was now in his eighth year.
And thus in great pomp and with merry cheer
Toward Saluzzo went they on their way,

And rode along together day by day.

Explicit quarta pars.
Sequitur pars quinta.

Meanwhile, according to his wicked way,
This marquis, still to test his wife once more,
Even to the final proof of her, I say,
Fully to have experience to the core
If she were yet as steadfast as before,
He on a day in open audience
Loudly said unto her this rude sentence:

"Truly, Griselda, I'd much joy, perchance,
When you I took for wife, for your goodness
And for your truth and your obedience,
Not for your lineage nor your wealth, I guess;
But now I know, in utter certainness,
That in great lordship, if I well advise,
There is great servitude in sundry wise.

"I may not act as every plowman may;
My people have constrained me that I take
Another wife, and this they ask each day;
And now the pope, hot rancour thus to slake,
Consents, I dare the thing to undertake;
And truly now this much to you I'll say,
My new wife journeys hither on her way.

"Be strong of heart and leave at once her place,
And that same dower that you brought to me,
Take it again, I grant it of my grace;
Return you to your father's house," said he;
"No man may always have prosperity;
With a calm heart I urge you to endure
The stroke of Fortune or of adventure."

And she replied again, of her patience:
"My lord," said she, "I know, and knew alway,
How that between your own magnificence
And my poor state, no person can or may
Make a comparison in an equal way.
I never held me worthy or of grade
To be your wife, no, nor your chambermaid.

"And in this house, where lady you made me

(The High God do I take now to witness,
And as He truly may my soul's joy be),
I never held me lady nor mistress,
But only servant to your worthiness;
And ever shall, while my life may endure,
Beyond all worldly beings, that is sure.

"That you so long, of your benignity,
Have held me here in honour in this way,
Where I was never worthy, once, to be,
For that, thank God and you—to God I pray
He will reward you. There's no more to say.
Unto my father gladly will I wend
And dwell with him until my life shall end.

"Where I was fostered when an infant small,
There will I lead my life till I be dead,
A widow, clean in body, heart, and all.
For, since I gave to you my maidenhead,
And am your true and lawful wife, wedded,
May God forbid such a lord's wife to take
Another man for husband or love's sake.

"And of your new wife, may God of His grace
Grant you but joy and all prosperity:
For I will gladly yield to her my place,
Wherein so happy I was wont to be,
For since it pleases you, my lord," said she,
"Who have been all my heart's ease and its rest,
That I shall go, I'll go when you request.

"But whereas now you proffer me such dower
As first I brought to you, it's in my mind
That 'twas my wretched clothes and nothing fair.
The which to me were hard now for to find.
O my good God! How noble and how kind
You seemed then, in your speech and in your face
The day we married in that humble place.

"But truth is said—at least I find it true
For actually its proof is seen in me—
Old love is not the same as when it's new.
But truly, lord, for no adversity,
Though I should die of all this, shall it be
That ever in word or deed I shall repent

That I gave you my heart in whole intent.

"My lord, you know that, in my father's place,
You stripped from me my poor and humble weed
And clothed me richly, of your noble grace.
I brought you nothing else at all indeed,
Than faith and nakedness and maidenhead.
And here again my clothing I restore,
And, too, my wedding-ring, for evermore.

"The rest of all your jewels, they will be
Within your chamber, as I dare maintain;
Naked out of my father's house," said she,
"I came, and naked I return again.
To follow aye your pleasure I am fain,
But yet I hope it is not your intent
That smockless from your palace I be sent.

"You could not do so base and shameful thing
That the same womb in which your children lay
Should, before all the folk, in my walking,
Be seen all bare; and therefore do I pray
Let me not like a worm go on my way.
Remember that, my own lord, always dear,
I was your wife, though I unworthy were.

"Wherefore, as guerdon for my maidenhead,
The which I brought, but shall not with me bear,
Let them but give me, for my only meed,
Such a poor smock as I was wont to wear,
That I therewith may hide the womb of her
Who was your wife; and here I take my leave
Of you, my own dear lord, lest you should grieve.

"The smock," said he, "that you have on your back,
Let it stay there and wear it forth," said he.
But firmness in so saying the man did lack;
But went his way for ruth and for pity.
Before the folk her body then stripped she
And in her smock, with head and feet all bare,
Toward her father's hovel did she fare.

The folk they followed, weeping and with cries,
And Fortune did they curse as they passed on;
But she with weeping did not wet her eyes,
And all this while of words she said not one.

Her father, who had heard this news anon,
Cursed then the day and hour when from the earth,
A living creature, nature gave him birth.

For, beyond any doubt, this poor old man
Had always feared the marquis soon would tire,
And doubted since the marriage first began,
If when the lord had satisfied desire,
He would not think a wife of station higher,
For one of his degree, had been more right,
And send her thence as soon as ever he might.

To meet his daughter hastily went he,
For he, by noise of folk, knew her coming;
And with her old coat, such as it might be,
He covered her, full sorrowfully weeping;
But the coat over her he could not bring,
For poor the cloth, and many days had passed
Since on her marriage day she wore it last.

Thus with her father, for a certain space,
Did dwell this flower of wifely meek patience,
Who neither by her words nor in her face,
Before the people nor in their absence,
Showed that she thought to her was done offense;
Nor of her high estate a remembrance
Had she, to judge by her calm countenance.

No wonder, though, for while in high estate,
Her soul kept ever full humility;
No mouth complaining, no heart delicate,
No pomp, no look of haughty royalty,
But full of patience and benignity,
Discreet and prideless, always honourable,
And to her husband meek and firm as well.

Men speak of Job and of his humbleness,
As clerks, when they so please, right well can write
Concerning men, but truth is, nevertheless,
Though clerks' praise of all women is but slight,
No man acquits himself in meekness quite
As women can, nor can be half so true
As women are, save this be something new.

Explicit quinta pars.
Sequitur pars sexta.

Now from Bologna is Panago come,
Whereof the word spread unto great and less,
And in the ears of people, all and some,
It was told, too, that a new marchioness
Came with him, in such pomp and such richness
That never had been seen with human eye
So noble array in all West Lombardy.

The marquis, who had planned and knew all this,
Before this count was come, a message sent
To poor Griselda, who had lost her bliss;
With humble heart and features glad she went
And on her knees before her lord she bent.
No pride of thought did her devotion dim;
She wisely and with reverence greeted him.

He said, "Griselda, hear what I shall say:
This maiden, who'll be wedded unto me,
Shall be received with splendour of array
As royally as in my house may be,
And, too, that everyone in his degree
Have his due rank in seating and service,
And high pleasance, as I can best devise.

"I have not serving women adequate
To set the rooms in order as I would.
And so I wish you here to regulate
All matters of the sort as mistress should.
You know of old the ways I think are good,
And though you're clothed in such a slattern's way,
Go do at least your duty as you may."

"Not only am I glad, my lord," said she,
"To do your wish, but I desire also
To serve you and to please in my degree;
This without wearying I'll always do.
And ever, lord, in happiness or woe,
The soul within my heart shall not forgo
To love you best with true intent, I know."

Then she began to put the house aright,
To set the tables and the beds to make;
And was at pains to do all that she might,
Praying the chambermaids, for good God's sake,
To make all haste and sweep hard and to shake;

And she, who was most serviceable of all,
Did every room array, and his wide hall.

About mid-morning did this count alight,
Who brought with him these noble children twain,
Whereat the people ran to see the sight
Of their array, so rich was all the train;
And for the first time did they not complain,
But said that Walter was no fool, at least,
To change his wife, for it was for the best.

For she was fairer far, so thought they all,
Than was Griselda, and of younger age,
And fairer fruit betwixt the two should fall,
And pleasing more, for her high lineage;
Her brother, too, so fair was of visage,
That, seeing them, the people all were glad,
Commending now the sense the marquis had.

"O storm-torn people! Unstable and untrue!
Aye indiscreet, and changing as a vane,
Delighting ever in rumour that is new,
For like the moon aye do you wax and wane;
Full of all chatter, dear at even a jane;
Your judgment's false, your constancy deceives,
A full great fool is he that you believes!"

Thus said the sober folk of that city,
Seeing the people staring up and down,
For they were glad, just for the novelty,
To have a young new lady of their town.
No more of this I'll mention or make known;
But to Griselda I'll myself address
To tell her constancy and busyness.

Full busy Griselda was in everything
That to the marquis' feast was pertinent;
Nothing was she confused by her clothing,
Though rude it was and somewhat badly rent.
But with a glad face to the gate she went,
With other folk, to greet the marchioness,
And afterward she did her busyness.

With so glad face his guests she did receive,
And with such tact, each one in his degree,
That no fault in it could a man perceive;

But all they wondered much who she might be
That in so poor array, as they could see,
Yet knew so much of rank and reverence;
And worthily they praised her high prudence.

In all this while she never once did cease
The maiden and her brother to commend
With kindness of a heart that was at peace,
So well that no man could her praise amend.
But at the last, when all these lords did wend
To seat themselves to dine, then did he call
Griselda, who was busy in his hall.

"Griselda," said he, as it were in play,
"How like you my new wife and her beauty?"
"Right well," said she, "my lord, for by my fay
A fairer saw I never than is she.
I pray that God give her prosperity;
And so I hope that to you both He'll send
Great happiness until your lives shall end.

"One thing I beg, my lord, and warn also,
That you prick not, with any tormenting,
This tender maid, as you've hurt others so;
For she's been nurtured in her up-bringing
More tenderly and, to my own thinking,
She could not such adversity endure
As could one reared in circumstances poor."

And when this Walter thought of her patience,
Her glad face, with no malice there at all,
And how so oft he'd done to her offence,
And she aye firm and constant as a wall,
Remaining ever blameless through it all,
This cruel marquis did his heart address
To pity for her wifely steadfastness.

"This is enough, Griselda mine!" cried he,
"Be now no more ill pleased nor more afraid;
I have your faith and your benignity,
As straitly as ever woman's was, assayed
In high place and in poverty arrayed.
Now know I well, dear wife, your steadfastness."
And he began to kiss her and to press.

And she, for wonder, took of this no keep;

She heard not what the thing was he had cried;
She fared as if she'd started out of sleep,
Till from bewilderment she roused her pride.
"Griselda," said he, "by our God Who died,
You are my wife, no other one I have,
Nor ever had, as God my soul may save!

"This is your daughter, whom you have supposed
Should be my wife; the other child truly
Shall be my heir, as I have aye purposed;
You bore him in your body faithfully.
I've kept them at Bologna secretly;
Take them again, for now you cannot say
That you have lost your children twain for aye.

"And folk that otherwise have said of me,
I warn them well that I have done this deed
Neither for malice nor for cruelty,
But to make trial in you of virtue hid,
And not to slay my children, God forbid!
But just to keep them privily and still
Till I your purpose knew and all your will."

When she heard this, she swooned and down did fall
For pitiful joy, and after her swooning
Both her young children to her did she call,
And in her arms, full piteously weeping,
Embraced them, and all tenderly kissing,
As any mother would, with many a tear
She bathed their faces and their sunny hair.

Oh, what a pitiful thing it was to see
Her swooning, and her humble voice to hear!
"Thanks, lord, that I may thank you now," said she,
"That you have saved to me my children dear!
Now I am ready for my death right here;
Since I stand in your love and in your grace,
Death matters not, nor what my soul may face!

"O young, O dear, O tender children mine,
Your woeful mother thought for long, truly,
That cruel hounds, or birds, or foul vermin
Had eaten you; but God, of His mercy,
And your good father, all so tenderly,
Have kept you safely." And in swoon profound

Suddenly there she fell upon the ground.

And in her swoon so forcefully held she
Her children two, whom she'd had in embrace,
That it was hard from her to set them free,
Her arms about them gently to unlace.
Oh, many a tear on many a pitying face
Ran down, of those were standing there beside;
Scarcely, for sympathy, could they abide.

But Walter cheered her till her sorrow fled;
And she rose up, abashed, out of her trance;
All praised her now, and joyous words they said,
Till she regained her wonted countenance.
Walter so honoured her by word and glance
That it was pleasing to observe the cheer
Between them, now again together here.

These ladies, when they found a tactful way,
Withdrew her and to her own room were gone,
And stripped her out of her so rude array,
And in a cloth of gold that brightly shone,
Crowned with a crown of many a precious stone
Upon her head, once more to hall they brought
Her, where they honoured her as all they ought.

Thus had this heavy day a happy end,
For everyone did everything he might
The day in mirth and revelry to spend
Till in the heavens shone the stars' fair light.
For far more grand in every person's sight
This feast was, and of greater cost, 'twas said,
Than were the revels when they two were wed.

Full many a year in high prosperity
They lived, these two, in harmony and rest,
And splendidly his daughter married he
Unto a lord, one of the worthiest
In Italy; and then in peace, as best
His wife's old father at his court he kept
Until the soul out of his body crept.

His son succeeded to his heritage
In rest and peace, after the marquis' day,
And wedded happily at proper age,
Albeit he tried his wife not, so they say.

This world is not so harsh, deny who may,
As in old times that now are long since gone,
And hearken what this author says thereon.

This story's told here, not that all wives should
Follow Griselda in humility,
For this would be unbearable, though they would,
But just that everyone, in his degree,
Should be as constant in adversity
As was Griselda; for that Petrarch wrote
This tale, and in a high style, as you'll note.

For since a woman once was so patient
Before a mortal man, well more we ought
Receive in good part that which God has sent;
For cause he has to prove what He has wrought.
But He tempts no man that His blood has bought,
As James says, if you his epistle read;
Yet does He prove folk at all times, indeed,

And suffers us, for our good exercise,
With the sharp scourges of adversity
To be well beaten oft, in sundry wise;
Not just to learn our will; for truly He,
Ere we were born, did all our frailty see;
But for our good is all that He doth give.
So then in virtuous patience let us live.[1]

But one word, masters, hearken ere I go:
One hardly can discover nowadays,
In all a town, Griseldas three or two;
For, if they should be put to such assays,
Their gold's so badly alloyed, in such ways,

---

1. It seems to have been Chaucer's intention, in the first instance, to end this Tale here. Hence, we find, in Mss. E. Hn. Cm. Dd., the following genuine, but rejected stanza, suitable for insertion at this point (a note of Walter W. Skeat)—

BEHOLD THE MERRY WORDS OF THE HOST

Now when this worthy clerk had told his tale,
'Our host remarked, and swore by God's own bones:
"I'd rather than receive a keg of ale
My wife at home had heard this legend once;
This is a noble story, for the nonce,
And to my purpose, if you knew my will;
But that which cannot be, let it lie still."

With brass, that though the coin delight the eye,
'Twill rather break in two than bend, say I.

But now, for love of the good wife of Bath,
Whose life and all whose sex may God maintain
In mastery high, or else it were but scathe,
I will with joyous spirit fresh and green
Sing you a song to gladden you, I ween;
From all such serious matters let's be gone;
Hearken my song, which runs in this way on:

ENVOY OF CHAUCER

Griselda's dead, and dead is her patience,
In Italy both lie buried, says the tale;
For which I cry in open audience,
That no man be so hardy as to assail
His own wife's patience, in a hope to find
Griselda, for 'tis certain he shall fail!

O noble wives, full of a high prudence,
Let not humility your free tongue nail,
Nor let some clerk have cause for diligence
To write of you, so marvelous detail
As of Griselda, patient and so kind;
Lest *Chichevache*[2] swallow you in her entrail!

Nay, follow Echo, that holds no silence,
But answers always like a countervail;
Be not befooled, for all your innocence,
But take the upper hand and you'll prevail.
And well impress this lesson on your mind,
For common profit, since it may avail.

Strong-minded women, stand at your defence,
Since you are strong as camel and don't ail,
Suffer no man to do to you offence;
And slender women in a contest frail,

---

2. Chichevache: a fabulous monster, in medieval satires, that fed on patient wives, and was therefore very lean. *Bicorne* was the contrasting monster that had grown fat from eating patient husbands.

Be savage as a tiger there in Ind;
Clatter like mill, say I, to beat the male.

Nay, fear them not, nor do them reverence;
For though your husband be all armed in mail,
The arrows of your shrewish eloquence
Shall pierce his breast and pierce his aventail.
In jealousy I counsel that you bind,
And you shall make him cower as does a quail.

If you are fair to see, in folks' presence,
Show them your face and with your clothes regale;
If you are foul, be lavish of expense,
To gain friends never cease to do travail;
Be lightsome as a linden leaf in wind,
And let him worry, weep and wring and wail!

HERE ENDS THE CLERK OF OXFORD'S TALE

THE MERCHANT'S PROLOGUE

"Of weeping and wailing, care and other sorrow
I know enough, at eventide and morrow,"
The merchant said, "and so do many more
Of married folk, I think, who this deplore,
For well I know that it is so with me.
I have a wife, the worst one that can be;
For though the foul Fiend to her wedded were,
She'd overmatch him, this I dare to swear.
How could I tell you anything special
Of her great malice? She is shrew in all.
There is a long and a large difference
Between Griselda's good and great patience
And my wife's more than common cruelty.
Were I unbound, as may I prosperous be!
I'd never another time fall in the snare.
We wedded men in sorrow live, and care;
Try it who will, and he shall truly find
I tell the truth, by Saint Thomas of Ind,
As for the greater part, I say not all.
Nay, God forbid that it should so befall!
    "Ah, good sir host! I have been married, lad,
These past two months, and no day more, by gad;
And yet I think that he whose days alive
Have been all wifeless, although men should rive
Him to the heart, he could in no wise clear
Tell you so much of sorrow as I here
Could tell you of my spouse's cursedness."
    "Now," said our host, "merchant, so God you bless,
Since you're so very learned in that art,
Full heartily, I pray you, tell us part."
    "Gladly," said he, "but of my own fresh sore,
For grief of heart I may not tell you more."

THE MERCHANT'S TALE

Once on a time there dwelt in Lombardy
One born in Pavia, a knight worthy,
And there he lived in great prosperity;
And sixty years a wifeless man was he,
And followed ever his bodily delight
In women, whereof was his appetite,
As these fool laymen will, so it appears.
And when he had so passed his sixty years,
Were it for piety or for dotage
I cannot say, but such a rapturous rage
Had this knight to become a wedded man
That day and night he did his best to scan
And spy a place where he might wedded be;
Praying Our Lord to grant to him that he
Might once know something of that blissful life
That is between a husband and his wife;
And so to live within that holy band
Wherein God first made man and woman stand.
"No other life," said he, "is worth a bean;
For wedlock is so easy and so clean
That in this world it is a paradise."
Thus said this ancient knight, who was so wise.

      And certainly, as sure as God is King,
To take a wife, it is a glorious thing,
Especially when a man is old and hoary;
Then is a wife the fruit of wealth and glory.
Then should he take a young wife and a fair,
On whom he may beget himself an heir,
And lead his life in joy and in solace,
Whereas these bachelors do but sing "Alas!"
When they fall into some adversity
In love, which is but childish vanity.
And truly, it is well that it is so
That bachelors have often pain and woe;
On shifting ground they build, and shiftiness
They find when they suppose they've certainness.
They live but as a bird does, or a beast,
In liberty and under no arrest,
Whereas a wedded man in his high state
Lives a life blissful, ordered, moderate,
Under the yoke of happy marriage bound;

Well may his heart in joy and bliss abound.
For who can be so docile as a wife?
Who is so true as she whose aim in life
Is comfort for him, sick or well, to make?
For weal or woe she will not him forsake.
She's ne'er too tired to love and serve, say I,
Though he may lie bedridden till he die.
And yet some writers say it is not so,
And Theophrastus is one such, I know.
What odds though Theophrastus chose to lie?
"Take not a wife," said he, "for husbandry,
If you would spare in household your expense;
A faithful servant does more diligence
To keep your goods than your own wedded wife.
For she will claim a half part all her life;
And if you should be sick, so God me save,
Your true friends or an honest serving knave
Will keep you better than she that waits, I say,
After your wealth, and has done, many a day.
And if you take a wife to have and hold,
Right easily may you become cuckold."
This judgment and a hundred such things worse
Did this man write, may God his dead bones curse!
But take no heed of all such vanity.
Defy old Theophrastus and hear me.

   A wife is God's own gift, aye verily;
All other kinds of gifts, most certainly,
As lands, rents, pasture, rights in common land,
Or moveables, in gift of Fortune stand,
And pass away like shadows on the wall.
But, without doubt, if plainly speak I shall,
A wife will last, and in your house endure
Longer than you would like, peradventure.

   But marriage is a solemn sacrament;
Who has no wife I hold on ruin bent;
He lives in helplessness, all desolate,
I speak of folk in secular estate.
And hearken why, I say not this for naught:
It's because woman was for man's help wrought.
The High God, when He'd Adam made, all rude,
And saw him so alone and belly-nude,
God of His goodness thus to speak began:
"Let us now make a help meet for this man,

Like to himself." And then he made him Eve.
Here may you see, and here prove, I believe,
A wife is a man's help and his comfort,
His earthly paradise and means of sport;
So docile and so virtuous is she
That they must needs live in all harmony.
One flesh they are, and one flesh, as I guess,
Has but one heart in weal and in distress.

A wife! Ah, Holy Mary, *ben'cite!*
How may a man have any adversity
Who has a wife? Truly, I cannot say.
The bliss that is between such two, for aye,
No tongue can tell, nor any heart can think.
If he be poor, why, she helps him to swink;
She keeps his money and never wastes a deal;
All that her husband wishes she likes well;
She never once says "nay" when he says "yea."
"Do this," says he; "All ready, sir," she'll say.
O blissful state of wedlock, prized and dear,
So pleasant and so full of virtue clear,
So much approved and praised as fortune's peak,
That every man who holds him worth a leek
Upon his bare knees ought, through all his life,
To give God thanks, Who's sent to him a wife;
Or else he should pray God that He will send
A wife to him, to last till his life's end.
For then his life is set in certainness;
He cannot be deceived, as I may guess,
So that he act according as she's said;
Then may he boldly carry high his head,
They are so true and therewithal so wise;
Wherefore, if you will do as do the wise,
Then aye as women counsel be your deed.

Lo, how young Jacob, as these clerics read,
About his hairless neck a kid's skin bound,
A trick that Dame Rebecca for him found,
By which his father's benison he won.

Lo, Judith, as the ancient stories run,
By her wise counsel she God's people kept,
And Holofernes slew, while yet he slept.

Lo, Abigail, by good advice how she
Did save her husband, Nabal, when that he
Should have been slain; and lo, Esther also

By good advice delivered out of woe
The people of God and got him, Mordecai,
By King Ahasuerus lifted high.

   There is no pleasure so superlative
(Says Seneca) as a humble wife can give.

   Suffer your wife's tongue, Cato bids, as fit;
She shall command, and you shall suffer it;
And yet she will obey, of courtesy.
A wife is keeper of your husbandry;
Well may the sick man wail and even weep
Who has no wife the house to clean and keep.
I warn you now, if wisely you would work,
Love well your wife, as Jesus loves His Kirk.
For if you love yourself, you love your wife;
No man hates his own flesh, but through his life
He fosters it, and so I bid you strive
To cherish her, or you shall never thrive.
Husband and wife, despite men's jape or play,
Of all the world's folk hold the safest way;
They are so knit there may no harm betide,
Especially upon the good wife's side.
For which this January, of whom I told,
Did well consider, in his days grown old,
The pleasant life, the virtuous rest complete
That are in marriage, always honey-sweet;
And for his friends upon a day he sent
To tell them the effect of his intent.

   With sober face his tale to them he's told;
He said to them: "My friends, I'm hoar and old,
And almost, God knows, come to my grave's brink;
About my soul, now, somewhat must I think.
I have my body foolishly expended;
Blessed be God, that thing shall be amended!
For I will be, truly, a wedded man,
And that anon, in all the haste I can,
Unto some maiden young in age and fair.
I pray you for my marriage all prepare,
And do so now, for I will not abide;
And I will try to find one, on my side,
To whom I may be wedded speedily.
But for as much as you are more than I,
It's better that you have the thing in mind
And try a proper mate for me to find.

"But of one thing I warn you, my friends dear,
I will not have an old wife coming here.
She shan't have more than twenty years, that's plain;
Of old fish and young flesh I am full fain.
Better," said he, "a pike than pickerel;
And better than old beef is tender veal.
I'll have no woman thirty years of age,
It is but bean-straw and such rough forage.
And these old widows, God knows that, afloat,
They know so much of spells when on Wade's[1] boat,
And do such petty harm, when they think best,
That with one should I never live at rest.
For several schools can make men clever clerks;
Woman in many schools learns clever works.
But certainly a young thing men may guide,
Just as warm wax may with one's hands be plied.
Wherefore I tell you plainly, in a clause,
I will not have an old wife, for that cause.
For if it chanced I made that sad mistake
And never in her could my pleasure take,
My life I'd lead then in adultery
And go straight to the devil when I die.
No children should I then on her beget;
Yet would I rather hounds my flesh should fret
Than that my heritage descend and fall
Into strange hands, and this I tell you all.
I dote not, and I know the reason why
A man should marry, and furthermore know I
There speaks full many a man of all marriage
Who knows no more of it than knows my page,
Nor for what reasons man should take a wife.
If one may not live chastely all his life,
Let him take wife whose quality he's known
For lawful procreation of his own
Blood children, to the honour of God above,
And not alone for passion or for love;
And because lechery they should eschew
And do their family duty when it's due;
Or because each of them should help the other
In trouble, as a sister shall a brother;

---

1. Wade: in Teutonic mythology, a giant, regarded as a storm or sea demon. On his ship he could pass from place to place instantaneously.

And live in chastity full decently.
But, sirs, and by your leave, that is not I.
For, God be thanked, I dare to make a vaunt,
I feel my limbs are strong and fit to jaunt
In doing all man's are expected to;
I know myself and know what I can do.
Though I am hoar, I fare as does a tree
That blossoms ere the fruit be grown; you see
A blooming tree is neither dry nor dead.
And I feel nowhere hoary but on head;
My heart and all my limbs are still as green
As laurel through the year is to be seen.
And now that you have heard all my intent,
I pray that to my wish you will assent."

Then divers men to him diversely told,
Of marriage, many an instance known of old.
Some blamed it and some praised it, that's certain,
But at the last, and briefly to make plain,
Since altercation follows soon or late
When friends begin such matters to debate,
There fell a strife between his brothers two,
Whereof the name of one was Placebo
And verily Justinus was that other.

Placebo said: "O January, brother,
Full little need had you, my lord so dear,
Counsel to ask of anyone that's here;
Save that you are so full of sapience
That you like not, what of your high prudence,
To vary from the word of Solomon.
This word said he to each and every one:
'Do everything by counsel,' thus said he,
'And then thou hast no cause to repent thee.'
But although Solomon spoke such a word,
My own dear brother and my proper lord,
So truly may God bring my soul to rest
As I hold your own counsel is the best.
For, brother mine, of me take this one word,
I've been a courtier all my days, my lord.
And God knows well, though I unworthy be,
I have stood well, and in full great degree,
With many lords of very high estate;
Yet ne'er with one of them had I debate.
I never contradicted, certainly;

I know well that my lord knows more than I.
Whate'er he says, I hold it firm and stable;
I say the same, or nearly as I'm able.
A full great fool is any councillor
That serves a lord of any high honour
And dares presume to say, or else think it,
His counsel can surpass his lordship's wit.
Nay, lords are never fools, nay, by my fay;
You have yourself, sir, showed, and here today,
With such good sense and piety withal
That I assent to and confirm it all,
The words and the opinions you have shown.
By God, there is no man in all this town,
Or Italy, it better could have phrased;
And Christ Himself your counsel would have praised.
And truthfully, it argues high courage
In any man that is advanced in age
To take a young wife; by my father's kin,
A merry heart you've got beneath your skin!
Do in this matter at your own behest,
For, finally, I hold that for the best."
 Justinus, who sat still and calm, and heard,
Right in this wise Placebo he answered:
"Now, brother mine, be patient, so I pray;
Since you have spoken, hear what I shall say.
For Seneca, among his words so wise,
Says that a man ought well himself advise
To whom he'll give his chattels or his land.
And since I ought to know just where I stand
Before I give my wealth away from me,
How much more well advised I ought to be
To whom I give my body; for alway
I warn you well, that it is not child's play
To take a wife without much advisement.
Men must inquire, and this is my intent,
Whether she's wise, or sober, or drunkard,
Or proud, or else in other things froward,
Or shrewish, or a waster of what's had,
Or rich, or poor, or whether she's man-mad.
And be it true that no man finds, or shall,
One in this world that perfect is in all,
Of man or beast, such as men could devise;
Nevertheless, it ought enough suffice

With any wife, if so were that she had
More traits of virtue than her vices bad;
And all this leisure asks to see and hear.
For God knows I have wept full many a tear
In privity, since I have had a wife.
Praise whoso will a wedded man's good life,
Truly I find in it but cost and care
And many duties, of all blisses bare.
And yet, God knows, my neighbours round about,
Especially the women, many a rout,
Say that I've married the most steadfast wife,
Aye, and the meekest one there is in life.
But I know best where pinches me my shoe.
You may, for me, do as you please to do;
But take good heed, since you're a man of age,
How you shall enter into a marriage,
Especially with a young wife and a fair.
By Him Who made the water, earth, and air,
The youngest man there is in all this rout
Is busy enough to bring the thing about
That he alone shall have his wife, trust me.
You'll not be able to please her through years three,
That is to say, to give all she desires.
A wife attention all the while requires.
I pray you that you be not offended."

    "Well?" asked this January, "And have you said?
A straw for Seneca and your proverbs!
I value not a basketful of herbs
Your schoolmen's terms; for wiser men than you,
As you have heard, assent and bid me do
My purpose now. Placebo, what say ye?"

    "I say it is a wicked man," said he,
"That hinders matrimony, certainly."

    And with that word they rose up, suddenly,
Having assented fully that he should
Be wedded when he pleased and where he would.

    Imagination and his eagerness
Did in the soul of January press
As he considered marriage for a space.
Many fair shapes and many a lovely face
Passed through his amorous fancy, night by night.
As who might take a mirror polished bright
And set it in the common market-place

And then should see full many a figure pace
Within the mirror; just in that same wise
Did January within his thought surmise
Of maidens whom he dwelt in town beside.
He knew not where his fancy might abide.
For if the one have beauty of her face,
Another stands so in the people's grace
For soberness and for benignity,
That all the people's choice she seems to be;
And some were rich and had an evil name.
Nevertheless, half earnest, half in game,
He fixed at last upon a certain one
And let all others from his heart be gone,
And chose her on his own authority;
For love is always blind and cannot see.
And when in bed at night, why then he wrought
To portray, in his heart and in his thought,
Her beauty fresh and her young age, so tender,
Her middle small, her two arms long and slender,
Her management full wise, her gentleness,
Her womanly bearing, and her seriousness.
And when to her at last his choice descended,
He thought that choice might never be amended.
For when he had concluded thus, egad,
He thought that other men had wits so bad
It were impossible to make reply
Against his choice, this was his fantasy.
His friends he sent to, at his own instance,
And prayed them give him, in this wise, pleasance,
That speedily they would set forth and come:
He would abridge their labour, all and some.
He need not more to walk about or ride,
For he'd determined where he would abide.

Placebo came, and all his friends came soon,
And first of all he asked of them the boon
That none of them an argument should make
Against the course he fully meant to take;
"Which purpose pleasing is to God," said he,
"And the true ground of my felicity."

He said there was a maiden in the town
Who had for beauty come to great renown,
Despite the fact she was of small degree;
Sufficed him well her youth and her beauty.

Which maid, he said, he wanted for his wife,
To lead in ease and decency his life.
And he thanked God that he might have her, all,
That none partook of his bliss now, nor shall.
And prayed them all to labour in this need
And so arrange that he'd fail not, indeed;
For then, he said, his soul should be at ease.

"And then," said he, "there's naught can me displease,
Save one lone thing that sticks in my conscience,
The which I will recite in your presence.

"I have," said he, "heard said, and long ago,
There may no man have perfect blisses two,
That is to say, on earth and then in Heaven.
For though he keep from sins the deadly seven,
And, too, from every branch of that same tree,
Yet is there so complete felicity
And such great pleasure in the married state
That I am fearful, since it comes so late,
That I shall lead so merry and fine a life,
And so delicious, without woe and strife,
That I shall have my heaven on earth here.
For since that other Heaven is bought so dear,
With tribulation and with great penance,
How should I then, who live in such pleasance,
As all these wedded men do with their wives,
Come to the bliss where Christ Eternal lives?
This is my fear, and you, my brothers, pray
Resolve for me this problem now, I say."

Justinus, who so hated this folly,
Answered anon in jesting wise and free;
And since he would his longish tale abridge,
He would no old authority allege,
But said: "Sir, so there is no obstacle
Other than this, God, of high miracle
And of His mercy, may so for you work
That, ere you have your right of Holy Kirk,
You'll change your mind on wedded husband's life,
Wherein you say there is no woe or strife.
And otherwise, God grant that there be sent
To wedded man the fair grace to repent
Often, and sooner than a single man!
And therefore, sir, this is the best I can:
Despair not, but retain in memory,

Perhaps she may your purgatory be!
She may be God's tool, she may be God's whip;
Then shall your spirit up to Heaven skip
Swifter than does an arrow from the bow!
I hope to God, hereafter you shall know
That there is none so great felicity
In marriage, no nor ever shall there be,
To keep you from salvation that's your own,
So that you use, with reason that's well known,
The charms of your wife's body temperately,
And that you please her not too amorously,
And that you keep as well from other sin.
My tale is done now, for my wit is thin.
Be not deterred hereby, my brother dear" —
   (But let us pass quite over what's said here.
The wife of Bath, if you have understood,
Has treated marriage, in its likelihood,
And spoken well of it in little space) —
"Fare you well now, God have you in His grace."
   And with that word this Justin and his brother
Did take their leave, and each of them from other.
For when they all saw that it must needs be,
They so arranged, by sly and wise treaty,
That she, this maiden, who was Maia hight,
As speedily indeed as ever she might,
Should wedded be unto this January.
I think it were too long a time to tarry
To tell of deed and bond between them, and
The way she was enfeoffed of all his land;
Or to hear tell of all her rich array.
But finally was come the happy day
When to the church together they two went,
There to receive the holy sacrament.
Forth came the priest with stole about his neck,
Saying of Rebecca and Sarah she should reck
For wisdom and for truth in her marriage;
And said his orisons, as is usage,
And crossed them, praying God that He should bless,
And made all tight enough with holiness.
   Thus are they wedded with solemnity,
And at the feast are sitting, he and she,
With other worthy folk upon the dais.
All full of joy and bliss the palace gay is,

And full of instruments and viandry,
The daintiest in all of Italy.
Before them played such instruments anon
That Orpheus or Theban Amphion
Never in life made such a melody.
　With every course there rose loud minstrelsy,
And never Joab sounded trump, to hear,
Nor did Theodomas, one half so clear
At Thebes, while yet the city hung in doubt.
Bacchus the wine poured out for all about,
And Venus gaily laughed for every wight.
For January had become her knight,
And would make trial of his amorous power
In liberty and in the bridal bower;
And with her firebrand in her hand, about
Danced she before the bride and all the rout.
And certainly I dare right well say this,
That Hymenaeus, god of wedded bliss,
Ne'er saw in life so merry a married man.
Hold thou thy peace, thou poet Marcian
Who tellest how Philology was wed
And how with Mercury she went to bed,
And of the sweet songs by the Muses sung.
Too slight are both thy pen and thy thin tongue.
To show aright this wedding on thy page.
When tender youth has wedded stooping age,
There is such mirth that no one may it show;
Try it yourself, and then you well will know
Whether I lie or not in matters here.
　Maia, she sat there with so gentle cheer,
To look at her it seemed like faëry;
Queen Esther never looked with such an eye
Upon Ahasuerus, so meek was she.
I can't describe to you all her beauty;
But thus much of her beauty I can say,
That she was like the brightening morn of May,
Fulfilled of beauty and of all pleasance.
　January was rapt into a trance
With each time that he looked upon her face;
And in his heart her beauty he'd embrace,
And threatened in his arms to hold her tight,
Harder than Paris Helen did, that night.
But nonetheless great pity, too, had he

Because that night she must deflowered be;
And thought: "Alas! O tender young creature!
Now would God you may easily endure
All my desire, it is so sharp and keen.
I fear you can't sustain it long, my queen.
But God forbid that I do all I might!
And now would God that it were come to night,
And that the night would last for ever—oh,
I wish these people would arise and go."
And at the last he laboured all in all,
As best he might for manners there in hall,
To haste them from the feast in subtle wise.

    Time came when it was right that they should rise;
And after that men danced and drank right fast,
And spices all about the house they cast;
And full of bliss and joy was every man,
All but a squire, a youth called Damian,
Who'd carved before the knight full many a day.
He was so ravished by his Lady May
That for the very pain, as madman would,
Almost he fell down fainting where he stood.
So sore had Venus hurt him with her brand,
When she went dancing, bearing it in hand.
And to his bed he took him speedily;
No more of him just at this time say I.
I'll let him weep his fill, with woe complain,
Until fresh May have ruth upon his pain.

    O parlous fire that in the bedstraw breeds!
O foe familiar that his service speeds!
O treacherous servant, false domestic who
Is most like adder in bosom, sly, untrue,
God shield us all from knowing aught of you!
O January, drunk of pleasure's brew
In marriage, see how now your Damian,
Your own trained personal squire, born your man,
Wishes and means to do you villainy.
God grant that on this household foe you'll spy!
For in this world no pestilence is worse
Than foe domestic, constantly a curse.

    When traversed has the sun his arc of day,
No longer may the body of him stay
On the horizon, in that latitude.
Night with his mantle, which is dark and rude,

Did overspread the hemisphere about;
And so departed had this joyous rout
From January, with thanks on every side.
Home to their houses happily they ride,
Whereat they do what things may please them best,
And when they see the time come, go to rest.
Soon after that this hasty January
Would go to bed, he would no longer tarry.
He drank of claret, hippocras, vernage,
All spiced and hot to heighten his love's rage;
And many an aphrodisiac, full and fine,
Such as the wicked monk, Dan Constantine,
Has written in his book *De Coitu*;
Not one of all of them he did eschew.
And to his friends most intimate, said he:
"For God's love, and as soon as it may be,
Let all now leave this house in courteous wise."
And all they rose, just as he bade them rise.
They drank good-night, and curtains drew anon;
The bride was brought to bed, as still as stone;
And when the bed had been by priest well blessed,
Out of the chamber everyone progressed.
And January lay down close beside
His fresh young May, his paradise, his bride.
He soothed her, and he kissed her much and oft,
With the thick bristles of his beard, not soft,
But sharp as briars, like a dogfish skin,
For he'd been badly shaved ere he came in.
He stroked and rubbed her on her tender face,
And said: "Alas! I fear I'll do trespass
Against you here, my spouse, and much offend
Before the time when I will down descend.
But nonetheless, consider this," said he,
"There is no workman, whosoe'er he be,
That may work well, if he works hastily;
This will be done at leisure, perfectly.
It makes no difference how long we two play;
For in true wedlock were we tied today;
And blessed be the yoke that we are in,
For in our acts, now, we can do no sin.
A man can do no sin with his own wife,
Nor can he hurt himself with his own knife;
For we have leave most lawfully to play."

Thus laboured he till came the dawn of day;
And then he took in wine a sop of bread,
And upright sat within the marriage bed,
And after that he sang full loud and clear
And kissed his wife and made much wanton cheer.
He was all coltish, full of venery,
And full of chatter as a speckled pie.
The slackened skin about his neck did shake
The while he sang and chanted like a crake.
But God knows what thing May thought in her heart
When up she saw him sitting in his shirt,
In his nightcap, and with his neck so lean;
She valued not his playing worth a bean.
Then said he thus: "My rest now will I take;
Now day is come, I can no longer wake."
And down he laid his head and slept till prime.
And afterward, when saw he it was time,
Up rose this January; but fresh May,
She kept her chamber until the fourth day,
As custom is of wives, and for the best.
For every worker sometime must have rest,
Or else for long he'll certainly not thrive,
That is to say, no creature that's alive,
Be it of fish, or bird, or beast, or man.
    Now will I speak of woeful Damian,
Who languished for his love, as you shall hear;
I thus address him in this fashion here.
I say: "O hapless Damian, alas!
Answer to my demand in this your case,
How shall you to your lady, lovely May,
Tell all your woe? She would of course say 'Nay.'
And if you speak, she will your state betray;
God be your help! I can no better say."
    This lovesick Damian in Venus' fire
So burned, he almost perished for desire;
Which put his life in danger, I am sure;
Longer in this wise could he not endure;
But privily a pen-case did he borrow
And in a letter wrote he all his sorrow,
In form of a complaint or of a lay,
Unto his fair and blooming Lady May.
And in a purse of silk hung in his shirt,
He put the poem and laid it next his heart.

The moon, which was at noon of that same day
Whereon this January wedded May
Half way through Taurus, had to Cancer glided,
So long had Maia in her chamber bided.
As is the custom among nobles all.
A bride shall not eat in the common hall
Until four days, or three days at the least,
Have fully passed; then let her go to feast.
On the fourth day, complete from noon to noon,
After the high Mass had been said and done,
In hall did January sit with May
As fresh as is the fair bright summer day.
And so befell it there that this good man
Recalled to mind his squire, this Damian,
And said: "Why holy Mary! How can it be
That Damian attends not here on me?
Is he sick always? How may this betide?"
His other squires, who waited there beside,
Made the excuse that he indeed was ill,
Which kept him from his proper duties still;
There was no other cause could make him tarry.
"That is a pity," said this January,
"He is a gentle squire, aye, by my truth!
If he should die, it were great harm and ruth;
As wise and secret, and discreet is he
As any man I know of his degree;
Therewith he's manly and he's serviceable,
And to become a useful man right able.
But after meat, as soon as ever I may,
I will myself go visit him, with May,
To give him all the comfort that I can."
And for that word they blessed him, every man,
Because, for goodness and his gentleness,
He would so go to comfort, in sickness,
His suffering squire, for 'twas a gentle deed.
"Dame," said this January, "take good heed
That after meat, you, with your women all,
When you have gone to chamber from this hall,—
That all you go to see this Damian;
Cheer him a bit, for he's a gentleman;
And tell him that I'll come to visit him
After I've rested—a short interim;
And get this over quickly, for I'll bide

Awake until you sleep there at my side."
    And with that word he raised his voice to call
A squire, who served as marshal of his hall,
And certain things he wished arranged were told.
    This lovely May then did her straight way hold,
With all her women, unto Damian.
Down by his bed she sat, and so began
To comfort him with kindly word and glance.
This Damian, when once he'd found his chance,
In secret wise his purse and letter, too,
Wherein he'd said what he aspired to,
He put into her hand, with nothing more,
Save that he heaved a sigh both deep and sore,
And softly to her in this wise said he:
"Oh, mercy! Don't, I beg you, tell on me;
For I'm but dead if this thing be made known."
This purse she hid in bosom of her gown
And went her way; you get no more of me.
But unto January then came she,
Who on his bedside sat in mood full soft.
He took her in his arms and kissed her oft,
And laid him down to sleep, and that anon.
And she pretended that she must be gone
Where you know well that everyone has need.
And when she of this note had taken heed,
She tore it all to fragments at the last
And down the privy quietly it cast.
    Who's in brown study now but fair fresh May?
Down by old January's side she lay,
Who slept, until the cough awakened him;
He prayed her strip all naked for his whim;
He would have pleasure of her, so he said,
And clothes were an encumbrance when in bed,
And she obeyed him, whether lief or loath.
But lest these precious folk be with me wroth,
How there he worked, I dare not to you tell;
Nor whether she thought it paradise or hell;
But there I leave them working in their wise
Till vespers rang and they must needs arise.
    Were it by destiny or merely chance,
By nature or some other circumstance,
Or constellation's sign, that in such state
The heavens stood, the time was fortunate

To make request concerning Venus' works
(For there's a time for all things, say these clerks)
To any woman, to procure her love,
I cannot say; but the great God above,
Who knows there's no effect without a cause,
He may judge all, for here my voice withdraws.
But true it is that this fair blooming May
Was so affected and impressed that day
For pity of this lovesick Damian,
That from her heart she could not drive or ban
Remembrance of her wish to give him ease.
"Certainly," thought she, "whom this may displease
I do not care, for I'd assure him now
Him with my love I'd willingly endow,
Though he'd no more of riches than his shirt."
Lo, pity soon wells up in gentle heart.
    Here may you see what generosity
In women is when they advise closely.
Perhaps some tyrant (for there's many a one)
Who has a heart as hard as any stone,
Would well have let him die within that place
Much rather than have granted him her grace;
And such would have rejoiced in cruel pride,
Nor cared that she were thus a homicide.
    This gentle May, fulfilled of all pity,
With her own hand a letter then wrote she
In which she granted him her utmost grace;
There was naught lacking now, save time and place
Wherein she might suffice to ease his lust:
For all should be as he would have it, just.
And when she'd opportunity on a day,
To visit Damian went this lovely May,
And cleverly this letter she thrust close
Under his pillow, read it if he chose.
She took him by the hand and hard did press,
So secretly that no one else could guess,
And bade him gain his health, and forth she went
To January, when for her he sent.
    Up rose this Damian upon the morrow,
For gone was all his sickness and his sorrow.
He combed himself and preened his feathers smooth,
He did all that his lady liked, in sooth;
And then to January went as low

As ever did a hound trained to the bow.
He was so pleasant unto every man
(For craft is everything for those who can),
That everyone was fain to speak his good;
And fully in his lady's grace he stood.
Thus Damian I leave about his need
And forward in my tale I will proceed.

Some writers hold that all felicity
Stands in delight, and therefor, certainly,
This noble January, with all his might,
Honourably, as does befit a knight,
Arranged affairs to live deliciously.
His housing, his array, as splendidly
Befitted his condition as a king's.
Among the rest of his luxurious things
He built a garden walled about with stone;
So fair a garden do I know of none.
For, without doubt, I verily suppose
That he who wrote *The Romance of the Rose*
Could not its beauty say in singing wise;
Nor could Priapus' power quite suffice,
Though he is god of gardens all, to tell
The beauty of that garden, and the well
Which was beneath the laurel always green.
For oftentimes God Pluto and his queen,
Fair Proserpine and all her faëry
Disported there and made sweet melody
About that well, and danced there, as men told.

This noble knight, this January old,
Such pleasure had therein to walk and play,
That none he'd suffer bear the key, they say,
Save he himself; for of the little wicket
He carried always the small silver clicket
With which, as pleased him, he'd unlock the gate.
And when he chose to pay court to his mate
In summer season, thither would he go
With May, his wife, and no one but they two;
And divers things that were not done abed,
Within that garden there were done, 'tis said.
And in this manner many a merry day
Lived this old January and young May.
But worldly pleasure cannot always stay,
And January's joy must pass away.

O sudden chance, O Fortune, thou unstable,
Like to the scorpion so deceptive, able
To flatter with thy mouth when thou wilt sting;
Thy tail is death, through thine envenoming.
O fragile joy! O poison sweetly taint!
O monster that so cleverly canst paint
Thy gifts in all the hues of steadfastness
That thou deceivest both the great and less!
Why hast thou January thus deceived,
That had'st him for thine own full friend received?
And now thou hast bereft him of his eyes,
For sorrow of which in love he daily dies.

    Alas! This noble January free,
In all his pleasure and prosperity,
Is fallen blind, and that all suddenly.
He wept and he lamented, pitifully;
And therewithal the fire of jealousy
Lest that his wife should fall to some folly,
So burned within his heart that he would fain
Both him and her some man had swiftly slain.
For neither after death nor in his life
Would he that she were other's love or wife,
But dress in black and live in widow's state,
Lone as the turtle-dove that's lost her mate.
But finally, after a month or twain,
His grief somewhat abated, to speak plain;
For when he knew it might not elsewise be,
He took in patience his adversity,
Save, doubtless, he could not renounce, as done,
His jealousy, from which he never won.
For this his passion was so outrageous
That neither in his hall nor other house
Nor any other place, not ever, no,
He suffered her to ride or walking go,
Unless he had his hand on her alway;
For which did often weep this fresh young May,
Who loved her Damian so tenderly
That she must either swiftly die or she
Must have him as she willed, her thirst to slake;
Biding her time, she thought her heart would break.

    And on the other side this Damian
Was now become the most disconsolate man
That ever was; for neither night nor day

Might he so much as speak a word to May
Of his desire, as I am telling here,
Save it were said to January's ear,
Who never took his blind hand off her, no.
Nevertheless, by writing to and fro
And secret signals, he knew what she meant;
And she too knew the aim of his intent.

 O January, what might it now avail
Could your eyes see as far as ships can sail?
For it's as pleasant, blind, deceived to be
As be deceived while yet a man may see.
Lo, Argus, who was called the hundred-eyed,
No matter how he peered and watched and pried,
He was deceived; and God knows others too
Who think, and firmly, that it is not so.
Oblivion is peace; I say no more.

 This lovely May, of whom I spoke before,
In warm wax made impression of the key
Her husband carried, to the gate where he
In entering his garden often went.
And Damian, who knew all her intent,
The key did counterfeit, and privately;
There is no more to say, but speedily
Some mischief of this latch-key shall betide,
Which you shall hear, if you but time will bide.

 O noble Ovid, truth you say, God wot!
What art is there, though it be long and hot,
But Love will find it somehow suits his turn?
By Pyramus and Thisbe may men learn;
Though they were strictly kept apart in all,
They soon accorded, whispering through a wall,
Where none could have suspected any gate.
But now to purpose: ere had passed days eight,
And ere the first day of July, befell
That January was under such a spell,
Through egging of his wife, to go and play
Within his garden, and no one but they,
That on a morning to this May said he:
"Rise up, my wife, my love, my lady free;
The turtle's voice is heard, my dove so sweet;
The winter's past, the rain's gone, and the sleet;
Come forth now with your two eyes columbine!
How sweeter are your breasts than is sweet wine!

The garden is enclosed and walled about;
Come forth, my white spouse, for beyond all doubt
You have me ravished in my heart, O wife!
No fault have I found in you in my life.
Come forth, come forth, and let us take our sport;
I chose you for my wife and my comfort."
    Such were the lewd old words that then used he;
To Damian a secret sign made she
That he should go before them with his clicket;
This Damian then opened up the wicket,
And in he slipped, and that in manner such
That none could see nor hear; and he did crouch
And still he sat beneath a bush anon.
    This January, blind as is a stone,
With Maia's hand in his, and none else there,
Into his garden went, so fresh and fair,
And then clapped to the wicket suddenly.
    "Now, wife," said he, "here's none but you and I,
And you're the one of all that I best love.
For by that Lord Who sits in Heaven above,
Far rather would I die upon a knife
Than do offence to you, my true, dear wife!
For God's sake think how I did choose you out,
And for no love of money, beyond doubt,
But only for the love you roused in me.
And though I am grown old and cannot see,
Be true to me, and I will tell you why.
Three things, it's certain, shall you gain thereby;
First, Christ's dear love, and honour of your own,
And all my heritage of tower and town;
I give it you, draw deeds to please you, pet;
This shall be done tomorrow ere sunset.
So truly may God bring my soul to bliss,
I pray you first, in covenant, that we kiss.
And though I'm jealous, yet reproach me not.
You are so deeply printed in my thought
That, when I do consider your beauty
And therewith all the unlovely age of me,
I cannot, truly, nay, though I should die,
Abstain from being in your company,
For utter love; of this there is no doubt.
Now kiss me, wife, and let us walk about."
    This blooming May, when these words she had heard,

Graciously January she answered,
But first and foremost she began to weep.
"I have also," said she, "a soul to keep,
As well as you, and also honour mine,
And of my wifehood that sweet flower divine
Which I assured you of, both safe and sound,
When unto you that priest my body bound;
Wherefore I'll answer you in this manner,
If I may by your leave, my lord so dear.
I pray to God that never dawns the day
That I'll not die, foully as woman may,
If ever I do unto my kin such shame,
And likewise damage so my own fair name,
As to be false; and if I grow so slack,
Strip me and put me naked in a sack
And in the nearest river let me drown.
I am a lady, not a wench of town.
Why speak you thus? Men ever are untrue,
And woman have reproaches always new.
No reason or excuse have you, I think,
And so you harp on women who hoodwink."

And with that word she saw where Damian
Sat under bush; to cough then she began,
And with her slender finger signs made she
That Damian should climb into a tree
That burdened was with fruit, and up he went;
For verily he knew her full intent,
And understood each sign that she could make,
Better than January, her old rake.
For in a letter she had told him all
Of how he should proceed when time should fall.
And thus I leave him in the pear-tree still
While May and January roam at will.

Bright was the day and blue the firmament,
Phoebus his golden streamers down has sent
To gladden every flower with his warmness.
He was that time in Gemini, I guess,
And but a little from his declination
Of Cancer, which is great Jove's exaltation.
And so befell, in that bright morning-tide,
That in this garden, on the farther side,
Pluto, who is the king of Faëry,
With many a lady in his company,

Following his wife, the fair Queen Proserpine,
Each after other, straight as any line
(While she was gathering flowers on a mead,
In Claudian you may the story read
How in his grim car he had stolen her)—
This king of Faëry sat down yonder
Upon a turfen bank all fresh and green,
And right anon thus said he to his queen.

  "My wife," said he, "there may no one say nay;
Experience proves fully every day
The treason that these women do to man.
Ten hundred thousand stories tell I can
To show your fickleness and lies. Of which,
O Solomon wise, and richest of the rich,
Fulfilled of sapience and worldly glory,
Well worth remembrance are thy words and story
By everyone who's wit, and reason can.
Thus goodness he expounds with praise of man:
'Among a thousand men yet found I one,
But of all women living found I none.'

  "Thus spoke the king that knew your wickedness;
And Jesus son of Sirach, as I guess,
Spoke of you seldom with much reverence.
A wild-fire and a rotten pestilence
Fall on your bodies all before tonight!
Do you not see this honourable knight,
Because, alas! he is both blind and old,
His own sworn man shall make him a cuckold;
Lo, there he sits, the lecher, in that tree.
Now will I grant, of my high majesty,
Unto this old and blind and worthy knight,
That he shall have again his two eyes' sight,
Just when his wife shall do him villainy;
Then shall he know of all her harlotry,
Both in reproach to her and others too."

  "You shall," said Proserpine, "if will you so;
Now by my mother's father's soul, I swear
That I will give her adequate answer,
And all such women after, for her sake;
That, though in any guilt caught, they'll not quake,
But with a bold face they'll themselves excuse,
And bear him down who would them thus accuse.
For lack of answer none of them shall die.

Nay, though a man see things with either eye,
Yet shall we women brazen shamelessly
And weep and swear and wrangle cleverly,
So that you men shall stupid be as geese.
What do I care for your authorities?

"I know well that this Jew, this Solomon
Found fools among us women, many a one,
But though he never found a good woman,
Yet has there found full many another man
Women right true, right good, and virtuous.
Witness all those that dwell in Jesus' house;
With martyrdom they proved their constancy.
The *Gesta Romanorum* speak kindly
Of many wives both good and true also.
But be not angry, sir, though it be so
That he said he had found no good woman,
I pray you take the meaning of the man;
He meant that sovereign goodness cannot be
Except in God, Who is the Trinity.

"Ah, since of very God there is but one,
Why do you make so much of Solomon?
What though he built a temple for God's house?
What though he were both rich and glorious?
So built he, too, a temple to false gods,
How could he with the Law be more at odds?
By gad, clean as his name you whitewash, sir,
He was a lecher and idolater;
And in old age the True God he forsook.
And if that God had not, as says the Book,
Spared him for father David's sake, he should
Have lost his kingdom sooner than he would.
I value not, of all the villainy
That you of women write, a butterfly.
I am a woman, and needs must I speak,
Or else swell up until my heart shall break.
For since he said we gossip, rail, and scold,
As ever may I my fair tresses hold,
I will not spare, for any courtesy,
To speak him ill who'd wish us villainy."

"Dame," said this Pluto, "be no longer wroth;
I give it up; but since I swore my oath
That I would give to him his sight again,
My word shall stand, I warn you that's certain.

I am a king, it suits me not to lie."
    "And I," said she, "am queen of Faëry.
Her answer shall she have, I undertake;
No further talk hereof let us two make.
Forsooth, I will not longer be contrary."
    Now let us turn again to January,
Who in the garden with his lovely May
Sang, and that merrier than the popinjay,
"I love you best, and ever shall, I know."
And so about the alleys did he go
Till he had come at last to that pear-tree
Wherein this Damian sat right merrily
On high, among the young leaves fresh and green.
    This blooming May, who was so bright of sheen,
Began to sigh, and said: "Alas, my side!
Now, sir," said she, "no matter what betide,
I must have some of these pears that I see,
Or I may die, so much I long," said she,
"To eat some of those little pears so green.
Help, for Her love Who is of Heaven Queen!
I tell you well, a woman in my plight
May have for fruit so great an appetite
That she may die if none of it she have."
    "Alas!" said he, "that I had here a knave
That could climb up, alas, alas!" said he,
"That I am blind."
                          "Yea, sir, no odds," said she,
"If you'd but grant me, and for God's dear sake,
That this pear-tree within your arms you'd take
(For well I know that you do not trust me),
Then I could climb up well enough," said she,
"So I my foot might set upon your back."
    "Surely," said he, "thereof should be no lack,
Might I so help you with my own heart's blood."
    So he stooped down, and on his back she stood,
And gave herself a twist and up went she.
Ladies, I pray you be not wroth with me;
I cannot gloze, I'm an uncultured man.
For of a sudden this said Damian
Pulled up her smock and thrust both deep and long.
    And when King Pluto saw this awful wrong,
To January he gave again his sight,
And made him see as well as ever he might.

And when he thus had got his sight again,
Never was man of anything so fain.
But since his wife he thought of first and last,
Up to the tree his eyes he quickly cast,
And saw how Damian his wife had dressed
In such a way as cannot be expressed,
Save I should rudely speak and vulgarly:
And such a bellowing clamour then raised he
As does a mother when her child must die:
"Out! Help! Alas! Oh, help me!" he did cry,
"Outlandish, brazen woman, what do you do?"
    And she replied: "Why, sir, and what ails you?
Have patience, and do reason in your mind
That I have helped you for your two eyes blind.
On peril of my soul, I tell no lies,
But I was taught that to recover eyes
Was nothing better, so to make you see,
Than struggle with a man up in a tree.
God knows I did it with a good intent."
    "Struggle!" cried he, "but damme, in it went!
God give you both a shameful death to die!
He banged you, for I saw it with my eye,
Or may they hang me by the neck up, else!"
    "Then is," said she, "my medicine all false;
For certainly, if you could really see,
You would not say these cruel words to me;
You catch but glimpses and no perfect sight."
    "I see," said he, "as well as ever I might—
Thanks be to God!—and with my two eyes, too,
And truth, I thought he did that thing to you."
    "You are bewildered still, good sir," said she,
"Such thanks I have for causing you to see;
Alas!" she cried, "that ever I was so kind!"
    "Now, dame," said he, "put all this out of mind.
Come down, my dear, and if I have missaid,
God help me if I'm not put out indeed.
But by my father's soul, I thought to have seen
How Damian right over you did lean
And that your smock was pulled up to his breast."
    "Yes, sir," said she, "you may think as seems best;
But, sir, a man that wakens out of sleep,
He cannot suddenly take note and keep
Of any thing, or see it perfectly,

Until he has recovered verily;
Just so a man that blinded long has been,
He cannot say that suddenly he's seen
So well, at first, when sight is new to him,
As later, when his sight's no longer dim.
Until your sight be settled for a while,
There may full many a thing your mind beguile.
Beware, I pray you, for, by Heaven's King,
Full many a man thinks that he sees a thing,
And it is other quite than what it seems.
And he that misconstrues, why, he misdeems."
And with that word she leaped down from the tree.
    This January, who is glad but he?
He kissed her and he hugged her much and oft,
And on her belly stroked and rubbed her soft,
And home to palace led her, let me add.
And now, good men, I pray you to be glad.
For here I end my tale of January;
God bless us, and His Mother, Holy Mary!

HERE ENDS THE MERCHANT'S TALE OF JANUARY

EPILOGUE
TO THE MERCHANT'S TALE

"Eh! By God's mercy!" cried our host. Said he:
"Now such a wife I pray God keep from me!
Behold what tricks, and lo, what subtleties
In women are. For always busy as bees
Are they, us simple men thus to deceive,
And from the truth they turn aside and leave;
By this same merchant's tale it's proved, I feel,
But, beyond doubt, as true as any steel
I have a wife, though poor enough she be;
But of her tongue a babbling shrew is she,
And she's a lot of other vices too.
No matter, though, with this we've naught to do.
But know you what? In secret, be it said,
I am sore sorry that to her I'm wed.
For if I should up-reckon every vice

The woman has, I'd be a fool too nice,
And why? Because it should reported be
And told her by some of this company;
Who'd be the ones, I need not now declare,
Since women know the traffic in such ware;
Besides, my wit suffices not thereto
To tell it all; wherefore my tale is through."

THE SQUIRE'S PROLOGUE

"Squire, come nearer, if your will it be,
And speak to us of love; for certainly
You know thereof as much as any man."
  "Nay, sir," said he, "but I'll do what I can
With hearty will; for I will not rebel
Against your wishes, but a tale will tell.
Hold me excused if I say aught amiss,
My aim is good, and lo, my tale is this."

THE SQUIRE'S TALE

At Sarai, in the land of Tartary,
There dwelt a king who warred on Russia, he,
Whereby there died full many a doughty man.
This noble king was known as Cambinskan,
Who in his time was of so great renown
That there was nowhere in the wide world known
So excellent a lord in everything;
He lacked in naught belonging to a king.
As for the faith to which he had been born,
He kept its law to which he had been sworn;
And therewith he was hardy, rich, and wise,
And merciful and just in all men's eyes,
True to his word, benign and honourable,
And in his heart like any center stable;
Young, fresh, and strong, in warfare ambitious
As any bachelor knight of all his house.
Of handsome person, he was fortunate,
And kept always so well his royal state
That there was nowhere such another man.

This noble king, this Tartar Cambinskan
Had got two sons on Elpheta, his wife,
Of whom the elder's name was Algarsyf,
And that same second son was Cambalo.
A daughter had this worthy king, also,
Who was the youngest, and called Canace.
But to describe to you all her beauty,
It lies not in my tongue nor my knowing;
I dare not undertake so high a thing.
My English is quite insufficient for
What must require a finished orator
Who knew the colours needful to that art
If he were to describe her every part.
I am none such, I must speak as I can.

   And so befell that, when this Cambinskan
Had twenty winters worn his diadem,
As he was wont from year to year, I deem,
He let the feast of his nativity
Be cried throughout all Sarai, his city,
The last *Idus* of March, as 'twas that year.
Phoebus the sun right festive was, and clear;
For he was near his exaltation grown
In face of Mars, and in his mansion known
In Aries, the choleric hot sign.
Right pleasant was the weather, and benign,
For which the wild birds in the sun's gold sheen,
What of the season and the springing green,
Full loudly sang their love and their affection;
It seemed that they had got themselves protection
Against the sword of winter keen and cold.

   This Cambinskan, of whom I have you told,
High in the palace, mounted on his throne
With crown and royal vestments sat alone,
And held his feast, so splendid and so rich
That in this world its like was not, of which,
If I should tell you all of the array,
Then would it occupy a summer's day.
Besides, it needs not here that I apprise
Of every course the order of service.
I will not tell you of their each strange sauce,
Nor of their swans, nor of their heronshaws.
Moreover, in that land, as tell knights old,
There are some foods which they for dainties hold.

Of which in this land the esteem is small;
There is no man that can report them all.
I will not so delay you, for it's prime,
And all the fruit of this were loss of time;
Unto my first theme I will have recourse.
    And so befell that, after the third course,
While this great king sat in his state that day,
Hearing his minstrels on their instruments play
Before him at the board, deliciously,
In at the hall door, and all suddenly,
There came a knight upon a steed of brass,
Holding in hand a mirror broad of glass.
Upon his thumb he had a golden ring,
And by his side a naked sword hanging;
And up he rode right to the highest board.
In all the hall there was not spoken word
For marvel of this knight; him to behold,
They stared and stretched and craned, both young and old.
    This stranger knight, who came thus suddenly,
Armed at all points, except his head, richly,
Saluted king and queen and those lords all,
In order of rank, as they sat there in hall,
Showing such humble courtesy to each
In manner of behaviour and in speech,
That Gawain, with his old-time courtesy,
Though he were come again from Faëry,
Could not have bettered him in any word.
And after this, before the king's high board,
He with a manly voice said his message,
After the form in use in his language,
Without mistake in syllable or letter;
And, that his tale should seem to all the better,
According to his language was his cheer,
As men teach art of speech both there and here;
Albeit that I cannot ape his style,
Nor can I climb across so high a stile,
Yet say I this, as to his broad intent,
To this amounts the whole of what he meant,
If so be that I have it yet in mind.
    He said: "The king of Araby and Ind,
My liege-lord, on this great and festive day
Salutes you as he now best can and may,
And sends to you, in honour of your feast,

By me, that am prepared for your behest,
This steed of brass, that easily and well
Can, in one natural day ('tis truth I tell),
That is to say, in four and twenty hours,
Where'er you please, in drought or else in showers,
Bear you in body unto every place
To which your heart wills that you go apace,
Without least hurt to you, through foul or fair;
Or, if you please to fly as high in air
As does an eagle when he wills to soar,
This self-same steed will bear you evermore
Without least harm, till you have gained your quest,
Although you sleep upon his back, or rest;
And he'll return, by twisting of a pin.
He that made this could make full many a gin;
He waited, watching many a constellation
Before he did contrive this operation;
And he knew many a magic seal and band.
    "This mirror, too, which I have in my hand,
Has power such that in it men may see
When there shall happen any adversity
Unto your realm, and to yourself also;
And openly who is your friend or foe.
More than all this, if any lady bright
Has set her heart on any kind of wight,
If he be false she shall his treason see,
His newer love and all his subtlety
So openly that nothing can he hide.
Wherefore, upon this pleasant summertide,
This mirror and this ring, which you may see,
He has sent to my Lady Canace,
Your most surpassing daughter, who is here.
    "The virtue of the ring, if you will hear,
Is this: that if she pleases it to wear
Upon her thumb, or in her purse to bear,
There is no bird that flies beneath the heaven
But she shall understand his language, even
To know his meaning openly and plain,
And answer him in his own words again.
And every herb that grows upon a root
She shall know, too, and whom 'twill heal, to boot,
Although his wounds be never so deep and wide.
    "This naked sword that's hanging by my side

Such virtue has that any man you smite,
Right through his armour will it carve and bite,
Were it as thick as is a branching oak;
And that man who is wounded by its stroke
Shall never be whole until you please, of grace,
To strike him with the flat in that same place
Where he is hurt; which is to say, 'tis plain,
That you may with the flat sword blade again
Strike him upon the wound and it will close;
This is the truth, I seek not to impose,
For it shall fail not while it's in your hold."

    And when this knight had thus his message told,
He rode out of the hall and did alight.
His steed, which shone as sun does, and as bright,
Stood in the courtyard, still as any stone.
This knight was to a chamber led anon,
And was unarmed, and there at meat sat down.

    The gifts were brought and royally were shown.
That is to say, the sword and glass of power,
And borne anon into the donjon tower
By certain officers detailed thereto;
The ring to Canace was borne also
With ceremony, where she sat at table.
But certainly, it is no lie or fable,
The horse of brass could no way be removed;
It stood as it were glued to ground. 'Twas proved
There was no man could lead it out or drive
With any windlass that he might contrive.
And why? Because they hadn't craft to heave it.
And therefore in that place they had to leave it
Until the knight had taught them the manner
Of moving it, as you'll hereafter hear.

    Great was the press of people to and fro
Swarming to see this horse that stood there so;
For it so high was, and so broad and long,
So well proportioned as to be most strong,
Just as it were a steed of Lombardy;
Therewith as horselike and as quick of eye
As if a gentle Apulian courser 'twere.
For truly, from his tail unto his ear
Nature nor art could better nor amend
In any wise, as people did contend.
But evermore their greatest wonder was,

How it could go, being made all of brass;
It was of Faëry, as to people seemed.
And divers folk diversely of it deemed;
So many heads, so many wits, one sees.
They buzzed and murmured like a swarm of bees,
And played about it with their fantasy,
Recalling what they'd learned from poetry;
Like Pegasus it was that mounted high,
That horse which had great wings and so could fly;
Or else it was the horse of Greek Sinon
Who brought Troy to destruction, years agone,
As men in these old histories may read.
"My heart," said one, "is evermore in dread;
I think some men-at-arms are hid therein
Who have in mind this capital to win.
It were right well that of such things we know."
Another whispered to his fellow, low,
And said: "He lies, for it is rather like
Some conjured up appearance of magic,
Which jugglers practise at these banquets great."
Of sundry doubts like these they all did treat,
As vulgar people chatter commonly
Of all things that are made more cunningly
Than they can in their ignorance comprehend;
They gladly judge they're made for some base end.
    And some much wondered on the mirror's power,
That had been borne up to the donjon tower,
And how men in it such strange things could see.
Another answered, saying it might be
Quite natural, by angles oddly spaced
And sly reflections thus within it placed,
And said, at Rome was such a one, men know.
They spoke of Alhazen and Vitello
And Aristotle, who wrote, in their lives,
On mirrors strange and on perspectives,
As all they know who've read their published word.
    And other folk did wonder on the sword
That had the power to pierce through anything;
And so they spoke of Telephus the king,
And of Achilles with his magic spear,
Wherewith he healed and hurt too, 'twould appear,
Even as a man might do with this new sword
Of which, but now, I've told and you have heard.

They spoke of tempering metal sundry wise,
And medicines therewith, which men devise,
And how and when such steel should hardened be;
Which, nevertheless, is all unknown to me.

Then spoke they of fair Canace's gold ring,
And all men said that such a wondrous thing
They'd ne'er heard of as being in ring-craft done,
Except that Moses and King Solomon
Had each a name for cunning in such art.
Thus spoke the people and then drew apart,
But notwithstanding, some said that it was
Wondrous to make fern-ashes into glass,
Since glass is nothing like the ash of fern;
But since long since of this thing men did learn,
Therefore they ceased their gabble and their wonder,
As sorely wonder some on cause of thunder,
Of ebb, of flood, of gossamer, of mist,
And each thing, till they know what cause exist.
Thus did they chatter and judge and thus surmise
Until the king did from the board arise.

Phoebus had left the angle meridional,
And yet ascending was that beast royal,
The noble Lion, with his Aldiran,
When that this Tartar king, this Cambinskan
Rose from his board where he had sat full high.
Before him went the sounding minstrelsy,
Into a room hung with rich ornaments,
Wherein they sounded divers instruments
Till it was like a heavenly thing to hear.
And now danced merry Venus' children dear,
For in the Fish their lady sat on high
And looked upon them with a friendly eye.

This noble king sat high upon his throne.
And this strange knight was brought to him anon,
And then to dance he went with Canace.
Here was such revel and such jollity
As no dull man is able to surmise;
He must have known and served love's high emprise,
And be a festive man as fresh as May
Who could for you describe such an array.

Who could tell you the figures of the dances,
So odd and strange and the blithe countenances,
The subtle glances and dissimulation

For fear of jealous persons' observation?
No man but Launcelot, and he is dead!
I therefore pass the joyous life they led
And saw no more, but in this jolliness
I leave them till to supper all did press.

 The steward bade them serve the spices, aye,
And the rich wine through all this melody.
The ushers and the squires got them gone;
The spices and the wine were come anon.
They ate and drank, and when this had an end,
Unto the temple, as was right, did wend.

 The service done, they supped while yet 'twas day.
What needs it that I tell all their array?
Each man knows well that at a kingly feast
There's plenty for the greatest and the least,
And dainties more than are in my knowing.
Then, after supper, went this noble king
To see the horse of brass, with all the rout
Of lords and ladies thronging him about.

 Such wondering was there on this horse of brass
That, since the siege of Troy did overpass,
When once a horse seemed marvellous to men.
Was there such wondering as happened then.
But finally the king asked of this knight
The virtue of this courser, and the might,
And prayed him tell the means of governance.

 This horse anon began to trip and dance
When this strange knight laid hand upon the rein
And said: "Sire, there's no more I need explain
Than, when you wish to journey anywhere,
You must but twirl a peg within his ear,
Which I will show you when alone with you.
You must direct him to what place also,
Or to what country you may please to ride.
And when you come to where you would abide,
Bid him descend, and twirl another pin,
For therein lies the secret of the gin,
And he will then descend and do your will;
And there he'll stand, obedient and still.
Though all the world the contrary had sworn,
He shall not thence be drawn nor thence be borne.
Or, if you wish to bid him thence be gone,
Twirl but this pin and he'll depart anon

And vanish utterly from all men's sight,
And then return to you, by day or night,
When you shall please to call him back again
In such a fashion as I will explain
When we two are alone, and that full soon.
Ride when you choose, there's no more to be done."
    Instructed when the king was by that knight,
And when he'd stablished in his mind aright
The method and the form of all this thing,
Then glad and blithe this noble doughty king
Repaired unto his revels as before.
The bridle to the donjon tower they bore,
And placed among his jewels rich and dear.
How I know not, the horse did disappear
Out of their sight; you get no more of me.
But thus I leave, in joy and jollity,
This Cambinskan with all his lords feasting
Well nigh until the day began to spring.

Explicit prima pars.
Sequitur pars secunda.

The nurse of good digestion, natural sleep,
Caused them to nod, and bade them they take keep
That labour and much drinking must have rest;
And with a gaping mouth all these he pressed,
And said that it was time they laid them down,
For blood was in the ascendant, as was shown,
And nature's friend, the blood, must honoured be.
They thanked him, gaping all, by two, by three,
And every one began to go to rest,
As sleep them bade; they took it for the best.
But here their dreams shall not by me be said;
The fumes of wine had filled each person's head,
Which cause senseless dreams at any time.
They slept next morning till the hour of prime,
That is, the others, but not Canace;
She was right temperate, as women be.
For of her father had she taken leave,
To go to rest, soon after it was eve;
For neither pale nor languid would she be,
Nor wear a weary look for men to see;
But slept her first deep sleep and then awoke.
For so much joy upon her heart there broke

When she looked on the mirror and the ring
That twenty times she flushed, and sleep did bring—
So strong an impress had the mirror made—
A vision of it to the slumbering maid.

Wherefore, ere up the sun began to glide,
She called her mistress, sleeping there beside,
And said to her that she was pleased to rise.

Old women like this governess are wise,
Or often so, and she replied anon,
And said: "My lady, where will you be gone
Thus early? For the folk are all at rest."
"I will," said she, "arise, for I've no zest
For longer sleep, and I will walk about."

Her mistress called of women a great rout,
And they rose up, a dozen more or less,
And up rose lovely Canace to dress,
As ruddy and bright as is the warm young sun
That in the Ram now four degrees has run;
He was no higher when she all ready was;
And forth she sauntered at an easy pace,
Arrayed according to the season sweet,
Lightly, to play and walk on maiden feet;
With five or six girls of her company
All down an alley, through the park, went she.
The morning mists that rose from the damp earth
Reddened the sun and broadened it in girth;
Nevertheless it was so fair a sight
That it made all their hearts dance for delight,
What of the season and the fair morning,
And all the myriad birds that she heard sing;
For when she heard, she knew well what they meant,
Just by their songs, and learned all their intent.

The point of every story, why it's told,
If it's delayed till interest grow cold
In those who have, perchance, heard it before,
The savour passes from it more and more,
For fulsomeness of its prolixity.
And for this reason, as it seems to me,
I should to my tale's major point descend
And make of these girls' walking a swift end.

Amidst a dry, dead tree, as white as chalk,
As Canace was playing in her walk,
There sat a falcon overhead full high,

That in a pitiful voice began to cry,
Till all the wood resounded mournfully.
For she had beaten herself so pitiably
With both her wings that the red glistening blood
Ran down the tree trunk whereupon she stood.
And ever in one same way she cried and shrieked,
And with her beak her body she so pricked
That there's no tiger, nor a cruel beast
That dwells in open wood or deep forest,
Would not have wept, if ever weep he could,
For pity of her, she shrieked alway so loud.
For never yet has been a man alive—
If but description I could well contrive—
That heard of such a falcon for fairness,
As well of plumage as of nobleness
Of shape, and all that reckoned up might be.
A falcon peregrine she was, and she
Seemed from a foreign land; and as she stood
She fainted now and then for loss of blood,
Till almost she had fallen from the tree.

   This king's fair daughter, Princess Canace,
Who on her finger bore the magic ring
Whereby she understood well everything
That any bird might in his language say,
And in such language could reply straightway,
She understood well what this falcon said,
And of her pity well-nigh was she dead.
So to the tree she went right hastily,
And on this falcon looked she pitifully,
And held her lap up wide, for she knew now
The falcon must come falling from the bough
When next it swooned away from loss of blood.
A long while waiting there the princess stood,
Till at the last she spoke, in her voice clear,
Unto the hawk, as you'll hereafter hear.

   "What is the cause, if it be one to tell,
That you are in this furious pain of hell?"
Said Canace unto this hawk above.
"Is this for sorrow of death or loss of love?
For, as I think, these are the causes two
That torture gentle heart with greatest woe;
Of other ills there is no need to speak,
Because such harm upon yourself you wreak;

Which proves right well that either love or dread
Must be the reason for your cruel deed,
Since I can see no one that gives you chase.
For love of God, come, do yourself some grace,
Or say what thing may help; for west nor east
Have I before now seen a bird or beast
That ever treated self so wretchedly.
You slay me with your sorrow, verily,
Such great compassion in my heart has grown.
For God's dear love, come from the dry tree down;
And, as I am a monarch's daughter true,
If I but verily the real cause knew
Of your distress, if it lay in my might,
I would make you amends before the night,
As truly help me God of human kind!
And even now will I look out and find
Some herbs to heal your hurts with, speedily."
    Then shrieked this falcon the more piteously
Than ever, and to ground fell down anon,
And lay there, swooning, deathlike as a stone,
Till Canace within her lap did take
And hold the bird till she began to wake.
And when from out her fainting fit she made,
All in her own hawk's language thus she said:
"That pity wells up soon in gentle heart,
Feeling its likeness in all pains that smart,
Is proved, and day by day, as men may see,
As well by deeds as by authority;
For gentle heart can spy out gentleness.
I see well that you have on my distress
Compassion, my fair Princess Canace,
Of truly womanly benignity
That nature in your character has set.
Not that I hope much good therefrom to get,
But to obey the word of your heart free,
And so that others may be warned by me,
As by the whelp instructed is the lion,
Just for that cause and reason shall I fly on,
While yet I have the leisure and the space,
The story of my wrongs to you I'll trace."
    And ever, while the one her sorrow said,
The other wept, as she to water'd fled,
Until the falcon bade her to be still;

And with a sigh, right thus she said her will.
   "Where I was born (alas, that cruel day!)
And fostered on a rock of marble grey
So tenderly that nothing troubled me,
I knew not what it was, adversity,
Till I could soar on high under the sky.
There dwelt a handsome tercelet[1] there, hard by,
Who seemed the well of every nobleness;
Though he was full of treason and falseness,
It was so hidden under humble bearing,
And under hues of truth which he was wearing,
And under kindness, never used in vain,
That no one could have dreamed that he could feign,
So deeply ingrained were his colours dyed.
But just as serpent under flower will hide
Until he sees the time has come to bite,
Just so this god of love, this hypocrite
With false humility for ever served
And seemed a wooer who the rites observed
That so become the gentleness of love.
As of a tomb the fairness is above,
While under is the corpse, such as you know,
So was this hypocrite, cold and hot also;
And in this wise he served his foul intent
That (save the Fiend) no one knew what he meant,
Till he so long had wept and had complained,
And many a year his service to me feigned,
That my poor heart, a pitiful sacrifice,
All ignorant of his supreme malice,
Fearing he'd die, as it then seemed to me,
Because of his great oaths and surety,
Granted him love, on this condition known,
That evermore my honour and renown
Were saved, both private fame and fame overt;
That is to say, that, after his desert
I gave him all my heart and all my thought—
God knows, and he, that more I gave him naught—
And took his heart in change for mine, for aye.
But true it is, and has been many a day,
A true man and a thief think not at one.
And when he saw the thing so far was gone

---

1. Tercelet: the male of the peregrine falcon.

That I had fully granted him my love,
In such a way as I've explained above,
And given him my faithful heart, as free
As he swore he had given his to me,
Anon this tiger, full of doubleness,
Fell on his knees, devout in humbleness,
With so high reverence, and, by his face,
So like a lover in his gentle grace,
So ravished, as it seemed, for very joy,
That never Jason nor Paris of Troy—
Jason? Nay, truly, nor another man
Since Lamech lived, who was the first began
To love two women (those that write have sworn),
Not ever, since the primal man was born,
Could any man, by twenty-thousandth part,
Enact the tricks of this deceiver's art;
Nor were he worthy to unlace his shoe,
Where double-dealing or deceit were due,
Nor could so thank a person as he me!
His manner was most heavenly to see,
For any woman, were she ever so wise;
So painted he, and combed, at point-device,
His manner, all in all, and every word.
And so much by his bearing was I stirred
And for the truth I thought was in his heart,
That, if aught troubled him and made him smart,
Though ever so little bit, and I knew this,
It seemed to me I felt death's cruel kiss.
And briefly, so far all these matters went,
My will became his own will's instrument;
That is to say, my will obeyed his will
In everything in reason, good or ill,
Keeping within the bounds of honour ever.
Never had I a thing so dear—ah, never!—
As him, God knows! nor ever shall anew.

"This lasted longer than a year or two
While I supposed of him no thing but good.
But finally, thus at the last it stood,
That Fortune did decree that he must win
Out of that place, that home, that I was in.
Whether I felt woe, there's no question, none;
I can't describe my feelings, no, not one;
But one thing dare I tell, and that boldly,

I came to know the pain of death thereby;
Such grief I felt for him, none might believe.
So on a day of me he took his leave,
So sorrowfully, too, I thought truly
That he felt even as deep a woe as I,
When I had heard him speak and saw his hue.
Nevertheless, I thought he was so true,
And that to me he would come back again
Within a little while, let me explain;
And 'twas quite reasonable that he must go
For honour's sake, for oft it happens so,
That I made virtue of necessity,
And took it well, because it had to be.
A look of cheer I felt not I put on,
And took his hand, I swear it by Saint John.
And said to him: 'Behold, I'm yours in all;
Be you to me as I have been, and shall.'
What he replied it needs not I rehearse,
Who can say better than he, who can do worse?
When he had well said, all his good was done.
'It well behooves him take a lengthy spoon
Who eats with devils,' so I've heard folk say.
So at the last he must be on his way,
And forth he flew to where it pleased him best.
When it became his purpose he should rest,
I think he must have had this text in mind,
That 'Everything, returning to its kind,
Gladdens itself'; thus men say, as I guess;
Men love, and naturally, newfangledness,
As do these birds that men in cages feed.
For though you night and day take of them heed,
And fairly strew their cage as soft as silk,
And give them sugar, honey, bread, and milk,
Yet on the instant when the door is up,
They with their feet will spurn their feeding cup,
And to the wood will fly and worms will eat;
So are they all newfangled of their meat,
And love all novelties of their own kind;
Nor nobleness of blood may ever bind.
So fared this tercelet, oh, alas the day!
Though he was gently born, and fresh and gay,
And handsome, and well-mannered, aye and free,
He saw a kite fly, and it proved a she,

And suddenly he loved this she-kite so
That all his love for me did quickly go,
And all his truth turned falsehood in this wise;
Thus has this kite my love in her service,
And I am love-lorn without remedy."
And with that word the hawk began to cry,
And after, swooned on Canace's fair arm.

   Great was the sorrow for the falcon's harm
That Canace and all her women made;
They knew not how they might this falcon aid.
But Canace home bore her in her lap,
And softly her in poultices did wrap
Where she with her own beak had hurt herself.
Now Canace dug herbs more rich than pelf
Out of the ground, and made up ointments new
Of precious herbs, all beautiful of hue,
Wherewith to heal this hawk; from day to night
She nursed her carefully with all her might.
And by her bed's head she contrived a mew
And lined the cage with velvets all of blue,
Symbol of truth that is in women seen.
And all without, the mew was painted green,
And there were painted all these treacherous fowls
As are these titmice, tercelets, and these owls,
While for despite were painted there beside
Magpies, that they might cry at them and chide.

   Thus leave I Canace her hawk keeping,
I will no more, just now, speak of her ring,
Till I come back with purpose to explain
How this poor falcon got her love again
Repentant, as the story tells to us,
By mediation of that Cambalus,
The king's son, of whom I've already told.
But henceforth I a straightened course will hold
Great battles and adventures to relate,
Whereof were never heard such marvels great.

   First will I tell you of King Cambinskan
Who won so many a town and many a man;
And after will I speak of Algarsyf,
How he won Theodora for his wife,
For whom full oft in peril great he was,
Had he been helped not by the steed of brass;
And after that I'll speak of Cambalo,

Who in the lists fought with the brothers two
For Canace, before he could her win.
And where I left off, I'll again begin.

Explicit secunda pars.
Incipit pars tercia.

Apollo in his chariot whirled so high
That in the God Mercurius' house, the sly——

(*unfinished*)

HERE FOLLOW THE WORDS OF THE FRANKLIN TO THE SQUIRE, AND THE WORDS OF THE HOST TO THE FRANKLIN

"In faith, sir squire, you have done well with it,
And openly I praise you for your wit,"
The franklin said, "Considering your youth,
So feelingly you speak, sir, in good truth!
In my opinion, there is none that's here
In eloquence shall ever be your peer,
If you but live; may God give you good chance
And in all virtue send continuance!
For, sir, your speech was great delight to me.
I have a son, and by the Trinity
I'd rather have, than twenty pounds in land,
Though it were right now fallen to my hand,
He were a man of such discretion shown
As you, sir; fie on what a man may own,
Unless the man have virtue therewithal.
I've checked my son, and yet again I shall,
For he toward virtue chooses not to wend;
But just to play at dice, and gold to spend,
And lose all that he has, is his usage.
And he would rather talk with any page
Than to commune with any gentle wight
From whom he might learn courtesy aright."

   "A straw for courtesy!" exclaimed our host;
"What, franklin? Gad, sir, well you know, I trust,
That each of you must tell us, at the least,
A tale or two, or break his sworn behest."

   "I know it," said the franklin; "I am fain,
And pray you all, you do not me disdain,
Though to this man I speak a word or two."

   "Come, tell your tale, sir, without more ado."

404

"Gladly, sir host," said he, "I will obey
Your will, good host; now hearken what I say.
For I'll not be contrary in any wise,
At least so far as my wit shall suffice;
I pray to God that it may please you; rough
Though it may be, I'll know 'tis good enough."

THE FRANKLIN'S PROLOGUE

These ancient gentle Bretons, in their days,
Of divers high adventures made great lays
And rhymed them in their primal Breton tongue,
The which lays to their instruments they sung,
Or else recited them where joy might be;
And one of them have I in memory,
Which I shall gladly tell you, as I can.
    But, sirs, because I am an ignorant man,
At my beginning must I first beseech
You will excuse me for my vulgar speech;
I never studied rhetoric, that's certain;
That which I say, it must be bare and plain.
I never slept on Mount Parnassus, no,
Nor studied Marcus Tullius Cicero.
Colours I know not, there's no doubt indeed,
Save colours such as grow within the mead,
Or such as men achieve with dye or paint.
Colours of rhetoric I find but quaint;
My spirit doesn't feel the beauty there.
But if you wish, my story you shall hear."

THE FRANKLIN'S TALE

In old Armorica, now Brittany,
There was a knight that loved and strove, did he
To serve a lady in the highest wise;
And many a labour, many a great emprise
He wrought for her, or ever she was won.
For she was of the fairest under sun,
And therewithal come of so high kindred

That scarcely could this noble knight, for dread,
Tell her his woe, his pain, and his distress.
But at the last she, for his worthiness,
And specially for his meek obedience,
Had so much pity that, in consequence,
She secretly was come to his accord
To take him for her husband and her lord,
Of such lordship as men have over wives;
And that they might be happier in their lives,
Of his free will he swore to her, as knight,
That never in his life, by day or night,
Would he assume a right of mastery
Against her will, nor show her jealousy,
But would obey and do her will in all
As any lover of his lady shall;
Save that the name and show of sovereignty,
Those would he have, lest he shame his degree
    She thanked him, and with a great humbleness
She said: "Since, sir, of your own nobleness
You proffer me to have so loose a rein
Would God there never come between us twain,
For any guilt of mine, a war or strife.
Sir, I will be your humble, faithful wife,
Take this as truth till heart break in my breast."
Thus were they both in quiet and in rest.
    For one thing, sirs, I safely dare to say,
That friends each one the other must obey
If they'd be friends and long keep company.
Love will not be constrained by mastery;
When mastery comes, the god of love anon
Beats his fair wings, and farewell! He is gone!
Love is a thing as any spirit free;
Women by nature love their liberty,
And not to be constrained like any thrall,
And so do men, if say the truth I shall.
Observe who is most patient in his love,
He is advantaged others all above.
Patience is virtue high, and that's certain;
For it does vanquish, as these clerks make plain,
Things that oppression never could attain.
One must not chide for trifles nor complain.
Learn to endure, or else, so may I go,
You'll have to learn it, whether you will or no.

For in this world, it's certain, no one is
Who never does or says sometimes amiss.
Sickness, or woe, or what the stars have sent,
Anger, or wine, or change of temperament
Causes one oft to do amiss or speak.
For every wrong one may not vengeance wreak;
Conditions must determine temperance
In all who understand good governance.
And therefore did this wise and worthy knight,
To live in quiet, patience to her plight,
And unto him full truly did she swear
That never should he find great fault in her.

    Here may men see an humble wise accord;
Thus did she take her servant and her lord,
Servant in love and lord in their marriage;
So was he both in lordship and bondage;
In bondage? Nay, but in lordship above,
Since he had both his lady and his love;
His lady truly, and his wife also,
To which the law of love accords, we know.
And when he was in this prosperity,
Home with his wife he went to his country,
Not far from Penmarch, where his dwelling was.
And there he lived in bliss and all solace.

    Who could relate, save those that wedded be,
The joy, the ease, and the prosperity
That are between a husband and a wife?
A year and more endured this blissful life,
Until the knight, of whom I've spoken thus,
Who at Kayrrud[1] was called Arviragus,
Arranged to go and dwell a year or twain
In England, which was then known as Britain,
To seek in arms renown and great honour;
For his desire was fixed in such labour;
And there he lived two years (the book says thus).

    Now will I hold from this Arviragus,
And I will speak of Dorigen his wife,
Who loved her husband as her heart's own life.
For all his absence wept she and she sighed,
As noble wives do at a lone fireside.
She mourned, watched, wailed, she fasted and complained;

---

1. Probably modern Karru. The meaning is, literally, red house.

Desire for him so bound her and constrained,
That all this wide world did she set at naught.
Her friends, who knew her grief and heavy thought,
Comforted her as they might do or say;
They preached to her, they told her night and day
That for no cause she killed herself, alas!
And every comfort possible in this pass
They gave to her, in all their busyness,
To make her thus put by her heaviness.

   With passing time, as you know, every one,
Men may so long with tools engrave a stone
That thereon will some figure printed be.
And so long did they comfort her that she
Received at last, by hope and reason grown,
Imprinted consolations as her own,
Whereby her sorrow did somewhat assuage;
She could not always live in such a rage.

   And, then, Arviragus, through all her care,
Had sent her letters home, of his welfare,
And that he would come speedily again;
Otherwise had this sorrow her heart slain.

   Her friends saw that her grief began to slake,
And prayed her on their knees, for dear God's sake,
To come and wander in their company
And drive away her gloomy fantasy.
And finally she granted that request;
For well she saw that it was for the best.

   Now stood her castle very near the sea,
And often with her good friends wandered she
For pleasure on the cliffs that reared so high,
Whence she saw many a ship and barge go by,
Sailing their courses where they wished to go;
But that was part and parcel of her woe.
For to herself full oft, "Alas!" said she,
"Is there no ship, of many that I see,
Will bring me home my lord? Then were my heart
Recovered of its bitter pains that smart."

   At other times there would she sit and think,
And cast her two eyes downward from the brink.
But when she saw the grisly rocks all black,
For very fear her heart would start aback
And quake so that her feet would not sustain
Her weight. Then on the grass she'd sit again

And piteously upon the sea she'd stare,
And say, with dull sighs on the empty air:
    "Eternal God, Who by Thy providence
Leadest the world with a true governance,
Idly, as men say, dost Thou nothing make;
But, Lord, these grisly, fiendish rocks, so black,
That seem but rather foul confusion thrown
Awry than any fair world of Thine own,
Aye of a perfect wise God and stable,
Why hast Thou wrought this insane work, pray tell?
For by this work, north, south, and west and east,
There is none nurtured, man, nor bird, nor beast;
It does no good, to my mind, but annoys.
See'st Thou not, Lord, how mankind it destroys?
A hundred thousand bodies of mankind
Have died on rocks, whose names are not in mind,
And man's a creature made by Thee most fair,
After Thine image, as Thou didst declare.
Then seemed it that Thou had'st great charity
Toward mankind; but how then may it be
That Thou hast wrought such means man to destroy,
Which means do never good, but ever annoy?
I know well, clerics gladly do attest,
By arguments, that all is for the best,
Though I can never the real causes know.
But O Thou God Who made'st the wind to blow,
Keep Thou my lord! This is my argument;
To clerks I leave disputing on what's meant.
But O would God that all these rocks so black
Were sunken down to Hell for my lord's sake!
These rocks, they slay my very heart with fear."
Thus would she say, with many a piteous tear.
    Her friends saw that to her it was no sport
To wander by the sea, but discomfort;
And so arranged to revel somewhere else.
They led her along rivers and to wells,
And such delightful places; and told fables,
And danced, and played at chess, and played at tables.[2]
    So on a day, all in the morningtide,
Unto a garden which was there beside,
Wherein they'd given command that there should be

---

2. Tables: backgammon.

Food and whatever else was necessary,
They went for pleasure all the livelong day.
And this was on the morning sixth of May,
And May had painted with his soft warm showers
This garden full of foliage and of flowers;
And work of man's hand had so curiously
Arrayed this lovely garden, truthfully,
That never was another of such price,
Unless it were the very Paradise.
The scent of flowers and the fair fresh sight
Would have made any heart dance for delight
That e'er was born, unless too great sickness
Or too great sorrow held it in distress;
So full it was of beauty and pleasance.
After their dinner all began to dance,
And sing, also, save Dorigen alone,
Who made alway her same complaint and moan.
For him she saw not through the dancing go,
Who was her husband and her love also.
Nevertheless, she must a time abide,
And with good hope held, let her sorrow slide.

   Amid these mazes, with the other men,
There danced a squire before this Dorigen,
That was more blithe, and prettier of array,
In my opinion, than the month of May.
He sang and danced better than any man
That is, or was, since first the world began.
Therewith he was, description to contrive,
One of best conditioned men alive;
Young, strong, right virtuous, and rich, and wise,
And well beloved, and one to idealize.
And briefly, if I tell the truth withal,
Unknown to Dorigen—nay, least of all—
This pleasant squire, servant to Queen Venus,
The name of whom was this, Aurelius,
Had loved her best of anyone alive
Two years and more (since she did first arrive),
But never dared he tell her of his state;
Without a cup he drank his draught of fate.
He had despaired, for nothing dared he say,
Save that in songs he would somewhat betray
His woe, as of a general complaint;
He loved, but none loved him, though he went faint.

Of such a subject made he many lays,
Songs and complaints, rondels and virelays,
How that he dared not his deep sorrow tell,
But languished, as a fury does in Hell;
And die he must, he said, as did Echo
For her Narcissus, daring not tell her woe.
In other manner than you hear me say
Dared he not unto her his woe betray;
Save that, perchance, there would be times at dances,
Where young folk honoured all that makes romances,
It may well be he looked upon her face
In such wise as a man who sued for grace;
But nothing knew she of his love's intent.
Nevertheless it chanced, ere thence they went,
Because it happened he was her neighbour,
And was a man of worship and honour,
And she had known him in the time of yore,
They fell to talking; and so, more and more,
Unto his purpose drew Aurelius,
And when he saw his time addressed her thus:
    "Madam," said he, "by God Who this world made,
So that I knew it might your sad heart aid,
I would, that day when your Arviragus
Went overseas, that I, Aurelius,
Had gone whence never I should come again;
For well I know my service is in vain.
My guerdon is the breaking of my heart;
Madam, have pity on my pains that smart;
For with a word you may slay me or save,
Here at your feet would God I found my grave!
Time to say more, at present naught have I;
Have mercy, sweet, or you will make me die!"
    So then she looked upon Aurelius:
"Is this your will?" asked she, "And say you thus?
Never before have I known what you meant.
But since, Aurelius, I know your intent,
By that same God Who gave me soul and life,
Never shall I become an untrue wife
In word or deed, so far as I have wit:
I will remain his own to whom I'm knit;
Take this for final answer as from me."
But after that she said thus, sportively:
    "Aurelius," said she, "by God above,

Yet would I well consent to be your love,
Since I hear you complain so piteously,
On that day when, from coasts of Brittany,
You've taken all the black rocks, stone by stone,
So that they hinder ship nor boat—I own,
I say, when you have made the coast so clean
Of rocks that there is no stone to be seen,
Then will I love you best of any man;
Take here my promise—all that ever I can."

    "Is there no other grace in you?" asked he.

    "No, by that Lord," said she, "Who has made me!
For well I know that it shall ne'er betide.
Let suchlike follies out of your heart slide.
What pleasure can a man have in his life
Who would go love another man's own wife,
That has her body when he wishes it?"

    Deep sighs Aurelius did then emit;
Woe was Aurelius when this he heard,
And with a sorrowful heart he thus answered:

    "Madam," said he, "this were impossible!
Then must I die a sudden death and fell."
And with that word he turned away anon.
Then came her other friends, and many a one,
And in the alleys wandered up and down,
And nothing knew of this decision shown,
But suddenly began to dance anew
Until the bright sun lost his golden hue;
For the horizon had cut off his light;
This is as much as saying, it was night.
And home they went in joy and with solace,
Except the wretch Aurelius, alas!
He to his house went with a woeful heart;
He saw he could not from his near death part.
It seemed to him he felt his heart grow cold;
Up toward Heaven his two hands did he hold,
And on his bare knees did he kneel him down
And in his raving said his orison.
For very woe out of his wits he fled.
He knew not what he spoke, but thus he said;
With mournful heart his plaint had he begun
Unto the gods, and first unto the sun.

    He said: "Apollo, governor and god
Of every plant, herb, tree, and flower in sod,

That givest, according to thy declination,
To each of them its time of foliation,
All as thy habitation's low or high,
Lord Phoebus, cast thy merciful bright eye
On wretched Aurelius, who is lost and lorn.
Lo, Lord! My lady has my swift death sworn,
Without my guilt, save thy benignity
Upon my dying heart have some pity!
For well I know, Lord Phoebus, if you lest,
You can thus aid me, save my lady, best.
Now vouchsafe that I may for you devise
A plan to help me, telling in what wise.

"Your blessed sister, Lucina, serene,
That of the sea is goddess chief and queen
(Though Neptune is the deity in the sea,
Yet empress set above him there is she).
You know well, Lord, that just as her desire
Is to be quickened and lighted by your fire,
For which she follows you right busily,
Just so the sea desires, and naturally,
To follow her, she being high goddess
Both of the sea and rivers, great and less.
Wherefore, Lord Phoebus, this request I make—
Without this miracle, my heart will break—
That at the time of your next opposition,
Which will be in the Lion, make petition
To her that she so great a flood will bring
That full five fathoms shall it over-spring
The highest rock in Armoric Brittany;
And let this flood endure two years for me;
Then truly to my lady may I say:
'Now keep your word, the rocks are gone away.'

"Lord Phoebus, do this miracle for me;
Pray her she run no faster course, being free—
I say, Lord, pray your sister that she go
No faster course than you these next years two.
Then shall she be even at the full alway,
And spring-flood shall endure both night and day.
And save she vouchsafe, Lord, in such manner
To grant to me my sovereign lady dear,
Pray her to sink, then, every rock far down
Into that region dark and cold, her own,
Under the earth, the place Pluto dwells in,

Or nevermore shall I my lady win.
Thy temple in Delphi will I, barefoot, seek;
Lord Phoebus, see the tears upon my cheek,
And on my pain be some compassion shown."
And with that word in swoon he tumbled down,
And for a long time lay there in a trance.

   His brother, who knew all his suppliance,
Found him, and took him, and to bed him brought.
Despairing in the torment of his thought,
Let I this woeful fellow-creature lie,
To choose, for all of me, to live or die.

   Arviragus, with health, in honour's hour,
As he that was of chivalry the flower,
Came home again, with other gentlemen.
O happy are you now, my Dorigen,
Who have your pleasant husband in your arms,
The vigorous knight, the worthy man-at-arms,
That loves you as he loves his own heart's life.
Nothing he chose to question of his wife
If any man had said, while he was out,
Some words of love; of her he had no doubt.
He tended not that way, it would appear,
But danced and jousted, made for her good cheer;
And thus in joy and bliss I let them dwell
And of love-sick Aurelius will I tell.

   In weakness and in torment furious
Two years and more lay wretched Aurelius
Ere foot on earth he went—aye, even one;
For comfort in this long time had he none,
Save from his brother, who was a good clerk;
He knew of all this woe and all this work.
For to no other human, 'tis certain,
Dared he his cause of illness to explain.
In breast he kept more secret his idea
Than did Pamphilius for Galatea.
His breast was whole, with no wound to be seen,
But in his heart there was the arrow keen.
And well you know that of a sursanure[3]
In surgery is difficult the cure,
Unless they find the dart or take it out.
His brother wept, and long he sought about

---

3. Sursanure: a wound healed or healing outwardly only.

Till at the last he called to remembrance
That while he was at Orléans in France—
For many young clerks are all ravenous
To read of arts that are most curious,
And into every nook and cranny turn
Particular strange sciences to learn—
He thus recalled that once upon a day,
At Orléans, while studying there, I say,
A book of natural magic there he saw
In a friend's room, a bachelor of law
(Though he was there to learn another craft),
Which book he'd privately on his desk left;
And which book said much of the operations
Touching the eight and twenty variations
That designate the moon, and such folly
As is, in our days, valued not a fly;
For Holy Church provides us with a creed
That suffers no illusion to mislead.
And when this book came to his remembrance,
At once, for joy, his heart began to dance,
And to himself he said in privacy:
"My brother shall be healed, and speedily;
For I am sure that there are sciences
Whereby men make divers appearances,
Such as these prestidigitators play.
For oft at feasts, have I well heard men say
That jugglers, in a hall both bright and large,
Have made come in there, water and a barge,
And in the hall the barge rowed up and down.
Sometimes there seemed to come a grim lion;
And sometimes flowers sprang as in a mead;
Or vines with grapes both red and white indeed;
Sometimes a castle built of lime and stone;
And when they wished it disappeared anon.
Thus seemed these things to be in each man's sight.

   "Now, then, conclude I thus, that if I might
At Orléans some old school-fellow find,
Who has these mansions of the moon in mind,
Or other natural magic from above,
He could well make my brother have his love.
For with a mere appearance clerks may make
It seem in man's sight that all rocks that break
The seas of Brittany were banished, so

That right above them ships might come and go,
And in such wise endure a week or two;
Then were my brother cured of all his woe.
For she must keep the word she gave at feast.
Or he'll have right to shame her, at the least."
    Why should I longer speak of this event?
He to the bedside of his brother went,
And urged him eagerly to get him gone
To Orléans; he started up anon
And forward on his way at once did fare
In hope to be relieved of all his care.
    When they were come almost to that city,
Perhaps two furlongs short of it, or three,
A young clerk walking by himself they met,
Who, in good Latin, heartily did greet,
And after that he said a wondrous thing.
"I know," said he, "the cause of your coming."
And ere a farther foot the brothers went,
He told them all the soul of their intent.
    This Breton clerk asked after school-fellows
Whom he had known through former suns and snows;
And he replied to this that dead they were,
Whereat he wept, for sorrow, many a tear.
    Down from his horse Aurelius leaped anon,
And onward with this wizard he was gone
Home to his house, where he was put at ease.
To him there lacked no victuals that might please;
So well appointed house as was that one
Aurelius in life before saw none.
    He showed him, ere he went to supper here,
Forests and parks full of the dim wild deer;
There saw he harts of ten with their horns high,
The greatest ever seen by human eye.
He saw of them a hundred slain by hounds,
And some with arrows bled, with bitter wounds.
He saw, when vanished all were these wild deer,
Some falconers by river flowing clear,
Who with their hawks had many herons slain.
And then he saw knights jousting on a plain;
And after this he did him such pleasance
That he showed him his lady in a dance
Wherein he also joined, or so he thought.
And when this master who this magic wrought

Saw it was time, he clapped his two hands, lo!
Farewell to all! the revels out did go.
And yet they'd never moved out of the house
While they saw all these sights so marvelous,
But in his study, where his books would be,
They had sat still, and no one but they three.

Then unto him this master called his squire,
And asked him thus: "Is supper ready, sir?
Almost an hour it is, I'll undertake,
Since I bade you our evening meal to make,
When these two gentlemen came in with me
Into my study, wherein my books be."

"Sir," said this squire then, "when it pleases you
It is all ready, though you will right now."

"Then let us sup," said he, "for that is best;
These amorous folk must sometime have some rest."

After the supper they discussed, they three,
What sum should this said master's guerdon be
For moving all rocks Breton coasts contain
From the Gironde unto the mouth of Seine.
He played for time, and swore, so God him save,
Less than a thousand pounds he would not have,
Nor eagerly for that would take it on.

Aurelius, with blissful heart, anon
Answered him thus: "Fig for a thousand pound!
This great wide world, the which, men say, is round,
I'd give it all, if I were lord of it.
The bargain is concluded and we're knit.
You shall be truly paid, sir, by my troth!
But look you, for no negligence or sloth,
Delay no longer than tomorrow morn."

"Nay," said this clerk, "upon my faith I'm sworn."

To bed went this Aurelius and undressed,
And well-nigh all that night he had his rest;
What of his labour and his hope of bliss
The pain had left that woeful heart of his.

Upon the morrow, when it was full day,
To Brittany took they the nearest way,
Aurelius, with this wizard at his side,
And thus they came to where they would abide;
And that was, as the books say, I remember,
The cold and frosty season of December.

Phoebus was old and coloured like pale brass,

That in hot declination coloured was
And shone like burnished gold with streamers bright;
But now in Capricorn did he alight,
Wherein he palely shone, I dare explain.
The bitter frosts, with all the sleet and rain,
Had killed the green of every garden-yard.
Janus sat by the fire, with double beard,
And drained from out his bugle[4] horn the wine.
Before him stood the brawn of tuskèd swine,
And "Noël!" cried then every lusty man.

Aurelius, in all that he could plan,
Did to this master cheerful reverence,
And prayed of him he'd use all diligence
To bring him from his pains that so did smart,
Or else with sword that he would slit his heart.

This subtle clerk such ruth had for this man,
That night and day he sped about his plan,
To wait the proper time for his conclusion;
That is to say, the time to make illusion,
By such devices of his jugglery
(I understand not this astrology)
That she and everyone should think and say
That all the Breton rocks were gone away,
Or else that they were sunken underground.
So at the last the proper time he found
To do his tricks and all his wretchedness
Of such a superstitious wickedness.
For his Toletan Tables forth he brought,
All well corrected, and he lacked in naught,
The years collected nor the separate years,
Nor his known roots, nor any other gears,
As, say, his centres and his argument,
And his proportionals convenient
In estimating truly his equations.
The eighth sphere showed him in his calculations
How far removed was Alnath, passing by,
From head of that fixed Aries on high,
That in the ninth great sphere considered is;
Right cleverly he calculated this.

When he the moon's first mansion thus had found,
The rest proportionally he could expound;

---

4. A drinking horn, made from the horn of the bugle, or buffalo.

And knew the moon's arising-time right well,
And in what face and term, and all could tell;
This gave him then the mansion of the moon—
He worked it out accordingly right soon,
And did the other necessary rites
To cause illusions and such evil sights
As heathen peoples practised in those days.
Therefore no longer suffered he delays,
But all the rocks by magic and his lore
Appeared to vanish for a week or more.

    Aurelius, who yet was torn by this,
Whether he'd gain his love or fare amiss,
Awaited night and day this miracle;
And when he knew there was no obstacle,
That vanished were these black rocks, every one,
Down at the master's feet he fell anon
And said: "I, woeful wretch, Aurelius,
Thank you, my lord, and Lady mine Venus,
That have so saved me from my dreadful care."
And to the temple straightway did he fare,
Whereat he knew he should his lady see.
And when he saw his opportunity,
With fluttering heart and with an humble cheer
He greeted thus his sovereign lady dear.

    "My own dear lady," said this woeful man,
"Whom I most fear and love best, as I can,
And whom, of all this world, I'd not displease,
Were it not that for you I've such unease
That I must die here at your feet anon,
I would not tell how I am woebegone;
But I must either die or else complain;
You slay me, for no crime, with utter pain.
But on my death, although you have no ruth,
Take heed now, ere you break your promised troth,
Repent you, for the sake of God above,
Ere me you slay, because it's you I love.
For well you know your promise apposite;
Not that I challenge aught, of my own right,
In you, my sovereign lady, save your grace;
But in a garden, in a certain place,
You know right well what you did promise me;
And in my hand you plighted troth," said he,
"To love me best, God knows you promised so,

Howe'er I may unworthy be thereto.
Madam, I say it for your honour's vow
More than to save my heart's dear life right now;
I have done all that you commanded me;
And if you will, you may well go and see.
Do as you please, but hold your word in mind,
For quick or dead, as you do, me you'll find;
In you lies all, to make me live or die,
But well I know the rocks are vanished, aye!"

He took his leave, and she astounded stood,
In all her face there was no drop of blood;
She never thought to have come in such a trap.
"Alas!" said she, "that ever this should hap!
For thought I never, by possibility,
That such prodigious marvel e'er might be!
It is against the way of all nature."
And home she went, a sorrowful creature.
For utter terror hardly could she go,
She wept, she wailed throughout a day or so,
And swooned so much 'twas pitiful to see;
But why this was to not a soul told she;
For out of town was gone Arviragus.
But to her own heart spoke she, and said thus,
With her face pale and with a heavy cheer,
All her complaint, as you'll hereafter hear:

"Of thee," she cried, "O Fortune, I complain,
That, unaware, I'm bound within thy chain;
From which to go, I know of no succour
Save only death, or else my dishonour;
One of these two I am compelled to choose.
Nevertheless, I would far rather lose
My life than of my body come to shame,
Or know myself untrue, or lose my name;
By death I know it well, I may be freed,
Has there not many a noble wife, indeed,
And many a maiden slain herself—alas!—
Rather than with her body do trespass?

"Yes, truly, lo, these stories bear witness;
When Thirty Tyrants, full of wickedness,
Had Phido slain in Athens, at a feast,
They gave command his daughters to arrest,
And had them brought before them, for despite,
All naked, to fulfill their foul delight,

And in their father's blood they made them dance
Upon the pavement—God give them mischance!
For which these woeful maidens, full of dread,
Rather than they should lose their maidenhead,
Unseen they all leaped down into a well
And drowned themselves therein, as old books tell.
   "They of Messina did require and seek
From Lacedaemon fifty maids to take,
On whom they would have done their lechery;
But there was none of all that company
Who was not slain, and who with good intent
Preferred not death rather than give consent
To be thus ravished of her maidenhead.
Why should I then hold dying in such dread?
   "Lo, too, the tyrant Aristoclides,
Who loved a maiden called Stimphalides.
Whenas her father had been slain by night,
Unto Diana's temple she took flight
And grasped the image in her two hands so
That from this image would she not let go.
No one could tear her hands from that embrace
Till she was slaughtered in that self-same place.
Now since these maidens showed such scorn outright
Of being defiled to make man's foul delight,
Well ought a wife rather herself to slay
Than be defiled, I think, and so I say.
   "What shall I say of Hasdrubal's fair wife,
Who in Carthage bereft herself of life?
For when she saw that Romans won the town,
She took her children all and leaped right down
Into the fire, choosing thus to die
Before a Roman did her villainy.
   "Did not Lucretia slay herself—alas!—
At Rome, when she so violated was
By Tarquin? For she thought it was a shame
Merely to live when she had lost her name.
   "The seven maidens of Miletus, too,
Did slay themselves, for very dread and woe,
Rather than men of Gaul should on them press.
More than a thousand stories, as I guess,
Could I repeat now of this matter here.
   "With Abradates slain, his wife so dear
Herself slew, and she let her red blood glide

In Abradates' wounds so deep and wide,
And said: 'My body, at the least, I say,
No man shall now defile,' and passed away.
  "Why should I of more instances be fain?
Since that so many have their bodies slain
Rather than that they should dishonoured be?
I will conclude it better is for me
To slay myself than be dishonoured thus.
I will be true unto Arviragus,
Or else I'll slay myself in some manner,
As did Demotion's virgin daughter dear
Because she would not violated be.
  "O Cedasus, it rouses great pity
To read of how your daughters died, alas!
That slew themselves in such another case.
  "As great a pity was it, aye and more,
That a fair Theban maid, for Nicanor,
Did slay herself in such a kind of woe.
  "Another Theban maiden did also;
For one of Macedonia her had pressed,
And she, by death, her maidenhead redressed.
  "What shall I say of Nicerates' wife,
Who, for like cause, bereft herself of life?
  "How true, too, was to Alcibiades
His love, who chose to drain death to the lees
And would not let his corpse unburied be!
Lo, what a wife was Alcestis," said she.
  "What says Homer of good Penelope?
The whole of Hellas knew her chastity.
  "*Pardieu*, of Laodamia they wrote thus,
That when at Troy was slain Protesilaus,
No longer would she live after his day.
  "The same of noble Portia may I say;
Without her Brutus could she no wise live,
To whom in youth her whole heart she did give.
  "The perfect wifehood of Artemisia
Was honoured throughout all old Caria.
  "O Teuta, queen! Your wifely chastity,
To all wives may a very mirror be.
The same thing may I say of Bilia,
Of Rhodogune and of Valeria."
  Thus Dorigen went on a day or so,
Purposing ever that to death she'd go.

But notwithstanding, upon the third night
Home came Arviragus, this worthy knight,
And asked her why it was she wept so sore.
And thereat she began to weep the more.
    "Alas!" cried she, "that ever I was born!
Thus have I said," quoth she, "thus have I sworn"—
And told him all, as you have heard before;
It needs not to re-tell it to you more.
    This husband, with glad cheer, in friendly wise,
Answered and said as I shall you apprise:
"Is there naught else, my Dorigen, than this?"
    "Nay, nay," said she, "God help me, as it is
This is too much, though it were God's own will."
    "Yea, wife," said he, "let sleep what's lying still;
It may be well with us, perchance, today.
But you your word shall hold to, by my fay!
As God may truly mercy have on me,
Wounded to death right now I'd rather be,
For sake of this great love of you I have,
Than you should not your true word keep and save.
Truth is the highest thing that man may keep."
But with that word began he then to weep,
And said: "I you forbid, on pain of death,
That ever, while to you last life and breath,
To anyone you tell this adventure.
As I best may, I will my woe endure,
Nor show a countenance of heaviness,
That folk no harm may think of you, or guess."
    And then he called a squire and a maid:
"Go forth anon with Dorigen," he said,
"And bring her to a certain place anon."
They took their leave and on their way were gone,
But nothing knew of why she thither went
Nor would he to a soul tell his intent.
    Perhaps a lot of you will certainly
Hold him a wicked man that wilfully
Put his wife's honour thus in jeopardy;
Hearken the tale, ere you upon her cry.
She may have better luck than you suppose;
And when you've heard all, let your judgment close.
    This squire I've told you of, Aurelius,
Of Dorigen he being so amorous,
Chanced, as it seems, his lady fair to meet

In middle town, right in the busiest street,
As she was going forth, as you have heard,
Toward the garden where she'd pledged her word.
And he was going gardenward also;
For he was always watching when she'd go
Out of her house to any kind of place.
But thus they met, by chance perhaps or grace;
And he saluted her with good intent,
And asked her, now, whither it was she went.

   And she replied, as if she were half mad:
"Unto the garden, as my husband bade,
My promise there to keep, alas, alas!"

   Aurelius then pondered on this case,
And in his heart he had compassion great
On her and her lamenting and her state,
And on Arviragus, the noble knight,
Who'd bidden her keep promise, as she might,
Being so loath his wife should break with truth;
And in his heart he gained, from this, great ruth,
Considering the best on every side,
That from possession rather he'd abide
Than do so great a churlish grievousness
Against free hearts and all high nobleness;
For which, and in few words, he told her thus:

   "Madam, say to your lord Arviragus
That since I see his noble gentleness
To you, and since I see well your distress,
That he'd have rather shame (and that were ruth)
Than you to me should break your word of truth,
I would myself far rather suffer woe
Than break apart the love between you two.
So I release, madam, into your hand,
And do return, discharged, each surety and
Each bond that you have given and have sworn,
Even from the very time that you were born.
My word I pledge, I'll ne'er seek to retrieve
A single promise, and I take my leave
As of the truest and of the best wife
That ever yet I've known in all my life.
Let every wife of promises take care,
Remember Dorigen, and so beware!
Thus can a squire perform a gentle deed
As well as can a knight, of that take heed."

Upon her bare knees did she thank him there,
And home unto her husband did she fare,
And told him all, as you have heard it said;
And be assured, he was so pleased and glad
That 'twere impossible of it to write.
What should I further of this case indite?

Arviragus and Dorigen his wife
In sovereign happiness led forth their life.
Never did any anger come between;
He cherished her as if she were a queen;
And she to him was true for evermore.
Of these two folk you get from me no more.

Aurelius, whose wealth was now forlorn,
He cursed the time that ever he was born;
"Alas!" cried he, "Alas! that I did state
I'd pay fine gold a thousand pounds by weight
To this philosopher! What shall I do?
I see no better than I'm ruined too.
All of my heritage I needs must sell
And be a beggar; here I cannot dwell
And shame all of my kindred in this place,
Unless I gain of him some better grace.
And so I'll go to him and try, today,
On certain dates, from year to year, to pay,
And thank him for his princely courtesy;
For I will keep my word, and I'll not lie."

With sore heart he went then to his coffer,
And took gold unto this philosopher,
The value of five hundred pounds, I guess,
And so besought him, of his nobleness,
To grant him dates for payment of the rest,
And said: "Dear master, I may well protest
I've never failed to keep my word, as yet;
For certainly I'll pay my entire debt
To you, however after I may fare,
Even to begging, save for kirtle, bare.
But if you'd grant, on good security,
Two years or three of respite unto me,
Then all were well; otherwise must I sell
My heritage; there is no more to tell."

Then this philosopher soberly answered
And spoke in this wise, when these words he'd heard:
"Have I not fairly earned my promised fee?"

"Yes, truly, you have done so, sir," said he.
"Have you not had the lady at your will?"
"No, no," said he, and sighed, and then was still.
"What was the reason? Tell me if you can."
    Aurelius his tale anon began,
And told him all, as you have heard before;
It needs not I repeat it to you more.
    He said: "Arviragus, of nobleness,
Had rather die in sorrow and distress
Than that his wife were to her promise false."
He told of Dorigen's grief, too, and how else
She had been loath to live a wicked wife
And rather would that day have lost her life,
And that her troth she swore through ignorance:
"She'd ne'er before heard of such simulance;
Which made me have for her such great pity.
And just as freely as he sent her me,
As freely sent I her to him again.
This is the sum, there's no more to explain."
    Then answered this philosopher: "Dear brother,
Each one of you has nobly dealt with other.
You are a squire, true, and he is a knight,
But God forbid, what of His blessed might,
A clerk should never do a gentle deed
As well as any of you. Of this take heed!
    "Sir, I release to you your thousand pound,
As if, right now, you'd crept out of the ground
And never, before now, had known of me.
For, sir, I'll take of you not one penny
For all my art and all my long travail.
You have paid well for all my meat and ale;
It is enough, so farewell, have good day!"
And took his horse and went forth on his way.
    Masters, this question would I ask you now:
Which was most generous, do you think, and how?
Pray tell me this before you farther wend.
I can no more, my tale is at an end.

HERE IS ENDED THE FRANKLIN'S TALE

THE SECOND NUN'S PROLOGUE

That servant and that nurse unto the vices
Which men do call in English Idleness,
Portress at Pleasure's gate, by all advices
We should avoid, and by her foe express,
That is to say, by lawful busyness,
We ought to live with resolute intent,
Lest by the Fiend through sloth we should be rent.

For he, that with his thousand cords and sly
Continually awaits us all to trap,
When he a man in idleness may spy
He easily the hidden snare will snap,
And till the man has met the foul mishap,
He's not aware the Fiend has him in hand;
We ought to work and idleness withstand.

And though men never dreaded they must die,
Yet men see well, by reason, idleness
Is nothing more than rotten sluggardry,
Whereof comes never good one may possess;
And see sloth hold her in a leash, no less,
Only to sleep and eat and always drink
And to absorb all gain of others' swink.

And so, to save us from such idleness
Through which great trouble and distress have grown,
I have here done my faithful busyness,
Translating the old legend, to make known
All of that glorious life which was thine own,
Thou ever with the rose and lily crowned,
Cecilia, for virtues high renowned.

Invocatio ad Mariam

And Thou that art the flower of virgins all
Of whom Saint Bernard loved so well to write,

To Thee at my beginning do I call;
Thou comfort of us wretches, help me indite
Thy maiden's death, who won through her merit
The eternal life, and from the Fiend such glory
As men may read hereafter in her story.

Thou Maid and Mother, Daughter of Thy Son,
Thou well of ruth, of sinful souls the cure,
In Whom, for goodness, God was embryon,
Thou humble One, high over each creature,
Thou did'st ennoble so far our nature
That no disdain God had of humankind
His Son in blood and flesh to clothe and wind.

Within the blessed cloister of Thy sides
Took human shape eternal love and peace
Who all the threefold world as sovereign guides,
Whom earth and sea and heaven, without cease,
Do praise; and Thou, O stainless Maid, increase
Bore of Thy body—and wert kept a maid—
The mighty God Who every creature made.

Assembled is in Thee magnificence,
With mercy, goodness, and with such pity
That Thou, Who art the sun of excellence,
Not only keepest those that pay to Thee,
But oftentimes, of Thy benignity,
Freely, or ever men Thy help beseech,
Thou goest before and art their spirits' leech.

Now help, Thou meek and blessed, Thou fair Maid,
Me, banished wretch, in wilderness of gall;
Think how the Canaanitish woman said
That even dogs may eat of the crumbs all
Which from the master's laden table fall;
And though I, now, unworthy son of Eve,
Am sinful, yet accept me, who believe.

And since all faith is dead divorced from works,
That I may do the right, O give me space
To free me from that darkness of deep murks!
O Thou, Who art so fair and full of grace,
Be Thou my advocate in that high place
Where without ever end is sung "Hosanna,"
Thou, Mother of Christ and daughter of Saint Anna!

And of Thy light my soul illuminate,
That troubled is by the contagion sown
Here in my body, also by the weight
Of earthly lust and false loves I have known;
O haven of refuge, O salvation shown
To those that are in sorrow and distress,
Now help, for to my work I'll me address.

Yet pray I all who read what I do write,
Forgive me that I do no diligence
By subtle change to make the story right;
For I have taken both the words and sense
From him who wrote the tale in reverence
Of this one saint; I follow her legend
And pray you that you will my work amend.

Interpretacio Nominis Caecilie

Quam Ponit Frater Iacobus

Ianuensis in Legenda Aurea.

First would I you the name of Saint Cecilia
Expound, as men may in her story see.
It is to say, in English, "Heaven's lily," a
Symbol of pure and virgin chastity;
Or, since she had the white of modesty,
And green of good conscience, and of good fame
The savour sweet, so "lily" was her name.

Or else Cecilia means "path for the blind,"
For she example was, by good teaching;
Or else Cecilia, as I written find,
Is made, after a manner of joining,
Of "Heaven" and "Lia"; and, in figuring,
The "Heaven" is put for "thought of holiness"
And "Lia" for enduring busyness.

Cecilia may mean, too, in this wise,
"Lacking in blindness," for her shining light
Of sapience, and for good qualities;
Or else, behold! this maiden's name so bright
From "Heaven" and *"leos"* comes, for which, by right,
Men well might her the "Heaven of people" call,
Example of good and wise works unto all.

Leos is folk in English, so to say,
And just as men may in the heavens see
The sun and moon and stars strewn every way,
Just so men ghostly, in this maiden free,
See of her faith the magnanimity,
And the whole glory of her sapience,
And many actions, bright of excellence.

And just as these philosophers do write
That heaven is round and moving and burning,
Just so was fair Cecilia the white
Eager and busy ever in good working,
Large and whole-hearted, steadfast in each thing,
And shining ever in charity full bright;
Now have I told you of her name aright.

Explicit

THE SECOND NUN'S TALE

OF THE LIFE OF SAINT CECILIA

This maiden bright, Cecilia, her life saith,
Was Roman born and of a noble kind,
And from the cradle tutored in the faith
Of Christ, and bore His gospel in her mind;
She never ceased, as written do I find,
To pray to God, and love Him, and to dread,
Beseeching Him to keep her maidenhead.

And when this maiden must unto a man
Be wedded, who was a young man in age,
And who had to his name Valerian,
And when the day was come for her marriage,
She, meek of heart, devout, and ever sage,
Under her robe of gold, well-made and fair,
Had next her body placed a shirt of hair.

And while the organ made its melody,
To God alone within her heart sang she:
"O Lord, my soul and body guide to Thee
Unsoiled, lest I in spirit ruined be."

And for His love Who died upon a tree,
Each second or third day she used to fast,
And ever prayed she till the day was past.

The night came, and to bed she must be gone
With her young husband, but she had no fear,
And privately to him she said anon:
"O sweet and well-beloved spouse so dear,
There is a secret, if you will to hear,
Which I am fain enough to you to say,
So that you swear that me you'll not betray."

Valerian to her his oath did swear
That evermore, whatever thing might be,
He never would betray what she said there
And so beginning straightway thus said she:
"I have an angel lover that loves me,
And with a great love, whether I wake or sleep,
He will my body ever guard and keep.

"And if he feels (and this is truth," she said)
"That you will touch or love me vulgarly,
At once he'll slay and leave you with the dead,
And in your days of youth thus shall you die;
And if you love me cleanly, so say I,
He'll love you as now me, for your cleanness,
And show you all his joy and his brightness."

Valerian, checked thus as God would mould,
Replied: "If I'm to trust you, let me see
That angel with my eyes and him behold;
And if that it a very angel be,
Then will I do as you have asked of me;
And if you love another man, forsooth
Right with this sword then will I slay you both."

Cecilia replied right in this wise:
"If you so wish, that angel shall you see,
So you believe in Christ and you baptize.
Go forth to Via Appia,"[1] said she,
"That from this town is distant but miles three,
And to the poor folk who in that place dwell
Say to them what I'll now proceed to tell.

---

1. A district near Rome (not the famous highway) where the earliest catacombs were located.

"Tell them that I, Cecilia, have sent
You to the good man Urban, who is old,
For secret need, and with a good intent.
And when this holy Urban you behold,
Tell him the thing that I to you have told;
And when he shall have purged you of your sin,
That angel shall you see ere thence you win."

Valerian to that place got him gone,
And just as he'd been told about the thing,
He found this ancient saint, Urban, anon,
Among the holy catacombs lurking.
And he anon, with never tarrying,
Told him his errand; and when it was told,
Urban for joy his two hands did uphold.

Some teardrops from his two eyes he let fall—
"Almighty Lord, O Jesus Christ," said he,
"Sower of counsel chaste, herd of us all,
The fruit of that same seed of chastity
Which Thou sowed'st in Cecilia, take to Thee!
Lo, like a busy bee, and without guile,
Thy thrall Cecilia serves Thee all the while!

"For that same spouse that lately wedded she,
Who was like lion fierce, she sends him here,
As meek as ever was a lamb, to Thee!"
And with that word anon there did appear
An old, old man, clothed all in white clothes clear,
Who had a golden-lettered book in hand,
And who before Valerian did stand.

Valerian for fear fell down as dead
When him he saw, who raised him from the floor,
And from his book (whereof I told) he read—
"One Lord, one faith, one God with never more,
One Christian Church, One Father of all to adore,
Above all, over all, and everywhere"—
These words in very gold were written there.

When this was read, then said the ancient man:
"Do you believe or not? Say 'Yea' or 'Nay.'"
"I do believe this," said Valerian,
"For truer thing than this, I dare well say,
Under the heavens none can think, nor may."

Then vanished the old man, he knew not where,
And Pope Urban baptized him even there.

Valerian, going home, Cecilia found
In chamber, wherein did an angel stand;
This angel had two coronals, woven round
Of roses and of lilies, in his hand;
And to Cecilia, as I understand,
He gave the one, and gave the other straight
Unto this said Valerian, her mate.

"With body clean and with unsullied thought
Keep well these crowns for ever," then said he;
"To you from Paradise have I them brought,
Nor ever shall they fade or withered be,
Nor lose their perfume sweet, so you trust me;
And never man shall see them with his eye,
Save he be chaste and hate depravity.

"And you, Valerian, since you so soon
Consented to accept the Faith also,
Say what you will and you shall have your boon."
"I have a brother," said Valerian, "Oh,
And in the wide world I love no man so.
I pray you that my brother may have grace
To know the truth, as I do in this place."

The angel answered: "God likes your request,
And both of you, with palm of martyrdom,
Shall come at last unto His blessed rest."
Whereon his brother Tibertius was come.
And when he smelled the sweet perfume that from
The roses and the lilies filled the air,
In heart he wondered much how came it there,

And said: "I wonder much, this time of year,
Whence comes the sweetness that arises so,
Of rose and lily, to my senses here?
For though I held them in my two hands—no
The savour could in me no deeper go.
The gentle scent that in my heart I find
Has changed me to a man of other kind."

Valerian replied: "Two crowns have we,
Snow white and rose red, and they're bright and fair,
The which your two eyes have no power to see;

And as you smell them, brother, through my prayer,
So shall you see them also, brother dear,
If you but will, without delay forsooth,
Rightly believe and know the very truth."

Tibertius answered: "Say you this to me
In truth? Or do I dream I hear all this?"
"In dreams," replied Valerian, then, "have we
Lived to this time, O brother mine, ywis.
In truth now for the first time our life is."
"How know you?" asked Tibertius: "In what wise?"
Valerian said: "You will I now apprise.

"God's angel unto me the truth has taught,
Which you shall see, if only you'll put by
All idols and be clean, else you'll learn naught."
(And of these crowns miraculous, say I,
Saint Ambrose of the two does testify
In his Preface; this noble doctor dear
Commends the story, making it all clear:

The palm of martyrdom, thus to receive,
This Saint Cecilia, filled with God's gift,
The world and even her chamber did she leave;
Witness Tibertius' and Valerian's shrift,
To whom the good God sent by angel swift
Two crowns of flowers fair and sweet smelling,
And bade the angel take them as fitting.

The maiden brought these men to bliss above;
The world has learned what it is worth, 'tis plain,
Devotion to fair chastity to love.)
Then did Cecilia show him and explain
That every idol is a thing all vain;
For they are dumb, and they are deaf also,
And charged him that his idols he forgo.

"Whoso believes not this, a beast he is,"
Said then Tibertius, "if I shall not lie."
And then she kissed his breast, when she heard this,
And was full glad that truth he could espy.
"This day I take you for my own ally,"
So said this blessed, lovely maiden dear;
And after that said on as you shall hear:

"Lo, even as the love of Christ," said she,

"Made me your brother's wife, just in that wise
I take you now my close ally to be,
Since you'll forgo your idols and despise.
Go with your brother, let them you baptize
And make you clean; so that you may behold
The angel's face whereof your brother told."

Tibertius answered, saying: "Brother dear,
First tell me where to go and to what man."
"To whom?" said he, "Come forth, and with good cheer,
For I will lead you unto Pope Urban."
"To Urban? Brother mine, Valerian,"
Tibertius said, "and thither will you lead?
I think this were a wondrous thing indeed.

"Surely you mean not Urban!" he cried out,
"Who's been so often ordered to be dead,
And lives in corners, dodging ever about,
And dares not once by day to show his head?
Why, men would burn him in a fire right red
If he were found, or any him could spy;
And us, if we should bear him company.

"And while we seek for that Divinity
Who is in Heaven where we may not see,
Burned in this world to ashes shall we be!"
To whom Cecilia answered, and boldly:
"Men might well dread, and very reasonably,
This life on earth to lose, my own dear brother,
If this alone were living, and no other.

"But there's a better life in other place,
That never shall be lost, nay, fear you naught,
Whereof God's Son has told us, through His grace;
That Father's Son all things that He has wrought,
And all that is has made with reasoned thought,
The Spirit which from Father did proceed
Has given a soul to each, fear not indeed.

"By word and miracle God's only Son,
When He was in this world, declared us here
There was another life that could be won."
To whom replied Tibertius: "Sister dear,
Did you not say, just now, in manner clear,
There's but one God, the Lord in truth, no less;

And now to three, how can you bear witness?"

"That will I tell," said she, "before I go.
Just as a man has kinds of wisdom three,
Memory, genius, intellect also,
So in one Being of Divinity
Three Persons, truly may there right well be."
Then she to him full earnestly did preach
Of Jesus' coming, and of His pain did teach,

And many points His agony had shown:
How God's Son in this world a time did hold
To man a full remission to make known,
Who had been bound in sin and care of old:
All these things to Tibertius first she told.
And then Tibertius, with a good intent,
He with Valerian to Pope Urban went,

Who thanked God; and with a glad heart and light
He christened him, and made him in that place
Perfect in knowledge, and God's very knight.
And after this Tibertius got such grace
That every day he saw, in time and space,
God's angel; aye, and every kind of boon
He asked of God, the same was granted soon.

'Twere hard in proper order to explain
How many wonders Jesus for them wrought;
But at the last, to tell it short and plain,
They by the sergeants of Rome town were sought,
And to Almachius the prefect brought,
Who questioned them and learned their whole intent,
And unto Jupiter's image had them sent,

Saying: "Who will not go and sacrifice,
Strike off his head, that is my sentence here."
These martyrs, then, of whom I do apprise,
One Maximus, who was an officer
Of the prefect's, and his corniculer,
Took them; and when the saints forth he had led,
Himself he wept, for pity that he had.

When Maximus had learned their creed and lore,
Of executioners obtained he leave,
And to his house he led them, without more;
And by their preaching, ere it came to eve,

They from the executioners did reave,
And Maximus and from his folk, each one,
The false faith, to believe in God alone.

Cecilia came, when it was fully night,
With priests, who christened them together there;
And afterward, when day came with its light,
Cecilia them bade, with steadfast cheer:
"Now Christ's own knights together, lief and dear,
The works of darkness cast you all away,
And arm you in the armour of the day.

"You have indeed fought the good fight—all hail!
Your course is done, your faith you have preserved,
Go to the crown of life that shall not fail;
The Righteous Judge, Whom you have so well served,
Will give it to you, since you've it deserved."
And when, as I have told this thing was said,
To make the sacrifice they forth were led.

But when before the image they were brought,
Briefly to tell the end as it is known,
They'd not incense, and sacrificed they naught,
But on their knees they reverently knelt down,
With humble heart and firm devotion shown,
And so they lost their heads there in that place.
Their spirits went unto the King of Grace.

This Maximus, who saw this thing betide,
With pitying tears he told folk then, forthright,
That he their souls had seen to Heaven glide
With angels full of glory and of light,
And by his words converted many a wight;
For which Almachius had him beaten so,
With whips of lead, he did his life forgo.

Cecilia him buried with the others,
Valerian and Tibertius, quietly.
Thus in the tomb he rested with the brothers;
And after this Almachius speedily
Ordered his servants fetch him openly
Cecilia, that she might in his presence
Make sacrifice to Jove and burn incense.

But since they were converted by her lore,
They wept, and to a full belief they came

In what she said, and cried out more and more,
"O Christ, God's Son, Whose substance is the same,
Thou'rt very God, and blessed be Thy name,
Who hast so good a servant Thee to serve;
This with one voice we say, nor will we swerve."

Almachius, who heard of this same thing,
Commanded that they bring her him to see,
And when she came, this was his questioning:
"What manner of woman are you?" then asked he.
"I am a noblewoman born," said she.
"I ask," said he, "though to your harm and grief,
Of your religion and of your belief."

"You have begun your questions foolishly,"
Said she, "who would two answers so include
In one demand; you asked me ignorantly."
Almachius answered that exactitude:
"Whence comes your answering so rough and rude?"
"Whence?" asked she, when that she was thus constrained,
"From conscience and from simple faith unfeigned."

Almachius said: "And do you take no heed
Of power I wield?" And she replied like this:
"Your might," said she, "is scarce a thing to dread;
For power of every mortal man but is
Like to a bladder full of wind, ywis.
For with a needle's point, when it is blown,
Prick it, and all the pride of it comes down."

"Erroneously have you begun," said he,
"And deep in error do you still remain;
Know you not how our mighty princes free
Have ordered us such error to restrain,
That every Christian man shall suffer pain,
Unless his Christianity he deny?
He shall be free if he'll do that, say I."

"Your princes err, and your nobility,"
Cecilia said, "and with a mad sentence
Condemn our guilt all guiltless though we be;
And you, who know full well our innocence,
Merely because we do our reverence
To Christ and bear ourselves the Christian name,
You thus impute to us a crime and blame.

"But we, who know far better than can you
Its virtue, will not once the name gainsay."
Almachius said: "Choose one of these things two:
Deny that faith, or sacrifice today,
That you may now escape from death that way."
Whereat the holy, blessed, lovely maid
Began to laugh, and to the judge she said:

"O judge, convicted by your own folly,
Will you that I deny my innocence
And make myself a criminal?" asked she.
"Lo, he dissimulates in audience,
He glares and rages in his violence!"
To whom Almachius: "O unhappy wretch,
Do you not know how far my might may stretch?

"Did not our mighty princes to me give,
Aye, both the power and authority
To give to people death or make them live?
Why do you speak so proudly then to me?"
"I speak to you but steadfastly," said she,
"Not proudly, for I say, upon my side,
We've deadly hatred for the vice of pride.

"And if to hear a truth you do not fear,
Then will I show, all openly, by right,
That you have said a full great falsehood here.
You say, your princes have you given the might
Both to condemn and give life to a wight;
But you can merely him of life bereave,
You have no other power or other leave!

"You may but say, your princes did declare
You were death's officer; if more you claim,
You lie, for of more power you are bare."
"This bold speech drop!" Almachius did exclaim,
"And do your sacrifice in our gods' name.
I care not what you wrongfully impute;
Like a philosopher I'll bear it, mute;

"But those same wrongs which I cannot endure
Are those you speak against our gods," said he.
Cecilia replied: "O vain creature,
You've nothing said, since speaking first to me,
That I've not learned thereby your great folly,

And that you were and are, in every wise,
An ignorant officer and vain justice.

"There is no proving, by your outward eye,
That you're not blind; what can be seen by all,
That it is stone—that men see well, say I—
Yet that same stone a god you think and call.
I charge you, let your hand upon it fall,
And test it well, and 'twill be stone, you'll find,
Since you can see it not with your eyes blind.

"It is a shame that all the people shall
So scorn you, judge, and laugh at your folly;
For commonly men know it above all
That mighty God is in His heaven high,
And idols such as these, they testify,
May bring no profit to themselves or you—
They have no power, nothing can they do."

These words and many other such said she,
And he grew wroth and bade she should be led
Home to her house. "And in her house," said he,
"Boil her in bath heated by great flames red."
And as he bade, so was it done, 'tis said;
For in a bath they locked her and began
(All night and day) a great fire there to fan.

The long night through, and a long day also,
For all the fire and all the bath's great heat,
She sat there cool and calm and felt no woe,
Nor did it make her any drop to sweat.
But in that bath her life should she lose yet;
For he, Almachius, with bad intent,
To slay her in the bath his headsman sent.

The executioner three times her smote
Upon the neck, and could not strike again,
Although he failed to cut in two her throat,
For at that time the ordinance was plain
That no man might another give the pain
Of striking four blows, whether soft or sore;
This executioner dared do no more.

But half dead, with her neck cut three times there,
He let her lie, and on his way he went.
The Christian folk that all about her were,

With sheets caught up the precious blood she spent;
And three days lived she in this same torment,
But never ceased at all the faith to teach,
That she had fostered; dying did she preach;

To them she gave her goods and everything,
And of Pope Urban put them in the care,
And said: "This much I asked of Heaven's King,
A respite of three days, that you might share
With me these souls; and too I would prepare
Before I go my house a church to make,
That it be kept forever for my sake."

Saint Urban, with his deacons, privately,
The body took and buried it by night
Among his other saints, right honourably.
Her house is Church of Saint Cecilia hight;
Saint Urban hallowed it, as well he might;
Wherein in noble wise unto this day
To Christ and to His saint men service pay.

HERE IS ENDED THE SECOND NUN'S TALE

THE CANON'S YEOMAN'S PROLOGUE

When Saint Cecilia's Life was done, and whiles
We had not farther gone a good five miles,
At Boughton-under-Blean us did o'ertake
A man, who was clothed all in clothes of black,
And underneath he had a surplice white.
His hackney was of dappled-grey, so bright
With sweat that it was marvelous to see;
It seemed that he had spurred him for miles three.
The horse too that his yeoman rode upon
So sweat that scarcely could it go; and on
The breast strap of the harness foam stood high,
Whereof he was as flecked as is a pie.
A double wallet on his crupper lay,
And as it seemed, he went in light array.
Lightly, for summer, rode this worthy man,
And in my heart to wonder I began
What he could be, until I understood
The way he had his cloak sewed to his hood;
From which, when long I had communed with me,
I judged at length some canon he must be.
His hat hung on his back down by a lace,
For he had ridden more than trot or pace;
He had spurred hard, indeed, as madman would.
A burdock leaf he had beneath his hood
To curb the sweat and keep his head from heat.
But what a joy it was to see him sweat!
His forehead dripped as a distillatory
Were full of plantain and of pellitory.
And this man when he came began to cry:
"God save," said he, "this jolly company!
Fast I have spurred," said he then, "for your sake,
Because I wanted you to overtake,

To ride on in this merry company."
His yeoman too was full of courtesy,
And said: "Good sirs, all in the morningtide
Out of your hostelry I saw you ride,
And warned my lord and master, full and plain,
And he to ride with you is truly fain
For his amusement; he loves dalliance."
    "Friend, for your warning, God give you good chance,"
Said then our host, "for truly it would seem
Your lord is wise, and so I may well deem;
He is right jocund also, I dare lay.
Can he a merry tale tell, on the way,
Wherewith to gladden this our company?"
    "Who, sir? My lord? Yea, yea, without a lie,
He knows of mirth and of all jollity
Not but enough; and also, sir, trust me,
If you but knew him as well as do I,
You'd wonder much how well and craftily
He can behave, and that in different wise.
He's taken on him many an enterprise
That were right hard for anyone that's here
(Unless he learned it) to effect, I fear.
As plainly as he rides, here among you,
It would be to your profit if you knew
Him well; you'd not give up his acquaintance
For much of wealth, I dare lay in balance
All that I have of goods in my possession.
He is a man of wondrous high discretion,
I warn you well, he's a surpassing man."
    "Well," said our host, "then pray tell, if you can,
Is he a clerk, or not? Tell what he is."
    "Nay, he is greater than a clerk, ywis,"
This yeoman said, "and briefly, if you'll wait,
Host, of his craft a little I'll relate.
    "I say, my lord has so much subtlety
(But all his art you cannot learn from me,
And yet I help by working at his side),
That all this pleasant land through which we ride,
From here right into Canterbury town,
Why, he could turn it all clean upside-down
And pave it all with silver and with gold."
    And when this yeoman had this story told
Unto our host, our host said: *"Ben'cite!*

This thing is wondrous marvelous to me,
Since your lord is a man of such science,
For which men should hold him in reverence,
That of his dignity his care's so slight;
His over-garment is not worth a mite
For such a man as he, so may I go!
It is all dirty and it's torn also.
Why is your lord so slovenly, pray I,
And yet has power better clothes to buy,
If but his deeds accord well with your speech?
Tell me that, sir, and that I do beseech."

"Why?" asked this yeoman, "Why ask this of me?
God help me, wealthy he will never be!
(But I will not stand back of what I say,
And therefore keep it secret, I you pray).
He is too wise, in faith, as I believe;
That which is overdone, as I conceive,
Won't turn out right, clerks say, and that's a vice.
In that, I hold him ignorantly nice.
For when a man has overmuch of wit,
It often happens he misuses it;
So does my lord, and this thing grieves me sore.
May God amend it, I can say no more."

"No matter then, good yeoman," said our host;
"Since of the learning of your lord you boast,
Tell how he works, I pray you heartily,
Since he's so clever and withal so sly.
Where do you dwell, if you may tell it me?"

"Within the suburbs of a town," said he,
"Lurking in corners and in alleys blind,
Wherein these thieves and robbers, every kind,
Have all their privy fearful residence,
As those who dare not show men their presence;
So do we live, if I'm to tell the truth."

"Now," said our host, "let me go on, forsooth.
Why are you so discoloured in the face?"

"Peter!" cried he. "God give it evil grace!
I am so wont upon the fire to blow
That it has changed my colour, as I trow.
I'm not wont in a mirror, sir, to pry,
But I work hard to learn to multiply.[1]

---

1. Multiply: to increase gold or silver in amount by alchemy.

We stir and mix and stare into the fire,
But for all that we fail of our desire,
And never do we come to our conclusion.
To many folk we bring about illusion,
And borrow gold, perhaps a pound or two,
Or ten, or twelve, or any sum will do,
And make them think, aye, at the least, it's plain,
That from a pound of gold we can make twain!
It is all false, but yet we have great hope
That we can do it, and after it we grope.
But that science is so far us before,
We never can, in spite of all we swore,
Come up with it, it slides away so fast;
And it will make us beggars at the last."

The while this yeoman chattered on like this,
The canon nearer drew and did not miss
A thing he said; suspicion always woke
In him, indeed, when anybody spoke.
For Cato says suspicion's ever fed
In any guilty man when aught is said.
That was the reason why he drew so near
To his yeoman, his gossiping to hear.
And thus he said unto his yeoman then:
"Now hold your peace and do not speak again,
For if you do you'll pay it ruefully;
You slander me, here in this company,
And you uncover that which you should hide."

"Yea?" said our host, "Tell on, whate'er betide;
For all his threatening do not care a mite!"

"In faith," said he, "my caring is but slight."

And when this canon saw how it would be,
That his yeoman would tell his privity,
He fled away for very grief and shame.

"Ah," said the yeoman, "hence shall come a game.
All that I know anon now will I tell.
Since he is gone, the Fiend take him to Hell!
With him hereafter I'll have naught to do
For penny or for pound, I promise you!
He that first brought me into that ill game,
Before he die, sorrow have he and shame!
For it's no game to me, sirs, by my fay;
That I feel well, whatever men may say.
And yet, for all my smart and all my grief,

For all the sorrow, labour, and mischief,
I never could leave off, in any wise.
Now would to God that my wit might suffice
To tell of all pertaining to that art!
Nevertheless, I will relate a part;
Since now my lord is gone, I will not spare;
The things I know about I will declare."

HERE ENDS THE PROLOGUE
TO THE CANON'S YEOMAN'S TALE

THE CANON'S YEOMAN'S TALE

Prima pars

Seven years I've served this canon, but no more
I know about his science than before.
All that I had I have quite lost thereby;
And, God knows, so have many more than I.
Where I was wont to be right fresh and gay
Of clothing and of other good array,
Now may I wear my old hose on my head;
And where my colour was both fresh and red,
Now it is wan and of a leaden hue;
Whoso this science follows, he shall rue.
And from my toil yet bleary is my eye,
Behold the gain it is to multiply!
That slippery science has made me so bare
That I've no goods, wherever I may fare;
And I am still indebted so thereby
For gold that I have borrowed, truthfully,
That while I live I shall repay it never.
Let every man be warned by me for ever!
And any man who casts his lot thereon,
If he continue, I hold his thrift gone.
So help me God, thereby he shall not win,
But empty purse and have his wits grow thin.
And when he, through his madness and folly,
Has lost his own, by willing jeopardy,
Then will he incite others, many a one,
To lose their wealth as he himself has done.

For unto scoundrels it's a pleasant thing
Their fellows in distress and pain to bring,
Thus was I taught once by a learned clerk.
Of that no matter, I'll speak of our work.

   When we are where we choose to exercise
Our elvish craft, why, we seem wondrous wise,
Our terms are all so learned and so quaint.
I blow the fire till my heart's like to faint.

   Why tell you what proportions of things went
In working out each new experiment,
As five ounces, or six, it may well be,
Of silver, or some other quantity?
Or tell you all the names, my memory fails,
Of orpiment, burnt bones, and iron scales
That into powder we ground fine and small?
Or in an earthen pot how we put all,
And salt put in, and also pepper dear,
Before these powders that I speak of here,
And covered all these with a plate of glass,
And of the various other gear there was?
And of the sealing of the pot and glass,
So that the air might no way from it pass?
And of the slow fire and the forced also,
Which we made there, and of the care and woe
That we took in our matter's sublimating,
And in calcining and amalgamating
Quicksilver, which is known as mercury crude?
For all our skill, we never could conclude.
Our orpiment and sublimed mercury,
Our litharge that we ground on porphyry,
Of each some certain ounces—it is plain
Naught helped us, all our labour was in vain.
Neither the gases that by nature rose
Nor solid matter either—none of those
Might, in our working, anything avail.
For lost was all our labour and travail,
And all the cost, the devil's own to pay,
Was lost also, for we made no headway.

   There is also full many another thing
That to our craft pertains in labouring.
Though name them properly I never can,
Because, indeed, I am an ignorant man,
Yet will I tell them as they come to mind,

Though I'll not try to class each one by kind;
Armenian bole, borax, the green of brass,
And sundry vessels made of earth and glass,
Our urinals and all our descensories,
Vials and crucibles, sublimatories,
Cucurbites, and alembics, and such freaks,
All dear enough if valued at two leeks.
There is no need to specify them all,
The reddening waters and the dark bull's gall,
Arsenic, sal ammoniac, and brimstone;
And, too, of herbs could I name many a one,
Valerian, agrimony, and lunary,
And others such, if I but wished to tarry.
Our lamps that burned by day and burned by night
To bring about our end, if but we might,
Our furnace, too, white-hot for calcination,
And waters all prepared for albication,
Unslaked lime, chalk, and white of egg, I say,
Powders diverse, and ashes, dung, piss, clay,
Little waxed bags, saltpetre, vitriol;
And many a different fire of wood and coal;
Alkali, salt, potassium carbonate,
And our burnt matters, and coagulate,
Clay mixed with horses' or men's hair, and oil
Of tartar, alum, glass, yeast, wort, argoil,
Realgar, and our matters absorbent,
And with them, too, our matters resorbent,
And how we practised silver citrination
And our cementing and our fermentation,
Our moulds and testers, aye, and many more.
   I will tell you, as I was taught before,
The bodies seven and the spirits four,
In order, as my master named of yore.
The first of spirits, then, quicksilver is,
The second arsenic, the third, ywis,
Is sal ammoniac, the fourth brimstone.
The seven bodies I'll describe anon:
Sol, gold is, Luna's silver, as we see,
Mars iron, and quicksilver's Mercury,
Saturn is lead, and Jupiter is tin,
And Venus copper, by my father's kin!
   This wicked craft, whoso will exercise,
He shall gain never wealth that may suffice;

For all the coin he spends therein goes out
And is but lost, of which I have no doubt.
Whoso, then, will exhibit such folly,
Let him come forth and learn to multiply;
And every man that has aught in coffer,
Let him appear and be philosopher.
Perhaps that craft is easy to acquire?
Nay, nay, God knows! And be he monk or friar
Canon, or priest, or any other wight,
Though he sit at his books both day and night
In learning of this elvish, fruitless lore,
All is in vain, and by gad it's much more!
To teach an ignorant man this subtlety—
Fie! Speak not of it, for it cannot be;
And though he has booklore, or though he's none,
In final count he shall find it all one.
For both of them, and this by my salvation,
Come to one end seeking multiplication;
They fare the same when they've done everything;
That is to say, they both fail, sorrowing.

Yet I forgot to tell you in detail
Of the corrosive waters and limaille,
And of some bodies the mollification,
And on the other hand of induration,
Oils, and ablutions, metals fusible—
More than a bible it would need to tell,
The largest ever; therefore I think best
That of these names I say no more, but rest.
For I believe that I've told you enough
To raise a devil, be he never so rough.

Ah no! Let be; the old philosopher's stone
Is called elixir, which we seek, each one;
For had we that, then were we safe enow.
But unto God in Heaven do I vow,
For all our art, when we've done all things thus,
And all our tricks, it will not come to us.
The thing has caused us to spend all we had,
For grief of which almost we should go mad,
Save that good hope comes creeping in the heart,
Supposing ever, though we sorely smart,
The elixir will relieve us afterward;
The tension of such hope is sharp and hard;
I warn you well, it means go seeking ever;

That future time has made men to dissever,
Trusting that hope, from all that ever they had.
Yet of that art they cannot well grow sad,
For unto them it is a bitter-sweet;
So it appears; for had they but a sheet
With which to wrap themselves about by night,
And a coarse cloak to walk in by daylight,
They'd sell them both and spend it on this craft;
They can withhold naught till there's nothing left.
And evermore, wherever they'll be gone,
Men know them by their smell of foul brimstone;
For all the world they stink as does a goat;
Their savour is so rammish and so hot
That, though a man a mile away may be,
The odour will infect him, trust to me!
Thus by their smell and their threadbare array,
If men but wish, these folk they'll know, I say.
And if a man but ask them privately
Why they do go clothed so unthriftily,
They right away will whisper in his ear
And say that if they should be noticed here,
Why, men would slay them, what of their science;
Lo, thus these folk impose on innocence!

   Pass over this; unto my tale I'll run.
Before the pot upon the fire be done,
Of metals in a certain quantity
My lord it tempers, and no man save he—
Now he is gone I dare say this boldly—
For, as men say, he can work artfully;
Always I well know he has such a name,
And yet full often has he been to blame;
And know you how? Full oft it happens so,
The pot broke, and farewell! All vanished, O!
These metals have such violence and force
That crucibles cannot resist their course
Unless they are built up of lime and stone;
They penetrate, and through the wall they're gone,
And some of them sink right into the ground—
Thus have we lost, at times, full many a pound—
And some are scattered all the floor about,
Some leap up to the roof. Beyond a doubt,
Although the Fiend's to us not visible,
I think he's with us, aye, that same scoundrel!

In Hell, wherein he is the lord and sire,
There's not more woe, nor rancour, nor more ire.
For when our pot is broken, as I've said,
Each man will scold and think that he's been bled.
One said that it was due to fire-making,
One said it was the blowing of the thing
(There I was scared, for that was what I did);
"O straw! You silly fool!" the third one chid,
"It was not tempered as it ought to be."
"Nay," said the fourth, "shut up and list to me;
It was because our fire was not of beech,
That's why, by all the wealth I hope to reach!"
I cannot tell where one should put the blame;
There was a dreadful quarrel, just the same.

   "What!" cried my lord, "there's no more to be done,
Whatever 'twas, I'll know the reason soon;
I am quite certain that the pot was crazed.
Be as it may, do not stand there amazed;
As always, sweep the floor up quickly, lad,
Pluck up your hearts and be both blithe and glad."

   The rubbish in a heap then swept up was,
And on the floor was spread a large canvas,
And all this rubbish in a sieve was thrown,
And sifted, picked, and whirled, both up and down.

   "By gad," said one, "something of our metal
There is yet here, although we have not all.
Although this thing has gone awry for now,
Another time it may be well enow.
We must put all our wealth at adventure;
A merchant's luck, gad! will not aye endure,
Believe me, in his high prosperity;
Sometimes his freight will sink beneath the sea,
And sometimes comes it safely unto land."

   "Peace," said my lord, "next time I'll understand
How to proceed and with a better aim;
And, save I do, sirs, let me be to blame;
There was defect in something, well I know 't."

   Another said the fire was far too hot.
But were it hot or cold, I dare say this,
That we concluded evermore amiss.
We fail of that which we desire to have,
And in our madness evermore we rave.
And when we're all together, then each one

Seems as he were a very Solomon.
But everything that glisters like fine gold
Is not gold, as I've often heard it told;
And every apple that is fair to eye
Is yet not sound, whatever hucksters cry;
And even so, that's how it fares with us:
For he that seems the wisest, by Jesus,
Is greatest fool, when proof is asked, in brief;
And he that seems the truest is a thief;
That shall you know ere I from you do wend,
When of my tale I've made at length an end.

Explicit prima pars.
Et sequitur pars secunda.

There is a canon of religion known
Among us, who'd contaminate a town,
Though 'twere as great as Nineveh the free,
Rome, Alexandria, Troy, and others three.
His tricks and all his infinite treacherousness
No man could write down fully, as I guess,
Though he should live unto his thousandth year.
In all this world for falsehood he's no peer;
For in his terms he will so twist and wind
And speak in words so slippery of kind,
When he communicates with any wight,
That he soon makes a fool of him outright,
Unless it be a devil, as he is.
Full many a man has he beguiled ere this,
And will, if he may live a further while;
And yet men walk and ride full many a mile
To seek him out and have his acquaintance,
Naught knowing of his treacherous simulance.
And if you care to listen to me here,
I'll make the proof of what I say quite clear.
    But most religious canons, just and true,
Don't think I'm slandering your house, or you,
Although my tale may of a canon be.
Some rogue's in every order, pardon me,
And God forbid that for one rascal's sake
Against a group we condemnation make.
To slander you is nowise my intent,
But to correct what is amiss I'm bent.
This tale I tell here not alone for you,

But even for others, too; you know well how
Among Christ's twelve disciples there was not
One to play traitor, save Iscariot.
Then why should all the rest be put to blame
Who guiltless were? Of you I say the same.
Save only this, if you will list to me,
If any Judas in your convent be,
Remove the man betimes, I counsel you,
Lest shame or loss or trouble should ensue.
And be displeased in nothing, I you pray,
But hear what on this matter I may say.

In London was a priest, an annualeer[2]
Who had therein dwelt many a quiet year,
A man so pleasant and so serviceable
To the goodwife who shared with him her table,
That she would never suffer him to pay
For board or clothing, went he ever so gay;
Of spending-silver, too, he had enow.
No matter; I'll proceed as I said, now,
And tell about the canon all my tale,
Who gave this priest good cause to weep and wail.

This canon false, he came, upon a day
Into the chaplain's chamber, where he lay,
Beseeching him to lend him a certain
Amount in gold, the which he'd pay again.
"Lend me a mark," said he, "for three days, say,
And when that time's done, I will it repay.
And if you find me false, I shall not reck
If, on a day, you hang me by the neck!"

This priest brought him a mark, and quickly, too,
Whereat this canon thanked him, said adieu,
And took his leave and went forth on his way,
And brought the money back on the third day,
And to the priest he gave his gold again,
Whereof this priest was wondrous glad, 'tis plain.

"Truly," he said, "it no wise bothers me
To lend a man a noble, or two, or three,
Or any modest thing that is my own,
To him who has the disposition shown
That in no wise will he forgo to pay;
To such a man I never can say nay."

---

2. A priest employed in singing anniversary masses.

"What!" cried this canon, "Should I be untrue?
Nay, that for me would be a thing quite new.
Truth is a thing that I will ever keep
Unto that day, at last, when I shall creep
Into my grave, or elsewise God forbid!
Trust this as surely as you trust your creed.
I thank God, and in good time be it said,
That there was never yet man ill repaid
For gold or silver that to me he lent,
Nor ever falsehood in my heart I've meant.
And, sir," said he, "out of my privity,
Since you have been so very good to me,
And showed to me so great a nobleness,
Somewhat to quit you for your kindliness,
I'll show to you, and if you'd learn it here,
I'll teach you plainly all the methods dear
I use in working at philosophy.
Give it good heed, for you'll see with your eye
I'll do a masterpiece before I go."

    "Yes?" asked the priest, "Yes, sir, and will you so?
Mary! Thereof I pray you heartily."

    "Right at your service, sir, and truthfully,"
Replied the canon, "else, may God forbid!"
Service this thief could offer, and he did!
Full true it is that service in this guise
Stinks, as take witness of these old men wise;
And soon enough I will this verify
By this canon, the root of treachery,
Who always had delight, nor could refrain—
Such devilish thoughts within his heart did reign—
When he brought Christian folk to tribulation.
God keep us from his false dissimulation!

    Naught understood this priest with whom he dealt,
And of his coming harm he nothing felt.
O hapless priest! O hapless innocent!
Blinded by avarice malevolent!
O luckless one, full blind is your conceit,
Nothing are you aware of the deceit
Which this sly fox arranges here to be!
His wily stratagems you cannot flee.
Wherefore, at once to make the ending known,
By which your troubles will be clearly shown,
Unhappy man, I'll hasten on to tell

The folly into which you blindly fell,
And, too, the treachery of that other wretch,
As far as what I know of him may stretch.

    This canon was my lord, you think I mean?
Sir host, in faith, and by the Heaven's Queen,
It was another canon, and not he,
Who has a hundred-fold more subtlety!
He has betrayed the people many a time;
Of his deceit it wearies me to rhyme.
Whatever of his falsehood I have said,
For shame of him I feel my cheeks grow red;
At any rate, my cheeks begin to glow,
For redness have I none, right well I know,
In all my visage; for the fumes diverse
Of metals, whereof you've heard me rehearse,
Have all consumed and wasted my redness.
Now take heed of this canon's wickedness.

    "Sir," this to the priest, "let your man be gone
For quicksilver, that we have some anon;
And let him bring us ounces two or three;
And when he comes, just so soon shall you see
A wondrous thing you've never seen ere this."

    "Sir," said the priest, "it shall be done, ywis."
He bade his servant go to fetch them all,
And since the lad was ready at his call,
He got him forth and came anon again
With this quicksilver, truly to explain,
And gave these ounces three to the canon;
And he took them and laid them fairly down,
And bade the servant coals to go and bring,
That he might get to work with everything.

    The coals at once were brought, and all was well;
And then this canon took a crucible
Out of his bosom, showing it to the priest.
"This instrument," said he, "you see—at least
Take in your hand, and put yourself therein
An ounce of quicksilver, and here begin,
And in God's name, to be philosopher!
There are but few to whom I would proffer
To make my science clear and evident.
For you shall learn here, by experiment,
That this quicksilver will I mortify
Right in your sight anon, without a lie,

And make it as good silver and as fine
As any that's in your purse or in mine,
Or elsewhere, aye, and make it malleable;
Otherwise hold me false, unfit as well
Among good folk for ever to appear.
I have a powder here that cost me dear,
Shall do all this, for it's the root of all
My craft; you'll see what shall therewith befall.
Dismiss your man and let him stay without,
And shut the door fast while we are about
Our secret work, that no man may espy
The way we work in this philosophy."

All was then done as canon had decreed;
This servant took himself straight out, indeed,
Whereat his master barred the door anon,
And to their labour quickly they were gone.

The priest, at this damned canon's ordering,
Upon the fire anon did set this thing,
And blew the fire and busied him full fast;
Within the crucible the canon cast
A powder (I know not whereof it was
Compounded, whether of chalk, or maybe glass,
Or something else—it was not worth a fly)
To blind the priest with; and he bade him high
The coals to pile the crucible above.
"In token of how much I bear you love,"
This canon said, "your own two hands, and none
Other, shall do this thing that shall be done."

"Thank you," the priest replied, and was right glad,
And heaped the coals up as the canon bade.
And while he laboured thus, this fiendish wretch,
This canon false—may him the foul Fiend fetch!—
Out of his bosom took a beechen coal,
Wherein right cunningly he'd bored a hole
In which, before, he'd put of silver limail
An ounce, and which he'd stopped up, without fail,
With blackened wax, to keep the filings in.
And understand you well that this false gin
Was not made there, but it was made before;
And there were other things I'll tell you more
About hereafter, which with him he'd brought;
Ere he came there, to cheat he'd taken thought,
And ere they parted he did even so;

Till he had skinned him he could not forgo.
It wearies me when of him I do speak,
For on his falsehood I myself would wreak,
If I knew how; but he is here and there:
He is so restless he abides nowhere.
    But take heed now, sirs, for God's very love!
He took this coal whereof I spoke above,
And in his hand he bore it privily.
And while the priest did pile up busily
The burning coals, as I told you ere this,
This canon said: "My friend, you do amiss;
This is not piled up as it ought to be;
But soon I shall amend all that," said he.
"Now let me thereof have a hand the whiles,
For I've great pity on you, by Saint Giles!
You are right hot, I see well how you sweat,
Take here a cloth and wipe away the wet."
And while the simple priest did wipe his face,
This canon took his coal, and with grave grace,
Laid it above and well to middleward
Upon the crucible, and blew it hard
Until the flames did blaze up hot again.
    "Now give us drink, sir," said the canon then,
"For soon all shall be well, I undertake;
Let us sit down, and let us merry make."
And when this treacherous canon's beechen coal
Was burnt, then all the filings from the hole
Into the crucible fell down anon;
As so, in reason, it must needs have done,
Since so well centred over it it was;
But thereof nothing knew the priest, alas!
He deemed that all the coals alike were good,
For of the trick he nothing understood.
And when this alchemist was ready, he
Said to the priest: "Rise up and stand by me;
And since I know that metal mould you've none,
Go sally forth and bring here a chalk-stone;
For I will make one of the very shape
That ingot moulds have, if I can them ape.
And, too, bring in with you a bowl or pan
Full of clear water, and you'll see, dear man,
How well our business here shall thrive, in brief.
And yet, that you may have no unbelief,

Or think that somehow I'm not doing right,
I'll never be a moment out of sight,
But go with you and come with you again."
　　The chamber door, then, briefly to explain,
They opened and they shut, and went their way.
And as they went they took the key, I say,
And came again, without a long delay,
Why should I tarry here the livelong day?
He took the chalk and shaped it in such wise
As moulds are made, as further I'll apprise.
　　I say, he took, then, out of his own sleeve
A tain[3] of silver (Hell the man receive!)
Which was an ounce, no more or less, in weight;
Now here's the trick, the way of which I'll state!
　　He shaped his mould in length and breadth to be
Like to the tain of silver, as you see,
So slyly that the priest this never spied;
And in his sleeve did then the model hide;
And from the fire he took his crucible
And poured it in the mould, for all went well,
And in the bowl of water then did cast
The mould and all, and bade the priest, at last:
"Seek what there is, put in your hand and grope,
And you shall find there silver, as I hope;
What—devils out of Hell!—should it else be?
Filing of silver silver is!" cried he.
　　He put his hand in and a tain took out
Of silver fine, and glad, you cannot doubt,
Was this priest when he saw that it was so.
"God's blessing, and His Mother's dear also,
And all the saints', too, may you have, my friend,"
The priest replied, "and may they curse my end
Unless you will vouchsafe to teach to me
This noble craft and all this subtlety;
I will be yours in all that ever I may!"
　　Said then the canon: "Yet will I essay
A second time, that you may take good heed
And be expert in this, and at your need
When I am absent on another day,
You may this science and its arts essay.
Quicksilver take," said he, "one ounce, no more,

---

3. Tain: a thin slice.

As you'll remember that we did before,
And as you treated that, so do with this
And like the first 'twill change, which silver is."
    The priest then followed carefully the plan,
As he'd been bidden by this cursed man,
The canon; long and hard he blew the fire
To bring about the thing he did desire.
And this said canon waited all the while,
All ready there the poor priest to beguile,
And, for assurance in his hand did bear
A hollow stick (take heed, sirs, and beware!),
In end of which an ounce was, and no more,
Of silver filings put, all as before
Within the coal, and stopped with wax, a bit,
To keep the filings in the hole of it.
And while the priest was busy, as I say,
This canon, drawing close, got in his way,
And unobserved he threw the powder in
Just as before (the Devil from his skin
Strip him, I pray to God, for lies he wrought;
For he was ever false in deed and thought);
And with his stick, above the crucible,
Arranged for knavish trickery so well,
He stirred the coals until to melt began
The thin wax in the fire, as every man,
Except a fool, knows well it must, sans doubt,
And all that was within the stick slipped out,
And quickly in the crucible it fell.
Good sirs, what better do you wish than well?
When now the priest was thus beguiled again,
Supposing naught but truth, I should explain,
He was so glad that I cannot express,
In any way, his mirth and his gladness;
And to the canon he did proffer soon
Body and goods. "Yea," was the canon's tune,
"Though I am poor, I'm artful as you'll find;
I warn you plainly, there's yet more behind.
Is there some copper in your place?" asked he.
    "Yea," said the priest, "I think there may well be."
    "If not, go buy us some, and quickly too,
Good sir, make haste and fetch us it, pray do."
    He went his way, and with the copper came,
And in his hands this canon took the same,

And of the copper weighed out but an ounce.
My tongue is far too simple to pronounce,
As servant to my wit, the doubleness
Within this canon, root of wickedness.
Friendly he seemed to those that knew him not,
But he was fiendly both in heart and thought.
It wearies me to tell of his falseness,
Nevertheless yet will I it express
To end that all men may be warned thereby,
And for no other reason, truthfully.
    Within the crucible he puts the ounce
Of copper which upon the fire he mounts,
And casts in powder, making the priest blow,
And at his labouring to stoop down low,
All as before, and all was but a jape;
Just as he pleased, he made the priest his ape.
And afterward into the mould he cast
The copper; into the water pan at last
Plunging the whole, and thrust therein his hand.
And in his sleeve (as you did understand
Before) he had a certain silver tain.
He slyly took it out, this damned villain,
While still the priest saw nothing of the plan,
And left it in the bottom of the pan;
And in the water groped he to and fro
And very stealthily took up also
The copper tain, of which the priest knew naught,
And hiding it, he by the breast him caught,
And spoke to him, thus carrying on his game:
"Stoop lower down, by God, you are to blame!
Come, help me now, as I did you whilere,
Put in your hand and search and learn what's there."
This priest took up the silver tain anon,
And then the canon said: "Let us be gone
With these three plates, the which we have so wrought,
To some goldsmith, to learn if they're worth aught.
For by my faith, I wouldn't, for my hood,
Have them, save they are silver fine and good,
And that immediately proved shall be."
    Unto the goldsmith, then, with these tains three,
They went, and put the metal in assay
By fire and hammer; no man could say nay,
But they were silver, as they ought to be.

This foolish priest, who was more glad than he?
Never was gladder bird for dawn of day,
Nor nightingale in season of the May,
Nor was there ever one more fain to sing;
Nor lady happier in carolling
Or speaking much of love and woman's meed;
Nor knight in arms to do a hardy deed
To stand in graces of his lady dear—
Than was the priest this sorry craft to hear;
And to the canon thus he spoke and said:
"For love of God, Who for us all was dead,
And as I may requite it unto you,
What shall this recipe cost? Come, tell me now?"

"By 'r Lady," said this canon, "it is dear,
I warn you well; for now in England here
One friar and I are all who can it make."

"No matter," said he, "now, sir, for God's sake,
What shall I pay? Oh, tell me this, I pray!"

"Truly," said he, "it is right dear, I say;
Sir, in one word, if this thing you will have,
You shall pay forty pounds, so God me save!
And were it not for friendship shown ere this
To me, you should pay more than that, ywis."

This priest the sum of forty pounds anon
In nobles fetched, and gave them, every one,
To this said canon for this said receipt;
His business was all fraud and all deceit.

"Sir priest," he said, "I do not care to lose
My secret craft, and I would 'twere kept close;
So, as you love me, keep it privily;
For if men knew all of my subtlety,
By God above, they'd have so great envy
Of me, because of my philosophy,
I should be slain, there'd be no other way."

"Nay, God forbid!" replied the priest. "What say?
Far rather would I spend all coin, by gad,
That I possess (and else may I grow mad!)
Than that you fall in any such distress."

"For your good will, I wish you all success,"
Replied the canon, "farewell, many thanks."

He went, and ne'er the priest this mountebank's
Face saw thereafter; and when this priest would
Make his own test, at such time as he could,

Of this receipt, farewell! it would not be!
Lo, thus bejaped and thus beguiled was he!
And thus he had his introduction in
The way men fall to ruin and to sin.
   Consider, sirs, how that, in each estate,
Between men and their gold there is debate
To such degree that gold is nearly done.
This multiplying blinds so many a one
That in good faith I think that it may be
The greatest cause of this said scarcity.
Philosophers they speak so mistily
About this craft, plain men can't come thereby
With any wit that men have nowadays.
They may well chatter, as do all these jays,
And in vague cant set their desire and pain,
But to their purpose shall they ne'er attain.
A man may easily learn, if he have aught,
To multiply, and bring his wealth to naught.
   Lo, such a gain is in this pleasant game
A man's mirth it will turn to grief and shame,
And it will empty great and heavy purses,
And causes alchemists to get the curses
Of all of those who thereunto have lent.
O fie! For shame! Those who the fire resent,
Alas! can they not flee the fire's fierce heat?
If you have tried it, leave it, I repeat,
Lest you lose all; better than never is late.
Never to thrive at all were a long date.
And though you prowl, you never gold shall find;
You are as bold as Bayard[4] is, the blind,
That blunders forth and thinks of danger, none;
He is as bold to run against a stone
As to go ambling down the broad highway.
And so fare you who multiply, I say.
If your two fleshly eyes can't see aright,
Look to it that your mind lack not for sight.
For, though you look about and though you stare,
You shall not win a mite in traffic there,
But you shall waste all you may scrape and turn.
Avoid that fire, lest much too fast it burn;
Meddle no more with that base art, I mean,

---

4. Bayard: common name for a horse.

For if you do, you'll lose your savings clean.
    And now I'll tell you briefly, if I may,
What the philosophers about this say.
    Arnold of Villanovana I will cite.
In his *Rosarium* he brings to light
These facts, and says—in this I do not lie:
"No man can mercury ever mortify,
Unless its brother's aid to it he bring,
And also he who first did say this thing
Was father of philosophers, Hermes;
He said the dragon, doubtless, takes his ease
And never dies, unless there's also slain
His brother, which, to make the matter plain,
Means, by the dragon, mercury, none other,
And brimstone's understood to mean the brother,
That out of *Sol* and *Luna* we can draw.
And therefore," said he, "give heed to my saw,
Let no man busy him ever with this art
Unless philosophers to him impart
Their meaning clearly, for unless he can
Their language grasp, he's but an ignorant man.
This science and this learning, too," said he,
"Must ever the most secret secrets be."
    Also there was a student of Plato
Who on a time said to his master so,
As his book *Senior* will bear witness;
And this was his demand, in truthfulness:
"Tell me the name, sir, of the Secret Stone."
    And Plato answered in this wise anon:
"Take, now, the stone that Titanos men name."
    "What's that?" asked he.
                                    "Magnesia is the same,"
Plato replied.
                        "Yea, sir, and is it thus?
This is *ignotum per ignotius*.
What is magnesia, good sir, I do pray?"
    "It is a water that is made, I say,
Out of four elements," replied Plato.
    "Tell me the root, good sir," said he, "if so,
What then, is water, tell me if you will."
    "Nay, nay," said Plato, "and now peace, be still."
Philosophers are sworn, aye, every one,
That they will thus discover it to none,

Nor in a book will write it for men here;
For unto Christ it is so lief and dear
That He wills that it not discovered be,
Save where it's pleasing to His deity
Man to inspire, and also, to defend
Whom that He will; and lo, this is the end.
  And thus do I conclude: Since God in Heaven
Wills that philosophers shall not say even
How any man may come upon that stone,
I say, as for the best, let it alone.
For whoso makes of God his adversary,
To work out anything that is contrary
To what He wills, he'll surely never thrive,
Though he should multiply while he's alive.
And there's the end; for finished is my tale.
May God's salvation to no good man fail! Amen.

HERE IS ENDED THE CANON'S YEOMAN'S TALE

THE MANCIPLE'S PROLOGUE

Do you not know where stands a little town
That's called by all about Bob-up-and-down,
Under the Blean, down Canterbury way?
There did our host begin to jape and play,
And he said: "Sirs, what! Dun is in the mire![1]
Is there no man, then, who, for prayer or hire,
Will wake our comrade who's so far behind?
A thief might easily rob him and bind.
See how he's nodding! See, now, by Cock's bones,
As if he'd fall down from his horse at once.
Is that a cook of London, with mischance?
Make him come forward, he knows his penance,
For he shall tell a tale here, by my fay,
Although it be not worth a bunch of hay.
Awake, you cook," cried he, "God give you sorrow!
What ails you that you sleep thus? It's good morrow!
Have you had fleas all night, or are you drunk?
Or did you toil all night in some quean's bunk?
So that you cannot now hold up your head?"

The cook, who was all pale and nothing red,
Said to our host: "So may God my soul bless,
As there is on me such a drowsiness,
I know not why, that I would rather sleep
Than drink a gallon of best wine in Cheap."

"Well," said the manciple, "if 'twill give ease
To you, sir cook, and in no way displease
The folk that ride here in this company,
And if our host will, of his courtesy,
I will, for now, excuse you from your tale.
For in good faith, your visage is full pale,
Your eyes are bleary also, as I think,
And I know well your breath right sour does stink,

---

1. The name of an old rustic game.

465

All of which shows that you are far from well;
No flattering lies about you will I tell.
See how he yawns. Just look, the drunken wight,
As if he'd swallow all of us outright.
Now close your mouth, man, by your father's kin;
Ah, may Hell's devil set his foot therein!
Your cursed breath will soon infect us all;
Fie, stinking swine, fie! Evil you befall!
Ah, take you heed, sirs, of this lusty man.
Now, sweet sir, would you like to ride at fan?[2]
It seems to me you're in the proper shape!
You've drunk the wine that makes a man an ape,
And that is when a man plays with a straw."

   The cook grew wroth, for this had touched the raw,
And at the manciple he nodded fast
For lack of speech, and him his horse did cast,
And there he lay till up the rest him took,
Which was a feat of riding for a cook!
Alas! That he had kept not to his ladle!
For ere he was again within his saddle,
There was a mighty shoving to and fro
To lift him up, and hugeous care and woe,
So all unwieldy was this sorry ghost.
And to the manciple then spoke our host:
"Since drink has got such utter domination
Over this fellow here, by my salvation,
I think that badly he would tell his tale.
For whether wine or old or musty ale
Is what he's drunk, he speaks all through his nose;
He snorts hard and with cold he's lachrymose.
Also he has more than enough to do
To keep him and his nag out of the slough;
And if he fall down off his horse again,
We'll all have quite enough of labour then
In lifting up his heavy drunken corse.
Tell on your tale, he matters not, of course.

   "Yet, manciple, in faith, you are not wise
Thus openly to chide him for his vice.
Some day he'll get revenge, you may be sure,

---

2. Fan: a vane or quintain. To ride at fan (or at quintain) was to tilt at a board at one end of a pivoted crossbar, at the other end of which was suspended a sandbag. The object was to strike the board with the lance and to escape being hit by the sandbag.

And call you like a falcon to the lure;
I mean he'll speak of certain little things,
As, say, to point out in your reckonings
Things not quite honest, were they put to proof."
    "Nay," said the manciple, "that were ill behoof!
So might he easily catch me in his snare.
Yet would I rather pay him for the mare
Which he rides on than have him with me strive;
I will not rouse his rage, so may I thrive!
That which I said, I said as jesting word;
And know you what? I have here, in a gourd,
A draught of wine, yea, of a good ripe grape,
And now anon you shall behold a jape.
This cook shall drink thereof, sir, if I may;
On pain of death he will not say me nay!"
    And certainly, to tell it as it was,
Out of this gourd the cook drank deep, alas!
What need had he? He'd drunk enough that morn
And when he had blown into this said horn,
He gave the manciple the gourd again;
And of that drink the cook was wondrous fain,
And thanked him then in such wise as he could.
    Then did our host break into laughter loud,
And said: "I see well it is necessary,
Where'er we go, good drink with us we carry;
For that will turn rancour and all unease
To accord and love, and many a wrong appease.
    "O Bacchus, thou, all blessed be thy name
Who canst so turn stern earnest into game!
Honour and thanks be to thy deity!
Concerning which you'll get no more from me.
Tell on your tale, good manciple, I pray."
    "Well, sir," said he, "now hear what I will say."

THUS ENDS THE MANCIPLE'S PROLOGUE

THE MANCIPLE'S TALE
OF THE CROW

When Phoebus once on earth was dwelling, here,
As in the ancient books it is made clear,

He was the lustiest of bachelors[3]
In all this world, and even the best archer;
He slew Python, the serpent, as he lay
Sleeping within the sunlight, on a day;
And many another noble, worthy deed
He with his bow wrought, as all men may read.

He played all instruments of minstrelsy,
And sang so that it made great harmony
To hear his clear voice in the joyous sun.
Truly the king of Thebes, that Amphion
Who, by his singing, walled that great city,
Could never sing one half so well as he.
Therewith he was the handsomest young man
That is or was since first the world began.
What needs it that his features I revive?
For in the world was none so fair alive.
Compact of honour and of nobleness,
Perfect he was in every worthiness.

This Phoebus, of all youthful knights the flower,
Whom generous chivalry did richly dower,
For his amusement (sign of victory
Over that Python, says the old story),
Was wont to bear in hand a golden bow.

Now Phoebus had within his house a crow,
Which in a cage he'd fostered many a day,
And taught to speak, as men may teach a jay.
White was this crow as is a snow white swan,
And counterfeit the speech of any man
He could, when he desired to tell a tale.
Therewith, in all this world, no nightingale
Could, by a hundred-thousandth part, they tell,
Carol and sing so merrily and well.

Now had this Phoebus in his house a wife,
Whom he loved better than he loved his life,
And night and day he used much diligence
To please her and to do her reverence,
Save only, if it's truth that I shall say,
Jealous he was and so did guard her aye;
For he was very loath befooled to be.
And so is everyone in such degree;
But all in vain, for it avails one naught.

---

1. Bachelor: a young knight.

A good wife, who is clean in deed and thought,
Should not be kept a prisoner, that's plain;
And certainly the labour is in vain
That guards a slut, for, sirs, it just won't be.
This hold I for an utter idiocy,
That men should lose their labour guarding wives;
So say these wise old writers in their lives.

But now to purpose, as I first began:
This worthy Phoebus did all that a man
Could do to please, thinking that by such pleasures,
And by his manhood and his other measures
To make her love him and keep faithful, too.
But God knows well that nothing man may do
Will ever keep restrained a thing that nature
Has made innate in any human creature.

Take any bird and put it in a cage
And do your best affection to engage
And rear it tenderly with meat and drink
Of all the dainties that you can bethink,
And always keep it cleanly as you may;
Although its cage of gold be never so gay,
Yet would this bird, by twenty thousand-fold,
Rather, within a forest dark and cold,
Go to eat worms and all such wretchedness.
For ever this bird will do his business
To find some way to get outside the wires.
Above all things his freedom he desires.

Or take a cat, and feed him well with milk
And tender flesh, and make his bed of silk,
And let him see a mouse go by the wall;
Anon he leaves the milk and flesh and all
And every dainty that is in that house,
Such appetite has he to eat a mouse.
Desire has here its mighty power shown
And inborn appetite reclaims its own.

A she-wolf also has a vulgar mind;
The wretchedest he-wolf that she may find,
Or least of reputation, she'll not hate
Whenever she's desirous of a mate.

All these examples speak I of these men
Who are untrue, and not of sweet women.
For men have aye a lickerish appetite
On lower things to do their base delight

Than on their wives, though they be ne'er so fair
And ne'er so true and ne'er so debonair.
Flesh is so fickle, lusting beyond measure,
That we in no one thing can long have pleasure
Or virtuous keep more than a little while.
    This Phoebus, who was thinking of no guile,
He was deceived, for all his quality;
For under him a substitute had she,
A man of little reputation, one
Worth naught to Phoebus, by comparison.
The more harm that; it often happens so,
Whereof there come so much of harm and woe.
    And so befell, when Phoebus was absent,
His wife has quickly for her leman[4] sent.
Her leman? Truly, 'tis a knavish speech!
Forgive it me, I do indeed beseech.
    The wise old Plato says, as you may read,
The word must needs accord well with the deed.
And if a man tell properly a thing,
The word must suited be to the acting.
But I'm a vulgar man, and thus say I,
There is no smallest difference, truly,
Between a wife who is of high degree,
If of her body she dishonest be,
And a poor unknown wench, other than this—
If it be true that both do what's amiss—
The gentlewoman, in her state above,
She shall be called his lady, in their love;
And since the other's but a poor woman,
She shall be called his wench or his leman.
And God knows very well, my own dear brother,
Men lay the one as low as lies the other.
    Between a tyrant or usurping chief
And any outlawed man or errant thief,
It's just the same, there is no difference.
One told to Alexander this sentence:
That, since the tyrant is of greater might,
By force of numbers, to slay men outright
And burn down house and home even as a plane,
Lo! for that he's a captain, that's certain;
And since the outlaw has small company

---

4. Leman: formerly applied to either sex.

And may not do so great a harm as he,
Nor bring a nation into such great grief,
Why, he's called but an outlaw or a thief.

But since I'm not a man the texts to spell,
Nothing at all from texts now will I tell;
I'll go on with my tale as I began.

When Phoebus' wife had sent for her leman,
At once they wrought all of their libertinage.

And the white crow, aye hanging in the cage,
Saw what they did, and never said a word.
And when again came Phoebus home, the lord,
This crow sang loud "Cuckoo! Cuckoo! Cuckoo!"

"What, bird?" asked Phoebus, "What song now sing you?
Were you not wont so merrily to sing
That in my heart it was a joyful thing
To hear your voice? Alas! What song is this?"

"By God," said he, "I do not sing amiss;
Phoebus," said he, "for all your worthiness,
For all your beauty and your nobleness,
For all your song and all your minstrelsy,
For all your watching, bleared is your bright eye
By one of small repute, as well is known,
Not worth, when I compare it with your own,
The value of a gnat, as I may thrive.
For on your bed your wife I saw him swive."

What will you more? The crow thereafter told,
In sober fashion, giving witness bold,
How that his wife had done her lechery
To his great shame and with great villainy;
Repeating that he'd seen it with his eyes.
Then Phoebus turned away in sad surprise;
He thought his wretched heart would break for woe;
His bow he bent and set there an arrow,
And in his angry mood his wife did slay.
This the result; there is no more to say;
For grief of which he ceased his minstrelsy,
Broke harp and lute, gittern and psaltery;
And, too, he broke his arrows and his bow.
And after that he spoke thus to the crow.

"Traitor," cried he, "with tongue of scorpion,
You have brought me to ruin, treacherous one!
Alas, that I was born! Why died I not?
O my dear wife, jewel of joy, God wot,

Who were to me so trusty and so true,
Now you lie dead, with face all pale of hue,
And you were guiltless, I dare swear to this!
O hasty hand, to do so foul amiss!
O stupid brain, O anger all reckless,
That unadvisedly struck the guiltless!
O ill distrust that jealousy had sown!
Where were your thought and your discretion flown?
O every man, beware of hastiness,
Do not believe without a strong witness;
Strike not too soon, before you reason why,
And be advised full well and soberly
Ere you do any execution thus
In your wild anger when it is jealous.
Alas! A thousand folk has hasty ire
Ruined, and left them bleeding in the mire.
Alas! I'll slay myself forthwith for grief!"
     And to the crow he said, "O you false thief!
I will anon requite you that false tale!
You sang but lately like a nightingale;
Now, you false thief, your songs are over and done,
And you'll all those white feathers lose, each one,
Nor ever in your life more shall you speak.
Thus men on traitors shall their justice wreak;
You and your offspring ever shall be black,
Nor evermore sweet noises shall you make,
But you shall cry in tempest and in rain
In token that through you my wife was slain."
And on the crow he leaped, and that anon,
And plucked out his white feathers, every one,
And made him black, and stilled for evermore
His song and speech, and flung him out the door
Unto the devil, where I leave this jack;
And for this reason, now all crows are black.
     Masters, by this example, I do pray
You will beware and heed what I shall say:
Never tell any man, through all your life,
How that another man has humped his wife;
He'll hate you mortally, and that's certain.
Dan Solomon, as these wise clerks explain,
Teaches a man to keep his tongue from all;
But, as I said, I am not textual.

Nevertheless, thus taught me my good dame:
"My son, think of the crow, in high God's name;
My son, keep your tongue still, and keep your friend.
A wicked tongue is worse than any fiend.
My son, from devils men themselves may bless;
My son, high God, of His endless goodness,
Walled up the tongue with teeth and lips and cheeks
That man should speak advisedly when he speaks.
My son, full oftentimes, for too much speech,
Has many a man been killed, as clerics teach;
But, speaking little and advisedly,
Is no man harmed, to put it generally.
My son, your foolish tongue you should restrain
At all times, save those when your soul is fain
To speak of God, in honour and in prayer.
The first of virtues, son, if you'll but hear,
Is to restrain and to guard well your tongue—
Thus teach the children while they yet are young—
My son, of too much speaking, ill advised,
Where less had been enough and had sufficed,
Much harm may come; thus was I told and taught.
In fluent speaking evil wants for naught.
Know you of where a rash tongue has well served?
Just as a sword has cut deep and has carved
A many an arm in two, dear son, just so
A tongue can cut a friendship, well I know.
A gossip is to God abominable.
Read Solomon, so wise and honourable,
Or David's Psalms, what Seneca has said.
My son, speak not, but merely bow your head.
Dissemble like one deaf, if you but hear
A chatterer speak what's dangerous in your ear.
The Fleming says, and learn it, for it's best,
That little prattle gives us all much rest.
My son, if you no wicked word have said,
To be betrayed you need not ever dread;
But he that has missaid, I dare explain,
He may not aye recall his words again.
That which is said, is said, and goes, in truth,
Though he repent, and be he lief or loath.
A man's the slave of him to whom he's told
A tale to which he can no longer hold.

My son, beware and be not author new
Of tidings, whether they be false or true.
Where'er you come, among the high or low,
Guard well your tongue, and think upon the crow."

HERE IS ENDED THE MANCIPLE'S TALE OF THE CROW

THE PARSON'S PROLOGUE

What time the manciple his tale had ended,
The sun down from the south line had descended
So low that he was not, unto my sight,
Degrees full nine and twenty yet in height.
Four of the clock it was then, as I guess:
Four feet eleven, little more or less,
My shadow was extended then and there,
A length as if the shadow parted were
In six-foot equal parts, as I have shown.
Therewith the moon's high exaltation known,
I mean the sign of Libra, did ascend
As we were entering a village-end;
Whereat our host, since wont to guide was he,
As in this case, our jolly company,
Said in this wise: "Now, masters, every one,
We lack no tales except a single one.
My judgment is fulfilled and my decree,
I think that we have heard from each degree.
Almost fulfilled is all my ordinance;
I pray to God to give him right good chance
Who tells to us this story pleasantly.
Sir priest," he asked, "can you a vicar be?
Are you a parson? Tell truth, by your fay!
Be what you will, break not our jolly play;
For every man, save you, has told his tale,
Unbuckle, show us what is in your mail;
For truly, I think, judging by your cheer,
You should knit up a mighty matter here.
Tell us a fable now, by Cock's dear bones!"
    This parson then replied to him at once:
"You'll get no foolish fable told by me;
For Paul, when writing unto Timothy,
Reproves all those that veer from truthfulness
And tell false fables and such wretchedness.
Why should I sow chaff out of my own fist

475

When I may sow good wheat, if I but list?
But if, I say, you something wish to hear
In which the moral virtues will appear,
And if you now will give me audience,
I will right gladly, in Christ's reverence,
Give you such lawful pleasure as I can.
But trust me, since I am a Southern man,
I can't romance with 'rum, ram, ruff,'[1] by letter,
And, God knows, rhyme I hold but little better;
But if you wish the truth made plain and straight,
A pleasant tale in prose I will relate
To weave our feast together at the end.
May Jesus, of His grace, the wit me send
To show you, as we journey this last stage,
The way of that most perfect pilgrimage
To heavenly Jerusalem on high.
And if you will vouchsafe, anon shall I
Begin my tale, concerning which, I pray,
Choose what you will, I can no better say.
Yet this my meditation is, I own,
Perhaps not free from errors to be shown
By clerks, since I am not a learned man;
I do but grasp the meaning as I can.
Therefore, I do protest, I shall prepare
To take what comes, and all correction bear."
    When he had spoken thus, we all agreed,
For, as it seemed to us, 'twas right indeed
To end with something virtuous in its sense,
And so to give him time and audience.
We bade our host that he to him convey
The wish of all that he begin straightway.
    Our host, he had the very words for all.
"Sir priest," said he, "may good to you befall!
Say what you wish, and we will gladly hear."
And after that he added, for his ear:
"Tell us," he said, "your meditation grown,
But pray make haste, the sun will soon be down;
Be fruitful, tell us in a little space,
And to do well God send to you His grace!"

Explicit prohemium

---

1. Rum, ram, ruff: nonsense words, to imitate and mock at alliteration.

THE PARSON'S TALE

Jer. 6°. State super vias et videte et interrogate de viis antiquis, que sit via bona; et ambulate in ea, et inuenietis refrigerium animabus vestris, &c.

Our sweet Lord God of Heaven, Who will destroy no man, but would have all come unto the knowledge of Him and to the blessed life that is everlasting, admonishes us by the Prophet Jeremiah, who says thus: "Stand ye in the ways, and see, and ask for the old paths (that is to say, the old wisdom) where is the good way, and walk therein, and ye shall find rest for your souls," etc. Many are the spiritual ways that lead folk unto Our Lord Jesus Christ and to the Kingdom of Glory. Of which ways there is a right noble way and a proper one, which will not fail either man or woman who through sin has gone astray from the right way to the Heavenly Jerusalem; and this way is called penitence, as to which man should gladly hear and inquire with all his heart, in order that he may learn what penitence is, and why it is called penitence, and in how many ways penitence functions, and how many kinds of penitence there are, and what things appertain and are necessary to penitence, and what things hinder it.

Saint Ambrose says that "penitence is the mourning of man for the sin that he has done, and the resolve to do no more anything for which he ought to mourn." And another doctor says: "Penitence is the lamenting of man, who sorrows for his sin and punishes himself because he has done amiss." Penitence, under certain circumstances, is the true repentance of a man that goes in sorrow and other pain for his misdeeds. And that he shall be truly penitent, he shall first regret the sins that he has done, and steadfastly purpose in his heart to make oral confession, and to do penance, and nevermore to do anything for which he ought to feel regret or to mourn, and to continue on good works; or else his repentance will avail him nothing. For, as says Saint Isidore: "He is a mocker and a liar and no true penitent who does again a thing for which he ought to repent." Weeping, when not accompanied by a refusal to sin, shall not avail. But, nevertheless, men should hope that every time a man falls, be it never so often, he may arise through penitence, if he have grace; but certainly there is great doubt of this. For, as Saint Gregory says: "With difficulty shall he arise out of sin who is burdened with the burden of evil habit." And therefore repentant folk, who keep from sin and abandon sin ere sin abandon them, Holy Church holds them to be sure of their salvation. And he that sins and verily repents in his last moments, Holy Church yet hopes for his salvation, what of the great mercy of Our Lord Jesus Christ, because of his repentance; but take you the certain way.

And now, since I have declared unto you what penitence is, now shall you understand that there are three deeds required by penitence. The first deed is that a man be baptized after he has sinned. Saint Augustine says: "Save he be repentant for his former sinful life, he shall not begin to lead the new clean life." For truly, if he be baptized without repentance for his old offence, he receives the sign of baptism but not the grace nor the remission of his sins, until he have true repentance. Another defect is this, that men do deadly sin after they have received baptism. The third defect is that men fall into venial sins after their baptism, and from day to day. Thereof Saint Augustine says that "penitence of good and humble folk is the penitence of every day."

The kinds of penitence are three. One of them is public, another is general, and the third is private. That form of penitence which is public is of two kinds: as to be expelled from Holy Church in Lent, for the slaughter of children and such-like things. Another is, when a man has sinned openly, of which sin the shame is openly spoken of in the community; and then Holy Church, by judgment rendered, constrains him to do open penance. Common or general penitence is when priests enjoin men collectively in certain cases, as, peradventure, to go naked on pilgrimages, or barefoot. Private penitence is that which men do continually for their sins, whereof we confess privately and receive a private penance.

Now shall you understand what is necessary to a true and perfect penitence. And this stands upon three things: contrition of heart, confession by word of mouth, and restitution. As to which Saint John Chrysostom says: "Penitence constrains a man to accept cheerfully every pain that is put upon him, with contrition of heart and oral confession, with restitution; and in doing of all acts of humility." And this is a fruitful penitence for three things wherein we anger Our Lord Jesus Christ; that is to say, by delight in thinking, by recklessness in speaking, and by wicked sinful works. And over against these wicked offences is penitence, which may be likened unto a tree.

The root of this tree is contrition, which hides itself away in the heart of him who is truly repentant, just as the root of another tree hides within the earth. From the root contrition springs a trunk that bears branches and leaves of confession and the fruit of penance, As to which Christ says in His gospel: "Bring forth therefore fruits meet for repentance." For by this fruit may men know this tree, and not by the root that is hidden in the heart of man, nor by the branches, nor by the leaves of confession. And therefore Our Lord Jesus Christ says thus: "By their fruits ye shall know them." From this root, too, springs a seed of grace, the which seed is the mother of security, and this seed is eager and hot. The grace of this seed springs from God, through remembrance of the day of doom and the pains of Hell. Of this matter says Solomon: "Fear the Lord, and depart from evil." The heat of this seed is the love of God and the desiring of the joy everlasting. This heat draws the heart of man unto God and causes him to hate his sin. For truly there is nothing that tastes so well to a child as the milk of its nurse, nor is there anything more abhorrent to it than this same milk when it is mingled with other food. Just so, to the sinful man who loves his sin, it seems that it is sweeter than anything else; but from the time that he begins to love devoutly Our Lord Jesus Christ, and desires the life everlasting, there is to him nothing more abominable. For truly the law of God is the love of God; whereof David the prophet says: "Ye that love the Lord, hate evil." He that loves God keeps His law and His word. The Prophet Daniel saw this tree in spirit following upon the vision of King Nebuchadnezzar, when he counselled him to do penance. Penance is the tree of life to those who receive it, and he that holds himself in true penitence is blessed, according to the opinion of Solomon.

In this penitence or contrition man shall understand four things, that is to say, what contrition is, and what the causes are that move a man to contrition, and how he should be contrite, and what contrition avails the soul. Then it is thus: that contrition is the real sorrow that a man receives within his heart for his sins, with firm purpose to confess them and to do penance and nevermore to do sin. And this sorrow shall be in this manner, as says Saint Bernard: "It shall be heavy and grievous and sharp and poignant in the heart." First, because man has offended his Lord and his Creator; and more sharp and poignant because he has offended his Heavenly Father; and yet more sharp and poignant because he has angered and offended Him Who redeemed him, Who with His precious blood has delivered us from the bonds of sin and from the cruelty of the Devil and from the pains of Hell.

The causes that ought to move a man to contrition are six. First, a man should remember his sins, yet see to it that this same remembrance be not to him in any wise a delight, but only great shame and sorrow for his guilt. For Job says: that sinful men do things that ought to be confessed. And therefore Hezekiah says: "I will remember all the years of my life, in bitterness of heart." And God says in the Apocalypse: "Remember from whence thou art fallen." For before that time when first you sinned, you were the children of God and members of the Kingdom of God; but because of your sin you are become slavish and vile, and the children of the Fiend, hated of the angels, the slander of Holy Church, and food of the false serpent. You are perpetual fuel for the fire of Hell. And yet more vile and abominable, for you offend often and often, like the dog that returns to his vomit. And you are even yet more vile, for your long continuation in sin and your sinful habits, for which you are as filthy in your sin as a beast in its dung. Such thoughts cause a man to take shame to himself for his sinning, and not delight, as God says by the Prophet Ezekiel: "Thou shalt remember thy ways and be ashamed." Truly, sins are the ways that lead folk unto Hell.

The second reason why a man ought to have contempt for sin is this: that, as Saint Peter says, "He that sinneth is the slave of sin." And sin puts a man into deep thraldom. And thereupon the Prophet Ezekiel says: "I went sorrowfully, in abhorrence of myself." And truly, well ought a man to abhor sin and to release himself from that thraldom and degradation. And see what Seneca says about this matter. He says thus: "Though I knew that neither God nor man should ever be cognizant of it, yet would I disdain to commit a sin." And the same Seneca also says: "I am born to greater things than to be thrall to my body, or than to make of my body a thrall." Nor a viler thrall may man or woman make of his or her body than by giving that body over to sin. And were it the lowest churl, or the lowest woman, that lives, and the least worth, yet is he or she then more vile and more in servitude. Ever from the higher degree than man falls, the more is he enthralled, and by so much the more to God and to the world is he vile and abominable. O good God! Well ought a man to have disdain of sin; since, because of sin, whereas he was once free, now is he in bondage. And thereupon Saint Augustine says: "If thou have disdain for thy servant, if he offend or sin, have thou then disdain that thou shouldest do any sin." Have regard of your worth, that you be not foul unto yourself. Alas! Well ought they then to disdain to be servants and thralls to sin, and to be sorely ashamed of themselves, when God of His endless goodness has set them in high place, or given them understanding, bodily strength, health, beauty, prosperity, and redeemed them with His heart's blood, who now so unnaturally, in face of His nobleness, requite Him so vilely as to slaughter their own souls. O good God! You women, who are of so great beauty, remember the proverb of Solomon, who says: "A fair woman who is the fool of her body is like a gold ring in the snout of a sow." For just as a sow roots deep into every ordure, so does she root her beauty into the stinking filth of sin.

The third cause that ought to move a man to contrition is fear of the day of doom and of the horrible pains of Hell. For as Saint Jerome says: "Every time that I remember the day of doom I quake; for when I eat or drink or do whatever thing, ever it seems to me that the trump sounds in my ear, bidding the dead arise and come to judgment." O good God! Greatly ought a man to fear such a judgment, "Where we shall be all," as Saint Paul says, "before the throne of Our Lord Jesus Christ." And there we shall compose a general congregation, whence no man shall absent himself. For truly there shall avail neither essoin nor excuse. And not only shall our faults be judged, but all our deeds shall openly be made known. As Saint Bernard says: "There shall no pleading avail, and no trickery; we shall give reckoning for every idle word." There shall we have a judge that cannot be corrupted or deceived. And why? Because, in truth, all our thoughts are known unto Him; nor for prayer nor for bribing shall He be corrupted. And therefore says Solomon: "The wrath of God will spare no one, either for prayer or gifts." Therefore, at the day of doom, there shall be no hope of escape. Wherefore, as says Saint Anselm: "Great anguish shall all sinful folk have at that time; there shall the stern and angry judge sit above, and under Him the horrible pit of Hell, open to destroy him who must acknowledge his sins, which sins shall be openly showed before God and before all creatures. And on the left side more devils than any heart can think, to harry and to draw the sinful souls to the punishment of Hell. And within the hearts of folk shall be the tearing of conscience and without shall be the world all burning. Whither then shall the wretched sinful man flee to hide himself? Certainly he shall not hide; he must come forth and show himself." For truly, as says Saint Jerome: "The earth shall cast him forth and the sea also; aye, and the air, which shall be filled with thunders and with lightnings." Now, indeed, whoso well thinks of these things, I suppose that his sin shall not be a delight within him, but a great sorrow, for fear of the pain of Hell. And therefore said Job to God: "Let me take comfort a little, before I go whence I shall not return, even to the land of darkness and the shadow of death; a land of darkness as darkness itself: and of the shadow of death, without any order, and where the light is as darkness." Lo, here may it be seen that Job prayed for respite to weep and to bewail his trespass; for indeed one day of respite is better than all the treasure of the world. And for as much as man may acquit himself before God by penitence in this world, and not by treasure, therefore should he pray to God to grant him respite for a while to weep and to bewail his sins. For truly, all the sorrow that a man might feel from the beginning of the world is but a little thing in comparison with the sorrows of Hell. As to the reason why Job called Hell the "land of darkness," it is to be understood that he called it "land" or "earth" because it is stable and never shall fail; "dark" because he that is in Hell lacks the materials for light. For truly the dark light that shall come out of the fire that burns for ever shall turn him all to pain who is in Hell; for it shall show unto him the horrible devils that torment him. "Covered with the darkness of death:" that is to say, that he who is in Hell shall lack the sight of God; for truly, to see God is life everlasting. "The darkness of death" is the sin which the wretched man has done, which hinders his seeing the face of God; just as does a cloud that comes between us and the sun. "Land of ill ease:" because there are three kinds of pains against three things that folk of the world have in this present life, that is to say, honours, delights, and riches. Over against honours they have in Hell shame and confusion. For well you know that men call "honour" the reverence that man gives to man; but in Hell is no honour or reverence. For indeed no more reverence shall be done there to a king than to a knave. As to which God says, by the Prophet Jeremiah: "They that scorn me shall be scorned." "Honour" is also called great lordship; but there no man shall serve another, save to his harm and torment. "Honour," again, subsists in great dignity and rank; but in Hell all they shall be trodden upon by devils. And God says: "The horrible devils shall go and come upon the heads of the damned." And this is because the higher they were in this life, the lower shall they lie and be defiled in Hell. Against the riches of this world shall they have the misery of poverty; and this poverty shall be of four kinds: lack of treasure, whereof David says: "They that trust in their wealth, boast themselves in the multitude of their riches, they shall sleep in the darkness of death, and nothing shall they find in their hands of all their treasure." And, moreover, the misery of Hell shall consist of lack of food and drink. For God says thus, through Moses: "They shall be wasted with hunger, and the birds of Hell shall devour them with bitter death, and the gall of the dragon shall be their drink, and the venom of the dragon their morsels." And, furthermore, their misery shall be for lack of clothing, for they shall be naked of body save for the fire wherein they burn, and for other filth; and naked shall they be of soul, devoid of all virtues, which are the clothing of the soul. Where shall be then the gay robes and the soft sheets and the soft shirts? Behold what God says by the prophet Isaiah: "Under them shall be strewed moths and their covering shall be of the worms of Hell." And still further, their misery shall lie in lack of friends; for he is not poor who has good friends; but there is no friend; for neither God nor any other shall be friend to them, and each of them shall hate all others with a deadly hatred. "The sons and the daughters shall rebel against father and mother, and kindred against kindred, and each of them shall curse and despise the others," both day and night, as says God through the Prophet Micah. And the loving people that once loved each other so passionately, each of them would eat the other if he might. For how should they love in the torments of Hell who hated each other in the prosperity of this life? For trust it well, their carnal love was deadly hate; as says the Prophet David: "Whoso loveth wickedness hateth his own soul." And whoso hates his own soul, truly he may love no other, in any wise. And therefore, in Hell is no solace nor any friendship, but ever the more fleshly relationships there are in Hell, the more cursings and the more deadly hates there are among them. And, again, they shall lack every kind of pleasure; for truly, pleasures are according to the appetites of the five senses, sight, hearing, smell, taste, and touch. But in Hell their sight shall be full of darkness and of smoke, and therefore full of tears; and their hearing full of wailing and the gnashing of teeth, as says Jesus Christ; their nostrils shall be full of a stinking smell. And, as the Prophet Isaiah says, "their savouring shall be of bitter gall." And as for touch, all the body shall be covered with "fire that never shall be quenched and with worms that never shall die," as God says by the mouth of Isaiah. And for as much as they shall not think that they may die of pain, and by death thus flee from pain, then may they understand the words of Job, who said, "There is the shadow of death." Certainly a shadow has the likeness of that whereof it is the shadow, but the shadow is not the substance. Just so it is with the pain of Hell; it is like unto death because of the horrible anguish. And why? Because it pains for ever, and as if they should die at every moment; but indeed they shall not die. For as Saint Gregory says: "To these wretched captives shall be given death without death, and end without end, and want without ceasing." And thereupon says Saint John the Evangelist: "They shall seek for death and they shall not find it; and they shall desire to die and death shall flee from them." And Job, also, says: "Death, without any order." And though it be that God has created all things in right order, and nothing at all without order, but all things are ordered and numbered; yet, nevertheless, they that are damned have no order, nor hold to any order. For the earth shall bear them no fruit. For, as the Prophet David says: "God shall destroy the fruits of the earth from them." No water shall give them moisture, nor the air refreshment, nor the fire a light. For, as Saint Basil says: "The burning of the fire of this world shall God send into Hell unto the damned souls there, but the light and the radiance thereof shall be given in Heaven unto His children" — just as the good man gives flesh to his children and bones to his dogs. And since they shall have no hope of escape, Saint Job says at the last that horror and grisly fear shall dwell there without end. Horror is always the fear of evil that is to come, and this fear shall dwell for ever in the hearts of the damned. And therefore have they lost all their hope, and for seven causes. First, because God their judge shall be without mercy to them; they may not please Him, nor may they please any of His saints; they can give nothing for their ransom; they shall have no voice wherewith to speak to Him; they cannot flee from pain; and they have no goodness within themselves which they might show to deliver them out of pain. And therefore says Solomon: "The wicked man dieth; and when he is dead he shall have no hope of escaping from pain." Whosoever, then, will well understand these pains, and bethink him well that he has deserved these very pains for his sins, certainly he shall have more longing to sigh and weep than ever to sing and play. For, as Solomon says: "Whoso shall have the wisdom to know the pains that have been established and ordained for the punishment of pain, he will feel sorrow." "This same knowledge," says Saint Augustine, "maketh a man to bewail within his heart."

The fourth point that ought to cause a man to feel contrition is the unhappy memory of the good that he has left here on earth; also the good that he has lost. Truly, the good deeds that he has left are either those that he wrought before he fell into mortal sin, or the good deeds he did while he lived in sin. Indeed the good deeds he did before he fell into sin have been all deadened and stultified and rendered null and void by the repeated sinning. The other good deeds, which he wrought while he lay in mortal sin, they are utterly dead as to the effect they might have had on his life everlasting in Heaven. And then the same good deeds that have been rendered null by repeated sinning, which good works he wrought while he stood in a state of grace, shall never quicken again without an utter penitence. And thereof God says, by the mouth of Ezekiel: "If the righteous man shall turn again from his righteousness, and do wickedness, shall he live?" Nay, for all the good works that he has wrought shall never be held in memory, for he shall die in his sin. And thereupon, as to that same chapter, Saint Gregory says thus: "That we shall understand this principally: that when we do mortal sin it is for naught that we tell of or draw from memory the good works that we have wrought before." For, certainly, in the doing of mortal sin there is no trusting to the help of good that we have wrought before; that is to say, as it affects the everlasting life in Heaven. But notwithstanding this, the good deeds quicken again and return again, and help and are of avail in attaining the everlasting life in Heaven, when we have contrition. But indeed the good deeds that men do while they are in deadly sin, because they are done in deadly sin, shall never quicken again. For truly, that thing which never had life may never quicken; nevertheless, albeit these deeds avail nothing as to the perdurable life, yet they help to lighten the pains of Hell, or else to acquire temporal riches, or else, because of them, God will enlighten and illumine the heart of the sinful man to be repentant; and also they avail in accustoming a man to the doing of good deeds, to the end that the Fiend has less power over his soul. And thus the compassionate Lord Jesus Christ wills that no good work be utterly lost; for in somewhat it shall avail. But for as much as the good deeds that men do while they are in a state of grace are all stultified by sin ensuing; and, also, since all the good works that men do while they are in mortal sin are utterly dead, in so far as the life everlasting is concerned, well may that man who does no good work sing that new French song, *J'ai tout perdu mon temps et mon labeur.* For certainly, sin bereaves a man of both goodness of nature and the goodness of grace. For indeed the grace of the Holy Ghost is like fire, which cannot be idle; for fire fails anon as it forgoes its working, and even so does grace fail immediately it forsakes its work. Then loses the sinful man the goodness of glory, which is promised only to good men who suffer and toil. Well then may he sorrow, who owes all his life to God, as long as he has lived and as long as he shall live, and who yet has no goodness wherewith to repay his debt to God. For trust well, "he shall give account," as Saint Bernard says, "of all the good things that have been given him in this present life, and of how he has used them; in so much that there shall not perish a hair of his head, nor shall a moment of an hour perish of all his time, that he shall not be called upon to give a reckoning for."

The fifth thing that ought to move a man to contrition is remembrance of the passion that Our Lord Jesus Christ suffered for our sins. For, as Saint Bernard says: "While I live I will keep in remembrance the travail that Our Lord Christ suffered in preaching; His weariness in travail; His temptations when He fasted; His long watchings when He prayed; His tears when He wept for pity of good people; the grievous and the shameful and the filthy things that men said of Him; the foul sputum that men spat into His face; the foul buffets that men gave Him; the foul grimaces and the chidings that men said; the nails wherewith He was nailed to the cross; and all the rest of His passion, which he suffered for my sins and not for his own guilt." And you shall understand that in man's sin is every order or ordinance turned upsidedown. For it is true that God and reason and sensuality and the body of man have been so ordained and established that, of these four things, the next higher shall have lordship over the lower; as thus: God shall have lordship over reason, and reason over sensuality, and sensuality over the body of man. But, indeed, when man sins, all of this order or ordinance is turned upside-down. Therefore, then, for as much as the reason of man will not be subject to nor obedient to God, Who is man's Lord by right, therefore it loses the lordship that it should hold over sensuality and also over the body of man. And why? Because sensuality rebels then against reason; and in that way reason loses the lordship over sensuality and over the body. For just as reason is rebel to God, just so is sensuality rebel to reason, and the body also. And truly, this confusion and this rebellion Our Lord Jesus Christ suffered upon His precious body, and paid full dearly thus, and hear you now in what wise. For as much, then, as reason is rebel to God, therefore is man worthy to have sorrow and to die. This Our Lord Jesus Christ suffered for mankind after He had been betrayed by His disciple, and secured and bound "so that the blood burst out at every nail of His hands," as says Saint Augustine. Moreover, for as much as reason of man will not subdue sensuality when it may, therefore man is worthy of shame; and this suffered Our Lord Jesus Christ for man when they spat in His face. Furthermore, for as much, then, as the wretched body of man is rebel both to reason and to sensuality, therefore is it worthy of death. And this Our Lord Jesus Christ suffered for man upon the cross, where there was no part of His body free from great pain and bitter passion. And all this Jesus Christ suffered, Who never did any wrong. And therefore it may be reasonably said of Jesus thus: "Too much am I tortured for things the punishment of which I do not deserve, and too much disgraced for shame that belongs to man." And therefore may the sinful man well say, as says Saint Bernard: "Accursed be the bitterness of my sin, for which there must be suffered so much bitterness." For truly, according to the diverse discordances of our wickedness, was the passion of Jesus Christ ordained in divers ways, as thus. Certainly sinful man's soul is betrayed unto the Devil by covetousness of temporal prosperity, and scorned by deceit when he chooses carnal delights; and it is tormented by impatience under adversity, and spat upon by servitude and subjection to sin; and at the last it is slain for ever. For this confusion by sinful man was Jesus Christ first betrayed and afterwards bound, Who came to loose us from sin and pain. Then was He scorned, Who should have been only honoured in all things. Then was His face, which all mankind ought to have desired to look upon, since into that face angels desire to look, villainously spat upon. Then was He scourged, Who had done nothing wrong; and finally, then was He crucified and slain. So was accomplished the word of Isaiah: "He was wounded for our misdeeds and defiled for our felonies." Now, since Jesus Christ took upon Himself the punishment for all our wickedness, much ought sinful man to weep and to bewail that for his sins the Son of God in Heaven should endure all this pain.

The sixth thing that ought to move a man to contrition is the hope of three things; that is to say, forgiveness of sin, and the gift of grace to do well, and the glory of Heaven, wherewith God shall reward a man for his good deeds. And for as much as Jesus Christ gives us these gifts of His largess and of His sovereign bounty, therefore is He called *Iesus Nazarenus rex Iudeorum*. Jesus means "saviour" or "salvation," in whom men shall hope to have forgiveness of sins, which is, properly, salvation from sins. And therefore said the angel to Joseph: "Thou shalt call His name Jesus, Who shall save His people from their sins." And thereof says Saint Peter: "There is no other name under Heaven given to any man, whereby a man may be saved, save only Jesus." *Nazarenus* is as much as to say "flourishing," wherein a man may hope that He

Who gives him remission of sins shall give him also the grace to do well. For in the flower is hope of fruit in time to come; and in forgiveness of sins is hope of grace to do well. "Behold, I stand at the door and knock," says Jesus: "if any man hear my voice, and open the door, I will come in to him, and will sup with him, and he with Me." That is to say, by the good works that he shall do, which good works are the food of God; "and he shall sup with Me"—by the great joy that I shall give him. Thus may man hope, for his deeds of penitence, that God shall allow him to enter His Kingdom, as is promised unto him in the gospel.

Now shall a man understand in what manner shall be his contrition. I say, that it shall be universal and total; that is to say, a man shall be truly repentant for all the sins that he has done in delight of his thought; for delight is very dangerous. For there are two ways of acquiescence; one is called acquiescence of the affections, when a man is moved to do sin, and delights in long thinking thereon; and his reason well perceives that it is sin against the law of God, and yet his reason restrains not his foul delight or appetite, though he see well that it is opposed to the reverence that is due to God; although his reason consent not to do that sin in very deed, yet some doctors say that dwelling long on such delight is full dangerous, be it ever so little. And also a man should sorrow for all that he has ever desired against the law of God with perfect acquiescence of his reason; for there is no doubt of it, there is mortal sin in acquiescence. For truly, there is no mortal sin that was not first in man's thought, and after that in his delight, and so on unto acquiescence and unto deed. Wherefore I say, that many men never repent for such thoughts and delights, and never confess them, but only the actual performance of great sins. Wherefore I say that such wicked delights and wicked thoughts are subtle beguilers of those that shall be damned. Moreover, a man ought to sorrow for his wicked words as well as for his wicked deeds; for truly, the repentance for a single sin, unaccompanied by repentance for all other sins, or else repentance for all other sins and not for a single sin, shall not avail. For certainly God Almighty is all good; and therefore He forgives all or nothing. And thereupon says Saint Augustine: "I know certainly that God is the enemy of every sinner." And how then? He that continues to do one sin, shall he have forgiveness for the rest of his sins? No. Furthermore, contrition should be wondrous sorrowful and full of suffering; and for that God gives fully His mercy; and therefore, when my soul was suffering within me, I had remembrance of God, that my prayer might come unto Him. Moreover, contrition must be continual, and a man must keep and hold a steadfast purpose to shrive himself and to amend his way of life. For truly, while contrition lasts, man may continue to have hope of forgiveness; and of this comes hatred of sin, which destroys sin within himself and also in other folk, according to his ability. For which David says: "Ye that love God hate wickedness." For trust this well, to love God is to love what He loves and to hate what He hates.

The last thing that man shall understand about contrition is this: What does contrition avail him? I say, that at times contrition delivers a man from sin; as to which David says: "I said I will confess my transgressions unto the Lord; and Thou forgavest the iniquity of my sin." And just as contrition nothing avails without firm purpose of shrift, if man have opportunity, just so shrift itself is of little worth without contrition. Moreover, contrition destroys the prison of Hell and makes weak and feeble all the strength of all the devils, and restores the gifts of the Holy Ghost and of all good virtues; and it cleanses the soul of sin, and delivers the soul from the pain of Hell and from the company of the Devil, and from the servitude of sin, and restores it unto all spiritual good and to the company and communion of Holy Church. And furthermore, it makes of him who was formerly the son of anger to be the son of grace; and all these things are proved by holy writ. And therefore he that would set his understanding to these things, he were full wise; for truly, he should not then, in all his life, have desire to sin, but should give his body and all his heart to the service of Jesus Christ, and do Him homage. For truly, Our sweet Lord Jesus Christ has spared us so graciously in our follies that, if He had not pity on man's soul, a sorry song indeed might all of us sing.

Explicit prima pars penitentie;
Et sequitur secunda pars eiusdem

The second part of penitence is confession, which is the sign of contrition. Now shall you understand what confession is, and whether it ought to be used or not, and which things are necessary to true confession.

First, you shall understand that confession is the true discovery of sins to the priest; I say "true," for a man must confess all the circumstances and conditions of his sin, in so far as he can. All must be told, and nothing excused or hidden, or covered up, and he must not vaunt his good deeds. And furthermore, it is necessary to understand whence his sins come, and how they increase, and what they are.

Of the birth of sins, Saint Paul says thus: that "as by one man sin entered into the world, and death by sin; . . . so death passed upon all men, for that all have sinned." And this man was Adam, by whom sin entered into the world when he broke the commandment of God. And therefore, he that at first was so mighty that he should never have died became such a one as must needs die, whether he would or no; and all his progeny in this world, since they, in that man, sinned. Behold, in the state of innocence, when Adam and Eve were naked in Paradise, and had no shame for their nakedness, how that the serpent, which was the wiliest of all the beasts that God had made, said to the woman: "Yea, hath God said, ye shall not eat of every tree of the garden?" And the woman said unto the serpent: "We may eat of the fruit of the trees of the garden: but of the fruit of the tree which is in the midst of the garden, God hath said, 'Ye shall not eat of it, neither shall ye touch it, lest ye die.'" And the serpent said unto the woman: "Ye shall not surely die: for God doth know, that in the day ye eat thereof, then your eyes shall be opened; and ye shall be as gods, knowing good and evil." And when the woman saw that the tree was good for food, and that it was pleasant to the eyes, and delectable in the sight, she took of the fruit thereof and did eat; and gave also unto her husband, and he did eat. And the eyes of them both were opened. And when they knew that they were naked, they sewed fig-leaves together into a kind of breeches to hide their members. There may you see that mortal sin had first suggestion from the Fiend, who is here figured by the serpent; and afterward the delight of the flesh, as shown here by Eve; and after that the acquiescence of reason, as is shown by Adam. For trust this well, though it were that the Fiend tempted Eve, that is to say, the flesh, and the flesh delighted in the beauty of the forbidden fruit, certainly until reason, that is, Adam, consented to the eating of the fruit, yet stood he in the state of innocence. From that same Adam caught we all that original sin; for we are all descended from him in the flesh, engendered of vile and corrupt matter. And when the soul is put into a body, immediately is contracted original sin; and that which was at first merely the penalty of concupiscence becomes afterwards both penalty and sin. And therefore are we all born the sons of wrath and of everlasting damnation, were it not for the baptism we receive, which washes away the culpability; but, forsooth, the penalty remains within us, as temptation, and that penalty is called concupiscence. When it is wrongly disposed or established in man, it makes him desire, by the lust of the flesh, fleshly sin; desire, by the sight of his eyes, earthly things; and desire high place, what of the pride of his heart.

Now, to speak of the first desire, that is, concupiscence, according to the law for our sexual parts, which were lawfully made and by rightful word of God; I say, for as much as man is not obedient to God, Who is his Lord, therefore is the flesh disobedient to Him, through concupiscence, which is also called the nourishing of and the reason for sin. Therefore all the while that a man has within himself the penalty of concupiscence, it is impossible but that he will be sometimes tempted and moved in his flesh to do sin. And this shall not fail so long as he lives; it may well grow feeble and remote by virtue of baptism and by the grace of God through penitence; but it shall never be fully quenched so that he shall never be moved within himself, unless he be cooled by sickness or my maleficence of sorcery or by opiates. For behold what Saint Paul says: "The flesh lusteth against the spirit, and the spirit against the flesh: and these are contrary, the one to the other; so that ye cannot do the things that ye would." The same Saint Paul, after his great penance on water and on land (on water by night and by day, in great peril and in great pain; on land in famine, in thirst, in cold, and naked, and once stoned almost unto death), yet said he: "O wretched man that I am! Who shall deliver me from the body of this death?" And Saint Jerome, when he had long lived in the desert, where he had no company but that of wild beasts, where he had no food but herbs, with only water to drink, and no bed but the naked earth, for which his flesh was black as an Ethiopian's with heat and well-nigh destroyed with cold, yet said he that the heat of lechery boiled through all his body. Wherefore I know well and surely that they are deceived who say that they are never tempted in the flesh. Witness Saint James the apostle, who says that everyone is tempted in his own concupiscence. That is to say, each of us has cause and occasion to be tempted by the sin that is nourished in the body. And thereupon says Saint John the Evangelist: "If we say that we have no sin, we deceive ourselves, and the truth is not in us."

Now shall you understand in what manner sin waxes or increases in man. The first thing to be considered is this same nurturing of sin, whereof I spoke before, this same fleshly concupiscence. And after that comes the subjection to the Devil, that is to say, the Devil's bellows, wherewith he blows into man the fire of concupiscence. And after that a man bethinks himself whether he will do, or not, the thing to which he is tempted. And then, if a man withstand and put aside the first enticement of his flesh and the Fiend, then it is no sin; and if it be that he do not, he feels anon a flame of delight. And then it is well to be wary, and to guard himself, else he will fall anon into acquiescence to sin; and then he will do it, if he have time and place. And of this matter Moses says that the Devil says thus: "I will pursue, I will overtake, I will divide the spoil; my lust shall be satisfied upon them; I will draw my sword, my hand shall destroy them." For certainly, just as a sword may part a thing in two pieces, just so acquiescence separates God from man. "And then will I slay him in his sinful deed." Thus says the Fiend. For truly, then is a man dead in soul. And thus is sin accomplished by temptation and by acquiescence; and then is the sin called actual.

Forsooth, sin is of two kinds; it is either venial or mortal sin. Verily, when man loves any creature more than he loves Jesus Christ our Creator, then is it mortal sin. And venial sin it is if a man love Jesus

Christ less than he ought. Forsooth the effect of this venial sin is very dangerous; for it diminishes more and more the love that man should have for God. And therefore, if a man charge himself with many such venial sins, then certainly, unless he discharge them occasionally by shriving, they may easily lessen in him all the love that he has for Jesus Christ; and in this wise venial sin passes over into mortal sin. Therefore let us not be negligent in ridding ourselves of venial sins. For the proverb has it: "Mony a mickle mak's a muckle." And hear this example. A huge wave of the sea comes sometimes with so great violence that it sinks a ship. And the same harm is caused sometimes by the small drops of water that enter through the little opening in the seam into the bilge of the ship, if men be so negligent that they do not discharge it in time. And therefore, though there be a difference between these two ways of sinking, nevertheless the ship is sunk. Just so it is sometimes with mortal sin, and with vexatious venial sins when they multiply in a man so greatly that the worldly things he loves, for which he venially sins, have grown as great in his heart as the love for God, or greater. And therefore, the love for everything that is not fixed or rooted in God, or done principally for God's sake, though a man love it less than he love God, yet is it venial sin; and it is mortal sin when the love for anything weighs in the heart of man as much as the love for God, or more. "Mortal sin," as Saint Augustine says, "is when a man turns his heart from God, Who is the truly sovereign goodness and may not change, and gives his heart unto things that may change and pass away." And true it is that if a man give his love, the which he owes all to God, with all his heart, unto a creature, then certainly so much of his love as he gives unto the said creature he takes away from God; and thereby does he sin. For he, who is debtor to God, yields not unto God all of his debt, which is to say, all the love of his heart.

Now since man understands generally what venial sin is, it is fitting to tell especially of sins which many a man perhaps holds not to be sins at all, and for which he shrives not himself; yet, nevertheless, they are sins. Truly, as clerics write, every time a man eats or drinks more than suffices for the sustenance of his body, it is certain that he thereby sins. And, too, when he speaks more than it is necessary it is sin. Also, when he hears not benignly the complaint of the poor. Also, when he is in health of body and will not fast when other folk fast, and that without a reasonable excuse. Also, when he sleeps more than he needs, or when he comes, for that reason, too late to church, or to other places where works of charity are done. Also, when he enjoys his wife without a sovereign desire to procreate children to the honour of God, or when he does it without intention to yield to his wife the duty of his body. Also, when he will not visit the sick and the imprisoned, if he may do so.

Also, if he love wife or child or any other worldly thing more than reason requires. Also, if he flatter or blandish more than, of necessity, he ought. Also, if he diminish or withdraw his alms to the poor. Also, if he prepare his food more delicately than is needful, or eat it too hastily or too greedily. Also, if he talk about vain and trifling matters in a church or at God's service, or if he be a user of idle words of folly or of obscenity; for he shall yield up an accounting of it at the day of doom. Also, when he promises or assures one that he will do what he cannot perform. Also, when he, through thoughtlessness or folly, slanders or scorns his neighbour. Also, when he suspects a thing to be evil when he has no certain knowledge of it. These things, and more without number, are sins, as Saint Augustine says.

Now shall men understand that while no earthly man may avoid all venial sins, yet may he keep them down by the burning love that he has to Our Lord Jesus Christ, and by prayer and confession, and by other good deeds. For, as Saint Augustine says: "If a man love God in such manner that all that he ever does is done in the love of God, and truly for the love of God, because he burns with the love of God: behold, then, how much a drop of water falling in a furnace harms or proves troublesome; and just so much vexes the venial sin a man who is perfect in the love of Christ." Men may also keep down venial sins by receiving deservingly the precious body of Jesus Christ; also by receiving holy water; by almsgiving; by general confession of *confiteor* at mass and at compline; and by the blessings of bishops and of priests, and by other good works.

> *Explicit secunda pars penitentie*
> *Sequitur de septem peccatis mortalibus*
> *et eorum dependenciis*
> *Circumstanciis et speciebus*

Now it is a needful thing to tell which are the mortal sins, that is to say, the principal sins; they are all leashed together, but are different in their ways. Now they are called principal sins because they are the chief sins and the trunk from which branch all others. And the root of these seven sins is pride, which is the general root of all evils; for from this root spring certain branches, as anger, envy, acedia or sloth, avarice (or covetousness, for vulgar understanding), gluttony, and lechery. And each of these principal sins has its branches and its twigs, as shall be set forth and declared in the paragraphs following.

DE SUPERBIA

And though it be true that no man can absolutely tell the number of the twigs and of the evil branches that spring from pride, yet will I show forth a number of them, as you shall understand. There are disobedience, boasting, hypocrisy, scorn, arrogance, impudence, swelling of the heart, insolence, elation, impatience, strife, contumacy, presumption, irreverence, obstinacy, vainglory; and many another twig that I cannot declare. Disobedient is he that disobeys for spite the commandments of God, of his rulers, and of his spiritual father. Braggart is he that boasts of the evil or the good that he has done. Hypocrite is he that hides his true self and shows himself such as he is not. Scorner is he who has disdain for his neighbour, that is to say, for his fellow Christian, or who scorns to do that which he ought to do. Arrogant is he who thinks he has within himself those virtues which he has not, or who holds that he should so have them as his desert; or else he deems that he is that which he is not. Impudent is he who, for his pride's sake, has no shame for his sins. Swelling of heart is what a man has when he rejoices in evil that he has done. Insolent is he that despises in his judgments all other folk in comparing theirs with his worth, and with his understanding, and with his conversation, and with his bearing. Elated is he who will suffer neither a master nor a peer. Impatient is he who will not be taught nor reproved for his vice, and who, by strife, knowingly wars on truth and defends his folly. *Contumax* is he who, because of his indignation, is against all authority or power or those that are his rulers. Presumption is when a man undertakes an enterprise that he ought not to attempt, or one which he cannot accomplish; and that is called overconfidence. Irreverence is when men do not show honour where they ought, and themselves wait to be reverenced. Obstinacy is when man defends his folly and trusts too much in his own judgment. Vainglory is delight in pomp and temporal rank, and glorification in this worldly estate. Chattering is when men speak too much before folk, clattering like a mill and taking no care of what they say.

And then there is a private species of pride that waits to be saluted before it will salute, albeit the one who has it is of less worth than is the other, perchance; also, when he attends services in church he desires to sit, or else to go, before his neighbour in the aisle, or to kiss the pax before him, or to be censed before him, or to make offering before his neighbour, and similar things; all against his necessity, peradventure, save that in his heart and his will is such proud desire to be magnified and honoured before the people.

Now there are two kinds of pride; one of them lies within the heart of man, and the other lies without. Whereof, truly, these aforesaid things, and more than I have named, appertain to that pride which is within the heart of man; for that other species of pride lies without. But notwithstanding, one of these species of pride is a sign of the existence of the other, just as the fresh bush at the tavern door is a sign of the wine that is in the cellar. And this second kind of pride shows itself in many ways: as in speech and bearing, and in extravagant array of clothing; for truly, if there had been no sin in clothing, Christ would not have noted and spoken of the clothing of that rich man in the gospel. And, as Saint Gregory says, that same precious clothing is culpable for the glory and beauty of it, and for its softness. and for its strange new modes, and its fantastic ornamentation, and for its superfluity, and for the inordinate scantiness of it. Alas! May not men see, in our days, the sinfully costly array of clothing, especially in the matter of superfluity, or else in inordinate scantiness?

As to the first sin, it lies in the superfluity of clothing, which makes cloth so dear, to the harm of the people; not only the cost of embroidering, the elaborate notching or barring, the waved lines, the stripes, the twists, the diagonal bars, and similar waste of cloth in vanity; but there is also the costly furring of gowns, so much perforating with scissors to make holes, so much slashing with shears; and then the superfluity in length of the aforesaid gowns, trailing in the dung and in the mire, a-horseback and afoot, as well of man's clothing as of woman's, until all this trailing verily, in its effect, wastes, consumes, makes threadbare and rotten with dung the superfluity that rather should be given unto the poor; to the great harm of the aforesaid poor. And that in sundry wise: this is to say, the more that cloth is wasted, the more it costs the people because of its scarcity; and furthermore, if they would give such perforated and slashed clothing to the poor folk, it would not be suitable for their wearing, what of their state, nor sufficient to help their necessity to keep themselves from the fury of the elements. On the other hand, to speak of the horrible inordinate scantiness of clothing, let us notice these short-cut smocks or jackets, which, because of their shortness, cover not the shameful members of man, to the wicked calling of them to attention. Alas! Some of them show the very boss of their penis and the horrible pushed-out testicles that look like the malady of hernia in the wrapping of their hose; and the buttocks of such persons look like the hinder parts of a she-ape in the full of the moon. And moreover, the hateful proud members that they show by the fantastic fashion of making one leg of their hose white and the other red, make it seem that half their shameful privy members are flayed. And if it be that they divide their hose in other colours, as white and black, or white and blue, or black and red, and so forth, then it seems, by variation of colour, that the half of their privy members are corrupted by the fire of Saint Anthony, or by cancer, or by other such misfortune. As to the hinder parts of their buttocks, the thing is horrible to see. For, indeed, in that part of their body where they purge their stinking ordure, that foul part they proudly show to the people in despite of decency, which decency Jesus Christ and His friends observed in their lives. Now, as to the extravagant array of women, God knows that though the faces of them seem chaste and gentle, yet do they advertise, by their attire, their lickerousness and pride. I say not that a moderate gaiety in clothing is unseemly, but certainly the superfluity or inordinate scantiness of clothing is reprehensible. Also, the sin of adornment or apparel lies in things that appertain to riding, as in too many fine horses that are kept for delight, that are so fair, fat, and costly; in many a vicious knave who is kept because of them; in too curious harness, as saddles, cruppers, poitrels, and bridles covered with precious caparison and rich, and with bars and plates of gold and silver. As to which God says by Zechariah the prophet: "I will confound the riders of such horses." These folk have but little regard for the riding of God of Heaven's Son and of His trappings, when He rode upon the ass and had no other caparison than the poor cloaks of His disciples; nor do we read that ever He rode upon any other beast. I say this against the sin of superfluity, and not against reasonable display when the occasion requires it. And further, certainly pride is greatly shown in keeping up a great household, when such servants are of little profit, or of no profit. And this is especially so when such an array of servants is mischievous and injurious to the people, by the insolence of high rank or by way of office. For truly, such lords sell then their lordships to the Devil of Hell when they sustain the wickedness of their following. And when folk of low degree, as those that keep and run hostelries, sustain the thievery of their servants, which is done in many ways. This kind of folk are the flies that seek honey or the dogs that seek carrion. Such folk strangle spiritually their lordships; as to which thus says David the prophet: "Wicked death shall come upon such masters, and God will give that they descend into Hell; for in their houses are iniquities and evil deeds." And God of Heaven is not there. And truly, unless they mend their ways, just as God gave His blessing to Laban for the service of Jacob and to Pharaoh for the service of Joseph, just so will God give His curse to such lordships as sustain the wickedness of their servants, unless they shall make amendment. Pride of the table is often seen; for truly, rich men are bidden to feasts and poor folk are turned away and rebuked. The sin of pride lies also in excess of divers meats and drinks; and especially in certain baked meats and made-dishes, burning with spirituous liquors and decorated and castellated with paper, and in similar waste; so that it is scandalous to think upon. And also in too great preciousness of vessels and in curious instruments of minstrelsy, whereby a man is stirred the more to the delights of luxury; if it be that he thereby sets his heart the less upon Jesus Christ, certainly it is a sin; and certainly the delights might be so great in this case that a man could easily fall thereby into mortal sin. The varieties of sin that arise out of pride, truly, when they arise with malice imagined, advised, and aforethought, or from habit, are mortal sins, and of that there is no doubt. And when they arise out of frailty, unadvisedly and suddenly, and are quickly withdrawn again, albeit they are grievous sins, I think that they are not mortal. Now might men ask, whence pride arises and takes its being, and I say: sometimes it springs out of the good things of nature, and sometimes from the benefits of Fortune, and sometimes from the good of grace itself. Certainly the good things of nature consist of either physical well-being or riches of the soul. Certainly physical well-being consists of the weal of the body, as strength, activity, beauty, good blood, and generous candour. The benefits of nature to the soul are good wit, keen understanding, clever talent, natural virtue, and good memory. The benefits of Fortune are riches, high rank, and the people's praise. The good of grace consists of knowledge, power to suffer spiritual travail, benignity, virtuous contemplation, ability to withstand temptation, and similar things. Of which aforesaid things, certainly it is great folly in a man when he permits himself to be proud of any of them. As for the benefits of nature, God knows that sometimes we receive them naturally as much to our detriment as to our profit. As, to take bodily health, certainly it passes away lightly enough, and moreover it is often the reason for the wickedness of the soul; for God knows that the flesh is a great enemy to the soul; and therefore, the more sound the body is, the more are we in danger of falling into sin. Also, to feel pride in the strength of one's body is a great folly; for certainly the flesh lusts for that which is detrimental to the spirit, and ever the stronger the flesh is, the sorrier must the soul be: and above all this, strength of body and worldly boldness bring a man often into danger of mischance. Also, to be proud of his gentility is a great folly; for often the gentility of the body debases the gentility of the soul; and furthermore, we are all of one father and one mother; and we are of one nature, rotten and corrupt, both the rich and the poor. Forsooth, but one kind of gentility is praiseworthy, and that it is which clothes a man's heart with virtue and morality and makes of him Christ's child. For trust this well, that over whatsoever man sin has gained the mastery, that man is a very serf to sin.

Now there are general signs of gentility; as the eschewing of vice and ribaldry and servitude to sin, in word, in deed, and in conduct; and as the practising of virtue, courtesy, and purity, and being generous, which is to say, bounteous within measure; for that which goes beyond a reasonable measure is folly and sin. Another such sign is, when a man remembers and bears in mind the good that he has received from others. Another is, to be benign to his good inferiors; wherefore, as Seneca says: "There is nothing more becoming a man of high estate than kindliness, courtesy, and pity. And therefore the flies that men call bees, when they make their king, they choose one that has no prick wherewith he may sting." Another is, for a man to have a good heart and a diligent, to attain to high virtuous things. Now truly, for a man to pride himself on the gifts of grace is also an extravagant folly; for these same gifts of grace that should have turned him to goodness and to alleviation, turn him to venom and confusion, as says Saint Gregory. Certainly, also, whoso prides himself on the benefits of Fortune, he is a full great fool; for sometimes a man is a great lord at morning who is a captive and a wretch ere it be night; and sometimes the wealth of a man is the cause of his death; sometimes the pleasures of a man cause the grievous malady whereof he dies. Certainly the people's commendation is sometimes false enough and brittle enough to trust; today they praise, tomorrow they blame. God knows, desire to have commendation of the people has caused death to many a busy man.

REMEDIUM CONTRA PECCATUM SUPERBIE

Now, since it has come to pass that you have understood what pride is, and what the species of it are, and whence pride arises and springs, now you shall understand what is the remedy for the sin of pride, and that is, humility or meekness. That is a virtue whereby a man may come to have a true knowledge of himself, and whereby he will hold himself to be of no price or value in regard to his deserts, but will be considering ever his frailty. Now there are three kinds of humility: as humility of heart, and another humility is of the mouth, and the third is in a man's works. The humility of heart is of four kinds: one is, when a man holds himself to be of nothing worth before God in Heaven. Another is, when he despises no other man. The third is, when he recks not though men hold him as nothing worth. The fourth is when he is not sorry for his humiliation. Also, the humility of the mouth is of four kinds: temperate speech, meek speech, and when a man acknowledges with his own mouth that he is as he thinks himself to be, in his heart. Another is, when he praises the goodness of another man and nothing thereof belittles. Humility in deeds is in four manners: the first is, when a man puts other men before him. The second is, to choose the lowest place of all for himself. The third is, gladly to assent to good counsel. The fourth is, to abide gladly by the decision of his rulers, or of him that is of higher rank; certainly this is a great work of humility.

SEQUITUR DE INUIDIA

After pride I will speak of the foul sin of envy, which is, according to the word of the philosopher, sorrow for other men's prosperity; and according to the word of Saint Augustine, it is sorrow for other men's weal and joy for other men's harm. This foul sin is flatly against the Holy Ghost. Be it that every sin is in opposition to the Holy Ghost, yet, nevertheless, for as much as goodness appertains properly to the Holy Ghost and envy springs by nature out of malice, therefore is it especially against the goodness of the Holy Ghost. Now malice has two species, that is to say, a heart hardened in wickedness, or else the flesh of man is so blind that he does not consider himself to be in sin, or he cares not that he is in sin, which is the hardihood of the Devil. The other kind of malice is, when a man wars against the truth, knowing that it is truth. Also, when he wars against the grace that God has given to his neighbour; and all this is envy. Certainly, then, envy is the worst sin there is. For truly, all other sins are sometime against only one special virtue; but truly, envy is against all virtues and against all goodnesses; for it is sorry for all the virtues of its neighbour; and in this way it differs from all other sins. For hardly is there any sin that has not some delight in itself, save only envy, which ever has of itself but anguish and sorrow. The kinds of envy are these: there is, first, sorrow for other men's goodness and prosperity; and prosperity being naturally a thing for joy, then envy is a sin against nature. The second kind of envy is joy in other men's harm; and this is naturally like the Devil, who always rejoices in man's harm. From these two species comes backbiting; and this sin of backbiting, or detraction, has certain forms, as thus. A man praises his neighbour with a wicked intention, for he puts always a wicked twist into it at the end. Always he puts a "but" in at the end, which implies more blame than all the praise is worth. The second form is, when a man is good and does or says a thing to good intent, the backbiter turns all this goodness upside-down to his own evil end. The third is, to belittle the goodness of a neighbour. The fourth form of backbiting is this: that if a man say good of a man, then the backbiter says, "Faith, such or such a man is better than he," in disparagement of him that men praise. The fifth form is this, to assent gladly and listen gladly to the evil that folk speak of others. This sin is a great one; and it grows according to the wicked endeavours of the backbiter. After backbiting comes grumbling or murmuring; and sometimes it springs from impatience with God, and sometimes with man. Impatience with God it is when the man grumbles against the pains of Hell, or against poverty, or loss of chattels, or against rain or tempest; or else complains that scoundrels prosper, or else that good men have adversity. And all these things should men suffer patiently, for they come by the right judgment and ordinance of God. Sometimes grumbling comes of avarice; as Judas complained of the Magdalen when she anointed the head of Our Lord Jesus Christ with her precious ointment. This murmuring is such as when a man grumbles at good that he himself has done, or that other folk do with their wealth. Sometimes murmuring comes of pride; as when Simon the Pharisee murmured against the Magdalen when she approached Jesus Christ and wept at His feet for her sins. And sometimes grumbling arises out of envy; as when men discover a man's secret weakness, or swear of him a thing that is false. Murmuring, too, is often found among servants, who grumble when their masters bid them to do lawful things; and for as much as they dare not openly gainsay the commands of their masters, yet do they speak evilly of them and grumble and murmur privately, for very spite; which words men call the Devil's Paternoster, though the Devil never had a Paternoster, save that vulgar folk give these murmurings that name. Sometimes grumbling comes of anger or privy hate, that nurtures rancour in its heart, as I shall hereafter set forth. Then comes bitterness of heart, through which bitterness every good deed of one's neighbour seems to one to be but bitter and unsavoury. Then comes discord, which undoes all friendship. Then comes spite, as when a man seeks occasion to annoy his neighbour, though he do never so well. Then comes accusation, as when a man seeks occasion to offend his neighbour, which is like the guile of the Devil, who watches both night and day to accuse us all. Then comes malignity, through which a man annoys his neighbour privately, if he may; and if he may not, then nevertheless his wicked will shall not want for means to harm him, as by burning his house, or poisoning or slaying his beasts, and suchlike things.

REMEDIUM CONTRA PECCATUM INUIDIE

Now will I speak of the remedy for this foul sin of envy. First, is the love of God, and the love of one's neighbour as one's self; for indeed the one cannot be without the other. And trust well, that by the name of your neighbour you are to understand your brother; for certainly all of us have one fleshly father and one mother, that is to say, Adam and Eve; and even one spiritual father, and that is God in Heaven. Your neighbour you are bound to love and to wish all good things; and thereunto God says, "Love thy neighbour as thyself." That is to say, to the salvation both of life and soul. Moreover, you shall love him in word, and in benign admonition and in chastening; and comfort him in his vexations, and pray for him with all your heart. And you shall love him in deed and in such wise that you shall charitably do unto him as you would that it were done unto yourself. And therefore you shall do him no damage by wicked words, nor any harm in his body, nor in his goods, nor in his soul by the enticement of wicked example. You shall not covet his wife, nor any of his things. Understand also that in the word neighbour is included his enemy. Certainly man shall love his enemy, by the commandment of God; and truly, your friend shall you love in God. I say, you shall love your enemy for God's sake, and by His commandment. For if it were reasonable that a man should hate his enemies, then God would not receive us into His love, when we are His enemies. For three kinds of wrong that his enemy may do to a man, he shall do three things in return, thus: for hate and rancour, he shall love him in heart. For chiding and wicked words, he shall pray for his enemy. And for the wicked deed of his enemy, he shall do him kindness. For Christ says: "Love your enemies, bless them that curse you, do good to them that hate you, and pray for them which despitefully use you and persecute you." Lo, thus Our Lord Jesus Christ commands that we do to our enemies. For indeed, nature drives us to love our enemies, and, faith, our enemies have more need for love than our friends; and they that have more need, truly to them men ought to do good; and truly, in the deed thereof have we remembrance of the love of Jesus Christ Who died for His enemies. And in so much as that same love is the harder to feel and to show, in that much is the merit the greater; and therefore the loving of our enemy has confounded the venom of the Devil. For just as the Devil is discomfited by humility, so is he wounded to the death by love for our enemy. Certainly, then, love is the medicine that purges the heart of man of the poison of envy. The kinds of this degree of sin will be set forth more at large in the paragraphs following.

SEQUITUR DE IRA

After envy will I describe the sin of anger. For truly, whoso has envy of his neighbour will generally find himself showing anger, in word or in deed, against him whom he envies. And anger comes as well from pride as from envy; for certainly, he that is proud or envious is easily angered.

This sin of anger, according to Saint Augustine, is a wicked determination to be avenged by word or by deed. Anger, according to the philosopher, is the hot blood of man quickened in his heart, because of which he wishes to harm him whom he hates. For truly, the heart of man, by the heating and stirring of his blood, grows so disturbed that he is put out of all ability to judge reasonably. But you shall understand that anger manifests itself in two manners; one of them is good, the other bad. The good anger is caused by zeal for goodness, whereof a man is enraged by wickedness and against wickedness; and thereupon a wise man says that "Anger is better than play." This anger is gentle and without bitterness; not felt against the man, but against the misdeed of the man, as the Prophet David says: *Irascimini et nolite peccare.* Now understand, that wicked anger is manifested in two manners, that is to say, sudden or hasty anger, without the advice and counsel of reason. The meaning and the sense of this is, that the reason of man consents not to this sudden anger, and so it is venial. Another anger is full wicked, which comes of sullenness of heart, with malice aforethought and with wicked determination to take vengeance, and to which reason assents; and this, truly, is mortal sin. This form of anger is so displeasing to God that it troubles His house and drives the Holy Ghost out of man's soul, and wastes and destroys the likeness of God, that is to say, the virtue that is in man's soul; and it puts within him the likeness of the Devil, and takes the man away from God, his rightful Lord. This form of anger is a great joy to the Devil; for it is the Devil's furnace, heated with the fire of Hell. For certainly, just as fire is the mightiest of earth's engines of destruction, just so ire is mightiest to destroy things spiritual. Observe how a fire of smouldering coals, almost extinct under the ashes, will quicken again when touched by brimstone; just so will anger quicken again when it is touched by the pride that lies hidden in man's heart. For certainly fire cannot come from nothing, but must first be naturally dormant within a thing, as it is drawn out of flints with steel. And just as pride is often the matter of which anger is made, just so is rancour the nurse and keeper of anger. There is a kind of tree, as Saint Isidore says, which, when men make a fire of the wood of it, and then cover over the coals with ashes, truly the embers will live and last a year or more. And just so fares it with rancour; when it is once conceived in the hearts of some men, certainly it will last, perchance, from one Easter-day to another Easter-day, and longer. But truly, such men are very far from the mercy of God all that while.

In this aforesaid Devil's furnace there are forged three evils: pride that ever fans and increases the fire by chiding and wicked words. Then stands up envy and holds the hot iron upon the heart of man with a pair of long tongs of abiding rancour. And then stands up the sin of contumely, or strife and wrangling, and strikes and hammers with villainous reproaches. Certainly, this cursed sin injures both the man who does it and his neighbour. For truly, almost all the harm that any man does to his neighbour comes from wrath. For certainly, outrageous wrath does all that the Devil orders; for it spares neither Christ nor His Sweet Mother. And in his outrageous anger and ire, alas! full many a one at that time feels in his heart right wickedly, both as to Christ and as to His saints. Is not this a cursed vice? Yes, certainly. Alas! It takes from man his wit and his reason and all the kindly spiritual life that should guard his soul. Certainly, it takes away also God's due authority, and that is man's soul and the love of his neighbour. It strives always against truth, also. It bereaves him of the peace of his heart and subverts his soul.

From anger come these stinking engenderings: first hate, which is old wrath; discord, by which a man forsakes his old friend whom he has long loved. And then come strife and every kind of wrong that man does to his neighbour, in body or in goods. Of this cursed sin of anger comes manslaughter also. And understand well that homicide, manslaughter, that is, is of different kinds. Some kinds of homicide are spiritual, and some are bodily. Spiritual manslaughter lies in six things. First, hate; and as Saint John says: "He that hateth his brother committeth homicide." Homicide is also accomplished by backbiting; and of backbiters Solomon says that "They have two swords wherewith they slay their neighbours." For truly, it is as wicked to take away a man's good name as his life. Homicide consists also in the giving of wicked counsel deceitfully, as in counselling one to levy wrongful duties and taxes. And Solomon says that cruel masters are like roaring lions and hungry bears, in withholding or diminishing the wages (or the hire) of servants; or else in usury; or in withholding alms from poor folk. As to which the wise man says: "Feed him who is dying of hunger." For indeed, unless you feed him, you slay him; and all these are mortal sins. Bodily homicide is when you slay a man with your tongue is some manner; as when you give command to slay a man, or else counsel him to the slaying of another. Homicide in deed is in four manners. One is by law; as when a judge condemns a culpable man to death. But let the judge take care that he do it rightfully, and that he do it not for delight in the spilling out of blood, but only for the doing of justice. Another kind of homicide is that which is done by necessity, as when one man slays another in his own defence, and when he may not otherwise escape his own death. But certainly, if he may escape without killing his adversary, and yet slays him, he commits sin, and he shall bear the punishment for mortal sin. Also, if a man by force of circumstances, or by chance, shoot an arrow or cast a stone with which he kill a man, he commits homicide. Also, if a woman negligently overlie her child in her sleep, it is homicide and mortal sin. Also, when a man interferes with the conception of a child, and makes a woman barren by the drinking of poisonous drugs, whereby she cannot conceive, or slays an unborn child deliberately, by drugs or by the introduction of certain substances into her secret parts with intent to slay the child; or does any unnatural sin whereby man or woman spill his or her fluid in such manner or in such place as a child cannot be conceived; or if a woman, having conceived, so hurt herself that she slays her child, it is homicide. What do we say of women that murder their children for dread of worldly shame? Certainly, such a one is called a horrible homicide. Homicide it is, also, if a man approach a woman by desire of lechery, through the accomplishing of which her child is killed in the womb, or strike a woman knowingly in such manner that she is caused to miscarry and lose her child. All these constitute homicide and are horrible mortal sins. Besides, there come from anger many more sins, as well of word as of thought and of deed; as that of accusing God of, or blaming God for, a thing of which a man is himself guilty; or despising God and all His saints, as do wicked gamblers in divers countries. They do this cursed sin when they feel in their heart a great wickedness toward God and His saints. Also, they do it when they treat irreverently the sacraments of the altar, and then the sin is so great that scarcely may it be forgiven, save that the mercy of God passes all His works; it is so great and He is so benign. Then comes of anger, venomous anger; when a man is sharply admonished after confession to forgo his sin, then will he be angry and will answer scornfully and angrily, and will defend or excuse his sin as the result of the weakness of his flesh; or else he did it to keep the good will of his fellows, or else, he'll say, the Fiend enticed him; or else he did it because of his youth, or else his temperament is so mettled that he could not forbear; or else it was his destiny, as he says, until a certain age; or else, he says, it comes to him out of the breeding of his ancestors; and suchlike things. All this kind of folk so wrap themselves in their sins that they will not deliver themselves. For truly, no man that excuses himself for his sin may be shriven of it until he meekly acknowledges it. After this, then comes swearing, which is expressly against the commandment of God; and this comes often of anger and ire. God says: "Thou shalt not take the name of the Lord thy God in vain." Also, Our Lord Jesus Christ says, through Saint Matthew: "*Nolite iurare omnino:* neither by Heaven; for it is God's throne: nor by the earth; for it is His footstool: neither by Jerusalem; for it is the city of the great King. Neither shalt thou swear by thy head, because thou canst not make one hair white or black: but let your communication be, yea, yea, nay, nay; for whatsoever is more than these, cometh of evil." For Christ's sake, swear not so sinfully, thus dismembering Christ by soul, heart, bones, and body. For indeed it seems that you think that the cursed Jews did not dismember enough the precious body of Christ, since you dismember Him even more. And if it be that the law compel you to swear, then be governed by the rule of the law in your swearing, as Jeremiah says, *quarto capitulo: "Iurabis, in veritate, in iudicio et in iusticia:* thou shalt swear, the Lord liveth, in truth, in judgment, and in righteousness." That is to say, you shall swear truth, for every lie is against Christ. For Christ is utter truth. And think well on this, that every great swearer, not by law compelled to swear, the plague will not depart from his house while he continues to indulge in such forbidden swearing. You shall swear for the sake of justice also, when you are constrained by your judge to bear witness to the truth. Also, you shall swear not for envy, nor for favour, nor for reward, but for righteousness; for the declaring of it to the honour of God and the helping of your fellow Christian. And therefore, every man that takes God's name in vain, or falsely swears by word of mouth, or takes upon him the name of Christ that he may be called a Christian man, and who lives not in accordance with Christ's example of living and with His teaching, all they take God's name in vain. Behold, too, what Saint Peter says, *Actuum, quarto capitulo:* "*Non est aliud nomen sub celo, etc.* There is none other name under Heaven given among men whereby we must be saved." That is to say, save the name of Jesus Christ. Take heed also how in the precious name of Christ, as Saint Paul says *ad Philipenses secundo:* "*In nomine Iesu, etc.* In the name of Jesus every knee should bow, of things in Heaven, and things in earth, and things under the earth." For it is so high and so worshipful that the cursed Fiend in Hell must tremble to hear it named.

Then it appears that men who swear so horribly by His blessed name despise Him more boldly than all the cursed Jews, or even than the Devil, who trembles when he hears His name.

Now, certainly, since swearing, unless it be lawfully done, is so strictly forbidden, much worse is false swearing, and it is needless.

What shall we say of those that delight in swearing and hold it for an act of the gentry, or a manly thing, to swear great oaths? And what of those that, of very habit, cease not to swear great oaths, though the reason therefor be not worth a straw? Certainly this is a horrible sin. Swearing suddenly and thoughtlessly is also a sin. But let us pass now to that horrible swearing of adjuration and conjuration, as do these false enchanters or necromancers in basins full of water, or in a bright sword, in a circle, or in a fire, or in a shoulder-bone of a sheep. I can say nothing, save that they do wickedly and damnably against Christ and all the faith of Holy Church.

What shall we say of those that believe in divinations, as by the flying or the crying of birds, or of beasts, or by chance, by geomancy, by dreams, by creaking of doors, by cracking of houses, by gnawing of rats, and such kinds of wickedness? Certainly, all these things are forbidden by God and by all Holy Church. For which they are accursed, until they repent and mend their ways, who set their beliefs in such filth. Charms against wounds or maladies in men or in beasts, if they have any effect, it may be, peradventure, that God permits it that folk shall have the more faith in Him and the more reverence unto His name.

Now will I speak of lying, which generally is the using of words in false signification with intent to deceive one's fellow Christian. Some lying there is whereof there comes no advantage to anyone; and some lying is done for the ease and profit of one man, and to the uneasiness and damage of another man. Another kind of lying is done to save one's life or chattels. Another kind of lying is born of mere delight in lying, for which delight they will fabricate a long tale and adorn it with all circumstances, where all the groundwork of the tale is false. Some lying is done because one would maintain his previous word; and some lying is done out of recklessness, without forethought; and for similar reasons.

Let us now touch upon the vice of flattering, which comes not gladly from the heart, but for fear or for covetousness. Flattery is generally unearned praise. Flatterers are the Devil's nurses, who nurse his children with the milk of adulation. Forsooth, as Solomon says, "Flattery is worse than detraction." For sometimes detraction causes a haughty man to be more humble, for he fears detraction; but certainly flattery— that causes a man to exalt his heart and his bearing. Flatterers are the Devil's enchanters, for they cause a man to think of himself that he is like what he is not like. They are like Judas who betrayed God; for these flatterers betray a man in order to sell him out to his enemy, that is, to the Devil. Flatterers are the Devil's chaplains, that continually sing *Placebo*. I reckon flattery among the vices of anger; for oftentimes, if one man be enraged at another, then will he flatter some other to gain an ally in his quarrel.

Let us speak now of such cursing as comes from an angry heart. Execration generally may be said to embrace every kind of evil. Such cursing deprives a man of the Kingdom of God, as says Saint Paul. And oftentimes such cursing returns again upon the head of him that curses, like a bird that returns again to its own nest. And above all things men ought to eschew the cursing of their children, and the giving to the Devil of their progeny, so far as they may; certainly it is a great danger and a great sin.

Let us now speak of chiding and reproaching, which are great evils in man's heart; for they rip up the seams of friendship in man's heart. For truly, a man can hardly be reconciled with him that has openly reviled and slandered him. This is a terrible sin, as Christ says in the gospel. And note now that he who reproaches his neighbour, either he reproaches him for some painful evil that he has in his body, as with "leper" or "hunchbacked scoundrel," or by some sin that he does. Now, if he reproach him for a painful evil, then the reproach is turned upon Jesus Christ; for pain is sent as the righteous giving of God, and by His permission, be it of leprosy or malady or bodily imperfection. And if he reproach him uncharitably for sin, as with "you whoremonger," "you drunken scoundrel," and so forth, then that appertains to the rejoicing of the Devil, who is ever rejoiced when men sin. And truly, chiding may not come, save out of a sinful heart. For according to the abundance of what is in the heart the mouth speaks. And you shall understand that when any man would correct another, let him beware of chiding or reproaching. For truly, save he beware, he may easily quicken the fire of anger and wrath, which he should quench, and perhaps will slay him whom he might have corrected gently. For, as Solomon says, "the amiable tongue is the tree of life," which is to say, of the spiritual life; and in sooth, a foul tongue drains the vital forces of him that reproaches, and also of him that is reproached. Behold what Saint Augustine says: "There is nothing so like the Devil's child as he that chideth." Saint Paul says, too: "The servant of the Lord must not strive." And though bickering be a sinful thing as between all kinds of folk, certainly it is most unsuitable between a man and his wife; for there is never rest there. Thereupon Solomon says: "A continual dropping in a very rainy day, and a contentious woman, are alike." A man who is in a house, the roof whereof leaks in many places, though he avoid the dripping in one place, it finds him in another; and so fares he who has a chiding wife. If she cannot scold him in one place, she will scold him in another. And therefore, "Better is a dinner of herbs where love is, than a stalled ox and hatred therewith," says Solomon. Saint Paul says: "Wives, submit yourselves unto your husbands, as it is fit in the Lord. Husbands, love your wives, and be not bitter against them." *Ad Colossenses, tertio.*

After that, let us speak of scorn, which is a wicked sin; especially when one scorns a man for his good works. For truly, such scorners are like the foul toad, which cannot bear to smell the sweet odour of the vine when it blossoms. These scorners are fellow-partakers with the Devil; for they rejoice when the Devil wins and sorrow when he loses. They are adversaries of Jesus Christ; for they hate what He loves, that is to say, the salvation of souls.

Now will we speak of wicked counsel; for he that gives wicked counsel is a traitor. For he deceives him that trusts in him, *ut Achitofel ad Absolonem.* Nevertheless, his wicked counsel first harms himself. For, as the wise man says, every false person living has within himself this peculiarity, that he who would harm another harms first himself. And men should understand that they should take counsel not of false folk, nor of angry folk, nor of vexatious folk nor of folk that love too much their own advantage, nor of too worldly folk, especially in the counselling of souls.

Now comes the sin of those that sow discord amongst folk, which is a sin that Christ utterly hates; and no wonder. For He died to establish concord on earth. And more shame do they do to Christ than did those that crucified Him; for God loves better that friendliness be among men than He loved His own body, the which He gave for the sake of unity. Therefore they are like the Devil, who ever goes about to make discord.

Now comes the sin of the double-tongued; such as speak fairly before folk, and wickedly behind; or they make a semblance of speaking with good intention, or in jest and play, and yet they speak with evil intention.

Now comes betraying of confidence, whereby a man is defamed: truly, the damage so done may scarcely be repaired.

Now comes menacing, which is an open folly; for he that often menaces, he often threatens more than he can perform.

Now come idle words, which sin is without profit to him that speaks and also to him that listens. Or else idle words are those that are needless, or without an aim toward any profit. And although idle words are at times but a venial sin, yet men should distrust them; for we shall have to account for them before God.

Now comes chattering, which cannot occur without sin. And, as Solomon says, "It is a sin of manifest folly." And therefore a philosopher said, when men asked him how to please the people: "Do many good deeds and chatter but little."

After this comes the sin of jesters, who are the Devil's apes. For they make folk laugh at their buffoonery, as they do at the pranks of an ape. Such clownings were forbidden by Saint Paul. Behold how virtuous and holy words give comfort to those that labour in the service of Christ; just so the sinful words and tricks of jesters and jokers comfort those that travail in the service of the Devil. These are the sins that come by way of the tongue, and from anger and many other sins.

SEQUITUR REMEDIUM CONTRA PECCATUM IRE

The remedy for anger is a virtue which men call mansuetude, which is gentleness; and even another virtue which men call patience or tolerance.

Gentleness withholds and restrains the stirrings and the urgings of man's impetuosity in his heart in such manner that it leaps not out in anger or in ire. Tolerance suffers sweetly all the annoyances and wrongs that men do to men bodily. Saint Jerome says thus of gentleness, that "it does harm to no one, nor says harm; nor for any harm that men do or say does it chafe against reason." This virtue is sometimes naturally implanted; for, as says the philosopher: "A man is a living thing, by nature gentle and tractable to goodness; but when gentleness is informed of grace, then is it worth the more."

Patience, which is another remedy against anger, is a virtue that suffers sweetly man's goodness, and is not wroth for harm done to it. The philosopher says that "patience is that virtue which suffers meekly all the outrages of adversity and every wicked word." This virtue makes a man god-like and makes him God's own dear child, as Christ says. This virtue discomfits one's enemy. And thereupon the wise man says: "If thou wilt vanquish thy enemy, learn to endure." And you shall understand that man suffers four kinds of grievances from outward things, against the which he must have four kinds of patience.

The first grievance is of wicked words; this suffered Jesus Christ without grumbling, and patiently, when the Jews many times reproached Him and showed how they despised Him. Suffer patiently, therefore, for the wise man says: "If thou strive with a fool, though the fool be wroth or though he laugh, nevertheless thou shalt have no rest." Another outward grievance is to suffer damage in one's chattels. In that Christ endured patiently when He was despoiled of all that He had in the world, that being His clothing.

The third grievance is for a man to suffer injury in his body. That, Christ endured full patiently throughout all His passion. The fourth grievance is in extravagant labour. Wherefore I say that folk who make their servants labour too grievously, or out of the proper time, as on holidays, truly they do great sin. Thereof endured Christ full patiently, and taught us patience when He bore upon His blessed shoulder the cross whereon He was to suffer a pitiless death. Hereof may men learn to be patient; for certainly, not only Christian men should be patient for love of Jesus Christ, and for the reward of the blessed life everlasting, but even the old pagans, who never were Christians, commended and practised the virtue of patience.

Upon a time a philosopher would have beaten a disciple for his great misdoing, at which the philosopher had been much annoyed; and he brought a rod wherewith to scourge the youth; and when the youth saw the rod he said to his master: "What do you intend to do?" "I will beat you," said the master, "for your correction." "Forsooth," said the youth, "you ought first to correct yourself who have lost all your patience at the offence of a child." "Forsooth," said the master, weeping, "you say truth; take the rod yourself, my dear son, and correct me for my impatience." From patience comes obedience, whereby a man becomes obedient to Christ and to all to whom he owes obedience in Christ. And understand well that obedience is perfect when a man does gladly and speedily, with entire good heart, all that he should do. Obedience, generally, is to put into practice the doctrine of God and of man's masters, to whom he ought to be humble in all righteousness.

SEQUITUR DE ACCIDIA

After the sins of envy and of anger, now will I speak of the sin of acedia, or sloth. For envy blinds the heart of a man and anger troubles a man; and acedia makes him heavy, thoughtful, and peevish. Envy and anger cause bitterness of heart; which bitterness is the mother of acedia, and takes from a man the love of all goodness. Then is acedia the anguish of a troubled heart; and Saint Augustine says: "It is the sadness of goodness and the joy of evil." Certainly this is a damnable sin; for it wrongs Jesus Christ in as much as it lessens the service that men ought to give to Christ with due diligence, as says Solomon. But sloth has no such diligence; it does everything sadly and with peevishness, slackness, and false excusing, and with slovenliness and unwillingness; for which the Book says: "Accursed be he that serveth God negligently." Then acedia is the enemy to every state of man; for indeed the state of man is in three degrees. One is the state of innocence, as was the condition of Adam before he fell into sin; in which state he was maintained to praise and adore his God. Another state is the condition of sinful men wherein they are obliged to labour in praying to God for the amendment of their sins. Another state is the condition of grace, in which condition man is bound to acts of penitence; and truly, to all these things acedia is the enemy and the opposite. For it loves no busyness at all. Now certainly this foul sin of acedia is also a great enemy to the livelihood of the body; for it makes no provision for temporal necessity; for it wastes, and it allows things to spoil, and it destroys all worldly wealth by its carelessness.

The fourth thing is that acedia is like those who are in the pain of Hell, because of their sloth and their sluggardliness; for those that are damned are so bound that they may neither do well nor think well. First of all, from the sin of acedia it happens that a man is too sad and hindered to be able to do anything good, wherefore God abominates acedia, as says Saint John.

Then comes that kind of sloth that will endure no hardship nor any penance. For truly, sloth is so tender and so delicate, as Solomon says, that it will endure no hardship or penance, and therefore it spoils everything that it attempts to do. To combat this rotten-hearted sin of acedia or sloth, men should be diligent to do good works and manfully and virtuously to come by the determination to do well; remembering that Our Lord Jesus Christ rewards every good deed, be it ever so little. The habit of labour is a great thing; for, as Saint Bernard says, it gives the labourer strong arms and hard thews, whereas sloth makes them feeble and tender. Then arises the dread of beginning to do any good deeds; for certainly, he that is inclined toward sin, he thinks it is so great an enterprise to start any works of goodness, and tells himself in his heart that the circumstances having to do with goodness are so wearisome and burdensome to endure, that he dare not undertake any such works, as says Saint Gregory.

Now enters despair, which is despair of the mercy of God, and comes sometimes of too extravagant sorrows and sometimes of too great fear: for the victim imagines that he has done so much sin that it will avail him not to repent and forgo sin; because of which fear he abandons his heart to every kind of sin, as Saint Augustine says. This damnable sin, if it be indulged to the end, is called sinning in the Holy Ghost. This horrible sin is so dangerous that, as for him that is so desperate, there is no felony or sin that he hesitates to do; as was well showed by Judas. Certainly, then, above all other sins, this sin is most displeasing to Christ, and most hateful. Truly he that grows so desperate is like the cowardly and recreant combatant that yields before he is beaten, and when there is no need. Alas, alas! Needlessly is he recreant and needlessly in despair. Certainly the mercy of God is always available to every penitent, and this is the greatest of all God's works. Alas! Cannot a man bethink him of the gospel of Saint Luke, 15, wherein Christ says: "Joy shall be in Heaven over one sinner that repenteth more than over ninety and nine just persons which need no repentance." Behold further, in the same gospel, the joy of and the feast given by the good man who had lost his son, when his son, repentant, returned to his father. Can they not remember, also, that, as Saint Luke says, XXIII° *capitulo*, the thief who was hanged beside Jesus Christ said: "Lord, remember me when Thou comest into Thy Kingdom." "Verily," said Christ, "I say unto thee, today shalt thou be with me in Paradise." Certainly, there is no such horrible sin of man that it may not be, in his lifetime, destroyed by penitence, by virtue of the passion and the death of Jesus Christ. Alas! Why then need a man despair, since mercy is so ready and so great? Ask, and it shall be given unto you. Then enters somnolence, that is to say, sluggish slumbering, which makes a man heavy and dull in body and in soul; and this sin comes from sloth. And truly, the time that a man should not sleep, in all reason, is the early morning, unless there be a reasonable necessity. For verily the morningtide is most suitable for a man to say his prayers, and to meditate on God and to honour God, and to give alms to the poor person who first asks in the name of Christ. Behold what Solomon says: "Whoso would awake in the dawn and seek me, me shall he find." Then enters negligence, or carelessness, that recks of nothing. And if ignorance is the mother of all evil, certainly then negligence is the nurse. Negligence cares not, when it must do a thing, whether it be well done or badly.

As to the remedies for these two sins, as the wise man says: "He that fears God spares not to do that which he ought." And he that loves God, he will be diligent to please God by his works, and will exert himself, with all his might, to do well. Then enters idleness, which is the gate to all evils. An idle man is like a house that has no walls; the devils may enter on every side and shoot at him, he being thus unprotected, and tempt him on every side. This idleness is the sink of all wicked and villainous thoughts, and of all idle chattering, and trifles, and of all filthiness. Certainly Heaven is for those that labour, and not for idle folk. Also, David says: "They are not among the harvest of men and they shall not be threshed with men," which is to say, in Purgatory. Certainly, then, it appears that they shall be tormented by the Devil in Hell, unless they soon repent.

Then enters the sin that men call *tarditas,* which is when a man is too tardy or too long-tarrying before he turns unto God; and certainly this is a great folly. He is like one that falls in the ditch and will not arise. And this vice comes of a false hope whereunder a man comes to think that he shall live long; but that hope full often fails him.

Then comes laziness; that is when a man begins any work and anon forgoes it and holds his hand; as do those who have anyone to govern and who take no care of him as soon as they find any difficulty or annoyance. These are the modern shepherds who knowingly allow their sheep to run to the wolf in the briers, or have no care for their governing. Of this come poverty and the destruction of both spiritual and temporal things. Then comes a kind of dull coldness that freezes the heart of man. Then comes lack of devotion, whereby a man is so blinded, as Saint Bernard says, and has such languor of soul, that he may not read or sing in holy church, nor hear or think of anything devout, nor toil with his hands at any good work, without the labour being unsavoury and vapid to him. Then he grows slow and slumbery, and is easily angered and is easily inclined toward hate and envy. Then comes the sin of worldly sorrow, such as is called *tristicia,* which slays men, as Saint Paul says. For, verily, such sorrow works the death of the soul and of the body also; for thereof it comes to pass that a man is bored by his own life. Wherefore such sadness full often shortens a man's life before his time has naturally come.

REMEDIUM CONTRA PECCATUM ACCIDIE

Against this horrible sin of acedia, and the branches thereof, there is a virtue that is called *fortitudo* or strength; that is, a force of character whereby a man despises annoying things. This virtue is so mighty and so vigorous that it dares to withstand sturdily, and wisely to keep itself from dangers that are wicked, and to wrestle against the assaults of the

Devil. For it enhances and strengthens the soul, just as acedia reduces it and makes it feeble. For this *fortitudo* can endure, by long suffering, the toils that are fitting.

This virtue has many species; and the first is called magnanimity, which is to say, great-heartedness. For certainly a great heart is needed against acedia, lest it swallow up the soul by the sin of sadness, or destroy it by despair. This virtue causes folk to undertake hard things, or grievous things, of their own initiative, wisely and reasonably. And for as much as the Devil fights a man more by craft and by trickery than by strength, therefore men may withstand him by wit and by reason and by discretion. Then there are the virtues of faith and of hope in God and in His saints, to achieve and accomplish the good works in which one firmly purposes to continue. Then comes security and certainness; and that is when a man shall not doubt, in time to come, the value of the toil of the good works that he has begun. Then comes munificence, which is to say, that virtue whereby a man performs great works of goodness that he has begun; and that is the goal to reach which men should do good works; for in the doing of great good works lies the great reward. Then there is constancy, that is, stability of purpose, and this should be evidenced in heart by steadfast faith, and in word and in attitude and in appearance and in deed. Also, there are other special remedies against acedia or sloth, in divers works, and in consideration of the pains of Hell and of the joys of Heaven, and in faith in the grace of the Holy Ghost, that will give to a man the strength wherewith to perform his good purpose.

SEQUITUR DE AVARICIA

After acedia I will speak of avarice and of covetousness, of which sin Saint Paul says that "The love of money is the root of all evil:" *ad Timotheum, sexto capitulo*. For verily, when the heart of a man is confounded within itself, and troubled, and when the soul has lost the comforting of God, then seeks a man a vain solace in worldly things.

Avarice, according to the description of Saint Augustine, is the eagerness of the heart to have earthly things. Others say that avarice is the desire to acquire earthly goods and give nothing to those that need. And understand that avarice consists not only of greed for land and chattels, but sometimes for learning and for glory, and for every kind of immoderate thing. And the difference between avarice and covetousness is this. Covetousness is to covet such things as one has not; and avarice is to keep and withhold such things as one has when there is no need to do so. Truly, this avarice is a sin that is very damnable; for all holy writ condemns it and inveighs against that vice; for it does wrong to Jesus

Christ. For it takes away from Him the love that men owe to Him and turns it backward, and this against all reason; and it causes that an avaricious man has more hope in his chattels than in Jesus Christ and is more diligent in the guarding and keeping of his treasure than in the service of Jesus Christ. And therefore Saint Paul says, *ad Ephesios, quinto*, that "this ye know, that no . . . covetous man, who is an idolater, hath any inheritance in the Kingdom of Christ and of God."

What difference is there between an idolater and an avaricious man, save that an idolater, peradventure, has but one idol and the avaricious man has many? For verily, every florin in his coffer is his idol. And certainly the sin of idolatry is the first thing that God forbids in the ten commandments, as witnesses *Exodi, capitulo* XX°: "Thou shalt have no other gods before me, thou shalt not make unto thee any graven image." Thus an avaricious man, who loves his treasure more than God, is an idolater, by reason of this cursed sin of avarice. Of covetousness come these hard exactions whereunder men are assessed and made to pay taxes, rents, and payments in lieu of service, more than duty requires or reason demands. Also, they take from their serfs amercements that might more reasonably be called extortions than amercements. As to which amercements and fines of serfs, some lords' stewards say that it is just, because a churl has no temporal thing that does not belong to his lord, or so they say. But certainly these lordships do wrong that take away from their serfs things that they never gave them, *Augustinus de Civitate, libro nono*. The truth is that the condition of serfdom is a sin: *Genesis, quinto*.[1]

Thus may you see that man's sin deserves thralldom, but man's origin does not. Wherefore these lords should not greatly glorify themselves in their lordships, since by natural condition, or origin, they are not lords of thralls; but thralldom came into being first as the desert of sin. And furthermore, whereas the law says that the temporal effects of bondmen are the property of their lords, verily, by that is to be understood, the property of the emperor, who defends them in their rights, but who has no right to rob or to plunder them. And thereupon says Seneca: "Thy prudence should cause thee to live benignly with thy slaves." Those whom you call your serfs are God's people; for humble folk are Christ's friends; they are at home in the house of the Lord.

Think, also, that such seed as churls come from, from such seed come the lords. As easily may the churl be saved as the lord. The same death that takes the churl takes the lord. Wherefore I advise you to do unto your churl as you would that your lord should do unto you, if you were in the churl's plight. Every sinful man is a serf to sin. I advise you,

---

1. Probably the reference should have been to *Genesis, quarto.*

verily, that you, lord, act in such wise with your serfs that they shall rather love you than fear. I know well that there is degree above degree, and that this is reasonable; and reasonable it is that men should pay their duty where it is due; but, certainly, extortions and contempt for underlings is damnable.

And furthermore, understand well that conquerors or tyrants often make thralls of those who were born of as royal blood as those who have conquered. This word of thralldom was unknown until Noah said that his grandson Canaan should be servant to his brethren for his sin. What say we then of those that plunder and extort money from Holy Church? Certainly, the sword which men give to a knight when he is dubbed, signifies that he should defend Holy Church and not rob or pillage it; and whoever does so is a traitor to Christ. And, as Saint Augustine says: "They are the Devil's wolves that pull down the sheep of Jesus Christ." And they do worse than wolves. For truly, when the wolf has filled his belly, he ceases to kill sheep. But truly, the plunderers and destroyers of God's Holy Church do not so, for they never cease to pillage. Now, as I have said, since it was because sin was the first cause of thralldom, then it stands thus: that all the while all the world was in sin, it was in thralldom and subjection. But certainly, since the time of grace came, God ordained that some folk should be higher in rank and state and some folk lower, and that each should be served according to his rank and his state. And therefore, in some countries, where they buy slaves, when they have converted them to the faith, they set their slaves free from slavery. And therefore, certainly, the lord owes to his man that which the man owes to his lord. The pope calls himself servant of the servants of God; but in as much as the estate of Holy Church might not have come into being, nor the common advantage kept, nor any peace and rest established on earth, unless God had ordained that some men should have higher rank and some lower: therefore was sovereignty ordained to guard and maintain and defend its underlings or its subjects within reason and so far as lies in its power, and not to destroy or to confound them. Wherefore, I say that those lords that are like wolves, that devour the wealth or the possessions of poor folk wrongfully, without mercy or measure, they shall receive, by the same measure that they have used toward poor folk, the mercy of Jesus Christ, unless they mend their ways. Now comes deceit between merchant and merchant. And you shall understand that trade is of two kinds; the one is material and the other is spiritual. The one is decent and lawful and the other is indecent and unlawful. Of this material trade, that which is decent and lawful is this: that where God has ordained that a kingdom or a country is sufficient unto itself, then it is decent and lawful that of the abundance of this country men should help another country that is more needy. And therefore there are permitted to be merchants to bring from the one country to the other their merchandise. That other trade, which men barter with fraud and treachery and deceit, with lies and with false oaths, is accursed and damnable. Spiritual trade is properly simony, which is earnest desire to buy spiritual things, that is to say, things that appertain to the sanctuary of God and to the cure of the soul. This desire, if it be that man is diligent in accomplishing it, even though his desire have no effect, yet it is a deadly sin; and if he be ordained he sins against his orders. Simony is named for Simon Magus, who would have bought, with temporal wealth, the gift that God had given, by the Holy Ghost, to Saint Peter and to the other apostles. And therefore you should understand that both he that buys and he that sells spiritual things are called simonists; be it by means of chattels, or by entreaty, or by fleshly asking of his friends—fleshly friends or spiritual friends. Fleshly friends are of two kinds, as kindred and other friends. Truly, if they ask for one who is not worthy and able, it is simony if he take the benefice; but if he be worthy and able, it is not. The other kind is when a man or woman asks folk to advance him or her, only for wicked fleshly affection that they may have for that person; and that is vile simony. But certainly, in that service for which men give spiritual things unto their servants, it must be understood that the service is honest; and also that it be done without bargaining, and that the person be able. For, as Saint Damasus says: "All the sins of the world, compared to this sin, are as naught." For it is the greatest sin that may be done, after that of Lucifer and Antichrist. For by this sin God loses the Church and the soul that He bought with His precious blood, because of those who give churches to those who are not worthy. For they put in thieves, who steal souls from Jesus Christ and destroy His patrimony. By reason of such unworthy priests and curates have ignorant men the less reverence for the sacraments of Holy Church; and such givers of churches put out the children of Christ and put in the Devil's own sons. They sell the souls that they watch over as lambs to the wolf that rends them. And therefore they shall never have any part in the pasture of lambs, that is, the bliss of Heaven. Now comes hazardry with its appurtenances, such as backgammon and raffles;[2] whence come deceit, false oaths, chidings, and hatred for one's neighbours, waste of wealth, mis-spending of time, and sometimes homicide. Certainly, hazarders cannot be without great sin while they continue to practise their craft. Of avarice come also lying, theft, false witnessing, and false oaths. And you must understand that these are great sins, expressly against the

---

2. Raffles: an old game with three dice, in which that player wins the stakes who throws all three alike.

commandments of God, as I have said. False witnessing lies in word and also in deed. In word, as by taking away your neighbour's good name by bearing false witness against him, or by depriving him of his chattels or his heritage by such false witnessing when you, for anger or reward, bear false witness or accuse him by your false witnessing, or else when you falsely excuse yourself. Beware, you jurymen and notaries! Certainly, by false witness, was Susanna in great sorrow and pain, as have been many others. The sin of theft is also expressly against God's command, and that of two kinds, corporal and spiritual. Corporal, as taking your neighbour's chattels against his will, be it by force or by fraud, be it by short lineal measure or by short measure of capacity. By secret swearing, also, of false indictments against him, and by borrowing your neighbour's goods with intent never to return them, and by similar things. Spiritual theft is sacrilege, that is to say, injuring of holy things, or of things sacred to Christ, and is of two kinds; by reason of the fact that it is a holy place, as a church or a churchyard, every vile sin that men do in such places may be called sacrilege, or every violence done in such places. Also they who withhold what of right belongs to Holy Church are guilty of sacrilege. And plainly and generally, sacrilege is to steal a holy thing from a holy place, or an unholy thing from a holy place, or a holy thing from an unholy place.

REVELACIO CONTRA PECCATUM AVARICIE

Now shall you understand that the relief for avarice is mercy and pity in large doses. And men might ask why mercy and pity relieve avarice. Certainly, the avaricious man shows no pity nor any mercy to the needy man; for he delights in keeping his treasure and not in the rescuing or relieving of his fellow Christian. And therefore will I speak first of mercy. Mercy, as the philosopher says, is a virtue whereby the feelings of a man are moved by the trouble of him that is in trouble. Upon which mercy follows pity and performs charitable works of mercy. And certainly, these things impel a man to the mercy of Jesus Christ—that He gave Himself for our sins, and suffered death for the sake of mercy, and forgave us our original sins; and thereby released us from the pains of Hell and lessened the pains of Purgatory by means of penitence, and gives us grace to do good, and, at the last, gives us the bliss of Heaven. The kinds of mercy are: to lend, and to give, and to forgive, and to set free, and to have pity in heart and compassion on the tribulations of one's fellow Christian, and also, to chasten, as need may be. Another kind of remedy for avarice is reasonable largess; and truly, here it behooves one to give consideration to the grace of Jesus Christ, and to one's temporal wealth, and also to the perdurable wealth that Christ gave to us; and to remember the death that he shall receive, he knows not when, where, or how, and also that he must forgo all that he has, save only that which he has invested in good works.

But for as much as some folk are immoderate, men ought to avoid foolish largess, which men call waste. Certainly, he that is prodigal gives not his wealth, but loses his wealth. Truly, that which he gives out of vainglory, as to minstrels and to followers, in order to have his renown carried about the world, he does sin thereby rather than gives alms. Certainly, he shamefully loses his wealth who seeks in the gift thereof nothing but sin. He is like a horse that chooses rather to drink muddy or turbid water than the clear water of a well. And for as much as they give where they should not give, to them belongs that cursing which Christ will give at the day of doom to those that shall be damned.

SEQUITUR DE GULA

After avarice comes gluttony, which also is entirely against the commandment of God. Gluttony is immoderate appetite to eat or to drink, or else to yield to the immoderate desire to eat or to drink. This sin corrupted all this world, as is well shown by the sin of Adam and Eve. Read, also, what Saint Paul says of gluttony: "For many walk, of whom I have told you often, and now tell you even weeping, that they are the enemies of the cross of Christ: whose end is destruction, whose God is their belly, and whose glory is in their shame, who mind earthly things." He that is addicted to this sin of gluttony may withstand no other sin. He may even be in the service of all the vices, for it is in the Devil's treasure house that he hides himself and rests. This sin has many species. The first is drunkenness, which is the horrible sepulture of man's reason; and therefore, when a man is drunk he has lost his reason; and this is deadly sin. But truly, when a man is not used to strong drink, and perhaps knows not the strength of the drink, or is feeble-minded, or has toiled, for which reason he drinks too much, then, though he be suddenly caught by drink, it is not deadly sin, but venial. The second kind of gluttony is when the spirit of man grows turbid, for drunkenness has robbed him of the discretion of his wit. The third kind of gluttony is when a man devours his food and has no correct manner of eating. The fourth is when, through the great abundance of his food, the humours in his body become distempered. The fifth is, forgetfulness caused by too much drinking, whereby sometimes a man forgets before the morning what he did last evening, or the night before.

In another manner are distinguished the kinds of gluttony, according to Saint Gregory. The first is, eating before it is time to eat. The second is when a man gets himself too delicate food or drink. The third is when men eat too much, and beyond measure. The fourth is fastidiousness, with great attention paid to the preparation and dressing of food. The fifth is to eat too greedily. These are the five fingers of the Devil's hand wherewith he draws folk into sin.

REMEDIUM CONTRA PECCATUM GULE

Against gluttony abstinence is the remedy, as Galen says; but I hold that to be not meritorious if he do it only for the health of his body. Saint Augustine will have it that abstinence should be practised for the sake of virtue and with patience. Abstinence, he says, is little worth unless a man have a good will thereto, and save it be practised in patience and charity and that men do it for God's sake and in hope of the bliss of Heaven.

The companions of abstinence are temperance, which follows the middle course in all things; and shame, which eschews all indecency; and sufficiency, which seeks after no rich foods and drinks and cares nothing for too extravagant dressing of meats. Measure, also, which restrains within reason the unrestrained appetite for eating; sobriety, also, which restrains the luxurious desire to sit long and softly at meat, and because of which some folk, of their own will, stand, in order to spend less time at eating.

SEQUITUR DE LUXURIA

After gluttony, then comes lechery; for these two sins are such close cousins that oftentimes they will not be separated. God knows, this sin is unpleasing to God; for He said Himself, "Do no lechery." And therefore He imposed great penalties against this sin in the old law. If a bondwoman were taken in this sin, she should be beaten to death with rods. And if she were a woman of quality, she should be slain with stones. And if she were a bishop's daughter, she should be burnt, by God's commandment. Furthermore, for the sin of lechery, God drowned all the world by the deluge. And after that He burned five cities with thunderbolts and sank them into Hell.

Let us speak, then, of that stinking sin of lechery that men call adultery of wedded folk, which is to say, if one of them be wedded, or both. Saint John says that adulterers shall be in Hell "in the lake which burneth with fire and brimstone"—in the fire for the lechery, in brimstone for the stink of their filthiness. Certainly, the breaking of this sacrament is a horrible thing; it was ordained by God Himself in Paradise, and confirmed by Jesus Christ, as witness Saint Matthew in the gospel: "For this cause shall a man leave father and mother, and shall cleave to his wife; and they twain shall be one flesh." This sacrament betokens the knitting together of Christ and of Holy Church. And not only did God forbid adultery in deed, but also He commanded that "thou shalt not covet thy neighbour's wife." This behest, says Saint Augustine, contains the forbidding of all desire to do lechery. Behold what Saint Matthew says in the gospel: "Whosoever looketh on a woman to lust after her, hath committed adultery with her already in his heart." Here you may see that not only the doing of this sin is forbidden, but also the desire to do that sin. This accursed sin grievously troubles those whom it haunts. And first, it does harm to the soul; for it constrains it to sin and to the pain of everlasting death. Unto the body it is a tribulation also, for it drains it, and wastes and ruins it, and makes of its blood a sacrifice to the Field of Hell; also it wastes wealth and substance. And certainly, if it be a foul thing for a man to waste his wealth on women, it is a yet fouler thing when, for such filthiness, women spend on men their wealth and their substance. This sin, as says the prophet, robs man and woman of good name and of all honour; and it gives great pleasure to the Devil, for thereby won he the greater part of the world. And just as a merchant delights most in that trading whereof he reaps the greater gain, just so the Fiend delights in this filth.

This is the Devil's other hand, with five fingers to catch the people into his slavery. The first finger is the foolish interchange of glances between the foolish woman and the foolish man, which slays just as the basilisk slays folk by the venom of its sight; for the lust of the eyes follows the lust of the heart. The second finger is vile touching in wicked manner; and thereupon Solomon says that he who touches and handles a woman fares like the man that handles the scorpion which stings and suddenly slays by its poisoning; even as, if any man touch warm pitch, it defiles his fingers. The third is vile words, which are like fire, which immediately burns the heart. The fourth finger is kissing; and truly he were a great fool who would kiss the mouth of a burning oven or of a furnace. And the more fools they are who kiss in vileness; for that mouth is the mouth of Hell; and I speak specifically of these old dotard whoremongers, who will yet kiss though they cannot do anything, and so taste them. Certainly they are like dogs, for a dog, when he passes a rosebush, or other bushes, though he cannot piss, yet will he heave up his leg and make an appearance of pissing. And as for the opinion of many that a man cannot sin for any lechery he does with his wife, certainly that opinion is wrong. God knows, a man may slay himself with his own knife, and make himself drunk out of his own tun. Certainly, be it wife, be it child, or any worldly thing that a man loves more than he loves God, it is his idol, and he is an idolater. Man should love his wife with discretion, calmly and moderately; and then she is as it were his sister. The fifth finger of the Devil's hand is the stinking act of lechery. Truly, the five fingers of gluttony the Fiend thrusts into the belly of a man, and with his five fingers of lechery he grips him by the loins in order to throw him into the furnace of Hell; wherein he shall have the fire and the everlasting worms, and weeping and wailing, sharp hunger and thirst, and horror of devils that shall trample all over him, without respite and without end. From lechery, as I said, spring divers branches; as fornication, which is between man and woman who are not married; and this is deadly sin and against nature. All that is an enemy to and destructive of nature is against nature. Faith, the reason of a man tells him well that it is mortal sin, since God forbade lechery. And Saint Paul gives him over to that kingdom which is the reward of no man save those who do mortal sin. Another sin of lechery is to bereave a maiden of her maidenhead; for he that so does, certainly, he casts a maiden out of the highest state in this present life and he bereaves her of that precious fruit that the Book calls "the hundred fruit." I can say it in no other way in English, but in Latin it is called *centesimus fructus*. Certainly, he that so acts is the cause of many injuries and villainies, more than any man can reckon; just as he sometimes is cause of all damage that beasts do in the field, who breaks down the hedge or the fence, just so does the seducer destroy that which cannot be restored. For truly, no more may a maidenhead be restored than an arm that has been smitten from the body may return thereto to grow again. She may have mercy, this I know well, if she does penance, but it shall never again be that she is uncorrupted. And though I have spoken somewhat of adultery, it is well to show forth more dangers that come of adultery, in order that men may eschew that foul sin. Adultery, in Latin, means to approach another man's bed, by reason of which those that once were one flesh abandon their bodies to other persons. Of this sin, as the wise man says, follow many evils. First, breaking of faith; and certainly, in faith lies the key to Christianity. And when faith is broken and lost, truly, Christianity stands barren and without fruit. This sin is also a theft; for theft commonly is to deprive a person of his own thing against his will. Certainly this is the vilest thievery that can be when a woman steals her body from her husband and gives it to her lecher to defile her; and steals her soul from Christ and gives it to the Devil. This is a fouler theft than to break into a church and steal the chalice; for these adulterers break into the temple of God spiritually and steal the vessel of grace, that is, the body and the soul, for which Christ will destroy them, as Saint Paul says. Truly, of this theft Joseph was much afraid when his master's wife besought him to lie with her, and he said: "Behold, my master wotteth not what is with me in the house, and he hath committed all that he hath to my hand: there is none greater in this house than I; neither hath he kept any thing from me but thee, because thou art his wife: how then can I do this great wickedness and sin against God?" Alas! All too little is such truth encountered nowadays. The third evil is the filth whereby they break the commandment of God and defame the Author of matrimony, Who is Christ. For certainly, in so far as the sacrament of marriage is so noble and honourable, so much the more is it a sin to break it; for God established marriage in Paradise, in the state of innocence, in order to multiply mankind to the service of God. And therefore is the breaking thereof the more grievous. Of which breaking come oftentimes false heirs, that wrongfully inherit. And therefore will Christ put them out of the Kingdom of Heaven, which is the heritage of good folk. From this breaking it happens oftentimes, also, that people wed or sin with their own kindred; and specially the loose-livers who haunt the brothels of prostitutes, who may be likened to a common privy wherein men purge themselves of their ordure. What shall we say, also, of whoremasters who live by the horrible sin of prostitution, yea, sometimes by the prostitution of their own wives and children, as do pimps and procurers? Certainly these are accursed sins. Understand also that adultery is fitly placed in the ten commandments between theft and homicide; for it is the greatest theft that can be, being theft of body and of soul. And it is like homicide, for it cuts in twain and breaks asunder those that were made one flesh, and therefore, by the old law of God, adulterers should be slain. But nevertheless, by the law of Jesus Christ, which is a law of pity, He said to the woman who was taken in adultery and should have been slain with stones, according to the will of the Jews, as was their law: "Go," said Jesus Christ, "and have no more will to sin," or "will no more to do sin." Truly, the punishment of adultery is given to the torment of Hell, unless it be that it is hindered by penitence. And there are yet more branches of this wicked sin; as when one of them is a religious, or else both; or folk who have entered orders, as a sub-deacon, or deacon, or priest, or hospitaller. And ever the higher that he is in orders, the greater is the sin. The thing that greatly aggravates their sin is the breaking of the vow of chastity, taken when they received the order. And furthermore, the truth is that the office of a holy order is chief of all the treasury of God, and His special sign and mark of chastity, to show that those who have entered it are joined to chastity, which is the most precious kind of life there is. And these folk in orders are specially dedicated to God, and are of the special household of God; for which, when they do deadly sin, they are especially traitors to God and to His people; for they live on the people in order to pray for the people, and while they are such traitors their prayers avail the people nothing at all. Priests are angels, by reason of the dignity of their ministry; but forsooth, as Saint Paul says: "Satan himself is transformed into an angel of light." Truly, the priest that resorts to mortal sin, he may be likened to the angel of darkness transformed into the angel of light; he seems an angel of light, but, forsooth, he is an angel of darkness. Such priests are the sons of Eli, as is shown in the Book of the Kings, that they were the sons of Belial, that is, the Devil. Belial means, "without judge"; and so fare they; they think they are free and have no judge, any more than has a free bull that takes whatever cow pleases him on the farm. So act they with women. For just as a free bull is enough for all a farm, just so is a wicked priest corruption enough for all a parish, or for all a county. These priests, as the Book says, teach not the functions of priesthood to the people, and they know not God; they held themselves but ill satisfied, as the Book says, with the flesh that was boiled and offered to them and took by force the flesh that was raw. Certainly, so these scoundrels hold themselves not pleased with roasted flesh and boiled flesh, with which the people feed them in great reverence, but they will have the raw flesh of laymen's wives and of their daughters. And certainly these women that give assent to their rascality do great wrong to Christ and to Holy Church and all saints and all souls; for they bereave all these of him that should worship Christ and Holy Church and pray for Christian souls. And therefore such priests and their lemans also, who give assent to their lechery, have the cursing of all the Christian court, until they mend their ways. The third kind of adultery is sometimes practised between a man and his wife; and that is when they have no regard to their union, save only for their fleshly delight, as says Saint Jerome; and care for nothing but that they are come together; because they are married, it is all well enough, as they think. But over such folk the Devil has power, as said the Angel Raphael to Tobias; for in their union they put Jesus Christ out of mind and give themselves to all filthiness. The fourth kind is the coming together of those that are akin, or of those that are related by marriage, or else of those whose fathers or other kindred have had intercourse in the sin of lechery; this sin makes them like dogs that pay no heed to relationship. And certainly, kinship is of two kinds, either spiritual or carnal; spiritual, as when one lies with one's sponsor. For just as he that engenders a child is its fleshly father, just so is his godfather his spiritual father. For which reason a woman is in no less sin when she lies carnally with her godfather or her godson than she would be in if she coupled with her own fleshly brother. The fifth kind is that abominable sin whereof a man ought scarcely to speak or write, notwithstanding it is openly discussed in holy writ. This wickedness men and women do with divers intentions and in divers manners; but though holy writ speaks of such horrible sin, holy writ cannot be defiled, any more than can the sun that shines upon the dunghill. Another form of sin appertains to lechery, and that comes often to those who are virgin and also to those who are corrupt; and this sin men call pollution, which comes in four ways. Sometimes it is due to laxness of the body; because the humours are too rank and abundant in the body of man. Sometimes it is due to infirmity; because of the weakness of the retentive virtue, as is discussed in works on medicine. Sometimes it is due to a surfeit of food and drink. And sometimes it comes from base thoughts that were enclosed in man's mind when he fell asleep; which thing may not happen without sin. Because of this, men must govern themselves wisely, or else they may fall into grievous sin.

REMEDIUM CONTRA PECCATUM LUXURIE

Now comes the remedy for lechery, and that is, generally, chastity and continence, which restrain all the inordinate stirrings that come of fleshly desires. And ever the greater merit shall he have who restrains the wicked enkindlings of the ordure of this sin. And this is of two kinds, that is to say, chastity in marriage and chastity in widowhood. Now you shall understand that matrimony is the permitted coming together of man and of woman, who receive, by virtue of the sacrament, the bond of union from which they may not be freed in all their life, that is to say, while they both live. This, says the Book, is a very great sacrament. God established it, as I have said, in Paradise, and had Himself born into wedlock. And to sanctify marriage, He attended a wedding, where He turned water into wine, which was the first miracle that He wrought on earth before His disciples. The true result of marriage is the cleansing of fornication and the replenishing of Holy Church with believers of good lineage; for that is the end of marriage; and it changes deadly sin to venial sin between those who are wedded, and makes one the hearts of them, as well as the bodies. This is true marriage, which was established by God ere sin began, when natural law occupied its rightful position in Paradise; and it was ordained that one man should have but one woman, and one woman but one man, as Saint Augustine says, and that for many reasons.

First, because marriage figures the union between Christ and Holy Church. And another is, because the man is the head of the woman; at any rate it has been so ordained by ordinance. For if a woman had more men than one, then should she have more heads than one, and that were a horrible thing before God; and also, a woman could not please too many folk at once. And also, there should never be peace or rest among them; for each would demand his own thing. And furthermore, no man should know his own get, nor who should inherit his property; and the woman should be the less beloved from the time that she were joined with many men.

Now comes the question, How should a man conduct himself toward his wife? and specifically in two things, that is to say, in tolerance and reverence, as Christ showed when He first made woman. For He made her not of the head of Adam, because she should not claim to exercise great lordship. For wherever the woman has the mastery she causes too much disorder; there are needed no instances of this. The experience of every day ought to suffice. Also, certainly, God did not make woman of the foot of Adam, because she should not be held in too great contempt; for she cannot patiently endure: but God made woman of the rib of Adam, because woman should be a companion to man. Man should conduct himself toward his wife in faith, in truth, and in love; as Saint Paul says: "Husbands, love your wives, even as Christ also loved the Church, and gave Himself for it." So should a man give himself for his wife, if there be need.

Now how a woman should be subject to her husband, that is told by Saint Peter. First, by obedience. And also, as says the law, a woman who is a wife, as long as she is a wife, has no authority to make oath or to bear witness without the consent of her husband, who is her lord; in any event he should be so, in reason. She should also serve him in all honour, and be modest in her dress. I know well that they should resolve to please their husbands, but not by the finery of their array. Saint Jerome says that wives who go apparelled in silk and in precious purple cannot clothe themselves in Jesus Christ. Also, what says Saint John on this subject? Saint Gregory, also, says that a person seeks precious array only out of vainglory, to be honoured the more before the crowd. It is a great folly for a woman to have a fair outward appearance and inwardly to be foul. A wife should also be modest in glance and demeanour and in conversation, and discreet in all her words and deeds. And above all worldly things she should love her husband with her whole heart, and be true to him of her body; so, also, should a husband be to his wife. For since all the body is the husband's, so should her heart be, or else there is between them, in so far as that is concerned, no perfect marriage. Then shall men understand that for three things a man and his wife may have carnal coupling. The first is with intent to procreate children to the service of God, for certainly, that is the chief reason for matrimony. Another is, to pay, each of them to the other, the debt of their bodies, for neither of them has power over his own body. The third is, to avoid lechery and baseness. The fourth is, indeed, deadly sin. As for the first, it is meritorious; the second also, for, as the law says, she has the merit of chastity who pays to her husband the debt of her body, aye, though it be against her liking and the desire of her heart. The third is venial sin, and truly, hardly any of these unions may be without venial sin, because of the original sin and because of the pleasure. As to the fourth, be it understood that if they couple only for amorous love and for none of the aforesaid reasons, but merely to accomplish that burning pleasure, no matter how often, truly it is a mortal sin; and yet (with sorrow I say it) some folk are at pains to do it more and oftener than their appetite really demands.

The second kind of chastity is to be a clean widow and eschew the embraces of man and desire the embrace of Jesus Christ. These are those that have been wives and have lost their husbands, and also women that have fornicated and have been relieved by penitence. And truly, if a wife could keep herself always chaste with leave and license of her husband, so that she should thereby give him never an occasion to sin, it were a great merit in her. These women that observe chastity must be clean in heart as well as in body and in thought, and modest in dress and demeanour; and be abstinent in eating and drinking, in speech and in deed. They are the vessel or the box of the blessed Magdalen, which fills Holy Church with good odour. The third kind of chastity is virginity, and it behooves her to be holy in heart and clean of body; then is she the spouse of Christ and she is the beloved of the angels. She is the honour of this world, and she is the equal of martyrs; she has within her that which tongue may not tell nor the heart think. Virginity bore Our Lord Jesus Christ, and virgin was He Himself.

Another remedy for lechery is, specially to withhold oneself from such things as give rise to this baseness; as ease, and eating and drinking: for certainly, when the pot boils furiously, the best measure is to withdraw it from the fire. Sleeping long in great security from disturbance is also a nurse to lechery.

Another remedy for lechery is, that a man or woman eschew the company of those by whom he expects to be tempted; for though it be that the act itself is withstood, yet there is great temptation. Truly a white wall, though it burn not from the setting of a candle near it, yet shall the wall be made black by the flame. Often and often I counsel that no man trust in his own perfection, save he be stronger than Samson and holier than David and wiser than Solomon.

Now, since I have expounded to you, as best I could, the seven deadly sins, and some of their branches, and their remedies, truly, if I could, I would tell you of the ten commandments. But so high a doctrine I leave to the divines. Nevertheless, I hope to God that they have been touched upon in this treatise, each of them all.

DE CONFESSIONE

Now, for as much as the second part of penitence deals in oral confession, as I said in the first paragraph hereof, I say that Saint Augustine says: Sin is every word and every deed and all that men covet against the law of Jesus Christ; and that is, to sin in heart, in word, and in deed by one's five senses, which are sight, hearing, smell, taste or savour, and feeling. Now it is well to understand that which greatly aggravates every sin. You should consider what you are that do the sin, whether you are male or female, young or old, noble or thrall, free or servant, healthy or ailing, wedded or single, member of a religious order or not, wise or foolish, clerical or secular; whether she is of your kindred, bodily or spiritual, or not; whether any of your kindred has sinned with her, or not; and many other things.

Another circumstance is this: whether it be done in fornication, or in adultery, or otherwise; incest, or not; maiden, or not; in manner of homicide, or not; horrible great sins, or small; and how long you have continued in sin. The third circumstance is the place where you have done the sin; whether in other men's houses, or your own; in field, or in church or churchyard; in a dedicated church, or not. For if the church be consecrated, and man or woman spill seed within that place, by way of sin or by wicked temptation, the church is interdicted till it be reconciled by the bishop; and the priest that did such a villainy, for the term of all his life, should nevermore sing mass; and if he did, he should do deadly sin every time that he so sang mass. The fourth circumstance is, what go-betweens, or what messengers, are sent for the sake of enticement, or to gain consent to bear company in the affair; for many a wretch, for the sake of companionship, will go to the Devil of Hell. Wherefore those that egg on to or connive for the sin are partners in the sin, and shall partake of the damnation of the sinner. The fifth circumstance is, how many times has he sinned, if it be in his memory, and how often he has fallen. For he that falls often in sin, he despises the mercy of God, and increases his sin, and is ungrateful to Christ; and he grows the more feeble to withstand sin, and sins the more lightly, and the more slowly rises out of sin, and is the more reluctant to be shriven, especially by his own confessor. For the which reasons, when folk fall again into their old follies, either they avoid their old confessors altogether, or else they make parts of confession in divers places; but truly, such divided confessions deserve no mercy of God for one's sins. The sixth circumstance is, why a man sins, as by way of what sort of temptation; and whether he himself procured that temptation, or whether it came by the incitement of other folk; or whether he sin by forcing a woman or by her consent: or, if the sinner be a woman, despite all her efforts were she forced or not—this shall she tell; and whether for greed of gain or for stress of poverty, and whether it was of her own procuring, or not; and all such trappings. The seventh circumstance is, in what manner he has done his sin, or how she has suffered men to do it unto her. And the same shall the man tell fully, with all the circumstances; and whether he has sinned with common brothel-women, or not; or has done his sin in holy times, or not; in fasting times, or not; or before confession, or after his last shriving; and whether he has, peradventure, broken therefor his enjoined penance; by whose help and by whose counsel; by sorcery or cunning: all must be told. All these things, according as they are great or small, burden the conscience of a man. And, too, that the priest who is your judge shall be the better advised to his judgment in giving you penance, that is, according to your contrition. For understand well that after a man has defiled his baptism by sin, if he would gain salvation, there is no other way than by penitence and shrift and penance; and specifically by the two, if there be a confessor to shrive him; and by the third if he live to perform it.

Then shall a man reflect and consider that if he will make a true and profitable confession, there must be four conditions. First, it must be in sorrowful bitterness of heart, as said King Hezekiah to God: "I will remember all the days of my life in bitterness of heart." This condition of bitterness has five signs. The first is, that confession must be shamefaced, not to cover up nor to hide sin, for the sinner has offended his God and defiled his soul. And thereof Saint Augustine says: "The heart suffers for the shame of its sin." And if he has a great sense of shame, he is worthy of great mercy from God. Such was the confession of the publican who would not lift up his eyes to Heaven, for he had offended God in Heaven; for which shamefacedness he received straightway the mercy of God. And thereof says Saint Augustine that such shamefaced folk are near to forgiveness and remission. Another sign is humility in confession; of which Saint Peter says "Humble thyself beneath the might of God." The hand of God is mighty in confession, for thereby God forgives you your sins; for He alone has the power. And this humility shall be of the heart, and shall be manifested outwardly; for just as he has humility to God in his heart, just so should he humble his body outwardly to the priest that sits in God's place. Since Christ is sovereign and the priest is means and mediator between Christ and the sinner, and the sinner is the last, in reason, the sinner should nowise sit as high as his confessor, but should kneel before him, or at his feet, unless infirmity hinder it. For he shall care not who sits there, but only in whose place he sits. A man who has offended a lord, and who comes to ask mercy and to be at peace again, and who should sit down at once by the lord's side—men would hold him to be presumptuous and not worthy so soon to have remission or mercy. The third sign is, your confession should be made in tears, if a man can weep; and if a man cannot weep with his fleshly eyes, let him weep in his heart. Such was the confession of Saint Peter; for after he had forsaken Jesus Christ he went out and wept full bitterly. The fourth sign is, when the sinner forgoes not for shame to make his confession. Such was the confession of the Magdalen, who did not spare, for any shame before those who were at the feast, to go to Our Lord Jesus Christ and acknowledge to Him her sins. The fifth sign is, that a man or woman shall obediently receive the penance that is imposed for the sins; for certainly, Jesus Christ, for the sins of a man, was obedient unto death.

The second condition of true confession is that it be speedily done; for truly, if a man had a dangerous wound, the longer he waited to cure himself the more would it fester and hasten him toward his death; and also the wound would be but the harder to heal. And it is even so with sin that is long carried in a man unconfessed. Certainly a man ought to confess his sins without delay, for many reasons; as, for fear of death, which often comes suddenly and whereof no man can ever be certain when it will come or in what place; and also the prolonging of one sin draws a man into another; and further, the longer he delays the farther he is from Christ. And if he live until his last day, scarcely then may he shrive himself or then remember his sins, or repent of them, because of the grievous malady about to cause his death. And for as much as he has not in his life hearkened unto Jesus Christ when He has spoken, he shall cry to Jesus Christ at the last and scarcely will He hear him. And understand that this condition must have four elements. Your shrift must be considered in advance and well advised upon, for wicked haste gives no profit; and that a man shall be able to make confession of all of his sins, be they of pride, or of envy, and so forth, according to the kind and the circumstances; and that he shall have comprehended in his mind the number and the greatness of his sins; and how long he has lain in sin; and also that he shall be contrite for his sins, and have a steadfast purpose that never again, by the grace of God, shall he fall into sin; and also that he fear and keep watch upon himself, so that he shall flee the occasions whereof he is tempted to sin. And you shall also shrive yourself of all your sins to one man, and not of some of them to one man and some to another; when, it is to be understood, the intention is to split up your shriving out of shame or fear; for this is but the strangling of your soul. For indeed, Jesus Christ is wholly good; there is no imperfection in Him; and therefore He perfectly forgives all, or nothing. I do not say that if you are sent to the director for a certain sin you are bound to show unto him all the rest of your sins, whereof you have been shriven by your own curate, save and except you wish to do so out of humility; for this does not constitute dividing your shrift. Nor do I say, in speaking of divided confession, that if you have leave to shrive yourself to a discreet and honest priest, where you wish to do so and by leave of your curate, that you may not as well shrive yourself to him of all your sins. But let no blot remain behind, let no sin be untold, so far as you have remembrance of them. And when you shall be shriven by your curate, tell him as well all of the sins that you have done since last you were shriven; and then this will be no wicked intention to divide confession.

Also, true confession asks certain other conditions. First, that you shrive yourself of your free will, not by constraint, nor for shame, nor for illness, nor for any such things; for it is only reasonable that he who trespassed of his own free will shall as freely confess it, and that no other man tell his sin, but that he himself do it, nor shall he withhold or deny his sin, nor allow himself to become angry at the priest for admonishing him to leave sin. Another condition is that your shrift be lawful; that is to say, that you, who shrive yourself, and also the priest who hears your confession, be verily of the faith of Holy Church; and that a man be not deprived of hope of the mercy of Jesus Christ, as was Cain or Judas. And also a man must himself accuse himself for his own trespass, and not another; but he shall blame and reproach himself and his own malice for his sin, and not another; nevertheless, if another man be the occasion for or enticer to his sin, or the state of a person be such that because of that person the sin is aggravated, or else if he cannot fully shrive himself without telling of the person with whom he has sinned; then he may tell; so that the intention be not to backbite such a person, but only to declare fully the confession.

Also you shall tell no lies in your confession; as to seem humble, perchance, in saying that you have done sins whereof you were never guilty. For Saint Augustine says: if thou, by reason of thy humility, liest against thyself, though thou wast not in sin before, yet art thou then in sin because of thy lying. You must also confess your sin with your own mouth, unless you grow dumb, and not by letter; for you have done the sin and you shall have the shame thereof. Also, you shall not embellish your confession with fair and subtle words, the more to cover up the sin; for then you beguile yourself and not the priest; you must tell it plainly, be it ever so foul or so horrible. You shall also shrive yourself to a priest that is discreet in counselling you, and moreover, you shall not shrive yourself for vainglory, nor hypocritically, nor for any cause other than the fear of Jesus Christ and the well-being of your soul. Also, you shall not run suddenly to the priest to tell him lightly of your sin, as one would tell a jest or a tale, but advisedly and with great devotion. And, generally speaking, shrive yourself often. If you fall often, then you rise by confession. And though you shrive yourself more than once of sin for which you have been already shriven, it is the more merit. And, as Saint Augustine says, you shall thereby the more easily obtain release from and the grace of God, both as to sin and punishment. And certainly, once a year, at the least, it is lawful to receive the Eucharist, for truly, once a year all things are renewed.

> *Explicit secunda pars penitencie;*
> *et sequitur tercia pars eiusdem,*
> *de satisfaccione*

Now have I told you of true confession, which is the second part of penitence. The third part of penitence is expiation; and that is generally achieved through alms-giving and bodily pain. Now there are three kinds of alms-givings: contrition of heart, where a man offers himself to God; another is, to have pity on the weaknesses of one's neighbours; and the third is, the giving of good counsel, spiritual and material, where men have need of it, and especially in the procuring of men's food. And take note that a man has need of these things, generally; he has need of food, he has need of clothing and shelter, he has need of charitable counsel, and of visiting in prison and in illness, and sepulture for his dead body. And if you cannot visit the needy in person, visit him by your message and by your gifts. These are general almsgivings, or works of charity, by those who have temporal riches or discretion in counselling. Of these works you shall hear at the day of doom.

These alms-doings shall you do with your own proper things, and without delay, and privately, if you can; but nevertheless, if you cannot do it privately, you shall not forbear to do such works though men may see you, so long as they be done not for the world's approbation, but for the pleasing of Jesus Christ. For take witness of Saint Matthew, *capitulo quinto:* "A city that is set on a hill cannot be hid. Neither do men light a candle and put it under a bushel, but on a candlestick; and it giveth light unto all that are in the house. Let your light so shine before men, that they may see your good works, and glorify your Father which is in Heaven."

Now, to speak of bodily pain, it consists of prayers, of vigils, of fasts, of virtuous teaching of orisons. And you shall understand that orisons or prayers consist of a pious will of the heart that has made amends to God and expresses itself by spoken word, asking for the removal of evils and to obtain things spiritual and durable, as well as temporal things, sometimes; of which orisons, truly, in the prayer of the paternoster has Christ included most things. Certainly, it is invested with three things pertaining to His dignity, wherefore it is more dignified than any other prayer; Jesus Christ made it Himself; and it is short, so that it may be learned the more easily, and be held the more easily in the heart of memory, that man may the oftener help himself by repeating the prayer; and in order that a man may the less grow weary of saying it, and that he may not excuse himself from learning it; it is so short and so easy; and because it comprises within itself all good prayers. The expounding of this holy prayer I commit to these masters of theology; save that thus much will I say: that, when you pray that God forgive your trespasses as you forgive those that trespass against you, beware that you are not uncharitable. This holy orison diminishes each venial sin, and therefore it appertains specially to penitence.

This prayer must be truly said and in utter faith, in order that men may pray to God ordinately and discreetly and devoutly; and always a man shall subject his own will to the will of God. This prayer must also be said with great humility and all innocently; honourably and not to the annoyance of any man or woman. It must also be followed by works of charity. It is of avail also even against the vices of the soul; for, as Saint Jerome says, "By fasting we are saved from the vices of the flesh, and by prayer from the vices of the soul."

After the foregoing you shall understand that bodily pain lies in vigils; for Jesus Christ says, "Watch and pray, that ye enter not into temptation." You shall understand, also, that fasting stands in three things; in the forgoing of material food and drink, and in forgoing worldly pleasures, and in forgoing the doing of mortal sin; this is to say, that a man shall guard himself from deadly sin with all his might.

And you shall understand, also, that God ordained fasting; and to fasting pertain four things: Largess to poor folk, gladness of the spiritual heart in order not to be angry or vexed, nor to grumble because you fast; and also reasonable hours wherein to eat moderately; that is to say, a man shall not eat out of season, nor sit and eat longer at his table because he has fasted.

Then you shall understand that bodily pain lies in disciplining or teaching, by word or by writing, or by example. Also, in wearing shirts of hair or coarse wool, or habergeons next the naked flesh, for Christ's sake, and such other kinds of penance. But beware that such kinds of penance on your flesh do not make your heart bitter or angry or vexed with yourself; for it is better to cast away your hair shirt than to cast away the security of Jesus Christ. And therefore Saint Paul says: "Clothe yourselves as those that are the chosen of God, in heart of mercy, gentleness, long-suffering, and such manner of clothing." Whereof Jesus Christ is more pleased than of hair shirts, or habergeons, or hauberks.

Then, discipline lies also in beating of the breast, in scourging with rods, in kneelings, in tribulations, in suffering patiently the wrongs that are done unto one, and also in patient endurance of illnesses, or losing of worldly chattels, or of wife or of child or other friends.

Then shall you understand which things hinder penance; and these are four, that is to say, fear, shame, hope, and despair. And, to speak first of fear, since a man sometimes thinks that he cannot endure penance, against this thought may be set, as remedy, the thought that such bodily penance is short and mild compared with the pain of Hell, which is so cruel and so long that it lasts for ever.

Now against the shame that a man has in confession, and especially of these hypocrites that would be held so perfect that they have no need for shrift—against that shame should a man think, and reasonably enough, that he who has not been ashamed to do foul things, certainly he ought not to be ashamed to do fair things, and of such is confession. A man should also think that God sees and knows all his thoughts and all his deeds; from Him nothing may be hidden nor covered. Men should even bear in mind the shame that is to come at the day of judgment to those who are not penitent and shriven in this present life. For all the creatures on earth and in Hell shall openly behold all that sinners hide in this world.

Now to speak of the hope of those who are negligent and slow in shriving themselves—that is of two sorts. The one is, that he hopes to live long and to acquire riches for his delight, and then he will shrive himself; and as he tells himself, it seems to him that it will then be time enough to go to confession. Another is the over-confidence that he has in Christ's mercy. Against the first vice he shall think, that our life is in no security; and also that all the riches in this world are at hazard, and pass as does a shadow on the wall. And, as Saint Gregory says, it is part of the great righteousness of God that never shall the torment cease of those that would never withdraw themselves willingly from sin, but have always continued in sin; because, for the perpetual will to sin, they shall have perpetual torment.

Despair is of two sorts: the first is of the mercy of Christ; the other is the thought of sinners that they cannot long persevere in goodness. The first despair comes of the thought that he has sinned so greatly and so often, and has lain so long in sin, that he shall not be saved. Certainly, against that accursed despair should be set the thought that the passion of Jesus Christ is stronger to loose than sin is strong to bind. Against the second despair, let him think that as often as he falls he may rise again by penitence. And though he may have lain in sin ever so long, the mercy of Christ is ever ready to receive him into grace. Against that form of despair wherein he deems that he should not long persevere in goodness, he shall think that the feebleness of the Devil can do nothing unless men allow him to; and also that he shall have strength of the help of God and of all Holy Church and of the protection of angels, if he will.

Then shall men understand what is the fruit of penance; and according to the word of Jesus Christ, it is the endless bliss of Heaven, where joy has no opposite of woe or grievance, where all evils of this present life are past; wherein is security from the torments of Hell; wherein is the blessed company that rejoices evermore, each of the others' joy; wherein the body of man, that formerly was foul and dark, is more bright than the sun; wherein the body, that lately was ailing, frail, and feeble, and mortal, is immortal, and so strong and so whole that nothing may impair it; wherein is no hunger nor thirst, nor cold, but every soul is replenished with the ability to perceive the perfect knowing of God. This blessed Kingdom may man acquire by poverty of spirit, and the glory of humbleness, and the plenitude of joy by hunger and thirst, and the ease and rest by labour, and life by death and the mortification of sin.

HERE THE MAKER OF THIS BOOK TAKES HIS LEAVE

Now do I pray all those who hear this little treatise, or read it, that, if there be within it anything that pleases them, they thank Our Lord Jesus Christ, from Whom proceeds all understanding and all goodness. And if there be anything that displeases them, I pray them, also, that they impute it to the fault of my ignorance and not to my intention, which would fain have better said if I had had the knowledge. For our Book says, "All that is written is written for our instruction;" and that was my intention. Wherefore I meekly beseech you that, for the sake of God's mercy, you pray for me that Christ have mercy upon me and forgive me my trespasses—and especially for my translations and the writing of worldly vanities, the which I withdraw in my retractations: as, The Book of Troilus; also The Book of Fame; The Book of the Nineteen Ladies; The Book of the Duchess; The Book of Saint Valentine's Day, Of the Parliament of Birds; The Tales of Canterbury, those that tend toward sin; The Book of the Lion; and many another book, were they in my remembrance; and many a song and many a lecherous lay,—as to which may Christ, of His great mercy, forgive me the sin. But for the translation of Boethius's *de Consolatione*, and other books of legends of saints, and homilies, and of morality and devotion—for those I thank Our Lord Jesus Christ and His Blessed Mother and all the saints of Heaven; beseeching them that they, henceforth unto my life's end, send me grace whereof to bewail my sins, and to study for the salvation of my soul:—and grant me the grace of true penitence, confession, and expiation in this present life; through the benign grace of Him Who is King of kings and Priest over all priests, Who redeemed us with the precious blood of His heart; so that I may be one of those, at the day of doom, that shall be saved: *Qui cum patre, etc.*

HERE ENDS THE BOOK OF THE TALES OF CANTERBURY,
WRITTEN BY GEOFFREY CHAUCER,
ON WHOSE SOUL MAY JESUS CHRIST HAVE MERCY.
AMEN.